Garri, on the other side of the courtyard, yelled "Zigger!"

He dropped the bundle of dirty tablecloths he had been carrying and ran towards Donnick. "Close the gate! Close the blasted gate!"

But Donnick stood rooted, his mouth gaping foolishly at Garri, as if the danger was coming from his direction.

And the zigger flew into his mouth.

Terelle glimpsed it as a black blur the size of a man's thumb. The keening stopped abruptly, replaced by the shriek of Donnick's agony. He clutched at his throat and a gush of blood spewed from his mouth like water from an opened spigot. His screams faded into a choking gurgle. He fell to his knees, staring at Terelle, begging her for help she could not render. He clawed at his face, jammed his hand into his mouth, clutching for something he could not reach. She stared, appalled. His blood was splattered over her feet but she couldn't move.

Praise for Glenda Larke:

"A magnificent gift for world-building . . . one of the best imaginations in the business."

— specusphere.com

By Glenda Larke

ISLES OF GLORY
The Aware
Gilfeather
The Tainted

THE MIRAGE MAKERS
Heart of the Mirage
The Shadow of Tyr
Song of the Shiver Barrens

STORMLORD
The Last Stormlord
Stormlord Rising
Stormlord's Exile

WRITING AS GLENDA NORAMLY
Havenstar

THE LAST STORMLORD

STORMLORD BOOK 1

GLENDA LARKE

www.orbitbooks.net

Copyright © 2009 by Glenda Larke
Excerpt from *Stormlord Rising* copyright © 2009 by Glenda Larke
All rights reserved. Except as permitted under the U.S. Copyright Act of 1976, no part of this publication may be reproduced, distributed, or transmitted in any form or by any means, or stored in a database or retrieval system, without the prior written permission of the publisher.

Orbit
Hachette Book Group
237 Park Avenue, New York, NY 10017
Visit our website at www.orbitbooks.net

First published in Australia in 2009 by HarperCollins*Publishers* Australia Pty Limited.

Orbit is an imprint of Hachette Book Group. The Orbit name and logo are trademarks of Little, Brown Book Group Limited.

The publisher is not responsible for websites (or their content) that are not owned by the publisher.

Printed in the United States of America

First United States edition, March 2010

10 9 8 7 6 5

for
Sam Griffiths
May you always know the joy of reading

The Quartern

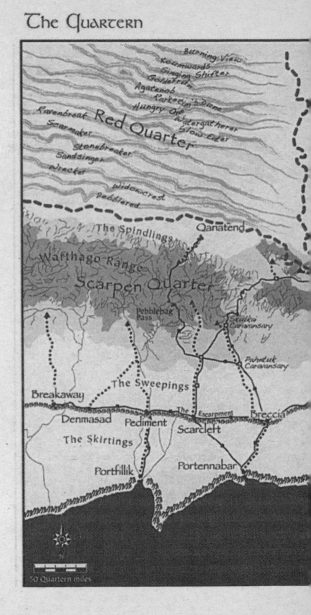

PART ONE

Prisons
without
Walls

CHAPTER ONE

Scarpen Quarter
Scarcleft City
Opal's Snuggery, Level 32

It was the last night of her childhood.

Terelle, unknowing, thought it just another busy evening in Opal's Snuggery, crowded and noisy and hot. Rooms were hazed with the fumes from the keproot pipes of the addicted and fuggy with the smell of the resins smouldering in the censers. Smoky blue tendrils curled through the archways, encouraging a lively lack of restraint as they drifted through the air.

Everything as usual.

Terelle's job was to collect the dirty plates and mugs and return them to the kitchen, in an endless round from sunset until the dark dissolved under the first cold fingering of a desert dawn.

Her desire was to be unnoticed at the task.

Her dream was to escape her future as one of Madam Opal's girls.

Once she'd thought the snuggery a happy place, the outer courtyard always alive with boisterous chatter and laughter as friends met on entry, the reception rooms bustling with servants fetching food from the kitchens or amber from the barrels in the cellar, the stairs cluttered with handmaidens as they giggled and flirted and smiled, arm in arm with their clients. She'd thought the snuggery's inhabitants lived each night adrift on laughter and joy and friendship. But she had only been seven then, and newly purchased. She was twelve now, old enough to realise the laughter and the smiles and the banter were part of a larger game, and what underlay it was much sadder. She still didn't understand everything, not really, even though she knew now what went on between the customers and women like her half-sister, Vivie, in the upstairs rooms.

She knew enough to see the joy was a sham.

She knew enough to know she didn't want any part of it.

And so she scurried through the reception rooms with her laden tray, hugging the walls on her way to the kitchen. A drab girl with brown tunic, brown skin, brown hair so dark it had the rich depth of rubies, a timid pebblemouse on its way back to its lair with a pouch-load of detritus to pile around its burrow entrance, hoping to keep a hostile world at bay. She kept her gaze downcast, instinctively aware that her eyes, green and intelligent, told another story.

The hours blurred into one another. Laughter devoid of subtlety drowned out the lute player's strumming; vulgar banter suffocated the soft-sung words of love. As the night wore on, Scarcleft society lost its refinement just as surely as the desert night lost its chill in the packed reception rooms.

Out of the corner of her eye, Terelle noted Vivie flirting with one of the younger customers. The man had a sweet smile, but he was no more than an itinerant seller of scent, a street peddler. Madam Opal wanted Vivie to pay attention to Kade the waterlender instead, Kade who was fat and had hair growing out of his nose. He'd come all the way downhill from the twentieth level of the city because he fancied the Gibber woman he knew as Viviandra.

Behind the peddler's slender back, Terelle made a face at Vivie to convey her opinion of her sister's folly with the peddler, then scurried on.

Back in the main reception room a few moments later, she heard nervous laughter at one of the tables. A man was drunk and he'd lost some sort of wager. He wasn't happy and his raised voice had a mean edge to it.

Trouble, she thought. Rosscar, the oil merchant's son. His temper was well known in the snuggery. He was jabbing stiffened fingertips at the shoulder of one of his companions. As she gathered mugs onto her tray, Terelle overheard his angry accusation: "You squeezed the beetle too hard!" He waved his mug under the winner's nose and slopped amber everywhere. "Cheat, you are, Merch Putter—"

Hurriedly one of the handmaidens stepped in and led him away, giggling and stroking his arm.

Poor Diomie, Terelle thought as she wiped the stickiness of the alcohol from the agate inlay of the stone floor. *He'll take it out on her. And all over a silly wager on how high a click beetle can jump.* As she rose wearily to her feet, her gaze met the intense stare of a Scarperman. He sat alone, a hungry-eyed, hawk-nosed man dressed in a blue tunic embroidered with the badge of the pedemen's guild.

"This is empty," he growled at her, indicating the

brass censer in the corner of the room. "Get some more resin for it, girl, and sharp about it. You shouldn't need to be told."

She ducked her head so that her hair fell across her face and mumbled an apology. Using her laden tray as a buffer, she headed once more for the safety of the kitchens, thinking she could feel those predatory eyes sliding across her back as she went. She didn't return to replenish the censer; she sent one of the kitchen boys instead.

Half the run of a sandglass later, she saw Vivie and Kade the fat waterlender heading upstairs, Madam Opal nodding her approval as she watched. The sweet-smiling, sweet-smelling peddler was nowhere in evidence. Terelle snorted. Vivie had sand for brains if she'd thought Opal would allow her to dally with a scent seller when there was a waterlending upleveller around. A waterlender, any waterlender, was richer than Terelle could even begin to imagine, and there was nothing Opal liked better than a rich customer.

Terelle stacked another tray and hurried on.

Some time later the bell in Viviandra's room was ringing down in the kitchen, and Madam Opal sent Terelle up to see what was needed. When she entered the bedroom, Vivie was reclining on her divan, still dressed. The waterlender was not there.

"Where's the merch?" Terelle asked.

"In the water-room," Vivie said and giggled. "Sick as a sand-flea that's lost its pede. Drank too much, I suspect. I was bored, so I rang down to the kitchen. Now you can have a rest, too." She patted the divan and flicked her long black hair over her shoulder. "And Kade's not a merchant, you know. He lends people water tokens. Which means you should address him as Broker Kade. Terelle, you *have* to learn that sort of thing. It's important. Keeps the customers happy."

"Vivie, if Opal catches us doing nothing, she'll be spitting sparks."

"Don't call me Vivie! You *know* I hate it. It's not a proper name for a Scarpen snuggery girl."

"It's your name. And you're not Scarpen. You're Gibber, like me."

"Not any more. Opal's right when she says 'Viviandra' has class and 'Vivie' doesn't. And why shouldn't we be lazy occasionally? I deserve a rest! You think it's easy pandering to the tastes of the men who come here? You'll find out when your turn comes."

"I'm not going to be a handmaiden," Terelle said. "I'm going to be an arta. A dancer, like the great Arta Amethyst. In fact, I am going to be greater than Amethyst." To demonstrate her skill, she bounced to her feet, undulated her hips in a slow figure of eight and then did the splits.

Vivie groaned. "You are *such* a child! You won't have any choice in the matter, you know. Why in all the Sweepings do you think Madam Opal paid Pa for the two of us? So as you could be a dancer? Not weeping likely!"

All hope vanished as Terelle glimpsed the darkness of her future, crouching in wait just around a corner not too far away. "Oh, Vivie! What sort of handmaiden would I make? Look at me!"

She hadn't meant to be literal, but Vivie sat up and ran a critical gaze over her. "Well," she said, "it's true that you're nothing much to look at right now. But you're only twelve. That will change. Look at how scrawny Diomie was when she first came! And now . . ." She sketched curves with her hands. "That jeweller from Level Nine called her luscious last night. A plum for the picking, he said."

"Even if I burst out of my dresses like Diomie, my face will still be the same," Terelle pointed out. "*I* think I have nice eyes, but Madam Opal says green is unnatural. And my skin's too brown, even browner than yours. And my hair's too straight and ordinary, not wavy and black like yours. No load of powder and paint is going to change any of that." She was not particularly upset at the thought. "I can dance, though. Or so everyone says. Besides, I don't *want* to be a whore."

"Opal will stick a pin in your backside if you use that word around here. Whores sell their bodies on the street for water. We are trained snuggery handmaidens. We are Opal's girls. We do much more than—well, much more than whores do. We are, um, *companions*. We speak prettily, and tell stories and sing and recite and dance, and we listen to the men as though they are the wisest sages in the city. We entertain and make them laugh. Do it properly, like I do, and no one cares if we don't have fair skin and blue eyes and straw hair like Scarpen Quarter folk."

"Opal says I'm the best fan dancer she's seen for my age."

"Maybe, but she can't teach you, not properly, you know that. You'd have to go to a professional dancer for lessons, and that'd cost tokens we don't have. Opal's not going to pay for it. She doesn't want a dancer, or a musician, or a singer—she just wants handmaidens who can also dance and sing and play the lute. There's a difference. Forget it, Terelle. It's not going to happen. When your bleeding starts, the law says you are old enough to be a handmaiden and Opal will make sure that's what happens."

Terelle lifted her chin. "I won't be a whore, Vivie. I *won't*."

"Don't say things like that, or Opal will throw you out."

"I wish she would. Ouch!"

Vivie, irritated, had leaned across and yanked a lock of her hair. "Terelle, she's given you water for more than five whole years, just on the strength of what you will become after your bleeding starts. You *know* that. Not to mention what she paid Pa. She *invested* in you. She will spit more than sparks if she thinks she's not going to get a return on her investment. She won't let you get away with it. Anyway, it's not such a bad life, not really."

But the crouching shape of her unwanted future grew in Terelle's mind. "It's—it's horrible! Like slavery. And even barbarian Reduners don't own slaves any more. We were *sold*, Vivie. Pa sold us to those men knowing we would end up in a brothel." The bitterness spilled over into her voice.

"This is *not* a brothel. It's a snuggery. A house for food and entertainment and love. We have style; a brothel is for lowlifes with hardly any tokens. And I am not a slave—I am paid, and paid well. One day I shall have enough to retire." She picked up her hand mirror from the divan and fluffed up her hair. The reddish highlights in the black gleamed in the lamplight. "I think I need another ruby rinse."

"I'll do it tomorrow."

"Thanks." Vivie smiled at her kindly. "Terelle, you're not a slave, either. For the odd jobs you do, you have water and food and clothes and a bed, not to mention the dancing and singing lessons. You've been taught to read and write and recite. When you start working properly, you'll be paid in tokens like the rest of us. You can leave any time you want, once you pay back what you owe."

"Leave? How can I leave unless I have somewhere else to go? I'd die of thirst!"

"Exactly. Unless you save enough tokens first."

Terelle slumped, banging her heels against the legs of the divan in frustration.

Vivie laid her mirror aside. "Terelle, Terelle, don't you remember what it was like in the Gibber Quarter before we came here? I do. It was *horrid*." She shuddered. "The only time we had enough water was when we stole it. I was *glad* when Pa sold us to the Reduner caravanners—"

She broke off as they heard footsteps in the passageway outside. Terelle jumped off the divan and grabbed up her tray. When the waterlender entered, she was picking up the empty mugs on the low table. She bobbed and scuttled past him. When she glanced back from the doorway, she saw Vivie smile shyly at Kade from under her lashes. One bare shoulder, all invitation, had slipped from the confines of her robe.

Terelle pulled the door shut.

Back in the main reception room, the crowd had thinned. Most of the handmaidens had gone upstairs with their first customers of the night. Men who had not secured a girl waited their turn. Opal, plump and painted, flirted shamelessly as she bargained prices with latecomers. Servants brought more amber, keproot and pipes. The air was thicker now, yet there was an edginess to the atmosphere. Terelle scanned the crowd, seeking the cause.

The pedeman in the blue tunic sat alone, and his eyes, still sheened with feral hunger, sought her—but he wasn't causing any trouble. On the other side of the room, Merch Rosscar glowered at Merch Putter, the man he had earlier called a cheat. He began another drunken tirade, his speech slurred, his words threatening, his nastiness growing more and more overt. Putter stirred uneasily. Terelle glanced at Opal, who gave the merest of nods. Terelle dumped her tray and slipped out of the room. She went straight to the unroofed courtyard where Garri the steward and Donnick the doorman controlled entry to the snuggery via a gate to South Way.

"Trouble," she told them. "Madam Opal wants Merch Rosscar removed."

"Drunk again, I s'pose," Garri said. "Look after the gate a moment, Terelle. Anyone comes, they'll have to wait a bit till we get back. Come on, Donnick."

Terelle sat down on the doorman's stool next to the barred gate. Outside in the street all seemed quiet; at this late hour, not too many people were still up and about. The city of Scarcleft tumbled down the slope known as The Escarpment in stepped levels and South Way was one of three roads that descended from the highlord's dwelling, on Level Two, to the southern city wall, on Level Thirty-six. During the day it was usually one of the busiest thoroughfares in the city.

She leaned back against the courtyard's mud-brick wall so she could look up at the sky. On those nights when Opal's was closed, once every ten days, she would take her quilt up to the flat roof so she could fall asleep watching the stars as they slid, oh so slowly, across the black depth of the sky. She liked not being surrounded on all sides by walls. She liked the feel of the wind gusting in from the gullies of the Skirtings in unpredictable eddies. She even liked it during the day when the air was so hot it crackled the hair on her head, and she had to rub rendered pede fat onto her lips to stop them drying out.

Whenever Terelle tried to explain such things to Vivie, the older girl would throw her hands up in incomprehension and remark that talking to her sister was as unsettling as having a stone in your sandal. So Terelle didn't try any more. She learned to accept the fact that she was odd and Vivie was the one who fitted in. Terelle wasn't comfortable in the snuggery; Vivie revelled in it like a birthing cat that had found silk cushions. Terelle sometimes cried real tears—and Vivie had never shed a tear in grief in her whole life.

Now, though, the oil lamps around the walled courtyard dulled the sky and made it hard to see the stars. A flame sputtered and shadows danced. Once more she saw the dark lump of a future crouching just out of reach, waiting to smother her.

I'm trapped, she thought. It had been her fate from the moment she had been included in the deal made with the caravanners passing through their settle. Her father had his tokens, enough for a year or two's water, and she had this. She took a deep breath, inhaling the scent of citrus flowers, a hint of perfume, the stale smoke of burned keproot.

She had to get out. She wasn't Vivie, and she never would be. Yet how to escape?

Garri and Donnick returned, hustling an irate Rosscar between them. Outside in the fresh air, he appeared less drunk and more dangerous. "I'll be back, Merch Putter!"

he shouted over his shoulder, even though the merchant was nowhere in sight. "You'll regret the day you cheated me!"

Terelle opened the gate, but when the steward attempted to guide the man through it, he lashed out with a kick, catching the older man in the knee. Terelle winced. Garri had swollen joints at the best of times. Donnick, a hulking youth of eighteen with few wits but a good heart, gently levered the drunken man through the gateway and closed the gate.

Terelle stepped back into the passage leading to the main reception room. Light flickered as some of the lamps guttered. There was someone coming the opposite way, and she politely flattened herself against the wall to let him pass. But he didn't pass. He stopped: the pedeman in the blue tunic. She turned to hurry on, but he barred her way, his arm braced against the wall at chest height.

Her heart scudded; fear broke through on her skin in goose bumps. She did not look at him but kept her head lowered. "Excuse me, pedeman. I have work to do."

He did not move the arm but lowered his head to whisper close to her cheek. "How much is your first-night price, child?" The tip of his tongue thrust into her ear, seeking to know her.

She tilted her head away, reminded of the forked tongue of a snake questing after prey. "I'm not a handmaiden. I'm a servant." Her voice sounded thin and frightened to her ears. Her terror was out of all proportion to her danger; after all, one way lay the security of Garri and Donnick, the other way Opal and her servants. No one would allow him to touch her. Not this night. Yet she shivered as if the cold of a desert night wind brushed her skin.

Madam Opal won't sell my first-night before my bleeding starts, will she?

"You're a lying Gibber child," he whispered. "And you should not try to deceive your betters. I will buy your first-night, and you'll pay for that lie." He placed a hand on the bud of her breast and squeezed, the touch a promise of horror. "It won't be long now, will it, sweetmeat?" She pushed him away, ducked under his arm and ran for the safety of the reception room at the end of the passage.

But the safety was illusory, her danger only postponed.

She was crying when she entered the room, and dipped her head to hide the tears.

The night was unending. The man in the blue tunic did not come back, but from one of the handmaidens she learned his name: Huckman. Pedeman Huckman, and worse still, he was a relative of Opal's. He owned a train of packpedes and ran cargoes from the coast to Scarcleft, bringing pressed seaweed briquettes to fuel the ovens and fireplaces and smelters of the city.

A wealthy man, and wealthy men bought what they wanted.

Fear fluttered at the edges of Terelle's thoughts for the rest of the evening. She still felt his hand on her breast, bruising her as he enjoyed her shock. Just thinking about him made her stomach churn.

At last the final dirty dishes and mugs were delivered to the kitchen and Opal indicated she could go to bed. Feet dragging with fatigue, she walked down the passage to the courtyard once more, on her way to the servants' stairs. Merch Putter was walking in front of her, on his way out after his time upstairs with one of the handmaidens.

Donnick opened the gate for the merchant, but before the man stepped through, he turned to press a tinny token into the youth's palm. And that was when they all heard it: a shrill keening, like a fingernail being dragged down a slate. No, more than that, a screech so horrible it shrieked of danger, of death on the move. Terelle had never heard such a sound before. She was terror-struck, rendered motionless. The merchant flung himself back into the courtyard, plunging sideways into the potted pomegranates.

Garri, on the other side of the courtyard, yelled "Zigger!" He dropped the bundle of dirty tablecloths he had been carrying and ran towards Donnick. "Close the gate! Close the blasted gate!"

But Donnick stood rooted, his mouth gaping foolishly at Garri, as if the danger was coming from his direction.

And the zigger flew into his mouth.

Terelle glimpsed it as a black blur the size of a man's thumb. The keening stopped abruptly, replaced by the shriek of Donnick's agony. He clutched at his throat and a gush of blood spewed from his mouth like water from an opened spigot. His screams faded into a choking gurgle. He fell to his knees, staring at Terelle, begging her for help she could not render. He clawed at his face, jammed his hand into his mouth, clutching for something he could not reach. She stared, appalled. His blood was splattered over her feet but she couldn't move.

Time slowed. She saw past Donnick through the gate to where a man stood on the opposite side of the street, his face muffled in a scarf. He held a zigger cage in one hand and a zigtube in the other.

She thought, her calm at odds with her shock, *I suppose it's Rosscar and he meant to kill Putter.* Her terror dissipated into numbing vacuity. Donnick fell sideways, his body twitching uncontrollably.

She moved then, to kneel at his side and stroke his arm, as if she could bring comfort.

Garri came to stand beside her, patting her shoulder in clumsy sympathy. "Go inside, Terelle. Nothing you can do here."

She stammered an irrelevance that suddenly seemed important: "He's from the Gibber, like Vivie and me. He tells me stuff. About the settle where he was born. His family." She started to tremble. "We must be able to do *something*—"

The steward shook his head. "Lad's already dead. His body just don't know it yet."

As if he heard the words, Donnick gave one last shuddering spasm that arched his back from the ground. His gaze fixed on Terelle's face, speaking his horror, his terror, his pain. When he collapsed it was with brutal finality. His eyes glazed, blank with death. The zigger crawled out through his open mouth and paused. Terelle hurled herself backwards, half sprawling as she levered herself away on her bottom, whimpering in fear.

The zigger sat on the plumpness of Donnick's lip, blood-covered and sated, purring softly while it used its back legs to clean its jagged mouthparts and brush the human flesh from its wing cases. Terelle's trembling transformed to shudders, racking her whole body.

"Kill it!" she begged, clutching at Garri's ankles. *Do something, anything, please . . .*

"I dare not, lass. That there beetle is a trained zigger, worth more tokens than I earn in a year, and someone'd blame me, sure as there's dust in the wind. 'S all right, though," he said, lifting her to her feet. "Won't hurt us. It's eaten now and won't want to feed again. In a while it'll fly back to its cage. That's what they're trained to do." He glared out through the gate to where the zigger's owner still waited, but didn't challenge him. With a sigh he turned back to her. "Go wash, child. Use the water in Donnick's day jar."

She looked down at her feet. Blood ran stickily down her legs and into her slippers. Shuddering, she kicked them off. Mesmerised, unable to stop herself, she stared at the zigger again. She wanted to flee, but couldn't bring herself to turn her back on it. Next to the gate, Merch Putter vomited messily into the pomegranate bushes.

"Remember that whining sound," Garri said, "and if you ever hear it again, take cover and hide your face. It's the wing cases sawing 'gainst each other in flight. Makes the victim turn his head, so all his soft bits and holes— eyes, nose, throat, ears—are facing the bleeding little bastard." He glanced at Merch Putter. "Go, Terelle. I'll take care of this, and tomorrow I'll report it to the highlord's guard. That's all I dare do."

"Would it—would it have made a difference if Donnick had closed the gate?" she asked.

He drew in a heavy breath. "No, I don't suppose so. It would've flown over the wall, wouldn't it?"

Just then the zigger spread its brightly veined wings and flew off, heading straight towards the cage held by the muffled figure on the other side of the street. Garri bolted the gate behind it, as if it was a departing guest.

Terelle fled towards the servants' rooms, leaving a line of bloody footprints across the courtyard.

It was hot up on the flat roof of the snuggery. Terelle pulled the day bed into the shade cast by the adjoining wall of the snuggery's uplevel neighbours, but the heat of the afternoon shimmered in the nearby sunlight, dragging her water from her with its ferocity. She sat cross-legged on the woven bab ropes of the bed, a stone mortar jammed against her shins while she pounded the pestle. When the rubyleaf powder was fine enough, she added water to make a paste. She puzzled over the oddity of how something green could end up staining things red-brown. She failed to come up with a satisfactory answer, but anything was better than remembering the way Donnick had died the night before. Or the words Huckman had murmured in her ear and the way he had squeezed her breast.

She considered instead what Vivie had said about them stealing water as children in a Gibber settle. Now that she thought about it, she dimly recalled sneaking out at night to fill jars from the wash when the water came down like a meddle of running packpedes. She remembered taking water from the open stone channels, too. What were they called? Slots, that was right. They had them here in Scarcleft as well, to irrigate the bab groves outside the city walls.

But most of all, she remembered being scared. Scared of the dark, scared of being caught by the reeve. Scared of Pa if they failed to return with water. Scared of his shouting.

She frowned, thinking back. She could remember the settle, every detail. She could have described each crack in the walls of their house, or the shape of the stains on Pa's baggy trousers, or the patterns on the water jars beside the fireplace and the way the water in them iced over on cold nights. Her memory of events had faded, but the place was imprinted on her mind, as unchanging as carvings in stone. *Other people don't remember things the way I do. Why not?* It worried her.

She wondered if forgetting the unpleasant happenings had been deliberate, the desperation of a child who had not wanted to remember. But she was no longer a child. Her future had challenged her childhood; Huckman's hand on her breast and Donnick's death had banished it forever.

"Oh good, you're ready." Vivie clambered onto the rooftop, fanning herself. She sank down on the day bed with a heartfelt sigh and leaned back so that Terelle could rub the paste into her scalp and comb it through the strands of her hair. *She is so like a cat*, Terelle thought. *Wanting to be stroked all the time.* Vivie demanding to be pampered was among her earliest memories.

"I hear Rosscar fled the city this morning," Vivie said, closing her eyes. "Opal's grinning like a frog in a day jar."

"What? *Why?*"

"Rosscar's pa, the oil merchant, paid Opal not to tell the highlord's guard how Donnick died. Luckily for Rosscar, Garri hadn't got round to reporting it. Opal will be in a good mood for days. She made a heap of tokens."

"But . . . what about Donnick?"

Vivie shrugged. "Makes no difference to him."

Upset, Terelle tightened her lips and tried not to think about it. Luckily Vivie lost interest in the subject. The heat of the afternoon mired conversation anyway. The monotonous click of cicadas sunning on top of the wall was comfortably familiar and it was pleasant not to be at the beck and call of every girl in the snuggery, helping to primp and preen them for the evening, running here and there fetching things, finding lost items.

If only she could forget the night before.

"That's good," Viviandra murmured as Terelle's fingertips massaged her scalp. She stretched, enjoying the first breath of a breeze that promised to cool the desiccating heat of the afternoon.

"It's been long enough, I think. You want shiny highlights, not bright red hair."

"Bit longer won't make any difference. It's so good just lying here with nothing to do."

Terelle took no notice. She started to wash away the rubyleaf paste, taking care to catch the water afterwards. "Vivie, why didn't we have a water allotment when we were kids?"

"Hmm? Oh, Pa lost his rights to land in the bab grove. Don't know why—a debt, maybe. And he couldn't find regular work."

Terelle took the comb and began to tease out the tangles. "Tell me about my mother."

Vivie sighed. "I have told you, countless times."

"No, you haven't. I don't know *anything*."

"You know everything I know. Father found her out on the plains when he was prospecting." She counted off the facts on her fingers, not bothering to conceal her impatience. "He guessed she'd been abandoned by a caravan. Her name was Sienna. She was dressed oddly, in colourful fabric. She spoke a strange language. Pa wanted her; he took her, she lived with us and later she had you and then she died. What more is there to tell?"

"You were eight or so then. She must have talked to you."

"Terelle, she could hardly speak our tongue! What could she say?"

"Where do *you* think she came from?"

"*I* don't know. I don't think anyone knew. And she couldn't tell us."

"Sienna is not a Scarpen name. Or a Gibber one. I've asked lots of people about that."

"Maybe she came from across the Giving Sea. Though we lived a long way from the sea."

"Was she happy?"

"Was anyone ever happy living with Pa? He made my ma bitter and unhappy by taking a second woman. He killed your ma because he was too mean to call the midwife when you were born." She was matter-of-fact, rather than angry. "Terelle, I scarcely knew her, and what I did know I've mostly forgotten. Looking back on it, I think she was weak and ill most of the time. Maybe because of her experience out on the Gibber Plains? She didn't say much, but then she probably didn't have the words anyway." She stood up. "I'm going to the baths now; do you want to come?"

Terelle shook her head. The women's bath house was a gossipy place, abounding with stories, and normally she loved it there. This time, though, she wasn't in the mood. "I'll clean up here," she said.

Vivie smiled her thanks and left, her scent floating behind her. She had spent days concocting a personal fragrance; Terelle found it over-sweet.

She poured the rinse water onto the fruit trees. Watering them was her job, and sometimes she used cooking water cadged from the kitchens or dirty wash water from the bedrooms. Her allotment of pure water for the plants she sold to the street waterseller for tokens, and used those to buy items in the bazaar. At first she'd thought

she was being clever, saving water like this and getting
money to spend on herself, but now she was wiser. Opal
knew perfectly well what she was doing and in fact intended for her to do just that. It was a lesson for every
child to learn: water was life; water was wealth. You
didn't throw away old water and you didn't waste drinking water. Ever.

As she watered a kumquat already coming into fruit,
she glanced down over the balustrade. Below, the lowest four levels of the city of Scarcleft merged into one
another, the outer walls of one building forming the
boundaries of the next a step below. From this angle,
the city looked lush, each terrace and roof crowded
with potted plants: dwarf figs and apricots and quan-
dongs, melons and peppers, herbs and spices, keproot
and hemp. The rock-hard daub of the stepped streets
between the houses was brown, as were the high windowless walls of mud-brick on either side, their sun-
baked clay as hard as iron. Gates set into the walls were
brilliant patterns in the drabness. Painted with family
colours and symbols, heavily studded with gemstones,
the gates varied from the garish scarlet paintwork and
amethysts of the snuggery to the subtle combinations
of ochre wash set with smoky quartz on a nearby potter's house.

Further down, on the buildings of the waterless inhabitants of the city's lowest level—the thirty-sixth—there
was neither paint nor studs. Nor much greenery sprouting
from rooftop pots, either. Terelle let her gaze linger for a
moment on the crumbling bricks and palmleaf weave of
the walls there and felt a familiar touch of fear.

To be waterless . . .

There could be no worse fate. Once it had been hers and could well be again if she didn't order her life wisely. She had been born without water allotment, owed none by any settle or town or city, all because at the time of her birth her father had been both landless and unemployed.

She drew a ragged breath, unbalanced even at the thought. *I won't let it happen again.* Useless to rely on Madam Opal or on Vivie, and certainly useless to think of her father, almost faceless now in her memory, who had sold them both. *Never again, I swear it,* she told the lurking dark. *But I'll earn a living my way, not Vivie's way.*

As she watered the last fruit tree, she kept back a finger-breadth of water in the bottom of the bucket, which she then poured into the sun pattern pressed into the clay of the flat rooftop. Her sacrifice to the Sunlord, the giver and taker of life. For a moment she knelt there in the heat of full sunlight, watching the rivulets spread outwards to fill the indentations. Greedily, the Sunlord sucked up the water.

"Lord of the sun, help me," she whispered, but she couldn't frame the words to specify her wants, even as the water began to vanish. Why would the Sunlord listen to a snuggery child? He, who was so great you couldn't even gaze at his true face as he moved across the sky? She addressed his emissary instead. After all, Gridelin the Watergiver was supposed to have once been human, until he was raised into the glory of eternal sunfire. *Watergiver, intercede for me*, she prayed, her eyes screwed up tight. *I need to escape snuggery service.*

When she opened her eyes again, only a damp patch

remained. She watched its edges contract. *Like magic*, she thought. People said that was proof a prayer had been heard.

But, the coldly sensible part of her head said in return, *that doesn't mean the prayer will be answered.*

CHAPTER TWO

Scarpen Quarter
Scarcleft City
Opal's Snuggery and the Cistern Chambers, Level 32

Terelle shifted to the shade and just in case the Sunlord withheld his aid, she schemed. Or tried to. Trouble was, nothing came to her. No sudden revelation, no miraculous idea. Her eyes watered with threatening tears. She rubbed at an eyelid, and then regarded the wetness there resentfully. No one else she knew ever shed tears when they wept. Tears only came to others when they had grit in the eye, or smoke. It was just a silly habit she had, absurdly pointless. Water wasn't supposed to be wasted.

A soft rhythmic drumming and tinkle of harness turned her attention to the street once more. A lone rider travelled downlevel past the snuggery, mounted on a myriapede hack, his face hidden by the brim of his hat. People in the street scattered out of his way. Nobody wanted to argue with a pede. Even the smaller hacks were taller than any man and had mouthparts as long and as sharp as scimitars.

When Terelle stuck her head through the balustrade to

see the rider better, she realised his mount was a particularly fine one: the segment scales were a burnished wine-red, edged with gold tassels. Two feelers, inlaid with gold wire in intricate patterns and each as long as three men lying end to end, touched the walls on either side of the street as the pede passed by. The embroidered saddle and gem-studded reins were richly ornate. The rhythmic undulations of its eighteen pairs of pointed legs—three pairs to a segment—did not miss a beat as the animal flowed down the steps. On its second segment, within reach of the rider at the front, were tied several zigger cages and a zigtube. Terelle's heart skipped a beat.

Ziggers . . .

No, don't remember. Don't remember any of it. Think about something else.

So she wondered who this Scarperman was who rode with his zigger cages so openly displayed. Ziggers were expensive to own and even more expensive to train. Yet despite his display of wealth, the rider himself was plainly dressed. The white desert tunic over loose pants gathered in at the ankle and the broad-brimmed palmubra hat woven of bab leaf were standard garb for desert riders. He wore no jewellery, nothing that drew attention to him, but the self-confident certainty with which he rode gave him an aura of power.

Perhaps, she thought, he wasn't a Scarperman. Perhaps he was a Reduner caravanner, travelling far from the quadrant he acknowledged as his own.

As he passed, he looked up, enabling her to see his swarthy face. She knew then that he was no Reduner. She'd seen him once before in the street, in fact, and the warden mistress had told her who he was: Taquar Sardonyx, one of the rainlords of the Scarpen Quarter and Highlord of Scarcleft City.

Why does he need ziggers? she wondered. As highlord, he answered to no one but the Cloudmaster, in Breccia City. As highlord, he had the power of life and death over every citizen in Scarcleft and controlled every drop of the city's water, of *her* water. As a rainlord, which all highlords were, he could kill or torture with his power, without ever having to resort to ziggers. He was known to be relentless in his pursuit and punishment of water thieves. As a rainlord, he took the water from the dead.

Like Donnick. *Oh, Donnick.*

Cold grey eyes did not flicker as his gaze met hers and then moved on. There could be nothing to interest him in a child poking her head through a snuggery balustrade, but she shivered nonetheless.

"Terelle! What are you doing out there in the sun without a hat?"

Startled, she jumped, bumping her head on the railing. Garri the steward had come into the courtyard below and was now frowning up at her, his face pinched into a picture of long-suffering.

"Weeding the pot plants," she lied. "I've finished now."

"We've bought a tenth of water and Reeve Bevran said they would channel it an hour before dusk. That's now, and everyone's too busy to attend to it. Go up to the Cistern Chambers and meet him."

"Me?" Garri had never before shirked the supervision of the channelling of water. However, he was limping heavily as he crossed the courtyard, and then she remembered the way Rosscar had kicked him the night before.

He stopped to stare at her, his heavy eyebrows drawn

into one of his many expressions of disapproval, which were generally accompanied by a mutter under his breath such as: "Why is it I have to tell everyone everything twice?" This time it was: "Yes, you! Get up to the chambers and meet the reeve before he gets tired of waiting. And take a hat!"

Terelle nodded and ran down the stairs into the house, pausing only to grab a palmubra from the stand by the door to the courtyard. Garri was waiting by the gate to let her out. "Remember," he said, "one tenth, already paid for. Make withering sure the Karsts next door don't siphon any off. Here's the snuggery seal. Bevran will show you how to press this into the wax to seal the cistern cover afterwards."

Terelle hid a smile and slipped through the gate into the street. Garri had maintained an acrimonious feud with the Karst family's steward for so long, no one remembered how it had started. She hurried up South Way to the chambers that housed the supply cistern serving their level. The gateman let her into the courtyard where Reeve Bevran was already waiting. He smiled a greeting as he raised a questioning eyebrow. "Terelle? *You* are coming with me? Where's Garri?"

"Limping," she said.

Bevran grinned. "For him to admit it, it must be bad."

She grinned back. "He didn't say a word."

"Ah. And he trusts you to do this, little one?"

"Would you cheat us, Reeve Bevran?" she asked pertly.

He tapped her on the nose. "Mind your manners, or you'll come to a dry end." He gestured her inside and led the way downstairs to the water tunnel. At the entrance, he picked up a lighted lantern and said, "Take your shoes off and put on a pair of these." He indicated a pile of rough-woven sandals. "We don't dirty the tunnel with street sandals. And keep to the walkway. We don't tread where the water runs."

Her daydreams had never included the possibility that she, a Gibber-born snuggery girl, would ever tread the sanctum of a water tunnel. She gazed around in awe at the ancient brickwork, as neat now as the day it was fashioned by unknown workmen. The reeve's oil lamp flickered and their shadows danced on the curve of walls interrupted only by a brick path built along one side of the tunnel. Only the bricks at the bottom were damp; she had expected it to be wetter.

"I don't see you as often as I used to," the reeve said. "You don't come to play with Felissa as often."

"I've got more chores now," she said. Her regret stirred; she liked his daughter and would gladly have knocked on the Bevran gateway more often if she'd had the time.

"Ah." He cleared his throat in an embarrassed fashion. "Hmm. Er, Madam Opal hasn't got you working in one of the upper chambers, has she?"

"No. I'm not old enough." Huckman the pedeman loomed in her thoughts. *How much is your first-night price, child? How much will Opal sell you for?*

"Good." He sounded relieved. "It is not legal for children. Remember that."

She was surprised at his tone and then realised with astonishment that he didn't like the idea of her working as a handmaiden any more than she herself did. Sensing an ally, she blurted, "I don't want to work in the upper rooms at all."

He stopped and turned to look at her, holding the lamp

up high so that he could see her face. Once again he cleared his throat. "Oh, Terelle . . ."

The regret in those words, coupled with his silence, told her more than anything Vivie had ever said. There was nothing anyone could do. Opal had watered her for five years; she was entitled to collect her dues.

"Couldn't the waterpriests—" she began in desperation, feeling the flutter of panic once more.

"Bargains over water and water debts are not the affairs of priests, Terelle. Their concern is with worship of the Sunlord and his Watergiver. If they bothered themselves with petty concerns and neglected their prayers, who knows what could happen?"

"What about rainlords, then? Don't they have some say in water debts?"

"Their job is to make sure that no one gets any water he is not entitled to. They would support Madam Opal. If she put you to work in the upper rooms before you reached your, um, womanhood, or if she forced you to pleasure men, you could protest, but she *is* entitled to have you pay off your water debt. You *could* work in the kitchens instead." He paused and then added softly, "Come and play with Felissa whenever you want."

His unspoken words lingered: *while you can.*

"Thank you." The reply sounded small and weak in the echo of the tunnel. She blinked back treacherous tears. It wasn't *fair*.

He walked on and she followed, her thoughts rebellious. She pictured the snuggery kitchen, with its huge ovens and fireplaces, and Dauvrid the cook with his foul temper. The kitchen maid started work each day before anyone else was up; the scullery maid went to bed only when the last dish had been washed. Neither of them ever had a day off. And they worked for little more than water and their keep. *No*, she thought fiercely. *I won't do that, either. I won't, I won't. Not ever.*

"This is the first of the inlets to houses between the level-supply cistern and the snuggery," Reeve Bevran said a moment later, and held the lantern up to show her the large metal sheet recessed into the floor of the tunnel. "Can you read the lettering on it?"

"*Bevran*," she said. "This is the cover for the inlet of your house."

"It is stamped with a wax seal, which tells me it has not been tampered with. When I buy water for my own family I have to get another reeve to open and re-seal the plate. When it comes to water distribution, we reeves must be above suspicion. Come, let's go on. There are four more outlets you have to inspect before the snuggery's: the Malachites', the Masons', the Karsts', and the myriapede livery's."

They stopped at each for Terelle to check the seal. When they finally arrived at the snuggery inlet, Bevran broke the seal and pulled the plate out, manoeuvring it to slip into a groove at the back of the hole.

"There's your snuggery cistern down there," he said. "Take a look."

She peered into the hole. The glint of lamplight on water seemed a long way down.

"Now we go back to release the water," he said.

"How can I be sure it won't spill over the plate and be lost to us?"

He smiled. "You are welcome to stay here and make

sure. But believe me, the amount of water released at any one time is carefully calculated. Anything that overshoots the hole splashes against the plate and then drains back into your cistern."

She nodded. Simple, yet clever. "Who built them? The tunnels, I mean. We didn't have any in the Gibber. Not that I remember, anyway."

"Well," he began as they walked back, "the story goes that once upon a time, water fell from the sky just anywhere, at any time. Random rain, they called it. Sometimes there was too much water, sometimes not enough. Folk never knew where or when to plant because they never knew when the rain would come. People would die of thirst or be drowned in water."

"Drowned?"

"Not able to breathe. Just as travellers sometimes choke on sand during spindevil storms. Anyway, then the Watergiver came, sent by the Sunlord himself. Some say he was a heavenly spirit, sent in the guise of a man. Others say he was just a nomad blessed with holy knowledge. One story says he got lost in the desert and walked into the sky, where the Sunlord taught him to control water and sent him back to teach us."

"At the temple, the priests say he was the first cloudmaster."

"Yes. He taught those who followed how to suck up fresh water from the salt sea to make clouds. He showed them how to bring the clouds to the Warthago Range. Forced high by the hills, they break open."

"And when they break, the water falls out?"

"Yes. They call that rain. Never seen it myself. It soaks into the ground. The Watergiver showed other sensitives—

who became our first stormlords and rainlords—how to
build wells in the Warthago Range and bring the water
from them to Breccia City by tunnel. And that was how
the Time of Random Rain ended."

"Why not just live in the Warthago Range if that's
where the water has to fall?"

"The best place to grow bab palms is in the good soils
at the base of the escarpment, that's why. Warthago Range
is just rock and stone and rough gullies."

"And the other cities?"

"They came later, one by one. Scarcleft, Qanatend,
Portfillik, Portennabar . . ."

"Breakaway, Denmasad and Pediment," she finished.
"The eight cities of the Scarpen Quarter."

"Yes. And there it stopped, because there is a limit
to how much rain can fall from the sky. The cloudmaster had to water the other quarters as well, you see." He
added sadly, "In all those hundreds of years, the tunnels
have supplied every city with exactly the right amount of
water. Until now."

Terelle drew in a sharp breath. His voice was grief-
filled, as if he spoke of something past and done with,
gone forever. In horror she realised that he was *afraid*.
He was a *reeve*, by all that was holy! One of the men and
women who controlled water, and therefore life. If he was
scared . . .

Apprehension rippled up her spine as they came to
a halt where the tunnel ended in a stone wall. Bevran
said, "Behind this wall is the cistern. Water enters it
from the level above." He pointed to a metal wheel in
the wall above a spout. "When I turn this, you'll get
your water."

"But how do you know how long to let it run?" she asked.

He reached into an alcove near the spout and removed one of the objects stowed there. "We use one of these." He showed her a glass timer filled with sand. Etched into the glass were numbers: 1/10. "One extra tenth," he explained. "I leave the valve open for the exact time that the sand runs. These timers are all made by the Cloudmaster's glass-smith, guaranteed accurate." Swiftly he turned the wheel and upended the timer. Water gushed out into the tunnel. "Of course," he continued, "it's more complicated when it is time for the quarterly free allotments to be dispensed. Then we have to make calculations based on how many persons in each household, how old they are and whether they have water allowances anyway. All that is a decision made by a committee of reeves."

She thought about that, then asked, "Who decided how much a day's free allotment was to be in the first place? The Watergiver?"

"Maybe. Certainly that was decided a long, long time ago and as far as I know the size of a personal day jar has never altered. Just as the amount of land under irrigation can never be altered, either. 'Each man shall have his sip and no more, lest the sky run dry,'" he quoted. "Any extra has to be bought, and the buyer has to explain why he needs extra."

She wanted to protest at the injustice done to those who had no free allowance, who were born without an entitlement because of what their parents didn't own or didn't do. She wanted to ask about those who lost their entitlement because of a change in their status.

But she didn't. She knew better. Who was she to question a representative of a highlord? She was a snuggery girl, born waterless, the lowest of the low, and lucky to be alive.

Instead she watched the water swirl out from the supply cistern and into the darkness of the tunnel.

CHAPTER THREE

Scarpen Quarter
Breccia City
Waterhall, Level 1, and Breccia Hall, Level 2

In the half-darkness of the vaulted waterhall, the water was black-surfaced and motionless, a mirror to the lamps lighted by the servants. Of the sixteen oblong cisterns, separated one from the other by stone walkways, twelve were full to the brim and reflected the teardrops of lamp flame.

To Nealrith Almandine—son of Granthon, Cloudmaster of the Quartern—the smell of water was overpowering. It doused any whiff of lamp oil, or any odour of sweat or dust or perfume that might have clung to his body or clothes. He shut his eyes and let its redolence seep into him: pure, cleansing, rejuvenating. For a moment in time he allowed himself to feel the connection: his body, the content of the cisterns around him. Water to water. Life—his life—calling to the source of all life.

If only—
"My lord?"
If only he could control it.

"Highlord?"

If only he had been born a stormlord.

He opened his eyes. With effort, he swallowed the bitterness, the sense that he had been the victim of an unjust fate. That was childish, and he was far from being a child.

Beside him the reeve waited, face impassive, even as the questioning intonation of the echo whispered through the vaults: "Highlord? . . . ighlord? . . . lord? . . . ord?"—until it was lost in the background tinkle of trickling water. "Should we take samples, my lord?"

Nealrith hauled his thoughts back to his responsibilities. "Yes, of course. All the cisterns, as usual."

The man moved to obey. The only other occupant of the hall stayed at Nealrith's side, regarding him with a cynical half-twist to his mouth. "Mist-gathering, Rith?"

Nealrith nodded, acknowledging his abstraction. "Sorry, Kaneth, I have much on my mind." And that was an understatement. Even as he spoke, he was watching the reeve kneeling at the cistern to fill the vials they had brought. The black glass of the water's surface shattered into half-moons of reflected lamplight and Nealrith felt the movement as a shiver across his skin.

"I've noticed," his friend said dryly. "You should talk more about what bothers you, you know. As my old granny used to say, 'A trouble shared is a trouble pared.'"

"From what I know of your old granny, I doubt she was ever given to uttering words of wisdom."

Unrepentant, Kaneth shrugged and grinned. "All right, so it was someone else's granny. But the sentiment remains. What's the matter, Rith?"

"You know what's the matter. And talking about it is

not going to solve anything. Let's see how much is in the overflow cisterns."

"You don't need to see," the other man said flatly.

Nealrith looked at him. The lamplight accentuated the deep grooves of a desert-etched face; even Kaneth's good looks were not immune. *We appear lined and older than our years*, Nealrith thought. And yet they weren't old, either of them, not really. Other men of thirty-five considered themselves in their prime. But Nealrith and Kaneth were both rainlords, and in these times, that made the difference. Kaneth had the advantage, though; he had a fighter's physique, broad shoulders and muscles that spoke of a more youthful strength and vitality. Nealrith was thinner and less toned. *Too much sitting at a desk dealing with city administration*, he thought, and envied his friend. Kaneth's fair hair still glinted straw-gold in the light, while his own was already salted with grey.

"No. I don't need to see," he agreed. The admission was surprisingly hard to make, and he heard his voice sag with the same grief that had aged him. "The two top cisterns are empty. The middle ones are half-full. The lower ones are fine."

"And at this time of the star cycle they should all be brimming."

"Yes." He began to walk up the slight slope between the oblongs of water. "I want to look at the intake."

Kaneth fell in step beside him. "I saw the inspection team return this morning," he remarked.

"Ryka Feldspar and Iani Potch?"

"Who else would I mean?"

"Yes, they are back."

"Will you stop making me drag information out of

you? Did they find anything wrong that would account for the drop in the amount of water arriving here?"

Nealrith knew his hesitation betrayed him. Worry seethed beneath his outward calm. Worry that was close to panic.

"Nothing. Ryka said they rode the whole course, checked the mother cistern, the intakes from the mother wells and every inspection shaft. There was nothing wrong. No signs of theft. Nothing except that the water flow is reduced from what is normal."

"Could she give a reason?"

"The highest well shafts in the Warthago Range do not reach the underground water any more. Which means less water for the mother cistern."

"She has enough water-sense to know that?"

"Granted, she's not much of a rainlord. But Iani? He's one of the best we have. Nothing wrong with *his* water-sense."

"He's also sandcrazy. Last time I saw him, he told me he thought Lyneth was with a nomadic tribe of pedemen who wandered the land, invisible to the rest of us."

Nealrith shook his head sadly. Iani's daughter Lyneth had disappeared in the desert and the rainlord had never been the same since.

"If the groundwater level has fallen . . ." Kaneth hesitated. "The information has implications."

"Do you think I don't know that?" Immediately he'd spat out the words, he wished he had not said them. There was no point in alienating a friend, and Kaneth was that. It was just so *hard* to bridle his worry.

Friend or not, Kaneth had never been one to accept rebuke mildly. He drawled, deliberately provocative, "On the contrary, I am quite sure you do. Your problem is not one of lack of understanding, but of will. The will to do something about it."

"And just what do you think I should do?" Nealrith's tone was still dangerously taut. "Slaughter half the city so there are fewer people who need to drink?"

They had reached the intake from the mother cistern tunnel. The splash of water through the heavy iron grille should have been comforting; instead it unsettled. Nealrith glanced through the bars. The rounded brick walls funnelled away into the darkness until they disappeared in a tiny pinpoint of light. That slim ray would have been sunlight entering at the first of the maintenance chimneys. There must be a crack in the cover. The tunnel did not end there, of course; it went all the way to the foothills of the Warthago Range, three days' ride distant, to the mother cistern, which was fed in turn by pipes from the mother wells.

"Kill some of our citizens . . . the lowlevellers perhaps. Now *there's* an idea," Kaneth replied, dryly sarcastic.

Nealrith grimaced and softened his tone. It was pointless to turn his anxiety into bad temper. He went back to Kaneth's original point. "Implications? Yes. The main one being that there wasn't enough rain last year."

"But there were the right number of rainstorms." Kaneth paused, and then asked, "Weren't there?"

"Oh yes." Nealrith turned to face him. "I haven't lied to you. My father hasn't failed in that regard. Nor will he . . . yet."

"So there was insufficient rain in each storm cloud."

"Obviously."

Kaneth's eyes narrowed.

Nealrith made an exasperated sound and lowered his voice to make sure the reeve could not hear. "All right, I'll say it, Kaneth. My father's powers are failing. You want it even blunter than that? Granthon, Cloudmaster of the Quartern, is gravely ill. Possibly dying. He is not lifting enough water vapour from the sea. Is that what you wanted to hear?"

"No, but I needed to hear you admit it, Nealrith. And I need to hear what you intend to do about it."

Nealrith ignored his words and waved a hand at the tunnel entrance. "Take a sample here."

Kaneth fumbled in his tunic pocket for one of the onyx vials he carried for the purpose. "Can you sense anything wrong?"

"I would say the water is just about as pure as when it came from the skies. Its essence is not wrong, just the amount." Nealrith thrust his hand under the water where it splashed through the grille. He kept it there for a moment before he added, "About half the flow of this time last year. And every star cycle before that. The city's mother cistern is not filling to capacity. Ryka said it is eight handspans too low. They had to adjust the siphon."

"How long before that translates into shortages on the streets?"

Nealrith shrugged. "Depends on when we start rationing."

"We can't wait until these cisterns are empty and the decrease becomes noticeable in the level-supply cisterns down in the city. We have to start rationing now."

"That's . . . drastic."

"Then what about deepening the mother well shafts?"

"It's not a solution, Kaneth. I've spoken to the engineers. The groundwater level needs to be maintained. And the only way to do that is to have sufficient rain."

"The engineers are fossilised old sand-grubbers, you know that." Kaneth turned back to the intake flow and caught some of it in the vial, which he then stoppered. "The city engineer wouldn't replace a single brick of the tunnel if it was left up to him, the sun-dried old fool. Rith, we can't just go jogging along pretending nothing is wrong! Deepen the shafts. Build more shafts. Tap into the groundwater elsewhere and bring water through a new tunnel. Be stricter about the enforcement of birth control—there are still rich folk who have more than two children because they can afford to buy their dayjars. Anything is better than sitting back and waiting for people to die of thirst. Better still—" He paused.

"Better still what?" Nealrith was willing to listen to anything, for how could you ration something that was already apportioned at its acceptable limit? There was no wastage of water in Breccia. Each man, woman and child received exactly what he or she needed for life. Every fruit tree, every palm grove, every jute and flax plant, every vegetable patch received exactly enough for growth and harvest. Ration water and food production would drop. Eventually people would die. They'd starve, if they hadn't already died of thirst.

But Kaneth backtracked. "Are you saying that the Cloudmaster cannot make good the lack?"

"You don't need me to tell you it is unlikely. You've seen him. My father is old beyond his years, and ill. I am going to the Sun Temple after this, to ask Lord Gold to make a heavier sacrifice to the Sunlord. Perhaps that will help."

Kaneth snorted. "Withering waste of water."

They looked at each other, two men who had been friends since the day they had first met as children, almost thirty years earlier. Nealrith's heart lurched. They were like sand grains at the top of a slope too steep for stability, waiting for the landslip, the irrevocable damage, the words that couldn't be taken back. He smothered a desire to change the subject rather than hear something he knew instinctively he would not be able to countenance.

"Spit it out, Kaneth," he said finally. "What is your solution? None of what you have suggested so far is practical. You can't tap into water that simply isn't there. More wells somewhere else would be accessing the same underground water as the present ones do; you know that. And I am assuming that you are not going to recommend wholesale slaughter of a number of our citizens so that the rest of us have enough to drink."

"As much as it might sometimes be tempting," Kaneth said with a flippancy that grated on Nealrith, "one has to draw the line somewhere."

"So?"

"We must let the other three quarters fend for themselves. Your father has more than enough strength to supply us here in the Scarpen Quarter; let the other three find their own water."

Nealrith drew in a sharp breath. "Sunlord help me—you *are* advocating wholesale slaughter! You *can't* be serious."

"I am perfectly serious." And indeed for once he appeared to be. The cynical half-smile, the insouciance, were gone. He was utterly sober. "Save ourselves. It's all we can do."

"It is *unthinkable*."

"Oh no, it's not, for I am thinking it. And I am not the only rainlord to do so."

"Taquar Sardonyx of Scarcleft, too, I suppose," Nealrith said bitterly. "But the idea is ridiculous. Quite apart from the sheer inhumanity, we would have the Reduners battering at our walls with an army of zealot tribesmen mounted on pedes and tapping out ziggers. Have you thought of that? A war on our hands at this time? You should, because you may be one of those who fall with a zigger burrowing up your nose. Although I suppose a war would indeed reduce the number of our citizens in need of water."

Kaneth shrugged dismissively. "All right, keep the Reduners supplied with water, although I suspect they may actually care the least. Many of them think they should return to a time of random rain anyway. But we should stop sending rain to the White's 'Basters and the Gibber grubbers. After all, what have they ever done for us? We don't need them, Rith. They are weeds, sucking up water and producing nothing we cannot do without in the short term."

He caught hold of Nealrith's sleeve. "Think of it. Your father need only supply half the amount of rain. He can do that much. It will buy us time to find other stormlords to help him, to find another to replace him as Cloudmaster when the time comes. He will live longer if he has fewer stresses on him."

"He wouldn't be able to live with himself if he had to do that! The shame and the guilt would kill him. What of those who would die in the White and Gibber quarters?

You are advocating the brutal eradication of two peoples, as if they were rats in the waterhall!"

He had raised his voice and the echoes faded out around them: "waterhall . . . hall . . . all." The reeve looked up from his work, curious. Nealrith lowered his voice to a furious whisper and shook off his friend's hand. "Kaneth, I didn't think even you would be so utterly without conscience."

"*Even* I?" Kaneth stood looking at Nealrith with a sharply raised eyebrow. "Well, *even I* don't want to see my fellow Scarpermen die of thirst. It is you—and your father—who would see us *all* die a lingering death as our gardens and groves wither and the cisterns empty. Tell me, Nealrith, Highlord of Breccia City, which is a better ending: to have all four quarters die slowly, or have two of them prosper and only two succumb to a waterless death? Yes, I'll admit it, I think of myself. Is there shame in that? I want to live! I am looking to settle down at last—to marry into the Feldspar family, actually. But that's neither here nor there. Rith, I want you to propose this solution to Granthon. He will listen to you."

"Never!"

"Then I will. Someone has to have a practical solution for a very real problem, and the Cloudmaster has got to listen. You're a dreamer, Rith, and your scruples will suffocate us all in sand." When Nealrith did not reply, he added, "I warn you, there will be those who will fight for this to the bitter end, and you may not like our methods. We will salvage something from this mess, with you—or in spite of you."

"You can't force my father to do something that goes

against all he has ever worked for: the unity of the four quarters and the prosperity of their peoples."

"That's just *words*, Rith. There has never been unity. Or prosperity, either, if you were to ask a Gibberman. It may have been Granthon's dream in his younger days, but he never achieved anything like it. And now we have a problem. And even you have to admit that there are only two possible solutions, at least in the long term. We either find several more stormlords—and we've had a singular lack of success there, you must admit—or we reduce the number of water drinkers. It is as simple as that."

Nealrith said nothing, knowing that it wasn't simple at all.

It was a choice between the apparently impossible and the totally unconscionable. He turned away so that Kaneth wouldn't see his revulsion, or his grief at the widening breach in a long-time friendship.

Breccia, like all Scarpen cities, was a single entity. Even though the narrow streets radiating downwards from Breccia Hall sliced through it, even though the winding lanes circling each level were cracks in its cohesion, every part of the city was linked. Houses and villas grew into one another, sharing walls, connected by their flat roofs, interlocked beneath the ground by arteries of brick tunnels supplying water.

The first and highest level contained only the water hall. On the next was Breccia Hall, and the remaining thirty-eight levels spilled down the escarpment slope in the shape of a fan. The lowest level at the base, inhabited by day labourers and the waterless, was a tattered flounce to the city. Although hemmed with a wall, parts of this dirty petticoat to Breccia seeped out through the gates in the form of foundries and liveries, kilns and furnaces, knackers' and slaughter yards. Another trimming to the city was more salubrious: the bab groves, the rows of trees interspersed with slots and cisterns and vegetable plots. Beyond them were only the drylands, the Sweepings to the north and the Skirtings to the south.

Level Three, where Nealrith headed after leaving the waterhall, was home to the city's richest inhabitants and the main house of worship, the Sun Temple, with its attached House of the Dead. After speaking with Lord Gold, the Quartern Sunpriest, Nealrith backtracked to Breccia Hall on Level Two. The hall was the traditional residence of the ruler of the Quartern, and was therefore now home to Granthon Almandine and the rest of the Almandine family. Granthon's father, Garouth, had preceded him in the post. When the old man had died ten years earlier, Granthon had succeeded to his father's position by virtue of his talent, not his birth. Unfortunately, Granthon was now not just the Cloudmaster of the Quartern, but the Quartern's only stormlord.

Nealrith Almandine knew his father's life had been far from easy. If the histories were correct, in some eras there had been several hundred stormlords scattered through the Quartern. Even during Nealrith's own childhood there had been ten or eleven, but one by one they had died, leaving only Granthon. For five years, the Cloudmaster had shouldered his responsibility without the help of another stormlord, a burden too great for any one man no matter how talented. Worse still, he'd been forced to acknowledge to the world that Nealrith, his only child, was not a stormlord and never would be. It had been a bitter blow to both father and son.

Granthon was kind enough never to mention his disappointment and wise enough never to reproach Nealrith for a lack beyond any man's power to remedy, but he could do nothing about the bleakness in his gaze. Nealrith saw it every time his father looked at him, and suffered that same blow again and again.

If only. If only.

When Nealrith entered the stormquest room of Breccia Hall, his father was reclining on a divan, propped up by cushions, while Ethelva hovered uncertainly behind her husband, wanting to fuss over a man who loathed fuss. Nealrith concealed a sigh. His mother was still tall and elegant, but her calm had long since become careworn, and the evidence was there in her prematurely white hair and the worry lines of her face. She was a water-blind woman renowned for her common sense, and Nealrith was not used to seeing her so indecisive, but Granthon's illness had lapped too long at her every thought. She had become prey to doubt, just as Nealrith had, filled with uncertainties about the future of the family and, indeed, the land itself.

Nealrith delivered his assessment of Breccia's water storage and the tale it told: his father had cut back too much on the size of his storms. Granthon said nothing at the news. His stillness was unnatural, as if he had even forgotten to breathe.

"Father?" Nealrith asked.

The Cloudmaster stirred. His gaze dithered around the room, lingering for a moment on the scroll racks and the rolled documents they contained. The lectern in front of him was spread with the parchment he had been considering when his son had entered the room.

"Father—"

"Open the shutters, Rith."

"Father, no. You have done too much today already. You can't drive yourself beyond—"

"Every day that I allow the levels to fall is another day I will not be able to make up."

That was true, and Nealrith knew it. He took a deep breath and pushed away thoughts of what should have been, of that insidious *if only*. "If you do too much, you will die, and where will we be then?"

"You have to find a replacement for me."

"We've been looking for as long as I remember." He concealed his frustration and tried to ease the tightness in his gut. Kaneth was right, damn him; they had to do something other than *talk*.

His father made a slight movement of his right hand, an opening out, as if he had just taken an unwelcome decision. "There's one place no one has looked. Two actually, although not even I would think of looking among the 'Basters."

Nealrith was confused. "In the White Quarter? Of course not! Where, then?"

"The Gibber."

Nealrith made a gesture of irritation. "A waste of time, surely. From what I've heard, there are very few water sensitives, and there's never been a rainlord or a stormlord from there. You know the saying, 'Wash a crow with rosewater and it still won't be pink.' They are a water-blind people. Worse, they are stupid and ignorant and dirty and dishonest."

His mother interrupted. "Don't judge, Rith. Perhaps they are dirty because they don't have enough water, ignorant because they have never been taught and dishonest because they are so poor. A thirsty man might steal to live."

"And what about the stupid part?" he asked wryly.

"Perhaps they are stupid merely because you haven't the wit to see them any other way."

He had the grace to laugh. "All right, all right. They are not as bad as I think and I displayed a bias that was both unjustified and unworthy of me; you are probably right about that. But that still doesn't make them water sensitive. They have never paid more than the barest of lip service to the Sunlord and the Watergiver, which might explain it. We would do better to look in the White Quarter; they at least are a pious people who have some water sensitives. Or so I'm told."

Granthon held up a hand. "We both know that the trouble with the White Quarter is not their sensitivity but their secrecy. We are not welcome there, and who can blame them? They have been spat upon for generations. Anyway, it takes more than sensitivity to make a rainlord, let alone a stormlord. We have more chance among the Gibber folk. At least they look up to the Scarpen. I suspect they would gladly give us their water-talented children."

"Fools," Nealrith muttered, but the remark said as much about his opinion of his own quadrant as it did about the people from the Gibber.

"I want you to go there," Granthon said. "A quest to find a potential stormlord. I want you to run the tests in every Gibber settle on the plains. Take Iani with you. It will give him something to focus his mind on."

Nealrith was appalled. "You want *two* rainlords out

searching the Gibber? *Why?* Anyone can conduct the tests for water sensitivity. It doesn't need a rainlord!" *And I have a city to run.*

"I may not be much of a storm gatherer nowadays, Nealrith, but I am still in full command of my senses."

"You must have a reason."

"Other than desperation? Yes, two, in fact. My passion for our land's history has rendered up a reward. A name and a place. I didn't do the actual research work; I passed that to Ryka Feldspar. She has a scholar's mind." He smiled at Ethelva. "I wonder sometimes if we don't underestimate our women, Nealrith. She found that one of my predecessors—from a very long time ago—bore a name that sounds as if it came from the Gibber. Gypsum Miner of Wash Drybarrow."

Nealrith stared, speechless.

"The long history of mining in the Gibber means they have more family names related to that ancient occupation than we do," his father continued. "Their constant fossicking has led them to use minerals and rocks as personal names all the time. And 'wash' is the Gibber word for dry riverbed, what we'd call a gully."

Nealrith was impatient. "Wash Drybarrow is an actual Gibber settle?"

"Well, Ryka found a Wash Dribarra, which has a settle. After that, I sent some of my people out to talk to Gibber folk down on Level Forty."

He was intrigued in spite of himself. "What did they find out?"

"Gibber reeves manage matters pertaining to water. However, unlike our reeves, who must have water skills, they usually have none. There *are* occasional water sensitives among Gibber folk, but they are regarded as potential water thieves. As a consequence, a child exhibiting water sensitivity usually has the tendency beaten out of him."

Ethelva gave an unladylike snort. "Or rather, they have the tendency to *admit* to it beaten out of them."

"Exactly. Rith, I want rainlords testing in the Gibber because I don't want the slightest chance that a water sensitive child, or an adult for that matter, is missed. I want more than standard tests. I want you to hunt for any sign of people there who may be hiding their talent deliberately."

Nealrith considered that. "I suppose it doesn't make sense that there should be water sensitives here but not in the Gibber. We are supposed to have had the same origins."

"Even Reduner sandmasters and tribemasters have some talent with water," Ethelva said, "and they aren't supposed to be related to us at all."

Granthon nodded. "We have searched the Red Quarter and the Scarpen—scoured them, more like—for the past twenty-five years, and found nothing. Think, Rith. The three new talents we identified in that time, we found right here at home. Your daughter Senya, Iani's Lyneth, and Ryka Feldspar. Ryka may be the daughter of a rainlord, but her power is weak. And Senya looks to be no better. Lyneth, now—but we all know what happened to Lyneth."

He fell silent, and Ethelva squeezed his hand. Even Nealrith was discomforted by the memory. How could he forget? She had been the hope of the Quartern, Iani's lovely six-year-old daughter. Dark-eyed and dimpled and plump, she had charmed them all with her lively inquisitiveness, her mischievous charm. And she'd been stormlord-talented. Then one day some fifteen years past, on a routine journey with her parents to attend a family wedding in another Scarpen city, she had wandered off into the desert. Nealrith felt sick about it even now. They had never found her body, and her father had never recovered from the shock. Iani the Sandcrazy—he had blamed himself because he was the rainlord of the group; he should at least have been able to follow the trace of her water.

Granthon stirred restlessly. "Only three children in almost thirty years—and we didn't even have to look for them, as they were all born to rainlords. What harm can it do to search the Gibber?"

"Father, it'll take a year or more! What about my duties here?"

"They can be shared by the city's other rainlords. This is important." Granthon lay back, fumbling for the support of the cushions. "Let's just say that we found a child in the Scarpen or the Red Quarter who has the potential to be a stormlord. It would be many more years before they would be skilled enough to help me." He gave a sick smile. "By that time we could all have died of thirst. On the other hand, if you find someone in the Gibber, they could perhaps be older and closer to attaining their full powers."

Nealrith grimaced. "I once had my purse cut by a waterless Gibberman, and I've seen how they live down on the last level. Hovels, reeking with vermin. And you should hear what caravanners say about travelling through the Gibber itself. They have to pay outrageous taxes just for passing through, whether they take water or not. If they don't pay up, they risk getting raided. Murdered even. Is that the kind of person we want as a new stormlord?"

"You are not usually so quick to judge!" his mother snapped. "Every pot is black on the bottom. They are not the only ones with a dark underside. There will be many good folk among them, too."

He forced a smile. "I'll try to remember that."

"Do so," she said with some asperity. "If there are ills on Level Forty, then ask yourself if that is not the fault of the city's ruler." Before he could retort, she added, "Perhaps the two of you should ask yourselves this: Why do we lack talented children all of a sudden?"

"What do you mean?" Nealrith asked, still smarting from her implied criticism of his rule.

"Just that. Never before has the Quartern been short of stormlords, let alone rainlords. Perhaps we should be looking for the reason."

It was Granthon who answered. "There's nothing so unusual in going for a time with so few stormlords born. My study of history has taught me that much. It will change; it always does. In the past it never mattered much if there was a gap in births, because there were enough older rainlords or stormlords to manage until a new generation came along. It's just that this time we have been unlucky. We lost a lot of young, talented people."

Nealrith nodded. He'd numbered good friends among them.

"Two were probable stormlords and the others were possibles. Such a tragedy. Iani's Lyneth was just the last," Granthon said.

"Garouth called the deaths an unnatural coincidence,"

Ethelva said thoughtfully, then reminded Nealrith, "Your grandfather put all you younger rainlords—those who might have developed into stormlords—under guard after that."

"Unnatural? They were just unfortunate accidents and illnesses," Granthon said, but his protest was hesitant, as if he doubted its truth. "Two disappeared during a spindevil windstorm, I remember. We nearly lost Taquar Sardonyx then, too." He shook his head sadly. "I had high hopes of Taquar. I thought he might just make a stormlord. He came so close, but never had quite enough pull. I wondered if what he suffered in the sandstorm might not have been the reason he lost the edge a stormlord needs. So close, so close, and he took it badly."

He shifted position, trying to get comfortable. "He offered me his aid recently, you know. He added his strength to mine, to see if it helped me."

Nealrith tried to quell the jealousy that raged through him at the thought. *It should have been me.* But then, what would have been the point? They both knew the limitations of Nealrith's rainlord skills.

"No, I didn't know. When was this?" he asked.

Ethelva came to rearrange the cushions at Granthon's back as he elaborated. "Last year when you were out inspecting the tunnels. I tried to teach him the knack of gathering a cloud out of the sea." He sighed. "He is stronger than you, certainly, but not as strong as I hoped. He had nothing to lend me that would make any difference."

"Oh. He wouldn't have been holding back deliberately, would he?"

His father lashed out with a hint of his old energy. "That suggestion is unworthy of you! And ridiculous."

Nealrith flushed. "Perhaps. Father, there's something you should know. Kaneth and, I suspect, Taquar, and maybe others as well, are saying that we should abandon the 'Basters and the Gibber folk. That you should bring rain only to the Red and Scarpen Quarters."

To his surprise, his father said merely, "Ah yes. Taquar mentioned that to me. Several years back, when it became clear that we were not going to find any more stormlords in a hurry. He regards both quarters as expendable. In a way, he is right. We don't need them for our survival. We'd be short of resin and salt and soda and some minerals, but we'd survive." He looked up at his son. "So he's persuaded Kaneth to his point of view, has he?"

"It's an . . . an evil idea. How can they even *consider*—"

"Nealrith, don't be a fool. This is exactly the sort of thing we may have to consider. I will have to decide soon which areas must get no rain at all so that I have the strength to bring rain elsewhere. Would you rather we die first?"

Nealrith stared at his father in horror.

"Ah, I see. You would have us all go down together, so that no one survives at all?"

"I can't believe you would—"

"Believe it!" his father growled in another display of his old strength. "Stop dreaming, Nealrith. Even if you find a potential stormlord or two in the Gibber Quarter, we may have to let whole parts of the Quartern die. There won't be a choice. My disagreement with Taquar is over *when* to do it, not *whether* to do it. He wants me to conserve my energies as long as possible by cutting down on cloudmaking. It's a wise strategy; I'm just not quite desperate enough to do it yet. But if you fail in the Gibber

Quarter, then yes, I will withhold rainstorms from that whole Quarter. And the White Quarter, too."

For a moment Nealrith stood, immobile, the blood drained from his face. Ethelva came and laid a hand on his arm. He turned to look at her and saw the acquiescence there, written in her eyes. His horror deepened, choking off thought. His *mother* could believe such a solution was necessary?

"Do as your father asked, dear. Open the shutters."

He strove for coherence. "Sandblighted eyes, Mother, he—"

"Nealrith, just do it."

He made a gesture of negation but threw open the shutters anyway. Light blasted in on a wave of dry heat, both so intense he winced.

Granthon did not bother to look down at the slopes of the city below; instead he squinted towards the horizon and waited for his eyes to adjust. Nealrith knew he was already assessing the distant water in the air, far beyond a mere rainlord's perception.

"The conditions are good," he said. "Can you see, Nealrith?"

It took a moment, but then he could indeed see wispy clouds dissolving and coalescing above where the Giving Sea bordered the southern limits of the Quartern. Not many, but enough to make Granthon's stormquest easier.

"Yes," Nealrith said heavily. *If only I could help!* Guilt rippled through him. Irrational, he knew. It wasn't his fault that he was no more than an average rainlord. Watergiver knew he tried.

Then his father's focus was gone from him, turned inwards, pushed outwards, whatever it was that he did at moments like this, with whatever power he possessed. Nealrith gazed at the cloud over the sea and tried to imagine that he could see the changes his father wrought, the gathering of water, the building of the dark storm clouds packed with the potential of life-giving rain.

For a long while there was nothing; then the storm clouds were there, growing larger and darker by the moment. Time passed; a servant entered the room twice to upend the sandglass. The clouds moved away from the sea, rose higher, slowly shifted closer across the Skirtings.

His father lay, propped up on the divan at the window, bathed in sweat. Giving up his own water in the effort. His own life seeping away as he reached the limits of his power. His skin was pale, his breathing shallow; his body shivered.

Nealrith shot a look at his mother, knowing he could not keep his fear out of the glance.

"Yes, it is too much," she whispered, the words soft, her voice resigned. "It was too soon. One day he will not come back." She held her son's gaze. "One day there will be one stormquest too many."

He tried to swallow, but his mouth was dry. "Could it be . . . today?"

"No, no, not yet. A year, two . . . who knows? Lord Gold makes sacrifices, the Sun Temple worshippers pray for him, the High Physician doses him; perhaps one of them will find the miracle they seek. We all do what we can. I no longer grow flowers. I bathe infrequently. I don't give my clothes to be washed so often."

He looked back at the clouds. They would bypass the city to the east, and they moved as if they rode winds across the sky. He knew there were no winds; there never were. Nothing except the force a stormlord sent from himself. All being well, soon they would reach the Warthago Range and be forced to rise and drop their rain.

Priests explained all water-power by saying the Sunlord had gifted it to his believers in order to mitigate the ferocity of his radiance. That made sense to Nealrith. A god by his very nature must always overwhelm, and water-power evened up the balance. What puzzled him was why the Sunlord had not helped as the stormlords disappeared one by one from the Quartern. Why had he not ensured the birth of others?

I mustn't question, he thought. *The Sunlord knows best and the priests say we must accept his will. Everything happens for a reason.*

He looked back at his father, the last stormlord in the land. He wanted to help him, yet he knew in his heart he was glad he didn't have to give up so much of himself to keep others alive. He was glad his whole life was not governed by the quest for storms. Still, he would have done it to help his father, to prevent the Cloudmaster's life seeping away from him, his strength draining drop by precious drop.

And then Granthon cried out, a heart-rending cry of pain and outrage and despair.

Ethelva gasped and dropped to her knees at his side, grabbing for his hand, but Granthon pushed her away.

"No!" he cried. "*No—*"

"Father, what is it?" Nealrith's heart was pounding. He couldn't even begin to guess what had gone wrong. He glanced at the storm clouds again. They were dark enough to carry rain and they were heading—as far as he could tell—in the right direction.

Granthon clutched at him. "Nealrith," he said, and shock made his voice quaver, "someone took it away from me. *Someone stole my storm.*"

CHAPTER FOUR

Scarpen Quarter
Breccia City
Feldspar House, Level 3

"Ryka, Ryka, come quickly!"

Ryka Feldspar looked up as her younger sister Beryll came skidding across the terracotta tiles into the room, grinning with a mixture of delight and mischief. "Quickly, change out of that horrible tunic thing and wear something pretty, for pity's sake. Your Destined One is here! Talking to Papa."

Ryka pushed away the document she had been translating and looked short-sightedly at Beryll, who was already rooting through her wardrobe. It shook alarmingly under the onslaught.

"What *are* you doing?" Her newest silk outfit, intended to be worn for the first time at the annual Temple Gratitudes, came sailing through the air and only her quick reflexes stopped it from overturning the ink jar. "Beryll, please! Stop and tell me what's going on."

Her sister's head ducked down into the cupboard, her voice muffled as she rummaged through footwear. "Lord

Kaneth Carnelian is here, asking to see you. Mama way-laid him and sent me to tell you to dress nicely."

She looked at Beryll blankly. "Uh?"

Her sister emerged triumphant, waving a pair of em-broidered slippers. "He's come as a suitor, you dryhead! Oh, Ryka—how did you manage to get ink all over your fingers? You'd better wash."

Ryka laughed, unbelieving, and went to return the dress to the wardrobe. "Whatever he's here for, it's cer-tainly not as my suitor. He might have an eye on you in a year or two, perhaps, if he wanted to marry a Feldspar. But I doubt he'll ever marry. He likes his women pretty and plentiful and playful, does Kaneth."

And he likes snuggery jades, too, from all accounts, she added sourly to herself.

Beryll laughed. "He's too *old* for me. At least thirty-five. Besides, I'm not a rainlord. You are. And so is he. Two rainlords: more chance of a stormlord child. Mama says there's a rumour that the Cloudmaster ordered Kaneth to marry if he wanted to continue to receive a rainlord al-lowance from the Quartern's coffers. The only other un-married rainlord female is Senya Almandine and she's a child, so what does that tell you?"

Ryka stilled, and the silk slid to the floor, unheeded. "Are you serious, Beryll?" she asked at last. "Cloudmas-ter Granthon *ordered* him?"

"After a fashion. Marry, or find tokens in short supply."

She felt the colour drain from her face and abruptly sat down again.

"You have a dowry you didn't even know about!" Be-ryll crowed.

"Even though I'm so low in talent I'm only a cat's whisker from being a mere reeve?" She pursed her lips, her anger growing. If Kaneth really was coming to propose, then he had a cheek! Suddenly willing to marry her because he needed a rainlord's allowance from the treasury? She'd have something to say about that.

"Maybe so, but you're the best the Quartern's got for Kaneth." Beryll grinned, enjoying her sister's discomfort. She did a little dance, scooped the outfit from the floor without breaking step and thrust it at Ryka with a flourish. "Like it or not, you're getting married!"

"Not if I can help it!" She snatched the dress and threw it back into the wardrobe with scant respect for its fragility. "I am certainly not wearing *that* to meet Kaneth. Spindevil take it, Beryll—we grew up together and if he doesn't know exactly what I look like by now, then he's a lot more dense than I thought." She refused to even glance in the polished surface of the mirror stone, and stalked out of the room, exactly as she was. She couldn't believe Kaneth was thinking of marriage to her anyway. The idea was ludicrous.

Plain Ryka, the other girls had called her in their younger years. The boys, still too young to appreciate her long legs and golden hair, had been even less kind. They'd taunted her with names like mangle-gangle or fumble-tumble, because a combination of short-sightedness and dreaminess meant she tended to trip over things a lot. Kaneth had been one of the worst of her tormentors.

When they were all older, the girls had—more kindly—encouraged her to improve her looks with powders and paints, but she'd always known the results were absurd. She was too solid of body, too mannish in the way she moved, too tall, too . . . un-dainty. Moreover, she had a habit of creasing her brow when she squinted to see better, which gave her an unjustified reputation for bad temper. As time passed, the boys, young men by then, had simply drifted away, indifferent, to marry others. And Ryka had shrugged and got on with her life. At least her eyesight didn't hamper her reading; it was only when things were more than a pace or two away that they started to go blurry.

Now, as she took the stairs two at a time on her way down to the reception room, Beryll following her, she frowned again, not caring if she appeared forbidding. By the time she entered the room where Kaneth waited with her parents, she felt thunderous and guessed it was obvious. She ignored the signal of her mother's desperately fluttering hands, and glared at Kaneth.

Her father said, "Ah, there you are. Kaneth has something to say to you. Come, my dear," he added, taking his wife's arm and ushering Beryll out at the same time, "we'll leave them to talk things over."

Kaneth, who had also risen, came across to her saying, "Sorry to disturb you. Your father said you were busy translating some Reduner scrolls for the Cloudmaster."

"Yes. And Beryll said you've been ordered to marry."

He looked taken aback. "News travels fast."

"And that you have me in mind."

"Blighted eyes, Ryka, can't you at least let me do the asking?"

She folded her arms. "All right. Go ahead."

"I was thinking of something more romantic. You know, out under a flowering orange tree or something. A stroll on the rooftop."

"Don't be ridiculous. This is *me* you're talking to, Kaneth. Ryka Feldspar. Tell me you have suddenly developed an overwhelming passion that necessitates a romantic proposal doused in the scent of orange blossom and I shall laugh in your face."

"You are not making this easy for me."

"Why in all the Scarpen should I? You are only proposing because you've been ordered to."

"There's more to it than that—"

"So I was informed. Cloudmaster Granthon threatened to cut your allowance."

"Er, well, yes, but—"

"But nothing! We fight like a couple of horned mountain cats every time we meet, you chase every female who bats her eyelids at you and you sleep with anyone who will have you, and then you expect me to fall into your arms because you take the trouble to arrange a romantic interlude for a proposal? I can only assume you are out of your sunfried mind. Have you been going outside without a hat on your head?"

He stared at her.

She kept her arms folded and glared back.

He said, "I take it that you are going to say no?"

"Did you doubt it?"

He looked uncomfortable. "Er, yes, I did. I thought that if the Cloudmaster ordered it and seeing the Quartern needs stormlord children—"

"Oh, so you don't *really* want to marry *me*. You just want my children. Lovely proposal."

He paused. Then, "Why do I get the idea that whatever I say, it will be the wrong thing?"

"Maybe because you're finally thinking straight. Granthon didn't speak to *me* about this, you know. As least not lately, and not naming you. And anyway, what difference would it make if he had? I am an inadequate rainlord at the best of times. You could marry Beryll and have just as much chance of talented children."

"I don't *want* to marry Beryll! I want to marry you."

She arched an eyebrow in disbelief.

"Curse it all, Ryka, you know the fix we are all in. We need stormlords, and we all have to make sacrifices—"

She gritted her teeth, her rage close to overwhelming her. "So marrying me would be a *sacrifice*, would it? Wonderful. I suppose giving up all your snuggery handmaidens would be a terrible sacrifice indeed. No, wait a moment. I don't suppose your idea of sacrifice goes *quite* that far."

He flushed, but she couldn't tell if it was anger or shame that put the colour in his face. "Ryka, I am willing to do whatever it takes to bring more water to the Quartern. And you should be, too. This is not about us—it's about the possibility of our children becoming the saviours of us all."

She made a sound of exasperated fury. "That's something you should have been thinking about ten years ago, Kaneth Carnelian. But no, you were having too much fun. And only *now* you are having an attack of guilty conscience?"

"All right, I admit it. I haven't been a model rainlord. And I always thought that if anyone was going to have stormlord children it would be Taquar or Nealrith, and I could leave it up to them. Well, for whatever reason, they haven't, and that leaves us, you and me. Ryka, I have been—well—yes, er, I do like women. I love women. I love bedding them. But the kind of women I bed aren't the kind I want to be the mother of my children. In fact, you and I, we—"

"Oooh!" She clenched her fists, quelling an almost overwhelming desire to punch him on the nose. Or better still, lower down. A lot lower down. "So I am good enough to have your children, but I'm not someone you'd ever want to *bed*? 'We' nothing, Kaneth Carnelian. There is no 'we' and there never will be!"

She turned on her heel and wrenched open the door, only to find herself face to face with Beryl, who'd had her ear pressed to the panelling. Ryka hissed at her in fury and stalked away.

Beryl, eyes bright with interest, watched her go and then turned her attention to Kaneth. "You are *such* a dryhead," she said. "You really messed that up, didn't you? Maybe you *should* think about marrying me instead."

"Marry an eavesdropping brat? Beryl, you are impossible. And you shouldn't listen at doors." He shouldered past her, grabbed up his palmubra in the hallway and let himself out.

Beryl grinned and made her way upstairs again.

Back in her room, Ryka plonked herself down at her desk and picked up her pen to continue the translation. Only this time, she dug the chitin nib into the flax paper with such force the ink spattered.

"Go away," she said when Beryl entered.

Beryl ignored the request. "Ryka, you're sandcrazy. You're twenty-eight—where do you think you are going to find another marriage partner at your age?"

"Why should I want one? What's so marvellous about

being married? I can be perfectly happy *un*married. I can even have children if I want." She dabbed furiously at the ink spatters with her sleeve.

Beryll came and sat on the edge of the desk, looking interested. "Oh?"

"What I ought to do is have a child with Taquar. There'd be a much better chance he would have a storm-lord offspring. His water sensitivity is as strong as it gets in a rainlord."

"I thought you didn't like Taquar."

She shrugged. "I wouldn't have to *live* with him. But he's handsome. I am sure he'd be a good lover. From what I've heard, he's just as experienced as Kaneth."

"I can't believe you just said that! Ryka, what's got into you? I know you and Kaneth argue a lot, but you once told me you liked it that way, because he was one of the few people who had the brains to think things through. A man who didn't have a hypocritical bone in his body, I think you said."

"Ah. I take that last one back, for sure."

Beryll cocked her head and considered all that had happened. Then her eyes widened. "Oh, my. You—oh my sandblighted wits—you're in *love* with him!"

Ryka rolled her eyes towards the ceiling. "With Taquar? Nonsense!"

"Stop being deliberately obtuse! Why didn't I see it? And don't deny it; it's written all over you. You're in love with Kaneth Carnelian."

She opened her mouth to deny it, then thought better of it. Her shoulders slumped. "Is—is it so obvious? He wouldn't have seen, would he?"

"I'm sure he went away convinced you loathe everything about him, right down to his delightful eyelashes. But Ryka, I don't understand—"

Her sister laid her work aside. "Oh, Beryll, think about it for a moment. You heard everything, after all. He doesn't want me! He wants his pretty snuggery handmaidens with their simpering ways. I'm large and clumsy and short-sighted. Ryka the reliable, good for a stimulating argument every so often. Kaneth doesn't *bed* women like me. He doesn't even look at me as if I am a woman! And he never has. All he wants now is a mother for his children, someone who will do a good job while he's off having fun with his jades."

She rubbed at her ink-stained fingers. "But I—I love him. I've loved him ever since we were half-grown kids playing water tricks on the priest in religious class."

Beryll tilted her head, still not understanding. "But *why*? What is it about him that is so loveable? All right, so he is witty and funny when he wants to be. And he's the best flirt I've ever met. Gorgeous to look at—not dark and mysterious like Taquar, but all muscles and that dimpled *smile* . . . oo-er. But you, you're Ryka Feldspar the scholar; how can you be in love with a man who has spent most of his life pinching the bottoms of snuggery girls? Father said the Cloudmaster thinks you have the best mind in Breccia. What can you possibly see in a light-weight nipple-chaser like Kaneth Carnelian?"

Ryka, suddenly tired of keeping secrets, wanted Beryll to understand. She said softly, "There is so much more to him than most people see. More than he sees in himself. But *I* see it. I see the man he could be, if only he would believe in himself. Have you ever noticed that he never shirks on his duties to Breccia? Who is it that Highlord

Nealrith turns to when he needs a job done well? Kaneth! Every time."

"You sure that isn't just wishful thinking? Because you find it hard to believe anyone with such a charming smile can be no more than an overstuffed prick?"

"That's horrible. Don't be so vulgar."

"Then tell me what you *really* see in him."

She stood and went to look out of the open shutter of her window. "So many things. His parents weren't even water sensitives, did you know that? They were artisans from one of the lower levels of Pediment City. Horrid people. I met them once when I was about, oh, eight, I suppose."

"How did that happen?"

"He was being granted rainlord status. They had to sign papers relinquishing their rights to his water or his earnings. He and I were standing with some of the other students in the academy courtyard when his father came stalking up and told him—in front of all of us—that his powers were an aberration that would never last because he was just a no-good layabout from downlevel Pediment. Kaneth tried to be polite, but his father cuffed him over the head and told him not to get too uppity because one day he'd be back on the lowest level, where he belonged, without any of those fancy-pancy water-powers he had no rights to. And he wasn't to come home when that happened because none of them would help. His mother stood there and nodded. It was horrible. Kaneth went as white as a 'Baster and didn't say a word."

"But that was years ago! He can't have been more than, um, fifteen, if you were eight. He's a *man* now, not a youth."

"Yes, but I think one part of him *believed* the horrible things they said, believed he had no right to be a rainlord, believed that his water sensitivity would never last, because it was an aberration. None of his family had ever had the slightest sensitivity as far back as anyone could remember. They had never even been reeves. And there's always been something peculiar about his powers, too. I remember when we were at the academy, he could tell if someone added or removed a single drop of water from his dayjar. That's a skilled stormlord's talent. Yet he couldn't always find a hidden dayjar full of water right under his nose, something even a mediocre reeve could do! Everyone teased him, of course. So he never took being a rainlord, or his powers, seriously."

She turned, leaning back against the window frame, to look at her sister, her gaze brimmed with pain. "Oh, Beryll, if only he could have loved me. I could have made him believe in himself. I could have shown him who he really is, what he is capable of, because inside him there is *such* a man."

Beryll blinked, openly mystified. "He just asked you to marry him! Or he would have, if you had given him half the chance. So why didn't you say yes?"

Ryka glanced at her. "You can't understand why?"

"No, I can't!"

"Then I can't explain it to you. Right now, I would rather marry anyone else other than Kaneth Carnelian. Anyone."

"Ryka," Beryll said seriously, "if they are so desperate to find new stormlords, you may *have* to."

The two sisters exchanged glances, and it was Ryka who looked away first.

CHAPTER FIVE

Gibber Quarter
Wash Drybone

A boy dug in a patch of sand in the drywash. A vertical crease between his eyebrows indicated the intensity of the concentration he applied to his task; this was not play. He was digging a hole, using only his hands and a short stick earlier stripped from the centre of a bab palm frond. Sensibly, he had chosen a dip where a boulder offered shade from the morning sun. A straggly saltbush had put down roots there, but the rest of the wash was a barren riverbed of stones and sand, a gully recessed into the gibber plain, a crack slashed across the flat face of the earth.

The boy was scaled with dirt, the grime as much part of him as his dark eyes or the strong square fingers that scrabbled in the sand. The rigid skull cap on his head was only matted hair, once brown, now darkened with the accumulated dirt of a lifetime. His skin, golden brown at birth, now blended into the background of the land. His feet were bare, the soles so thick and hard that the heat of the sand meant nothing to him. There was little left of the smock he wore. It had once belonged to a much larger child; now it hung in tatters and hindered him as he worked.

He didn't know his true name. His father, Galen Flint, had once sworn that his younger son was as useless as a heap of shale, and ever since he had been known as Shale, the most worthless lad in the settle. If he'd ever had a name before that, he could not remember it. However, thanks to the settle's reeve, who taught the boys their numbers, and a chance remark from his father that he was a year younger than his brother Mica, he was able to guess his age to be around twelve or thirteen.

He was desperately thirsty and scraped at the dry soil with the determination of a desert animal. As the hole went deeper, the sand dampened. He drew in a deep breath, willing the water to come, wanting a drink so badly he could feel the taste of it on his tongue. Finally, when the hole was about as long as his arm, water began to seep into the bottom. When the level was several inches deep, the seepage slowed and Shale stopped digging. He waited patiently for the sand to settle and the water to clear. Then he inserted a hollow grass stalk he had brought with him and used it to suck up the moisture. It was gone in two or three mouthfuls, and he had to wait again for the hole to refill—and repeat the process several times more—before he had drunk sufficient to satisfy his thirst. He then filled in the hole to preserve whatever moisture remained from the power of the sun.

Then he shied like a startled pede.

Somethin's botched. He blinked, unsettled, not knowing why he had startled, or why that thought had suddenly popped into his head.

Somethin's real broke.

He sniffed at the air, but what he sensed had nothing to do with smell and it raised the hair on his arms. He clambered nimbly up the side of the wash, even though it was three times his height, to stand at the edge of the plain.

The Gibber stretched to the horizon in all directions, a flat tableland, with small stones strewn across a shiny, crusted surface of gleaming deep mauve. Here and there a few tiny plants survived on moisture that condensed from the air at night. There wasn't much: saltbush, spiny beggarchild and gummy plant. None grew more than a few inches in height, preferring to creep along the ground rather than reach towards the desert sun. The earth in between glistened with tiny fragments of purple and pearl-coloured mica as if the plain was sheened with starlight. All that was normal, but he spared a moment to envy his brother as he absorbed the scene: he would have liked a name like Mica, named after something so shiny. By contrast, the rock shale around his settle was always so grey and dull and dirty.

Distant hills made humps along the horizon, and mirages moved in a shimmering dance in front of them. Nothing odd there: sand-dancers were always around in the heat of the day. And then his senses stirred once more, and his body tautened in response. His head was full of sensation, rough-edged and scratchy feelings that brought a thrill of excitement and a depth of unease.

Water. It was water, water in pieces, all broken up into bits that wouldn't stay still. He knew the feel of water, but not like this. He frowned in bewilderment as he searched for the source. Then he found it. A smudge blurring the clarity of the open sky above the rounded bumps of land. A cloud. He'd seen those before. He'd even felt them, all bursting with water. But not like this. Not all mucked up and on the verge of shattering. And not when it wasn't expected. Anxious, he returned to the wash, hefted his resin bag onto his shoulder and headed down the path along the dry riverbed.

The sun was directly overhead when he reached the top edge of the settle. Here the wash widened to contain two streets lined with houses, each with its walled garden. Both streets were no more than rock-hard earthen laneways running the same way as the wash. The garden walls had their sun-baked daub reinforced with stone, their only protection against the force of flash-flood stormwater that barrelled down the wash twice a year, as regular as the star cycle of the skies above.

Mica was waiting for him there. "What you been doin', you little wash-rat?"

Shale shaded his face with his hand, grinned up at his brother and shrugged. "Gettin' me some resin."

"Pa's lookin' for us. He's as wild as a spindevil."

Shale tensed. "Aw, Mica, what's he want now?"

"Rishan the palmier offered him tokens to crush the shell of the packpede that died way back. Pa says we got t'do it. Reckons he'll buy some meat with the tokens."

Shale found himself salivating just at the thought. It had been more than a year since he'd eaten meat. Gathar the butcher must have salted the dead pede. "You sure? Pa's more like to buy a calabash of amber and drink hisself stupid. I don't want t'work just so's he can belt me when he's slurped."

"Nah, it's all right. Ma told old man Rishan to pay direct to her. But we best hurry 'n' get started. I been lookin' all over for you." He grabbed his brother's arm and hauled him down the main street. "Sooner we start, sooner we get t'eat some meat."

Shale pulled himself free, then had to run to keep up. "Is Pa goin' t'help?"

Mica snorted. "Not bleedin' likely, the waterless bastard. Don't worry, he won't lam into you for bein' late, not if he wants you t'work."

Nonetheless they sped down the slope of the street to the lower end of the settle. Shale had rarely entered any of the houses to either side. Sometimes, when there was no one around, he would try and peek through the water slits to see into the gardens. It was easy enough at the top where Gravel the reeve lived on one side and Rishan the palmier on the other. Their water slits were the widest because they were entitled to the most water when it came down the wash and the streets became rivers. However, the slits narrowed as the street descended the slope towards the bab palm groves planted in the wash below the settle. You couldn't see anything at all if you peeped through the narrow slits for the last houses, where Stipple the potmender and Shard the jobman lived. He'd tried.

Emerging from the lower end of the settle, near the entrance to the underground cistern, he sent an anxious glance to the left-hand side of the wash, where a few sorry hovels huddled at the top of the bank. The first belonged to his pa, Galen the sot. Even from where they were, Shale could hear his pa shouting at his ma, Marisal the stitcher, although he could not make out the words.

Mica made a face. "We gotta go tell him you're here."

Ma, a thin, gaunt woman now heavily pregnant, stood outside the burlap curtain that was all the door the one-roomed hut possessed. To Shale, the contrast between her thin arms and legs and the bulge of her stomach was grotesque. He was vaguely sorry for the coming child: already unwanted and waterless, and the little grubber hadn't even been born yet.

The boys slowed and sidled up to her, warily eyeing their father. Galen was small and wiry and tough. Years of drunkenness had blurred his mind and twisted his spirit, as well as added a tremor to his hands. He was sober now, though, an indication more of the state of his purse than of inclination. Unfortunately, sobriety did not always mean evenness of temper; both his sons knew that.

He looked at Shale, his brow gnarled with anger. "Y'found him," he said to Mica. "Where you been this time, you spitless bastard?"

Long experience had taught Shale not to answer questions like that.

"Lazy little git; you're never around when there's work to do. Think we can feed and water you for nothin', eh? By all that's wet, I dunno why that stupid slut of a mother of yours ever had you to start with! You find any resin today?"

"Some," Shale mumbled, keeping his eyes downcast.

He swung the sack off his shoulder to the ground, and Galen hefted it to see how heavy it was. "That's *all*?" He raised his arm.

Mica went to pull Shale out of the way, but his mother prevented him, grabbing his shoulder. "Mind y'own business," she said, and then muttered in his ear, "You want him t'lam into you, too?"

Galen swung at his younger son, and Shale rode the blow, already moving away as hand and cheek connected.

He fell anyway, dropping as if the blow had been much worse.

"Now git yer blighted spit outta here, the two of you," Galen roared. "The carcass is down in the grove in Rishan's plot."

The two boys ran. Just before they scrambled into the wash once more, Shale looked back at the sky. The cloud had vanished, but he felt the water still. It niggled at him, in his mind, in his chest. *Botched*, he thought again. *I know it.*

"Pede piss," Mica muttered as they walked through the shade of the grove trees. "I didn't think the bastard would slam you one. You all right?"

"Yeah. Wasn't hard. Reckon you were right—he didn't want t'hurt me when there's work to do."

"I hate 'im, Shale. Sometimes I hate 'im so bad—"

Shale shrugged. "He don't hurt me half as much as he thinks he does. An' you know what? I reckon when we're growed, he'll be scared of us."

"Sometimes I reckon he'll kill you first if he goes on like this. And Ma never does nothin' to stop 'im. Bitch." He took a deep breath. "Shit, I don't want nothin' to happen to you. Not ever. You're a good littl'un."

Shale looked at him, surprised. Then he grinned, enjoying a pleasant warm feeling inside. "Not so little no more," he protested, but he walked straighter. As they reached the first trees of the palm grove, he added, "Mica, there's somethin' I got t'tell you. Sounds crazed, but it's not. The rush is comin' down."

Mica laughed. "That don't just sound crazed, that *is* crazed; the next rush must be, I dunno, a full quarter cycle away."

"Nah. Goin' t'be a rush through by star-shine."

"Blighted eyes, Shale. Where you get these ideas from? What makes you think there's a rush due? Take a look at the sky tonight, you daft brat—the Old Man cluster is only startin' on its journey 'bove the horizon!"

"Can feel it comin'."

Mica's grin faded. "Sure as the sand is hot better not tell Pa that, or he'll have you staked out in the sun to see if roastin' your brains makes any difference to your sense. Knowin' too much 'bout water? That's bad stuff. Shaman stuff."

"But hadn't we better warn folk?"

"You sunfried? No one'll believe it and you'll get belted for sayin' so! And look an idiot after, when it don't happen." He strode off through the palm trees, jumping the slots as he went. Shale followed, taking care not to tread on the ground crops that grew beneath the rows of palms. Not, he thought, that it would make much difference. If the rush came down in full spate, with most of the settle's cisterns still partly full, too much of the water was going to flow right out of the town and into the bab palm groves. The slots would never cope. The palms would not mind if they were flooded, but crops beneath the trees would be washed away. He bit down on his lip, worried. He had been hungry often enough to know catastrophe when it threatened.

Water came twice a star cycle, as regular as the cycle itself, and everyone lived by its coming. Normally the crops would have been harvested before the rush was due; normally the slots would have been cleaned; normally the water allotments would have been checked and family entitlements recalculated after taking births and deaths into account. The width of the water slits would have been adjusted accordingly. Most of the floodwater would either be channelled off through the slits to empty into underground house cisterns, or it would disappear down into the grove cistern at the bottom of the settle. Any overflow from that would enter the slots and be soaked away to irrigate the trees and crops. The poorer people who owned the last of the bab groves would count themselves lucky if any of the water even reached their palms bordering the last slot. The drywash continued on to the Giving Sea, but the water never did.

This time, everything was wrong. The knowledge swelled inside Shale's chest and churned there painfully, stirred by fear and a strange anticipation that excited him. He had always been aware when the rush was close by, but never this strongly. Never this clearly.

And never when it wasn't expected.

The remains belonged to a packpede, and a packpede was five times the size of a myriapede hack so there were plenty of chitinous remnants. They were piled under one of the last of Rishan's bab palm trees, close to where a dip in rocky ground made a natural mortar. Ants and beetles had already eaten away the last flesh; all that was left were the hundred or so legs, the feelers and mouth parts, and the curved plates. Crushing them to powder suitable for manure was a job better suited to a man with a sledgehammer, but Mica and Shale had long since learned to be grateful for any work. Work meant tokens; tokens bought food and water.

Not that water was going to be in short supply soon. "Dunno why we're doin' this," Shale grumbled. "It's all goin' t'be washed away 'fore star-shine. Mica, we got t'tell someone."

Mica looked worried. "Shale, don't *gab* things like that."

"Why not? 'Strue."

Mica hammered a large pede segment and sent pieces flying in all directions. "Think, you daft brat: who sends us the water?"

"Cloudmasters. Rainlords. The Watergiver. They's Scarpen gods." He considered what he had said. "Don't know where Scarpen is. Maybe up in the sky? The caravanners say that's where the rush comes from. Seems awful strange to me, but they say it's true. Water falls from the sky 'cause the thing it's inside of—which is a sort of grey water jar called a cloud—breaks. Then the water falls out and it's called rain. It falls into the wash and we get a rush. I saw one of them cloud things today."

"I don't think Scarpen's in the sky," Mica said doubtfully. "Anyways, it's not important. What you should be worryin' 'bout is them rainlords and stormlords. Have you ever knowed them to fail? Sometimes they might send less than we want, specially just lately, but have you ever knowed the rush not to come when it's 'spected, or to come when it's not?"

Shale shook his head.

"They are gods. Gods don't make mistakes," Mica said seriously. "And if you *say* they do, they'll maybe hear you and get real angry. And if Pa or any of the other folks hear you, they'll say you're funnin' stormlords and rainlords and the Watergiver. Then they'll blame you next time the bab crop shrivels or the sandgrouse get sick and die. They'll say it's 'cause gods don't like folks funnin' 'em.

'Sides, if you know too much 'bout water, they'll say you was born t'be a water thief."

Shale thought about that as he banged the shell pieces with his hammer. He'd had quite enough bad luck already, yet he hadn't ever mocked any of the rainlords. Why then had they never given him any *good* luck? He wouldn't have minded being Rishan's son, Chert, for instance. Chert got to live in the top house, with real walls and a cistern and a garden. It had an outhouse in the yard, just for them, and Chert said the house even had a separate room for sleeping in. Shale frowned, thinking of his own hovel of stones and palm fronds, with his pa peeing through a crack in the back wall because he was too slurped to find the collection pot.

"It's not me that's bringin' Wash Drybone Settle bad luck," he said finally. "The water was already on its way 'fore I told you. Not my fault." He scratched at his chest, as if that would relieve the feeling pressing in on him.

Mica heaved a sigh. "You're as stubborn as a rock stuck in a cistern pipe, Shale. Have you heard a word I've tole you?"

"You're not listenin' to what *I* say!" Shale protested. "Mica, when I say the rush is real close, will you climb up onto the bank with me, out of the wash?"

Mica started to say no, but Shale gave him a ferocious glare, so he rolled his eyes instead. "Oh, all right, if I have to. If only to show that you're gabbin' pebbles and nonsense."

Shale subsided, partially satisfied, and worked on in silence. He took the smaller pieces and crushed them to a fine powder, which he poured into the woven palm-frond basket Rishan had supplied. When the water came, he would at least be able to save that much.

In the midafternoon, Rishan's household servant brought them some bab bread stuffed with steamed bab fruit and a calabash of water. He let them drink their fill, then took the calabash back with him.

"Pede's piss, wish Ma cooked this good," Shale said as he stuffed the bread into his mouth. All he'd had to eat that day were two pomegranates he'd filched the day before from the garden belonging to Gamath the resiner, the gum collector. "Hope he don't cut the number of tokens we get 'cause we drank his water."

"Nah. Rishan's a soft 'un. He feels sorry for us." Mica dropped his voice. "Watch it. Here comes Pa."

Shale hurriedly finished the bread and picked up his hammer. Mica was already swinging his mallet to shatter yet another pede segment. One glance at their Pa was sufficient to tell them both that his mood was now more amiable. "Glad to see you hard at it," he said. "I'd help, but if I do drudge work like this, folk'll think it's all I'm good for. There's a Red caravan through tomorrow. I 'spect I'll have the unloading of that."

If you're not slurped after gettin' your hands on Rishan's tokens, Shale thought, and avoided catching Mica's eye.

Galen squatted next to the bulbous trunk of the closest palm and leaned back against the smooth grey surface. "Big'un, this caravan. Twenty packpedes and a couple of myriapedes. The pedemaster's offsider just rode in to warn us. They'll be buying water and resin and fossicked stuff. And selling us salt. Make sure you're there. There may be work for you boys." He laid a friendly hand on

Mica's shoulder, but the stare he gave Shale was flat and cold. "You—" he said finally. "You're old 'nough to earn your keep with a caravanner, if one of 'em asks. Understand me, boy?"

For a moment Shale didn't understand. And then he caught sight of the revulsion on Mica's face, and he did. He laid down his hammer. "Nah. Don't want t'do that," he said. "Not what Ore the stonebreaker makes his boys do. They say it hurts."

"*Hurts?* I'll give you *hurts* if you cheek me, boy! You'll do as you're tole." His pa stood up and came towards him.

"The rush is comin' down," he blurted out. "You got t'do somethin', Pa. Warn folk."

His Pa looked at him in astonishment. "You crazy as well as lazy, boy?"

Mica gave him an agonised look, but Shale couldn't keep quiet even though his hands had started to shake. "If the pedeman has his mount tied up in the street, he should get it inside someone's garden. The water'll be here 'fore the sun goes down."

Without warning his father back-handed him across the mouth, this time hard enough to send him flying. He hit the trunk of the nearest bab palm and slid to the ground, dazed.

Mica sat still, biting his lip.

"Your brother's got the brains of a sand-tick. What the pickled pede is the matter with him?" Galen asked him, without even bothering to look at Shale.

Mica shrugged and said nothing. His father walked away, grumbling. Mica waited until he'd disappeared through the palms, then went to kneel where Shale was trying to sit up.

"You all right?"

Shale touched his mouth gingerly. "S'pose so."

"What the withering spit did you have to tell him for?"

But Shale couldn't put into words the desire he felt—the stupid, childish *need* he had—to see approval in his father's eyes. He knew it was stupid, but couldn't help it. He mumbled, "'Cause it's true. Mica, it's almost here. I can feel it. We got to get to the top of the bank." When Mica opened his mouth to scold, Shale added reproachfully, "You *promised*."

"Pedeshit. All right. Though you're too messed up to go anywhere much."

Shale pushed the basket of crushed segment plates at him. "Take this."

"Someone'll say we're stealing if they see us makin' off with it."

The feeling in Shale's chest suffocated him, speeding up his breathing, quickening his sense of urgency. Roughly, he shoved the basket into Mica's arms. "Then hang it up high in the bab palm so's it won't get washed away."

Mica gave an exaggerated sigh of irritation, but slung the bag over his shoulder, hauled himself up over the bulge of the lower trunk, then shimmied up the narrower part above until he could reach the fronds. He hung the bag on the broken end of a stem and slid down again. Shale, his whole face aching, headed for the bank on the opposite side from where they lived, and Mica followed.

"Pa's right," he said as he pushed Shale up over the top lip of the wash a moment or two later, "You got no more brains than a wilting sand-tick."

"Folk should know," Shale said, stubborn to the last. He felt dizzy and sick. Blood dripped from his nose and lip and already his face was beginning to swell. "Mica, think. They won't have their garden cisterns open. Gravel won't have opened the grove cistern, neither. An' what if there's folk in the streets? The pedeman's pede, too. Even Pa might still be in the wash somewheres."

"But it's not goin' to happen," Mica protested. "You're as muddled as a legless pede!"

"It's comin'!"

Mica stood up and looked down the wash. He could see over the settle to where the riverbed cut north through the plains. "There's nothin' there." He glanced at his brother where he sat in misery, holding his head in his hands. "Shale, there really isn't." But even as he said the words, he gave an uneasy glance back up the wash.

Beside him, Shale struggled to stand up. His fear vanished, swamped in the excitement of feeling the power of water on the move. The water in his blood stirred in joyous response; his heart raced. "Listen," he said, and cocked his head to hear better. "I *tole* you so!"

Mica listened, then squinted against the light to look up the wash. His eyes went wide with horror.

"Weeping *shit*!" he said.

CHAPTER SIX

Gibber Quarter
Wash Drybone

The rush shot down the riverbed, filling it from side to side, riding up the banks on the curves and sloshing back down again. The front was a roaring brown monster topped with a ragged curl of foam. It consumed the gully, blasted it with sound that was at once familiar and exhilarating. The feral rage of water on the move. Life and death inextricably mixed.

Too late, the settle heard. Within the walls of their gardens, people scrambled to close gates, to open sluices that led to the cisterns, to scream for children, to make sure that all were safe within their yards and houses. In the street, a pede reared up on its multitude of legs, wailing. Shale could see its head above the walls as it attempted to climb over into one of the house gardens. He was glad they were too far away to see the terror in its myopic eyes.

From where they stood, they could not see the bore hit the strengthened garden walls of the first houses, but they heard the impact, the slap of a wave travelling as fast as a pede could run, slamming into stone.

"I'll be waterless," Mica muttered, awe-struck. "It's never been like this before."

"Much more water," Shale agreed, crossing his arms over his chest to hug himself, as if that would stop the turmoil gathering inside him from bursting out.

The bucking torrent—now parted by the first of the houses—streamed down the parallel streets of the settle. The streets became rivers; garden walls were riverbanks. From their vantage point, Shale watched as villagers flung back the stone covers to allow the water, already gushing into their gardens through the water slits, to flow into their underground cisterns. He watched as several people escaped from the streets by diving through gates or climbing across walls. He saw the pede try to follow them, and fail. Its great body fell back and it was borne away on the water.

He cried out, anguished, his elation diminishing.

The water thrashed out of the settle and into the palm groves, far too much for the slots to handle. Spreading out to cover the cultivated land, it submerged crops, battered the trees, slammed up against the banks of the wash. The pede came with it, head emerging briefly, then disappearing, then visible again. Black pointed claws raked one of the palm trunks, scrabbling for purchase. The saddle came untied and was swept into the torrent. The water, relentless, dragged at the beast until it lost its grip. It snatched at the trunk of the next tree. This time it used its mouth parts as well as the sharp tips of its feet.

Shale churned with conflicting emotions. He stood on land, but he felt he was caught up in the water, struggling for life. He was filled with power then buffeted by it, powerless. He couldn't control his feelings. Everything was too volatile, too turbulent. He found himself shouting to the pede, as if it could hear above the sound of the water. For an absurd moment he thought that if only he could save the animal, everything would be all right. Everything could go back to the way it should be.

The pede didn't give up. It clawed deep into the second bab palm and rested. Its long feelers—the length of its body—lifted out of the torrent and began to grope around. One of them hooked on to another tree, closer to the bank where Shale and Mica stood. Quite deliberately, the pede loosed its foothold, allowing its body to swing out into the flow. Torn by the current, the creature groped through the air with its second feeler until it too hooked on to a palm, this one closer still to the bank.

Shale surged with hope. "It's goin' t'work its way over to the edge," he said, awed.

Mica gaped. "I thought they were *dumb*."

Noise filled Shale's ears. Water was roaring past, but the sound he heard was inside his head. Everything was muddled up, pressing in on him, making his brain ache. *Later*, he thought. *I'll sort it all out later.* "Let's meet it," he said.

"What?" Mica asked, not understanding.

"Let's meet it. Once it gets to the bank I reckon it won't be able t'climb up without help. It's too muddy."

Already the beast had moved across another two rows. It clung to a tree, resting, gathering strength as water tugged at its body. Raising its first three segments out of the water, it clasped the trunk with all its front legs. The great head turned to look at them, blurry black eyes gazing out above mouthparts that fitted together like the pieces of a puzzle.

"Oh dust, it's *beautiful*," Shale said. He pulled away from Mica, who looked at him as if he was daft, and ran to a spot further down the wash. "Down here, I think," he called back over his shoulder. "Come, we gotta try t'catch him and help him up the bank."

"We can't haul somethin' that large," Mica protested, but already the pede had plunged through the water away from the last of the trees, struggling with all its pairs of legs, thrashing even with its feelers in an attempt to close the gap to the edge. "It'll never make it!"

"Yes, he will."

Shale started to scramble along the lip of the bank, looking for a way down. The flood bucked and plunged past in muddy skeins, and the closer he came to it, the more disoriented he was. He lost sight of himself, became at one with the water, unable to distinguish where he began and the river ended. He stumbled and sat down hard, clutching at his head, and felt himself begin to slide into the wash.

Too much water, he thought. *There's too much. And it won't stay still. If only it'd just stop so I can think.*

As the myriapede drew near, he slipped further down the slope and his feet plunged into the flood where it gouged at the bank. The flow tugged at him, plucking powerfully at his ankles and calves. His senses exploded. The hugeness of the expanse of water overwhelmed him; terror made incoherent nonsense of his thoughts. There was nothing that distinguished him from that expanse. He was part of it, not a boy any more. He was just water, unshaped, without boundaries.

When something touched his face, sliding across his skin in jags, he focused on it. The pede; it was the pede's feeler reaching out to him. He grabbed it and fixed all his attention on the physical reality clutched in the solidness of his hand. The water receded from his mind, and the turbulence within him ebbed. The beast scrabbled against the bank, its feet churning up mud. Shale held tight. He slipped further into the water and struggled to dig his heels and his elbows into the mud of the bank. Terror returned as he realised he was about to be swept away. He lost his footing and swung out into the current. He tightened his hold on the feeler. As long as he had that, he could also hold on to what was real. He could keep the terror at bay.

Water washed over his head and instinctively he held his breath and closed his eyes. The feeler, caught in the flow now that it was weighed down by his body, floated alongside the pede. Shale bumped hard against the body segments. Wincing, his head broke the surface and he opened his eyes. The black shiny side of the pede rose above him, slippery and wet and impossibly high. It blocked his view of the bank and of Mica, but even over the sound of rushing water, he heard his brother screaming his name.

He shuddered with shock. The water wanted to enter his mind again, but this time he wouldn't let it. He grasped the feeler tight and scrutinised the pede. *Mounting handles. It's got to have mounting handles somewhere.* He could pull himself up.

Towards the head, he thought, and began to haul himself along the feeler in that direction. The current tugged at him, but he ignored its clutch. The pede wasn't moving. *It's hooked itself 'gainst the bank*, he thought.

When he saw the toehold slot carved into one of the segments, he knew he had the right place. He first hooked his fingers, then a foot, into the slot and levered himself up out of the water far enough to reach for a mounting handle. He hung there for a moment, then clambered up, slipping and sliding, until he was on the top of the beast where the saddle had been.

His brother stared at him from the top of the bank. Mica was wet and covered in mud—and he held the pede reins in his hand. He was leaning back to keep them taut, braced against the weight of the pede in his effort to stop the animal drifting away. He swore at Shale, a nonstop string of obscenities.

Shale grinned sheepishly back.

The pede's feet found purchase on the floor of the wash as the water level dropped, and with Mica hauling on the reins it began to edge its way upwards. It dug the points of its feet into the earthen slope and finally humped its way over the top edge, Shale riding triumphantly on its back.

I'm a caravanner, he thought. *A pedeman ridin' me own beast 'cross the plains.*

For a precious never-to-be-forgotten moment of make-believe, he was free of the settle, independent of his father, unencumbered by poverty. He was Shale of the Gibber, leader of men, emerging victorious from an adventure.

As he slid reluctantly to the ground, reality returning, Mica punched him on the shoulder none too softly. "I'll *kill* you if you do anything so pissing *stupid* ever again, you sandwitted wash-rat!" he cried. "You could have *died* in there!"

Shale blinked. "Died?" He hadn't been afraid of dying. He'd been afraid of losing himself. Of not knowing what or who he was. Of becoming part of a larger whole, of being like a jug of amber spilled into a cistern until there was nothing of the original recognisable.

"Yeah," said Mica. "Don't you know you can suffocate in water? Like chokin', 'cause there's no air."

Shale furrowed his brow, thinking about that. He didn't remember choking. He didn't remember not being able to breathe. His fear had been that he was melting, disappearing as a person. He wanted to explain, but didn't think there were any words he could find that would make Mica understand.

Beside him, the pede shivered with a clatter of segment plates, sending water streaming out of the joints. Then it reached out a feeler and touched the two boys one after the other, running the tip over their faces and bodies as if it needed to assess them, and remember.

Tentatively, Shale reached out and touched the animal's head. For a moment it regarded him, then it slid its first segment down over its eyes, tucked its feelers back along its body and carefully rolled itself up into a tight ball, legs inside. The edges of the segments were embroidered with a lace fringe, tattered now, and several of the segments themselves were carved—a common custom among the Red Quarter people. They sculptured their personal myriapedes with pictures of all their journeys, so that the pede carried stories with it wherever it went, commemorating both its life and the life of its driver.

"Reckon it's gone to sleep," Mica said, after it had stayed that way for a while.

"I'm never goin' to eat pede again," Shale announced reverently.

Mica gaped at him, baffled, as if unable to see what had prompted that statement. About to ask, he was diverted by the indescribable sound of earth on the move. On the other side of the wash, where the squatter shanties huddled, the bank had been undermined by water. Shocked, helpless, they watched several houses—including their own—slip down the wall of the wash and vanish into the water.

"Ma," Mica whispered. "I'll be shrivelled, I hope Ma wasn't inside."

Shale's heart clenched painfully. He scanned the figures rushing to and fro in front of the remaining houses. "Nah," he said, relief loosening the tightness in his chest. "Look, that's her there. No one else has a belly like that."

Inwardly he thought, *But Pa will kill me anyways*.

If Galen the sot was still alive.

The Gibber Plains appeared to be flat all the way to the horizon. In truth, they were crazed through with cracks, each one a wash that started in the Border Humps to the north and then wandered southwards to the Edge. There, the plain stopped in a ragged tear as if a giant had ripped it away. A brave man could walk to the edge of the tear and peer over to see the Giving Sea several hundred paces below, the rolling surf pounding the cliff face in relentless lines.

In the Time of Random Rain, before the rainlords commanded the clouds—or so the storytellers said—water would occasionally reach the Edge and fall over, to be wasted, evaporated into mist until the foot of the cliffs disappeared behind a skirting of white spindrift and the sea below was lost to sight.

At dawn on the morning after the bore swept through the settle on Wash Drybone, water once again reached the Edge and plunged down towards the sea. There was no one to see it, no one to exclaim over the waste or be moved by the rainbow beauty of colour playing across the spindrift. Yet somewhere deep in their souls, several people felt that water fall and felt the loss of its purity when it hit the sea. Far away in Breccia City, Cloudmaster Granthon cried out in his sleep and woke, the sadness lingering from his dream subsumed in a larger grief he could not name. In Wash Drybone, Shale Flint felt a wave of pain pass through him, and foundered in the residue of sorrow it left behind. Beside him, Mica stirred uneasily. Highlord Taquar of Scarcleft, already awake, left his bed and opened the shutters, wondering what he'd just felt. In other parts of the Quartern, some of the rainlords stirred, distressed by an event they sensed but lacked sufficient power to interpret.

Shale and Mica had spent the night out under the stars. At sunset the water had still been running too high to cross the wash; later, when the water level fell, it was too dark to see. Once the sun had gone, the cold came, as always. Poorly clad and as wet as they were, they might have died in the open if it had not been for the myriapede. It curled its great body around them and although it lost heat as the night wore on, it trapped the boys' warmth within its encircling wall. Shale and Mica weren't comfortable, and Mica complained that all the water was making his head ache, but they were sheltered.

At first light they heard voices, and as they struggled to unwind themselves from a tangle of pede legs, a Reduner peered down on them. "Who the salted wells are you?" the owner of the face asked, in tones that were far from friendly. "What you doing with my pede?"

Shale felt his guts twist. The pedeman. He sat up saying, "We didn't hurt him!"

Beside him, the pede woke and, still sluggish with the cold, clicked its segments apart in an unhurried stretch.

The boys scrambled to their feet.

"Why, it's Galen's two lads!" another voice exclaimed. Rishan the palmier. "Your da thinks you two snuffed it." He turned to the Reduner in explanation. "They're just settle lads. They won't have harmed your pede."

The Reduner glared but didn't say anything. He was running his hand over his beast, checking for broken legs, frowning over a nick he found in the edge of a segment and fingering a torn embroidered fringe.

"He broke the tip of one of his feelers," Shale said.

The Reduner took a deep breath and Rishan hurriedly intervened. "Why don't you two lads run off. Your ma and pa'll be worrying."

Nodding, Mica grabbed hold of Shale and pulled him away. "Let's go," he muttered in his brother's ear. As they scrambled down the earthen bank to the sodden floor of the wash, he added, "You don't want t'come between a Reduner pedeman and his mount. They say that a caravanner w'druther lose his son than his pede. He probably thinks we wanted to steal it or somethin'."

"But we helped *save* it," Shale protested.

"Yeah, but he's not goin' t'believe that. Hey, look at all the water!" Mica looked around in amazement. A shallow stream trickled down the centre of the wash. The slots were all overflowing. Wherever there was a dip in the riverbed, water had pooled clean and clear, with the mud and sand sunk to the bottom. The crops were all gone, but most of the bab palms stood, battered but still anchored by their tortuous root systems.

Shale's eyes widened. "I never *seen* so much water lying round after a rush! And it's all goin' t'waste—just flowin' away."

"Tell you what, I'm going t'have the best drink I've ever had in all m'life."

"Me, too," Shale agreed reverently. He knelt at the edge of the flowing water, cupped his hands and drank deeply. When he finally looked up, chin dripping, he asked, "Do you think Pa saved enough water for the house?"

"In what? Our hut fell into the wash, remember? We must've lost all our jars. I wish Pa'd fallen in, too, and got washed all the way to the Edge." Mica smiled gleefully at the thought.

"You reckon Ma was worryin' herself 'bout us?"

"Her? Don't be daft. The bitch would be glad to get rid of us. 'Specially as she's having another brat soon." He wiped his face with a wet hand. "You know what I'm going t'do? Get in and wet myself all over."

Shale thought of the way the water had tried to swallow him up and frowned, doubtful. "Reckon we should?"

"Why not? Isn't no settle lower down the wash t'drink it." Mica waded out into the deepest pool he could find and sat down in water up to his neck.

Shale followed, but stopped when he was knee deep. This time it felt different. Not so overwhelming. Without the furious speed of the flood, the water was gentle, welcoming. The feeling of oneness was still there, but this time it didn't threaten; it was huge and immeasurable and it felt *right*. He waded in further and watched water swirl around his thighs.

"'S good, right?" Mica asked.

"Cold, but wunnerful! Like . . . like . . . I don't know what it's like. Like being happy and full of water an' food an' everything good all at once." He stripped off what was left of his smock and threw it aside. Then he flung himself face down in the pool.

The shock of being surrounded by water, of having it come up over his head, of absorbing its oneness with him: it was too much. The pleasure of its touch—the sensuality of it—threw him. He sank into the depths of the pool and his body responded to the joy. Warmth spread through his loins, swelling his stick, but in a way he'd never felt before. He gasped at the wonder of that and choked. He spluttered, pushing the water away from his face in irritation without even being aware of the impossibility of what he did. He wanted to concentrate on feeling so . . . so *good*. On the rising pleasure, the spreading heat, the rushing of his blood, the unbearable, unbearable moment of exquisite pressure when everything stood still. Then the warmth burst inside him. He shuddered, and shuddered again.

Just as he was beginning to revel in the mind-boggling wonder of that, he found himself grabbed and hauled upwards, to break the surface. Mica, white-faced, still dressed and dripping wet, was holding his arm, yanking him into the shallows. "You dryhead—didn't I tell yer you can suffocate in water?"

He blinked, clearing his vision, and wondered what Mica meant. Suffocate? He hadn't been suffocating, or choking. He'd been breathing, just as usual. He'd pushed the water away from his face. He flushed, remembering the rest, enjoying the memory, the glow left behind, the way it made him feel. So *that* was what it was like. Embarrassed, he avoided meeting Mica's gaze.

Rivulets of water trickled down his body, and idly he rubbed at his forearm. Dirt dissolved, leaving his skin lighter.

Mica remarked uneasily, "Folk say washin' a lot makes you sick."

"I don't feel sick." He felt wonderful. He rubbed some more of the dirt away. "Makes me look more like ord'nary folk. Didn't know I got that colour underneath."

Mica grabbed a handful of wet sand and scrubbed his own arm. His skin lightened as well and he started to laugh. "Let's get back in and wash all the dirt away," he said.

"Nah. Better get back and see if Ma and Pa's all right."

"Y'know what? I don't care. Neither of them cares as much as—as a grain of sand for us. And Pa will be in a real rotten temper. Come on, Shale. We'll prob'ly never see water like this, never again."

He waded back into the pool. Shale wavered and then followed. They played, washing away the accumulated dirt of a lifetime, laughing and giggling at the strangeness of their appearance, at the feel of it.

Only later, when his skin was soft and shiny and golden brown, did Shale suddenly sober up. "But we're not like ord'nary folk, are we? Not you 'n' me. Ord'nary folk live in real houses and have water allotments and don't get beat up by their pa." He looked up at his brother. "An' ord'nary folk don't know when the rush's comin' down. I felt it, Mica. A feeling inside my guts. Pa's goin' kill me."

Mica didn't reply.

"You reckon he'll make me go with a Reduner if one of them wants it?"

His brother wrung the water out of his clothing and wouldn't look at him. "He's never made me do it."

But Shale knew that didn't mean a thing. He pulled on the remains of his smock. "I won't do it," he said as they headed across the groves to where their house had once stood on the opposite bank. "Least of all for 'im."

"The bastard'll clobber you proper."

"Not this time. Not no more. 'Cause I'll clobber him right back. I'm done with his wallopings."

Mica stared at him, eyes wide.

Not all the shanty houses had been demolished by the force of the water. Further away from the bank, several huts belonging to other waterless families still stood, and they found Galen leaning against one of them, talking to Ore the stonebreaker and Parman the legless. He scowled at them as they approached.

"Where the waterless hell have you whelps been?" he yelled at them. "You know your mother's birthin' that new brat of hers and you two off enjoyin' yourselves somewheres, without a thought to what trouble we're in. We got no house, and no jars neither, just when there's water out there for the having!" He jerked a finger at Mica. "You, get back down into the wash. Pick up anything you can find that's of any use. There's wood there, Mica, washed down from the hills, I wouldn't wonder. You know how valuable wood is? Get back down there!"

Mica gave a despairing look at Shale but didn't dare say anything. He slunk away towards the wash.

Shale stood his ground, waiting for his father to speak

to him. *It weren't m'fault*, he thought. *None of this was my fault. The bastard's got no* right *t'be angry. I was the one what warned him.*

Ore laid a hand on Galen's arm. "Go easy on the lads. They could've been dead y'know."

"Mind your own damn business, Ore. Them's my get, and I'll deal with them my way." He grabbed Shale by the arm and pulled him around to the back of the shanty house where they couldn't be seen. He shoved Shale up against the stones of the wall, bruising his back with his roughness.

"Now you listen to me, Shale, and you listen good." He lowered his voice and hissed in the boy's ear. "That talk of knowin' 'bout the water comin' down aforehand? I don't want t'hear it. Not a word. That's shaman stuff, and nobody wants no shaman stuff. You talk 'bout that, and I'll beat you as you've never been beat before, till your tongue comes out your arse. You understand me?" He fitted his hand across Shale's cheeks, and pinched them inwards towards his nose. It hurt.

Fury bubbled up. Shale slammed his forearm against his father's. He was nowhere near as strong, but Galen was taken by surprise and his hold was broken. "You should of listened t'me," Shale said defiantly. "I tole you what was goin' t'happen, but you wouldn't listen! Weren't *my* fault the jars 'n' stuff was lost."

He raised his chin and met his father's gaze. His heart pounded as he waited for the inevitable blow.

It didn't come. Galen dropped his gaze and wiped his hands on his smock, as if he wanted to rid himself of taint. "You've even been in that water, haven't you? You sand-crazy?" He stepped back, his voice soaked with loathing.

There was panic there, too, and the shock of understanding left Shale shaken. Pa was *afraid*, deathly afraid, and his fear quivered his voice as he spat his words out.

"Shaman-taint! I wish you'd never seen the light of day, and that's the truth. Now get back down into the wash and help your brother. We got t'find some of our stuff. Or other folks' stuff. Unnerstand? We got no dayjars now!"

Shale ducked past his father and walked away, only too glad to have escaped so lightly, but the words echoed on in his head: *I wish you'd never seen the light of day.*

Rage welled up in his throat. *I didn't ask t'be his get,* he thought. *Weren't my fault I am.* And side by side with his anger, there was triumph. The beatings might continue, but even if they did, he knew he would never truly be afraid of his father again, not now that he had seen fear in his eyes.

That night he crept into the makeshift shelter they had built of stones and palm fronds, where Ma now lay with her new baby sleeping in the crook of her arm. The child, named Citrine, was tiny and perfect, and Shale thought her as beautiful as the gem she was named for. He tucked a finger into one tiny hand, and the babe tightened her grip around it. The flood of love he felt for something so small and fragile staggered him. Fiercely, he thought he would do anything to protect her. If ever Pa raised a hand to her, he would kill him. If *anyone* ever raised a hand against her he would kill them. She was his, his charge in this world that held so much pain and uncertainty. She, he decided, would never know what it was like to go thirsty or be hungry or be beaten. Never.

CHAPTER SEVEN

Red Quarter
Dune Watergatherer

Sandmaster Davim sat on his pede at the top of the dune they called the Watergatherer. To the east and west, the red line of the dune humped away as far as he could see. To the north, it fell sharply to the plains. This, the front edge of the Watergatherer, was a wall of fine red dust unsullied by any plants or growth, a slope steep enough to make walking difficult. Its top edge, towering five hundred paces up, was as sharp as a sword cut. An occasional playful gust of wind tore grains away from the cut in flurries.

The back side of the dune was different. There were gullies and dips and hollows and valleys carved into the long, more gentle descent of several miles to the distant plain. The red sand of this sculpted slope was dotted with vegetation: a prickly bush here, a sand-creeper there; a clump of smoke-bush behind that. Bare surface showed through, but the plants maintained a precarious existence, oblivious to the slow inching of the dune that carried them forward.

The red dunes of the quarter were waves swallowing

up the land in front only to discard it behind two or three decades later as lifeless as the skeletal remains of a masticated meal. The Red Quarter had sixteen such dunes, spaced equidistant from one another, all on their inexorable slither northwards to extinction, a long slow demise as they eased themselves into the expanse of the Burning Sand-Sea, a desert so hot and vast that not even a pede ventured there.

The dunes were birthed in the south, perhaps by the eroded red rock of the Warthago Range or the red earth of The Spindlings. The plain they traversed was also red, although the earth was coarser and its vegetation sealed it tight against the depredations of the wind. It was covered with low bushes, rocks, the odd waterhole that was sometimes no more than a bowl of dust—until the next parallel dune ten or fifteen miles away.

Davim scanned the country carefully from his vantage point, watching for the man he expected. His fellow conspirator, he supposed, but he preferred to think of the man as the Traitor, for such he was to his own kind. Once Davim had respected him, though not now. Conspirators they might be, but Davim despised the treachery, useful as it was, that was bringing the Scarperman to him again.

As yet, there was no sign of him. The only people he saw were his own followers, camped in one of the dune hollows on the gentler slope, together with the meddle of pedes that were the pride of his clan. He looked for a distant telltale plume of smoke or the glint of sunshine on metal—anything that would tell him there were other people out there somewhere—but he saw nothing. No man alone, no band on the move. Nothing.

Some things he did not expect. There were no buildings in the Red Quarter. No cities. It was pointless to build any, because sooner or later the next dune would come to devour them. Reduners were proudly nomadic, living in tribal camps on the dunes, near waterholes but never right next to them, for fear the pedes would pollute the water. Each dune had several tribes and when the situation demanded it, a tribe moved their camp from one water hole to another. They hunted game across their dune and the adjoining plains, and gathered roots, leaves, berries and seed pods for food. They sold pedes for tokens to buy other necessities. They ran caravans for trade. Together, the tribes of each dune made a clan and each clan paid homage to a single sandmaster. And, of course, to the god of the dune, who lived beneath the sands and moved the dune towards its eventual death.

Idly the Sandmaster of Dune Watergatherer wondered if the Scarpen fool had mistaken the dune. One dune was much like another to an outsider. Perhaps the fellow had gone to the Hungry One, the next dune to the north, or to the Sloweater, to the south. Or perhaps he had simply become lost along the Watergatherer itself. It extended from one side of the Red Quarter to the other, after all.

Davim waited patiently while the sun sank to the horizon and the sky reddened. His pede did not move and neither did he. He sat cross-legged on the saddle, at ease, and used the time to scheme. He knew he would appear at his best like this: a silhouette against a red sky, a man of destiny mounted on Burnish, a pede that some called the most magnificent beast ever captured from the wild herds of the Red Quarter. Its segment plates had since been intricately carved and inlaid with mica so that the sagas they told shone with a pearly glow. Each segment edge had been embroidered by Davim's wife and daughters and trimmed with blood-red lace along the outside rim. There was no other pede as beautiful as this one.

Davim knew he was deemed a handsome man. Like all Reduners, his hair and skin were permanently stained red by the dust of the quadrant. He was not particularly tall or even broad, but he was muscular; he took pride in participating in the games that occupied the leisure time of his dune tribes. And he was fastidious in his personal appearance. The neat plaits, twenty of them, the ends of which poked out from under the Reduner version of the palmubra, were rewoven with a new set of gemstone beads twice every star cycle. In the light of the setting sun, the red robes he wore were black in the folds, and the chrysoprase beads that decorated the collar glittered. Behind him in their cage, his ziggers rattled their wing cases and hummed. He knew he must appear to be what he was: a man of power. A leader who would one day take the Quartern by storm.

There will come a day when even the rainlords will sink to their knees before me.

In the slanting rays of the sun, he saw a speck on the plain. As it approached, it became two dots, then a rider on a myriapede, packpede trailing behind; and they were on the steep side of the Watergatherer. Davim gave a smile. To arrive from that direction the Traitor must have indeed been lost and now, coming at the dune head on, he was denying himself a dignified entry.

He underestimated the man. The Traitor dropped the reins of the packpede at the base of the dune, but his own mount did not slow; in fact, he jabbed the animal with his riding prod to hasten it. The beast leaped at the slope and bounded upwards. Dust billowed and shifted beneath its feet, but before the fine-grained sand could slip, the animal had been prodded into yet another leap, and then another. It plunged up the slope, and the Scarperman rode out each bound with one arm held high in balance.

Davim had to admire the rider's skill. As a rider of renown himself, given to similarly flamboyant gestures, he knew exactly what was involved. The reins had to be separately controlled to tell the animal how to move, doubly hard if you did it all with one hand. One tug at the wrong rein and the pede would react wrongly; one wrong reaction and you'd be tumbling to the bottom of the slope. Behind him, the packpede started to plod slowly upwards with stoic indifference.

And so Davim watched and secretly admired, but never by as much as the twitch of a muscle indicated that he cared one way or the other. And then, deep inside the sands somewhere below his mount, the dune god started to sing a low soughing melody that slid from note to note as if in acknowledgement of the newcomer's arrival. Davim scowled. He did not know the language of the god; only the Watergatherer's shaman could interpret the message. He resented that ignorance, but there was nothing he could do about it. He would have to wait until he spoke to the holy man. For the moment, he dismissed the question from his mind, even as the song of the dune continued with melancholy sweetness.

When the rider topped the rise in a swirl of dust backlit by sunset—a dark figure pasted on a blood-red sky like a mythical god—Davim asked simply, in his own tongue, "What happened to the promised rain?"

He expected excuses, a tale of blameless woe. Instead the Traitor shrugged and said, "I failed."

He used the language of the Scarpen. Davim spoke it well enough, but he was in his own land now, and he refused to defile it with the outlander's tongue. "Failed, my lord?" he asked, still using Reduner, knowing the man understood. He raised an eyebrow, but balanced the subtle mockery with the polite use of the title. It didn't pay to be stupid. This man had powers that no sandmaster could match, and he could use them faster than any Reduner warrior could release a zigger. And the man carried ziggers as well; there was a cage strapped behind him on the pede.

The Traitor inclined his head and switched languages. He spoke Reduner well, although his outlander accent was strong. "Yes. I stole a storm as I said I would—with that I had no problem—but, alas, I lacked the power to bring it safely to the Red Quarter. I believe a wash and a settle or two in the Gibber must have received an unexpected water bore as a consequence." He shook some dust from his robe and edged his mount closer to Davim's. "Failure happens. There will doubtless be others. I need a rainlord to join his power to mine, Sandmaster Davim. At the very least. Better still, someone of stormlord level. If I had such, there would be no more failures."

Davim opened his hands in a gesture of lack. "I have found none. Heard of none. My men scoured the dunes, testing in the ways you suggested. No one. Not unexpected. After all, we did it not too long ago, for the Cloudmaster." His voice hardened. "Will you deliver on your promises, my lord?"

"In time. I never let a setback overturn the mount,

Sandmaster. If I cannot discover an unknown stormlord, if I cannot locate a rainlord child to train, then I can kidnap the remaining one there is."

"The Cloudmaster's granddaughter?"

"Yes. Senya. Or I can kidnap a grown rainlord and force him to do my bidding by threatening his wife or child or loved one. There are always ways."

"A rainlord is not a stormlord. You *claim* to be a potent rainlord yourself, yet you cannot make a storm."

"Because of my potency, if I have a rainlord at my call, to bind his or her power to mine, it may be sufficient." He shrugged. "Sooner or later there will be another child with the talent. It is just a matter of finding them before others do. Keep looking, Davim."

"I'm a patient man. I can afford to be. I am young yet." Davim smiled slyly, confident in his comparative youthfulness. He was not quite thirty years old, and the man he faced must surely have been closer to forty than thirty. "However, my patience is not limitless."

"Nor is mine. And yet I will not jeopardise our plans by precipitate action—I am not in my dotage yet. Listen, Sandmaster, Granthon grows weaker by the day. Weaker in physique and weaker in power. He is already failing to bring enough water for all life in the Quartern. You have seen this yourself in your reduced rainfall."

"That's true. I even heard random rain has fallen along The Spindlings. Granthon is not even capturing all the natural-born clouds."

"I hadn't heard that. I'm not surprised, though. Cloudmaster Granthon has even let the cisterns of his own city drop dangerously in level." He gave a snort of contempt. "He would let his own people suffer along with the rest of the Quartern. Did I walk his path, the Gibber or the White Quarter would have suffered first; but no, he tried to be fair. Fair! As if you can rule a land such as the Quartern fairly. He knows *nothing* about rule."

For the first time in their conversation he was showing emotion and Davim hid a smile. The Traitor had a weakness after all. It was worth remembering. "The Cloudmaster is a fool. Fortunately for us, you say he also birthed a foolish son," he added softly, soothing.

"Yes. When Granthon finally dies, you and I will be there to take his place, *not* Highlord Nealrith, never fear."

"I will have the Red *and* the White Quarters. You may do what you will with the rest." He could not help the joy of anticipation that edged his words. "Don't make it too long, lord."

"Granthon's death comes. Possibly even before the next star cycle completes itself. Already he is desperate. He now wants to send rainlords to the Gibber to look for potential stormlords." Once again his contempt broke through. "The Gibber, of all places! Next he will be sending us across the Giving Sea, searching lands where men have no water sensitivity!"

"He hopes to suck water from stone. I almost pity him."

The Traitor smiled. Behind him, his packpede arrived at the top of the slope and clattered its segment plates with a shake, in an attempt to rid itself of sand. "Not I, Sandmaster. Not I," he said.

"Will he further cut water to the Red Quarter?"

"No, I think not. He knows that would only rouse the dunes to frenzy. A number of people have, however, sown the idea that perhaps the Gibber and the White Quarters are not exactly as important. It will make our taking control of those two Quarters easier if they are thirsty."

"How long?"

"Hard to say. Granthon is weak, but there is a sinew of toughness in that old man that will hang on to life and power. And a senseless streak of softness that will keep him sending water to the Gibbermen and the 'Basters as long as he can." He paused as the sound from the heart of the dune thrummed in quickening rhythm. "What says your dune god?"

Davim gave an unpleasant smile. "He warns of treachery. Beware, brother. Do not cross us or you will learn to fear the power of the dune drovers."

The Traitor shrugged. "I have no reason to contemplate treachery. How goes the training of your men?"

"Well. They will be ready whenever the wind is right. They are loyal, utterly, to my leadership of the Watergatherer. And I build numbers by taking in the unwanted. We never refuse water to anyone. My men slit their throats if they do not prove their worth within ten days or so, but that is rarely necessary. We are warriors as great as the dunes have ever seen. True men see and admire and long to follow."

"The other dunes? Can you deliver them as promised, when the, er, wind is right?"

"Show them you control the rain and that you supply us with water at my bidding, and I could have them at my feet tomorrow. Already the weaker dunes offer their tribute to me wordlessly with fear in their eyes. If I could tell them I had a stormlord at my side to fill the waterholes to the brim as in the past, then they would come willingly, not dragging their feet through fear, and the larger dunes would follow. You understand the difference, I think?"

The Traitor shrugged. "Between threats and rewards? Oh yes. But one man's way is not another's. I demand nothing but loyalty. What prompts it is irrelevant."

Davim gestured with an upturned palm, indicating his indifference to the other's preference. "Just remember this: I prefer to bring the other dunes in with a bribe—a stormshifter, cloudbreaker, stormlord, whatever name you like—but I have other plans if you fail me. You may not like them as much as the present plan."

"Threats are unnecessary," the Traitor said coldly.

Davim smiled. "Do you stay the night in our camp? I offer the hospitality of my tribe."

"Another time perhaps."

"When do we meet again?"

"Not for a while, I think. If you have a message, you know how to contact me." Without farewell, he swung his pede around, picked up the reins of the packpede in passing, and set them both at the gentler slope. The animals gathered momentum, and the red dust rose in a cloud behind them, obliterating any view of their departure.

Davim remained where he was for a moment longer. The smile he directed after the travelling pede was brittle. "You are a worthy ally, my traitorous friend," he murmured, "and one day you will make an even worthier enemy. One day all the Quartern will be mine, and we will depend on rainlords and their filthy water magic no more."

Beneath his feet, the dune god growled.

CHAPTER EIGHT

Scarpen Quarter
Breccia City
Breccia Hall, Level 2

"Mercy! Has he gone mad?"

Nealrith braced himself for the tirade that was sure to follow. His wife, Laisa, stared at him, her dark blue eyes wide with unfeigned shock. She had just freed her long blond hair from its combs and it tumbled over her shoulders in thick waves, but for once she appeared to be oblivious to the impact of her sensual beauty.

He took her question literally. "No, no, not that." He was tired. Too much had happened. Too many things over the previous ten days, all worthy of worry. He sat down on the bedroom stool and chose to look up at his wife as he listened. Dispassionately he wondered just how she was going to react to all he had just told her, once she was beyond the initial surprise.

She said, obviously irritated, "It was bad enough to know that sick old man was sending you caravanning off on a fool's journey with Iani, but now he would send *me*, too? To the most water-forsaken cracks in the world, looking for a new stormlord—this when we couldn't find one after years of searching the most *likely* places?"

"Yes. You *and* Taquar."

"His head must be stuffed with sand. He has gone crazy since someone stole his storm. Why me? Why Taquar?"

"He says he's come to the conclusion that we are all needed to protect the sensitives we may find there. He feels that this rogue rainlord who stole the cloud wants all the potential stormlords dead. That he may have killed before. Remember all those deaths before we were married, when Taquar almost died?"

"That's ridiculous! They were accidents, illnesses—"

"So we thought. But then someone stole Father's storm. And, it seems, later dumped it into a drywash in the Gibber Quarter. Father sensed that much. He suspects the thief must be either a Gibberman, or someone who lives there. It's another reason he wants us all there—to look for this man. Or woman."

"This gets more and more silly. It must be fifteen years since Lyneth disappeared. And even longer since the others died. And he thinks the same person is responsible? And a Gibber plains-grubber at that? Your father is going senile. What's to say the rogue who stole the cloud is not one of us?"

She started pacing, long hungry strides that ate up the floor space, forcing her to turn and start back the opposite way. Her silks—imported from across the Giving Sea—swished and shimmered, as intense and as beautiful as she herself. A concealed split up one side of the skirt allowed tantalising glimpses of a shapely calf and thigh.

She stopped pacing abruptly and considered him, head

on one side. "Nealrith, could *you* do that? Seize a storm from him by force?"

He blinked, stupid with fatigue. "Of course not."

"Not *would* you, but *could* you."

"No."

"Neither could I. A stormlord could, but a real stormlord could call up his own storm anyway; he wouldn't need to steal one."

"It must be someone with talent who needed my father to create the storm because he couldn't do that part himself."

"Hmm. A rogue indeed. There are fifty-two rainlords in Scarpen to choose from, but it must be someone who is stronger in water-power than either of us. That narrows it down a bit. I can think of only four or five. Highlord Taquar, Lord Iani and that awful wife of his, Highlord Moiqa. Your cousin Highlord Tolven, over in Denmasad, although he's always struck me as the most unambitious man I've ever met. And then just possibly Lord Kaneth, whose power has always fluctuated from pathetically incompetent to flashes of remarkable skill, things even a stormlord might find difficult. Sunlord only knows why."

"None of us would have a reason! It has to be someone who has the talent but who has never been trained."

"Another kind of rogue, in fact." She sounded more intrigued than frightened and he experienced a momentary irritation. Didn't she realise how much his struggle to retain the storm had cost Granthon? Couldn't she see how much it had cost the cities of the Scarpen? It had been days before his father had summoned the strength to create another.

Laisa was apparently following a different train of

thought. "Why on earth would a rogue rainlord want to cast water on the Gibber?"

"Why would he want to steal it in the first place? Nothing about this makes sense."

"All that water dumped on those plains-grubbers instead of where we could use it. What a waste!"

Something in the way she said that alerted him. "Kaneth's been talking to you," he said flatly.

"About abandoning the Gibber? Yes. So has Taquar on his last visit. But it wasn't anything I haven't thought myself." She sounded matter-of-fact. "Your father is only delaying the inevitable. He's far too soft."

"Damn it, doesn't anyone see how wrong that would be? We have a responsibility to the whole of the Quartern!"

She looked at him in surprise. "Oh yes, in good times, perhaps. But Nealrith, would you see Senya and me die of thirst? Of course we should cut off water to the useless desert-grubbers first! And to the 'Basters as well. That's only logical. The Reduners are too dangerous to treat that way, unfortunately."

He felt suddenly nauseated, and turned away.

She didn't notice his repugnance. "How do we find this rogue?" she asked.

Another question he couldn't answer. *Laisa*, he thought tiredly, *you have a genius for making me feel inadequate.* "I've no idea. The only thing we can do is to put every rainlord on their guard."

She gave an unpleasant smile. "When all the time it could be one of us. Wonderful." Her smile thinned into calculation. "An intriguing problem, Nealrith."

"It's all I can suggest. There is no way we can trace just

who did this. He or she could have been many days away in any direction. Or in a house right here in Breccia."

"I'll give it some thought. I do so like to pit my wits against a worthy opponent."

"This is not a game, Laisa."

"I did not say it was. In fact, I look at it more as a—a battle of minds." She slanted an inquiring look in his direction. "And what of Senya?"

"Senya stays. I am not going to drag our daughter half-way across the Quartern."

"Who will look after her if we are both away?"

"Mother will, of course."

"Nealrith, stop that. You always get an idiotic smile on your face when you think of Senya. You spoil her with your—"

She was interrupted by a knock at the door, and the entry of a servant to tell Nealrith that Iani was waiting below to see him.

"I have to make arrangements," he said as the servant left. "Laisa—"

"Yes?" She came close and raised an innocent face to smile at him.

"Don't be difficult about this."

"No, of course not." She touched him, running her fingers over his crotch, arousing and tormenting as she moved her own body in a provocative gesture against his thigh. "When am I ever difficult?" Once she had elicited a response, she stepped back and waved him away in a swirl of silken sleeve. "Go, Nealrith, dear. You have more important things to do."

He thought, *You are always difficult, Laisa.* His throat

tightened and he mourned, although for what he wasn't sure.

As usual, she had left him baffled, not knowing what she wanted or why a deep anger inside her burned at him through her eyes. After fourteen years of marriage, he had no idea what she thought of him. No idea if her playful sensuality was part of her loving or part of a deeper need to humiliate and tease. Her bedroom behaviour alternated between a passion so intense it frightened him, and a scornful coolness that left him both frustrated and at a loss.

He sighed, loving her, hating her, despising himself as he left the room.

Iani was waiting in the entrance hall, admiring the water-painting that floated in the shallow tiled pool set into the floor. It showed a picture of a storm crossing the Warthago Range, of rain descending from a broken cloud—a picture of turbulence and plenty falling onto a barren landscape. It had been painted at Laisa's request by an outlander, a strange old man whose art had become fashionable in several of the Scarpen cities.

Its potency made Nealrith uneasy; the idea of wasting water on a piece of art reinforced his disquiet, especially as every now and then the water under the paint had to be topped up, otherwise the colours lost their vibrancy and the painting lost its impact.

He descended the stairs and clapped Iani on the back. "I'm glad you're here," he said simply. "I need to talk to you. Let's go sit in my study."

"You have another job for me?" One corner of his lips

quirked upwards. "I know you think keeping an eye on the tunnels and mother wells is what keeps me sane."

This was so close to the truth that Nealrith reddened. Left too much to his own devices, Iani became increasingly odd, muttering to himself, refusing to leave his room, forgetting to eat, shaking his fist at the sun and the sky, shouting blasphemies about the Watergiver or the Sunlord. Nealrith preferred to keep him busy.

"Father has set four of us a task," he said as he ushered the rainlord into his study.

Yet another man who has aged faster than anyone should, he thought as he told Iani all he needed to know. At fifty, the man looked twenty years older. His face was crisscrossed with a network of lines as fine as a crocheted jug cover, creases put there, perhaps, by the many years he'd spent riding the Scarpen Quarter looking for any trace of his beloved Lyneth. Worse still, a later apoplexy had left him with a sagging lip and a dribble, a left hand that had trouble grasping things, and a dragging left leg.

"Four rainlords?" he asked after Nealrith had finished explaining. "We can divide up the Gibber and have it all done in less than a hundred days."

"I'm afraid not. Father wants us to stay together. To protect and train the sensitives we find, for a start."

"Then it will take us the better part of a year."

Nealrith turned his face away. A whole star cycle: Senya would be a year older before he saw her again.

"That's a long time for you and Taquar to be away from your cities," Iani added.

"Merqual Feldspar will keep an eye on Breccia for me. Taquar has his rainlords and that shrivelled bastard of a seneschal of his, Harkel Tallyman. They are so well trained that Scarcleft just about runs itself."

"That's true."

"We might be back sooner than we think. If we find water sensitives in Wash Dribarra—"

"We won't be coming home early," Iani warned. "Even if we find a potential stormlord on the first day. If Granthon thinks this is worth doing, we have to scour the Gibber, every mud-cracked drywash and every dust-blown settle of it, from one side to the other. We need as many young stormlords and rainlords as we can find. None of us is going to live forever." His voice trailed away into a mumble. "Lyneth didn't."

Nealrith gave a heavy sigh. "I know. I just hate the idea of being away so long. Let's hope it produces results."

"Improbable. Reckon I have a better chance of finding Lyneth alive."

"Father has always thought we will find solutions in the histories he so loves to read."

A servant entered with a tray of drinks and sweet cakes; they paused the conversation until he had left. Nealrith poured a glass of lime juice for each of them. The servant had supplied a grass straw; everyone knew Iani found drinking a messy business without one.

Iani took the proffered drink, but his mind appeared to be elsewhere. "Granthon is dying . . ." His voice trailed away as if he'd started to think of something else.

"Yes. So?" Nealrith prompted.

"She was so beautiful, Lyneth. She had this way of ducking her head and then looking up at you from under her lashes—"

"I remember."

"Once we had quite a few young rainlords who were probably going to be stormlords when they were older, Nealrith."

Something inside Nealrith lurched in terror. Why was everyone harping back to what had happened in the past? "Don't tell me you, too, think they might have been murdered?"

"I don't know, really. But there was a time when I was confident that there would be a line of succession after Granthon." He sipped his drink and looked out of the open shutters. "My Lyneth responded well to her training, you know. And that's not just the hopes of a besotted father. She *was* a true stormlord." He put his glass down. "Do—do you remember how lovely and sweet she was, Nealrith?"

"I remember."

"She would be nearly twenty-one now, if she was alive." He looked back at Nealrith. "But she's not. I know that, even though her body was never found. Whatever got the others got her, too. Too many deaths, my friend. Far too many. And now there's only two rainlords under thirty. Your daughter and Merqual Feldspar's Ryka." His gaze held Nealrith's intently. "You have a beautiful daughter. I would be careful of her if I were you. *Very* careful."

Nealrith stilled. Iani couldn't be *threatening* her, could he? No. Not Iani. Never Iani. It was a warning, not a threat. The idea of anything happening to Senya chilled him beyond thought, became a darkness that loomed out of nowhere and swallowed him whole. He struggled free of the panic, seeking calm.

"I *am* careful," he said at last. *How to care for her when*

I won't even be here? A lot could happen in a year. "You will come on this . . . quest?" he asked.

"Of course. I am the Cloudmaster's to command, as are we all. Perhaps he is even right." He did not sound as if he shared the belief. "Anyway, I can look for Lyneth at the same time, can't I?"

Nealrith suppressed another sigh. "Yes, of course."

I know what that darkness is, he thought. *The future. It's our future. Our vision is obscured because we can't see solutions to present problems. All we do is clutch at dim possibilities. And that could doom us.*

Oh, Watergiver forgive me, what if Taquar and Kaneth are right?

Nealrith ran a finger down the line on the map. "About these eastern washes," he said to Kaneth, "we won't get to the last of them until a full year hence."

"I'll organise for supplies to be there for you on time," Kaneth said. "Water included, but—"

He didn't finish what he was going to say. Ethelva entered and waved aside their greetings, saying, "Granthon wishes to see you both. Now."

The two men exchanged glances and headed for the door. When the lady Ethelva used that sort of tone, it was best to obey first and ask questions later.

"I bet he found out I made a mess of my marriage proposal," Kaneth said, swallowing a sigh.

"Don't tell me Beryll turned you down?" Nealrith asked in surprise.

"Beryll?" He blinked. "You can't think I was wanting to marry *Beryll* Feldspar, surely? She's not a rainlord! Besides, she's barely seventeen, if that."

"You don't mean you proposed to *Ryka* Feldspar?"

Kaneth glowered defensively. "What's the matter with that?"

"Well, um, nothing. In fact, if that's what you did, it's the wisest move you've made involving a marriageable female since you were twelve. But Beryll's the empty-headed, pretty one."

"Thanks. Nice to know you have such faith in my judgement. But the point is academic at best; Ryka turned me down. In fact, she as good as told me that I have done a superb job of earning her absolute contempt."

"Oh." Nealrith digested that, bemused. "I thought you were friends."

"So did I. I was wrong. Her esteem for me is somewhere around the level of what she would give to a sand-tick on a pede's arse."

When they entered Granthon's room, it was to find the Cloudmaster lying on his divan. Although his cheeks and eyes were sunken, his expression was alert. And annoyed. To Nealrith's surprise, Kaneth was right; Granthon had choice words to direct at the rainlord and they all concerned his ineptitude at proposing to Ryka.

Even more surprising, Kaneth offered no excuses, and when he was dismissed he was uncharacteristically subdued.

"You were hard on him," Nealrith remarked as he closed the door after Kaneth's departure.

"No more than he deserved."

"I doubt he *intended* to be turned down or tried to make sure he was."

"He must have trampled on the woman's feelings.

Ryka is not a fool, and I thought I had impressed upon her that she has a duty to marry properly."

"You spoke to her about this?" *Sands*, he thought, *even after all these years, Father still surprises me. I never thought he would intervene in such personal matters.*

"Not lately, no. But years ago I made it quite clear to her that her duty lay with a rainlord. Or I thought I had." He fixed a sharp gaze on his son. "I expect you to see that the match goes ahead. And soon."

"*Me?* How do you expect me to do that?"

"I will order both of them to go with you on this Gibber expedition."

Nealrith stared at his father in disbelief. "Are you *serious?*"

"I want you to have plenty of rainlords with you. You may have need of them."

Granthon reiterated, at length, just how careful he wanted them to be if they found any potential rainlords or stormlords, while Nealrith groaned inwardly. He had thought the trip to the Gibber Quarter already offered every unpleasantness possible, but he began to wonder if he'd been overly optimistic. Now that the journey included persuading a woman known for her plain-spoken stubbornness to marry a man she apparently despised as husband material—with some justification, given Kaneth's history—it was shaping up to be even more of a nightmare.

"I'll do my best," he said when his father's rambling finally came to a halt. He had a horrible idea he might lose a friend on this trip. He just wasn't sure which one: Kaneth Carnelian or Ryka Feldspar.

CHAPTER NINE

Scarpen Quarter
Scarcleft City
Level 32 and Level 10

The snuggery courtyard, normally a place of still and quiet in the heat of the late afternoon, was filled with the sound of outraged voices. Terelle, who had been snatching a few moments' sleep while she was supposedly folding linen in the upstairs storeroom, jerked into wakefulness. She hurriedly smoothed out the imprint of her head from the top of the pile of clean bedding and looked out the door.

"What's going on?" she asked.

The mistress of the chambers, waking from a doze at her post at the head of the stairs, shook her head. "I don't know. Go and find out and come back and tell me."

Terelle gladly left her task half done and ran downstairs. Out in the courtyard five or six handmaidens were gathered around Madam Opal, Garri the steward and Linsia the warden mistress. Everyone was talking at once. Just as Terelle stepped out of the house, Madam Opal raised her voice above the din and snapped, "Quiet! All of you! I have never heard such a caterwaul. Warden Linsia, tell me—quietly and calmly if you can—just what happened."

The girls all knew it did not pay to upset Madam Opal, and the silence was instant. Linsia, a plump middle-aged woman with a lizard-like stare, said primly, "I was taking these girls to the baths, madam. But when we got there, it was shut. There was a crowd in the street, so I asked someone what time it was going to open again. He said it wasn't going to reopen. Not today, not ever. That the reeve had closed it down."

"I saw the notice on the door," one of the handmaidens piped up. "It said it was done by order of Highlord Taquar."

"There was a man standing guard outside," Vivie added. "He wore a blue uniform I haven't seen before."

Opal swore. "That is ridiculous. Where are we going to bathe? Where will our laundress wash the linens and clothes? We'd have to go right to the other side of the level! Garri, go to Reeve Bevran and find out what is going on, and all you girls, go back inside. Your skins will blemish if you stand around in the sun like this."

As the girls began to disperse, Garri pointedly rubbed his knee and cleared his throat. More than forty days had passed since the night Donnick had died, but he still complained he could not walk up and down steps without pain.

Opal pursed her lips. "Oh very well." She glanced around and caught Terelle's eye. "Child, you go. Ask Reeve Bevran to explain what is going on. And don't forget to wear a palmubra. I don't want a dark face to lower your first-night price. Scarpen men prefer pale girls, and don't you forget it." She turned back to Garri. "I don't know what to do with you. If your joints are so bad you can't do your job, then why should I be paying you tokens? Tell me that."

Garri glared at his employer. "Because I'm the only person in this establishment who knows a troublemaker when one comes to the gate and who remembers every troublemaker who *ever* came to the gate. And when are you going to get a replacement for Donnick, eh? Tell me that!" Terelle grabbed up a hat and left the snuggery without hearing Opal's reply. Arguments between her and Garri were legion and she had no wish to hear another.

As the doorman at the Cistern Chambers opened the gate to Terelle, he was already saying the words to deny her entry. "The reeve is not seeing anybody—" Then he saw he was addressing Terelle and said ungraciously, "Oh, it's you. You've come to play with Felissa, I suppose. She's upstairs in the house."

Terelle hung up her palmubra and headed to the door that led to the reeve's house adjoining the chambers. Fortunately for her errand, just at that moment Bevran came out of the entrance to the Cistern Chambers and saw her. "Ah, Terelle. It's only you. Come to see Felissa?"

"No, Reeve. Not really. Madam Opal sent me. She wants to know why the women's baths are closed."

He sighed and it seemed to Terelle that his shoulders slumped in sympathy with the sound. "Everyone has been hounding me about the same thing." He gave a reluctant smile. "You are the only one clever enough to get in. Tell Madam Opal that all baths below the tenth level are closed till further notice, on the orders of Seneschal Harkel, in the name of Highlord Taquar."

Terelle blinked, astonished. "All?"

He nodded.

"But why?"

"To conserve water."

"We can't bathe?"

"Not unless you use your normal water supply, no."

She thought about that, frowning. "But that's silly. Rinse water from the baths is sold to the livery for the pedes; it's not wasted. Soapy water is used to wash clothes. And then it's resold. That's what I was told, anyway."

"Yes, to the smiths and the stone polishers and the metalworkers, for use in their trades. I know. But some is lost each time, too. Scarcleft must reduce that waste now, because there is not enough water coming in from the mother cistern. Bathing and washing clothes are not deemed essential. It is a wise decision."

"But the upper levels still have their bath houses. What's so special about uplevellers?"

He gave a slight smile. "Ah, still the Terelle who thinks that life should be fair and wants to argue the case!" He reached out and tilted her chin up. "Don't ever lose those illusions, child. Hold on to those dreams." He turned her around to face the gate. "Now go and tell Opal what I have just told you."

"Who are those men in the blue tunics?" she asked.

"They are called enforcers. It is their job to see that all the new water laws are obeyed. Especially as the highlord is away for some time."

"Highlord Taquar? Is he? Why?"

"Gone looking for new stormlords in the Gibber, or so I heard. That's the wind-whisper, anyway. The seneschal, Harkel Tallyman, manages Scarcleft now, backed by the enforcers. And there's the highlord's rainlords as well, of

course, to help at the House of the Dead and to check on
water matters. Oh, you'd better tell Opal there's a reward
offered to anyone who turns in water-wasters to the enforcers. You snuggery girls need to take care."

Terelle hesitated on the doorstep, remembering the
clamour in the snuggery courtyard. "Everyone is going to
be very angry about the new law," she said.

She looked back to meet his eyes, and knew he thought
the remark impertinent. She turned away so he wouldn't
see her flush.

It's true, though, she thought stubbornly. *People will
be angry—and they will blame the reeves.*

The days flew by, too fast for Terelle. Each one brought
her closer to her first bleeding, yet did not seem to offer
her a way out of the snuggery. Her evenings were a tor-
ment spent trying to evade the attention of men who expressed an interest in her first-night.

Almost a full year after Donnick's death, and not long
after her thirteenth birthday, she found out exactly where
Arta Amethyst the dancer lived: the tenth level, a pres-
tigious address for someone not from one of the better-
known families. Terelle had never been as high as that
in the city, but she was determined to see the arta if she
could.

She chose her time carefully, selecting early morning
before most of the snuggery was awake. She took all the
tokens she had, which were pitifully few when she counted
them, and put on her best tunic, of mauve-dyed cloth with
embroidery around the neck, and matching leggings. A
swathe of purple silk tied with a bow at the back belted
the outfit. Opal had been paying much more attention to

what Terelle had been wearing lately and had started to replace her drab brown clothing with more expensive garments. Terelle didn't like to think about why.

She left the snuggery unseen, via the back delivery gate. It was too early to knock on Amethyst's door, so she ambled from level to level, enjoying the chance to look about. She soon realised how little she knew about life outside the snuggery walls. She'd had no idea, for example, that on the twenty-seventh level there was a salt market where many sellers were 'Basters from the White Quarter, dressed in their strange garments adorned with mirrors. Or that on the twenty-third level, inns and snuggeries were used exclusively by traders from outside the Scarpen Quarter. Or that Level Eighteen had streets consisting entirely of jewellery shops. Or, that from Level Fifteen upwards children went to temple schools run by waterpriests. Or that on Level Fourteen there was an outdoor market in a square where it was possible to buy goods from across the Giving Sea, things she'd never dreamed existed. She lingered there, fascinated by the oddly dressed men who sold everything from strange foods to board-books. When they spoke, their accents were so thick she could scarcely understand. They came from lands with names like the ringing of wind chimes.

One of them, a young man with a beard and gingery hair—both attributes proclaiming his origins outside of the Quartern—delighted in teasing her when she stopped to look at his goods. He was selling necklaces and bracelets and rings and she thought them the most beautiful things she had ever seen.

He called her "lovely lass" and bantered with her, trying to entice her into buying.

"What are they made of?" she asked.

"Why, little love, they is corals, black 'n' red 'n' white corals o' the sea. Things that grow in the sea 'n' leave these lovely skel'tons behind when they die. And sure 'tis a lovely thing to be gracing a neck as long 'n' smooth as yours, my sweetling."

"I've never seen the sea," she said wistfully. "Is it as beautiful as they say? Does it go on forever? Is it really made all of salt water?"

"Lovely? Sure! Go on forever? Why, not so! Else how could I live on the other side of it? And yea, 'tis salt all right. Too salt for the drinking of."

"They say there are lands across the sea where plants grow without being watered. Is that true? Do you live in a place like that?"

"Sure I do! There's grass and trees and bushes and no one ever waters them except the sweet God in heaven. Ah, lass, it's not a dust hole like your land here, where a decent man finds it hard to get a drink of water, even. And where is it you're from, my precious?"

"From a snuggery on the thirty-second level."

The merch in the stall next door guffawed. "A snuggery, eh? Would have thought you a little young for that trade, girl!" He turned to the coral seller and added, "Watch it, lad, she lives in a whorehouse. She'll have the pants off yer before yer say yer name."

The first man looked revolted.

Terelle reddened in humiliation and turned away. She would *not* be a whore. She *wouldn't*.

She hurried upwards, stopped now on every level by an enforcer asking what she was doing there, as if the higher one went, the stricter the enforcement of rules. It was a further humiliation to realise how easily they recognised her as being from a lower level. Perhaps her clothes betrayed her; the weave of her tunic was coarse compared with the clothing she saw around her. Fortunately, her explanation—that she had a message for Arta Amethyst the dancer about a new student for her classes—was accepted, and each time they sent her on her way, with a stern warning not to linger.

The way they looked at her, as if she was grubby and worthy only of contempt, brought back memories better forgotten: her stepmother Mauna, Vivie's mother, looking her up and down and saying, "Well, not sure anyone would want to buy a water-waster, but we don't want a useless rag like you in this house soakin' up our water, that's f'sure. You were born to a caravan whore, and it's a whore you should be." The words had cut deep, though not as deep as her own father's acquiescence. Vivie had wanted to leave the settle, but Terelle hadn't, and she'd pleaded with her father to let her stay. "Sell her as well," he'd told his wife. "Don't mind if Vivie wants to stay, but I've never been sure I fathered this one anyway." Terelle may have forgotten much of her early life in the Gibber, but she had never forgotten those words.

Useless. Whore. Water-waster. *Never been sure I fathered her anyway.*

And now, fuelled by rage, her own resolution: *I will not be a whore.*

She would *never* give up. If Yagon hadn't sired her, then good. She didn't want to be the daughter of a man who would sell his children. She blinked back tears, those unwelcome water-wasting tears, and continued on her way.

It wasn't as easy to see Amethyst as she had hoped. The steward of the dancer's house opened the door in answer to her pull on the bell, but refused her entry. "The arta is not in need of new students." A flat, uninterested remark uttered in bored tones.

But Terelle had come too far to turn back. Quickly she put her foot in the door, a strategy she had seen executed often enough by troublemakers at the snuggery. "Then I will dance in the street outside the door till Arta Amethyst comes to see," she said. "It will take only a few moments. If she says I am not good enough, I will say thanks and leave quietly."

The steward was silent for a moment while he leaned forward and peered at her in myopic appraisal. Terelle's dislike of him was instant. His gaze lingered around the level of her breasts. He was short and plump, with a round protruding stomach that started not far under his chin and a small thick-lipped mouth now pursed in disapproval. Sweat trickled down his face to pool in the folds of his neck. "Wait here," he said finally and eased her foot out of the door with his own. "I'll ask."

He was gone so long she thought he wasn't coming back, but when the door opened again, it was to let her in. "The arta has very charitably given you some of her precious time. This way."

He laboured upstairs, breathing noisily, while she trailed in his wake. He smelled, a sourish smell of unwashed armpits and greasy hair. At the top he had to catch his breath before ushering her into a large room with a smoothly tiled floor. At one end of the room a dancer stood dressed in her practice clothes. Standing alongside her there was another woman who held a dance flute.

Amethyst had been famous for many years, but Terelle hadn't considered what that must mean: the dancer was no longer youthful. Even though there was a suppleness about her still—her body moved like one much younger—it was a shock to see from her lined face that she must have been forty or more.

Terelle went down on one knee, acknowledging her reverence of Scarcleft's greatest dancer. Amethyst looked her up and down without moving. Then she said, addressing the steward, "You may go, Jomat. Come back in a quarter of a sandglass run. Get up, child. Where are you from?"

"Madam Opal's snuggery. On the thirty-second. But I don't want to be a handmaiden. I want to be a dancer."

Amethyst digested that, inclining her head to acknowledge that in those few words Terelle had told her all she needed to know. She indicated the flautist. "What music do you want Meriam here to play?"

"Loskin's 'Desert Wind.'" She had designed a short dance to fit that music. The routine incorporated many of the most difficult steps and contained all that Amethyst needed to see in order to judge her standard. She had been prepared to dance without music, and it was a relief to know that would not be necessary.

Amethyst nodded to the woman and waved her hand at the centre of the room. "Your chance, child."

Hurriedly Terelle bunched up her tunic under the belt to shorten the skirt and give her more freedom of movement. Her voice wavered as she said, "I have called this dance 'Born Waterless.'"

Her heart pounded. What if she stumbled?

Don't think about failing, you idiot. You can do this.

The woman lifted her flute and Terelle blotted out everything but the sound. Slowly she began to dance.

The early passages of the music were written to echo the peace and beauty of a windless desert. Terelle turned the tune into movement that captured—or so she hoped—the early life of a carefree child, still too young to realise what lay ahead. The first toddling steps, the smiles, the unconscious grace of the very young. As the music changed, to signify the first gusts of wind and flurries of sand and to offer a warning of what might follow, Terelle changed the toddler into a growing child. The infant grace became the uncertain movements of a girl finding out that the world could be cruel and unfair, of a girl who sometimes thirsted. As the music built to the crescendo of a full desert storm, the girl became a young maiden, rebellious and thirsty, a cunning thief of water. Her steps became more intricate, full of passion and a love of life, interwoven with rage at life's unfairness.

Gradually the desert storm faded, and so did the young woman, dying of thirst and despair as she yearned for something she could never have: the right to water. When the tune returned to the beauty of the stilled desert, Terelle's movements reflected her last vision of hope as she glimpsed an afterlife where thirst and inequality had no place.

At the end of the piece, she unrolled from her crouch on the floor and raised her eyes to meet Amethyst's—and was unable to read the expression there. It wasn't that the dancer's face lacked expression; rather that it held too much.

"Who taught you that dance?" she asked eventually.

"No one. I mean, I made it up."

"I see. *Were* you born waterless?"

Terelle nodded.

"Ah." Amethyst took a deep breath. "I could take you in. I could teach you, if you had the money to pay me, which I think you have not. But I would be wasting my time and your money."

Terelle felt the shock of her disappointment as a physical blow, snatching her breath away. *No. Oh no*.

"True, your dancing is good. You have been well taught, for a snuggery girl. But you must realise that Scarcleft doesn't support too many full-time dancers. Most dancers earn the bulk of their income some other way; usually through a snuggery or a personal financial arrangement with a protector. As whores, if you like. It is as good a word as any. To earn enough as a dancer to support yourself independently, you would have to be more than just good. You would have to be special. You are not special."

The words battered her hope. *You are not special.* Good wasn't good enough. And there was that word again: *whore*.

"I'm only thirteen," she said, and knew immediately that it was the wrong thing to say. She may have been a child in years, but being childish was a luxury she could not afford.

Amethyst shrugged. "You will be better when you are older, of course. But you will never have the—the shining edge that makes a solo dancer. That indefinable something. It has nothing to do with looks, nothing to do with training. It is more than that. It is something you are either born with, or not. You were not."

Terelle wanted to cry. She wanted to protest. She wanted to beg.

She did none of those things. Instead she pulled her tunic down and retied her sash. "I'm sorry to have wasted your time, Arta."

"Oh, but you did not waste my time, child. Not at all. Wait, I want to show you something. Meriam, play the same tune again."

The flautist looked surprised but lifted her instrument to her lips. To Terelle's amazement, Amethyst started to dance, the same dance she had just been shown. She had remembered every step in its correct sequence, every nuance. Terelle watched spellbound. Every move was exactly how Terelle had envisioned it should be done. "Oh," she said when the dance was finished, "that was . . . beautiful. I could never have danced it like that."

"No. But you wrote it that way." Amethyst came across the floor and took her by the shoulders. "You have been looking in the wrong direction, child, chasing water when you can make the vessel."

"I—I don't understand."

"You are not a performer of dance; you are a creator. That is where your skill lies."

Terelle considered that. She had always thought that a performer *was* a creator, but she was not going to argue the point with Amethyst. "I'm not sure how that can help," she said finally.

"Neither am I, exactly. The problem is that there is not much call for new dances. I will buy one piece from you every quarter, though. A dance of about the same length for five tokens."

Terelle drew in a sharp breath. Enough water for five days just for a short dance! "That's . . . wonderful," she said at last.

"But it won't solve your problem, will it? You need more than that to separate yourself from the snuggery. For that, I can only offer advice. Look to making things, Terelle. That's where your destiny lies."

"What—what sort of things?"

"How should I know? Songs? Tunes? Pottery? Jewellery? Patterns for weavers or lace makers? Go and find out!" She sounded snappish but her next action belied her tone. She put an arm around Terelle as they went to the door, saying with a quiet passion, "Don't become a whore. It might make you a better artist in the end, but you will lose part of your soul."

Jomat the steward was hovering outside the door, and the smirk he gave her made Terelle want to slap him. She was sure he had overheard.

"Jomat," Amethyst said, "pay her five tokens and show her out. She will return in a quarter year; please admit her again then."

At the front door Jomat disappeared into a side room for a moment and returned with the tokens, which he ostentatiously counted into Terelle's hand. "I'm sure you dance very prettily, my dear," he said. "You mustn't let these little setbacks get you down."

He sounded sincere enough, and she tried not to step backwards as he patted her on the arm with a sweaty hand. She said, "The arta is a wonderful dancer, and she was very kind."

"Oh yes, she's the best there ever was. A perfectionist, of course, and perfectionists are difficult to live with, aren't they? Not, of course, that we would *ever* have her any other way."

He opened the door and Terelle slipped out, wondering

if the way his arm brushed her chest as she went past was accidental or not.

Her feelings in a turmoil, she started back to the thirty-second. Elation warred with despair. She had sold a dance to the famous Amethyst—there were five shiny tokens in her purse to prove it—but she herself would never make a dancer. So, she did have a talent for creation, but how was she going to put that to good use? She had just seen the country's most famous dancer perform something of hers, and do it beautifully, but it was something she herself would never do so well.

And she came away convinced of two things about Amethyst that she had not known before. The dancer had been born waterless, and at one time in her life she had sold her body for water.

Terelle knew the signs.

CHAPTER TEN

Scarpen Quarter
Breccia City
Breccia Hall, Level 2, and outside the city walls

"But I want to go!"

Rainlord Senya, granddaughter of the Quartern Cloud-master and eleven years old, came close to stamping her foot. She was stopped only by the memory of her grandmother telling her that when she behaved in such a manner she resembled a myriapede in heat. The comparison was unpleasant, so she tried not to stamp and not to grit her teeth, either. Her restraint, however, made no difference to her mood.

"I am *sick* of being cooped up in the palace. It's been almost a year since Mama and Papa left, and in all that time you haven't allowed me to go *anywhere*. Papa would let me go if he was here."

"I doubt it," her grandmother said evenly as she looked up from the gemstone she was carving. "Your father gave precise orders before he left for the Gibber. He said you weren't to be allowed out of Breccia Hall except under rainlord escort. None can be spared to take you to the

Gratitudes festivities until we all go this evening. That will have to suffice."

"But it's much more fun in the afternoon. They have a fair, and games. Tonight is just all the religious stuff." In parody, she mimicked the high-pitched wail of Lord Gold, the Quartern Sunpriest: " 'Praise be to the Watergiver for our water! Praise him, praise her, praise the whole darn parcel of sun-dried water prophets!' "

Ethelva's face tightened, but she said nothing.

"Why can't someone go with me this afternoon? Rainlord Merqual would take me."

"Your grandfather has sent Lord Merqual to investigate a water theft from the tunnel that supplies the dyemakers' street on the twenty-eighth level. It is a very serious matter."

Senya flounced into the chair next to Ethelva and glared at her. "Why do I have to be bothered with guards anyway? I can go with a servant. I am quite safe in Breccia, surely."

"We do not know that." With a sigh Ethelva laid her carving aside and took her granddaughter's hands in hers. "Senya, my dear, it is time you started to think a little more deeply about things."

"What do you mean?"

"Think: twenty or so years ago there were six other young rainlords or potential stormlords around your father's age, besides Taquar and Kaneth. None of them made it to twenty-two. Not one. I don't mean to scare you—no, I take that back. I *do* mean to scare you. I want to scare you silly because you don't seem to have the sense to know when you are threatened."

"By *who*? No one has ever tried to hurt me! None of

those people were murdered. They just had stupid accidents and things. Falling down stairs. Getting lost in the desert. Getting sick."

"Let's just say that we don't want any of those things to happen to you."

Senya pouted. "I am so *bored*! There is nothing to do here. I should have gone with Papa and Mama—"

"That's a change," Ethelva remarked, releasing her hands. "Before your parents left, you said you wouldn't want to set foot on the Gibber Plains for all the water in a mother well."

"I don't *want* to exactly, but anything would be better than sitting around doing *nothing*."

"Then work on your water sensitivity. Senya, you are growing up to be a very indifferent rainlord. No one comes into full powers unless they work at it; you know that. You hardly ever do the exercises."

"Oh, what's the point? I'll never be allowed to do any of the interesting things that a rainlord can do. If you are so worried about my safety, why don't you have someone teach me the rainlord way to kill? Then I could protect myself!"

"It is no light thing to learn to kill, child. That is reserved for men and women who have proved they can control their talents and who understand the implications of using those same talents to destroy life."

For once, Senya recognised that she had gone too far. Contritely she knelt on the tiles beside her grandmother's chair; sensibly she changed the subject. "Grandmama, Mama has always said that if they find a stormlord, I must marry him. Because there's only one other unmarried female rainlord, Ryka, and she's too old and useless anyway. Besides, she can't see past the end of her nose." She looked up woefully. "I won't have to marry someone from the Gibber, will I? They are horrid! I have seen them down in the market sometimes. They are always dirty and ragged and they have funny accents. Annas says that they beat their wives and get drunk on amber—"

"Annas is very silly, my dear. You should listen to your teachers, not your maid. There are good men and bad men in every quarter, and you may rest assured that no one is going to marry you off to someone who will beat you."

"I don't want to marry anyone who's dirty, either. In fact, I think I already know who I want to marry. I want to marry Taquar." She stood up and pranced around the room as if listening to music only she could hear.

"*Taquar?*"

"Yes. Why not? He's not married. I did think of Kaneth, because he's fun, but he's not really rich like Taquar. Taquar commands a city. I think I would like that. Everyone says Scarcleft is much more beautiful than Breccia. Besides, he is fearfully handsome, and . . . mysterious."

"He's also older than your father."

"Thirty-seven. That's not so very old."

"Too old for you. Listen, Senya, if you go up on the roof you can watch the festivities from there. Ask the servants to rig up a piece of silk to keep off the sun."

Senya pulled a sour face. "It won't be the same."

"No, it won't. But it is all I can offer, and at least it is safe."

Senya gave a heavy sigh and left the room dragging her feet, a picture of weary gloom.

"Giving you problems?"

Ethelva turned in her chair and smiled as her husband entered. It was an effort not to show her concern at his weakness, not to jump up and offer him an arm as he made his way carefully across to his chair. "Yes, in a way. I have come to know her better, without her father or mother around."

Granthon did not sit as much as lower himself into the chair. "And you find that upsetting?"

"I'm afraid I do. I had no idea she was so—so manipulative. Or so, *petty* with it."

He settled back into his seat. "She is beautiful. More so even than her mother. And like many beautiful people, she has been spoiled."

"I fear it is more than that."

He didn't answer, waiting for her to explain, but she said, "I can't explain it, Granthon, because I can't put my finger on it. There is just something *lacking* in her. And it disturbs me greatly."

"She is a child yet. Younger perhaps than her years. Irresponsible. Sooner or later events will catch up with her and she will have to grow up. Then she will come into her own."

"I hope you are right. Waterless soul, I hope so. The child wants to marry Taquar! The man would eat her for breakfast and not even hiccup."

"I'm right. You'll see. It is not Senya we should worry about. It is who is going to sit in my place when I am gone."

She stared at him, and her heart plunged. She knew him well enough to know she would not like whatever he was about to tell her.

"I had another letter from Nealrith today. They still haven't found a child who shows stormlord promise.

There's not going to be a stormlord ready to step into my shoes, Ethelva; even if we find a youngster who could become one with training. Someone has to rule this land in the interim."

"Granthon, we both know there won't *be* a Quartern if there is no stormlord. How can any of us live if there is no water? And how can there be water if there is no stormlord to bring it? If you die, we all die."

"No. That's an oversimplification." He leaned forward, resting his forearms on his thighs. "If there is no stormlord calling up storms and placing them exactly where they are needed, there will be rogue storms instead, dropping rain at random, the way it used to be. Without a stormlord, there will still be rain, sometimes, in some places, and rainlords can track it. Some people will survive."

"But not all," she said flatly.

"No. As far as I can discover from my reading, our population is about twenty times larger than it used to be in the Time of Random Rain."

"You're telling me nineteen in every twenty will die?"

He did not answer.

"And what happens on the route to such a catastrophe? Can you imagine it, Granthon? People will not go willingly to their deaths. It will be hell, and it won't be the gentle who survive."

He gave a grim smile. "Not a place I would want to live in."

She failed to appreciate the humour in his irony. "So—who?"

"Nealrith is not up to it," he said bluntly.

She was silent.

"I love our son; you know that. But I can't blind myself

to what will be. Nealrith is a good man, a gentle man. But the time after I have gone will not be a place for gentle men. Decisions will have to be made about the water we have in storage. About who will live and who will die. It will be the time for a hard man who has to make hard decisions. Nealrith . . . is not that man."

She felt the space inside her body contract, as if her own water was already disappearing. *This is a mistake*, she thought. *Don't make it, Granthon. Don't destroy our son.*

"Taquar Sardonyx," he said, answering her unspoken question.

She shrivelled still further. "Nealrith doesn't deserve that. You know they hate one another. Taquar lusted after Laisa, but Nealrith was the one who married her." Her thoughts added an uncharitable: *Because Laisa thought Nealrith, not Taquar, would be the heir to the Quartern.*

"I know."

"Have you mentioned this to Senya, by any chance?"

"No, of course not. Why?"

"She—she has her eye on that man."

"I would not wish Taquar on any woman, let alone a child."

"But you would wish him on the land?"

"He's the only person I can think of who could pull it through the turmoil to come. He has vision, Ethelva. And courage. He sees reality, not dreams. We need his pragmatism and the wisdom of his solutions."

"Have you told him?"

"Not yet. But I have left documents in case I fade out before they all return from the Gibber."

She paled but continued the conversation doggedly.

"As a matter of interest, what makes you think that once Taquar held administrative power he would ever relinquish it to a new stormlord?" *Can't you see what kind of man he is?*

"Perhaps he wouldn't have to. He could continue to rule, and the stormlord—please Sunlord that we find one—could bring rain. Ethelva, I *can't* ask Nealrith to take on a cloudmaster's task. It would kill him. He hasn't the . . . the cruelty for it."

Incredulous, she asked in dismay, "You'd put your land in the hands of a man you believe to be *cruel*?"

His answer was barely above a whisper. "Yes. Taquar is not gratuitously cruel, you know; just sufficiently callous to enact the solutions needed for some to be saved."

Before she could answer, the Breccia Hall seneschal, Mikael, entered the room and cleared his throat. They turned to look at him, relieved at the interruption, knowing it had saved them from a bitter argument that might have scarred their affection for each other.

"Your pardon, master," he said, "but there is a delegation of Reduners at the gates. They have set up camp outside the walls and sent you this." He held out a scroll cylinder.

Ethelva and Granthon exchanged glances.

"Doubtless it is just an update of the places in need of rain," Ethelva said, not believing her own words.

Granthon scanned it quickly and then started to translate it aloud for the benefit of Ethelva and the seneschal. "The representative of the Sandmaster of the Tribes of the Scarmaker bids the esteemed Cloudmaster of Quartern greetings and may his water be plentiful, with—"

"Yes, yes," Ethelva said. "Let's dispense with the flowery bits."

"Then there's nothing much else. He wants me to grace his encampment, being reluctant to cause me any discomposure by venturing to Breccia Hall, and so on, and so on." He gave a cynical laugh. "They care little for my discomposure, of course; they just hate to enter anything with solid walls and a roof."

"Oh, my dear," Ethelva said in concern, "for you to go all that way, when you have to sit through the religious ceremonies this evening—"

"I am not decrepit yet," he said mildly. He turned to Mikad. "Have a pede and driver made ready for me, with a chair saddle. I'll take ten men from the guard. In the meantime, send water to the Reduner camp. One dayjar for each man and beast. Do that every day they are our guests."

The seneschal bowed and retreated.

Ethelva looked at her husband in concern. "You didn't even ask how many of them there were before ordering the water! Granthon, we cannot spare—"

"Hush, Ethelva. Apart from our duty as hosts, we can ill afford to offend them now. I have been short-sending their storms for several years. They will have no reserves. All their waterholes will be operating at the bare minimum."

"Was that . . . wise?"

"Wise?" He snorted. "Wise to cut the allotment of a volatile quadrant of nomads who live just to the north of us, all well armed with ziggers, scimitars and spears, warriors renowned for their ferocity, mounted on the best pedes in the Quartern?" Troubled, he ran a hand through his thinning hair. "So far they have enough, but the cuts will have worried them."

He closed his eyes briefly. "It will be an awkward meeting at best. Fortunately for me it is the Scarmakers who have come and not that young hothead Davim from Dune Watergatherer. That lot would feed my eyeballs to their ziggers as an appetiser." He levered himself to his feet.

Ethelva rose immediately as well. "I wish one of the rainlords was available to accompany you."

He looked at her in affection. "I am hardly in danger from these men. And I am not defenceless, either. Not yet. I feel sure I can still take a man's water."

"I'll see that your clothes are laid out." She walked out without waiting for him, knowing he would bless her for it. He hated her to see just how slow he was nowadays. How *old*.

There was a strong smell in the nomad tent.

It wasn't that the Reduners never washed—they did in fact, often, because they liked to swim and had no qualms about doing so in the same waterhole that supplied their drinking water. The smell was exuded not by people but by the ziggers in their cages.

Granthon had long since had them banned from Breccia City. If he'd had his way, they would have been banned throughout the Quartern, but the Reduners regarded them as part of their heritage and would never have countenanced limitations on what they called their ancestral right to own and travel with ziggers. They had a point. As a hunting people, they might have starved without the use of their traditional hunting weapon.

Some cities of the Scarpen Quarter allowed ziggers

to be carried for protection or used for hunting for sport, even though the number of citizens who died as a consequence of zigger accidents was, to Granthon, astonishingly high. They also fell into the hands of criminals from time to time, and then there would be a spate of robberies where victims were threatened or killed by zigger-carrying bandits.

The smell of them in the tent was strong but not all that unpleasant, except that it reminded Granthon of his reluctance to impose his will on the Red Quarter.

He avoided looking at the cages and glanced around the tent. The man who came forward to greet him he knew: Tribemaster Bejanim, who carried the title Drover Son with the honorific Kher, because he was responsible for Dune Scarmaker's pedes. He was also the younger brother of the Scarmaker sandmaster and he spoke the language of the Quartern fluently. Granthon was pleased to see him and acknowledged his gesture of salutation before turning his attention to the rest of the tent. The usual mats and cushions: basic colour, red. Refreshments laid out. Four other tribemasters (he knew them all). At least they were still smiling. As he returned their greetings and spoke the usual Reduner set phrases of hospitality, he reflected that Nealrith wasn't the only one who was too weak to rule the Quartern; he himself had displayed weakness and a deeply rooted disinclination to do anything that would result in confrontation. He should have banned ziggers from the Scarpen Quarter at the very least.

With the formalities finally out of the way, including the ritual offering and acceptance of water, Granthon turned to the reason that the Reduners had crossed the Warthago Range and the Sweepings to come to Breccia.

"Well, Kher Bejanim, old friend," he said, "what is it that causes you to honour my city with your presence?" He stirred uneasily. His joints did not take kindly to sitting cross-legged on a carpet. *I'm too old for this*, he thought.

"Not a happy ride, m'lord. Our waterholes are little more than mud wallows. My brother, the Sandmaster, wishes to remind you of the ancient handclasp between the people of the Red Quarter and the stormlords of the Quartern. He says to inform you that the tribes of the Red Quarter have kept their clasp tight."

"Indeed they have. They are an honourable people." A lie, that. The Reduners were renowned more for their breaking of promises than for the honouring of them. However, Granthon was well aware of the terms of this particular agreement—the scribes of Breccia Hall had written it down even if the Reduners had not—and it was true that the Red Quarter had followed most of its clauses. They'd promised not to raid the other quarters as they had done with terrifying ruthlessness for generations. They'd acknowledged the cloudmaster as the head of all the Quartern with certain rights to taxes and privileges. In return, they'd received regular rain at places specified by the Reduners themselves.

Granthon added smoothly, "We, too, have followed the agreement."

Kher Bejanim's red face flushed still deeper in colour. "Not so. Our water is too little."

"We promised regular rain in sufficient quantities. We have done that. You do not thirst."

"No, not yet," Bejanim admitted. "But if the next storm around my dune's main waterhole was but a week or two late, the result would be unthinkable."

"Kher Bejanim, I'll not lie to you. I cannot maintain previous levels of rainfall, not when I have to do it alone. The reduced levels will continue until such time as another stormlord is found. This is not negotiable. I do not have the strength for it to be any other way. My reduced storms are still more dependable than rain based on the vagaries of nature. Believe me, you do not want a return of the Time of Random Rain."

The four men were silent and motionless.

"This is not good news," Bejanim said finally. "It grieves us."

Granthon found he had to suppress an involuntary shudder at the flint he heard in Bejanim's tone. He said quickly, "Even as we speak, our rainlords scour the Gibber for new blood to restore our ranks. We have every confidence of success."

"Cloudmaster, I hope you're right." More levels of meaning there, stacked one on the next. Bejanim gave a fleeting glance at the man next to him before continuing. "You've been honest with us; I'll be honest with you. We older tribesmen, those of us from dunes that follow the traditions closely, are losing control of some of the younger pede hunters and drovers on other dunes. They are angered by the diminishing rain. They blame you city dwellers. They speak of returning to the old ways."

"Old ways?"

" 'Free of the Scarpen harness' are the words they use. Free to raid and plunder when they feel like it."

"Free to steal water."

"Yes."

"They would be worse off."

"*I* believe you. But the young, as ever, prefer action

to waiting. I am not sure how long the wisdom of older heads will prevail. Take this as a warning, Cloudmaster, meant in friendship, not as a threat uttered by an enemy. Do not cut our water any further. Ever."

Granthon's heart sank as he bowed his head in acknowledgement. He knew the links between the dunes were even looser than those between Scarpen cities. There was an overall leader—traditionally the sandmaster of Dune Scarmaker—but he had little way of enforcing his rule unless there was consensus to begin with. "I will take an oath," he said carefully, "that I will never cut the Reduners' water one drop more than I cut that of Scarpermen. We will live or die together, Kher."

Once again there was a long silence. Then one of the older tribesmen spoke, a shrivelled ancient called Firman, if Granthon remembered correctly. "There be old story among drovers," he said, his desert accent thick, his words clipped short, "telling of nomad, name Ash Gridelin. Learned water-powers from Watergivers, became first stormlord."

"We have the same story," Granthon said, "although we believe there was but one Watergiver, Ash Gridelin himself, who now sits at the right hand of the Sunlord. Our waterpriests pray—"

"Pah!" Firman said dismissively. "What they know, men living inside dried mud, never feeling sand beneath feet? Watergivers not gods."

Granthon gave Bejanim a questioning look.

Bejanim looked embarrassed. "It's a legend of our people. In it, the Watergivers are many, not just a single god. It says they live in a place where there's all the water you could ever want—"

"I understand there are many such places," Granthon said, "across the Giving Sea. Unfortunately for us, people live there already."

Bejanim ignored the interruption. "The story says that the Watergivers have power over water, but that they hide their land from the greed of the thirsty. That there are guardians who prevent us from ever finding them or their land. Some think the shimmering sand-dancers of the plains are in fact the guardians, dancing to lead a man away when he strays too close to the paths that lead to the Watergivers' land. The tale says that the Watergivers took pity on Gridelin when he was lost and admired his courage so they gave him the power to be a stormbringer and cloudbreaker. They sent him on his way and hid their land again. Legend has it that someone will find the Watergivers once more, when the need is at its greatest. In the past, some of our young hotheads have searched. None ever returned. It's said that one must find the key to the guardians first."

Granthon hid his irritation. "The story might be of more value if it told us where to look."

"Be wisdom to listen old stories," Firman said. The words were bland, but the tone was layered with contempt.

"I do," Granthon replied. "But I can't see how this one helps us."

Firman grunted, barely concealing his disdain for the Cloudmaster.

"More water?" Bejanim asked, proffering the jug.

When he emerged from the tent some time later and straightened his tired body in the full heat of the afternoon sun, Granthon felt the grip of panic around his heart. How long could he hold on? He could feel power slipping away from him like water disappearing into desert sand.

Sunlord, he thought, *is that how you will end our era, having us slain by ziggers wielded by renegade nomads?* The thought was more a prayer for mercy than an accusation.

Oh, Ethelva, I have loved you so. And now I cannot even protect you from what is to come.

CHAPTER ELEVEN

Gibber Quarter
Wash Drybone

The distance shimmered in dance. From afar, the figure plodding across the Gibber Plain stretched and split and rejoined, now an elongated giant, now several thin-limbed sand-dancers. But there was no one to see it, no one to note that the illusion was larger than the reality: a boy of thirteen or fourteen, on foot, lugging a sack of resin on his back. Far beyond him, the sand-dancers swayed and cavorted . . .

Shale had spent three days collecting out on the plains; now he had run out of water and was desperately thirsty. He shifted the weighty sack from left shoulder to right. The harvest had been good and the resiner would pay him well. It riled Shale that he couldn't sell direct to the caravanners; he would get more tokens that way. But then, maybe not. Caravanners would try to cheat him. Besides, the resiner would make life unbearable, maybe even go to his father. No, it was better this way, at least for the time being. The last thing he wanted to do was rile Galen.

After the unexpected rush down the drywash, a full

year ago, his father had hated him with renewed vigour, even though he rarely raised a hand to him any more. Shale was as grateful as he was puzzled. Surely his father could not fear him as some sort of shaman simply because he had sensed the coming of the rush.

He stopped for a moment, long enough to taste the air with his senses. He had been feeling water from an unexpected direction for some time now. Wash Drybone Settle was ahead of him, in the south-east. The Giving Sea was to the south, a long way off, but large enough for him to feel its water as a vague mistiness. What he felt now, though, was to the north and it was coming closer. It wasn't a cloud this time, he was sure of that.

Uneasy, he turned to study the horizon behind. It was never wise to travel alone on the plains; some who travelled the desert regarded a lone fossicker as prey. And Shale had a sack of resin, laboriously collected from gummy plants, drop by precious drop. He strode on, quickening the pace a little in spite of his fatigue and thirst. He would be glad to reach the safety of the wash. In a wash, one could hide.

By the time he dropped down into the dry riverbed about two sandglass runs later, he was staggering with the light-headedness of water deprivation. His tongue stuck to the roof of his mouth, and it took physical effort to detach it. In spite of his disorientation, he took care to hide the sack in amongst the rocks. The water on the move was much closer now. From this distance, he could not differentiate water in jars, water in people or water in animals, so the presence he felt could have been a wild herd of pedes—rare outside of the Red Quarter but not unheard of—a caravan on the move or even people on foot. The latter he doubted. Whatever it was, it was moving fast and there was a lot of water present.

He ignored its approach and attended to his more immediate needs. He crouched for a moment and cast about for water close by. Concentrated.

A feeling, an awareness. Not something he could explain. It was just there: knowledge that there was water to be found a short walk up the wash. When he arrived at the place, the knowledge was even more pressing and he could narrow down the position. About five hand spans deep, there was a pocket of water caught in a basin of rock. He would have to dig down for it, but he had expected that. He set to work.

By the time his thirst was sated a little later, he could sense more about the form of the approaching water: some myriapedes with mounted riders, and two larger packpedes. A strange combination. Usually in a trade caravan there were far more packpedes, burdened with supplies and goods, than there were myriapede hacks. They were approaching fast; and once they hit the watercourse, if they wanted to reach Wash Drybone Settle they would have to pass by him, perhaps even descending into the wash to follow the path.

He was filling in the hole he had made when one of the stones he had uncovered caught his eye: a pebble polished smooth by aeons of tumbling along in the sand-filled waters of the rush; green coloured but flecked with blood-red streaks. He spat on it and rubbed the spit over the surface. The wetness made the green sparkle and the veins within gleam with ruby fire.

Jasper! he thought. His heart slipped, unbelieving. He'd seen such gems before; not raw like this but polished, in the rings and brooches the Reduner caravanners wore. His disbelief leaped into delight and hope. A fine jasper piece would buy him—no, buy the whole family—enough water for days. Caravanners paid well for good gems.

And they might steal 'em, too.

His head jerked up and he scanned the air once more. The moving water was closing the gap.

His stomach clenched as he enclosed the stone in his fist and ran back to where he had left his sack. A rough heap of boulders made it a suitable place to hide and he hunkered down, confident he was difficult to see. His smock, given to him by the palmier and much mended by his mother, blended in with the pale ochre of the rocks.

It never occurred to him that there were men who could sense him the same way he sensed them. That to such a man, a dirty desert urchin among the sand-eroded rocks was a body of water in a desert, and worth investigating.

Their water approached.

He peered through a narrow crack between the boulders, to see that they had already descended into the wash and would pass not more than a few paces from where he crouched. They had slowed down to a walk, probably resting their mounts now that they had found the path up the drywash. He stayed where he was, unmoving and silent, secure in the knowledge that they would be unlikely to catch a glimpse of a dust-covered boy blending into a background of dust-covered boulders.

As they passed, his jaw dropped. He had never seen such people. These were no Reduner or 'Baster traders. Nor were they marauders.

The first to ride past were armed men on several myri-apede hacks. On the first mount, one man stood on the back of the beast, perfectly balanced, holding the reins in one hand and an upright spear in the other. The base of the spear was slotted into a niche on the pede; a flag marked with colours fluttered from the haft. The point of the spear was wickedly sharp. At his back stood another man, similarly armed, facing the opposite way.

Shale had never seen such a thing. Two men standing upright to ride the same pede? They were dressed oddly, too. 'Basters wore white to match their salt-white hair, salt-white skin and salt-white pedes; Reduner caravanners were red men dressed in red. Some said the Red Quarter stained everything red that came its way, whether men or clothes or water.

These men were different. They had pale but not white skin, and golden or light brown hair, and they wore plain white loose trousers that gathered in at the ankle, with loose white tunics over the top. Their only ornamentation was an embroidered mark on the breast of the tunic. Their mounts were unadorned: no embroidery, no lace, no carved history, nothing apart from the same mark etched on the back segment with a number below. They all wore hats of woven palm fronds, but shaped differently to the red headgear of the people from the Red Quarter—these were broader brimmed, hardly the sort of headgear worn by people used to fast riding or accustomed to battle.

Shale stared and wondered.

His wonderment grew as he saw the next group of rid-ers. In front were five adults, seated cross-legged on myri-apedes. These animals were embroidered and ornately fringed; the saddle cushions were stuffed and equally ornate in their lace and straps. The riders themselves were plainly dressed, resembling the two guards in front except that they had no coloured marks on their robes. Two of them were women mounted on the same pede, both wearing hats draped with veils to exclude the sun and dust. Shale's eyes widened at the fineness of the clothes they wore, the fairness of their skins and the lightness of their accents. He was more thrilled than frightened, his excitement tickling his imagination, as stimulating as water trickling across his skin. Behind them on another myriapede were six boys and two girls mounted behind a man. They looked like Gibber folk, and he guessed they were all a little younger than himself.

As the two women passed, they chatted. He could barely understand them.

"Not much further," one said.

"What do we know about this place?" the other asked.

"Nothing," the first replied, her tone sour. "Another dirty hole in another dusty drywash."

Beside them, one of the men said, "May I remind you that it was just such a hole in a wash that produced no less than four water sensitives just six days ago? One of whom is a potential rainlord."

"Not one of them has stormlord potential," the second woman pointed out. "Not one. Sunblast it, a year on the saddle, Nealrith, and no new stormlord to show for it, not even at Wash Dribarra."

"We haven't finished yet, Laisa."

"No, damn it."

Shale heard, but hardly understood. The accents were too strange, the voices far from the guttural tones he was used to hearing.

They passed out of his view and it was a moment or two before several more riders appeared, all dressed similarly but riding mounts with less decoration and no fancy saddles or bridles. Servants, Shale guessed. Or guards. Some of them were armed. He knew about servants and guards from the Reduner caravans.

The next animals that came into his line of sight were two packpedes. Much larger than myriapedes, they were laden with baggage and a single rider on the first segment. The dozens of pointed feet undulated like a fringe lifting in the breeze, leaving the characteristic holed tracks in their wake.

There was one final rider yet to come. He had dropped behind. Shale remained hidden, waiting for him to pass, and he came into view a short while later. Not a servant, this one, Shale decided. He would have thought the same even if he had not noticed the decorated saddle and the inlaid bridle. There was something about the man himself. A regal assurance, the aura of a man who was certain of himself and of his power. Unlike the others who had passed by, he was swarthy, dark enough to be a Gibberman, with deep brown hair tied back at the nape. His face was sharp-planed, handsome, shrewd. There were no crinkle lines at the edges of his eyes; he was not a man who laughed much.

He reined in opposite Shale and sat motionless on his mount. Shale found himself holding his breath in growing terror. He saw boxes strapped to the back of the mount: zigger carriers. Shale knew about ziggers, too. All Reduner caravans were armed with ziggers, and most of the caravanners had a reputation for being willing to use them if they felt threatened. Still clutching his jasper, he dug the fingers of his free hand into the soil, as if holding tight to the earth would save him.

Slowly the man on the pede turned his head and stared right at the rocks where he was hidden.

It should have been impossible for the man to detect him. Shale had moved nothing but his hidden fingers, had not made a sound, and the slit he used as a spy hole was no more than a sliver of space between two boulders. And yet he knew, beyond doubt, that he had been seen.

"Come on out," the man said. His voice was deep, pleasant to listen to, like the regular booming of night-parrots. It contained no hint of threat, yet the command countenanced no refusal.

Slowly, Shale stood and stepped out from behind the boulders.

The man looked him up and down without expression. "You are from Wash Drybone Settle?" he asked.

Shale nodded.

"Answer properly, boy. You may address me as 'my lord.'" No anger; it was a neutral statement.

Shale stumbled over the word, not sure he understood. "L-lord?"

"What is your name?"

"Shale. My. Lord."

"Shale?" A hint of amusement this time, although the man did his best to hide it. "A true descendant of mining folk, eh? Would you like a ride back to your settle?" The man gestured at the rear of his mount.

Shale thought of his resin sack. "Nah. Um, my lord. I'll walk."

The man was apparently not offended by his refusal.

"As you wish," he said. "But do return, lad. You are wanted there this evening."

"Huh?" *Me?*

"What is it you hide in your hand, Shale?"

Shale's fist closed even tighter over his jasper, cursing himself for not having dropped it before he'd stepped out. "Bit o' pebble."

The man smiled. "Then you won't mind showing me, will you?"

Shale's whole body cried out his denial, yet under the unflinching gaze of those deep grey eyes he found himself holding out his hand, palm upwards, so that the jasper shone in the sunlight.

"Ah. That *is* a pretty gem. Give it here."

Shale was sure the man was going to steal it. And yet there was nothing he could do. A man on foot could not run from a pedeman; and no one could run from a zigger. If he refused, he would not only lose the gem; he could die. He approached the pede. "'S mine," he said, defiant.

"Did I say it wasn't? Give it here."

Shale eyed the ziggers one more time and then handed the jasper up.

The man turned it over and over in his fingers, then held it up to the light. "Jasper," he said. "Of the type they call bloodstone. You found it today?"

Shale nodded.

"What will you do with it?"

"Sell it to a red-man gem hunter."

"Hmm. He will cheat you, I think. It is a fine specimen, and fossickers don't find too many these days. They sometimes call it the martyr's stone. Legend says the red inside is the blood spilled by the Watergiver when he was attacked by Gibbermen. The blood splashed on desert jasper, and each stone so stained is now a piece of bloodstone. A gem like this is worth about five hundred day tokens to a gem polisher on the streets of my city, and he would sell it polished and set for three times that, probably to the waterpriests. They are not only rich enough, but they believe such a stone to be holy. A gem hunter from a caravan should pay you at least three hundred. Don't take a token less. And if they quibble, tell them Taquar, Highlord of Scarcleft, told you that."

Shale gaped, wits scrambled. *Highlord?* Did that make him a rainlord? Was he then a *god*? Three *hundred* tokens? He tried to think how much that could buy.

The man bent in the saddle to hand the gemstone back. "Take care of it, Shale of Wash Drybone. You're unlikely to find another as good in your lifetime." He noted Shale's awe, and the amusement was open this time.

Shale took back the jasper, still reeling under the impact of all he had been told.

Rainlord Taquar turned from him, manipulating his reins.

The myriapede responded to the complex signal and started off, picking up speed and tucking its long antennae under the lower edge of its segments. Another twitch on a rein and it had straightened its legs, bringing them in line with the edge of its segments. This mode raised its underbelly higher from the ground so it could now run faster, untroubled by bumps and unevenness in the terrain. Shale stood looking after it, admiring the quick parallel ripples of the wall of legs as they flowed through the sand.

One day, he thought, *I'm goin' t'get me a pede like that.*

As he turned back to collect his resin bag, he considered what the man had said. Highlord? Maybe he was, but he wasn't a god. He was just a man like any other. An honest man, kind even. He could so easily have stolen the jasper and who would ever have believed Shale if he said so? And he need not have given the advice about its value.

Kindly, perhaps—but never soft. A man like that reeked of power that expected instant obedience.

Shale was not sure he wanted their paths to cross again. A Gibber boy like himself could be no more than a grain of sand before the wind when he came face-to-face with such a lord, be he god or man.

"It's growing cold in here." Laisa looked around the tent with distaste. There were no chairs, just a heap of saddle cushions, a floor rug and the flat wooden circle of the low table they used when testing settlefolk. Iani placed covered water bowls on the table, his palsied hand shaking, while Taquar, Ryka and Kaneth watched and wondered if he would drop any.

No one said anything. They had become used to Laisa's complaints in the time since they had left the Scarpen, and had learned that it was unwise to agree with her. It only led to a litany of other complaints. It was even more unwise to contradict her because that either made her indignant or led to long sulks interspersed with sarcastic remarks aimed at the person who had uttered the contradiction.

"We should have a fire," Laisa added. "These desert nights are unbearable."

"I can't think of anything we could use to burn," Taquar

said pleasantly. "Except maybe some of the dresses in the extensive wardrobe you brought with you, my dear."

She gave him a sharp glance to see if he mocked her or merely joked, but she could make nothing of the look on his face.

He went on, "I for one would have no objections to you wearing less."

"Nealrith might have something to say about that."

"Really?"

She played with the folds of the dress she had donned the moment her own tent had been erected on their arrival in Wash Drybone Settle. It was midnight-blue silk and matched her eyes and the sapphires in the pendant at her neck. She knew it suited her; she also knew that the looseness of the neckline enticed men's eyes. The rest of the garment was decorous, with full sleeves, skirt just above the ankles and a high back; she had long known the value of never showing too much at any one time. She ducked her head and looked up at Taquar from under her eyelashes, leaning forward just a little so that the neckline gaped. A tiny smile played at the edge of her lips, but all her performance elicited from Taquar was one raised eyebrow.

From across the room, Ryka snorted.

"What's that supposed to mean?" Laisa asked her, eyes flashing.

Ryka shot her a scornful glance. "If you really want a fire, we'll get you some pede droppings to burn, Laisa. Shit makes good fuel."

What might have developed into a longstanding feud was cut short by the arrival of Nealrith. He entered rubbing cold hands, oblivious to the tension in the tent.

"Salted damn, but it's cold tonight. I have talked to the headman. Fellow called Rishan the palmier. And to the reeve as well. And you aren't going to believe this, but apparently the settlefolk think we are some kind of gods."

"Are you joking?" Ryka asked. She looked around at them all, her glance obviously adding up what she saw: Laisa's petulance, Iani with his stroke-ravaged face and limp, Kaneth's lazy insouciance, Taquar's sardonic grin. "*Us?* I must be the first short-sighted god in the history of mankind."

"Well, not exactly us. Rainlords and stormlords in general. They think—or they thought until we actually arrived—that rainlords are gods who supply water from the heavens."

Iani's eyes widened. "I'll be waterless! And where do the Sunlord and the Watergiver fit into all of this?"

"Minor gods of no importance, I gather."

Taquar gave a bark of laughter. "The waterpriests back in the Scarpen would love that. The Sunlord and his right hand reduced to an appendage of rainlords?"

"Not a bad concept, even so," Kaneth drawled. "I quite like the idea of being a deity. I fancy it would appeal to you, too, wouldn't it, Laisa—being a goddess?"

She ignored that. "And do they still think we are gods?"

"I've tried to disabuse them of the blasphemy, but among some of the more gullible it may not be so easy. On my way back to the tent, one of them prostrated himself in the street." Nealrith looked distressed. "I didn't know places as remote and as naively credulous as this could exist in the Quartern."

"And why not?" Taquar asked. "The Gibber folk in

outlying areas are illiterate and ignored. Who ever comes here, apart from trading caravanners? This will be the first visit that any official from the Scarpen or the Cloudmaster has ever paid them. The only time a stormlord's administration shows an interest in the Gibber is when we want something from them. What did you expect?"

Nealrith flushed. "It is not as simple as that, and you know it, Taquar. Our quarter has very limited jurisdiction in other quarters."

"And the Gibber is no more than a collection of poverty-stricken settles and dust-clad towns eking out a living from an unforgiving desert. If you wanted to help them, you could. Who's to stop you? The Gibber has no central government, no armed guards, no central priesthood even."

"We all know what kind of help you would give," Nealrith said savagely. "If my father hadn't stopped you, you would have been scouring those same deserts for gemstones, exploiting the fossickers without a thought for Gibber wellbeing."

"At least I am partially of Gibber ancestry. And being exploited is better than being ignored. Had I been allowed to regulate the gem trade as I wished to do, Gibbermen would have hired themselves out as workers, obtaining a steady, reliable income. They would have been exposed to outside contacts and been richer for the experience."

"They would have been enslaved and impoverished!"

Taquar raised an eyebrow sardonically. "Impoverished? More than they already are? Do you know, I would not have thought that was possible. And poverty *is* slavery. I offered them a way out. You prevented it."

Iani intervened. "That's enough. Let us get back to the

matter in hand. What did this Rishan say about the settlers? Are there any water sensitives?"

"He doesn't even know what a water sensitive is. However, he and the reeve are happy enough to have the whole settle tested. They are preparing dinner for us, by the way."

"Oh, wonderful," Laisa muttered, "another dreadful meal of bab fruit and bab sugar and bab liquor and bab paste."

"Our servants are supervising. They will see that it is edible," Nealrith told her mildly. "Is the initial test ready?"

Ryka nodded. The first test was a simple one: fifteen lidded bowls were placed on the table. Some were filled with sand, others with varying amounts of water. The test was to see who could say which contained water, merely by placing a hand on the lid of each bowl. Anyone who had enough water sensitivity to know the difference with reasonable accuracy was given further testing.

"How many people are there in this miserable sand hole?" Laisa asked.

"Rishan thinks about three hundred and fifty. He's never actually counted them. I said we'll see thirty tonight and the rest tomorrow morning."

"Did you inquire about the stolen storm?" Ryka asked. They had already found out from other settles further north that it was Wash Drybone that had benefited from the unexpected rainfall.

"Yes, I did. The water did indeed get this far."

"Nobody expected it?" Iani asked with quick interest.

"It took them by surprise. They suffered considerable loss of crops. There was no real benefit because none of them had enough holding capacity for extra water. Whoever did this wasn't doing it for Wash Drybone Settle, that's for sure. Or any of the other settles along the wash."

"A curious matter," Kaneth said. "It would be interesting to get to the bottom of it. Are you certain that your father didn't just imagine what happened? Perhaps he just *thought* the storm was stolen—"

"Or said it was stolen to cover up his own inability to bring the storm to where it was supposed to be?" Taquar added.

"That's enough!" Nealrith snapped.

"No, Kaneth and Taquar are right. You must consider all possibilities," Ryka said. "There is no point in hiding your head in the sand, Nealrith, just because you may not like the truth."

Taquar inclined his head in her direction. "Ryka, the voice of reason and scientific thought, as always. Cloudmaster Granthon has to recognise his limitations before it is too late. He has to stop expending his energies on Gibber dust holes like this place—or we'll *all* end up dead."

"Making the Gibber thirst while we drink is a disgusting idea," Ryka said.

Taquar shrugged. "Of course it is. Show me another way to resolve our dilemma, and I will be happy to support it."

Before anyone could answer, the first of the settlefolk arrived for testing.

CHAPTER TWELVE

Gibber Quarter
Wash Drybone Settle and the Gibber Plains

In the one-roomed shanty of Galen the sot, Shale was sitting with his sister, Citrine, on his lap. Her black eyes, so full of sharp intelligence and wonderment, regarded him with joy. Just over a year old, she was thin, this baby he had taken under his wing. His mother had little milk for her, and there was precious little food to spare. Nonetheless, her face was bright with life, and she liked nothing better than to play with her favourite brother, Shale.

Their mother was stirring dinner in the pot on the fire outside the hut, Mica was carving some bab-wood hairpins he hoped to sell to a caravan some time, and Galen had not yet returned from the settle, where he had gone to spend tokens on his usual jug of amber.

"Leastwise he won't be too slurped tonight," Mica said. "He only had a tinny-token to spend."

"There was a caravan in this evening," Shale warned. "Who knows what he's got from them."

"Yeah, I know. Real rich folk. Skin as light as milk opal. Never seen the like, meself."

"One of 'em said he was a highlord."

Mica laughed. "Is that sort of like a stormlord? He was scoffing you!"

Shale shrugged. "Maybe. But he's different all right."

"Your pa's comin'," his mother hissed from the doorway. "Watch yourselves."

Mica and Shale fell silent, although even silence might provoke Galen into unreasoning anger if he was drunk enough.

A moment later, he pushed past Marisal on his way inside. Once there, he fixed an angry gaze on Shale. "I want t'speak t'you, lad."

Shale hurriedly handed Citrine to his brother and stood up.

"There's rainlords in the settle."

Outside, Marisal dropped her stirring paddle into the pot and bit off an exclamation of surprise. Mica gaped and then attempted to draw attention away from Shale. "But aren't rainlords gods?" he asked.

"Just folk, seems like. Fancy folk from a place called Scarpen. Seems they are the ones who make sure we get water. Or don't get water, see? So we got t'keep in good with that lot." He turned his attention back to Shale. Reaching out with one hand, he pinned the boy against the back wall of the hut by his throat. "We don't want them t'think anyone here messes with their business, unnerstand me? We don't know a sand-flea's piddle 'bout water or when it comes, you get me, boy?"

Shale, choking, attempted to nod.

"We don't know anythin', never. I don't want you going nowhere near those Scarpen fancy-clothes with their pretty words and their stinkin' perfumes. Unnerstand?"

Shale spluttered and attempted another nod. He was choking, gasping for air, sure he was going to die. He clutched Galen's wrist and attempted to wrench his hand away. He tried to call Mica's name but his brother was rocking Citrine, his gaze deliberately averted. Citrine, however, stared at him, wide-eyed with distress. Her mouth turned down and she started to bellow.

Galen ignored her and went on, "I'll kill you if you bring trouble on us, see? And if *I* don't, then them fancy lords will. And if *they* don't, then the settlefolk will. So just shut your teeth down tight and keep your tongue at the back of 'em."

He loosened his hand from around his son's throat and Shale dropped to the floor, gasping. Losing interest, Galen turned to his wife. "Well, woman, where's my meal? Get me somethin' t'eat, or I'll take that stirring paddle to yer."

Mica helped Shale up and the two of them went to sit on the bedding in one corner of the room, taking the baby with them. They both knew there were times when it was better to be inconspicuous. Happy again, Citrine quietened.

"Sorry," Mica mumbled.

"It's all right," Shale said hoarsely, trying to smile at Citrine. "You couldn't have done nothin' anyways." But in the darkness he knew Mica was grieving—for all the things he could not do.

Nealrith stood watching and listening in the deep of a desert night. As always at this time, the Gibber Plains were alive with sound: faint scrabbling and soft slithers, clicks and chirps, booming songs and thin reedy warbling, emitted by the creatures that emerged from their burrows in the earth or their crannies under stones, creatures as diverse as pcbblcmicc, mole-crickets and night-parrots. All the life that was hidden during the heat of the day came into action at night: hunting one another, seeking the life-giving dew, sniffing out mates. Nealrith wondered if those creatures would go on living if there was no rain, and came to the conclusion that they probably would. They did not depend on the water that came down the wash.

We are the weak ones, he thought. *The ones who never belonged here in the first place.*

"Mist-gathering yet again?" Kaneth emerged out of the darkness, coming from the direction of the tents.

"More or less."

"Taquar is getting to you, isn't he? His poison is insidious—corrosive, nibbling at the edges."

"I thought you agreed with him."

"Oh, I do. Doesn't mean I love him, though. Or that we have the same goals. I just want to live, that's all. I want the Scarpen to survive. Taquar wants something more."

"Power."

"I suspect so. He puzzles me, though. Why is being a highlord not enough? I sometimes think there is something unnatural about him, Rith. As if all we see is the person acting a part—farsighted leader, future warrior, indefatigable lover. Never the real man. Sometimes I think he will be the salvation of us all—and sometimes I think he will destroy not just us but everything we stand for and everything we hold in trust."

"I thought you liked him."

Kaneth snorted. "Taquar is not a man one 'likes.'" Admire? Yes, often. But *like*? Never. The intricacies of his labyrinthine mind are beyond me. Don't underestimate him, my friend."

"I never have."

"And remember that just because you dislike him, that doesn't mean he is wrong and you are right. We are near the end of our journey, and we haven't found anyone that has the potential to be a stormlord. You are going to have to think more seriously about—"

"We have found hope, Kaneth. Those twelve minor water sensitives we sent back to Breccia for training, for a start."

Kaneth was dismissive. "Potential reeves at most."

"You can't say that about the other six we have with us still." He had hope for them. The most talented he had placed under his protection, closely guarded by his own personal guards at all times.

"Hmm, they have responded well to our training, I will admit," Kaneth said. "Possible rainlords, yes, but a stormlord among them? I think not, Rith. And in the meantime, your father could be on his deathbed."

"Blast you to a waterless damnation, Kaneth! Can't you keep your sand-rasp of a tongue still?"

"You'll hear only the truth from me. Whatever you think of me now, I am still a friend. The best friend you'll ever have."

"Watergiver help me."

"Now, that is not nice." Kaneth sounded hurt. "Oh, and one thing more," he added as Nealrith walked off. "Watch your back. As my old granny used to say, what use is a kiss on your lips if your back is clawed?"

Nealrith faltered, but he didn't turn around. He knew

exactly who Kaneth was warning him against, and it wasn't Taquar. He headed for his tent.

"You have a funny way of treating your friends, Kaneth Carnelian."

Kaneth spun around to face the speaker: Ryka, on her way to the main tent from her own.

"Would you rather I sounded like a mealy-mouthed woman?" he asked. "Speaking sugary-sweet platitudes to her friends until they believe everyone loves them?"

Her eyes glittered in the dark. "There you go again, denigrating women. For someone who professes to know so much about us, you're an expert at reducing us to ciphers."

"I haven't the faintest idea what you mean."

"You rarely have. What makes you think women are mealy-mouthed? Look at us female rainlords for a start. Laisa? She delights in nasty insinuation. Highlord Moiqa is as blunt as a miner's pick and prefers hammering out honesty to compliments. And I have a reputation for preferring fact over fancy. Then there's Anqia, over in—"

"By all that's wet, I was hardly saying *all* women are mealy-mouthed!"

"You implied it."

"Don't put words in my mouth that I didn't say."

"I don't have to. You can sound like an idiot without any help from me."

He gritted his teeth. "Blighted eyes, Ry, what do I have to do to show you I am not as rotten as you would have me smell? Have I been visiting every whore between Breccia City and here, or even flirting with settle girls? Have I once sneaked out of my tent at night to be pleasured by some matron who likes the idea of a rainlord in her bed? You're not blind—you've seen the number of opportunities I could have seized. I can even tell you the name of the settle whore right here in Wash Drybone. Her husband, the settle's drunk, just offered me his wife."

"Are you trying to tell me you haven't bedded a single girl since we left the Scarpen Quarter?"

"As a matter of fact, yes, I am."

"I don't believe you. I saw that hussy with the curls sneaking under the back wall of your tent back in Quartzgrain Settle—"

"I tossed her out. She didn't come at my invitation."

"And then there were those identical twins in Dopstik. They were boasting all over the settle that they'd shared your bed."

"I doubt it, because it didn't happen. If you heard a rumour, I suspect it referred to Taquar. I know he was eyeing them."

"I don't trust you, Kaneth. And anyway, if you haven't bedded anyone at all this trip, it's probably because you don't fancy Gibber women with their dark skins."

"Don't be ridiculous. The shade of her skin has nothing to do with a woman's bed skills or her desirability!"

She rolled her eyes.

Inwardly he cursed himself. Was he totally incapable of saying the right thing? Or even the sensible thing? He wanted to call after her as she walked away, but he wasn't sure what to say. That he had not bedded another woman out of respect for her? That as the days passed, he found her more and more desirable?

He suspected that if he did, she would throw it back at him, saying that abstinence had made him desperate. That any tent would do in a sandstorm. Or she would say that he wanted her because she was unattainable, that what he wanted was the victory, not the person.

Sighing, he wondered if any of that was true. All he knew for certain was that as he watched her now, her neat hips swaying beneath the loose weave of her traveller's trousers, he desired her with a longing he had rarely felt for any woman anywhere.

Shale did his best to obey his father.

He did not go near the main settle the next day, and he stayed away from the rainlord tents erected in the bab groves. When Rishan sent his son Chert to the shanty huts outside the settle to tell them all they were to come to the rainlords' main tent for testing, Shale felt his stomach turn to palm mash—and stayed at home.

When Mica came back, he questioned him closely about what had happened.

"Nothin' much really," Mica said. "We all went into the tent one at a time. There was all these bowls. One of them rainlords asked me to put my finger on the lid of each, then say if it got water inside."

"What did yer do?"

"Told the truth, of course! Said I didn't know. I mean, there was water all right, I knowed that, but which of them bowls had it? I dunno. So they said I could go. Hey, Shale, there's one woman who's—who's—salted wells, she's as beautiful as—" Lacking words to describe her, he traced curves in the air. "She's the best thing I ever laid eyes on. Better than ten full dayjars in a row."

Shale wasn't interested. "Come on, Mica, have sense! Did they say why they was doin' this test? Are they, um, are they lookin' for *me*? Did I do somethin' awful bad just 'cause I knew the rush was comin' down that day?" *And 'cause I know things 'bout water other folk don't know— like where to find it?*

"I dunno. They wasn't goin' t'tell me what they's doin' here, was they? Just said it was a test, and there was nothin' to be afraid of. They seemed all right."

Shale sat down on the bedding and put his head down on his arms. "I'm frit, Mica. One of those men saw me. He'll remember and know that I didn't come for the testin'."

"Then go. Go down there an' tell 'em you don't know what bowls have water in 'em." He looked curiously at Shale. "After all, you wouldn't know, would you?"

Shale was silent.

Mica clapped a hand to his forehead. "Oh, pedeshit. You would know."

Shale nodded miserably. "Yeah. Don't know how, but I'd know."

Mica floundered, unable to give advice because neither of them had any way of guessing what the reaction of the strangers would be. "I—I've gotta go," he said at last. "I'm supposed to be helpin' to gather feed for their pedes. If I'm not there, Pa'll be mad."

"That fellow on the pede that I met—you don't mess with the likes of him, not if you want t'keep a zigger out of your ear. Mica, I'm scared."

Mica bit his lip, hesitating. "Then you'd better hide. Get off into the Gibber. Take my water skin, an' y'own. Come back in a day or two when them lords have scarpered." He dug into the pocket of his smock. "Here, I got some palm fruit. That'll stop you gettin' too hungry. And I'll explain to Pa."

"Yeah, I think that's best." He took the food and Mica's water skin and went to fill it at the family jar Rishan the palmier had given them to replace the one they had lost in the flood. Now that he had made a decision, he was already feeling better.

"I'm off then," Mica said awkwardly. "See you in a day or two."

"Yeah. Thanks, Mica." He lifted a hand in farewell and Mica grinned and was gone.

Shale took a deep breath and looked around. He would need something warm for the nights, so he rolled up his sleeping sack and stuffed the full water skins into the middle of the bundle. He grabbed an empty sack; he might as well look for some more resin while he was out on the plains.

That night he lay awake for several turns of a sandglass, watching the stars. Even with the sleeping sack and the hollow he had made in some sandy soil, the cold of the sunless plains chilled him to the bone. His nose felt as cold as the dew riming on the plants around him. He listened to the sounds of the night: the soft scrabbling of scorpions and centipedes, the squeak of a pebblemouse, the far-off booming of a night-parrot. Nearby, an ant sipper trundled past, snuffling its long nose under the pebbles in search of food.

He drowsed, then slipped into a deeper sleep.

And woke when something sharp dug into his side, not once but several times.

He sat up in a hurry, shocked to realise someone was standing at his side, poking him with a foot.

"Going somewhere?"

Although the figure that addressed him was no more than a silhouette, he knew the shape of the water. He knew the voice. His mouth dried up and he couldn't have answered even if he had tried. *Highlord Taquar.*

The man squatted down, dumping a large basket beside him. Behind, a pede settled down to wait, its antennae scenting the air. Ziggers hummed in their cage tied to one of the saddle handles.

"I'm curious about you, Shale," the highlord said. "I'm wondering why you are so frightened of us. I am wondering if it is because you sense water, and you think that might make us angry."

Shale stared at him, mesmerised. His heart was pounding in his chest hard enough to hurt. "How—how did you know I were here?" he asked. How could the man have found him in the dark in the middle of the Gibber?

"I can feel you. I can feel your water. Just as I felt you the evening we arrived, hunkered down among the rocks of the drywash. Just as I knew there was someone up there alone in those huts when everyone else came down to the tent to be tested. And I wondered why that would be. Especially when I never saw the resin-hunter Shale down there at our tent. So maybe you wouldn't mind telling me why you didn't come?"

Shale wished he could see the man's face properly. Darkness obscured his features and blurred his outline, so it was hard to be sure if he was threatening or not.

Lies raced through his head: he'd been out resin collecting, he hadn't known he was supposed to go to the tent—but every single untruth died on his lips. Something told him that not one of them would be believed. "I was frit," he said at last.

"Frightened? Of us?"

He nodded. In fact, he was beyond terror, just wanting it all to be over, whatever "it" might be. There could be nothing worse than the fear he already knew. "Pa said that you lords'd be angry if anyone meddles in water business. That you'd kill me."

The highlord looked at him in disbelief. Then he shook his head in wonderment. A chuckle started in his throat and grew to a full-bodied laugh. Shale's unease increased. What was so funny?

When he finally had control of himself once more, Taquar said, "Lad, lad, if only you knew. A water-sensitive youth of your age is worth more than all the precious stones in the Quartern. Even your piece of bloodstone jasper is nothing to us. Nothing. No one in this caravan would harm a hair of such a boy's head. Kill you? You would be treated better than the Cloudmaster's granddaughter."

He was suddenly serious again. He put his hands on Shale's shoulders, holding tight as he tried to flinch away. "Now, you listen to me. Someone who can sense water, who can tell when people are coming because he senses the water within them, that person is called a water sensitive. There are differing degrees of water sensitivity. Some people have a lot, like me. Some have none at all, like the others in this settle, including your idiot reeve, who should never carry that title at all. And some have even more than me, enough to be a stormlord. We are here to find new rainlords, and perhaps even a new stormlord. Do you understand so far?"

"I—I think so. But them other rainlords—they didn't know I was hidin' in the wash. They rode on by."

Taquar gave a dismissive grunt of contempt. "They don't listen to their senses. Not the way I do. They weren't paying attention, so the feel of water from your settle overwhelmed that of one small lad in the drywash. What about you, Shale? I bet you do the same thing sometimes. Do you sometimes feel too much water—like in the settle? So you try not to feel any of it?"

Shale's jaw dropped. That was it exactly. This man knew. Knew what it was like. "Uhuh," he whispered.

"I thought so. I will not lie to you. There *are* people who might try to harm a water sensitive, for their own reasons. Who have done so in the past, in fact. But if you have such abilities, you have nothing whatever to be afraid of from *me*. You understand, Shale?"

He nodded, unable to let the tension slide out of his muscles. Was the man lying?

"Right. Now I am going to give you a small test. Just tell the truth. And remember, you have nothing to fear."

"Yes, lord."

The rainlord began to unpack his basket. It contained the bowls Mica had described, and Shale realised the lids were screwed on. Carefully Taquar laid them out in a row. "I want you to touch each one on the lid. I want you to tell me which contain water."

Shale took a deep breath. The moment had come when he had to make a decision. What he said next could determine the course of his whole life. He glanced at the highlord. Was he telling the truth? Shale couldn't be sure, but he thought he was. And he knew what his own life was like now. He knew the hunger, the beatings, the yearning for something better. Better for himself, for Mica, for Citrine. He touched his throat where his father's fingers had left purple bruises that pained him still. He remembered that Taquar had returned his jasper to him. And the highlord understood what it was like to *know* water . . .

Taquar said softly, "I think you and I have a path to walk together, lad. Trust me and you will lead a life you could never dream of, not in your wildest fantasies. Touch the bowls."

"Don't need to touch 'em." He pointed to the three bowls at one end of the row. "Them don't have water. The others do."

For a long while, the highlord sat motionless. Then he asked, and his voice was steady and unemotional, "Can you tell me which one has the least water?"

Shale tapped one of the bowls. "This'un." He tapped the one next to it. "And this'un has the most."

"So," Taquar murmured, "old Granthon was right. Who would have thought?" He gave an amused grunt. "Lad, it seems you and I will come to know each other well." He reached over and cupped Shale's face gently in one hand. "One day I believe you might just be a stormlord of the Quartern—and the irony is that right now you do not even know what that means. I want you to listen very, very carefully to what I have to say, Shale, because your life may depend on your obedience."

Shale's fear returned and he tried to twist his face away; the highlord's hold tightened, firm but not cruel. "In the past, there were a number of lads like you, girls too, all water sensitives. Many died. We do not know why. The Cloudmaster himself, Granthon Almandine, sent me on this quest to make sure no more are harmed. If it be-

comes common knowledge that you passed this test, you
could be the next. The best way for you to remain safe is
for no one to know that you did indeed pass. No one. Not
your father, nor your mother, nobody. Not even the other
rainlords. Do you understand?"

Shale licked his dry lips. "Uhuh."

"Don't be frightened. As long as no one knows you
are a water sensitive, you are as safe as a sand-leech in
its hole. Safer. Tomorrow I will ride on with the others
and you will go on with your life as if nothing happened.
Sometime after the end of this star cycle I will be back to
take you away from here for your training. Think on it,
boy—no more thirst. Water will be yours whenever you
want it, for the rest of your life. No more hunger; you
can eat when you will. You will wear fine clothes, have
whatever you wish for, whenever you wish." His hand
still cupped Shale's face, forcing the boy to meet his eyes
by the light of the stars.

Shale asked, "Ride a pede?"

"Ride one? Why, you will *own* one!"

"What—what about me brother and sister?"

"Would you like them to come, too?"

"Uhuh."

"Then they shall—but *only* if you swear not to tell anyone about all this. Not even them."

"Won't, I promise."

"Did they take the test?"

"Not me sister. She's only a baby. Mica did."

"Ah. And failed. Don't tell Mica about all this. Not
yet."

Shale nodded.

Taquar released his face. "Then I think we understand

one another." He piled the bowls into the basket and stood up. "We will meet again, Shale. And I, too, will make a promise. I will guard you with my life. There is *nothing* I will not do to keep you safe. Nothing."

He stood up and held out his hand. "Come, you can ride with me to the edge of the settle and walk back from there. I don't want anyone to see us together."

Shale hesitated, and then took the proffered clasp.

CHAPTER THIRTEEN

Scarpen Quarter
Scarcleft City
Level 32, Level 10 and Level 36

On the day she turned fourteen, Terelle finally became a woman, at least by the standards that governed Opal's snuggery. Her bleeding started.

All she felt at her change in status was fear; not sudden terror, but a nagging, sickening fear that slowly welled up out of the place in which it had lurked so long, waiting for this moment. She washed her undergarments to hide all signs of blood and sneaked some clean bleeding cloths out of the laundry to wear, but she knew that it was just a temporary reprieve. The sharp eyes of the snuggery women would not be deceived for long. For her, time had run out. She was face-to-face with the darkness of her future.

Madam Opal had, of course, been preparing for this moment. Terelle no longer collected the dirty dishes. She brought drinks to customers in the early evening and helped to serve the snuggery's late suppers. Opal had her dressed in adult clothing: soft, clinging imported silks designed to show the growing curves of her breasts and thighs, decorous yet suggestive. Every night she felt the caressing gaze of the men who watched her; she smelled the subtle lusts that lingered in the air as she passed.

Every time Huckman was in Scarcleft, he spent his evenings in the snuggery. Forced to bring him refreshments, she could not avoid the way his hands would brush her body or the way he whispered crudities in her ear, promising pain and humiliation on her first-night.

When she cringed, he complained to Opal, and Opal berated her. "He's a customer, Terelle, and he's offering good money for your deflowering. Tantalize him, child. Blush. If he wants to pinch the fruit before plucking, squeal and let him—it will put the price up. I don't expect to have him complain that you are rude!"

"He hurts the other girls when he buys their time," she muttered, dreading.

"Nonsense! They love to exaggerate. Anyway, if you don't want Huckman, encourage some of the other men who like their bedmates young and fresh, so that they will bid high for you."

Terelle was desperate. The fact that the men vying for her had to wait apparently only added more spice to the auction. Some of the regulars were even betting on the date of her first-night and on who the lucky man would be. In the meantime, Opal brushed aside her protests as childish modesty, soon to be forgotten.

Since the day she'd first met Amethyst the dancer, Terelle had searched for an arta or artisman who would take on an untried girl as an apprentice. She slipped out of the snuggery at every opportunity. She met several musicians from the musicians' guild first, even though she had been

doubtful that her talents lay in that direction. They had
listened politely enough to her lute playing, then shown
her the door. She tried the jewellery designers and makers next, followed by the stone polishers who collected
and prepared gemstones for the jewellers. They all said
they only employed family members. After that, she
spoke to the fine metal workers, who made the settings.
They laughed, saying it wasn't a child's job. She pestered
every potter in the city. They had no need of outside talent, they told her. She went to the bab palm carvers. They
shook their heads and said they only employed men. She
begged the tile-bakers, the lacemakers, the weavers and
the rug designers. Every single one turned her down and
the reason was always basically the same: these trades
were handed down within families. Who wanted to take
on an outside apprentice who had no experience and no
proven skill? Besides, it would mean having to pay off
Opal's snuggery.

And so her fourteenth birthday had dawned without
any sign of a future outside the snuggery—and with every
indication that the future within its walls was about to
plunge into horror. In her despair, she sneaked out the gate
once more that morning, and went to visit Amethyst.

For over a year now, she had been receiving five tokens
every quarter in exchange for a newly created dance. She
had saved the tokens, but it was the time she spent with
Amethyst that she treasured. The dancer always gave her
hope, hope that there was a way out. It was just a matter
of finding it. After all, Amethyst herself had been born
on the thirty-sixth level; in Scarcleft, that was the lowest.
And now, even though she was no longer young, the rich
of Scarcleft begged to see her dance. "It wasn't easy," the

dancer admitted once. "In fact, there were times when I wondered where my next sip of water was coming from, when I had to do things I didn't want to, just in order to survive."

"You sold your body."

Amethyst smiled slightly. "You *are* blunt, child. But yes, I sold myself. Oh, not as a street whore, or even in a snuggery. But there are other ways—more subtle, but just as destructive." She looked away from Terelle, as if unwilling to meet the sharpness of her gaze. And Terelle was glad of it. She had glimpsed something in the dancer's eyes that spoke of a deep self-loathing. "And it wasn't just for water, either. It was for the right to dance at all. It was as simple as that."

She stopped and Terelle thought she wasn't going to say any more, but then she added softly, "He was a young rainlord; and at that time it was within his power to give me a water allotment and allow me to perform uplevel— or not. He fancied me and made it clear that if I bedded him, my career and my water entitlement were assured. If I didn't . . . well, he never said what he could or would do. But knowing what he was like, I was afraid to find out. And so I slept with him. I was his mistress for ten years, until he tired of me."

She saddened. "One of many. He had a theory that he had a duty to have as many children as possible, in the hope that some of them would grow up to be rainlords. Not sure if he was successful, though, because we don't see too many rainlords these days.

"Fortunately he didn't require me to bear him a child. All I had to do was be his when he wanted it. And only his. For the water entitlement alone I might not have done it, but for the right to dance? Sometimes I think I would have sold my soul." But the look she gave Terelle then was one of devastation. "Sometimes a price can be too high, Terelle. Remember that."

Terelle did indeed remember as she climbed uplevel on the morning of her fourteenth birthday. How much, she wondered, was she willing to pay to be free of the snuggery?

As usual, Jomat the steward opened the door to her, but only with reluctance. He always resented her intrusion on Amethyst's time, although he had never actually refused her entrance. Every time, he would open the door a crack first, and wait for her to ask for entry. Then he would lean forward to stare at her with his myopic eyes, running his gaze over her body. And always, always, he would smile pleasantly and then lay down his poison, disguised as casual conversation.

"Arta Amethyst is such a kind lady," he might say as he pulled himself laboriously upstairs, wheezing as he went, with sweat beading along his forehead and running down his nose. "Always so generous to the girls who come for lessons or advice. Never turns anyone away, even when they are not worthy of her attention. She hasn't the heart to be honest."

Another time, as he ushered Terelle in through the front door, brushing his hand against her thigh, it was, "Arta Amethyst tells me she finds your dances delightfully naive. They remind her of when she was unskilled." On her previous visit he had remarked, "Arta Amethyst said yesterday she was so looking forward to the next time you came. She finds your downlevel simplicity so refreshingly *charming*." And he had smiled, his eyes glistening at her. "Your visits do her so much good, my dear. Do come whenever you can get away from your duties in the snuggery." She had come to hate his smile, his unctuous statements, the sting in the tail of every remark.

This time, as his gaze lingered on her budding breasts, he murmured, "How lovely you are looking today, my dear!" He smiled suggestively. "Quite the young lady now, eh? Please do go up. Arta Amethyst will be *so* sad when you are no longer able to come."

For once, Terelle could not keep her irritation in check. As she joined the dancer, she burst out, "Oh, that man is horrible! Why do you keep him on?"

Amethyst raised an eyebrow without saying a word.

Terelle's indignation dissolved into embarrassment. "I'm—I'm sorry. I shouldn't have said that."

"I hope that is not the kind of manners they teach you at Opal's, child."

"No, Arta. I'm sorry. It's just that—oh, it doesn't matter."

Amethyst looked at her shrewdly. "You are upset about something else. Sit down here beside me. What is it?"

To her shame, Terelle found her chin wobbling as she verged on tears. She fought the temptation to cry. "My bleeding has come," she said simply. "I've run out of time."

Amethyst looked away with a sigh. "Oh, Terelle, I don't know what to say to help you. It seems to me that you have tried hard. I have been to see a few people, too. I didn't want to tell you for fear you would be discouraged, but I couldn't find anyone who would take you on, not when it would mean paying back the snuggery for so many years of free water, plus your father's sale price. Opal even wants interest, and legally she can do that. That's a small fortune."

"You went to see Madam Opal?"

"I sent a friend to inquire. I was wondering if I could afford to pay off your debt. I can't. I must conserve what meagre wealth I have for my old age, once I can no longer dance."

Terelle's spirits sank. She had wondered if Amethyst could—or would—be prepared to buy the debt; it had not occurred to her that the dancer could not afford it.

"Then what will I do? I could run away, but where could I go? I might have just enough tokens to pay for a caravan seat to Breccia City or Pediment, but what would I do in another city? It would be the same there!"

"Opal can't *force* you into prostitution."

"No, but if I can't pay the debt, I can be forced to work it off. It would take my whole life if I was doing work that didn't involve the upper rooms." Even as she said the words, she hated the bitterness she heard in her own voice.

"And if you refused to work it off, you'd have to go to court and they'd sentence you to the city's labour force. Which would mean something far more unpleasant, like the lye-makers. I know."

Terelle nodded miserably. "It's not fair."

Amethyst looked at her in compassion. "Have you told Opal you don't want to be a whore?"

"Of course. She dismisses it as—as girlish qualms. She thinks I'll 'settle down' once I've had a few men." She shuddered. "I've seen the men who want me now. Water-giver have mercy, I don't want that! It's just not *fair*."

"No, it rarely is." She pondered, then added, "There are people who live without allowances or regular jobs, you know. Down on the thirty-sixth. Have you ever been there?"

Terelle shook her head.

"I was born there. There are ways to live. People who want casual labour often employ workers from the lowest level. It's worth a try. If it doesn't work out, well then, you can always go back to the snuggery."

"They'll come looking for me. I know it."

"Yes, no doubt. The important thing is for them not to find you for a while. If you can hide out for half a year, they may not bother to look any more."

"Is it possible to hide there?"

Amethyst gave a derisive laugh. "Every second person on the level is hiding from something! Go there. Have a look for yourself. Then decide. For now, let's forget your woes. We'll dance together. It will make you feel happier."

But later, when it was time for Terelle to leave, she added, "Be careful, my dear—don't trust anyone who lives on the thirty-sixth until they have proved themselves, and be careful of the highlord's enforcers as well. Those men love an excuse to use their swords on the waterless. However, there are better things to be found on the thirty-sixth level, too. It all depends on whether you want to take the risk involved in finding them."

I do, Terelle thought. *I'll risk anything.*

It was true, Terelle decided as she looked around the main thoroughfare of the thirty-sixth. Bad and good, all mixed up. Freedom, of a kind. That was the good. But then there was the poverty. And the dirt. And the *smell*.

She had never been curious to visit Level Thirty-six, believing what she had been told: that this was the lowest level not only of the city, but of humanity; here were the dregs that had sunk down from the city above. Thieves, criminals, murderers, the waterless, the undeserving. They clung to the hem of the city's robe like grime, impossible to brush off. They received no free water allotment, yet still they survived. They sucked up the city's moisture and held on to life.

Terelle had heard tales—the young bloods who came to the snuggery were full of stories of how they'd survived a night of debauchery down in the dregs—but nothing had prepared her for the reality. The lack of order, the commotion, the stench, the untidy milling movement of it all. She had never seen so many people in such a small space, never heard so much noise, never been assaulted by so many different odours all at once.

Yet it was the absence of colours that she noticed first. The drabness. The dreary shades of brown seeping into everything. Skin, clothes, buildings—all coated with the misery of a hue that had no spirit, no animation. The shade of dust, of dead leaves, of detritus, of a life sucked dry of beauty. The colour of dirt.

On the other levels, each homeowner paid taxes and in return the streets were kept clean, the tunnels and cisterns were kept in good repair, and the nightsoil was collected each morning and carted outside the walls to be dried and processed into manure. On the thirty-sixth, none of that happened. Street urchins collected rubbish uplevel to bring downlevel, where it was sold and re-used, and there were piles of it everywhere. Privies stank. Rats scampered up and down walls and through lanes, heedless of the daylight or the throng of people.

Houses were made of ancient mud-brick or woven bab palm leaves; some were hardly more than lean-tos against the city wall. It would have taken no more than one carelessly discarded ember to set the whole place on fire. Worse, the poor could not afford the seaweed briquettes brought into the city by the packpede load. They used instead a volatile mixture of pede dung and dead palm fronds for fuel. She understood now the plumes of smoke she had seen from time to time curling from the foot of the city. Here, buildings often burned.

Everywhere she looked, there were people. Bare feet, ragged clothes, skeletal thinness, skin diseases. Sunlord save them, such *poverty*. Men and women and children even lived at the edge of the roadway, their pitiful heaps of belongings next to them. On a corner, for a price, a waterseller dispensed water from a transport jar. Not far away, a woman lounged against a wall, eyeing the men in the street. Terelle had never seen a street whore before, but she didn't need to be told the woman's trade. Snuggery women may have had a veneer of class, but the signals were still the same.

A group of children sat in the dust behind her, weaving mats from palm fronds; another two children pounded bab kernels in a single stone mortar, each with wooden pestles as large as themselves. They had built up a rhythm: whump-whump, whump-whump, like the beat of a drum. A man walked past, bent double under a load of palm fruit. Another two hefted a body wrapped in a tattered mat that wasn't long enough to cover the skinny bare feet of the corpse. Several wailing women followed, with bare-foot children trailing behind. Someone pushed past with a bucket of liquid that smelled like stale urine. Another man was hanging sinucca leaves to dry on a line. Terelle was familiar with those: the snuggery bought them to make the paste that the handmaidens used to prevent pregnancy.

A child with no hair came up to her and tugged at her robe, holding out a grimy hand in supplication. It was a gesture she remembered from her childhood—an action of her younger self? She rather thought so, but the memory was vague and shameful—and she almost responded by digging into her purse. Then instinct told her that it wouldn't be wise to show she was willing to give up tokens to a beggar. She shook her head, her act of rejection bringing a lump to her throat.

As she turned away from the child, she saw that the whore on the corner was in luck: a young blood from the upper levels had come by, and he was leaning over her, staring down her blouse while he negotiated a price.

Terelle shuddered. *Oh, sweet water, is this how I will end up?*

She blundered away, the street blurred by her tears, and she had to stand still for a moment to try to regain her composure. She was next to the waterseller now, and he was eyeing her with interest. "Water?" he asked.

She shook her head, not trusting herself to speak, wishing she could stop the tears before anyone saw. A woman came up to buy water. She was carrying a standard dayjar, designed to contain a full day's water for an adult. To fill it would cost exactly one token. And yet as Terelle watched, she saw the woman hand over a full quarter as much again in payment. She blurted out, "How much is it?"

The waterseller replied as he poured, without looking up. "One and a quarter tokens for a dayjar. Regular price."

Terelle was incredulous. "Regular price? Since when has a day's worth been more than one token?"

This brought the full attention of both the seller and the buyer. The woman snorted. "Where you been all your life? On Level Two maybe? The poor pay more, don't y'know that?"

"But—that's illegal, isn't it?"

This naive remark resulted in a loud guffaw from the seller. "Nothing's illegal here, lass; you're on the thirty-sixth!"

"I don't understand," she said.

He finished filling the jar, handed it to the woman and put away the money. "No uplevel reeves will sell water to the waterless," he said as the woman left. "It's against the law. Water is only sold to licensed sellers like me—at one token a dayjar—direct from the waterhall on the first level. But I have to rent a packpede to bring the water down thirty-six levels, once a day. And I got to live. So I sell it at one and a quarter. That's business, lady. Here you got to have business, or you die. Course, if you piss for the watermaker, then you save a couple of tinny."

When she looked blank, he said, "Collect your pee every day; take it to the watermaker outside the groves. He heats it on top o' the smelters, it evaporates and he collects the water, which he sells. The rest becomes manure for the gardens. There ain't nothin' you can't do here, if it keeps you watered. Uplevel law stopped the moment

you took the last step down to the thirty-sixth." He gave
her a calculating look. "And what's an upleveller like you
doing mixing with the likes of us, anyway?"

But she had already turned away, her heart settling
like a stone within her. She'd have to sell her *pee* to survive? If she had to pay a quarter as much again for water,
her tokens were worth less than she had anticipated. She
felt ill.

She walked on a little further and found a quiet spot
against a blank wall. On one side, she was blocked from
the bustle of the street by a pile of broken hampers of the
kind used to carry bab fruits. On the other side, an oil
seller sat cross-legged on a palm mat, his clay jars of bab
oil heaped in front of him. He had his back to her, and
his customers were few and far between, so she had a
moment to adjust, unseen. She wanted to gather her wits;
instead she found herself crying, tears sliding down her
face, unstoppable. She was not sure what was causing
her such grief. Unattractive self-pity? Empathy for the
people here whose problems were even worse than her
own? Guilt because she cared more about her own problems than theirs? Despair because she was not sure she
was hard enough to survive outside the confines of the
snuggery? Everything melted into a pointless welter of
desperation and hopelessness. And that made her angry.
She was better than that.

She closed her eyes and leaned against the wall, willing herself to be inconspicuous while she strove to gain
control. She would *not* be weak. Weakness was for people
who gave up. Who settled for less.

I will never be like that!

What was it Amethyst had said? *It all depends on*

whether you want to take the risk. Well, she would take the risk. She took a few deep breaths, slowed herself down. Calmed. Stopped the stupid tears.

And opened her eyes.

There was a man seated on the ground between her and the oil seller. He hadn't been there before, surely, had he? Or maybe she had just not noticed him. He was staring at her. She stepped away from the wall and returned the stare, but her heart was thudding. Where had he come from?

He was elderly, wizened, small. By no means decrepit, though, or stupid. The eyes that gazed at her were deep blue-green and knowing; shrewd, assessing eyes. Quickly she brushed away the remaining tears.

Like the oil seller, he was seated cross-legged, but his seat was not a simple brown palm mat; it was a multi-coloured carpet. His clothes were woven from a type of thread she did not recognise, of varying colours: deep blues and greens, reds and yellows. They were strangely cut and appeared to have been wrapped around him, rather than sewn, so that he resembled an odd-shaped parcel out of which arms and legs emerged. Even his head was wrapped. The backs of his hands were painted or tattooed in intricate patterns that then snaked up his arms and disappeared under his wrappings.

At his side a dozen or so earthenware pots were lined up in a row. Each was as large as a pomegranate; each contained a spoon. If the stains around the pot lips were any indication, the contents of each were a different colour. In front of him sat a tray, perhaps twice the size of a normal serving tray, with a raised edge about three finger-widths high all the way around. It was two-thirds full of water.

Terelle's stare turned to one of astonishment. She had never seen anyone do such a thing—spread water out under the sun so that it could evaporate. Scarpen jars were always as narrow-lipped as a potter could make them. And all water containers were kept covered.

She looked up from the tray to meet his eyes once more. With one hand he beckoned, and against her will she found herself taking one step forward, then another and another until she was standing in front of him. With a simple gesture of his hand he indicated that she should sit at his side, facing the tray.

When she hesitated, he made the gesture again. She sat, not quite knowing why, except that she was touched by an odd sense of excitement, of childlike wonder. She wanted to know what he was going to do.

He filled one of the spoons from its pot and gently sprinkled the contents onto the water in the tray. Indigo-coloured powder spilled on the surface. It did not sink, and he spread it evenly with a spatula. When all the water was covered with a film of indigo, he followed it with other colours: yellow, then red, brown, white, black. These he applied with more precision and deliberation and yet with a fluidity of gesture, as if he knew exactly where each colour should go and his certainty lent him confidence of movement. Occasionally he used a small pointed stick to mix a top layer of colour into a lower one; other sections he left undisturbed. Some parts of the water had only one layer of colour sitting atop the indigo. Terelle was spellbound, although she couldn't have said why.

He had started at the top of the tray, working his way downwards. For a long time she could see no sense in what he did, and the way the powder reacted with the water was odd. It stayed where it was placed. Nothing sank. When a colour did bleed into another, it was intentional.

And then, in a flood of revelation, she saw what he was painting. There was a doorway in a wall. A broom resting against the daub. A heap of used bab husks piled up. A palm roof with a ragged edge. It was a representation of the building and the wall across from where they sat. A picture.

She had never seen such a thing before, not like this, not in any medium. In the Scarpen, pictures were woven into mats and cushions, cut into or painted on pottery and ceramics—but those pictures were always stylised. They were reality disguised as shapes and designs, two-dimensional, symbolic, precise, offering form and shape and, most of all, pattern. They never offered the suggestion of movement; they were never a raw representation of what existed. Never anything like this. They weren't *alive*.

She saw the way the shadow of the broom fell across the wall, the patterns of light and shade in the discarded husks, the dustiness of the street in front of the doorway. She saw the sunlight as it hit the wall; she could see the haziness of it, knew the dryness of it. It had depth, as if she could step into it. It had immediacy, as if the door was about to open and someone was going to step into the street. She could feel the heat, smell the dust, sense the weariness and poverty of the occupants. Here was the emptiness of a life felt, rather than seen, the portrayal of the husk rather than the contents.

The old man laid aside the pots and the spatula to survey the finished work.

The ache inside Terelle welled up into longing. She felt as if she was suspended in time, on the edge of some momentous point in history, and she had only to take a step to make it happen.

And then she became aware that someone was staring at her, even as she stared at the painting on the water. She turned her head. There was a man standing in the middle of the street. People pushed their way around him, and a passing packpede loaded with palm pith even brushed his elbow; he didn't notice.

She knew instantly that he was from the White Quarter. There was, after all, no mistaking a 'Baster. They were as white as the great saltpans of their own quadrant. Startlingly white, with skin that never burned or blemished in the sun, and white hair that never changed colour, from birth to old age. Their eyes were always the palest of blue, almost colourless, their lips and cheeks bloodless. There were some who said 'Basters did not have blood in their veins, but water.

He was middle-aged, this 'Baster, dressed in their usual garb: a white robe with tiny round pieces of mirror sewn on in red embroidery. The mirrors sparkled when they caught the sunlight.

His gaze was so intent, so intrusive, that Terelle scrambled to her feet, staring back.

Time continued to hang, snagged on the moment—the magic of the painting, the power of the stare, the ache within Terelle responding to something potent in the air around her.

It was the 'Baster who sent time spinning on. He made a gesture of blessing with his hand and walked away. Sunlight caught in the mirrors, a myriad of flashing sparks winked, and he was gone, lost into the crowd.

And the old man spoke for the first time, using a thickly

accented and clumsily worded version of the Quartern tongue she found hard to follow. "He smelled your tears. As did me. Which be why I came. Those, ye cannot be hiding from likes of us, Terelle."

She turned back to him, terror flooding her senses. "How do you know my name?"

He shrugged. "Who else ye be? Ye your mother's daughter."

It was a comment that made no sense. She opened her mouth to protest, but he gestured at his painting and said, "Watch." He lifted one side of the tray an inch from the ground, and then dropped it back down again. The water shivered, sending ripples through the colours. Terelle expected the paint to run and mix, the picture to disappear, but that did not happen. The ripples died away, and the painting remained, exactly as it had been when he had finished it.

Her eyes widened. "How . . ."

"Waterpainting be art," he said. "Secret of art be in paint-powder. That can learn. *Magic* of the art, ah—that must be born in blood of artist.

"Watch again."

She lowered her gaze from his face back to the tray.

He picked up one of the spoons and splashed some colour on the dusty road in the painting. Then another colour and another. This time, his work was slap-dash. Colours blended without real outline, edges blurred. He was painting a woman, but it was mere suggestion: a dress of indeterminate style and shadowed drabness, a face that was turned away so no features were clear, hair that was half-covered with a carelessly flung scarf. Even the shoes she wore were obscured by the length of her skirt.

Afterwards, Terelle was not sure how it happened—or, indeed, what happened. She was looking at the painted figure, admiring how a few touches of colour could suggest so much and wondering why he had used such a different technique to paint the woman, when the surface of the water blurred and shifted. Although she had not seen the old man touch the tray, the colours moved, and then re-formed. The blur focused; edges sharpened.

And the formless woman was formless no longer. Her dress was grubby and drab, and she had evidently just stepped out into the street from the house. Her shoes were woven palm slippers; her scarf was hardly more than a tattered rag, hastily donned. She had a puzzled expression on her face, as though she had forgotten why she had stepped outside.

Terelle's jaw dropped. How had the painted figure changed so? Had the details been hidden beneath the paint, to be released by the artist's movement of the water? Impossible, surely.

She looked across at the house opposite, the real one—and nearly screamed.

There was a woman there, dressed just as the woman in the painting was, with the same look of puzzlement on her face. Behind her the door was still swinging. She shrugged, turned and went back into the house.

Terelle looked down at the painting. The figure was still there, poised to move but caught in the stasis of paint.

"*How*—" But she did not know what to ask. "I saw *that* woman," she said finally, pointing at the painting. She gestured with her hand across the street. "She was *there*. The real woman. And the painting changed. To fit—to *fit* her."

The old man smiled. It was an expression not of friendliness but of sly pleasure. "Things change. Sometimes one thing be preceding another; sometimes not. And sometimes ye determine the order, if ye wish.

"Watch again."

Once more she looked at the picture, afraid this time of what she would see. He drew out a knife and used it to separate paint from the edge of the tray, as if he was loosening a bab-fruit pie from its dish. Then quite casually he picked up two corners of the painting and lifted it. It came up whole, like a sheet of cloth, dripping water. He rolled it up and handed it to her.

"Keep it," he said, "to remind ye of day ye met Russet Kermes the waterpainter. Sever painting from water, though, ye kill its soul."

She took hold of it, amazed that it showed no signs of falling apart or even cracking. It was supple and strong. "It is . . ." She had been going to say beautiful, then realised that would be a lie.

The painting was not beautiful. It was intense, even savage. It reeked of anger against the poverty of the life it portrayed. "Remarkable," she finished lamely.

This time his smile was sardonic. He said, "It be payment."

She was suffocating as if choking on the dust of a desert spindevil; she felt unstable, as if the power of the wind had swept her feet from under her. Desperately she wanted to touch ground, to feel that there was something solid beneath her feet.

"Payment? For what?"

"For soul of artist, Terelle. Payment for *ye*, of course. What else?"

CHAPTER FOURTEEN

The unsuccessful search for a stormlord was over.

Now that Taquar had returned to Scarcleft Hall, evening was the time when he pushed aside any thought of his duties or his worries over water and indulged himself. Sometimes he would venture out to a high-level snuggery or a public house where there were dancers and musicians. Sometimes his pleasure was more cerebral and he would read in his library, or more active and he would spend time sparring with his master-of-swords.

No one dropped by without an invitation, so when the steward came to him one evening with the news that there was someone to see him, he was surprised. When it proved to be Ryka Feldspar, he was utterly astonished.

He rose to his feet, put what he hoped was an urbane smile on his face and said, "Rainlord Ryka! This is an unexpected, um, pleasure. What brings you to Scarcleft? Or perhaps even more to the point, what brings you to my abode at this time of the night?" He turned to look at the steward, still hovering in the doorway, and said, "Refreshments. Some of our best amber, perhaps."

The steward bowed and departed. Taquar waved a hand towards a chair and schooled both his expression and tone to perfect neutrality. "Take a seat." Her broad shoulders trembled slightly, which interested him. Ryka? Scared? That wasn't in character. He'd always thought her about as nervy as a bab palm on a windless day.

She sat, but still didn't appear to be at ease. "This is difficult to talk about," she murmured.

"You intrigue me." He couldn't imagine what had brought this usually self-assured, arrogant woman to him, at night what's more, which was definitely broaching the etiquette for an unwed woman. He didn't like her and never had, but he had never cared enough to make that clear to her. He wondered if he was about to regret his lack of bluntness. She wanted a favour of him, that much was clear, one that she dare not commit to the written word.

"I shall speak plainly," she said after an uncomfortable pause. "Granthon is pressing Kaneth and me to marry because we must have more stormlords. He is right about that, of course, but why he imagines that someone with limited rainlord skills such as myself would ever give birth to potential stormlords is beyond me."

"It is puzzling," he agreed.

She gave him a sharp look but continued. "I do not want to marry Kaneth. You are the only other unattached rainlord."

He just caught himself in time to curtail an undignified desire to gape. "Waterless heavens, Ryka. You are not—surely—suggesting that you and I should wed?"

"Hardly. We would be scratching each other's eyes out before the ceremony was over. But I did wonder if—"

He raised an eyebrow when she paused, genuinely puzzled. And she blushed.

"—ifachildofoursmightnothaveabetterchance," she said in a rush.

He wasn't sure he'd heard correctly. "*What?*"

She took a deep breath. "If a child of ours—yours and mine—might not have a better chance. Of being a storm-lord, I mean. We wouldn't have to marry, or anything. Or even live together."

For the first time in years, someone had truly aston-ished Taquar Sardonyx. This staid, no-nonsense woman, who was normally so sensible that he found her pro-foundly boring, was sounding like an overly romantic girl of seventeen with a sandcrazy idea in her head. He could barely contain his distaste. "You're out of your mind," he told her.

"Why?"

"I *beg* your pardon?"

"Why is it so unthinkable? You know we need storm-lords. You are hardly shy about your numerous liaisons, so what difference will one more make to you?"

"My liaisons aim to be pleasurable. I can't imagine anything less to my taste than to bed Ryka Feldspar be-cause she wants to placate the Cloudmaster! I have not the faintest desire to bed you, Ryka. I have always found your snappish character and lack of femininity as unattractive as your face and as dull as the way you dress."

When she flushed, he took no notice and continued, "Anyway, what do you propose? Taking a room down-level somewhere and popping up here every night until such time as you are pregnant? You might have to wait a long time, my dear. To the best of my knowledge, I have never fathered a child, and I haven't taken precautions to prevent it for the past fifteen years. Nor, I imagine, have many of the women involved. Why do you think the Cloudmaster hasn't pressured me into a wedded state?"

He allowed a tinge of amusement to suffuse his tone. "As much as it saddens me to point this out to you, I fear I am destined never to have offspring. I *had* thought this fact was a matter of vulgar gossip throughout the Scarpen Quarter. It seems I was wrong, which pleases me, I will admit. Foolish pride, I know, but a man does not like his sterility to be a matter of common knowledge."

While he'd been speaking, she had slowly risen to her feet, her face reddening and then draining of colour until she was as white as a 'Baster.

She stood staring at him, unable in her embarrassment and humiliation to speak. Finally she managed a strangled, "Then I have been wasting time for both of us. My apologies."

He inclined his head. "Accepted. Ah," he added with deliberate heartiness, "here are the refreshments—"

"I beg to be excused."

Her departure was too abrupt to be polite.

Outside in the street, Ryka leaned against the villa wall to collect herself. She could still hear Taquar's low chuckle as she'd left his room. Damn it, the humiliation of his derision was going to haunt her.

You stupid, stupid woman! she thought. *How can you have been such a sand-brained idiot? Did it never occur to you* why *he had no children? And why, oh why, did you imagine he might find you attractive enough to bed?*

Her cheeks burned hot as she recalled his words. *Damn*

him. There'd been no need to tear her down like that. He had been so—so—downright *nasty*.

Watergiver take you, Taquar, I may have asked for that, but you are such *a bastard.*

She squared her shoulders. If Taquar had been within range she would have ripped into him. Instead, all she could do was grit her teeth and dream of what she should have said. Damn, damn, damn, how could she have been so *stupid*?

"Ryka?"

She whirled in surprise. A man came out of the darkness at the right of the gate, and she cursed herself for not paying attention to her surroundings. No one ought to have been able to creep up on her like that. Then, belatedly, she recognised him, and her eyes widened. "*Kaneth*?" she asked. "What are you doing here?"

"Here, meaning in Scarcleft, or here, meaning in front of Taquar's gate?" He glanced up to where a guard on the wall was staring at them in an interested way, his zigger hissing in the cage that was clipped to the shoulder of his uniform.

She allowed him to take her elbow and guide her away, but her tone was frosty. "Both," she replied.

"The answer's the same to both questions, anyway. Following you."

"Then you had better have a good excuse," she snapped. "Because it feels very much like being spied upon."

"Feels rather like spying to me, too," he said cheerfully as they headed down to the next level. "But my excuse is a good one. Granthon sent for the two of us. I went to your house to tell you, and your father said you'd come to visit your cousins here in Scarcleft. I told Granthon that, and he told me to go and get you. Not, mind, 'send her a message.' Oh, no. I had to come and get you. Which meant I had to drop everything and ride two days to get here. Then, when I arrive, what do I find? You aren't staying with your cousins at all. They hadn't even seen you. It was just as well I recognised your mount down in the pede livery when I was stabling mine or I would have been wondering if you were even *in* Scarcleft!"

"So how did you find me?"

"I walked the streets until I sensed your water."

She was dumbfounded. "You can recognise me *by my water?*"

He didn't reply.

"That's a *stormlord* skill."

"Ah—well. You know my powers have always been damned unpredictable. I can't do it from very far away, and not for anyone else. Just you. And don't ask me why, because I have no idea. I've been able to do that since we were children. Remember how I used to always know what you were up to?"

"Oh! That explains a lot. It used to drive me crazy."

"Which is why I never told you how I knew. I was glad of the skill tonight, because quite frankly, Scarcleft Hall was the last place I thought of looking. I was on Level Three, and I thought I must be imagining things when I sensed you up there. Although I suppose I should have guessed, the way you were fluttering your eyelashes at Taquar when we were in the Gibber Quarter. What the pickled pede do you think you are doing, going to Scarcleft Hall at night? Don't you know what sort of reputation he has with women?"

"*Fluttering my eyelashes?* I do not flutter my eyelashes! How dare you insinuate—" She halted, flustered by her recollection of how—eyelashes notwithstanding—she had at least tried to arouse Taquar's interest in her. Then her fury exploded at the last of what he had said. "And as for reputations, what about *yours*? I hear far more about Kaneth Carnelian's acquaintance with every snuggery girl from Breccia to Breakaway than I do about Taquar's! You are utterly *insufferable*!"

"Maybe, but that still doesn't explain what you were doing there. You *can't* think of marrying Taquar, surely. Even you can't be that foolish. You *do* know he has never sired a child, don't you, although it hasn't been for want of trying, believe me."

"*Even I?* Sunlord, save me, but you are insulting, Kaneth." Inside she thought miserably, *Damn it, am I the only person who didn't know Taquar was sterile?*

"Only when you deserve it."

She winced, and he changed his tone, suddenly gentle. "By all that's water-holy, what is it with us? Ryka, we used to be such good friends. What *happened*?"

She looked at him, straining to see his face in the dim light. "You really don't understand, do you?"

"No, I don't."

He sounded so genuinely mystified, she took him at his word. "Bedding a string of hussies and snuggery girls may be forgivable when you are eighteen and as randy as a street cat surrounded by a crowd of fluffy felines on heat. It even has a certain youthful charm. But in a man of thirty-five or so, it's just . . . vulgar. Immature. Tawdry. It makes me sick. And the idea that I am to be just one in that string makes me feel dirty. As though I am a body to be enjoyed, but never a mind to be respected. Or a face to be admired, or a friend to be appreciated, or a wife to be esteemed."

She stopped as Taquar's words resounded in her head, sour and hateful. And worrying. What if they were true? *Your snappish character and lack of femininity as unattractive as your face and as dull as the way you dress.* What if Kaneth felt the same way about her? *Oh Sunlord, Ry,* she thought, *you never used to care that you weren't pretty. What's* happened *to you? Why should it suddenly matter?*

Kaneth raised his eyebrows. "Oh? Then why did you go sneaking around to Taquar's? You *can't* think he's more chaste than I am, surely."

"Oh *bother* you, Kaneth. Go away."

"I'll escort you to wherever you're staying."

"I don't need company."

"No, I don't suppose you do. You are a rainlord, after all. But it's late and I'll do it nonetheless. And I'll escort you back to Breccia, too. Granthon still wants to see us. And quite frankly, I don't know what we are going to say."

" 'No.' At least that's what *I* am going to say. And if that is enough to stop our rainlord's allowance, then we shall just have to learn to do without it. It may curtail your popularity with the snuggery girls, but I'm sure you can learn to live with that."

"Easy to see you haven't faced Granthon when he's made up his mind about something," he said, and she heard genuine warning in his tone. "Do you really think that's all the persuasion he has in mind?"

She thought about it and went cold.

*   *   *

Ryka remembered Kaneth's words when they faced the Cloudmaster in the Breccia Hall dining room several days later. Granthon was apparently well enough to sit up and have dinner with the rest of his family, but she was shocked by the decline in his health since she had seen him last. His cheeks were sunken, his eyes deep-set and suffering. Moreover, he looked . . . unkempt. And this in a man who had always been faultlessly attired, a regal, proud man, not one who would informally interview a couple of rainlords in front of his family, let alone be seen with his vest stained and his tunic sleeves dirty.

Ryka shot a look at Ethelva and saw the tightness around the woman's eyes. They exchanged a wordless glance, and Ryka saw the pleading there, and the wisdom. Her expression said, as clearly as spoken words, "Don't thwart him. He's all we have."

Ryka looked away to give her attention to the others. Nealrith, who had risen when she and Kaneth were ushered in, was shifting his weight uncomfortably. He'd greeted them both, but now refused to meet Kaneth's gaze. Laisa watched with interest, smiling faintly, as if secretly amused, while Senya, the little brat, sparkled with an unpleasantly gleeful interest.

The kind of women men admire, Ryka thought. *Beautiful, and who cares what the inside is like? Or whether they have anything but sand in their skulls.* She sighed to herself, wryly aware that she did not much like the cynicism of her thoughts. She used to be a much nicer person before she'd fallen in love. *How ironic is that?* she mused. *And do we really have to stand here like a couple of naughty children while Granthon chastises us in front of these two bitches, mother and daughter? Sands, this is as humiliating as my interview with Taquar.*

"Laisa, Senya, let's go outside, shall we?" Nealrith said. "This is not a matter that concerns us."

"On the contrary!" Granthon barked, his white bushy brows drawn so tight they met over his nose. His voice was surprisingly strong. And angry, with a twist of deep emotion. "This is exactly something you should all hear, because you should all know the sacrifices you might be called upon to make in the future. Senya, particularly."

ˋ   He then directed his attention to Kaneth and Ryka, saying, "You both know the situation. The land could die with me. Probably will. And neither of you are doing your duty to prevent it. I have been patient far longer than I should have. I have threatened you with monetary loss. I have appealed to your sense of honour. I know nothing is certain—that any children you have may be water-blind—but we need to try everything, no matter the cost. If I can ruin my health and the quality of my life for you and this land, the very least you can do is marry for the good of it."

Ryka looked steadily at the floor, but heat spread from the back of her neck into her cheeks. Shame. Anger. Helplessness. She wasn't sure what was uppermost. Humiliation, perhaps, and not just because the Cloudmaster's family was listening, but because she couldn't imagine a worse humiliation, than marrying a man she loved who didn't care for her and would be rubbing her nose in his faithlessness every evening. What would he do: bed her then go off to his snuggeries? Or the other way around? She felt sick.

Granthon continued, "Now go into the next room and talk to one another, and don't come back until you have a solution that involves an attempt to bring another stormlord into the world. Is that clear?"

She and Kaneth glanced at each other, silently communicating their reluctance to even discuss the subject. Then Kaneth turned his gaze to look at the Cloudmaster. "The fault is mine. And I will not compound my errors by forcing myself on a woman who does not want me."

Granthon's eyes narrowed, but he did not comment.

"Would you really countenance such a thing, Lord Granthon?" Kaneth asked. "Since when did the Cloudmaster advocate rape?"

Nealrith winced. Senya smirked. And Granthon levered himself out of his chair in rage. "You think to play with me on this matter? It is the future of the Quartern we speak of here! Go discuss this, the two of you, and before you come back, think on this. If you will not marry—or set up a viable relationship in a home together—then one of you will be cast out of the gates as far as a pede can ride in three days, without water and away from a road. And the choice of which one of you that will be will rest on the selection of the shortest straw of two in my hand. Is that clear?"

Ryka felt the colour drain from her face. He would kill a rainlord—and never mind which one—just to make a point? And in such a cruel way: death by thirst. Neither she nor Kaneth had the kind of power that could retrieve water from the city over such a distance.

When he stared at her now, she could see none of his weakness, just the harsh look of a ruler who was determined to help his land the best way he knew how, no matter the cost to others.

There were no choices left, and she knew it. She

tensed to control the shiver that threatened to skitter down her spine.

She exchanged another glance with Kaneth, saw his compassion, and said, "Yes, it is clear. And we don't need time to think about it. I will do as you ask."

"Kaneth?" the Cloudmaster asked.

He nodded abruptly.

"Good. Then I will expect to see you living under one roof within ten days. Nealrith, show them the door." He slumped back against the chair, suddenly once again an old, tired man.

Outside the door, a servant came to show them out but Kaneth waved him away irritably. Ryka was already at the top of the stairs, where she had frozen, her attention caught by what she saw as she glanced over the banisters to the hall below. There was a new waterpainting set into the floor.

It measured perhaps ten paces long and seven wide, and it showed a young woman riding a black pede crossing a white landscape. The pede's many feet kicked up a white cloud as it went. The woman was dressed plainly, in travelling clothes, a palmubra hat on her head, her cloak billowing out behind her. Heat shimmers rose into a cloudless sky. All the immediate landscape was flat, featureless and white; in the distance, a range of blue and grey peaks rose, capped with white. They seemed to float in the sky, impossibly distant, yet appearing solid and real at the same time.

"That's new," Kaneth said at her elbow. He sounded upset, and she knew he was glad to find a neutral topic of conversation. "There used to be a picture of the clouds over Warthago Range, which was more appropriate for a cloudmaster's villa, I would have thought. This looks too, um, too personal. Although I'm damned if I know where it is. I've never seen a range like that one."

"I don't like it," she said, shuddering, not sure if it was the painting or the Cloudmaster's anger or the commitment she had been obliged to make that was making her so fearful. "In fact, I don't like waterpaintings."

"Why not?"

"They are too powerful. They . . . *dominate* the room they occupy. And you are right. This one is too personal. That has to be a real portrait of someone. And she looks . . ." She searched for the right word. "She looks *haunted*."

He glanced down at the painting again. "No, not haunted. Hunted. She looks hunted." He turned back to Ryka. "And I don't know why we are talking about a damned painting when we should be talking about what we are going to do."

She didn't look at him, but started on her way down the stairs. "There's nothing to talk about. We have to go through with it." She strove to sound cool, insouciant. "All we have to do is decide what we opt for: marriage or just a liaison."

"Marriage," he said.

She waved a careless hand, trying not to read anything into the choice. "As you wish."

Inside she wanted to weep.

CHAPTER FIFTEEN

Gibber Quarter
Wash Drybone Settle

Shale kept his promise to Taquar.

He told no one he had been tested and had passed the test. He even explained away all he had previously said to Mica. "I was making that up 'bout knowing which bowls had water in them," he said. "I wouldn't have known, no way. I *did* know the rush was comin' down the wash that time—I saw the grey things in the sky, that's all. Clouds. Anyone could tell the rush would come down after that."

Mica looked relieved, willing enough to believe the lie in place of the more inconceivable truth. "I'm glad there's not somethin' funny 'bout you. I was worried 'bout what Pa said. 'Bout the rainlords not liking anyone to meddle in their business."

"Yeah," said Shale. "Me, too."

In his heart, though, Shale wasn't sure he was doing the right thing, lying to Mica. The oddities of the conversation with Taquar had soon come to haunt him. First the rainlord had said a water sensitive was valuable and that Shale was in no danger, then he'd said water sensitives had been snuffed. First he had said no one in the rainlords' caravan would harm him, then he had told Shale it would be dangerous to tell any of the rainlords that he was a water sensitive.

The inconsistencies worried him, but by then the caravan had gone, leaving nothing except the unreality of the memory. He could not even ask anyone in the settle about just what a stormlord was, because no one knew. When a small Reduner caravan passed through a couple of weeks later, collecting the settle's resin, he asked several of the servants about stormlords, but the answers were unsatisfactory. "A Scarperman," he was told. "The sandmaster of the Scarpermen," another added. "The stormlord breaks the clouds to bring rain to the waterholes." But none of them had ever seen a stormlord, although they had all seen it rain.

Shale couldn't make sense of it. If a stormlord was a Scarperman or a sandmaster or powerful enough to bring rain—well, Shale was sure he was none of those things. Just knowing about water was a far cry from breaking clouds to make water fall from the sky. He continued to mull over the question, keeping his uncertainties to himself.

In the meantime, life went on. His caution stopped him from trying to sell the jasper to any of the caravanners or telling his father about it. He had a feeling he might need the tokens it would fetch at some future date. For now, he continued to wander the plains collecting resin.

Mica worked in the bab groves or the clay pit or the stone quarry, wherever there was casual work to be done that would earn them a few tokens to buy water and food. Marisal sold her embroidery—and perhaps her services as well—directly to the caravans, and then lied to her husband about how much she was paid. Galen did little except drink away as much of their earnings as he could.

But Shale had gained something from Rainlord Taquar's visit: hope. For the first time in his life he had a vision for the future that didn't include his father, or being scared of him. He had a confidence he'd never possessed before. He no longer cringed before Galen. If he could, he simply walked away; if he couldn't, he stood his ground. Galen's eyes would flash with anger, but he no longer beat his son. Nor did he again broach the idea of prostituting him for money. The idea was dropped as if it had never been suggested.

Patiently, Shale waited for the day when Taquar would return.

Life seemed better than ever before.

One morning early in the next star cycle, about a hundred days after the Scarpen rainlords' visit, a kick to Shale's ribs woke him from a troubled dream. He rolled over, aware only of a feeling of terrible wrongness. His head ached with the oppression of it.

"We're outta fronds to burn. Go get some from the grove." His father's voice, still thick with the results of a drinking bout the night before. Dawnbreak had not yet come, and Galen had lit a rush light. Shale knew what he was supposed to do: sneak down to the palm grove and steal some of the fallen fronds under the trees. Anything that fell from the tree was the property of the tree owner, and such fronds were valuable as fuel or roofing thatch or for the weaving of mats.

Shale could filch fruit from a garden orchard before the sandgrouse alerted the household, or shin up a palm tree and pinch the bab fruit from the back of the bunch without the owner ever realising it had been pilfered, or relieve settlefolk of their property in a hundred similar ways. But he didn't *like* doing it. It made him feel dirty inside. How could he feel right about stealing, say, from Rishan the palmier, when it was Rishan who occasionally gave him the leftovers from his kitchen or a few extra eggs from his sandgrouse?

He staggered out of bed rubbing the sleep from his eyes, unable to say why he felt so rotten. So heavy-headed, so suffocated. That feeling of something botched was back. He glanced over at Mica, still curled up asleep, and contemplated waking him, but a fierce look from his father sent him stumbling straight out into the morning cold. His breath made clouds in the air and he regretted not having picked up his blanket on the way out. He thought about returning to get it, but the memory of the anger in his father's voice banished that idea, so he plucked the empty burlap sack from where it hung on the outer wall to put around his shoulders in its place. As he headed for the edge of the wash, he decided he must be sickening with something.

The watercourse was black with night, the sun still hidden below the desert rim. A touch of colour tingeing the horizon indicated that dawn was on its way, but the bab palms were just indeterminate shapes barely rising to the level of the bank. It was too dark down there to be able to see anything.

Yet it was all wrong. His awareness of water was telling him things that didn't make sense.

He stood on the lip of the wash, knowing his world had been changed while he slept. There was water everywhere. The beginnings of panic finally snapped his eyes wide, tensed his muscles ready for flight, banished sleepiness.

He forced himself to concentrate, and the details came into focus. Too much water. Surrounding him. Surrounding the settle. Once he concentrated on the pieces instead of the whole, he was able to put a name to what was happening. *People.* Not water by itself, but water inside people. *Everywhere.*

The settle was surrounded by people and pedes, too many to count. Far more people than had ever visited Wash Drybone at any one time before, far more pedes than Shale had known could ever be gathered together in one place. The reality of it hit as hard as his father's fist in the stomach. This was all wrong. Caravans didn't sneak up in the pre-dawn and come on the settle from all sides. And caravan folk didn't sneak along the wash, either.

Vague tales of nomad raids and rumours about recent water thefts in some of the settles coursed through his mind, even though common sense told him that nomads raided cargo-rich caravans or gem-rich wash towns, not water-poor settles. Not Wash Drybone Settle.

His second thought grew with his fear: *it can't be because of me . . . can it? I didn't tell anyone, Lord Taquar!*

He shuddered and tried to convince himself that he wasn't that important. That no one surrounds a settle with tens and tens of people just to kill one boy. And yet his fear scudded into terror.

He was outlined against a sky that was getting lighter by the moment. He abandoned the sack and dropped down into the wash, where it was darker. He doubled over as he ran into the shelter of the grove. When he sensed strangers among the trees, he gave them a wide berth and dropped down still further, this time into an empty slot. He pelted up the narrow stone drain, his bare feet skidding on the sifting of sand that covered the stonework.

When he reached the grove's holding cistern, he climbed out and ran into the settle street. Arms pumping, he pounded upward to the top house in the settle: Rishan's. He desperately needed to pass on the problem to someone who would know what to do. Luckily no one in the settle ever barred their gates, so he was able to enter the garden and bang on the house door, yelling at the same time.

Rishan himself came to answer, bare-chested and yawning, his wife behind him uncovering the coals in the fireplace to light the candle she carried, his two sons hanging back, stupid with sleep. "*Shale*? What is it? What's the matter, lad? Your pa hasn't gone killed your ma, has he?"

"Somethin's botched, Palmier Rishan. There's folk all round the settle. More than I can count—they're sneakin' up through the wash, an' 'cross the plains!"

The two boys woke up properly at that and came up behind their father, full of questions. Rishan ignored them and took the lighted candle from his wife. "Is it a caravan, lad?"

Shale shook his head vigorously. "Too many folk. Tens 'n' tens of pedes. As many men as settlefolk. No—more. I'm scared, palmier."

"You saw them?"

He thought of explaining—and opted for an easier lie. "Yes."

"Who are they?"

"Dunno. Too dark t'tell."

Rishan didn't move. He was holding the candle high, as if to study Shale's face, but his eyes had gone blank.

Shale was panicking. Why didn't Rishan *do* some-thing? He began to hop up and down, unable to contain his agitation. He needed to get back home. He had to warn them. "I got t'go—" he began.

Rishan came alive and turned to his sons. "Warn every-one, quickly. *Run!*" His face was dead white.

Shale fled. As he ran down the street, he could hear Rishan and his sons beginning to pound on doors to wake their neighbours. He himself went straight back home, flung himself into the hut, shouting, not even sure what he was saying between his gasps for air. He was aware, horribly aware, of the people out there, all around him, closing in on the settle, getting closer. Waiting for the sun to come up, to do whatever it was they were going to do. He tried to explain to them all, to Mica, raising his tousled head from the filth of the blankets, to Galen who had gone back to his sodden sleep after Shale had left the hut, to his mother who just looked at him blankly, with no alarm or interest.

"What's it matter?" she asked. Citrine had woken screaming and she pushed the child at him. "You woke her with your noise, you can shut her up."

"Don't you unnerstand? Those folk out there, what-ever they want ain't good! They're sneakin' up on us like marauders—"

Galen propped himself up on one elbow. "So? What you reckon they goin' t'steal from us, boy? Half a jar of water? Fuel to light the cooking fire? Where's your sense? You got sand for brains? Let 'em come!" He flopped back onto the bed and turned his back.

Shale, Citrine in his arms, gave Mica a despairing look. "Please," he said. "Please."

To Shale's relief, Mica didn't question him. He nodded and grabbed two water skins from where they hung on the wall and went to fill them from the dayjar. In the Gibber Quarter, no matter what you did, you thought of water first. Shale hurriedly unearthed his piece of bloodstone from where he had buried it under his sleeping sack.

"We'll hide in the wash," Mica muttered.

Shale was already pushing his way through the sacking of the door, trying to hush Citrine's cries. She was calming and her screams became a few muffled sobs. He ran out, looking around, wanting to assess which way to go, which way was free of people.

And stopped dead.

In the few moments he had been inside, the sun had sent its first rays racing over the land. The shadows were long fingers stretching across the purple of the plains: shadows of men on pedes, each rider with his chala spear in his hand and his long-handled curved scimitar at his waist.

"I'll be bleeding withered," Shale whispered.

"Reduners," Mica said, expelling the breath he had been holding, as if he didn't know whether to be frightened or just puzzled. "Never seen so many. What could they *want*?"

Shale went cold all over. He ran around the corner of the hut, to look in the other direction. More men and pedes were silhouetted against the skyline there, too. Below, the wash was full of moving shapes.

"Nowhere to run," he said, coming back to Mica. "Got t'wait and see what they're after." He held Citrine tight, joggling her to keep her quiet. As more light poured across the plains, silhouettes sharpened into packpedes and myriapedes, riders became armed men, each with his lower face muffled, wrapped in the ends of a red head cloth. Each wore identical red robes without any adornment. There was nothing to show which tribe they were from or which dune.

"I'll get Pa," Mica whispered.

As Mica dived back into the hut, Shale saw one of the packpedes peel away from the waiting line and head their way. There were eighteen riders on its back, one to each segment. He wanted to run, to hide. Instead, he clutched Citrine still tighter. She squirmed and giggled, thinking it was a game, and then plucked at his fist. "Shalie," she crowed, spotting the piece of jasper, "Shalie give!" He relinquished the gem to her. The packpede slid to a halt thirty paces away. No one moved.

Mica came back with their parents. One glance and Galen's swearing faded, and Marisal reached to take Citrine back. They all knew there was nothing to be done. There was nowhere to hide on the plains and you couldn't outrun a zigger. Shale surrendered his sister and slipped his water skin over his shoulder.

Out of the air there arose an unearthly sound, a bull-roarer's buzz that settled into a deep fluctuating whirr as whoever held it twirled it faster and faster. Another began to sound in the wash, and the message was taken up by a third and a fourth, then another so far away it must have been on the other side of the settle.

Shale shivered. It must have been a signal for the Re-duners to move, because down in the drywash men rose out of hiding and raced towards the settle. Many clutched scimitars, others chala spears, and some lighted torches from smouldering tinder as they ran.

"Goin' t'fire the thatch," Galen said flatly.

Shale wondered how he knew.

As if in answer, Galen said, "My grandpa tole stories about nomad raiders. Back in the days when they took slaves. They'd light the thatch first, and when people ran into the streets . . ." He shrugged.

"They don't take slaves no more," Marisal said. She sounded more puzzled than frightened.

"Whadda they want, then?" Galen asked. He ducked back into the hut to fetch his skin of amber, then continued, "Whatever it is, we're dead meat, Marisal. They may take the young'uns, but they won't want us. And maybe they won't want t'leave any to tell the tale." He drank heavily and, ignoring Shale, offered the skin to Mica. "Here, drink. Better not t'know what's comin'."

Mica shook his head dumbly and slipped a hand into Shale's.

The men on the myriapede in front of them, following an unseen signal, dismounted and ran to surround the huts. When Gissek the forager rushed out of his door to see what was happening, one of the Reduners casually speared him through the chest. Rushing out behind him, his wife tripped over his body and fell. The toddler she carried, the little girl everyone called Sooks, went sprawling. She took a deep breath as a prelude to a wail, and another Reduner stamped on her throat before any sound emerged.

"Oh, waterful mercy," Marisal gasped, and clutched Citrine even closer.

"Don't move," Mica pleaded. He was shaking with fear and his voice wobbled. "Don't move."

Galen gave a sour smile and drank more amber. "That's not goin' t'make no difference."

Another pede approached, this time one man on a myriapede. His glance swept over the group of people in front
of the huts. Shale looked around, aware of his trembling
but unable to stop it. All their neighbours were outside now,
faces pale in the dawn light: Ore the stonebreaker and his
family; Demel the widow and her two children; Topaz the
scrubber; Parman the legless. They were all staring at Gissek and Sooks, so obviously dead. Gissek's wife was sitting up, her shock so deep she wasn't able to move.

The man on the myriapede looked them over and ordered, "No trouble!" His tone was hard. Uncaring. They
didn't need to be told he was in charge. And he didn't
need to threaten them further. He had a zigger cage tied
to the segment handle. The creatures were agitated, their
high-pitched humming frenzied. The Reduners who had
dismounted had their spears levelled.

None of the settlefolk moved.

The man spoke to several of his men in their own
tongue. As they scattered to enter the huts, he turned back
to the settlefolk saying, "Men search. Even sand-ant hiding, we find. Then fire roofs."

Marisal drew in a sharp breath; Galen dug her hard in
the back. "Shut up, woman," he growled.

Shale felt removed from what was going on around
him. Remote. Being detached was the only way he could
handle it; the only way he could stay silent. Stay *still*. He
wanted so badly to run, yet knew he would die if he did.

They had a good view of the settle from where they
were. Fires already flickered across the roofs of the
houses. Although the stone and mud-daub walls would
not burn, the roofs were another matter. There was no better fuel than bab fronds dried under a desert sun.

A while earlier, he had been about to look for fronds to burn. *Shit.*

As the villagers fled their homes, Reduners cut them down in the streets. The whirr of the bullroarers finally ceased. The screams went on. He knew he would never forget the screams. Images burned into his memory. Iolite the seamstress on fire. Gamath the resiner decapitated as he tried to reason with one of the raiders. Rishan thrown alive into a burning house. A woman, he didn't know who, raped on the back of a pede, then tossed to the ground like a sack of stones. Reeve Gravel being dragged through the street behind a pede.

It was then that Ore the stonebreaker went berserk. He picked up a heavy rock from the ground and leaped at the closest of the Reduners. His initial rush caught the man by surprise; his spear wavered and Ore slammed into him, battering him with the rock. The man went down, unconscious and bleeding heavily from the nose and eye. Ore's arm went up and punched down twice more, even as the first of three or four spears thudded into his back.

Shale drew in a shuddering breath. Refused to think. Refused to ask himself why. The answers were all too terrible. And much too personal.

Beside him Mica stood, wide-eyed and shivering, Marisal pressed Citrine's head into her shoulder so she wouldn't see what was happening and Galen drank himself into unthinking numbness.

The Reduner leader sat for a while on his mount, watching what was happening down in the settle. Then he turned his beast and came back to where Shale and the others huddled together in front of their burning homes.

He looked them all over and then homed in on Mica. "You," he said. "Name?"

"M-mica Galen, pedeman."

He switched his attention to Shale. "You?"

Shale's mouth went dry. "Chert," he said, giving the first name that popped into his head.

Fortunately the man was not looking at Mica, or he would have known Shale lied. He turned his attention to one of the younger boys in the group, Demel the widow's eldest son. "You?" he asked.

"Crag, pedeman."

"Crag, answer true, me not kill. Understand?"

No, Shale thought, scuffing a toe in the dirt as if he wasn't scared. *No. He's not going to ask about me. He's a Reduner. Reduners wouldn't be looking for me.*

The boy nodded, trembling. He was eight, and so frightened he'd wet himself.

"Who Shale Galen, Crag?"

Crag, trembling, pointed to Shale. "Th-that's Shale, p-pedeman."

The man gave a faint smile that scarified Shale with terror. "Babe?"

"Sh-sh-shale's s-s-sister, pedeman. Citrine."

The man turned to one of his followers. "Fanim?"

"*Veh, Pasirdam?*" Yes, Sandmaster? Shale understood enough Reduner to know that much.

The sandmaster jerked his head in Marisal's direction. "We play game of chala." He looked straight at Shale. "Davim hate liars." He gathered in his reins and flicked his mount into wakefulness.

Shale tried to remember what chala was. A Reduner game. Chala spears. He had seen caravanners play it.

They passed a ball from spear to spear. No, not a ball—they didn't use a ball. An animal, that was it. They used an animal, alive to start with. A large horny lizard, perhaps, or a desert cat. Once it was dead, they continued to pass its carcass from one to the other. If you let the carcass fall, then you had to retire from the game. Until there was only one person left: the winner.

But he didn't understand. Why play chala now?

The man called Fanim gave a broad grin. "*Veh, Pasirdam!*" With one swift movement he leaned forward, inserted the point of his spear into Citrine's clothing and yanked her out of Marisal's arms.

And Shale began to scream—not her name, but his own, over and over and over.

CHAPTER SIXTEEN

Scarpen Quarter
Scarcleft City
Level 32 and Level 10

"You can't do this to me," Vivie said flatly. "I won't let you."

"You can't stop me."

"Don't be stupid, of course I can. All I have to do is call for Garri." She waved a hand in the direction of her door, as if the steward was waiting outside. "Or Madam Opal. Terelle, you are honour-bound to serve the snuggery. You *owe* Opal."

"I didn't *ask* to be here."

"You've been glad enough to drink the water."

"I wish I hadn't told you now! I just didn't want you worrying about me."

"Waterless heavens! Terelle, are you out of your mind? You met a man down on the thirty-sixth—what were you doing down there anyway?—and on the strength of that one meeting, you want to live with him so he can teach you to *paint water*?"

"It's not like that."

"Have you any idea what Opal will say to me if you

vanish? She will think I knew and didn't tell her!" Even
as she spoke, she paled. "What if she makes me pay off
your debt as well as my own? Oh, mercy, of course that's
what she'll do! Terelle, you *can't* walk out!"

Terelle stayed stubbornly silent. Inside, her hopes
leaked away. Why had she told Vivie this much? She
should have just disappeared. Now she'd never be allowed out of the snuggery. They would watch her like
chameleons hunting prey.

Use your head, Terelle. Get out of this.

"I never thought of that," she said at last. "Of course,
that's exactly what Opal *would* do. Make you pay. Oh,
Vivie, that would be awful." She tried to look woebegone.
Vivie was probably right, at that.

"You can't do that to me," Vivie reiterated.

And what about me? Terelle asked silently, trying
to push away the guilt. Aloud she said, eyes downcast,
"I'm—I'm sorry. You're right. That would be awful. I
never thought of that." She flushed, and hoped that Vivie
wouldn't realise it was because she was lying.

Vivie looked relieved. "You won't go?"

Terelle slumped on the bed. "No. I guess not."

"That's all right, then. By all that's holy, you had me
worried, Terelle. I thought you'd taken leave of your
senses! And over nothing, too. You'll *like* working here
once you start upstairs."

Terelle looked at her curiously. "Do you, Vivie? Do
you really *like* it?"

She shrugged. "Some of the men are nice. Some aren't,
but Opal never lets them hurt us. If Huckman gets your
first-night, it may not be pleasant, but Opal will give you
part of what she makes him pay. She's very fair. Why do

you let it bother you so, Terelle? If we were back in the Gibber, Father would have married us off by now, and we could both be stuck with men we hated for the rest of our lives! That would be far, far worse."

"I'm sorry, Vivie. I guess I just didn't think."

Vivie smiled at her. "It's not so bad, don't worry. Here, look, I bought you a present in the bazaar." Smiling, she handed over a small parcel wrapped in a melon leaf.

When Terelle unfolded the wrapping, she found a mirror with a carved pede-shell back. "It's a 'Baster looking glass!" she said, astonished. They were much more expensive than the polished stone mirrors most people used. "It's lovely," she added, and meant it. "Thanks. I—I will treasure it."

"Hey, it's nothing. Run along now and help the servants with the preparations for tonight. I've got to dress. Hanri the trader said he was coming and I want him to choose me, so I've got to look especially nice."

Terelle left, but she didn't go downstairs. She went back to her own room, which she shared with several of the servants. As she expected, there was no one there. She took the waterpainting from under her bed, then gathered her spare set of working clothes and bundled them up with the painting and the mirror inside. She made sure that she had all her tokens safely in her coin pocket and took one last glance around the room. She had no regrets at leaving. The servants were all middle-aged; she had no close friends in the snuggery except for Vivie, and in the end they'd had nothing in common except a shared childhood, a vague sisterly affection and a father who had sold them.

She closed the door behind her and started down the

stairs. She knew the trick to dodging any added workload: you looked busy. So she hurried, clutching her bundle as if it was a pile of dirty bed linen. Once downstairs, she walked briskly past the kitchen and let herself out of the back door.

She was surprised at just how busy the streets were at night, surprised to find that the people of Scarcleft flung open their doors and brought chairs out to sit in front of their gateways. A young lad was trying to impress his friends with his dubious mastery of the intricacies of the lute as he sat on his doorstep. Residents ambled by, visiting their neighbours. A peddler, tray hanging from a strap around his neck, sold hot cakes rolled in honey for a tinny token.

She had feared people would think it odd for someone of her age to be out in the streets at this hour after sunset but she found she was just one of many. She used her bundle to make it look as if she was a servant on an errand and found it easy enough to slip by the occasional patrolling enforcer. With a pang, she realised how much she had missed, growing up in the snuggery. At this hour of the night, she had always been too busy working ever to wonder what ordinary people did with their lives.

I'm sorry, Vivie, she thought, *but I've got to do this.*

She did not go directly to Level Thirty-six. Instead, she climbed up to the tenth, to Amethyst's. As always, Jomat answered her pull of the bell with sour suspicion.

"What are you doing here?" he asked. "What makes you think that the arta will want to see *you* in the middle of the night?" Even in the cool of the evening, he was sweating. He reached out and pinched her cheek with damp fingers, but Terelle stood her ground. Fortunately, just at that moment Amethyst entered the courtyard and waved Jomat away.

"I've run away," Terelle explained once they were seated inside, away from Jomat's eavesdropping. "I'm going down to live on Level Thirty-six. But I'm scared to go there at night, so I wondered if I could stay here. Just for tonight."

However, by the time Terelle had told the whole story, Amethyst looked no more pleased than Viviandra had. "Have you seen where this old man lives?" she asked.

"He did show me. It's just a single room, but it's clean and large."

"Hmm. I have seen some waterpaintings. Perhaps they were his work. I've seen the one Kerkil the singer has in her front hall. She said the artist was a strange old man, an outlander. Did he tell you his name?"

"Russet Kermes."

"Russet, yes, that was him. Artisman Russet. It's the same person." Amethyst stirred uncomfortably. "Terelle, are you sure? What's that old saying . . . 'Don't hug the ghost out of fear of the corpse.'? You are not stepping out of one brothel door and into another, are you?"

"I—I don't think so. I spoke to some of the people who live in his building. They said he's been there about a year. Before that, he lived in other cities, or so he told them. They say he spends a lot of his time uplevel, where the rich pay him to do waterpaintings. And that he sometimes goes to the other cities, too."

"But?"

"They—they don't like him much. I think it's just because he is different. I don't think he's from the Quartern. He has a really funny way of speaking, his arms and legs are painted with patterns and his clothes are weird. And he's not terribly friendly."

"Wherever he comes from, he will be waterless here, dependent on what he can earn." She continued to look at Terelle in concern.

"He's old, Arta. Very old. He couldn't do anything to me that I didn't agree to; he wouldn't be strong enough."

"Few people make offers to complete strangers without wanting something. He told you he wanted an apprentice—why?"

"He's old. He needs help," Terelle replied defensively.

"I hope that's all."

Terelle shivered, but said nothing. *Hug a ghost . . .* One part of her knew that she was foolish, tucking her fears away in a corner of her mind instead of bringing them out and confronting them. *What did the old man do to the painting to make it change? How is it possible to make a portrait of a real person out of a few suggestive splashes of paint?* Scarier still: *Why had the woman he portrayed then stepped into the street? Coincidence? Or had the painting* made *her do that?* Her mouth went dry at the thought. And then, perhaps the scariest of all: *How did he know my name?*

"I have the painting he did," she said. She spread it out on the floor at her feet so that Amethyst could look at it. The dancer studied it, sipping her tea. "It is very powerful," she said at last. "I would not like to cross the man who did that."

Terelle regarded the artwork anew. The painted sunlight bathed the beaten earth of the roadway in heat, the door to the house hung loose in breathless air. She reached out a finger to touch the paint and it was a relief to find that it was not warmed by the sun. The feel beneath her fingertip was just paint, not dust. Powerful, true—but already the power was fading, just as he had said it would once it was cut away from the magic of water.

That night, bedded down on the divan in the reception room, Terelle did not sleep well. Her dreams were disturbing, her fears surfacing in vivid inanities, all horribly real while she was asleep and stupid when she was awake, but which left a residue of worry behind like dregs in a dirty glass.

Dream and reality merged halfway through the night when she awoke to the feeling that there was someone in the room. She opened her eyes a crack. A figure was moving around holding a glimmer nightlamp. It barely cast a glow, but it was enough for her to recognise Jomat; his bulbous stomach and suppressed wheezing were unmistakable. He placed the lamp on a table, shielding most of its light with his body. He stealthily rifled through the bundle she had brought with her. She opened her mouth to scream out a protest, but thought better of it. She didn't want to embarrass Amethyst. There was nothing for Jomat to steal; her tokens were all under her pillow. And his stealth told her he wasn't intending to molest her.

She held her breath and watched through slitted eyes while he pulled out her waterpainting and unrolled it. He picked up the lamp to look at it properly, then carefully rolled it up again. Even more carefully, he replaced everything the way it had been and crept out of the room.

Terelle expelled her breath.

He was spying, she thought. *But he can't be interested in me, not really. He knows why I come, and the reason is harmless enough. No, maybe he's just a snoop.* She knew handmaidens at the snuggery who were like that: girls who just wanted to stick their noses into everything, looking for secrets because secrets gave you power over those with something to hide. And then another thought came: *Maybe it's really Amethyst he spies on.*

She hadn't thought it was possible to dislike that man more than she already did. Uneasily, and for no reason she could define, she regretted that he'd seen the painting.

CHAPTER SEVENTEEN

From the Gibber Quarter to the Scarpen Quarter

Shale was in pain and the pain was everywhere.

He welcomed it. Pain kept him from thinking, and thinking would have been a worse agony.

He had been flung, stomach down, across the back of a myriapede. His hands were tied with hemp to one side of the beast, his legs anchored to the other side. The flexible multiple legs of the pede made for a smooth ride, but just being bent over in the middle for so long created tangled knots of agony in his sinews and cramp in his muscles. The black chitin of the pede heated up beneath him and the sun beat down on his back.

Every hour or two his captors stopped for a short rest. There were only two of them: two pedes, two men, still with their faces wrapped in their red cloths.

Why only two? Where were the rest?

Still killing a settle.

A whole settle.

Stop thinking.

Citrine . . .

Stop thinking.

Mica. They hadn't killed Mica. Or he hadn't seen them do so.

They had herded everyone who was still alive, including Mica, in one direction and taken Shale the opposite way, to load him onto the pede. But so many had died before that. He saw their deaths still. He remembered their screams.

Stop thinking, you sand-leech! Concentrate on the pain. On the aching muscles. On the heat. On your thirst. On anything.

Two men on pedes. Heading up the wash towards the next settle. With him tied up like a sack of salt. His head bumped on the saddle cloth. It was thickly embroidered with patterns and swirls. The kind of thing his mother had stitched.

She was dead. He had seen the spear in her stomach. She'd actually tried to attack the man who'd snatched Citrine. Who would have thought she would be so brave? She'd always cowered from Galen. She'd never made the slightest attempt to defend Shale from his father.

They had singled him out. They had known his name. That man, the leader, had been looking for him. But not to kill him. To take him away. To the Red Quarter?

I didn't tell anyone, Lord Taquar. I didn't tell anyone about knowing water!

So how then had the sandmaster known his name?

He stared at the carvings on the pede segment near his cheek. They showed some early event in the life of the pede: apparently he had fallen into a sinkhole and Reduners had pulled him out. And that was how he had been caught and tamed. Shale wondered about how the Reduners made the carvings. Did it hurt the pede? Did they use a knife? Did the owner do it himself, or did he employ a special person to do it for him?

Stupid questions when his sister's blood was drying on his clothes. He'd felt the stickiness of it on his skin, before they tied him down.

Citrine.

Don't think about it.

If they were going to kill him, why hadn't they done it back at Wash Drybone Settle?

And Mica. Blast the withering bastards, what were they going to do to Mica?

They stopped at nightfall. They untied him and gave him food to eat, a blanket from their packs to sleep in, a water skin. He asked them where they were going, what they were going to do with him, and they didn't reply. When they spoke to each other, they muttered in their own tongue. Even when he heard, he didn't understand much. He ate, even as he thought his hunger was a betrayal of those who had died that day. They tied his legs together then and pointed to the blanket. He wrapped it around himself and went to sleep. He thought he wouldn't be able to; he thought oblivion would be banned to him for the rest of his life; he believed that last scream of Citrine's would keep him awake forever. And yet he slept, fitful sleep studded with the spikes of tortured dreams, impaired sleep that left him weary and sick.

When he woke in the morning, he vomited; he had the worst headache he had ever had in his life. He didn't want to eat, so they gave him water. The next thing he knew, it was hours later and he was lying lengthwise on the back of a pede, a packpede this time. He was tied to a baggage pallet like a sack of bab fruit. Two Reduners rode the beast, one at the head, the other at the back. They had not bothered to wrap their faces. He didn't think these were the same men who had guarded him the day before. The myriapedes those first men had been riding had vanished, and now there was more baggage than there had been.

He tried to make sense of what had happened, but drowsiness overcame his senses.

After that, his conscious moments blurred into a series of vague images as confused as any dream. Sometimes he was in a camp, wrapped in a blanket; sometimes he was lying on the baggage pallet, and they were moving. During other half-lucid moments, aware of the agony of aching muscles and a bruised body, he ate, drank, relieved himself. Most of the time, though, he just slept. Every time he struggled awake, when he thought he was beginning to make sense of what was happening, the clarity would slip away once more. He tried to ask where they were taking him, but the men just laughed and said things he couldn't understand.

Several days passed before he made the connection between the water they gave him and his inability to stay awake. He tried to refuse to drink, but they forced it down his throat and he couldn't remember what happened next. Hours later, he woke on the back of the pede, muscles screaming.

Then one night, after accepting the food and water they gave him, he felt better, not worse. More alert, for the first time in days. When he slept, it was in snatches, lightly. He wondered if they had run out of whatever it was they had been putting in the water, and began to feel hope.

* * *

He was dreaming. Someone was shouting, but he couldn't see them. "What happened to the brother?" a voice growled, irate. "Where is he? Mica? Where is the one called Mica?"

Someone replied, but he didn't hear what they said.

Then, "Yes, I know she died! But there was a brother. Tell me, or—"

Something knocked against him. He woke, terrified. People were fighting around him. He struggled up, entangled in his blanket. He kicked himself free and scrambled to his feet, heart thudding in the suddenness of his terror. Two men, just dark shapes in the starlight, rolled past him. They were grunting, punching, wrestling. He didn't know why, and he didn't care. All it meant to him was an opportunity to escape.

He grabbed for what he thought was one of the packs—he would need food and untainted water if he was going to head off into the desert alone—but his hand closed around an ankle instead. In shock, he stumbled and thumped down on his backside next to a body. One of his captors, semiconscious, groaning. Who was the second man in the fight, then? He looked, just in time to see one of the fighters hit the other with a blow that lifted him off his feet.

The victor looked around, saw him, and said, "Shale?"

He was too stunned to answer.

"It's Highlord Taquar. Come on, quick, let's get out of here."

"How—how—" he began, but his mind wouldn't think. No, *couldn't* think.

"Later. My pede is this way." A hand closed over Shale's and pulled him around a rocky outcrop to where a myriapede waited. "Quick, up you get."

"But—"

"*Later.*" The voice gave every indication the owner of it would not tolerate further delay, so Shale stretched, hopping awkwardly, to shove his foot into the mounting slot and heave himself up. He settled cross-legged on the padded cushion-saddle. Experienced riders might be able to balance themselves without holding on, but Shale had no illusions. People could die falling off a pede. He held tight to the handle.

Taquar mounted in front of him and swung the pede away from the prostrate figures. Shale tried to sort out what had happened. How had Taquar known where to find him?

"Are you all right, lad? Hold on tight. I want to get out of here fast. Crouch down low."

He did as he was told and felt the pede lift up underneath him as it quickened. The ground blurred; the wind rushed by. He gripped so hard his fingers ached.

When the beast tired and slowed, Taquar settled it down into a steady pace, then twisted around in the saddle to look at Shale. "Don't worry, they won't find us even if they do wake up. The ground is hard here—there'll be no trail to follow."

"How did *you* find me?"

"Come now, people like you and me don't need marks on the ground to know a pede passed by. We can sense the trace of water ahead of us. I'm sorry it took so long, though." He patted Shale's arm. "And I'm so very, very sorry about what happened back there, in your settle."

"I didn't tell no one!"

"I fear it may have been my fault. I thought—never

mind that now. I was coming to fetch you, but I was just a day too late."

Memory flashed, unwelcome. "They s-spitted m'sister and Ma and then Pa. I saw that. My brother—they didn't k-kill him. Mica and some of the older'uns—they were still alive when I left." He started shaking and wasn't able to stop. They had played a *game* with Citrine. And she hadn't died until the third player had passed her back to the sandmaster and he had gutted her on his chala spear. Her blood had sprayed . . .

His stomach heaved.

For a moment Taquar was silent. Then he said, "Sometimes they take boys and youths back to the Red Quarter. Girls and the prettier women, too."

Shale's shudders went on. "As slaves?"

"No. Converts, more like."

"Don't unnerstand."

"They take them to make warriors out of them. Tribe members. Tribal women. To become Reduner. It's not a bad life."

His revulsion and denial were instant. "Mica'd *never* be one of them spitless bastards!"

"You'd better hope he's bright enough not to tell them that, then. Otherwise, he's already dead. I asked the Reduners about him, back at the settle, and just then, too, but no one could tell me anything. I did hear about your sister. I'm sorry." He fumbled in the saddlebag and then turned once more to press something into Shale's hand. "I found this," he said. "Your piece of jasper. It was lying on the ground near your hut."

Shale's hand closed around the stone, feeling its familiar shape. Citrine had held it in her hand and smiled. He was silent, grieving.

"I fear Mica will have to make his own choices. There's nothing you or I can do about what happened in your settle, Shale. At least not yet. Put your mind to other things."

He thought that over, and although it made sense, it just wasn't possible. How could he rip out the pictures in his head of Citrine dying? Of so many bloody deaths? The splitting-shrill-begging scream of dying. The blood-vomit-shit *stench* of it. Citrine turning in the air, her little hands opening and closing as if she wanted to clutch something, anything, the jasper spinning away to be trampled underfoot, unnoticed by the Reduners, forgotten by him until now.

He tried to swallow away his terror. His grief. He slipped the jasper into the seam of his tunic and held on to the segment handle tight to stop the shaking of his hands. "W-where you takin' me?"

"Somewhere safe. Very safe. I can't trust anyone. But we have a long ride tonight to get there. We'll be there sometime tomorrow morning. Now let me concentrate on guiding the pede—it's dark and it's not an easy ride at night."

He turned to pay attention to the way ahead. Shale huddled behind him and tried not to think too much.

By the time they reached their destination, the sun was blazing and the sand-dancers were blurring the horizon. It was more a cave than a building, a cavern carved into a steep hillside, just where the slope eased off to become an undulating rocky plain. Shale didn't understand the land. It looked as if it had been folded and pleated and torn by a giant hand, or crushed in the grip of a maniac god. Used to the flatness of the Gibber, that intrigued him—but what overwhelmed him was the smell, the feel, the presence of water.

Taquar halted the pede in front of the entrance and slipped down. Shale was so tired, so stiff, that he fell rather than dismounted. The rainlord had to grab his arm to stop him crashing to the ground.

"Take a good look, Shale. This is going to be your home for quite a while. Can you feel the water?"

He nodded.

"What do you think this place is?"

He thought about that. "It's got a cistern. A big 'un. There's water comin' into it all the time—and goin' out, too."

Taquar smiled in satisfaction. "It's the mother cistern for one of the Scarpen cities. A tunnel takes water from here to my city, Scarcleft."

Shale looked blank. "Tunhill?"

"Tunnel. Like an underground slot. A slot big enough to walk through."

"Like a mine adit?" Shale asked, brightening. "I seen those. There's lots of old mines near the settle."

"Exactly. Except our tunnels are round."

The rainlord unstrapped his pack and the two cages of ziggers from the back of his mount, passing the latter to Shale to carry. "You know what these are, what they can do?"

He nodded.

"Then be careful." The rainlord turned and walked to the entrance. There was no door, just a large grille across the opening. Taquar stood in front of it for a long while, not moving.

He is concentrating, Shale guessed, vaguely aware
of water moving, but against a background of so much
water, he could not be sure what was happening. He was
astonished to see the grille rise, apparently by itself,
and disappear up into the rock. It grumbled as it went,
slowly, in spasmodic shifts. When it was fully open,
Taquar walked inside and gestured for Shale to do the
same. "Leave the ziggers on the floor near the wall," he
said. He strode across the flat floor of the cavern, the
pede ambling after him, to where there were several
troughs. He unplugged a spigot on the cavern wall and
Shale blinked as water streamed out. He stepped back
uneasily. It seemed a careless way to deal with water.
The pede dropped its head to drink.

"While we are here, the care of my pede is one of your
chores," Taquar said. "Do you know how to groom one?"

He nodded again, still wide-eyed. Such odd jobs
had earned him and his brother tokens from Reduner
caravans.

"What about cupping blood from a pede for the
ziggers?"

Shale nodded yet again. It was easier than talking.

"You've done it before?"

"For Reduners. They all have ziggers."

"Good. Come with me into the inner rooms." Taquar
closed the spigot and went to open a door on the far side
of the cavern. Shale put the ziggers down carefully and
followed him through the doorway into a smaller cave.

Light filtered in from a long thin crack high overhead. Shale looked around: several raised platforms with
folded-up bedding, four chairs, a table and a pot-belly
stove—more items than in most homes of Wash Drybone

Settle. Taquar took out his flint and tinderbox to get a flame going.

"Those are beds," Taquar said when he saw Shale staring at the platforms, "to sleep on. It's better than a pallet on the floor." He indicated a recess in the wall. "That's the deep-earth privy. You'd probably call it an outhouse."

Shale nodded, but he had a hard time containing his astonishment. All the hovels along the top of the Drybone wash had shared a single outhouse, and privies in the settle were always built outside, in the garden, not inside the house. He sniffed cautiously, but couldn't smell anything. Still, he thought it stupid to put an outhouse in the room you wanted to live in.

"When you use it," Taquar said, pausing to apply the flame to the wick of a lamp on the table, "wash properly afterwards."

Shale's eyes widened further. *Wash?*

Taquar didn't notice his amazement. He continued, "The door on the left opens to the storeroom. This one here"—he picked up the lamp and walked to another door on the right—"goes to the waterhall." He stepped through, beckoning Shale to follow. The sense of water was suffocating.

At first Shale couldn't see anything in the dark. Then, as his eyes grew accustomed to the gloom, he saw that they were in another huge underground cavern. He'd seen such things before, below the surface of the Gibber. There was no direct opening to the outside world, and beyond the feeble light of the lamp and the light that entered through the door, there was only darkness. Close to where they stood, he could see the edge of an underground expanse of water, the surface of which was as smooth and as black as a starless sky. He gaped, overwhelmed.

Taquar gave a faint smile. "You'll get used to it, in time. Water flows into this lake from the mother wells, which are deep in the Warthago Range. The inlet pipe is over there."

He pointed. Shale could not see it in the dark, but he felt the flow.

"Over there"—Taquar pointed to the opposite side— "there's another pipe, through which water is siphoned off, to the tunnel that runs to Scarcleft. There's an overflow pipe there, too, which also runs down to the tunnel, just in case the lake level rises too high. Not that *that* happens these days," he added in disgust. "We in Scarcleft do our utmost to conserve water, yet are treated the same way as those cities that squander their water-wealth! I've had to adjust the siphon several times over the past year because the water entering has lessened."

"Scarcleft's a settle?" Shale asked, struggling to understand.

"Of sorts. If you were to walk to Scarcleft from here— without stopping from sunup to sundown—it would take you six days or more. And it is a very *large* settle, called a city." Taquar's tone implied he expected Shale to retain all this information because he wouldn't be told again. Then the rainlord reached into the darkness behind him and picked up a bucket, which he filled to the brim from the lake.

"One thing I will not tolerate, Shale, is filth. And you are a filthy child. You are going to wash, using soap, and I am going to shave your head. Then I am going to burn that smock of yours. I have several sets of clean clothes for you. You will wear them, and you will keep them clean. You will brush your hair—once it grows again—every day. You will clean your teeth every day. Every day you will use a bucket of clean water for washing. When you have finished with the water, you will pour it into the pede trough. Those are orders. Understand me?"

Shale stared at the rainlord in amazement, one part of him horrified. "Use w-water for washin' m'*body*?" he asked. "*Every day?*"

"That's right." Taquar's voice was as hard as iron, making it clear there was to be no argument. Without pausing, he went on, "Right now, you will wash, dress in clean clothes, then you will eat, and only then can you go and rest. This evening, after you have napped, we will begin work."

Shale did not dare ask what kind of work.

The twist of fear inside made him feel as if his father was still there, haunting him.

CHAPTER EIGHTEEN

Scarpen Quarter
Scarcleft City
Level 36

After a few weeks on Level Thirty-six, Terelle knew everyone who lived or worked nearby. She and Russet lived on the upper floor of a mud-brick building. Lilva, a gaunt, mean-minded woman who rented out the sexual favours of her son and daughter, lived in the room next door. On the other side was Cilla, who wove bab-leaf sleeping mats for sale, and next to her, Rhea, the wife of a thief who was missing most of the time. Directly below them on the ground floor was old Ba-ba the humpback, bent double with swollen joints, who made and sold sinucca-leaf paste for whores—and for respectable married women, too—to prevent pregnancy. His wife, Fipiah, a buxomly handsome woman at least twenty years younger than him, was known to fix any problems that arose when the paste failed to do its job.

Sometimes she "fixed" more than she intended; twice Terelle had seen women enter Fipiah and Ba-ba's rooms only to see them leave as bodies wrapped in palm-leaf shrouds. Both times, Terelle had expected someone to make a fuss. Both times, the body was quietly carted away and nothing was said. Terelle had made sacrifices of water for their souls. It wasn't right that anyone should vanish into death without someone telling the Sunlord to look out for them on their journey to eternal life within the glory of His sunfire.

Next to Ba-ba and Fipiah, there was a family of stone-breakers who sometimes found work mending roads on the higher levels. In a lean-to in front of them was Qatoo the madman, who had a habit of stripping off all his clothes and jumping up and down on top of them, wailing, until his ten-year-old son came and led him away. The boy earned his living as a catamite for the pede grooms who lived in the stables outside the walls, men rich by the standards of the Thirty-sixth because they had regular jobs and water allocations.

The waterseller on the street outside, Vato, was the same man who had spoken to her on her first visit to the level about the cost of filling a dayjar. One of Terelle's duties now was to buy water from him every morning. She obtained the latest gossip at the same time, which she then relayed to Russet. Vato, who made daily journeys to Level One, was known as a good source of the kind of information that kept the inhabitants of Level Thirty-six alive: whether there was going to be a raid that day, perhaps, or whether the enforcers were looking for anyone in particular.

When Opal sent a party of professional searchers into the level looking for Terelle, Vato warned her they were coming. She spent three days hiding in a storeroom that Russet rented several streets away. The searchers made no less than five visits to Russet's room, two of them in the middle of the night, before they gave up. None of Russet's neighbours would admit to ever having seen Terelle, even when offered money.

"Vivie must have told Opal about you," she said to Russet. She was so annoyed with her sister that she felt like cracking a water jar over her head.

After that, Russet anonymously sent Opal water tokens every week. Vivie sent word back—in a letter addressed to Terelle àt Russet's room, showing that nobody had been fooled—that the snuggery owner would be placated as long as the payments continued.

Russet smiled with smug gratification. "Ye not worth much to snuggery, eh?"

For the time being, Terelle was safe—although remembering Huckman, she avoided all caravans from the south that passed through the level.

Half a year passed and for the average dweller on the thirty-sixth level, the situation worsened. Raids and arrests became a daily occurrence as laws tightened. No waterless woman was allowed to have children now; the enforcers came to every lane, dressed in their blue uniforms with a swirl of sand glued on the breast to symbolise their office, and read the proclamation. The following week they were back, scouring the streets for visibly pregnant women and demanding proof that both they and their unborn child were entitled to water allotments. If they couldn't produce proof, or if they couldn't show that they or their husband had regular employment, they were taken away.

Some never returned. Some came back the next day, pale, bleeding and no longer pregnant.

One morning, Terelle watched the husband of one such woman buying some herbs from Fipiah to stop the bleeding. Terelle said to Vato, shocked, "I saw his wife last week. She was at least two-thirds of the way into her pregnancy!"

"Yes. My wife was with her last night. Says that like as not, she'll die."

"It wasn't her fault! A woman can't always prevent a baby. I know that from the snuggery. Is it the Cloudmaster who makes such terrible laws?"

Vato shrugged. "He's certainly the one who doesn't send us enough water. But it's our very own highlord who has the decision on how to make water last. Taquar Sardonyx the Splendid, of Scarcleft City, who else?"

"Then he is wicked!"

Ba-ba, spreading his sinucca leaves to dry on his doorstep, heard her indignation and waggled a crippled finger at her. "I heard say he's been away, and it's Harkel the seneschal been runnin' things. And he's a right proper bastard, no mistake. But wicked? Are they, child? Either of 'em? Tell me this, by what right does a woman bring a child into a world when she has no water for him? That's a crime as heinous as murder, for the child is born to die— or to steal life-givin' water from someone else. You mark my words, m'dear, if folk are let do what they will, then there'll come a day when Vato here goes uplevel to find the reeves won't sell him a drop for us. Not a drop, 'cause there won't *be* no more water. Taquar does what he has to, and he's *right*. 'Tis fools like the Cloudmaster in Breccia

City with their bleedin' hearts that'll bring us to a thirst that can't be quenched."

"You silly old fool," Vato told him, "one day Taquar is going to throw people like us out into the Sweepings. We're the dregs of the thirty-sixth. Who cares 'bout us?"

"They *need* us workers," Ba-ba protested. "We do the dirty work for 'em. The dangerous work. That's why they nivver cut off our water altogether. They could if they wanted. They could stop you from sellin' it to us, for a start!"

"Yeah, well, it might happen one day," Vato shook his head. "I've heard tell hoarding water is punishable by desert exile now, and we both know what that means."

"*I* don't," said Terelle.

"Dumped far out into the Sweepings or the Skirtings," Ba-ba told her. "And yesterday I saw some waterless illegals from other cities being chucked out the city gates under penalty of execution if they return. Good riddance, I say!"

Vato glared at Ba-ba, but he didn't notice. Terelle turned away abruptly. She and Russet were waterless illegals born elsewhere. True, Russet had work of sorts—he sold his paintings to uplevellers—but she didn't know if that counted as regular employment entitling him to a water allotment. Certainly he didn't collect one. She gave a worried frown as she walked up the stairs to their room.

She entered their living quarters and put the water jars into the storage slots. Russet was there at the fire, heating up some resin over burning seaweed briquettes.

"Ye go bazaar this morning," he said, not looking up from his task. "Abel the bigger's shop. Buy·eight sea urchin skeletons, sort used for purple dye."

Terelle hid a sigh. She had thought her apprenticeship would start with painting; instead she laboured to produce the paints while Russet did the artwork. She had also learned that it was no use complaining, or even asking Russet what he planned for her. He told her nothing about himself, either. After the half-year she had lived with him, she knew no more than she'd told Amethyst or Vivie. He paid her an allowance, gave her food, bought her water. He gave her orders, which he expected her to obey immediately, yet he never scolded. He never had to: all he had to do was look at her with his sharp little eyes, as green as her own, to have her scurrying to do his bidding. One part of her feared him, even though he never gave her overt cause.

He had strung a curtain of bab-leaf matting across one corner of the room, given her a pallet to sleep on there, and never violated her privacy once she retreated behind the curtain. When his eyes did linger on her body, it was with a shrewd assessing look, not with lust.

And still she feared, with an uneasy, uncomfortable feeling, that all was not well. That Russet Kermes the waterpainter was not to be trusted. She hated the feeling, knowing that she should be grateful to him. He had *saved* her with his generosity. Why could she not like him in return? Why could she not trust him?

Always her thoughts returned to the same thing: how had he known her name?

"How much will the sea urchins be?" she asked.

"Two tinny each." He reached into his belt and extracted sufficient coins. "No paying more, although he sure to ask. Come straight back after; no loitering. Need purple for painting I make for merch on fourth level."

"Can I come with you?"

He shook his head. He had not taken her uplevel once, and she wondered if he ever would.

She said, "They say that there are enforcers on the streets looking for waterless outlanders."

His features sharpened in distaste. "Barbarians," he muttered. Once again he dug into his purse. "Here." He gave her a squashed piece of parchment, much folded and grubby about the edges.

"What is it?"

"Pass for an artisman's assistant. I bought. Anyone be stopping ye, show, yes?"

Relieved, she took the parchment, and her palmubra hat from the hook, and left the room. There was a skip in her step as she went down the stairs. She enjoyed the freedom of being out in the streets and no matter how many times she went to the bazaar, she always saw something new. Not even the thought that there might be blue-uniformed enforcers out looking for outlanders could dim her enjoyment, not with the parchment safe in her waist pouch.

The bazaar was a haphazard conglomeration of stalls, all roofed with bab-leaf thatch and separated into narrow alleyways. Goods spilled out on the ground or were stacked up to the thatching or even hung from a network of ropes that looped across the laneways. Away from the sun, it was cool and dim in the heart of the bazaar, and it was easy enough to lose one's way. The laneways smelled of spices, bab-palm oil, herbs and medicines—a tangle of odours and perfumes jostling for dominance. Gunny sacks of speckled fire-peppers, blue stamen spice, dried fruit and roots were jammed in with dried lizard skins, pebblemouse fur and fish bones. Globs of amber-coloured resin, for glues and turpentine and lacquer, were heaped up with shards of desert crystals said to cure bad luck, back ache and skin diseases.

And through it all came the sounds of stallholders enticing customers: "Look, madam, would you not like a ribbon for those lovely curls?" "Unguent to grow back hair on that bald head, merch?" "A shred of keproot to drive away your cares, broker?" "Ointment to whiten the skin, girlie?"

Terelle found Abel the bigger's stall tucked between a barber's shop and a fortune teller's. Abel sold sea produce: salted fish, pungent shrimp paste, fermented crabmeat, dried seaweed. In amongst seashells and cuttlefish skeletons—said to be nourishing food for ziggers—she found the urchins, but it took much bargaining before he would part with them for two tinnies each.

"You're from that old codger with the funny clothes, aren't you?" he asked as he wrapped the urchin shells in a yam leaf. "He's 'bout the only person who wants these things nowadays. T'other folk stopped buying frivolities like purple urchins long ago." He handed over the parcel, then exclaimed, "Lord above! What's that racket?"

Terelle turned to see. In the covered laneway between the stalls, several of the stallholders and a number of customers were trading insults with six people dressed in the robes of waterpriests.

"Good folk, make sacrifices," one of the younger priests was saying with youthful earnestness, "for if you do not return a little of your daily water to the soil, the Sunlord will surely punish you!"

The barber, a portly man with no hair at all on his head, waggled a finger at the man who had spoken. "'S all very well for you—you're not waterless like us Thirty-sixers! Every drop we can buy is precious. We don't have any to chuck away. Water sacrifice is for the rich." He turned his head and spat into the dust.

"Hand in jar with the reeves, you wilting waterpriests," a woman agreed.

The oldest of the priests raised a hand in protest. "Madam, madam, please. We counsel you all for the good of your souls. Do not the Watergiver's writings say that 'he who shares his water with the land will live'? But it's more than that, for the Watergiver also speaks of times of drought when every man, woman and child must give water to the sun lest the Sunlord turn on them to chastise their lack of faith. And has he not turned on us, good people? Not enough rain falls in the hills—"

"Ain't that the Cloudmaster that's turned on us then?" someone called from the back of the crowd that was gathering.

There was scattered laughter.

"Go take your preaching back to those that can afford you!" someone cried.

Abel the bigger leaned forward and said quietly in Terelle's ear, "Best be gone, lass. These things have a way of turning ugly these days, alas. Neither priests nor reeves nor enforcers have many friends on the Thirty-sixth of late."

Terelle thanked him and pushed her way back to the open streets beyond. The last thing she wanted was trouble. Uneasy, she turned her thoughts to what was really bothering her: Russet. His secrecy. His refusal to tell her how he had known her name. *Sands*, she thought, *there are no shadows in my future now. Why can't I be satisfied?*

But she wasn't. That night she asked Russet yet again how he had known her name, and whether he had known her mother.

"Be not time for ye to know such things," he said.

"I need to know," she said.

His sharp little eyes glared at her. "Trust your teacher," he said.

"I'd trust him more if he told me the truth!"

Infuriatingly, his next words were laced with condescension. "All in good time. When ye be older."

"I am old enough right now."

"Ye be old enough when I say so, child!"

She returned his glare with one of her own.

Soft-voiced, he reminded her, "Ye can't be leaving. Nowhere to go."

The petty meanness of his statement left her furious. Trouble was, it was true. She needed him, and because of that, he could do what he pleased. She fell asleep that night thinking that her future was still a place where freedom was an illusion. All she had done was exchange a decorative cage for another, plainer one.

Several hours later she woke, aware she was alone in the room. She raised herself on one elbow, not knowing what had awoken her. The door was open a crack and the sliver of light that squeezed through told her someone had lit an oil lamp in the communal hallway that ran past all the upstairs rooms. Broad and airy, it overlooked the road through a series of archways. Terelle and Russet prepared their paints there, Lilva the madam sat there when her daughter or her son brought home clients to their room,

Cilla did her weaving, Rhea sewed the beadwork she sold uplevel.

Terelle peeped around the curtain to look at Russet's sleeping pallet. It was empty. She padded to the door and put her eye to the crack. He was painting by the light of a lamp, totally absorbed in what he was doing. She stood, watching him, baffled. In the dim light, she could not make out the subject matter, and in the end she returned to her bedding knowing only that this must be a painting he wanted to keep secret.

When she finally went back to sleep, she had a nightmare in which Huckman and Russet were inextricably blended into a single menacing customer of Opal's snuggery. He was demanding that Terelle be made to paint her own first-night in graphic detail. She was protesting, her terror absolute, her heart beating wildly—and then it was morning.

CHAPTER NINETEEN

Scarpen Quarter
Warthago Range
Scarcleft mother cistern

Shale slept most of the day and woke in the late afternoon with the memory of turbulent dreams in which Mica was killed, over and over again. And then came his memory of the reality, worse because it was true.

Citrine.

He touched his chest, expecting to feel again the stickiness of her blood. And woke more fully when his hand encountered the unfamiliarity of his clothes.

The clothes felt odd. Soft and fine. And the bed was too soft; he was used to a gunny sack stuffed with dried grass on the earthen floor. He ran a hand over his shaved head. He wasn't used to that, either.

When Taquar turned his head and saw Shale was awake, he said, "Well, get up, lad. The day's almost over, but there are still things to be done."

Shale obeyed wordlessly.

"Come, I want you to clean the pede." He showed Shale where the brushes and cleaning picks were kept and Shale set to willingly. While working, it was easier not to think.

Taquar inspected the beast afterwards and nodded his approval. "Now let me see you cup blood for the ziggers."

Still silent, Shale set about the task. The metal cup Taquar gave him had a grooved lip with a sharpened edge, and it was just a matter of forcing the edge into the skin between two of the segments of the pede and waiting for the cup to fill. The pede didn't stir. The blood was such a deep red it appeared black; as it flowed out, the ziggers began to throw themselves against the bars of their cage. Shale grimaced.

"That's enough," Taquar said as the blood rose towards the brim. "Withdraw the lip . . . Good. The cut seals itself; that's it. Use a different segment each time." He indicated the cage of ziggers. "Never underestimate the danger of a zigger. If you release one, someone is going to die. Always. Make a mistake, and it could be you."

Shale nodded. He knew that much already.

"As you can see, the cage is divided into two, and all the ziggers are in one side. You open it at the empty end, slide in the cup, close the door." He waited until Shale had followed these instructions and then continued, "Now pull out the divider between the two sides of the cage." Shale had done all this before, but he was still careful. The ziggers, frenzied, flew straight to the cup, inserted their sharp mouth tubes into the blood and began to drink. When they flew, their hind gauzy wings shimmered in rainbow colours like oil on water.

"Beautiful, but deadly," Taquar murmured, echoing his thoughts. "At rest, or when a zigger tears its way into flesh, those delicate wings are sealed tight under the hard cover of the forewings. You can close the divider again now. There's an empty cup in the vacant section—take it out and wash it, ready for the next meal. You must always keep one end empty. You must always check that the doors on both ends are securely latched before you touch the cage at all. Understand me?"

"Yes, lord."

"Feed them twice a day."

"Don't like ziggers," Shale said, the words spilling out without thought.

"What you like is irrelevant, but they do have a purpose. It is dangerous for a man to ride the Quartern alone without them. I do not expect to have to use them; merely having them is enough to keep me safe. I can use water-powers instead, of course, but that can be tiring."

"Why don't ziggers attack their owners?"

"They never attack the man who feeds them. That's why I want you to do this, so you'll be safe. They are also trained not to attack men who wear the same perfume I do. That way I keep my guards safe—I give them the scent especially concocted by my perfumer for me. Most zigger owners do that. Once a zigger is released from a zigtube, it flies straight to feed on the nearest person who smells different.

"Now come and have your supper. I wish to talk to you."

Supper was bread, bab fruit and nut cakes made from bab kernels. As Taquar cleared the table to lay out the food, he asked, "I presume you cannot read?"

Shale shook his head. "Nobody in Wash Drybone Settle knows 'bout reading. I know what it *is*, but," he added with a hint of pride. "A 'Baster caravanner showed me a board-book once. I can figure and write m'figures too. Gravel taught us that. I'm real good at it. He reckoned we all ought t'do figuring, if we was goin' buy and sell to the caravanners. Gravel's the reeve."

Was the reeve. He'd died being dragged behind a pede.

"Good. That's something." Taquar poured himself some amber from a calabash and offered Shale water. He sat down and gestured to the chair opposite. "I want to tell you a story, Shale. To explain your place in the world."

He broke the round of bread and gave Shale half. "The present Cloudmaster is a man called Granthon Almandine. He lives in Breccia, which is a city in the Scarpen Quarter. His house is as large as the whole of Wash Drybone Settle. His son, Nealrith Almandine, is the highlord. A highlord rules a city. I am a highlord because I rule Scarcleft. Granthon is the Cloudmaster and the most powerful ruler in the Quartern, but it is Nealrith who rules Breccia City. Are you following?"

Shale nodded.

Taquar continued, "Nealrith and I were friends when we were boys." He took a deep breath, as if he didn't want to go on, and then said, "Back then, it was Nealrith's grandfather who was the Cloudmaster. I was just a lowleveller from a crumbling city in the west called Breakaway. My mother was from a Gibber family. Fortunately, when I was about five, I was identified as a water sensitive, and I went to Breccia to be trained.

"One day, when Nealrith and I were both about fifteen or so, I went into the desert on what was to be an eight-day training trip with two other rainlords of about my own age.

"We were all possible stormlords and were young enough to think ourselves invulnerable. We were not, of course. We had food for the pedes with us, but it was poisoned, or so I now believe. The animals died when we were miles from anywhere. We had to walk, carrying as much water as we could. The two other boys insisted on walking the wrong way. They followed the smell of the larger, more distant source of water, when they should have sought the closer, smaller one. I nearly died myself, and only survived because I went in the right direction.

"My water skills were better, you see, but I couldn't convince the other two to come with me." He took a deep draught of amber. "Nealrith publicly blamed me for what happened. I blamed myself; I didn't need my closest friend to turn on me like that. I came to the conclusion that he was riven through with jealousy, but I still thought he had the best interest of the Quartern at heart. Until now."

Shale shivered. There was something grimly intent about Taquar.

"At the time, though, I suspected several other young rainlords, including Laisa, now Nealrith's wife, of being responsible for the poisoning of the pedes. I never, ever thought it was Nealrith. Later, there were several other deaths that were odd. One was particularly sad: a young girl called Lyneth, daughter of one of the rainlords who rode with us to Wash Drybone Settle. Perhaps you saw him. The man with the limp." He paused a moment.

Shale hazarded a guess. "You think someone was tryin' to snuff out rainlords?"

"Snuff out?" he asked, his contempt for the expression obvious. "Kill them, yes. At least, kill the ones who might one day be stormlords."

"What—what's the difference 'tween a rainlord and a stormlord?"

Taquar shook his head in wonderment. "Holy Water-giver, I can hardly believe there exist places as backward as Wash Drybone! Don't you know *anything*?" He evidently did not expect an answer, because he continued, "A reeve—at least in any place that counts—is someone who can sense water, its movement and shape, but not move it. A rainlord is a water sensitive who can both sense and move water. Not huge amounts, and not over very long distances. A stormlord goes one step further. He can move bodies of water longer distances than a mere rainlord. He recognises people by their water. Best of all, he can create storm clouds, move them, then break them open to release the rain they contain."

"It's true then? A *person* brings the water to us? Not a god?"

"A stormlord keeps us alive, Shale. He makes freshwater clouds from salt water and sends rain to places where it can make its way to our wells or waterholes. Usually there are many stormlords, and the task is not that difficult. At the moment we have only one: Cloudmaster Granthon. If he dies, everyone—or most of us—will die, from Wash Drybone to Breccia to the Red Quarter to the salt quarries of the Whiteout."

"Then no one would ever wanna hurt such a person," Shale said sensibly. "He'd be too important."

"Want to."

"What?"

Taquar frowned. "Speak properly. Want to, not wanna."

Shale blinked. "I don't speak proper?"

"You surely do not. Copy me in the future. Speak proper*ly*."

Shale tensed. This was getting more and more difficult by the moment.

Taquar leaned forward, fixing Shale's gaze with his own. "To continue: I think that there is a person, or people, who want there to be no stormlords. Possibly because rain will then be random, and if rain is random, the people who will be in most demand are those who can sense and find water. Someone who is not a stormlord, can never be a stormlord, but wants the power to rule the Quartern anyway. A rogue rainlord. At least, that's one possibility."

It sounded mad to Shale, but he nodded anyway and avoided Taquar's gaze by helping himself to a kernel cake.

"All of which brings me to you, boy. And why you weren't killed."

Shale refused to cringe. He lowered the cake so that he could concentrate.

"Cloudmaster Granthon sent us to the Gibber Quarter searching for water sensitives. Against all expectations, we found many. Six of the older ones may possibly be good enough to be rainlords. I started to worry. What if they, too, died young? What if there was another rash of mysterious accidents? I did not know who to trust with my unease. They travelled with us—four boys and two girls—and we taught them as we journeyed. I protected them as best I could, but I worried.

"That was why, when I found you, I decided not to tell the other rainlords, except one. The one I most trusted. The one I thought would never be so indifferent to the wellbeing of the Quartern that he would want to prevent us obtaining a stormlord to follow his father."

He took a deep breath. "I don't know whether Nealrith betrayed us, Shale. Or whether he told his wife, Laisa, or one of his friends—Kaneth maybe—and they betrayed us. I *did* tell him not to tell anyone. Anyway, whether the guilt is wholly his or not, whether he is a murderous madman or just a credulous instrument in the hands of his wife or advisors—whatever happened, the result was tragic for you and your settle."

Shale, meal now forgotten, sat rooted. Cold. "Don't unnerstand," he said at last. "What's this to do with Reduners? It weren't no rainlord who led those men to our settle! They was *Reduners*, and they was looking for me. They knew me name!"

"Yes. I believe our rogue rainlord has an ally among the dune tribes. I think he asked the sandmaster of that tribe—his name is Davim—to capture you and to hide your capture by killing the adults. What the sandmaster did with the young was up to him, and he chose to kill the babes and seize the older children as slaves or converts to their way of life."

Shale was unable to speak. It was *true*. It was because of *him*. Citrine. Pa, Ma, Rishan—almost every adult he had ever known in his life—were *dead*. Mica and the other children taken. Because of him. He saw the picture in his head again, the image he wanted desperately never to see again: Citrine tossed into the air, too shocked to scream at first, turning, oh-so slowly. The sandmaster on his pede, manipulating the reins, whirling his steed. The beast rearing up, a magnificent beautiful animal, burnished red-on-black in the rays of the rising sun, great black shadow cast across the plains like a monster out of nightmares; Davim holding his seat, extending his spear in a fluid movement of grace, the ululation of triumph ripping from him, catching Citrine's robe on his spear . . .

Davim.

The piece of jasper from her hand turning in the air, catching the light like an arc of bloodied green fire.

Taquar leaned forward and slapped him across the face. "Stop it!"

Shale was gasping for breath, his chest heaving, his eyes wild.

Taquar was relentless. "You are our only hope for the future, boy. *You.* Granthon is old, close to death. You are the only person we have who can possibly be the next cloudmaster. The only one who has enough power within to be trained."

Stormlord. "No," he said, shaking his head. "No." He stood, hands up, palms outwards, as if to ward off an attack. "Noooo."

Then he whirled and ran. There was no sense to it, no plan, nothing but a desire to run from a trouble too great to bear, from thoughts that were, in fact, unbearable.

There was nowhere to run, of course. He shot across the entrance hall, past the pede, and came up against the metal squares of the grille that separated the underground building from the outside. It was closed once more. And because there was no exit, he climbed. Even then, there was nowhere to go. He reached the top of the grille; above, there was only rock wall, far too smooth to offer a handhold. He hung there on the bars, facing outwards, lit by the last rays of a setting sun, like a spider's prey caught spread-eagled in a web.

"Come down," Taquar said. He did not sound angry, just exasperated.

Slowly, Shale did just that. When he stood on the cave floor again, Taquar added, "There's nowhere to run,

Shale. Nowhere. You were born to be what you are. It is your duty. Accept it."

"You don't unnerstand. They all died 'cause of me," he whispered. "They *died*."

Taquar heaved a sigh. He came forward and pulled Shale into his embrace, Shale's cheek to his shoulder. For once, his tone was gentle, threaded with regret and concern. "Yes, that's right. I'm not going to lie to you. You are more important than any one of them. If you die, thousands of people die. From now on, Shale, you think of nothing but making yourself into a stormlord. Nothing else is important. *Nothing.* Not one of those people mattered by comparison."

Shale's jaw tightened with anger. *Citrine mattered.*

Taquar felt his tension and released him. "All right," he said, voice hardening, "if you don't believe that, then believe this. Your only chance of ever finding and freeing your brother is to have the power of a stormlord. Then you can do *anything.*" He turned Shale back towards the inner room. "Go and finish your meal," he said. "Then we will start the first of your lessons."

Shale returned to the table. He took the piece of jasper from where he had put it in his tunic pocket and rubbed it with his thumb. For a long time, he didn't speak; the lump in his throat didn't allow it. Finally, he closed his hand over the gemstone, holding it tight. He would keep it forever, to remember Citrine.

He raised his head to meet Taquar's gaze. "Why didn't they snuff *me* out?" he asked. "Why did this—this rogue rainlord ask the Reduners to find me if not to kill me? They bunched all the rest together, those they didn't kill.

But me—me they asked for by name. They put me on the pede and took me away 'stead of snuffing me. *Why?*"

"I don't know. It may have something to do with that water that came down your wash. Remember that? It was stolen from Granthon by someone who has water-powers. It's unlikely that he intended your settle to be the recipient of it. I suspect he was trying to send it elsewhere, and he failed. Perhaps that told him he is not as powerful as he thought. Perhaps his Reduner ally is angry with him as a result. Perhaps the Reduners have begun to wonder if they will have enough rain for themselves after Granthon dies.

"They were taking you to the Red Quarter, that's what I found out when I went to Wash Drybone to collect you. You were to be a prisoner on one of the dunes."

"They tole you that?"

Taquar smiled, a touch of nastiness in his satisfaction. "A rainlord can be very persuasive, Shale. Anyway, what I learned leads me to suspect that you were to be their secret stormshifter, the one who could save them if their Time of Random Rain didn't work out to be as successful as they hoped." He shrugged. "It's the only thing I can think of that even begins to explain what happened."

Shale stared at the two bowls on the table. One was filled with water; the other was empty.

"Look," said Taquar.

Shale watched as the water in the first bowl flowed out, seemingly of its own accord, into the second bowl.

"That," said Taquar, "is the simplest of all exercises. Learn that, then you will move on to these others." He indicated a jumble of items on the table. He selected one, a twist of glass tubing that stood several handspans high.

It was made up of tubes of a variety of sizes and shapes, connected one to another by a series of open bowls and chutes and stepped slides. "You have to get the water from top to bottom and back again without spilling it," Taquar said as he poured water into the top. "As you can see, that means either pushing it uphill or controlling its speed as it comes down. Not as easy as it looks." As he spoke, water began to move at a measured pace through the tubes.

Shale gazed, mesmerised by its passage. "*You* are doing that?" he asked, awed.

"Indeed. Any rainlord can do this. As will you, in a matter of weeks. You will learn to manipulate water, not just move it. Like this . . ."

A drop detached itself from the water in the bowl. It moved into the air and hovered above the table. Then it jumped to the left, slowly skated sideways to the right and moved in a loop before it dropped back into the bowl. "Control, Shale, is just as important as the ability to move it. Before I leave, I will run through every piece of apparatus here. That will give you enough to work on while I am gone."

Shale's heart lurched. "Leave? *Gone?*"

It had never occurred to Shale that he was going to be *left* in this place. On his own.

Taquar looked at his horrified face and gave an exasperated hiss. "Shale, I *can't* take you to Scarcleft. You must be strong in water-power and able to defend yourself against attack before we reveal your existence to the world. I don't know how old you are, but you must be at least fourteen by now, surely. Quite old enough to manage on your own. You will be safe. No one knows you are here. If anyone does come, you will feel them coming because you can sense their water, and you can retreat into this inner room with the door closed. No one can open the grille except rainlords, and none will come this way."

"Defend myself? How, by chuckin' water at them?" Shale asked, saying the first words that came into his head.

One of Taquar's eyebrows shot up. "So," he drawled, amused, "the Gibber cub has a modicum of spirit, after all, eh? No, Shale. There are other ways we have of defending ourselves. Ways you will eventually learn when you are old enough. Until such time, you will remain here. Safe."

"And you reckon I'll be able to move clouds one day?" Doubt and elation jostled in his mind.

"If you work hard at the exercises I give you, certainly."

"I'll be pissing waterless!"

Taquar glared. "Watch your language. Vulgarity is the mark of the inarticulate. We will start on the exercises tomorrow. I will leave the following day. Do you have any questions?"

"Uhuh, yeah. I wanna know why this rogue rainlord asked for help from a Reduner sandmaster, and why a sandmaster gave it. Don't make sense t'me. I reckon Reduners don't much like anyone but themselves. That's what they say—used to say—in m'settle."

Taquar's grey eyes flashed, but Shale could not read what the emotion was.

"Not so dumb, are you?" he said flatly. "Good." He leaned forward, once more pinning Shale down with his stare. "A rainlord is only one man. He can only do so much by himself. He needs powerful friends. Armed men to back his ambition. Yet no sane Scarperman would follow him if he told them he planned to kill other rainlords and prevent the training of a new stormlord. But there are other people out there who aren't so sensible, underlings who are discontented about their status, who will listen."

"Reduners?"

"*Some* Reduners, yes. The men who attacked Wash Drybone are from a tribe on the dune they call the Watergatherer. Sandmaster Davim is a young warrior with ambition. We in the Scarpen have heard rumours that this man hankers to free all the dunes from any reliance on the rainlords or stormlords of the Scarpen. He thinks the dune tribes are better off in a Time of Random Rain. He seeks to lead all the Reduner people as nomads, the way they were once before. We thought no one would want to follow a man with so foolish a dream. But if he was allied to a rogue rainlord and they had in their hands the next stormlord—yourself—well, that could be another tale."

And Mica was in the hands of this man. Shale felt he was suffocating in horror. *Mica, how will I ever save you?*

"When I arrived at Wash Drybone Settle, I saw Davim's men still looting. He'd gone, though."

Shale struggled to understand. "They didn't snuff you?"

"Obviously not."

"Why not?"

"A rainlord with a cage full of ziggers and the powers of his rank is a man to be feared. I could have killed any one of them. In fact, I did, to make the others talk. That was how I knew what direction you had been taken in and where you were headed. That's how I knew they were Davim's men."

Shale looked disbelieving. "You speared them all?"

"I have no need of such bloody methods. I merely took

their water. And killed the ziggers they were rash enough to threaten me with. But enough of this conversation. It is time for you to go to sleep. Tomorrow we will start your teaching in earnest."

He stood, indicating Shale's bed. "Don't forget to clean your teeth as I showed you."

Shale nodded absently. Somewhere in the back of his mind a thought troubled him, something about his rescue by Taquar, but he shrugged it away. He was just grateful that it had happened.

Took their water.

He would remember those words. Just as he would remember the name Davim. And Nealrith. Nealrith, highlord. And one day he would seek his revenge.

His *justice.*

CHAPTER TWENTY

That night, Shale cried himself to sleep.

He took care Taquar did not hear him, as he was sure that the rainlord would not approve. Shale was not afraid of Taquar, not the way he had feared his father. The man had no wish to hurt him, he felt sure. But he could wither with a look, and Shale dreaded seeing disapproval in that judgemental gaze. At the first sign of a quivering lip or indecision or fragility, Taquar would raise an eyebrow and look at him—and it was a look that quelled emotion, that forced the masking of fears. Inside, he felt as if he had been reduced to a toddling child once more. In private, he cried, tearless sobs of grief. He'd lost all the family he had ever had. Even Mica was gone. The thought of that swelled inside him like a canker about to burst.

In the morning, Taquar looked at him in distaste as he swung himself out of bed. "You are feeling sorry for yourself, lad," he said. "Be grateful that you live when others have died."

"They were m'fam'ly," he muttered.

Taquar's expression was pure surprise. "You don't *grieve* for them, surely? You said your father beat you and your mother never did much for you, either. Your brother still lives, as far as you know. Your sister was just a babe."

Shale frowned at him. "She was m'*sister*," he said, thinking that was sufficient explanation.

Taquar shrugged. "Doubtless I do not know how you feel. I do not have a sister. And please remember not to slur your words. Copy the way I speak."

Shale pressed his mouth closed and went to wash.

After breakfast, Taquar sat him down at the table with the two bowls of water.

Shale stared at them resentfully. "What am I s'posed to do?"

Taquar sat opposite and reached across to tilt the boy's face up with his hand. "Before we start, I think I know what's bothering you. You think it's all your fault people died, don't you?"

Shale nodded, but in his heart he knew it was a lot more than that. It was *everything*. It was losing the only two people who had ever loved him: Mica and Citrine. It was fear of dying, fear of being hunted like an animal, fear of being gutted on a spear. It was fear of becoming what he was supposed to become, a stormlord.

Taquar did not notice his hesitation. "Well, it wasn't your fault. Nealrith or some other traitor was responsible, plus Sandmaster Davim and the men who followed them. You did nothing to deserve what happened to you, nor are you responsible for what happened. The only thing you have to do is to be worthy, so that they didn't die in vain.

If you become a stormlord, then you become the saviour of a nation—of all the Quartern. And you can't even *begin* to imagine how many people that is. More than you've ever seen in your whole life."

Shale couldn't control himself well enough to risk speaking. He wanted desperately to please this man who had saved him. Who had such expectations. And yet . . .

"Shale," Taquar continued, more gently this time, "we who are rainlords or stormlords, we have to make sacrifices. For without us, thousands of people would die of thirst and hunger. We have to put them before our selfish needs. What I ask of you—what the Quartern asks of you—will never be easy. If I appear hard or unfeeling, that is the reason. You are one of us and must grow up to be a man of honour."

Shale wasn't quite sure that he understood the meaning of the word "honour," but he nodded anyway.

He was glad when Taquar changed the subject and returned to his lessons on moving water.

He tried. He worked at it all day, trying to send the water from one bowl to another. For the first two hours, nothing happened, except that he became frustrated and helpless. He didn't know how he was supposed to do it, and the water never budged.

Halfway through the morning, Taquar came to sit at the table. "Close your eyes, Shale, for a moment," he said.

Shale did as he was asked.

"What am I doing with the water?"

"You're pourin' it into that plate thing."

"Not into the other bowl?"

"Nah."

"*No*, not nah. And yes, you are right. How do you know?"

He thought about that. "I can feel the shape of the water."

"Good. You can open your eyes." Taquar poured the water back into the bowl. "From now on I want you to think of the water as a shape, not as something in a container. I want you to change the shape, with your mind. Change it so that it will come out of this bowl and drop into the other."

Shale sighed and tried again.

He still had not raised as much as a ripple on the surface of the water by lunchtime.

When Taquar once again approached him, he cringed.

"It will come," Taquar said. "You can't expect to have it happen all at once. It takes years to learn how to be a rainlord, years more to be stormlord. One step at a time."

Shale looked at him in wonderment.

Taquar must have understood something of his surprise because he added, "You won't get beaten by me, lad. Not when you do your best to please. Anyway, take a rest. Here, eat this." He handed him food in a bowl.

Shale stirred the mixture and tasted it carefully. "That's real good. Highlord, what's—what's Scarcleft like?"

"Large. Larger than anything you've ever seen."

Shale reduced the idea of large to something he could understand. "Twice as large as Wash Drybone Settle?"

Taquar threw up his hands. "Waterless heavens, lad, but you are ignorant." He rose and went into the store-room and came back with a book. He undid the ties that kept the parchment pages in place between the end-boards, and turned the first pages over to find what he was looking for. "Here, this is Scarcleft." He pushed the page over to Shale. It had a woodcut picture and some writing underneath.

Shale studied it but had trouble understanding the drawing. Finally he realised he was looking at a settle of enormous proportions, tipped down a hill slope that was many times higher than the banks of the wash back home. He had seen slopes like that only on his journey to the waterhall. "Whassit say unnerneath?"

"What does it say underneath?" Taquar corrected.

Carefully Shale repeated the words.

"It says that this is Scarcleft, a city of the Scarpen Quarter."

Shale wanted to ask more, but he sensed that there was a limit to the amount he could pester Taquar at any one time and have him remain pleasant. The rainlord was already beginning to sound bored. He abandoned the idea of another question and said instead, "I wanna—"

"I want to—"

"I . . . want . . . to learn how t'read."

Taquar stared for a moment, considering. "That's an excellent idea. It will give you something else to keep you occupied while I am gone. It's easy enough." He indicated some of the writing on the open page. "Each one of these marks is the sign for a sound. We call them letters. There are forty-eight of them. Learn them all, and you can read. Look." He dipped a finger in one of Shale's bowls of water and drew a letter in water on the table. "This is the letter we call 'shi.' It says the first sound in your name. And this symbol is the second sound, and this the third. Sh . . . ay . . . el. Shale."

Shale's mind blossomed with the concept. So that's what reading was! Suddenly something that had always seemed so arcane was within his reach. He pointed to the words under the picture. "Which one says Scarcleft?"

"That one," Taquar said, pointing. "There are quite a few books in the storeroom. You may look at them while I am gone. Make sure your hands are always clean, and always tie the end-boards back on when you finish." Quickly he sketched four more letters on the table and explained the sounds they represented. "I'll teach you some more tomorrow before I leave, *if* you can remember these," he said. "Now, finish your meal."

The next morning, when Taquar left, Shale watched him ride away with a growing sense of disbelief. The rainlord really was leaving, taking his ziggers with him. And he, Shale, was going to have to spend his time alone, unprotected.

It felt strange.

It wasn't that he had never been alone. He had, often— whenever he went into the Gibber to collect resin. The open space of the Gibber he had regarded as friendly; even its trackless and waterless nature had not scared him. He could always sense where the settle and the wash were. He could sense the water in the cisterns, in the ground. The familiar had never been far away. Sometimes he had worried about the people he might meet out there, but he'd never feared the place itself or the loneliness of it.

But now he felt trapped.

The grille was closed and he had no idea how to open it. What if Taquar never came back? The food would not last forever, and he had nothing he could use to force open the grille.

And what if his enemies came? What if *Davim* came?

He stood at the grille and watched as the speck that

was Taquar and his pede grew smaller and finally vanished into the stony soil and dry gullies of the Scarpen.

I have got to find the way out of here, he thought. He considered the pipes into the—what was it called? Tunnel?—and shivered. If he tried that and got stuck halfway . . . *No, I have to find out how to lift that grille.*

But as hard and as long as he studied it, he couldn't see how it was done. All he knew was that it had something to do with moving water. Controlling water, that was the key. He had to learn, and learn quickly.

He went back to the table and the two bowls, one full, one empty.

Taquar had actually not given him good advice: he had told him to concentrate, but in concentrating, he lost his affinity with water. It was not until he realised that the secret was focus and relaxation, not concentration and stress, that he could ripple the water at will. The next day, he slopped some of it from one bowl into the other, and he smiled for the first time since Citrine had died.

After that he relaxed still more. No one came to threaten him; there was no pressure from anyone to perform. Taquar was not there to watch his every move; he could advance at his own pace, to suit himself.

He *was* lonely. Without Mica he was bereft, and the pain of loss was welded onto him, part of his being. He knew what Taquar had said was true: the horror at Wash Drybone Settle had not been his fault. Yet it was still a tragedy that was undeniably linked to his gift, and *that* motivated him. If he could become a stormlord, then he could undo some of the damage. He could free Mica.

He spent hours moving water drop by drop from one

bowl to the other. He slopped it, dribbled it, splashed, wasted it—but gradually he moved it. The day he moved the entire contents from the first bowl to the second in a steady stream he celebrated by going for a swim.

Within a day of Taquar's departure, he had found being cooped up in the rooms a physical irritation. He wanted more space, and so he gravitated towards the waterhall every evening. The rock walls of the cavern rose sheer from the water's surface in several places, which meant he couldn't walk around the lake. He could sense its depths—cold, bleak and dark—and one part of him was wary. He remembered the power of the rush down Wash Drybone, the way he had lost himself. Mostly, though, this still water held no fears for him. It fascinated. Its power, its weight, its immensity—his bodily *need* of it. He understood it, recognised it so easily, felt kinship with it. He knew, without consciously dwelling on it, that he himself was mostly water.

For the first few days he just looked. The lake, so large and still, seemed a sacred thing, not to be taken lightly. Now, though, he was a *mover* of water, a rainlord, and he saw it differently. He remembered how good it had been to submerge himself in water that day with Mica, and now it felt right to do it again. And so, to celebrate his success, he walked into Scarcleft's drinking supply.

The cold water moved over his naked body like a living thing, connecting with him and yet not blending with him. Toughened by a lifetime of desert nights covered only by burlap sacking, he was not bothered by the temperature. He waded in waist-deep, crouched down and let the water lift him, hold him, cradle him in the gentle, arousing embrace of a lover. This time, though, he controlled his urge.

This time, it seemed right to accord respect to something that allowed him to have power over its very movement, to respect something that could have killed him with its own power. He remembered every moment of being hurled this way and that in the surge of the rush.

This time he didn't sink in the water like a token dropped into a dayjar, either. He splashed around on the surface, discovering that if he thrashed his arms and kicked his legs, he could move as he willed. He ducked his head under and tried to move water away from his nose and mouth, the way he had in the wash pool, but found he couldn't duplicate the effect now that there was no urgency.

Never mind, he thought. *I can practise.*

When the cold finally did drive him out, he felt cleansed. Uplifted. Jubilant. He was surely a water-mover. A rainlord.

I was born for this, he thought.

Then: *Mica, one day I will use my power to save you.*

That same evening, he thoroughly explored the storeroom. As he uncovered one treasure after another, he found himself the possessor of an abundance of riches—more, surely, than any one person could ever want. There were extra blankets to keep out the cold of desert nights. There were supplies of oil and salt and amber. There was dried bab mash for pedes. There was the food that Taquar had left behind for him: strips of dried pede meat—which Shale refused to touch—nuts and nut paste, bab fruit, pickled kumquats, dried figs and apricots, salted eggs, raisins, honey and yam biscuits. There were odd items of clothing, both for adults and for children of different ages, and there was even a child's gold bracelet.

Reduner caravan women occasionally wore gold bangles, but Shale had never seen one with metalwork as finely executed as this. The centrepiece was a flat gold disc intricately carved with a word—which he could not read—surrounded by fruit-tree blossoms. It was obviously valuable, and Shale could not imagine why it was so carelessly tossed in amongst a pile of clothing. He laid it aside and turned his attention to other items. Extra pede harnesses, water skins, saddle cloths and cushions, pede packs, zigger-feeders . . . and books.

He opened every one of the books that night, looking at them by lamplight. He took exaggerated care not to knock over the lamp and spill the oil, or worse, set fire to the parchment sheets. Most of the writing was just strings of words he couldn't read. Fortunately there were eight or nine books with pictures, including one that had page after page of drawings, each carefully labelled, of living things—beetles, moths, sand crawlers, pebble speeders and pebblemice, ant sippers, night-parrots and the like— most of which Shale recognised. He grinned, delighted.

Before he had left, Taquar had taught him a total of twenty letters, twenty out of forty-eight, and Shale was desperate to learn the remainder. Once he knew each letter and the sound it made, he believed, he would be able to read, and that excited him. He had *seen* the city of Scarcleft, simply because there was a picture in the book; how much more could he learn if he knew what people *wrote* about the city? And now here was a chance to learn all the letters without waiting for Taquar to come back.

He knew what an ant sipper looked like, and the drawing he had in front of him definitely portrayed that little desert-living creature: long tail, furry nose, strong feet for digging, long tongue for eating ants. He traced out the letters underneath, two words, as should be expected. Ant sipper. And the letters he already knew were exactly where they should have been. His grin broadened: he *could* teach himself to read.

That night he fell asleep smiling.

After a while he developed a routine. He kept the rooms, and himself, as clean as possible, just as Taquar had insisted he do. He couldn't see the point of sweeping up the dust (it was going to blow right back in again) or folding his blankets every morning (he would just have to unfold them again at night) or cleaning his teeth (he was going to eat with them again, after all)—but Taquar had wanted him to do these things, so he did. He came to like the feel of all this cleanliness. No grit beneath his bare feet, no greasiness on his skin, no coating on his teeth. It was pleasant, and there had never been much that was pleasant in his life before.

The water exercises tended to become boring after a while, and he didn't proceed nearly as fast as he would have liked. The gains he made were small ones: a little more control, a little more precision, one tiny step at a time. Fortunately, life in Galen's erratic household had taught him patience, and the son of a drunkard learned never to expect miracles, never, in fact, to expect.

Still, the loneliness continued. He started to feed a pouched mouse that came each evening at dusk, looking for insects in the hallway, but it remained shy. Sometimes he talked to Mica, telling him everything that happened, as if he could hear. He found himself longing for Taquar to return.

* * *

When the rainlord did return, it was a disappointment. After a few hours, Shale was remembering the man's remote coolness. He brought food and more books and more clothing, although Shale thought that last an unnecessary extravagance. He appeared content with Shale's progress with regard to water sensitivity. He complained that the floor hadn't been kept clean enough and scolded him for not washing his clothes.

"I've learned a lot of readin'," Shale told him. "I can read whole pages—"

"Yes, yes, I'm sure," Taquar said. "Now go and brush my pede." Shale subsided, hurt by the rainlord's indifference, and went to perform the task.

That evening, after the sun had set, Shale noticed a light out in the desert. He stared, so startled by the idea of someone being out there that it was a moment before he could even think straight. *A fire,* he thought. It was the flickering of flames from a distant camp fire. He blocked out the idea of the water behind him in the waterhall— which he had once found impossible to do—so that he could concentrate on whatever was beyond the grille. Finally he isolated one person, only one, and a pede.

He went back into the main room. "There's someone out there," he said. He was shaking, but flattened his tone so Taquar would not hear the fear he felt.

The rainlord's head swung up and he paused, focusing. "Ah. I have been expecting a visitor. Doubtless this is he." He laid down the book he had been reading by lamplight and stood. "That was well-sensed, Shale. I am pleased with your progress. I will ride out to meet him alone. There is no point in him knowing you are here."

"Whossit?" Shale asked.

For a moment he thought Taquar would refuse to answer. Then he said, "Who is it? I rule a city, Shale. There are matters that concern me that are better dealt with away from Scarcleft. Sometimes with men from other Scarpen cities, even Reduners. The man is a messenger, merely."

When Shale glared, he said, "Not all Red drovers are evil men, you know. There are moderate men among them who need to be cultivated. But who this is and why he is here is none of your concern."

Shale concentrated when the rainlord lifted the grille, trying to sense what happened. He thought Taquar moved water from one place inside the rock wall to another, through a pipe of some kind, and as a result the barrier opened. However, the rock blocked his feeling for the water within, so he found it difficult to understand precisely how it worked. *I will in time*, he thought. *I must.*

Taquar closed the grille behind him, and Shale watched him walk away. He had a loaded zigtube swinging at his side, and the insects screamed with rage at their close confinement. In their agitation, the odour they exuded was sharply tangy, the smell of toxins that kill with unimaginable agony.

He still didn't like them.

"But how d'you *know* I am a stormlord?" Shale asked the next morning over breakfast. "And not just a rainlord?"

"Because you sense water with such ease. I knew right from the beginning, when we were in Wash Drybone Settle." He leaned back in his chair, rolling his mug between his hands. "One day you will bring all the water we need, from the sea, just as Granthon used to do."

"Is he still alive? Y'said he was almost snuff—er, you said he was dyin'."

"He is. And taking a long time about it, too. Fortunately for us."

"How long 'fore I can help him?"

"That depends on how hard you work. Several years at least. I don't know. I've never trained a stormlord before."

"Why don't y'take me to Granthon then? He'd know the best way t'train me. He went through it hisself."

The rainlord's face became curiously blank. "Because he is Nealrith's father. How long do you think you would be safe? Use your head."

Shale swallowed unhappily. Arguing with Taquar always made him feel vaguely threatened. *He's not Pa*, he told himself. *He's not going to lam you.* He said, "If he's snuffed it, he can't teach me nothin' and we're all in a heap of pedeshit."

The highlord's expression changed from blankness through exasperation to something else Shale could not quite read, but the stare was unsettling. "You will stay here," Taquar said finally, "until you learn enough to look after yourself. Then I will take you to Scarcleft. Now go and feed the ziggers."

Shale obeyed.

As he lay in bed that night, his discontent grew. He wanted to rebel, but wasn't sure what he wanted to rebel against. His imprisonment in the mother cistern? Not being taken to meet the Cloudmaster? Not being able to search for Mica? His fate generally? Something was not right.

I got t'know things, he thought. *Them books aren't enough, specially if I can't read proper.* He wanted more. Much more.

The next day, he begged still more books from Taquar and continued to pester him with questions. Finally, the rainlord said, more in exasperation than in a spirit of help-fulness, "I'll ask a few of the Scarcleft Academy teachers to select books for you. In fact, I'll ask them to set you some written work to do and then I'll take it back for them to mark. That should keep you happy. You can ask them questions in writing instead of asking me in person. I'm no teacher."

"But I can't write! Can't read proper, neither."

"I can't read properly," Taquar corrected.

"Can't read proper*ly*, neither."

Taquar sighed. "Then you will have to learn, won't you? I'll teach you more letters and words today and you can practise writing them. However, if you have written contact with teachers, I will need your promise that you will not tell them who you are or where you are."

"Course not," Shale said.

Inside, his mind was already bubbling with ideas and questions to ask, answers he wanted. Something told him that the key to his future lay in how much he could under-stand of things he had never seen.

That first visit of Taquar's set the temper of all his vis-its. He came bringing books, food and other necessities; he tested the progress of Shale's water sensitivity, made sure that the state of the rooms was to his liking and criticised if it wasn't. He started to bring lessons from Scarcleft Academy teachers and take back the completed exercises. He'd glance at them, but their content did not seem to interest him much. He was more concerned that Shale learn to speak properly; sloppy speech he corrected without fail. Shale soon learned to mimic Taquar's accent and grammar, until his speech was no longer an issue between them.

At first, Taquar came every ten days; then the time between visits began to lengthen, until it was usually thirty days. He never stayed more than four days, usually less. And on some visits, he walked out towards the light of a distant fire in the desert. He never mentioned the reason for it again, and Shale did not ask. He always loaded his zigtube before he went, but whether he ever had cause to use it, Shale never knew.

The water exercises became more complex and difficult. He had to move plain water through coloured water without mixing the two. He had to move water through a maze without letting it touch the sides or base. He had to identify which out of a number of different-shaped containers held more water—and sometimes the difference could only be measured in drops.

Gradually his knowledge of the Quartern increased as his reading improved and he learned to write sufficiently well to communicate with his teachers. A map he found in the storeroom was invaluable. The only other maps he had ever seen were temporary things drawn in the dirt by caravanners; this one was an entry point into another world that he had not known existed. He'd had no idea that the Quartern was so *large*. That Wash Drybone Settle was so small. That distances were so vast.

Or that he could be important in such a huge world.

Shale was aware of the passage of time: he could see much of the sky through the bars of the grille, and he watched the constellations move. The way his arms stuck out of the bottom of his tunic sleeves told him he was growing fast. His clothes were becoming too tight.

He rummaged through the clothes in the storeroom, only to find there was nothing there that fitted. The garments were for women or children, and he was no longer a child. He held one of the tunics he found and fingered the intricate embroidery along the hem—finer embroidery than his mother had ever done—and thought of Citrine. Sadly, he reflected that he had already begun to forget what his little sister looked like.

And Taquar seemed to have forgotten all about her, and Mica, too. How could he ever rescue Mica if he never got to leave the mother cistern?

By the time the stars told him he had been there for about half a cycle, his frustration was a boiling cauldron of emotion in his chest, and he knew he had to do something, or go mad. He waited until Taquar came and went once more, and then started to work on opening the grille to the outside world.

He thought he knew now, at least in principle, how it was done. He had sensed Taquar do it often enough. He already knew about pulleys and weights from watching the building and repair of houses in Wash Drybone Settle, and observing some of the mine diggings maintained by a few settle fossickers. He now had enough water sense to understand that the grille was opened by transferring water at each end from full tanks to empty ones through pipes in the hollows of the cavern wall. As the empty ones filled up, they dropped down. The falling weight worked pulleys to open the grille. To close it, it was just a matter of moving the water back again. What scared him was the possibility of moving the grille up but not being able to bring it back down again before Taquar returned.

He wondered why he was so afraid. He wasn't even sure whether the rainlord would regard the opening of the grille as something worthy of anger. Maybe Taquar expected him to try. Maybe he wanted him to try. Maybe it was a test.

Shale sighed. Why did he understand so little of what was in Taquar's head? And why, when he thought of the rainlord, was it with a mixture of niggling fear of his ire and desire for his approval—of wanting to have the man look at him with pride the way Rishan looked at his son, Chert.

He took a deep breath and focused on the wall of the entrance hall, feeling the water inside. He was slow, much slower than Taquar. He was sweating by the time the containers started on their way down and the grille began its slow rumble upwards. He was weak at the knees by the time it disappeared into the wall above the entrance.

But he was free.

His initial steps outside were hesitant, as if he half-expected Taquar to come bellowing in a fury over the nearest hill. A ridiculous thought, and he grinned at the image. Then in a moment of wild exuberance he flew down the slope in loping strides, going faster and faster until his feet barely seemed to touch the ground. He was a desert elan escaping a hunter, a hawk liberated from a cage winging into the sky. He was *free*.

At the bottom of the slope, he tripped and rolled into a somersault. He sat up, brushing the dust from his knees, and laughed.

The liberation, the release, was so profound it brought a flash of brilliance and clarity to his thoughts. *I've been*

a prisoner, a sandgrouse in a cage. All the stuff Taquar
had been talking about? Safety, protection, responsibility,
duty, the need to learn—it was all just words. He had been
a prisoner, and it was Taquar who had latched the cage.

His shift in perception was so fundamental that it had
a physical dimension, as if his shoulders were suddenly
broader, his spine strengthened, his height taller. He stood
up and took a deep breath.

His heart pounded in his chest. *Outside. Under the
sky. Free, the way I was once, wandering the Gibber.* He
began to climb the hill above the cavern entrance so that
he could look out over the Scarpen.

Half a year earlier, still confused and torn with grief,
still wearing clothes fouled with Citrine's blood, he had
not absorbed much of his journey or the surroundings of
the cavern in the hill slope.

Now he saw it all with wondering eyes. The brightness of full sunlight and the brilliance of the late morning
sky assailed him, leaving him blinking like a night-parrot
dragged out of its hole into the light. Heat baked the skin of
his arms and seared through the cloth of his tunic to warm
his back. The soles of his feet had lost their tough armoured
skin, so the stones were sharp and rough beneath his sandals. The muscles of his calves, unused now to anything but
a flat floor, shrieked their pain. Every time he looked up at
the vault of the sky directly above he felt vulnerable, as if
he was naked. When he disturbed a lizard and it exploded
out from under his feet, he jumped and had to halt until
his heart steadied. Part of him even wanted to turn back, to
return to the sanctuary of the cavern, like a pebblemouse
scurrying back to the protection of its hole.

He resisted the temptation and climbed to the top of

the hill. And found himself looking out at the Warthago Range. When he had ridden in from the Gibber with Taquar, the lower foothills had blocked the view. Now he could see the rugged red walls and the fierce jags of its ridges and he could gaze on the height of the peaks that were a snare to the clouds when they came. He could contemplate the deep forbidding folds of its fissures, where the rains fell and drained into the mother wells. The sight robbed him of breath, rooted him in silent awe. What he had seen before only in woodcut prints became real.

He felt as if he had spent years looking only at shadows and reflections, and now he had stepped into the sunlight. *Life is out here*, he thought. *Not down there in the cavern.* Life outside might be ready to claw and rip at him, to tear through to his heart yet again—but at least it was real. He took a deep breath and smiled.

At last he turned his back and looked south, in the direction of Scarcleft and the sea, both too far distant to see. Even in that direction, the Scarpen was not flat. Nor was it a plain strewn with pebbles and crazed with washes, like the Gibber. There were gullies and fissures and hillocks. The soil was a different colour. Not purplish and shiny with mica, but sometimes yellowish, sometimes brown. The plants were different, too, not cautious miserable things that crept along the ground, reluctant to reach for the sun, but small bushes and the occasional tree reaching upwards on a crippled trunk, spreading arthritic limbs and gnarled fingers to the wind, from which it gathered life-giving moisture. He stood under the meagre shade of one and marvelled. A tree that was not a bab palm or a fruit tree. Growing out in the open, not in a grove or a pot in someone's yard, not jealously guarded and lovingly tended to yield its fruit and its wood, or its nuts and its bark.

His gaze scoured the flatter land in front of the hill and lit on a squat tower crouching like an obese toad on the landscape: a maintenance shaft, signalling the presence of the tunnel burrowing beneath the land to escape the sun. One book had described the structures built over the shafts as brick chimneys. He had asked one of his teachers what those two words meant, and as a result, he now knew what he was seeing. Thoughtfully, he retraced his footprints back to the cavern.

The next afternoon he left the waterhall again, this time with water skins, a battered palmubra, a blanket and a knife stuffed into a pack, all from the storeroom.

He picked his way down the hill once more and set off to take a closer look at the first of the maintenance shafts. It was further away than he thought, and the sun set long before he reached it. At dusk, he ate some of the food he had brought and then wrapped himself in his blanket against the gathering cold. In the early part of the night he slept without stirring, but as the desert lost its heat, he awoke shivering and spent the rest of the night huddled into a ball, dozing fitfully. He had forgotten how the desert chill could creep into your bones in the time just before the dawn.

At first light he set off again.

The maintenance shaft rose up out of the ground to twice his height, built to discourage the entry of desert creatures or wind-blown sand. It was bulbous at the base, narrowing as it rose, just like a bab palm. He marvelled at its construction, the neat pattern of clay blocks—no, bricks, harder than the sun-dried daub they used in Wash

Drybone Settle. The top of the shaft was covered by a wooden lid. Footholds to suit a man had been excavated into the brickwork so that it was possible to climb to the top. When he did so, though, the result was disappointing. He could slide the wooden cover open, but underneath was a locked grating, the iron lock covered by a seal. There was no way in without breaking it open, and he had no means to do so.

He climbed down and sat in the shade cast by the structure, waiting for the midday sun to illuminate the interior.

When the shade shrank to nothing, he climbed up to peer inside again. Lit by sunlight, the tunnel running below the shaft was much larger than he expected, large enough for a man to walk upright. A narrow brick walkway along one side ensured there was no need to wade in the water that ran sluggishly down the middle. A ladder led down the inside of the shaft, to provide access to anyone who could open the grating.

Shale took it all in, then replaced the wooden lid once more and returned to the mother cistern. Each step back was a step away from freedom, but he took it nonetheless.

I must have patience, he thought. *The time will come, and I will be ready for it.*

If I stay, he thought, *it will be because I want to, not because someone bars the door.*

CHAPTER TWENTY-ONE

Scarpen Quarter
Breccia City
Level 2 and Level 3

Ethelva came out of Granthon's study carrying a tray. The food in the dishes was hardly touched and she stopped a moment to regard it with the eloquent arch of an eyebrow. From his seat at the dining table, Nealrith saw the look and pursed his lips.

"Still not eating?"

"Barely nibbling. Nealrith, he can't go on like this."

Senya, on the other side of the table, next to Laisa, looked up from her food. "Is Grandpa dying?" she asked.

"He is certainly not well," Ethelva replied. She put the tray down and slipped into her own seat at the table.

"I suppose we should be grateful he still lives," Laisa said. "When we returned from the Gibber, I thought he was about to take his last breath any moment—yet here he still hangs on, making clouds, shifting storms. One has to admire his stubborn tenacity."

Ethelva murmured, her voice full of pain, "He's not eating enough to restore the energy he expends."

"If he takes too much, he vomits," Nealrith said.

Senya pulled a face. "Oh, horrid," she said. She dabbed at her lips with her napkin.

Laisa washed her fingers in the lemon water of the finger bowl. "Senya is right, Nealrith. This is not a subject for the dinner table."

Nealrith's face tightened, but he did not comment. Instead he said, "A finger bowl is a waste of water, Laisa. Please instruct the servants not to put them on the table." He turned back to his mother and added, "Father told me today that he has decided to reduce still further the supply of water to the Gibber and the White Quarter."

Laisa gave a sigh of satisfaction. "That decision was long overdue. He has been wasting his energies on them far too long."

Ethelva dropped the bread she had been about to eat. "Watergiver have mercy," she murmured. "That decision will have cost him more than any of you can possibly understand." She glanced at the closed study door, as if she wanted to go back to him, but Nealrith placed his hand over hers.

"No, Mother. You, too, need to eat."

She took a deep breath and turned back to him. "All right, all right. And Nealrith, there is something else—"

"Yes?"

"You aren't going to like it."

"There can't be anything much worse than the thought of 'Basters and Gibbermen dying of thirst."

"That's not going to happen overnight," Laisa said carelessly. "Many will have enough water in their cisterns for a year or so. They will just have to stop irrigating the groves. What is it you want to tell us, Ethelva?"

"Granthon has decided to draw up the succession declaration this week. He has asked Mikael to prepare it."

Nealrith stared at her in silence for a long time. Even Senya was stilled. When he finally spoke, his tone was flat. "And it is not me."

"No."

"What?" Laisa looked shocked, then furious. "Why, how *dare* he—"

"It is his privilege," Nealrith said tightly. "But the Council of Rainlords can overturn his decision after his death if they wish. Who *is* named?"

"Taquar."

Nealrith paled. "*Taquar?* No, Father wouldn't do that. Not Taquar!"

"Oh, goody," Senya said, oblivious to her father's shock. "If Taquar's going to be the next ruler of the Quartern, maybe you will let me marry him!"

At first Nealrith didn't take in her words. He was still staring at his mother. "He wouldn't do that, surely. *Taquar?* The man is despicable! He has the morals of a waterhall rat. He runs Scarcleft like it was one of the punishment quarries. Did you know he has introduced enforced abortion? And I heard he is nailing people—alive—on the city gates for water theft! And dumping Watergiver knows how many others out in the desert to die. By all that's holy, Father would give the Quartern to such a monster?"

"He's *not* a monster!" Senya said hotly. "Those are just stories to scare people into conserving water."

Laisa's eyebrows shot up and she turned her head to stare at her daughter.

Ethelva, as pale as her son, sat unmoving. "He does

think harsh policies are the only ones that will work in the times to come, Nealrith. Since you all returned from the Gibber without a potential stormlord, we will return to a Time of Random Rain once your father has passed away. He does not think you could, um, *cope* with the kind of decisions that would have to be made."

"See, Taquar's not a monster!" Senya cried, heedless of Laisa's frown. "He's only doing what has to be done."

"Like enforced abortion?" Nealrith stood up abruptly and strode off, but in the doorway he turned once more to look at the three women at the table. "Senya," he said, and his voice was so suffused with pain and anger it was unrecognisable, "you will *never* marry Taquar while I am alive. *Never*." He turned and left the room, his back rigid with fury.

Ethelva looked down at her plate, grieving.

"It's not fair!" Senya wailed. "I'm never going to be allowed to marry anyone! There *are* no rainlords of my age."

"On the contrary," Ethelva said, "I've heard there are several among the water sensitives your parents found in the Gibber."

"Gibbermen? You would have me marry a *Gibberman*? They are dirty! They never bathe! Besides, that lot of water sensitives are only *children*."

"And you are not?" Laisa asked. "The eldest of those lads is but two years younger than you. Anyway, you have just turned twelve and you're far too young to think of marriage. If you think I would support this absurd desire to marry Highlord Taquar, you are quite mistaken. He is your father's age, older in fact, and thoroughly unscrupulous. The only thing that could possibly be said in his favour is that he does not run after silly little girls. So I am quite sure this foolishness never came from him."

Senya glared, then threw her napkin on the floor and ran from the room. Laisa calmly selected a piece of the pede steak from the chafing dish, dipped it into the sweet pickle sauce and ate it.

Across the table, Ethelva glanced at her in distaste. "Is that all you can say? Nealrith needs you now," she said. "This will have shattered him."

"Nealrith brought this on himself by his foolishness. He is weak. We all know that. I do not approve of what Granthon wants to do, of course, but I appreciate why he has deemed it necessary." She wiped her fingers on her napkin. "I would suggest, though, that you try to dissuade him from doing it, Mother Ethelva. For the moment Granthon dies and Taquar rules the Quartern, the present highlord of Breccia is a dead man."

Ethelva started in shock. "Wha— what do you mean?"

"Watergiver save me from you all. You are worms burying yourselves in the sand thinking you'll be safe! People won't be happy with Taquar's rule once we run short of water, and the discontented will look to Nealrith for leadership. Taquar will not tolerate such a rival. You don't play with a man like him, unless you are prepared to face the consequences. If you want your precious son to live, and for all of us to be safe, you had better persuade Granthon to rethink his plan. In the meantime, I trust he does not intend to make this succession document public." She rose, shaking out the wide sleeves of her dress and smoothing down the skirt. "Permit me to take my leave. I have an appointment with my dressmaker for the final fitting of the dress I am wearing to Kaneth and Ryka's wedding tomorrow."

With regal composure, she went out, leaving Ethelva alone with her knowledge that Granthon had indeed every intention of making the succession issue public.

Feeling bereft, she said to herself, "Oh, merciful Sun-lord, where did we go wrong?"

This, Ryka thought, *is going to be the most ridiculous ceremony there ever was. Neither of us wants to wed, and yet we are having the largest wedding since . . . I guess since Nealrith and Laisa married.*

She looked at herself in the polished mirror stone with mixed feelings and wondered who had decreed that wedding dresses had to sweep the floor. No one ever wore such a silly garment at any other time. She preferred leggings and tunic. Lowleveller women wore tunics and short breeches to save on material and make work easier; uplevellers wore skirts to mid-calf. Yet every woman wanted to wear a dust-gathering heavy curtain around her legs when she married. She'd heard it said that a woman down on Level Forty made a living renting out the only wedding dress on the whole level.

Sandblast, but it was heavy and confining. And the wrong colour for her, too. Wedding yellow made her look sallow, as if she'd just had a good dose of desert fly fever. Turning to look at her profile, she snorted. She didn't belong in this elaborately woven garment or the silly frothy veil; she looked like someone pretending to be something they were not, and failing miserably. Her legs were her most attractive asset—long and perfectly proportioned, with a hint of muscular strength—and they were hidden. Her only other physical asset was her luxuriant light brown hair streaked gloriously blonde, and Beryll had just covered that with the veil. But not her face. No, her face had to be exposed to the critical crowd: long nose, nondescript eyes that had to squint to see better, too prominent a jawbone, an atrocious number of freckles even though she was careful to always wear a palmubra.

"You look lovely," Beryll said cheerfully at her side, as she contemplated the mirror image.

"Liar."

"All right, not lovely. Wrong word. But . . . interesting. Intriguing."

"Stop trying so hard, Beryll. You are making me sound like an unusual rock formation. I'm not pretty or even attractive, and right now I look horrible. A bit like a rockslide, come to think of it."

Beryll screwed up her face at her sister. "You are *so* hard to compliment sometimes, Ry. I thought you would be happy today, marrying the man you love, but you look as if you are going to his funeral. Or your own."

Ryka's expression tightened to match the lump in her throat. "He's only marrying me because he has to," she pointed out. "Think about that sometime, Beryll. Think about how that makes me feel."

"He'll come to love you," Beryll replied with her usual youthful optimism. "After all, I do, and I can't think of many reasons why I should, because there's nothing you and I seem to agree about. Except maybe that Kaneth is gorgeous, at least to look at." She tapped her buttocks with both hands meaningfully. "Stand him up on a pede with the reins in his hands and I just melt. He's not only the best pedeman in the whole Quartern, but he's the most delicious to look at, too."

Ryka blushed, which was odd. She had not thought she was the blushing sort.

"I wish you were happier about this, Kaneth," Nealrith told him as they waited in the temple for the waterpriests and the bride to arrive.

"So do I," Kaneth agreed morosely. "I've always liked Ry, you know that. And she was the one who changed, not me. In fact, I suppose in the back of my head I always had the thought that if I was going to marry anyone, it would be her. I always wanted a—a *sensible* woman to raise any offspring of mine. It's one thing to have a pretty, empty-headed doxy in your bed, but you want quite another person to raise your sons and daughters. If there are any."

"Do you have reason to doubt your fertility? Is *that* why it took my father's intervention to bring you to your wedding?"

"No. That was just—I don't know, laziness, I guess. A disinclination to spoil my fun. I'm not a particularly *good* man, Rith, for all that you stubbornly believe otherwise. Perhaps Ryka has the right of it when she calls me immature. But unlike Taquar, I took care not to burden any woman with a child I wasn't prepared to be a father to. Ironic, isn't it? He's tried so hard and it's got him nowhere. The Sunlord has a sense of humour, after all." He turned to look at the archway through which the waterpriests and Ryka would enter the courtyard. "Are brides *ever* on time?"

"Not that I know of. Laisa kept me waiting so long I thought she'd changed her mind and run off with Taquar.

Kaneth, may I ask, you aren't thinking of circumventing my father's orders are you, by not consummating the marriage?"

"Neither of us are that sandcrazy. We both know this has got to be real. He's placed someone in my household, hasn't he? Two of my servants resigned last week for no reason I could discern. Finally got them to admit they'd been offered a job at Breccia Hall, and hardly had they vanished than two more were knocking at the door with just the right qualifications."

"Water sensitives. Not my doing, I assure you. They'll be hanging outside your bedroom door until you two convince them your marriage is real."

Kaneth grimaced. "I thought as much. I don't suppose it will do much good to protest the distasteful intrusion into our privacy?"

"I'd take your word, you know that. But Father won't."

"I feel as I did when we were at the academy and on probation after some prank or other."

"You deserve it. I heard you were at the Level Three snuggery last night." Nealrith shook his head in a troubled way. "For someone who purports to know women, you can be exceptionally silly sometimes."

"I was just settling up my tab there and saying goodbye to the girls," he protested. "That was *all*."

Nealrith rolled his eyes in disbelief. "If you are wise, you will devote some time to convincing Ryka that you didn't just marry her to save your water and your wealth. And you'll stay away from snuggeries and that pretty hussy on the sixteenth that you've been sharing with those rich gem merchants from the fourth."

"Dammit, you appear to know a heap about my personal affairs, Rith."

"This is my city. It's my business to know what all the influential people are up to, and that includes both you and the gem merchants. Ah, hush up, here's your bride."

Kaneth turned.

Oh, blast, he thought and his stomach lurched oddly. She looked like a corpse all fancied up for the taking of her water at the funeral ceremony.

The emotion he felt, taking him by surprise, was pity.

"She's ugly," Senya said to her mother in a whisper heard by everyone within a radius of five or six paces.

"Hush," Laisa replied, pinching her daughter's arm.

As rainlords, they had front-row seats along the curving balcony. It overlooked the temple's ceremonial court where weddings, funerals, prayers and services took place. Ethelva was seated next to Laisa, but Granthon had not come. Lesser dignitaries sat at the back and had poor views of what went on, in spite of the heavily raked seating. By contrast, Senya and her mother could see everything.

They sat in the shadow of woven bab shades. Kaneth, Nealrith, Ryka and the waterpriests stood in the full sunlight on the bare beaten earth below, and were not permitted even to wear a hat. They had to be exposed to the full light of the Sunlord, of course. Senya did not envy them. It was hot and airless down there in the courtyard, and she'd heard that even the priests fainted sometimes.

Recessed in the centre of the court, in the full sun, was a long, narrow tiled pool, now empty. Under the stern eye of the robed waterpriests, Kaneth, then Ryka, came forward and each poured half a dayjar into it at either end. The other half of the dayjars, Senya knew, would have been donated to the priesthood. Everyone knew that the priests took care of their own first, even though they all received a water allowance from the city.

Covetous parasites, her mother called them.

Deserving servants of the Quartern, spending hours praying in the sun for our wellbeing, was the way her father put it.

Senya eyed the water from Kaneth and Ryka intermingling in the middle of the pool and dwelt on the symbolism with a prurient fascination that would have shocked her grandparents.

Next came the ceremonial words that began with a long and tiresome speech from Lord Gold, the Quartern Sunpriest, on the sanctity of vows made before the Sunlord in his temple. Senya fidgeted. Finally, Ryka and Kaneth vowed, before the Sunlord above, to cherish one another. Lord Gold then linked them by wrapping a yellow cloth around their clasped hands as they stood on either side of the pool. Then he stepped away, joining a group of lesser waterpriests in the shade. Kaneth and Ryka remained where they were, hands joined over the water, not speaking. They had to stay like that until the water—their sacrifice to honour the Sunlord and invoke his blessing on their marriage—had evaporated from the pool. Only then would they truly be wed.

Bored, Senya glanced around to where Highlord Taquar sat at the end of their row. Because of the way the balcony curved, she had a good view of the interesting planes of his face. He was perhaps darker than she liked, but that made him interesting, too. Forbidding. Mysterious. Dangerous. And so-ooo handsome.

He looked her way, smiled and winked. Then he rose and threaded his way through the other guests to the exit. Her heart thumped faster. He had smiled at *her*.

"Mother," she whined, "do *we* have to wait until all that water's gone?"

"Sunlord be thanked that's over," Ryka said. "I swear, I thought that water would never dry up. My nose must be as red as a ripe bab fruit, being out in the sun for so long."

"I never understood why those in the ceremonial courtyard are not permitted palmubras," Kaneth replied.

"Me, neither. As though wearing a hat indicates impiety."

"And discomfort and worship must go hand in hand."

"Exactly."

They fell silent, until she looked around in desperation to find something to say. "You swear this is all new?" she asked with a wave at the room furnishings.

They had compromised on where to live. Ryka had agreed to move into Carnelian House, as long as all the bedrooms were totally refurbished and rearranged. She would not, she had informed him, sleep where he had once bedded his succession of hussies. Rather to her surprise, he'd swallowed the humiliation of that with good grace, even though the new furniture had taken fifty days to be made and he'd been compelled to beg the Cloudmaster for an extension of the deadline for their marriage.

"I swear," he said. "In fact, this used to be my sitting room."

"And no hussies in the house in the future. You want to be unfaithful, you do it somewhere else. And now, let's get this over and done with. I am going to need you to unlace this stupid dress for me, unless you'd prefer me to ring for a maid."

"Oh, I think I have plenty of experience in undressing women," he said dryly, "as you so frequently remind me." He hesitated, then continued, "Ryka, I don't like this. It's not something that should be got 'over and done with' like taking a dose of kalo oil for indigestion. I've never taken a woman against her will, and I sure as the sands are hot don't want to start now. Especially not with you. I value your friendship too much, for a start, but even without that—" He shook his head unhappily. "It's distasteful, and I object to the position you have been placed in."

"There's someone waiting outside the door, isn't there? Granthon's man? A water sensitive waiting to see if we mingle our water today?"

He nodded apologetically. "I'm sorry. Um, we could fake it."

He sounded doubtful, though, and she shook her head. Blighted eyes, the idea that he could die, thrown out into the desert, because of her foolish scruples gave her the shivers. "No," she said, more forcefully than she intended. Modulating her tone, she added more quietly, "We are not going to take such stupid risks."

"You don't deserve to have your first experience forced on you like this. We could probably fool the fellow—"

She blinked at him in startled surprise. "You're scoffing me!"

He stared back. "We could try—"

"Not that! No, I mean—you can't possibly think this is my first experience, surely!"

"Why, y—" He stopped and reddened in embarrassment as the silence lengthened; her eyebrows were raised so high they disappeared under her fringe. "Er—I guess not."

"I'll be damned. You did. Kaneth, I'm *twenty-nine years* old!"

He was silent.

"You arrogant, condescending, ridiculous *male*! You can bed women from one end of the land to the other, but I am expected to forgo all such pleasures simply because I am a woman?"

"Well, you made such a fuss about *my* pleasures—"

"Not the fact that they occurred but that they were so promiscuous, so blatant and—and—so *commercial*!"

"I grant you that no one can say you were blatant. I have no idea who you favoured. Can I ask why you didn't marry him?"

"Who?" she asked, puzzled, and then started to laugh when she realised what he was thinking, but there was a bitter edginess to her mirth. "You really are impossible! Whatever makes you think there could only ever have been *one*? You have insulted me in just about every possible way in the past few moments. Am I so unattractive that you can't imagine anyone wanting to bed me? Should we wait until it's dark, perhaps, so that you find all this more . . . palatable because you can't see the body in your bed?"

"Oh, *shit!*" He turned away from her, throwing his hands up in the air, then spun to face her again, anguished. "Blighted eyes, Ry, why is it I have a genius for spewing forth turds instead of sense when you are around? You are the *last* person I want to hurt and yet I have an aptitude for doing just that. Forgive me, please. What I said was thoughtless and insulting, you're right. And I am a fool."

She took a deep breath, torn between loathing and loving him. "It's just as well I have a sense of the ridiculous, isn't it?" she asked at last. "Or that water sensitive outside the door would be running back to the Cloudmaster with a tale to tell. Even now, he's probably wondering just why we are standing on opposite sides of the room."

"We can rectify that," he said diffidently and rounded the bed to stand in front of her. "I have a mind to rid you of that cumbersome garment, for a start. Ry, we may not be lovers, but I would very much like to bed a friend. To build something worth keeping, especially if we have children. I can't think of anyone I would prefer to bear a child of mine than you, you know."

"I can live with that, I suppose." The words were ungracious, sharpened by her need to have him look at her as a lover, not as a necessary wife or prospective mother. She tried to soften them with a smile, but it came a shade too late to be convincing.

He held out a hand to her and struggled on. "I don't really want to wait for dark," he said. "I've always wanted to see your legs without the benefit of clothing. I don't think there's another woman in the Quartern who can match them."

She raised an eyebrow. "Lord Kaneth, are you attempting to charm me?"

"Er . . . yes. I guess I am. Trying to charm the breeches, um, the dress off you. Ry, I do think we can make this work, if we try."

She took his hand. "Especially as the alternative is a little grim, eh? All right, let's give that spy outside the door something to think about." And she lifted her face to receive his kiss, hoping he would not feel the wild beating of her unruly heart.

CHAPTER TWENTY-TWO

Red Quarter
Dune Scarmaker

Vara Redmane had been born on the dune called the Scarmaker and expected to die somewhere along its mighty length. She was sixty-four years old and the furthest she had ever been from the red sands of the dune was the edge of a nearby waterhole, to fill dayjars, as she was doing now. It was a task she and the other women performed every morning, in the cool of the long dune shadows, carting the dayjars in panniers on the back of two packpedes.

It was Vara's favourite job and collecting the water was a pleasant time between waking in her tent and facing the true work of the day. At the edge of the waterhole, where bab palms grew and flame creeper insinuated itself like a thread-snake among the rocks, she was at peace, in harmony with life and the water of life. Here she could, with trueness, offer up a prayer to the god of Dune Scarmaker; here she really did feel grateful for the gift of living water and life. And here, when she spilled the water in sacrifice to their dune god, she took pleasure in the idea that the precious drops would find their way back into the cool greenness of the pool where they belonged and not be sucked up into the greediness of the dry air.

Vara was old enough to remember many different dune camps and waterholes. It didn't seem so very long ago that this hole had been at the foot of the dune. Now the round trip and the filling of the jars took far too long. If it had been up to her, the camp would already have moved somewhere east or west along the length of the dune, after finding and digging out a new waterhole that the dune had recently left behind as it moved. All it took was a message to Breccia to tell the Cloudmaster where to send the next rains.

As though she had read Vara's thoughts, one of the other women grumbled, "Vara, when are you going to ask that husband of yours to move camp? I swear, the dune is moving away from us as we speak! The trip back is longer than the one out, and every day it's longer than the day before."

"Fully the length of your big toe," Vara agreed, seeping sarcasm. "If you lost weight, Irinat Redlander, the walk would be easier."

"And if you'd talk to Makdim, we'd have it easier still!" Irinat shot back.

A new voice intervened. "Makdim is not going to take any notice of what Vara says." Zuzan, of course, her voice carefully neutral, even as her words stung. She was an ancient, almost beyond making the trip for water, and known for her forthright opinions now that her great age had bestowed her with status. "He is a leader who does not consult his womenfolk."

"No? Maybe that's because we're asking the wrong one of his womenfolk. Maybe we should ask *her*," Irinat said, her tone full of spite, as she nodded towards the girl who was filling her jars at a distance from the others. "Maybe he'll take notice of the pretty little bauble Davim dropped in his lap."

Her head is filled with sand, Vara thought without rancour. *She hasn't the wits to see how Davim's bribery attempts have angered Makdim.*

Sandmaster of the Scarmaker and the most senior of all the dune leaders, Makdim loathed the upstart sandmaster of the Watergatherer, but he was finding himself increasingly powerless to stop the excesses of the man. The gift of a girl that Davim had seized on one of his forays into the Gibber had not pleased Makdim; it had infuriated him. Scarmaker did not deal in slaves and had not done so since before the days of Stormlord Garouth. To present Makdim with the gift of a human being was an insult; worse still, Davim had known that. He argued that the anti-slave laws were a Scarpen innovation and should not be followed by the Red Quarter. And he had presented Makdim with a dilemma: if the Scarmaker sandmaster refused the gift, then Davim could say that Makdim was a lackey of the Cloudmaster and his laws, and that he, Davim, had been gravely insulted. He could even insist on a zigger duel to avenge his honour. On the other hand, if Makdim accepted the gift, then he was giving tacit agreement to Davim's espousal of slavery and his slave raids.

Vara had thought Makdim should refuse, but he hadn't. He was an old man and he had long since lost a warrior's ability to kill a zigger with a sweep of the sword. He was vulnerable. However, neither had he accepted the gift of a slave and thus lost his honour. Instead, he had welcomed

the woman as a guest and taken her in. But the incident
had diminished him. He ought to have confronted Davim;
he hadn't, thus he had lost face among the men of the
Reduner tribes. The other women might not have realised
that, but Vara did.

She had married the youthful and headstrong Makdim
when she was fourteen, and in the lifetime of years since
then, she sometimes thought she had moved no further
in her life than the dune had travelled on its slow journey across the plains. She had borne Makdim's children,
fetched his water, cooked his meals, embroidered his robes
and hooked the lace for his mount's trimmings. Under her
supervision, his sons had grown up to be strong and noble
warriors. They had learned the science of battle and the
art of pede carving—but she might as well have been a
grain of sand beneath his feet for all the public recogni-
tion he had given her. In fifty years of marriage he'd never
offered her praise or thanks. And yet he loved her; she
knew that. And she loved him, understood him. And now
she grieved for him. For his loss of integrity.

When Vara thought of the girl Davim had captured in
the Gibber, it was with pity.

"Speak of the spiny devil and his eye will find you,"
Zuzan said suddenly. "He comes."

Vara looked up from her work. At first she thought it
was their own menfolk back from the hunting trip that had
sent them out over the plains the day before; then she saw
what the old woman had already seen: the red banners
carried by the first of the myriapede riders, the blood-red
banners of the Watergatherer dune. Her heart pounded as
she straightened from her task to take in the lines of myri-

apedes as they flowed down the dune in black rivulets, joining at the base behind the fluttering banners.

Dune god save us, she thought. *Makdim, you should be here now.*

"What shall we do?" Zuzan asked. Although she was older than Vara, she rightfully looked to Makdim's wife for leadership.

"Nothing," Vara said calmly. "Fill your jars." She topped up the last of her own jars and closed the pannier. Then she went to the head of the beast, gathering up the reins. Reduner women did not ride pedes, except sometimes as passengers behind their menfolk. When the women fetched water, they led the animals, as was proper.

Patiently she waited for the others to finish their tasks, but the Watergatherer party was upon them before they were ready to move off. Vara had hoped that Davim was not among them, but she soon recognised his mount, the formidable beast he called Burnish, reputedly the strongest and most intelligent of pedes ever born. And Davim himself, tall and straight and handsome—and arrogant.

He urged his mount right up to hers, until he was just a body length away, facing her.

"I have a gift for you, woman," he said. His voice was without expression.

"It is not meet that I should receive a gift from a man of another dune," she said evenly. Her voice lied; it was her pounding heart that told the truth. She *feared*. She feared the flatness of his tone, the fanaticism of his eyes.

"This one belongs to you," he said. He signalled one of his men, who then opened a pannier on his mount and began to throw out the contents at the feet of Vara's pede.

At first, absurdly, she thought he was throwing down bunches of overripe bab fruit. They spattered onto the crust of sand, scattering tiny crowns of red drops where they fell. Drops of blood.

Not fruit bunches. *Heads.*

One rolled and came to rest against Vara's toes. She stared, seeing and yet not comprehending. How could it be her son's eyes looking up at her from the ground? How could it be? He had ridden out with his father and brothers and friends, a hunting trip. Just a hunting trip, after the desert elans, or tasty night-parrots. Her eyes went from head to head as they rolled—but her mind lagged behind, and her ears hardly heard the keening of the other women.

"Your husband and his brother and your sons," Davim said. "We left the others in the desert for the spindevil winds to cover."

Stricken, Vara began to shake. Makdim's head had fallen face down, but his hat had come off and she knew that balding patch and the way his braided hair curled around his ears. And that over there was Bejanim. Gentle Bejanim, Makdim's brother, who had travelled to the great Scarpen cities and returned with such tales of wonder. His head had landed on its neck, so that he appeared to be buried chin-deep in sand. Impossibly, he seemed at peace, sleeping. She dragged her gaze away, her attention snagged by the voice that was still speaking words to her, meaningless words concerning a world that no longer existed.

"The Watergatherer rules here now, woman. Submit to us—or die. The choice is simple. Join with us as your menfolk would not, and we will take you to a victory in which you need never fear for your water again, in a world where we need never bow again before those who blot out the sky with their buildings. Or you can defy us, and die now."

Vaguely she was aware of Irinat, fat stupid Irinat, throwing herself at Davim's feet in submission, sobbing. Vaguely she was aware of others looking at her for leadership. The old woman's sharp eyes saying things that spoke deep in Vara's soul. The girl from the Gibber looking at her with indifference.

"Respect not the spindevil wind and you reap its wrath," she said. "That is my prophecy to you, drover. You have stirred the sand of the dunes; your time will come to receive just harvest." Without haste she wrapped her shawl tight around her head and shoulders, gathered the reins together and pulled herself up onto the lead segment of her pede. One of the women gasped. Several of Davim's men stirred angrily and would have intervened except that Davim made no move to stop her.

She turned the head of the beast away, clumsily because she had never before controlled the reins from the back of a mount. Then she jabbed the riding prod between the segments, pushing deep into the vulnerable flesh. The animal—unused to such abuse—responded immediately. It raised itself up onto the points of its feet and leaped forward, plunging straight into the waiting group of Reduner warriors. Mounts scuttled sideways to dodge and Vara broke free of the encircling group.

Behind her one of the men gave a snort of disparagement. There was no way that a transport packpede laden with water could outrun a myriapede hack. "Shall I run her down?" he asked Davim, his eyes gleaming at the thought.

"Send a zigger," Davim said.

With a disappointed shrug, the man reached behind to his zigger cage. When he allowed a single zigger to crawl into his zigtube, the other ziggers went into a frenzy of frustration at having missed out on the opportunity of a meal. The man turned to face the direction that Vara had taken. The riders around him drew back to give him an open view of her flight, even though they doubtless all wore the perfume of the tribe.

The man raised the tube, sighted along its length, and tapped on the side to release the cover.

The zigger flew.

There was a collective sigh from the women as the animal flew true: straight at the first moving thing it saw when the tube opened. And then it was gone, gathering speed until it was a blur against desert sands, invisible to the naked eye, a tiny missile with deadly intent.

Davim did not even wait to see it hit. He turned back to the women. "Your menfolk no longer exist," he said. "The Scarmaker tribe no longer rules the Red Quarter. Choose your fates."

In the distance, the red of Vara's shawl momentarily flared as if caught in the wind, then the figure on the back of the packpede faltered and slumped. One by one the women dropped to their knees on the red sands, until the only person standing was the old woman, Zuzan, finding her final dignity.

Davim shrugged. "Kill her," he said indifferently. Then, as someone speared her with casual skill, he turned to the man who had sent the zigger after Vara. "Go get that packpede back," he said. "Leave the woman out there for the desert cats to fight over."

He turned to the rest of his men, smiling. "The Red Quarter is ours," he said. "The woman was right: there will be those who reap the wrath of the spindevil winds— but it is *we* who are the spindevils." He grabbed one of the Watergatherer banners from the saddle of another rider and waved it high. "The Quartern will feel the greatness of the wind sweeping out of the dunes!"

Vara would have said he was a man who wasted his water on flamboyant gestures, but Vara was not there to see. Far away, still slumped over the back of the running pede, her shawl clutched in her hand, she gave a smile, part grimace—and all hatred. She came from a long line of sandmasters, and in her family, everyone knew how to deal with a lone zigger. Her shawl, thrown like a bird catcher's net and then slammed against the pede's back with the zigger caught in its folds, was now soiled.

Playing dead, she clutched a dagger in her hand and waited for the warrior she knew Davim would send after her. By the time they realised he was not coming back, she would be on the next dune.

PART TWO

Escape
without
Freedom

CHAPTER TWENTY-THREE

"This is not good enough."

The tone of Taquar's words was as sharp as a well-honed knife and cut Shale just as deep. Slowly he rose to his feet to face the highlord.

After more than three years in the mother cistern waterhall, he was as tall as Taquar and almost as broad in the shoulder. His daily swimming and frequent forays outside to climb the surrounding hills and explore the gullies had built muscles to match those of the man he faced. Shale wondered sometimes what Taquar thought about that; did he ever ask himself how Shale had come by his strength?

"I can do no better," he said in answer, his voice deep and even. He indicated the first three of a series of bowls on the table. A grain or two of salt stuck to the bottom of each. "See? I have no trouble creating vapour when there is not much else dissolved in the water. But those—" Frowning, he pointed to the remaining four bowls, all still full. "There's too much dissolved salt, and it anchors the water in place. Or that's the way it feels."

The appalling truth had been growing inside him like a gall for some time now: if he couldn't lift vapour from a salty solution in a bowl under his nose, how ever was he going to lift a cloud from the sea?

In frustration, he tried to lift the water with the salt still in it, and earned the rainlord's cynical amusement. "We have power over water, you imbecile, not salt. Nor anything else that happens to be in the water. When you move water, that's *all* you move."

His fury was controlled, but Shale heard it in the viciousness of his next words. "You have to be able to extract vapour from the salt water of the sea! Yet you can't even extract *liquid* water from a solution right in front of you. Even rainlords can do that much."

"Then perhaps I am not even a rainlord." Blood, ink, piss, fruit juice or even dead bodies—it made no difference to rainlords, he knew that. They could extract the water. And he could not.

"The trouble is that you came to training too late and we are running out of time." Taquar began to pace up and down. "Things have deteriorated throughout the Quartern. Gibber settles are raiding one another now. Davim has most of the Reduner tribes behind him as their water holes shrink. He rides out mounted on that great pede of his— Burnish—his men following like a huge red dust storm, and puts the fear of the dune drovers into every settle in the northern Gibber, not to mention 'Baster caravans."

Shale sat down again. When Taquar was in a mood like this, it was pointless to say much, because he rarely listened.

"Water theft is increasing across the Scarpen. The measures I take in Scarcleft do not make me popular—some fool had the audacity to throw a stone at me from a rooftop last week! At least Granthon has finally ceased sending regular storms to the Gibber and White Quarters."

Shale stared, unbelieving. "Storms aren't regular in the Gibber any more?" He went cold all over, unable to comprehend the enormity of the tragedy in the making. "You think people of the White Quarter and the Gibber Plains should die?" he asked finally, his rage building.

"No, of course not. I think they should learn to live without our storms. They did once." He did not sound particularly concerned. "With Granthon not able to make full use of all the natural clouds, they will have to go somewhere and some will drop rain. Those two quarters will revert to a Time of Random Rain. In fact, I have heard rumours that there has been unexpected rainfall in both quarters already.

"If Granthon and Nealrith had any sense whatsoever," he continued, "they would have stopped trying to please everybody long ago and spent more time learning how to save the Scarpen. And the Reduners, of course. We have no choice there—if we don't supply *them* with water, they'll be on our doorsteps with their ziggers. Even now, they are restless. If I ruled in Breccia, I would give them the White Quarter to do what they liked with, to placate them for the reduction in water. Leave the north to the Reduners and the south to us."

"You mean split control of the Quartern?"

"Exactly."

Taquar's callousness was beyond Shale's understanding. Was this, he wondered, some kind of test? Was he supposed to protest?

His burning thirst for change—for any change—flared. He could not bear his imprisonment any more. He couldn't.

Taquar stopped pacing and came to sit opposite him. "You have to try harder, Shale. I *know* you have the capability of a stormlord. No rainlord can manipulate water the way you do, in such large quantities, with such control. No rainlord can move water such long distances. You can, therefore you are more than a rainlord. You can make vapour from fresh water. You just have to practise more and you'll be able to do it from salt water."

"No."

"I beg your pardon?"

"No. Practice is not going to make any difference. I have not been improving for a while now. It is time you took me to the Cloudmaster. It is time he taught me. Besides, I am tired of living here, of never meeting anyone but you."

And I don't trust you. And why do you never mention Mica?

It was more than three years since Wash Drybone Settle had died. More than three years since he had seen his brother. He met Taquar's hard gaze and refused to flinch. "My time here is over."

If it had not been for his studies, he thought he might have gone mad. At first, his three teachers from the Scarcleft Academy had all assumed he was much younger than he was, possibly because his writing was so poor. He hadn't minded that because he needed to be taught at the most childish of levels.

Now their mistake amused him, because they still

thought him younger than he was and were unable to contain their delight at the rapid advances he made. One taught him arithmetic, geometry and water dynamics; another history, literature and—lately, at Shale's request and without Taquar's knowledge—basic Reduner vocabulary; and the third, natural history and geography. He knew his teachers' names but nothing more about them, and he had no idea what Taquar had told them about him. He knew he must puzzle them with his strange ignorance at times.

"What's a temple?" he'd asked his history teacher once, prompting the horror-struck man to pen a reply lamenting the gap in his religious education. He also had to have explained to him things as diverse as staircases and ships and silk and bath houses and trade across the Giving Sea. He'd soaked up the knowledge like desert sand thirsty for the evening dew, and asked for more.

As his horizons expanded, though, his discontent had grown. And now he knew the time had come to change things.

"You cage me," he accused. "I want to go to Breccia City."

The highlord frowned. When he spoke, it was without overt anger, but Shale shivered at the frost in the soft tones of his voice. "Shale, accept that I know what is best for you. I have many years of experience and a knowledge of both my fellow man and water-power. You have to trust me. I know the loneliness you must experience here, but our land demands it. The rewards will be huge, you know. And you will still be alive, because of me."

"If you do not take me, then I shall go alone. There is no way you can keep me here against my will. None."

Taquar stared at him, and for a long, uncomfortable

moment, Shale wondered if he was in danger. There was something in Taquar's eyes that spoke of a rage so deep he was capable of doing anything. Then, unexpectedly, he laughed.

"Why, I believe you would indeed walk all the way to Scarcleft! I knew you worked out how to raise the grille, of course. And perhaps you are right—it is time. Very well, but allow me to go and make arrangements first, if you will. Next time I come, I will take you away from here. That is a promise, the word of a highlord. Perhaps I should take you to the sea. If you confront the ocean, you may do better at water extraction."

Shale let out the breath he had been holding. "I would like that."

"We will need to be cautious. We still do not know who the rogue rainlord is. I have come to the conclusion that Kaneth is more likely than Nealrith. He certainly has more opportunity to speak to Reduners, as he travels a lot. He leads a group of young warriors who hunt down the Reduner marauders, yet the raids continue. Who knows if that is all he does?"

They stared at one another, youth and man. Shale remembered the collared lizards around the settle, flexing their neck ruffs, circling one another before a fight. *We're like that*, he thought. *We don't like each other. Not really.* He looked away, wondering if they would ever come to a full-scale argument. He hoped not, because he was not sure he would win.

As far as Taquar was concerned, they left the matter of his future there, but Shale's thoughts raged on. Discontent needled him. The rewards Taquar had mentioned meant little. He already had all he could eat and drink, and once that had been a dream of untold riches. What he wanted most was to look for Mica, to free Mica—if he was still alive. Controlling water for a whole land meant nothing unless he could make amends for the suffering his possession of water-powers had provoked.

The thought of rewards had never crossed his mind. And Taquar had apparently forgotten Mica ever existed.

Sometimes, he thought, *we don't speak the same language.*

He went to clean Taquar's pede, wanting the rhythm of grooming the animal to calm him. Besides, he needed to think. Now that he had the promise of freedom before him, he felt as much trepidation as elation. In spite of all his lessons, he knew so little and it was all theoretical.

Perhaps Nealrith would make life miserable for him. Perhaps he would hate city life. Perhaps the Cloudmaster would despise him.

He knew now that Granthon was more than just a stormbringer. He actually ruled. True, the cities and settles and tribes of the Quartern managed their own daily affairs, but some things were controlled from Breccia City. Water was guaranteed, but only in exchange for services. There were taxes to be paid; laws to be observed and enforced; in some areas there were trade roads or docks or roadside cisterns to be maintained.

The tribes of Reduner were obliged to supply a certain number of pedes to Scarpen markets each year. The quarries of the White Quarter were expected to send a fixed quota of salt and soda and gypsum. The mines of Scarpen were required to tender a certain weight in metals. The fossickers of the Gibber supplied gemstones and resin to pay their taxes. It was a whole network of obligations and trade and tax agreements supervised from the offices of the Cloud-master, and Shale had gleaned enough from his teachers and his reading to know that he didn't know half of it.

Even an idle question had ramifications beyond anything he expected. He once asked Taquar who made the tokens and why they didn't make more of them so that no one needed to be waterless. This careless query laid Shale open to Taquar's scorn and a lecture on the whole concept of the debasing of coinage. He found out that the minting of tokens was done under strict supervision in Breccia, and the number of tokens was rigidly controlled according to the amount of water available for sale each year.

"But isn't that amount of water actually the same from year to year?" he asked. "At least in the past, if not now. You shouldn't have needed *any* new tokens made, in that case."

Taquar looked exasperated. "Tokens get lost, or people hide them under the bed and forget about them, or they get traded on the other side of the Giving Sea. Somehow or another, you have to keep the right amount of tokens in circulation, and that means minting new coins every year. Otherwise people won't be able to buy water."

"How do they know how many to make?"

"Oh, there are ways," he answered vaguely. "The Breccia Hall treasurer does that. Something to do with whether people are buying water at prices higher than—or lower than—one token per dayjar. And something to do with the ratio of old coins to newer ones in the marketplace. Each year's minting has a number, and the accountants can calculate how many of the old tokens have been lost—I don't know the details. I do know it works differently here from other countries. Over on the Other Side—"

"The Other Side?"

"The outlander countries on the other side of the Giving Sea. They keep growing, getting bigger and bigger. More people born each year. But we can't do that. Our population has to stay the same because there is no water to spare." He gave a disgusted grunt. "And still there are people who can't see that truth. Idiots who will have more children than they should, even though they know the extra ones will be born waterless and that most of them will end up on the lowest level, one step away from death by thirst. I have no patience with those people. Not with the poor who breed like pouched mice because they can't be bothered to stop, nor with the rich who try to buy a place for their extra children. They have no right to take away *my* water—the water of a hard-working citizen. The waterless, rich or poor, are the curse of this land. They live by thieving; they are either poor and diseased and useless and filthy, or rich and useless parasites."

Shale felt he was standing on shifting sand. He looked straight at Taquar. "I was born waterless," he said.

There was a long silence. Then, "Yes. So you were. And I thank the Watergiver you were born, but it does not change my opinion. A succession of stormlords have been too weak to make the birth of waterless progeny a crime, as it should be. Instead they just deny the children water allotment. Where is the good in that? It takes the crime away from the parent and punishes those born through no fault of their own."

"I didn't know it was possible to—well, to stop the children coming. My mother never knew how. Most of them died, anyway."

"Of course there are ways! But why are we talking

of such matters? Monetary policies and the lack of birth laws are no concern of yours."

No concern of yours.

As he remembered that conversation, Shale knew that Taquar did not ever think of him as being a cloudmaster one day, ruling as Granthon did. The rainlord was not teaching him the duties of a ruler. What Shale knew about those things he gained from his reading or the academy teachers.

He wasn't sure exactly what Taquar did intend, but he suspected the highlord thought he, Shale, was going to be doing little more than move storms all his life.

Maybe I don't understand all I read, or what I am taught, he thought. *But I am not as stupid as Taquar thinks, either. I am sure I'm not.*

As they were about to eat their midday meal, Shale felt the arrival of people outside. Not a few, but a large group. "Men and pedes," he said urgently. "Coming up the slope."

Swiftly Taquar was on his feet, his hand going to the loaded zigtube he had put down on the table. "Wait here," he rasped and went out.

Shale, however, followed, pushing his water senses outwards. He felt most of the pedes and men stop at the bottom of the slope. Two men riding myriapedes continued up towards the grille.

He saw them arrive. Two dune tribesmen. *Reduners.*

Shale began to unravel. Breathing became an effort. His hands felt clammy. His stomach churned.

They dismounted and the first man gave his reins to the second. "It is time," he said to Taquar without greeting. "I want to meet him."

The way Taquar held himself told Shale that the rainlord was angry, but nothing of the emotion came through in his voice. "As you wish," he said smoothly. "Perhaps you will join me for a meal?"

As the highlord manipulated the grille, Shale saw the Reduner more clearly. Red-skinned, lean, hawk-nosed, his red-stained braids poking out under the cloth extensions of his woven cap, he was a striking man. His red-dyed tunic was lavishly embroidered in matching thread in a panel down the front. Even though he wasn't large, he held himself tall; everything about him spoke of power and prestige.

Taquar turned to Shale. "Help the servant clean the pedes," he said abruptly, indicating the animals. "Get them food and water."

But Shale couldn't move. He was pinned to the wall by a welter of emotion and memory.

"And who is this?" the first man asked, eyeing him with an intense gaze as he entered the cavern. Something told Shale the question was redundant; the man knew exactly who he was.

Taquar ushered the Reduner towards the living quarters. "Shale Flint," he replied. "He does the chores around the place for me. We live simply here," he added, "but I can offer you the finest of Scarpen pickles and preserves, and some bread I brought from Scarcleft." He looked back over his shoulder as they entered the inner room, frowning his disapproval at Shale's lack of response to his order. "Get to it, lad."

Shale moved then. The Reduner servant wordlessly handed Shale the reins of his pede, making it clear that he did not intend to indulge in idle conversation now they were alone. Shale made himself busy, while the man tended to his master's pede. It was a magnificent creature, larger than most, the deep red-black colour of the darkest of rubies. Shale stared at it with covetous eyes before turning to the servant's pede. He worked without thinking, calming the turbulence of his thoughts in the steady cleaning and polishing. Antennae first, for without the sensitivity of clean feelers it was purblind. Then the head and mouthparts, next the thorax, brushing out the irritating grains of sand caught in between or under the segments. Next he fetched the herbal polish and began to work on the segments themselves, shining them till they gleamed. Alongside him, the man worked on similar tasks but said nothing, often deliberately turning his back. It didn't take Shale long to realise he was being snubbed.

He was still wondering about that when he came to the fifth segment on the pede he was cleaning. Like all the others, it was carved with pictures. And as Shale ran the polishing cloth over the carvings, the pictures seemed familiar. A pede being pulled out of some kind of sinkhole.

He stared. Everything stopped: his heart, his breath, his throat.

He had last seen those pictures close up, with his cheek pressed down into the carvings as the pede—the very same pede—had flowed across the desert in the heat of the day with its burden, a boy still bathed in his sister's blood.

CHAPTER TWENTY-FOUR

Scarpen Quarter
Scarcleft City
Level 36

A few weeks before her eighteenth birthday, Terelle was buying water from Vato when a man raced past and almost knocked her water jars flying. Several armed men pounded after him, followed a moment or two later by riders on a myriapede. The driver and those seated behind him were zigtube-wearing enforcers.

"What is all that about, at this time of the morning?" Terelle asked Vato, grateful that she had saved the jars from being smashed.

"There's a lot of raids lately. Be careful, lass. That fleeing man was Wilsent the beggar from Dung Street. He's a water thief. Used to be a beggar on the uplevels, but they've got a lot stricter now. It's hard to even go upwards any more, let alone beg there." He frowned unhappily. "And water goes up in price again tomorrow."

"Not *again*! Why?"

"Not enough water coming in from the Warthago Range, why else? Same old story: Highlord Taquar says the Cloud-

master isn't making enough rain. That he's old and dying."
He shrugged. "But he's been dying for the past four years
or more. People say Highlord Taquar has to do something
because he's the heir, you know. The Quartern heir. Did
you know that? Granthon announced it ages back. What
nobody cares about is that we waterless are always the first
to suffer. After the cats, that is." He spat, shedding his own
water to show the depth of his contempt.

"Cats?"

"People don't keep pets when times are bad."

She thought about that. It had been a long time since
she had seen a cat. The idea that people killed their cats
rather than feed them, or worse, that they killed them for
the cupful of water they could obtain if they took the body
to one of the houses of the dead for water extraction, appalled her more than anything else he'd said. She felt ill,
sick in the stomach and heartsick in spirit.

"And if the Cloudmaster does die?" she asked at last.

"Who knows? We are taught that we owe everything to
stormlords. That without them, there would be no water.
If that's true, and we've only got one stormlord now—
which is definitely true—I think we could all be in trouble
before much longer. But, Terelle, it may all be a lie. After
all, what better way to stay in power than to tell everyone
that they get their water because of you? Seems a mighty
clever way to rule to me."

She stared at him in horror. "Surely no one can think
the Cloudmaster lies!"

He shrugged. "The waterpriests say the rainlords are
the living proof that the Sunlord exists and aids us. People
who believe them bow low to the rainlords. But me? I
reckon Highlord Taquar has a nasty smell to his water.

There's not much holy about that wilted bastard. And if you tell anyone I said that, I'm dead, lass."

He hawked and spat yet again. "Withering lords. Grind us down into the dust of the Scarpen, while they live in their fancy uplevel houses and drink all the water they want. If I had my way, I'd slit all their throats. Then we'd find out, wouldn't we?"

Terelle tried to suppress her unease.

"Don't look so worried!" He grinned at her. "You're coated with dew, you are! Because of that old man you've hooked up with. Never short of tokens to buy water, you are!"

She reddened at the insinuation behind his words, but resisted the temptation to deny what he had not openly said. "Russet says that in troubled times people are less likely to buy artwork, and it's true, I think. Especially ones that use water. Lately we've been getting less work."

"Eh, I heard tell he did one for the Cloudmaster himself!"

"Yes, but that was ages ago."

He turned away to serve Ba-ba and she plodded her way upstairs lugging the water jars and wondering about her life. She hated the unfairness of the idea that she could one day be struggling with water problems again.

This was her fourth year with Russet, and the old man had finally done what he had promised: he had taught her how to paint. In addition, she had learned nearly all there was to know about making the paints. She knew where to procure the ingredients, how to grind them and mix them and add the resins and additives that made waterpainting possible. She knew all the tricks of what Russet called artistry: perspective, depth, foreshortening, texture, shadow. The sort of things anyone could learn. But she was aware, too, that she had something that he could never have taught her. She could do more than reproduce the reality of a scene in paint; she could suggest the feel and movement, the smell and mood of it as well. Just as Russet could. Painting was a joyous thing, a whole experience, not just the layering of colour on water. It was better than dancing had ever been. She could no longer imagine a life without it.

But one thing Russet had never shown her: how to make a suggestion of a painted figure change the way he had done that first day.

More to the point, was he ever going to tell her? After all, he'd never explained how he had known her name. She'd asked—no, begged—him to tell her who she was, but his reply was always the same: "When I be ready."

At first she had been both defiant and persistent, threatening to leave him, but her arguments with the old man always had the same result: she ended up in the outhouse, throwing up her last meal, doubled over with cramp. For days afterwards she would feel listless.

The sharp-eyed Lilva had cornered her about it one day. She had been fifteen at the time. "You got a young'un in your baby jar that's making you sick, have you, love?" she asked.

Terelle, blushing, denied it.

"Ah, then maybe you have one of them delicate stomachs that don't like arguments," she said with a derisive snort. "Specially arguments you'll never win. That old man? He's pure poison, child. The more you defy him, the more his eyes glint with the joy of battle. But you? You just get sick to the stomach."

Terelle had dismissed the idea as fanciful at the time, but now, when she thought about it, she wondered if Lilva was right. Defying Russet did seem to upset her stomach, which was infuriating and such a stupid weakness to have when he so often annoyed her.

She bit her lip as another nagging thought niggled at her. That first waterpainting she had seen Russet do . . . the confused expression on the face of the woman, as if she'd stepped out of the house without knowing why. As if she had been *compelled* . . .

Compelled. Could Russet force someone to do something simply by painting them doing it?

No, of course not. The idea was preposterous. And he couldn't make her sick simply by arguing with her, either. Besides, she was sometimes sick like that when she hadn't been arguing with him. Why, she'd been sick just the other day, when she had been doing nothing more than daydreaming about going to Breccia City or Denmasad or somewhere to be a waterpainter there, all on her own . . .

That memory trailed away and was replaced by another: the time she had seen Russet painting in the middle of the night. She frowned uneasily as she stowed the dayjars, not liking the way her mind seemed to be drifting.

"I be going uplevel now," Russet said. He wound his coloured cloth around his bald head and tucked in the ends. "To collect a debt owed for a painting. Ye can make stew for dinner."

She nodded and started to gather the ingredients as he left the room and set off along the hallway. Even though her mind wasn't on the task, it didn't take long before she had the pot hanging on the hook over a low-burning fire. She continued to think about the painting she had seen him do in secret, when he'd thought she was asleep.

Once the stew was gently simmering, she studied the

room. There weren't many places to hide anything, let alone something as large as a painting severed from its water. She knew it wasn't under his pallet because she always moved it to sweep. The only other place it would fit was under the box where the seaweed briquettes were kept.

Carefully, she took out all the briquettes and lifted the woven box from its corner. Ten or so paintings lay flat underneath. Her hands trembled as she carried them to the table.

They were all pictures of her. Several portrayed the girl she had been when she'd first come to live on the thirty-sixth level, showing her right here in this room or out in the hallway. In one of them she was doing a waterpainting, in another she was eating at the table, in a third she was pounding something up to make paint-powder. Because they looked so much like moments she had known, she assumed he must have done them from memory.

Other paintings showed her older, year by year, doing similar things, still living in this same building. Then there were three sheets portraying her at an age she had not yet reached. She looked in bewilderment at these versions of herself. In one, she was mounted on a pede, and the land the animal was crossing was pure white. The White Quarter, perhaps? She'd heard there was a place called the Whiteout, where the soil was as white as salt. Strapped behind her was a bundle of what looked to be Russet's clothes.

In another painting, she was in a camp, and Russet's belongings were strewn around her feet on that white soil.

In the third, she was standing on some kind of green plants, and there was water—water exposed to full sunlight—sliding in profligate abandon across the green. She gasped to see even a painted depiction of so much waste. In the background, the land tilted, ending in jagged shapes of blue and purple. The picture was the imaginings of a fever dream, surely, not reality.

Yet when she touched the paint, an overwhelming desire to be there, in that place, uncurled inside her, until she was gasping from a need she could not understand. The desire wasn't hers; she was sure it wasn't. *I don't want it.* And if it wasn't hers, it had to be his.

That was the moment, with cold clarity, that she began to make sense of it all. Terror ripped through her then, tearing all her peace of mind apart. She skimmed through the paintings again, staring, shaking, not believing, grasping a thought only to lose it again when it seemed too unbelievable to be true.

And always, always that memory she had: the woman stepping out into the street as if she had been compelled to do so. Compelled, because he had painted her there. Another memory: she had been uncertain after she had first met him whether she should take up his offer—until a day or two had passed, when she had become certain.

She knew then what had been done to her, and it was unspeakable. Those early portraits had not been painted from memory at all. He had done them before she had agreed to become his apprentice, not afterwards. *He made my future by painting it.*

She let the paintings fall from nerveless fingers and could not bring herself to touch them again. She sank down onto the chair and sat huddled there, not moving.

That was the way Russet found her several runs of the sandglass later.

He glanced at her, then at the paintings lying where she had dropped them. "So now ye know," he said.

She struggled to sit straight, to contain the rawness of her emotions, her rage. "What have you done?" she asked. But she knew. In her heart, she knew.

"Trapped ye," he said. His complacency was both chilling and streaked through with a gloating malice. "For y'own good. Y'future be painted, and ye never be changing it. If ye be wise, ye'll not struggle against it, because will get ye nowhere. Ye cannot leave me."

"And what is my future?" she asked in a whisper. "What life have you decided I must live?"

He smiled. "That is for you to find out by living it."

Oh, Sunlord help me, she thought. She had believed she'd escaped an unwanted future when she'd left the snuggery. Now the menace of it was back, lying in wait, inevitable in its arrival, unchangeable, its outcome unknowable—at least to her.

"No!" She jumped up, snatched the heap of paintings and leaped for the fireplace. He moved faster than she thought possible. As she went to fling all the paintings into the fire, he struck downwards across her forearms, sending the sheets scattering across the floor instead.

"Ye'll die!" he cried, panting. "That be y'future, ye silly frip. Burn them, and ye'll be burning with them!"

Terelle stood, her hands dropping to her sides, her passion draining away.

"And ye already know, I think: fighting a painted future means ye'll be ill."

She began to weep, the tears born not of defeat but of fury.

CHAPTER TWENTY-FIVE

Scarpen Quarter
From Scarcleft mother cistern to Scarcleft City

"Are you *sandcrazy*?" Taquar hissed, his temper only just under control.

He had closed the door to the outside cavern, where Shale and the Reduner pedeman were busy with the pedes, but he used the Reduner tongue just in case Shale could hear.

Davim looked around, frowned at the table and chairs, and settled for a bed instead, where he sat crossslegged. "You have played with me long enough, Taquar," he replied in the same tongue. "I came to see the lad myself. I want to see his power. I want to be sure you really have a stormlord as you claim, because I have seen none of your promised rain."

"If he recognises you, he will never cooperate with me again. You're sun-fried to come here like this—your visit taints me in his eyes! Have you any idea how much he hates Reduners? You wiped his settle off the face of the Gibber!"

Davim shrugged. "He won't recognise me. He saw me

only in the cold light of dawn with the sun behind me and my face swaddled. He won't recognise my chalaman out there, either—the boy was drugged out of his senses. Anyway, it was almost four years ago. Besides, as planned, we have the means to persuade him should he prove reluctant to help our cause. I have his brother still."

"We would have his sister as well, if you hadn't been so damned set on teaching him a lesson. She shared his blood and might even have been a stormlord. You jeopardised everything I've been working towards."

"She was too young to be bothered with, and he needed to know my nature in case we ever need to threaten him. *You* are the one who jeopardised our agreement. You were to supply me with water until such time as all the tribes were behind me. Instead of their willing cooperation, I have had to fight some of them because I had nothing to offer them!"

Taquar's eyes gleamed at the opportunity to ridicule the sandmaster. "I've heard rumours there's active rebellion against your leadership. I hear Makdim's *wife* leads it from one of the northern dunes. An old woman!"

"Vara Redmane is a shrivelled bag of bones, no more danger than a sand-leech," he snapped. "Do you think we drovers fear a wrinkled old hag with no more children in her womb?"

"If she's so harmless, why haven't you killed her and her followers?"

"That is dune business, none of yours!"

Taquar did not bother to hide his smile.

"The lad. Tell me about the lad! When does he begin to cloudshift?"

"Shortly. He must be eighteen soon, and that's when

most stormlords begin to shift." He forbore to say that previous stormlords had always been able to extract vapour from salted water at a much younger age.

"If I don't see evidence of it within another year, then I will use other methods to bring water to the dunes. We don't get enough random rain yet because Granthon is still stealing many of the natural-born clouds. I must placate those tribes who resist my rule, and I will do it one way or another. I do not carry all my wealth on the back of one pede, my friend. Remember that, if you choose to betray our agreement."

"You threaten me? I could take your water right now and leave you a dry husk on the floor."

"You'd never get out of here alive. Even you can't kill *all* the ziggers out there in the hands of my men." He smiled pleasantly. "Now show me what the lad can do."

Shale stood, dragging air into his chest, staring at the carvings on the segment plates of the servant's myriapede. Memory renewed, raw and anguished: a bag roughly pulled over his head, the pain of the ride, the searing agony of Citrine's death, despair at being parted from Mica.

The Reduner servant did not notice his abstraction. The man was still working on his sandmaster's pede, sharpening the roughened points at the end of the feet with a file.

Shale inhaled once more, forced himself to think. Forced his thudding heart to slow. With awful clarity, he knew exactly how much depended on the rest of this day. If he made one wrong move, he risked his chance of freedom, perhaps even his life.

He cleared his mind of emotion and thought back. Was

this man, supposedly a servant, one of those who had initially carried him away from Wash Drybone Settle? He could not be sure, even though he was sure about the pede. He'd been too drugged, too sick, and during the day both men had kept their faces covered. Certainly the man Taquar was now talking to had not been either of them— but he could have been the leader who'd suggested a game of chala.

Davim. Dressed in red, all but his eyes obscured by the red cloth he wrapped around his head, mount rearing up . . . a reddish pede. A sandmaster. Catching Citrine— thrown to him as if she was a ball in a game—on his chala spear and laughing as the blade pierced her dress but not her body . . . not then. They kept her alive as long as they could, those chala players.

Shale cleared his throat and risked everything. *He had to know.* Quietly, and hoping the man understood, he asked in the language of the Quartern, "That's a magnificent pede you're working on. Does it have a name? Do Reduners name their pedes?"

"Has, yes," came the answer, thickly accented, but understandable. "Burnish."

Davim. The man in the inner room, it was *him.* The man who had killed Citrine . . . sitting there in the other room talking to Taquar, like an old friend.

Davim and Taquar. Together. Planned all this.

Davim uniting the Reduner tribes, raiding the Gibber. Slaughtering Citrine. Enslaving Mica.

Taquar the betrayer, who had killed Citrine as surely as if he had been the one who had held the chala spear. Who had tricked Shale into gratitude by "rescuing" him from his captors. No wonder something about the rescue had bothered Shale: Taquar had not killed the two kidnappers. He could have done so easily. *Should* have done so, to ensure they weren't followed. It was hardly the kind of thing that would have bothered his conscience.

Automatically, Shale's shaking hands went on polishing the plates of the pede. He didn't notice that he was working on the same spot, over and over. His mind darted after facts, skimming all that had been said and not said. And in between it all, he heard Citrine's last scream of terror.

Power. All for power. Split the Quartern. A man who couldn't be stormlord, but who wanted the power of the Scarpen ruler.

Pede piss, but you are a fool, Shale. All Taquar ever wanted was the skills he thinks you have. He wants a stormlord. A man could do anything if he owned the only stormlord in the Quartern.

The thought choked him, lumped somewhere in the throat. The teaching, the patience, even the small kindnesses—all a sham. And he, Shale, had tried to please him. He, Shale, had ached to be liked, ached to see respect in Taquar's eyes. To make the rainlord proud of the lad he had rescued. *Rescued!*

His stomach heaved, and he had to choke back the vomit. He grabbed up the file and began to work on the feet of the pede, savagely filing away the rough edges and sharpening the points. How could he have been so dumb? So credulous? Had he learned *nothing* from all that had happened at Wash Drybone Settle? Sun-fried, sandcrazy *dryhead*!

He looked up briefly when Davim's servant switched over to the near side of the pede, and was glad to note that the man kept his face averted.

Making sure I don't recognise him, Shale thought savagely. *But I wouldn't have. It's been too long, and I was too crazed to think then anyway. He's probably not a servant, of course. He's a warrior. A chalaman.*

As he worked, his eyes lit on the zigger cage against the wall. Ziggers. If he could load a zigtube, one of Taquar's, he could kill Davim and this man. But not Taquar. For that he'd need Davim's zigger. Too difficult. Besides, Shale wasn't wearing the correct perfume, so he could be the victim. No, he couldn't use ziggers.

But these men deserved death. Deserved it over and over again.

Citrine, Mica, all of Wash Drybone Settle—either dead or enslaved.

What kind of men are they?

The pede stirred restlessly, unused to quite so much passion applied to its foot maintenance.

The door of the inner room opened. "Shale, haven't you finished out there yet?" Taquar called out to him.

He straightened, laying down the file.

Don't let your thoughts show. "Coming, Highlord." He washed his hands in the pede trough and went through into the other room.

"Bring us some amber, there's a good lad," Taquar said. He and Davim were just about to seat themselves at the table. "And something to eat."

"Yes, Highlord." He didn't know how he could keep his voice calm, expressionless—and yet he could, and did. He walked into the storeroom, collected the amber and mugs, came back, poured the drinks. His hands shook slightly, but his nerves showed no more than that. This red man in his embroidered red tunic and breeches, his braided and beaded hair swinging around his face, had been the one who had played a deadly game with Citrine. Deliberately. To punish Shale for lying. To show him who had the power.

For no good reason at all.

As he handed the Reduner a food platter a little later, he deliberately looked him straight in the eye.

Davim smiled. "What you name?" he asked, demonstrating a clumsy, heavily accented command of the Quartern tongue.

As if you don't know, you murderous bastard. "Shale Flint of Wash Drybone Settle." His voice was steady enough—a little hoarse, perhaps, but that was all. The next words he addressed to the sandmaster were silent ones: *Remember that name, Davim. It is the name of the man who will kill you.*

"How old?"

He shrugged in reply. "Seventeen, eighteen perhaps. Thereabouts."

"Shale serve master good?"

"I do not have a master," he said quietly. "If you mean Highlord Taquar, he is my teacher."

Taquar gave the faintest of smiles and spoke in Reduner. Shale struggled to comprehend. "The boy is sharp, Sandmaster. I would not play mind games with him, if I were you." He looked at Shale and switched to the Quartern tongue. "The Sandmaster would like a demonstration of your water-power. Bring some water in from the mother cistern."

Shale continued to put food on the table as he worked his water skills. He bundled up a ball the size of a man's head, pulled it up out of the lake and brought it to hover low over Davim's head. "What would you like me to do with it, my lord?"

Taquar sent a questioning look to the Reduner.

"Send it back," the man snapped in Reduner. He must have known Shale could empty the water all over him any time he wanted. He stared hard at Shale as he spoke, and Shale was taken aback by the hatred he thought flashed there only to vanish a moment later under the fakery of a bland smile.

"The lad is too clever," Davim growled.

"Shale has not had the best of experiences with Reduners, my friend," Taquar said and switched languages once more. "Send the water back, Shale. And remember that not all men from the Red Quarter are coloured with the same dust. Please do not insult my guest by asking after those of your settle who were taken to the Red Quarter."

"No, my lord." Shale removed the water and cut some bread. His fury swelled in his throat.

Davim spoke again, and this time Taquar translated. "He asks if you can bring up a storm yet."

Scrupulously polite to cover his rage, Shale said, "I do not know, Sandmaster. I have never tried."

"I expect Shale to come into his full powers soon," Taquar added.

"And how much longer will Granthon last?" Davim asked.

"It is nothing short of a miracle that he is still alive now."

They were speaking in Reduner once more, ignoring Shale. He strove to grasp the gist of the conversation while appearing oblivious.

Davim sat back in the chair and regarded Shale through

narrowed eyelids. "It will all depend then, won't it, on which comes first? A stormshifter's power or a stormlord's death. We are prepared either way. We Reduners have no fear of a Time of Random Rain."

Shale did not understand all that speech, but he did hear the threat lurking behind every word.

Taquar addressed him directly again. "That will be all, Shale. The grille is still open; why don't you go for a walk outside? My friend here and I have much to speak about." With that, he turned his attention to the food.

Shale moved to obey. It was only when he was outside that he started to shake.

Davim and his companion left about the run of a sandglass later.

Taquar called Shale in to tell him that he too was leaving, going back to Scarcleft.

"Who was that man?"

"A sandmaster. He was concerned about the growing extremism among some of the Reduners, so I told him about you. He came for reassurance that there will indeed soon be another stormlord." The untruth was easily said, without inflection.

Shale stilled the tremor in his fingers. Blind rage turned his vision red, and he strove to subdue it. *The salted bastard!* Was there no end to his gall? The withering lies flowed from him like water from a calabash.

Taquar had been allied with the Reduners of Dune Watergatherer all along. Not Nealrith or Kaneth or one of the other rainlords. *Taquar*, rogue rainlord, and the sandmaster who had burned Wash Drybone Settle.

Part of Shale wanted to fall on the highlord and rend him

to pieces with his bare hands. Rip his heart out and hold it in his hands. The image, detailed in his mind, shocked him, and the corrosiveness of the hate that had inspired it made him jerk back from the edge of the precipice that had opened up, black and forbidding, before him.

I'm not like that. I will not be consumed by hate or revenge. And then the afterthought: *Though one day I will have justice.*

Oblivious, Taquar said, "While I am away this time, I want you to concentrate on two exercises for me. The first is changing water to vapour. Remember what I have told you: the secret is to saturate the air with droplets within the cloud at a faster rate than water evaporates at the edge. The amount of droplets that the air will hold depends on temperature, so do not expect it to be constant.

"The other exercise is, of course, simply to continue trying to extract fresh water from a salt solution. Next time I come, I will take you down to the sea to begin to practise on the real thing: clouds."

Absurdly, Shale's heart surged. The sea. He couldn't even *imagine* such a huge body of water.

He quelled the longing he felt. He wasn't going anywhere with the highlord, ever. *Damn you, Taquar. You sent Davim and his men to get me, but my family was just an encumbrance. Blast you to a dry end and a waterless hell.*

He watched the rainlord leave.

One day, Taquar, he promised, *I will have justice for them.*

That night, alone again, Shale did not sleep.

He lay awake shivering. Thinking. Trying to make

sense of all that had happened. One thing he knew for certain: Davim was deceiving Taquar, and Taquar was too arrogant to see it. Shale was sure he had not mistaken the look in Davim's eyes. He had seen it too often on his father's face: a flash of loathing and contempt, warring with a murderous rage. Davim hated both him and Taquar.

Worse, though, was the ache Taquar's betrayal had left behind. The emptiness that swamped him as a result. He felt a sense of loss, but wasn't sure what it was that made him grieve. He had never *liked* Taquar, yet he felt bereft. Perhaps that was what betrayal was: the creation of a hole inside the betrayed. The loss of part of oneself.

You dryhead, he thought.

He could have prevented the massacre of Wash Drybone had he not listened to Taquar in the first place. Why had he not gone to Highlord Nealrith and taken the sensitive's test in front of all the rainlords? Citrine might still be alive and Mica safe if he had.

His stupidity had killed or enslaved his whole settle.

His fault. Because he had feared the wrong people and trusted where he should have feared. *Never again*, he thought. *Never again.*

In the morning, he rose, tired and dulled, and prepared to leave the mother cistern.

He packed a cloth bag with food and his best clothing, a bottle of lamp oil and a lamp, some candles, his flint and striker and tinderbox, a couple of empty water skins and—after a moment's further thought—six books. He scoured the storeroom for anything of value he could convert to tokens, but the only thing he found was the gold bracelet with the carved name. He had forgotten all about it and now he packed it without a qualm, together with his piece of jasper. The last thing he added to his makeshift pack was a length of hempen twine.

He raised the grille, closed it behind him and set off for the maintenance shaft. He walked quickly, scarcely aware of his surroundings, anger driving him forward.

Once there, he climbed up to the top of the shaft and removed the wooden cover. He made no attempt to break the lock; instead, he emptied his belongings out of the cloth bag and threaded the twine through the shoulder strap. The other end of the twine he tied to the grating. Then he pushed the bag through the bars. He had chosen to bring only items that would fit through the grating and could therefore be reinserted into the bag now that it was on the inside of the inspection shaft. Once the bag was full again, he lowered it down and left it hanging there, within easy reach of someone walking along the tunnel below. He went to close the wooden cover, but changed his mind. He left it half open to let in a shaft of light. Then he retraced his steps to the mother cistern.

Perhaps the long walk helped calm him, for he managed to sleep a little that night. The next morning, carrying a lighted candle, a bucket of water and an old cloth, he walked to the overflow outlet. Designed to drain water into the tunnel if the lake ever rose too high, it was covered with a metal mesh filter, easily removed. He peered into the pipe, as he had done several times before on his previous explorations of the lake, but could see nothing. It disappeared into a darkness as deep as a starless patch of night sky.

He set fire to the cloth and dropped it into the outlet. It slid down and dropped out of sight as he watched its progress. For a few moments longer he could see the glow of the flames somewhere below the end of the pipe. Then he poured the bucket of water into the pipe and followed the water with his senses. He had done that before, too, but he wanted to double-check exactly how long the pipe was, that it did not get any narrower, that the water gushed out of the other end without any impediment to its flow. He wanted to confirm that it then plunged only a body length before it hit ground again. His main worry was that his shoulders were nearly as broad as the pipe itself.

He stripped off all his clothing, took a deep breath and entered the pipe feet first. The lower part of his body slipped in easily, but when he tried to wriggle in still further, his upper torso became wedged. He curled his shoulders inwards, crossing his arms in front.

For one terrifying moment he was trapped, then he was plunging down, burning his bare skin against the sides of the pipe. He had a brief sensation of flying unimpeded through total darkness before his feet hit the brickwork at the base of the tunnel. He was free of the pipe, crouching in the blackness, his feet stinging from the impact. There was water underfoot because the inlet from the siphon was somewhere behind him.

He took a deep breath, trying not to think too much. There was no way out now, until he reached Scarcleft, five or six days' walk away. The only light was a pinprick in the far distance. He remained still for a moment, sensing the water: ankle deep, flowing gently in a straight line for as far as his senses would allow him to perceive.

Blighted eyes, he thought, *how many people are there in this city of Scarcleft that they need more than this amount of water all day, every day, flowing into their cisterns?*

He allowed another moment to try to detect any other forms of life anywhere ahead, but there were none. Not even the smallest of sand-leeches, as far as he could tell. He started to walk towards that far-off star of light.

It enlarged as he approached, going from a pinpoint to a shaft falling as a half-moon on the brick floor of the tunnel. His bag hung at the end of the twine, waiting for him. He was glad to dress. Naked and stripped of any material possessions, he had felt not only chilled but vulnerable.

His cold fingers had trouble striking the flint to the tinder, but he finally lit the lamp and placed it on the walkway. Then he hauled himself up the ladder to the top of the shaft. It was a moment's work to reach through the grating and manoeuvre the wooden cover back into place. He was far too much the son of the Gibber to have been comfortable leaving water exposed to the sun and wind-blown sand, or to any small desert creature seeking the dark and a drink.

Down in the tunnel again, he began his long walk to Scarcleft.

Now he could see what he was doing, he used the walkway built along the side. When he was tired or hungry, he stopped. He slept fitfully at intervals, stretched out on the walkway in the smothering dark with the lamp extinguished. When he awoke it was always into panic at the utter blackness, and the panic remained until his fumbling with flint, striker and tinder produced enough of a flame to light the lamp or a candle.

He passed other maintenance shafts, where light filtered in through cracks or knot holes in the wooden covers: tiny slivers of light visible from far, far away if he turned out the lamp and walked in the darkness. He had little idea of the passing of time. Disconnected from the rest of the world, he felt as if he was the only person left alive, destined to walk this straight line in the dark forever.

He'd hoped the tunnel would turn into a slot and he would simply emerge at the end of the journey into the light and the open air. A silly idea, on reflection: all this water was precious and had to be protected, of course. And so, at the end of the tunnel, he was left staring at another grille, trying to see into the darkness beyond.

The light cast by the meagre stub of his sole remaining candle did not show him much. His water senses told him that there were a number of cisterns in the room and that water ran from one to another. A waterhall, he guessed. Those same senses told him that the room was empty of people. The grille had a door, but it was locked. He had come so far only to be stopped by more iron bars; he would have been better off trying to walk to Scarcleft in the desert heat above ground, stealing water from the maintenance shafts as he went.

And now what, anyway? This was Taquar's city, and the rainlord was here somewhere. If a strange youth was found in the tunnel, would Taquar be told?

His heart jerked, his breathing quickened. He would *not* allow himself to be taken again. He slid down to sit on the walkway right where he was, back hunched up against the curving wall. Surely there had to be someone in regular attendance in the waterhall. They couldn't just let water run like that all the time without checking on it, could they? They had to make sure cisterns didn't overflow, perhaps even divert the water into different tunnels from time to time. He had read enough to know a little

about how water distribution worked in Scarpen cities. It
was just a matter of waiting.

He ate some of his food, refilled his water skins,
checked how much oil there was left in the lamp—not
much—and watched while his last candle burned itself
into oblivion and dropped him into suffocating darkness.

CHAPTER TWENTY-SIX

Scarpen Quarter
Scarcleft City

It was several hours before someone opened the entrance to the waterhall and two liveried men entered with torches, which they set in wall brackets. They were followed by a man and a woman, who came in chatting to one another.

". . . so I said to him he ought to report the family. That kind of behaviour borders on misuse of allotments," the woman said as she led the way, heading off to the left. Shale remained where he was, silent and still.

"Will he, do you think, Reeve Dennil?" the man asked.

"I don't know. He's fond of his sister and the fact that she may be a water-waster is not going to make any difference. So I reported her to the enforcers myself. Sandblast it, every single person in the city has to try to cut water consumption still further, or we starve. The farmers are complaining the bab fruit won't be plump next harvest. A tenth of the trees have already died. And it near broke my heart when Highlord Taquar ordered more pedes to be slaughtered. Sorquis, we need this spigot opened till sunset. But close two and seven first."

This last remark was addressed to one of the men carrying a torch. He nodded his acquiescence and bent to fiddle with something at the end of one of the cisterns. "Do you want it opened full turn, Reeve?"

Shale stood up, hoisting his bag onto his shoulder. "Excuse me," he said loudly, "but could you let me out of here?"

All four people turned in his direction, spigots and conversation forgotten.

"Watergiver above! There's someone in the tunnel!" exclaimed a servant, seizing a torch from the wall and approaching the grille.

The reeve followed and peered at Shale by the light of the flames. "I'll get the key," she said finally.

"Shouldn't we call the highlord first?" the man asked, his voice hostile. "He can only be a water thief, surely."

"I think you had better let me out first," Shale said hurriedly, submerging his fear under a plaintive whine made all the more convincing by its truth. "I don't want to foul the water and I need to—you know . . ."

"He's only a lad. I'll be back in a moment," the reeve said.

The man stared at Shale. His expression danced in the flame light, but there was no mistaking the suspicion in his tone. "How did you get into the tunnel? Have you been stealing water? Did you break into one of the inspection shafts? Where did you come from? What's your name?"

Of all these questions, Shale decided to answer the last, and that with a lie. "My name's Chert," he said.

"Well, Chert, you little rat, you have a great deal of explaining to do. No one is allowed into *any* tunnel without a rainlord or a reeve at their side." Outrage seeped through the words. "How long have you been in there? You've been contaminating our water, haven't you?"

Shale hung his head. "I did my best not to," he mumbled. "I, um, used the walkway."

The man gave a grunt of disgust and continued to fire questions, which Shale did not answer.

It was several moments before the reeve returned with the key and opened the half-door in the grille. Shale had to stoop to walk through. As he straightened up, both the servants—at a sign from the reeve—went to grab his arms. Shale deliberately stumbled. At the same time he pushed at the water in the nearest cistern. A wave splashed over the edge onto the floor.

"What the—" The woman's face was a picture first of incomprehension and then horror at the wastage. "How the salted damn did *that* happen?"

Distracted, both servants turned away from Shale, and in that moment of inattention, he was up and running. He raced between the cisterns, heading for the closest exit. It led into another room, empty of people, with several doors, all closed. He wrenched at the handle of the nearest as the two servants pounded through the doorway behind him. Their hands brushed the back of his tunic sleeve as he plunged into the sunlight.

Blinded by the sudden brightness, he sped on. He squinted, eyes watering. A low parapet loomed in front of him. He sailed over it without hesitation. And fell, his heart lurching at the unexpected depth of the drop on the other side. His feet hit a flat surface hard, jarring his spine and driving his breath out. Fortunately, his followers thought better of making the jump, and when he was

able to look up, it was to see them turning away from the
parapet above to find another route down.

Gasping, he spared a moment to look around. He was
on a flat area studded with fruit trees in pots. He dived
into them, skidding between the plants as shouts of alarm
rose on all sides. Glimpsing guards in uniform off to his
left, he veered right. Then footsteps pounded behind. He
dashed headlong through the greenery until his way was
blocked by another parapet. He scrambled over this one,
hung from fingers over another drop, then fell again. This
time he landed on the bab webbing of an outdoor bed.
Unable to keep his footing, he tumbled to his knees and
bumped his chin on the bed frame. Swearing, he picked
himself up and raced towards another low wall. This time
the fall wasn't so soft. He plunged straight into a kumquat
tree in a pot, shattering both plant and container. Pain shot
up one of his legs. For a moment, he lay on the spilled
earth and pot shards, staring up at the blueness of the sky,
too stunned to move, his chin aching, pain in his calf stabbing at him. He rolled over to look. His trousers were torn
and his leg was bleeding, pierced by part of a branch. He
pulled out a long splinter of wood, then wasted a moment
clutching his leg above the knee, rocking to and fro until
the pain subsided.

Only when he stood and grabbed his bag once more
did he realise there was a body of living water nearby. He
whirled to see a girl staring at him. She had been using
a flat paddle to bang at a rug hung over a railing and the
dust still drifted in the air, a puff of brown in the blinding
sunlight. He stared back, shocked, trying to make sense
of everything.

In a rush of understanding, he realised what he had

done. He had not exited the waterhall building through its main entrance. He had gone out onto a balcony and had jumped onto a roof the next level down. He was not in a street at all but on the stepped rooftops of Scarcleft.

He remembered the woodcuts he had seen of the city, and with a sick feeling knew he must have crossed the roof of Scarcleft Hall, where Taquar lived. No wonder there had suddenly been so many people after him; they were guards. Taquar's guards. He looked back to where he had jumped from: there was no one there. Yet. But he could hear shouts from above; they weren't giving up the chase.

His head was throbbing with his sense of water. For an instant he floundered, struggling with the assault. Water was everywhere, in every direction he cared to turn. In jars, in people, in cisterns, running everywhere in lines beneath him, around him, all of it jostling for his attention. So much water, so many people, so much noise, so many new smells. He was under attack. He took a deep breath, pushed away the invasion of his senses and tried to concentrate on his immediate surroundings.

The girl did not move or speak, so he ignored her and began to run again. This time he looked before he jumped. The villa below had a stack of empty oil jars conveniently placed against the wall and he clambered down using those as a ladder. This house was two-storeyed, so it was easy. He took steps leading down to the next level two at a time, ignoring the throbbing of his wound. Blood stained his trousers, but the amount was not enough to alarm him.

The shouting behind intensified and spread out. He could hear the excited gabble of the girl adding to the din. This time, instead of running directly to the roof edge in front of him, he peered over the edge to his right. He looked down into a narrow street. There were houses opposite, their outer doors studded and coloured. And people. People walking, talking. And several people running, beating on doorways. He could hear the words they yelled: "'Ware, water thief! Up on your roof! Stop him in the name of the high reeve!"

Think, Shale.

His best chance lay not in a continued downwards descent. He had to lose his pursuers in the maze of housing by doing the unexpected—and they wouldn't expect him to be on the other side of the street. He measured the distance with his eyes. Too far to make it across in a standing leap; he needed a run-up. He considered the mud-brick parapet that bordered the roof he was standing on. It was broad and flat on top: a pathway pointing directly to the house opposite.

He hurled his bag across the gap first, so that it landed on the flat rooftop across the lane, then hoisted himself up onto the parapet. He gave himself a long run-up, ignoring the narrowness of his chosen path and the steep drop on one side, then dashed along the top of the wall, arms pumping, legs sprinting. At the corner, he took off, flailing, his terror transforming time into a strangely lengthened interlude of silence and grace as he arced across space. The impression of slow motion ceased in a rush as his left foot landed on the parapet of the flat roof he was aiming for. He strove for balance—and lost. He grabbed for the parapet as he fell, and managed to hook his fingers over the top. His body slammed hard against the outside of the house, knocking the breath from him.

He hung there, above the street, partially winded, terror welding his fingers to the parapet. Dragging in air, he scrabbled with his feet for purchase, and found it: the top of a window frame. Inch by torturous inch, he moved his hands until he had a better hold. Then, pushing off with his feet, he managed to swing first one leg, then the other, up to straddle the parapet. From there he tumbled down onto the roof.

He was panting, bruised and bleeding. He lay flat on his back for a moment to recover, then stood and risked a peep down into the street. To his relief, no one was looking up. No one had seen his jump, or its near-disastrous consequences.

Hurriedly, he picked up his bag and limped across the roof to the opposite side, where potted fruit trees grew thickly. He glanced around, but there was no one to be seen. He took the opportunity to relieve himself into a potted fruit tree and catch his breath.

The roof of the house next door adjoined, so he crossed this as well, until he was looking down into a different street. This was more of a thoroughfare, thronged with people. He waited awhile, hoping for a period when there was no one around, but it never happened. As he waited, he managed to push his overwhelming awareness of water into the background, but he had trouble grappling with the size of everything. The houses, the city stepping down in stages below him, the crowd in the street, the volume of noise: packpedes clattering by, creaking handcarts, people chatting and laughing, the chanting of children reciting lessons somewhere.

He peeked down into the roadway again. If he waited too long, he might be found by another servant, so he decided to seek the anonymity of the crowd below, even if there was a risk he would be seen descending. He lowered himself over the side of the house to the top of an architrave above the entrance. From there it wasn't too hard to clamber down using the decorative studs of milky quartz embedded in the double doors. He ignored the stares he was given from passers-by. As soon as he reached the street, he straightened his clothing and walked away. No one moved to stop him.

He soon discovered that his troubles were not over. People looked at him oddly as he passed. His leg had stopped bleeding, but the torn trousers and the blood attracted attention. Even his colouring was out of place: the people around him were more fair-skinned than he was, with hair that glinted gold in the sun.

He managed to descend several more levels before he was stopped. A uniformed man approached him to ask who he was and what he was doing there on Level Six. The man evidently knew nothing of the commotion Shale had caused on the roof, but still Shale panicked and ran, dodging through the crowd. He pelted on down through another two levels before he slowed to a walk once more, panting.

All he knew of the hierarchy of Scarcleft levels was that the highest were the most prosperous, but he didn't need that kind of knowledge to know he was out of place. The house gates were too lavish with their decorative stone inlays, the people in the streets were too well dressed, and he received too many odd glances for him to feel that he blended in. There were servants and delivery boys going about their business, but he didn't look like them, either, not with a bloodied leg. The best he managed to do was find a quiet corner near a brass market where he was able to put a makeshift bandage on his leg using a spare undershirt from his bag. After that he did not attract quite as much attention.

He continued to wend his way downwards, hoping to get to an area that felt more familiar to someone brought up in the poverty of the Gibber. Out in the palm groves, perhaps. He'd read something once about cities having fringe dwellers and the waterless.

It was nightfall by the time he reached the thirty-sixth level. It didn't take long for him to recognise it for exactly what it was: home for people similar to those who lived in the hovels outside Wash Drybone Settle. On a large scale of course, but the same for all that. He saw replicas of the house he had lived in, doubles of Marisal the stitcher, of Galen the sot. He glimpsed people who could have been family to Demel the widow and Ore the stonebreaker. Grubby thin children with hungry eyes not unlike the child he had once been.

He didn't know whether to be relieved that Taquar's harsh rule had not rid the world of the obviously waterless, or distressed that right here in a rainlord's city were people as poor as his own family had been. He recognised the smell of poverty and hopelessness, of the dirt and the decay that wallowed in its wake. It had been there in Wash Drybone Settle. Here it was just bigger, dirtier, more violent.

I am not the only one Taquar has failed, he thought, depressed.

He looked around for somewhere to rest.

*   *   *

He slept that night behind a heap of discarded bab husks, his bag serving as a pillow.

In the morning, he sold one of the books for five tokens. He had no idea of its real value, but he had learned enough from the bargaining of Reduner caravanners to be aware that the Scarperman who bought it was probably robbing him blind.

He used part of one of the tokens to buy hot food served on a yam leaf, and he squatted right there in front of the stall to eat. The woman selling the food was a motherly soul and, on finding out during a lull in her trade that Shale was new to Scarcleft, indeed to the Scarpen, she took it upon herself to give him advice on where to live and how to take care of himself. Her name, she said, was Illara. She suffered from what they called desert peel back in Wash Drybone Settle. She had no eyelashes and no eyebrows, and her skin flaked. Rendered pede fat was needed to cure that, but he doubted she had the money to buy any.

"Don't you trust nobody," she said. "Nobody. Not me, neither. In this place, a man or a woman or a child will sell his granny for water, and don't you never forget it."

From her, he found out that for just three tinnies a night, you could rent a place to sleep on a rooftop, along with a palliasse stuffed with bab husks, and have your safety guaranteed by the owner's bodyguards. He found out there were labouring jobs to be had in the bab groves or at the city's pede stables; or at the pede market, shovelling manure; or at the metal smelters or the knackery—all of which were situated just outside the city gates. He learned where to buy the cheapest food, where to leave his bag (for a price) so that it would be safe until he came to collect it, where to sell stolen goods. She warned him which people never to deal with, which employers never to work for, and which places and street women to avoid. She told him how to identify authorities: the reeves, and—worse, or so she said—the enforcers in blue with the sand swirls on their chests.

"You break a law here on Level Thirty-six, no one cares, unless it concerns city water. You can steal or cheat or kill, and no one will come after you. But if you break a law on another level, or if you steal the water that belongs to the city or the groves or an upleveller—then you had better find a good place to hide because sooner or later someone will come after you. And there's never no mercy for outlanders." She looked at him critically. "That's a bit of a disadvantage to start with."

"What is?" he asked.

"You look like a Gibberman. Lately the reeves have been throwing waterless Gibber folk out of the city gates and not letting 'em back in again, 'specially the ones that look real poor or dirty or diseased." She rubbed at the flaking skin on her face. "They're dying out there. The Highlord of Scarcleft wants to save water for those Scarpermen entitled to water allotments. Us waterless count for even less than usual now that water is short. And Gibber waterless are as hated as 'Baster waterless. So you'd better watch yourself. You go outside to work, you make sure the employer gives you an employment chit. That will entitle you to sleep in the city for a night. You got a job, they need you. They don't need you, you're dead. Get it?"

Shale nodded, wondering if life was playing a joke on him. Was his imprisonment going to be the high point of comfort in what promised to be a short existence? Had he been sandcrazy to run away? Taquar would never have *hurt* him, after all, just used him.

And then he thought of Mica.

And Citrine.

His heart hardened. *I don't know what to do*, he thought, *but I do know what I* don't *want to do. I don't want to work for the Highlord of Scarcleft. Ever.*

He left the city that morning and found work shovelling sand out of a dry slot in the palm groves. Hard, aching work under a hot sun. Payment for the whole day's labour was half a token plus a day's water ration, drawn from the employer's cistern. At the end of the day, he was sore all over from the unaccustomed labour. And he had seen for himself what happened to Scarcleft water thieves.

Zigger-wielding officials on their way into the desert had led a couple past, their arms ending at the wrist, the fresh cuts dipped into heated resin to stop the bleeding. They stumbled by, moaning, tied by a length of hemp to the pedes the officials rode. Shale doubted they would be alive even at sunset, let alone find a way to survive till they reached another city. This wasn't punishment; it was brutal execution.

He rested awhile under the palm trees once he was paid—eyed suspiciously by the palm-grove guards before he started to walk back towards the city through the grove. He had lingered deliberately because he wanted to be on his own. He'd heard about an irrigation slot that would be flooded at sunset, and he wanted to steal enough water to refill his water skin. Being waterless all his life had left him without guilt when it came to stealing a drink. Still, it was hard not to think of the fate of the two thieves.

It was easier for him not to get caught, of course. All

he had to do was walk along the irrigation slots with his container uncorked, then move water out of the flow, a few unnoticed drops at a time, until the skin bulged.

Taquar did at least teach me something useful, he thought as he ambled back in the twilight, filching water as he went.

When a mounted rider approached him from behind, he took extra care to hide what he was doing, apparently in vain, because as the pede drew level, a perplexed voice addressed him, "Well, young man, just what might ye be up to?"

He jumped and nearly dropped the skin. He turned to see a 'Baster mounted on a white myriapede, leading a packpede, also white, behind him.

CHAPTER TWENTY-SEVEN

Scarpen Quarter
Scarcleft City
Level 36 and the bab groves

The 'Baster, obviously a trader, was alone. The white
packpede was piled high with roped cargo, still dusty
from desert travel. Although the goods were covered with
woven matting, their shape suggested blocks of rock salt.
Like all 'Basters, the man was pale, as pale as a mother's
milk, with eyes as light as star-shine. He wore white robes
and a loose twist of white cloth encased his head; both
were sewn with tiny mirrors that reflected the red light of
the setting sun in sparkles as he rode. The red thread that
held the mirrors in place could have been crazed runnels
of blood on the white cloth.

The man smiled as he drew his hack up opposite Shale.
"Let me offer ye a ride back into the city," he said.

Shale, surprised, found himself stuttering.

"But perhaps ye had better cork your skin first."

In a mixture of embarrassment and fear, Shale fumbled
to close his water skin.

The 'Baster reached out a hand to pull him up onto the

saddle behind and because he didn't know how to refuse, Shale took it and climbed up.

"What's your name?" the man asked. He spoke with the lilting accent of the White Quarter, chopping his vowels short and almost singing the words.

"Jasper, pedeman," Shale said, changing his name yet again.

"And would Jasper like to be telling me why a water sensitive of considerable skill finds it necessary to be stealing water from a slot?"

"I—" But Shale's inventiveness failed there, and he didn't know what to say.

"I would have thought that the Scarpen Quarter, in need of all the water sensitives it could get, would pay them well enough that they didn't have to steal." The words might have carried an element of accusation, but the tone was mild, even friendly.

Shale, not trusting, stayed silent.

"Don't worry, young Jasper," the man said softly, "I'll not tell the reeves. Are ye waterless?"

Shale nodded. "Who—who are you, pedeman?"

"Feroze Khorash, salt merchant of Alabaster."

"Alabaster?"

"Yes, the place ye call the White Quarter. But we are a quarter of nothing. We are our own entirety."

"Oh, you mean you're a 'Baster." He wasn't sure he understood the rest.

"That is not a word we appreciate. We are Alabasters."

"Forgive me, pedeman. Um, merch. I did not mean to be rude." That was true. He'd no idea that inhabitants of the White Quarter regarded the term 'Baster as derogatory.

As they reached the city gates, Shale prepared to slip down from the mount, but Feroze stopped him with a hand on the knee. "I am going to Level Twenty-seven, where there is a salt trading house. I shall pay ye a token to be helping me unload the salt. Easier work than whatever it was ye were doing in the grove, I'll wager ye."

Shale weighed the idea carefully. He felt vulnerable leaving the lowest level for a higher one, but a token was a token. "All right," he said.

They were stopped by the gate guards, as expected. Shale produced the employer's chit from the grove owner while Feroze was asked to pay an import tax on the salt. "And you are only permitted to stay three nights in the city now, 'Baster," one of the gatekeepers told the merchant. "New rule for all outlander traders. And you must leave by this gate." Feroze made the required payment and they were waved on into the city.

It was obvious that Feroze had been to Scarcleft before. He guided the pedes straight up to the twenty-seventh level and then on to the salt merchant's yard through a maze of streets and alleys. On several of the lower levels, men spat at the feet of the pede as they passed. On the thirtieth level, some boys pelted them with discarded bab husks and called them bastard 'Basters and dirty foreign water-wasters. Feroze ignored them all.

At the salt yard gate, he pulled the bell and waited patiently until the summons was answered. The gatekeeper greeted him by name, the salt trader was sent for, and Feroze and Shale dismounted to lead the pedes into the yard. The trader arrived, profuse in his greetings as he offered the ritual drink of water to an arriving traveller. Then, when the formalities were over, a specimen block of salt was unloaded and examined, and the bargaining began. Shale stood to one side, holding the pede reins, listening and watching and taking the opportunity to study Feroze.

He was tall and thin, and to Shale's eyes ugly. The pale skin was sickly; the bloodless lips unattractive and the faded eyes lifeless. In fact, his general lack of hue suggested coldness or an absence of passion, and reminded Shale of something dead. It was hard to guess his age, but he was no longer a young man.

"They say they have water in their veins," a voice murmured in his ear. He turned to see one of the salt merchant's lads standing behind him. "'Stead of blood, and that's why they're that funny colour. That right, you reckon?"

"I don't know," he said, and then added carefully, "I don't think it matters much. He is a man, no matter the colour of his blood." Inside, he wondered if it was true.

The youth looked at him scornfully. "Yeah, I s'pose you would say that. You're a dirty desert-grubbin' Gibberman, after all. You might think you're as good as us, but you're not. No Gibber sand-grubber nor 'Baster is as good as the lick of a tongue of a Scarperman!"

"No? Well, I can't say I think much of either your manners or your brains," Shale returned. "At least I know how to be polite, and I have enough brains to know it's not sensible to insult the people your master does business with."

The youth opened his mouth to retort, and Shale raised his eyebrows, which was enough to make the fellow think twice about saying anything more. He swaggered off.

The negotiations came to an end, the two men shook hands on the deal, and Feroze came back to Shale. "Time to be unloading," he said. "I'll see ye afterwards."

He went off with the salt trader to be paid, and Shale turned back to the pede. To his surprise, the beast was now surrounded by the salt trader's workers, who had the ropes untied and the big blocks of wrapped salt unloaded in just a few moments. It dawned on Shale that Feroze must have known that the salt trader's men would unload the cargo; why, then, had he asked for help? He thought about that and began to feel uncomfortable. He wondered if it was wise to wait for his token, especially when he had done nothing yet to earn it.

He had just made up his mind to leave when Feroze emerged from the merchant's office. He was smiling, but Shale wondered if there was not something grim about the expression. The good humour seemed forced.

The merchant was saying, "That's what I've heard, merch. Beware. Scarcleft is no longer a place safe for you or your kind." It was not a threat he uttered, but a warning, reinforced by his worried tone.

Feroze nodded and took the pede reins from Shale. "Let's go, Jasper."

"I have to get back to Level Thirty-six," Shale said as they left the yard, still leading the pedes. "That's where I live. And I was not needed to unload the salt—the trader's men did that. All I did was coil and repack your rope."

"Oh? Never mind, ye shall have your token anyway. I have taken your time needlessly. Would ye share my evening meal?" The look he gave Shale was kindly and his eyes were gentle, but Shale's discomfort increased.

"I think I should go, merch. I have to find a bed for the night." And then, abruptly aware of what he had just said, he flushed.

Feroze stared at him for a long moment, assessing. "Ah.

Jasper," he said at last, "I think you have mistaken my intentions. True, I like my pallet partners young and virile, much as you are. But I also like them to be hankering after a man such as myself, which I suspect ye do not. And so I am prepared to confine myself to an interest in your water abilities rather than your body, as attractive as it is."

Shale's flush deepened.

Feroze dug into his purse and extracted a token. "Here is the token I promised. And now I want ye to listen carefully to what I have to say." He took Shale by the arm and pulled him to the side of the street, leaving the pedes to stand alone. "I saw what ye did at the slot because I am water sensitive, rather like one of your reeves. I know ye have great talent, and such talent is needed in the Quartern, gentle God knows. Ye must not squander it living a feral life on Level Thirty-six. Do ye hear me, Jasper?"

Shale nodded.

"And do ye *understand* what I am saying?"

Shale nodded again, and he did understand. His inner voice told him, had been telling him ever since he had arrived in Scarcleft, exactly what Feroze meant: *You are a stormlord. You could possibly help bring water to a whole land. You have no right to hide your talent out of fear.*

"I don't know what to do," he whispered. He felt momentarily helpless, a grain of sand caught up in the spindevil wind.

"And ye don't trust me, either?"

Shale did not answer.

Feroze sighed. "That would be too much to expect, I suppose. Very well, listen to some advice first: do not go to Highlord Taquar. He is a harsh man. If ye want, I will take ye to Breccia. To the Cloudmaster himself, Granthon."

Shale still did not answer, but hope flared—then wavered. Could this man help him? Or was it a trap? He vacillated, sick with raw anxiety, desperate for help yet unable to snatch at it. He had trusted once, and learned to regret it.

Feroze continued, "I shall stay in Scarcleft for the three nights allowed me. At dawn on the following day, I shall leave for Breccia City. If ye need my help to be leaving this place, meet me at the gateway we used today, with your belongings, just as the sun rises. I will take ye with me. No charge."

Suspicion overwhelmed the hope. "Why would you do that?"

Feroze released his hold on Shale's arm. "We need water, Jasper. We *all* need water. The Cloudmaster, Granthon, has recently stopped most storms to the Gibber and Alabaster, because he has not the strength needed. When cisterns run dry, there will be no more water for your people and mine. Anyone who can pull water out of a slot with his powers is needed by us all."

"Are you—are you exactly what you say you are?" The question was naive. Silly, even. What kind of answer was he expecting to that? He felt foolish, childish.

"Am I a salt trader?" Feroze considered his answer carefully. "I do sell salt, but I am more than just a trader. I seek information. I am also an emissary for my people. I go from here to Breccia to be pleading our cause."

They looked at each other, man and youth. Had the face that stared back at Shale been that of a Scarperman or a Gibberman, he might have trusted. But it wasn't. It was the face of a man so white he would have blended in with the salt he had just sold. A man whose eyes and skin and hair were so pale they could have foreshadowed death itself.

"I'll think about it," Shale mumbled and walked away. Part of him still felt shamed; the Alabaster had given him no cause to distrust him.

He did think about it.

The next day, he found more work in the groves; the day after that, he helped out in the pede knacker's yard, outside the city walls. He hated the work; stripping pede carcasses reminded him too much of the day the unexpected rush had come down Wash Drybone. The day Citrine was born.

Still, he was earning tokens. He was *free*. He looked at the calluses he was developing on his hands and was proud of them.

At night he paid for a bed on the rooftop doss house that desert-peeled Illara had told him about; during the day, he paid for his belongings to be kept safe at a storage house. Because he stole his water—a few drops at a time from many different sources—he had enough money to eat well without selling any more of the books. And all the while, he listened and thought about what he should do.

By the end of the third day, he knew he had to leave Scarcleft. All the talk on the level indicated that soon there was not going to be a place for a waterless Gibberman anywhere. People were targeting outlanders as the source of their problems, and Shale was an outlander. When a further increase in the price of water was rumoured, there was no mistaking the resentful looks some people sent his way. The baseless hate in people's eyes as they found someone to blame was intimidating.

And so, on the morning Feroze was due to depart, Shale waited at the gate for him.

He waited till mid-morning, but there was no sign of the Alabaster with the white pedes.

Angry, he left the gateway, and went to find work, knowing he had wasted half a day. As it was already too late to hope for anything in the groves, he returned to the knacker's yard. He was welcomed; the knacker had just taken delivery of two dead pedes. The butcher had already taken the meat he wanted, but there was still flesh to be scraped out.

Shale looked at the two huge corpses. A myriapede and a packpede. Both all white. They had been bludgeoned, battered until their carapaces were cracked and broken. "They were attacked," he said, dumbfounded. "I mean, it's like they were . . . *murdered*."

"Yeah, well, they were white, so who cares? You want the job or not?"

He nodded, stricken. "Who owned them?" he asked.

"Don't know. Don't care. Must have been a 'Baster, though. They are the only ones who use white animals. And there's all that red embroidery on the carapace."

And Feroze had not turned up at the gate.

Shale laid a hand on the shuttered eyes of one of the beasts, and the anger he'd felt towards the Alabaster melted into grief.

He spent what was left of the day at the knacker's, toiling over the remains of the pedes. By sunset, most of the segments had been scraped clean. "Tomorrow there'll be more work for you if you want it," the knacker said as he paid him that evening. "Got to get the meat out of the feet and send it off to the fish growers. Day after that, you can help unpick all that blasted stitchery and lay out all the segment pieces for the ants to clean."

"All right," Shale said and felt like a traitor. They had to have been Feroze's animals. As he slipped the token the knacker had just given him into his purse, a packpede flowed past. An enforcer directed the beast, and another rode the end segment. In between sat a line of roped men, shoulders hunched in hopeless defeat.

"Outlander waterless," the knacker said, seeing Shale's interest. "You want to make damned sure you get work every day, grubber, or you'll end up like them, too. Thrown out onto the Sweepings half a night's ride distant, without any water and forbidden to return. Not much chance any of 'em will make it through tomorrow."

"That's horrible," he protested, looking at the men as they passed.

"Hmph! People are asking why Scarcleft babies should be killed instead of the outlanders. You and I know the answer to that one: Scarcleft babies don't do the dirty work—but try telling that to someone whose wife's told she's got to scrape their babe out 'fore it's born."

Shale was about to turn away, sickened, when he saw that the first prisoner, the one riding behind the driver, had turned his head to stare at the remains of the pedes. His robe had been stripped from him and he wore only a loin cloth. Even in the dimming light of dusk, Shale recognised him. The face may have been battered and bloody, and the white skin of his body may have been covered with abrasions and purple bruises, but it was unmistakably Feroze.

The Alabaster turned his face away as the pede moved on, gathering speed.

The knacker turned to pay the next worker. Shale waited until neither of the men was looking his way, then picked up a flensing knife and slipped it inside his tunic before strolling away into the palm trees. Out of sight of the knackery, he raced after the pede. He had not the slightest idea what he was going to do. He just knew that this man had tried to help him, and he had to do *something* or Feroze was going to die.

Just before they reached the last of the bab palms, he became aware of the run of water starting down the irrigation slot. They were watering the grove, or part of it. With a half-formed thought of stopping the pede, he reached out and seized the water, lifted it from the channel and skeined it through the air above. There was a scream of anguish from several of the grove owners as they realised their allotment was being stolen.

"Thieves! Water thieves!" someone yelled.

Others began shouting, but no one knew what to do. The enforcer on the packpede drew rein. He looked back over his shoulder to see what was happening. A grove worker ran up to him waving his hands in distress. "Enforcer—some bastard's stealing our allotment!"

The man swore and slid from the pede, shouting to his companion at the rear to join him. As he tied the reins to the nearest palm tree, Shale wheeled the water past the pede and then away through the trees. The two enforcers ran after it, shouting contradictory advice to each other. The pede stayed where it was, and so did the men on its back. There was little they could do, as each prisoner had his wrists tied tightly to the mounting ring bolted to each segment. One, however, immediately started to work at the knots with his teeth.

Shale might not have had a coherent plan to start with, but he could not have asked for a better chance. He climbed onto the back of the packpede and worked his way along, slashing the twine that tied each of the prisoners. "Run!" he told them. "Try to get back into the city!"

They were quick to obey. Around them there was no one to notice. Shale still controlled the water, twirling and flicking it through the grove at a distance, and the enforcers and the grove workers were keeping it in sight, trying to discover who was manipulating it. Fortunately, it didn't occur to any of them that the culprit did not have to be in close proximity to the water.

Shale freed the last of the Gibbermen and reached Feroze. "You will have to take this beast and flee," he said as he slashed the cords binding the man. He thrust his water skin into the saddlebag. "Take this," he said, "it's full. You may make it to Breccia, if you are lucky."

"Come with me," Feroze mumbled through his swollen mouth. "We'll both go."

Shale hesitated. The temptation was almost overwhelming. Then he shook his head. "Two of us would never make it. There's only one water skin. I'm not sure whether I could steal water from a long distance away; I've never tried. Maybe you can tell the Cloudmaster about me, though." He dug out his purse. "Take this as well. You might need tokens when you get there. There's not much." He shoved it into the saddlebag.

Feroze grabbed his arm as he was about to drop to the ground. "Thank ye," he said simply. "I'll not forget. In Alabaster, we say that a cloth given is returned embroidered. Remember that, and remember my name. Feroze Khorash."

Shale nodded. "Good luck." He slid down from the pede and ran back towards the knacker's yard. He needed to return the flensing knife before it was missed, and then he wanted to manipulate the water further away through the grove, to give Feroze more time to escape.

He didn't look back. The rest was up to the Alabaster now.

He returned to the city without trouble some time later, wryly reflecting that he was back where he had started. He had just given Feroze all his water tokens. He would have to sell another book to pay for food and lodging for the night and to buy a new water skin. Fortunately, he was now more experienced and he knew someone who would offer him a better price for a book.

Later that night, with tokens rattling in a second-hand purse, he made inquiries about how to get to Breccia and found out that it was going to cost forty tokens to join a passenger caravan of pedes. He could save a little every day because he stole his water, but forty tokens was impossibly remote.

The next day, after putting in a full day at the knacker's, he investigated the possibility of working as a pedehand on one of the caravans leaving Scarcleft, only to find too many others had the same idea. Day by day, the city was becoming more and more dangerous for a waterless outlander, and they were all trying to leave. There was no place for Shale.

He thought of selling the gold bracelet or the jasper to raise enough tokens to buy a passenger seat, but when he went to Illara for advice, she told him to lie low. "The enforcers are cleaning out this cesspit," she warned. "People who deal in stolen property are vanishing, Jasper. Wait a while."

"They're not stolen," he protested, bending the truth a little.

She snorted. "It doesn't matter how you got them. What matters is what folk will believe."

She was probably right at that. And then he realised— although the bracelet was still safely tucked away among the things he had paid to store—the bloodstone jasper had been at the bottom of his purse. The same purse he had given to Feroze.

He cursed himself.

It had been his last link to Citrine, and now it was gone.

He tried not to be unrealistic in his hopes. Feroze might die. The man had not even had a robe or a hat as protection against the sun. If he did manage to reach Breccia and talk to the Cloudmaster, he might not be believed. Taquar was one of *them*, a ruler, a high rainlord, a friend perhaps.

As the days passed and there was no sign of anyone coming to look for him, his hopes faded.

Then, fifteen days later, he was in trouble again. He was looking for work one morning when he came face-to-face with a group of uniformed enforcers accompanied by someone he guessed to be a reeve. He looked away and went to walk on by, but the reeve stopped him with a curt, "Wait, you." He unrolled a parchment he carried, looked at it, looked up at Shale and said, "This is the one. Arrest him."

Shale didn't wait to hear anything more; he took to his heels. He was young and his quick reactions gave him a head start. He made straight for the twisted alleyways around the market area. He pelted up the street, skidded around the first corner to his right and hurdled a pile of refuse in the middle of the lane.

The reeve's men followed, and one of them—a young man of about his own age—could run like wind whistling up the wash. A quick glance behind told Shale that he was in trouble: the man was gaining. It was only a matter of time. He raced on, shoving people out of the way.

At the next corner, instead of dashing on down the street, he swung hard to the left, vaulted a wall and crashed across the tops of some sandgrouse cages stored in the yard beyond. By the time his pursuer had realised where he'd gone, Shale was already climbing the wall on the other side. He jumped down, knowing he had only a few seconds to disappear unseen. A frantic glance around told him he was in another street, and luck was with him. There was a waterseller's cart laden with supply jars and a number of people milled around helping themselves to the water. It looked as if they were stealing it. Which didn't make sense, but he had no time to think about it. He raced up a set of stairs on his right, hoping that they would lead to some kind of hiding place.

At the top, he swung into a hallway and tripped over something on the floor before he noticed it was there. He took another few steps and then stopped, realising that there was only a blank wall ahead of him. On his right there were archways that overlooked the street, on his left a number of closed doors. There was only one person in the hallway, a girl—young woman?—of about his own age. She was standing looking at him with an odd expression on her face that he couldn't read.

"Can you hide me?" he asked. "Please?"

She stared at him, wordless.

"I'm desperate. *Please.*" In his urgency, he couldn't think of the right words to say to persuade her.

She opened her mouth to speak but was then distracted by something behind him. He whirled to see what it was and glimpsed a man crawling across the tiles of the sloping roof of the building opposite. The fellow looked as scared as Shale felt.

He looked back at the girl. Already he could hear sounds of running feet below, people shouting. He could feel the water of his pursuers. Someone would soon think to come up the stairs. He glanced at the closed doors to the side. Useless to try hiding behind one of those if the girl was only going to give him away.

"Please," he whispered. "Otherwise I could be a prisoner for the rest of my life."

CHAPTER TWENTY-EIGHT

Scarpen Quarter
Scarcleft City
Level 36

Earlier that morning, Russet had told Terelle he wanted her to do a painting for him. "Out in the hallway," he said, "where the light be better."

"A picture of what?" she asked.

"Oh, anything ye can see. Cover the water with layer of motley first, then picture on top." He shoved a pot into her hand. The paint powder it contained was a bruised purple colour.

"Motley?"

"Special mix. All colours in one."

He nodded and flapped his hands at her in a gesture of dismissal. She knew better than to ask questions; they were never answered.

She set up the materials in the hallway and got to work. As she covered the water with the powder, she tried to remember why this reminded her of something. She sighed, reflecting on how little concerning Russet made sense to her. And she hated the way his eyes followed her about as she painted or ate or cleaned the house. The gaze was not prurient or even speculative; he just watched her as if he wanted to know everything about her. He *studied* her, as a pede auctioneer might study the animals he was about to sell or a palmier would study the trees in his grove to make sure they thrived.

"He's not as bad as Huckman," she told herself, not for the first time. The trouble was, she was no longer sure that was true.

She painted the view from where she sat: a puzzle of interlocking rooftops, patterns in light and shadow, thatched fronds and clay pantiles, uneven daub walls with holes for windows. She worked steadily for the rest of the morning, striving for a combination of reality and suggestion, trying to convey the heat, and the aura of poverty and dilapidation and of timelessness.

Neighbours came and looked, spoke a few words, and moved on. When she was painting she tended to be vague in her replies, and most of them had become accustomed to that. Only when she was cleaning the paint spoons in sand did she realise that Russet now sat on his coloured mat peering over her shoulder watching her work.

She jumped and laughed nervously. "I didn't know you were there," she said.

His sharp green eyes, small now with age, examined her picture. "Interesting perspective," he said. "I be doubting anyone will ever want to buy a picture of rooftops."

She shrugged. "I did it for myself. You did say to paint anything."

He gave an odd smile that didn't make any sense to her. "Ah, I did, yes? Serves me right." He glanced around, as if to make sure they were not overheard. "I be taking your lessons one step further. Show ye how to move the paint."

"What paint?"

"The motley. To make painting . . . different. To add an element. Or elements."

"I don't understand." But her heart thudded uncomfortably. She realised now. Motley—that was how he had started the first painting she had ever seen him do, the one that had changed. She had thought the colour was indigo.

"Watch. Watch very carefully." He picked up a paint spoon and dropped some sienna brown on the ridge of one of the roofs. Using the paint skewer, he swirled it gently to define the shape he wanted, then added a touch of umber, some ochre, a spot of yellow. A few more deft strokes and she could see the shape of a large bird perched on the ridge of the roof. When he put down the spoon and skewer, however, the painting was still unfinished, with the details of the plumage, head and beak left vague. He sat and gazed at the picture, his hands loosely clasped in his lap.

She thought she identified the moment when something changed, when the merest of shivers rippled the water beneath the paint and the surface moved. There was a shifting of colour, a blurring around the bird, a darkening of the reddish tiles. She tried to isolate the detail and yet watch the whole too. Even so, she almost missed the precise moment when the blurriness sharpened and the indefinite impression of a bird became something else: a scavenger hawk, every line sharply defined. It coalesced out of the splash of browns, becoming a real portrait of one of the birds that soared around the city waiting for the moment when something died. Its shadow deepened the colour of the tiles next to it, yet she was sure he had not painted its shadow at all.

"That's impossible," she said softly, knowing that it was not, for he had just done it.

He gave a quiet laugh that chilled her to the tips of her fingers. "Just as stormlords moving clouds be impossible, to the commoner."

"You used the colours in the motley," she said. "You took the colours you needed and pushed them up through the paint, mixed them with the colour you had already added, to make the detail of a painting on top of mine. How is that possible?"

"The affinity of water and man," he said. "Water is the key, always. Hook paint to water and move the water."

"Only sensitives can move water," she said.

"No, child, only rainlords and stormlords and water-painters move water. Stormlords move the sea, rainlords a cistern, ye and I—a few drops in a tray."

"I'm not water sensitive."

"Never said ye were. I said ye can also move water. Fact, we do more even than stormlords, for we be moving the paint as well. If it be motley powder. Tomorrow, ye learn how to make motley. All colours in one mix. Special resin keeps each separate."

She shook her head. Her tongue was dry against the roof of her mouth and her skin felt stretched tight. "Is that what all this is about? You think I can move paint and water?" She meant: Is that why you have taken me in and compelled me to stay?

"All Watergivers who cry water can move water," he said. "And ye are your mother's daughter."

She was swept with panic. "You knew my mother," she whispered, confirming what she had long believed, though not knowing why the thought shattered her so. "And you knew my name. How? Who am I?"

Once again he casually dismissed her need. "Be of no matter. Matters ye be learning how to change a painting. I want ye to put another hawk there, on the roof, beside mine. The way I did it."

"I can't do that!"

"Ye can and ye shall." He dashed several more spoonfuls of paint-powder on top of the painting, in the shape of a similar bird. Then one scrawny arm reached out and took hold of her wrist. She stared at the marks that covered his hands and forearms. She had once thought the patterns were just painted on; she knew better now. The marks were permanent. "Look deep into the painting."

The power in his voice reverberated through his arm and into her body. "Connections," he whispered. "Water to water, life to life. Look deep. See beneath to layers of colour. See bird there, bring to life. Not with paint spoon, but using your mind. Connect to water, Terelle. Each grain of colour be floating in bubble of water. Take the grains ye need, the colours ye want, float them up. Re-form them, make your bird with your mind, see its colours, cruel beak, taloned claws, yellow eye, each feather. Move the colours, *move* them . . ."

His voice murmured on, saying words that no longer had individual meaning but built an entire idea. Her mind was not her own; she felt drugged; and yet she saw the bird. She saw it, beneath the paint. Under the painted roof tiles. And she moved it upwards.

The second bird sat on the roof ridge in the painting, next to the first.

She shuddered, cried out in denial. "You did that! It wasn't me!"

"Was ye," he said, and she hated him. She hated his manipulation. She hated what he had done, and why. Her heart told her that this was something he had done not for her, but for himself.

"Who are you?" she asked. "*What* are you?"

"One day I be telling ye. But not yet."

"And *why*?" she asked. Remembering the woman who had appeared in both the street and his painting at the same time, her gaze flew upwards to the rooftop, but there were no hawks sitting there.

He followed her gaze and smiled. "Be long way to go, child, journey we be making, ye and me. At journey's end, ye know exactly who ye be and *what* ye be. And when I die, your future be yours to choose. That's what ye be wanting, no? Ability to choose your own fate. Then ye no longer be saying life not fair."

He's mocking me, she thought. *Laughing at my childish desire for fate to be both impartial and just.*

He stood up, hitching his wrapped robes about him as if he was chilled, and walked back into their room. She stretched, needing to unwind, to feel the tension dissipate from her muscles and tendons. Finally, when she reached a semblance of normality again, she looked down at the painting once more. The hawks were still sitting there, side by side, Russet's better-made than hers. His bird regarded her with a living intensity in its yellow eye, all predator, with a predator's hunger—and impartiality. She could almost hear it telling her: Life isn't fair. It is harsh and unkind and cruel.

Why couldn't she accept that?

Because even if it's true, it's not acceptable, she thought.

Against her will, she found herself drawn into the painting again, entangled in its strands of light and dark, aware of the colours beneath the superficiality. She heard a whisper in her mind: *You could do anything. You could make life fair.* Her inner desire manifesting itself. Tempting her.

Anything? Could I?

Half in anger, half in defiance, she splashed more colours onto the roof ridge over the top of the hawks, obliterating them, and then manipulated the new colours with the paint skewer. A few lines: the suggestion of a face, an arm, a leg flung across the peak of the tiles. A man sitting up there where the birds had been.

Then she sat back and regarded the painting through half-closed eyes. She summoned up the colours beneath without even thinking about what she was doing. Not a bird this time but Vato the waterseller. She pulled him out with loving detail: his sardonic, bitter smile, the sadness of his eyes, the lines of his face. His worn clothes. His mended bab sandals. The rough way someone had cut his hair. His chipped nails. She melded the colour beneath with the colour she had painted on top and formed the picture of the man.

As she did it, she realised something that scared her: the details were not coming from her conscious mind but from somewhere else. Yes, she had noticed the nails before and the hair and his expression and the mended

sandals—but she had never looked at his feet closely
enough to know that one of his sandals was mended with
hempen twine and the other with catgut, or that the mark
on his cheek was not a scar but a birthmark. Yet those
details had been filed away inside her memory.

She drew in a shuddering breath, immeasurably frightened. She might have done this, but the power that fuelled
it, that filled in the details, went far beyond what was normal. As she drew in the breath, the smell of water was
suffocating. What was it Russet had said? Water to water,
life to life.

The power of water. Her affinity to water. She *knew*
Vato's water. In some strange way, she *remembered*
water—or its lack. And that was why she could dredge up
such detailed memories of her past whenever she wanted.
She could have painted the kitchen of her childhood, or
the face of the caravanners who had brought her to the
Scarpen when she was seven, or the patterns on the highlord's pede. A glance was all it took to etch a memory.

Once more she looked across at the real building opposite: no birds, no waterseller, either, of course. Yet as
she gazed, a shadow crossed the tiles, wings spread, tail
fanned. She was riveted, horrified. The shadow banked,
bird and shadow fusing as a scavenger kite came in to
land on the ridge of the roof. "Watergiver help me," she
whispered. "It's true. He can make things come true."

Her own voice spoke in her head: *Of course he can. He
trapped you in his painting.*

Down in the street below, people were shouting, but
she couldn't hear the words. It sounded like another raid
was in progress, but she took no notice. She looked back
at her painting, her horror growing. Vato. Dear sweet

halls of water, Vato wasn't suddenly going to appear on the roof, was he? In revulsion, she slid the tray away from her, pushing it across the hallway, slopping the water.

She stood up and stared at the bird, the real one. As she looked, a second bird dropped down to stand beside it. *Please, Watergiver, no. Don't make Vato climb onto the roof.* She hesitated, part of her wanting to run to Russet to ask him to stop it happening, part of her rooted to where she was, refusing to believe it *could* happen.

Sunlord save me, he could die if he suddenly found himself high above the street.

But that wouldn't happen, would it? Ridiculous to think it.

Oh Sunlord, I will sacrifice a whole dayjar of water if you stop this! I've learned my lesson, I truly have.

Even as she hesitated, even as she choked on her indecision, she was overtaken by events.

The sound of running on the stairs: a single person's racing footsteps. She turned, only half-focused. A youth. Well dressed, better than most lowlevellers, although one of his trouser legs was torn and his tunic was dirty. Dark Gibber colouring, untidy hair, sweating. Panicked. Fear in his face. Still running, he swept around the corner at the top of the stairs and kept on coming, oblivious to what was in front of him. One sandaled foot planted itself squarely in the painting tray, destroying the picture.

She felt the destruction as a shock of possibilities, all illogical: what if he had killed Vato? Knocked him off the roof? Squashed him? She glanced back at the buildings opposite. The two kites had raised their wings and launched themselves into the sky. Vato wasn't there. *Stu-*

*pid, of course he isn't there. Why by all that is sun-holy
would he be on the roof?*

The youth skidded to a halt, suddenly aware that there
was no way out of the hallway except back the way he had
come. He whirled around, saw the row of closed apart-
ment doors and turned back to her. His chest heaved; his
breath came in ragged gasps. His left sandal was covered
in paint and dripped water in a pool at his feet.

"Can you hide me?" he asked. "Please?"

She stood still, staring, unable to think.

"I'm desperate. *Please.*"

She opened her mouth to speak—although she didn't
know what to say—then saw movement behind the young
man. It was Vato, crawling across the roof pantiles of the
building opposite, his face a picture of fear and bewilderment as he clambered up towards the ridge.

From below came the sound of running feet; the youth's
pursuers at the base of the stairs, or so she guessed. She was
caught in a nightmare from which she could not wake.

"Please," he whispered. "Otherwise I could be a prisoner for the rest of my life."

What a strange thing to say, she thought. *The whole
world's gone mad.* She looked back at him and focused.
If he was a waterless Gibberman, they might kill him. His
troubled eyes begged her, without a hint of expectation
or threat.

"Take off your shoes," she said and held out her hand.

Shale looked down at his feet. The sandals were wet and
streaked with colour. He had only seconds to make up his
mind. He took them off and handed them to her.

"Go into that room there," she said calmly, gesturing to

one of the closed doors. "Tell Artisman Russet that I said you were to wait there for me. My name's Terelle."

For once he didn't hesitate, didn't consider whether he should trust or not. He had no choice. He could already hear someone coming up the stairs. He ran and opened the door. As he stepped inside, he did spare one backward glance at the girl. She'd put on his sandals and run diagonally across to the balustrade under the archways, leaving a wet and paint-smeared trail. There she stripped the shoes off and threw them over the balustrade. She stood there, back to him, shaking her fist and yelling. Hurriedly, he closed the door and turned around. An old man with a wrinkled brown face and penetrating green eyes was regarding him with a look that was sharp enough to see through to his soul.

Shale took a deep breath and wondered if he had just made the biggest mistake of his life. He leaned back against the door and listened to what was happening outside. The old man, who had been stirring something over the fire, stood perfectly still, glaring at him. Shale's immediate impression was one of great age: the man was ancient, not just old. He was not frightened or even alarmed. On the contrary, the annoyed look he gave Shale was also one of calculation and assessment.

Outside, someone shouted, "Which way did he go?"

"That way." The girl's voice. She sounded angry. "He stepped in my waterpainting! He spoiled it and wasted the water!"

Shale closed his eyes and waited. He had no way of knowing whether she was pointing towards the door or down into the street. He tried to believe that she would help him, but couldn't think of any reason why she should—

and there was one very good reason she shouldn't. If they found out she lied, she could be in real trouble.

He opened his eyes, swallowed the panic and blanked his face. He said quietly, "Terelle said I was to wait here for her."

"Did she, now?" The old man's eyes, although shrunken by age, continued their shrewd assessment. "Presumptuous of her, no?" He put the ladle down and pulled the pot off the fire. Smoke wisped up into a makeshift metal chimney that poked out through the lattice along the top of the outer wall. The pot was heavy but the age-spotted hands were still strong and manoeuvred it effortlessly onto the stone hearth. In its place he hung a kettle, then turned back to Shale. "*I* pay for this room." His back may have already been bent with age, but his voice was strong and even.

"My—my apologies." Shale looked around. There were no windows, no other exit. Light and air entered through the latticework. A few strategically hung pieces of woven bab-leaf matting divided the room into living space and sleeping quarters, but the only solid furniture was a table and two chairs made of poor quality bab wood. His glance roved back to the kettle. Hot water could be a weapon. And there were two dayjars—not that flinging cold water at someone would do much harm.

He said, keeping his voice low, "I shall be gone as soon as the men out there have stopped looking."

"And if I, Russet Kermes, choose to say ye be here?"

Shale said nothing. He did not think the man was threatening him but rather mocking him, and he didn't know how to answer.

Outside the door there was more conversation and then the sound of footsteps hurrying away. A moment later, the girl Terelle opened the door and stepped inside. She looked flustered. "He's gone. I told him you jumped down onto the awning and then into the street. One of your sandals is on the awning. The other was in the street, but someone picked it up. I think you can say goodbye to them."

"The man on the roof?" Shale asked. "What happened to him?"

"Nothing. He climbed down again." At his words she had gone as white as salt.

Russet looked up sharply. "What man?"

What she said next did not make sense to Shale. "I pulled Vato out of the motley and put him on the roof."

"*Sand-witted*!" he exclaimed. "Ye foolish frip—didn't ye understand what be happening if ye shuffled?"

"No. No, I didn't!" She was almost shouting at him. "I didn't. I don't. I don't even know what it is to—to *shuffle*. Perhaps you had better *explain* something for a change. How is it possible?"

"I told ye once, sometimes be possible for us to fix the future."

"*Us*? Just who is . . . us?"

Shale was acutely uncomfortable. He hadn't the faintest idea what he had walked into and wasn't sure he wanted to know. He stood next to the door, still holding his bag, barefoot and feeling out of place.

"People like us."

Shale thought about that. Who were they, these people? He had never seen anyone dressed like the old man. His clothes were wrapped around him rather than made to fit; the colours of the cloth were startlingly vivid, the weave rough and knotted. His arms and hands were covered in red-brown tattoos, patterns of swirls and waves that were possibly only the beginning of designs hidden under his wrap. And Shale had never seen anyone with eyes that colour—except the girl.

She was striking. Dusky-complexioned enough to be from the Gibber, but different, too. Already taller than most Gibber women. And more . . . he searched for a word. Regal. Something about the structure of her face, the inner strength in the gaze. He shuffled his feet in embarrassment. "Er, I, um, I'm sorry to have disturbed you," he said. "And thank you, um, Arta, for hiding me. I'll go now."

That switched their attention to him immediately. Terelle said nothing, but Russet came forward, smiling. It was not a smile that gave Shale confidence in his benevolence.

"No, no, Gibberman, ye will not. Going out there when reeve's men be looking for ye? Enforcers, no?"

Shale nodded dumbly.

"Seneschal Harkel of Scarcleft Hall—his men. They keep looking all day. You leave tonight."

"But I have to find work," he said.

"No one take ye today, not when Harkel's men be asking about ye." The mockery was back; the old man was laughing at him.

"They don't know my name."

The man's shrewd eyes pierced him with contempt. "Gibber youth wearing noble livery? They find ye."

He looked down at the clothes he was wearing, a tunic and breeches Taquar had given him. "Livery?" he asked stupidly.

"That's right. Worn by servants in Scarcleft Hall."

"No one else has remarked on my clothes."

"Not too many lowlevellers know uplevel livery. I be one of them. Reeves and enforcers too. They have the name ye use by now." He chuckled, a high-pitched sound that grated on Shale. "Safer staying here." He was still grinning, his small, ageing eyes disappearing into the filigree of wrinkles on his cheeks and eyelids.

He turned to Terelle. "Give him meal, while I be finding out what I can." He picked up a length of coloured cloth and wrapped it around his head, took up a staff of wood and went to the door. "Take advice, Gibberman: be here when Russet comes back, eh?" The sharpness of the warning was reinforced by the hint of malice in his tone. The man was not sympathetic; he was gleefully amused at Shale's predicament and left chuckling.

Terelle went to the pot that had been keeping warm at the back of the fireplace and ladled out some of its contents into two bowls. She gestured towards the table and chairs. "Sit down, why don't you?" She sounded distracted, not really interested in whether he stayed or not.

"He won't sell me to them, will he?"

That got her attention. "Russet? No. He hates all Scarpermen, particularly anyone connected with the rainlords and water sensitives. Do you want some amber?"

He shook his head. "I have my own water." He sat down at the table, and she sat opposite.

She pushed a plate of yam biscuits towards him. "Help yourself."

He took one and picked up the spoon in his bowl. "I'm sorry about your painting. I didn't see it when I came around the corner. Will you be able to do it again?"

"It doesn't matter."

He struggled on, knowing he sounded inept. Spoken words did not come easily to him. "I—I want to say thank you, for doing what you did. That was brave."

She waved a dismissive hand. "Who are we, we waterless, if we can't help one another?" She still seemed preoccupied, and he was perversely offended.

"Is that old man your grandfather?"

"What makes you say that?"

"You look like him."

"You think *I* look like *him*?"

Her eyes blazed at him, and he knew he had just said something stupid. The man was old and wizened; of course it would hardly be flattering to be compared to him. "Um, no, of course not. Not really. I mean, he's old. And you're—but—"

"But *what*?"

"It's your eyes; you have the same eye colour." Now that he had her attention, he rather wished he didn't.

"Not everyone with the same colour eyes is related."

"No, of c-course not," he stuttered. He bent over the food and ate, wishing she would stop looking at him as if he was a sand-leech.

"What's your name?" she asked.

He opened his mouth to say Jasper, and then closed it again. Pointless to continue the lie; the reeves weren't stupid. They were looking for Shale. He thought he knew what had happened. The waterhall reeves had told the highlord what had occurred in the waterhall. Taquar had gone to check if he was still in the Scarcleft mother cistern. When he'd found him missing, he had instituted a thorough search of Scarcleft. And he wasn't going to give up until Shale was found.

"My name's Shale," he said.

"What do they want you for?"

"It's a long story."

She shrugged, accepting the rebuff as if she didn't care. "I am the apprentice of Russet the waterpainter."

"He sells waterpaintings?" he asked, intrigued.

"Uplevellers commission them for their hallways; some have even built special recesses into their floors for them."

"Why?"

"Why, what?"

"Why would someone want such a painting?" The thought of water being wasted like that was repugnant to him.

She stared at him blankly. Finally she said, "Because they are beautiful. Because they stir the senses. Because a good painting can speak to you, can say many things about life, about the world, about your place in the world. Like . . . poetry. Or dance."

He thought about that with a sense of wonder. People *paid* to have their water wasted? Just to make something beautiful or interesting that had no purpose?

"You don't know what I'm talking about, do you?"

He shook his head.

"Watergiver's heart! Is the Gibber really such a wretched place that its people have no—no *soul*?"

"We have beautiful things in the Gibber," he said defensively. "My mother used to embroider. And the potter in our settle made designs on his pots. But they made useful things first. Making them beautiful afterwards never used any extra water."

She stared at him some more, one eyebrow raised as if

in disbelief, and then looked away to continue eating her meal. He took his cue from her and bent over his bowl. He didn't think he liked her much. She made him feel clumsy, as if his body was too large for grace and his tongue too stupid to make sense of his thoughts.

They ate the rest of the meal in silence.

When Russet came back, he was rubbing his hands in a self-satisfied way, a gesture that disturbed Shale even more than Terelle's flat stare. "Have something to show ye," he said to Shale. "Look!" He reached into a fold of his wraps and withdrew a piece of rough parchment. He unrolled it on the table and showed them both.

Shale stared at it. It was a picture of a youth, a Gibberman. Underneath, there was writing he had no trouble deciphering.

REWARD for the capture ALIVE AND UNHURT of the above Gibberman, aged 17 or 18. Anyone delivering this youth UNDAMAGED and in GOOD HEALTH to any reeve or water enforcer will, if waterless, receive honorary water allotment for life, otherwise a reward of 5,000 tokens.

Only then did he realise the picture was of himself. He stared at it, shocked, fascinated. *That* was him? That serious young man, with the calm expression that told no one anything?

Then the information sank in. *Water allotment for life.* How many waterless men or women would be able to resist that? He looked at Terelle, dismayed.

"I'll be desert-fried," she said, apparently impressed, "whatever did you do?"

"W-w-where did you get this?" Shale asked Russet.

"Pasted up on a wall. People say they are on every level." He considered Shale thoughtfully. "Imagine trouble to copy so many pictures of ye, boy. And the reward. Ye be valuable to highlord, yes?"

But Shale was speechless. He felt as if all the water inside him was being replaced by sand. Why had he ever thought he could escape Taquar? He should have foreseen this. He should have risked escaping with Feroze. What a dryhead he'd been.

"Better say who ye be," Russet said. He reached out and ran a dry hand down Shale's face. His fingers had the roughness of saltbush leaves. "Water-sense spills out of ye like water from storm cloud."

Shale shuddered and pulled away. "Are you going to claim your reward?" he asked bitterly.

Russet cackled. "I be having enough tokens for my needs." He leaned forward and his breath was stale against Shale's cheek. "But here be another truth: step out that door, ye soon be prisoner hauled uplevel, liking it or not. Be no choice except trust Russet. So, who be ye, eh?"

Shale slumped down on his stool, capitulating. "Shale Flint," he said at last. "From the Gibber Quarter. I'd better tell you the whole story, I suppose."

Russet and Terelle exchanged glances. "Let me sit down," Russet said gleefully. "Be lengthy tale coming, no?"

CHAPTER TWENTY-NINE

Scarpen Quarter
Scarcleft City
Arta Amethyst's house, Level 10

Arta Amethyst always strolled around the rooftop at dusk. She loved the day at its close, when the slant of liquid sunlight, hugging the last of the day's warmth within itself, poured across the buildings. A time when shadows purpled and people gathered on rooftops to eat their evening meals before the business of the night began. If she looked across at the temple opposite, she could see the priests in the last of their daily rituals, pouring the final libation to the Sunlord, splashing the water carelessly onto the daub of the rooftop.

Fine for them, she thought. *They've never been waterless.* She leaned on the parapet and looked down into the street as the crowd diminished and the lull, the hiatus between day and night, began.

To her surprise, the last of the pedestrians stopped before her gate and pulled at the bell rope. Two people. She leaned over a little more and recognised Terelle's hair, so deeply rich brown it was close to black. It had been a while since the girl had come to see her, and she felt a rush of pleasure, quickly smothered. Not wise to expect too much of anyone.

Strange, though, that the girl—no, not girl; woman—had someone with her.

Amethyst watched as the gate was opened and the usual argument started between Jomat and Terelle. No matter how many times she instructed her steward to let Terelle in without question, he always tried to hinder her entry with his nastiness. Amethyst wondered whether she would ever have the courage to dismiss him. But how could she? What was the old saying? *He who pays for the water determines the patterns on the dayjar.* Something had told her long ago that she wasn't the only one paying for Jomat's water and she had never dared to protest. *Cowardice*, she thought. *That has always been your problem, Amethyst. Terror of being waterless again.*

Patiently she waited.

A few moments later, Jomat ushered Terelle and her companion to the rooftop. The steward was breathing with difficulty, his face blotched maroon on paste-white. The hair that drooped over his forehead dripped sweat; his skin oozed the stink of stale perspiration. Amethyst suppressed her distaste.

"The waterpainter is here to see you, madam. Again." The last word was soaked with vitriol. His puffy eyes turned from her to Terelle to the young man, his gaze devouring them all hungrily in his search for information he could use for his own ends.

It was difficult to be polite. "Thank you, Jomat."

He wasn't finished. "With *another* outlander waterwaster."

"That will be all," she said firmly and waved him away.

He went with reluctance, wheezing all the while. No one spoke until he had lumbered down the stairs.

Terelle indicated the red-skinned youth with her. "Arta, I have brought someone to meet you."

He was dressed in loose red clothes and his red hair was braided with beads. He wore a scimitar at his side. Although she had never met a Reduner face-to-face, she assumed he must be one, until Terelle added, "His name is Shale. He's not really a Reduner. That's just a disguise. Russet painted his skin and we dyed a tunic and breeches for him, and his hair, too. I braided it."

Amethyst stared at him, frowning. "You did a good job. I would never have known. But why was it necessary?"

"Enforcers are searching for him, and this was the only way we could think of to hide him. I used Russet's pass to bring him uplevel, but no one even asked to see it. Russet says enforcers have been told to treat all Reduners with respect."

"And why are they searching for him?" Amethyst wasn't happy with what she was hearing, and she didn't bother to hide her unease.

"He has a story I—we—want you to hear. We need your advice."

Amethyst stared at the youth but could not come to any conclusions. He was as closed to her as a shuttered pede. His eyes were intelligent but lacked expression; he held his whole body as if he was quietly waiting for something to happen—but whether he was happy or sad, frightened or tense, she could not say.

"Take a seat," she said. She indicated the cushions on the mud-brick benches around the edges of the roof. "There is still mint infusion in the pot, I believe, and plenty of savouries left over from my dinner. Will you both not join me?" She walked to the top of the stairs and called down for more hot water. While waiting, she chatted with Terelle, probing as tactfully as she could to find out if she was happy and safe. She remained unconvinced by Terelle's cheerful but evasive answers.

Oh Sunlord, she thought, *why did I ever become embroiled in the doings of this child? I see trouble round the corner for me in this.*

Jomat brought the water, still wheezing, his mouth pinched in disapproval at the water-waste involved in serving a drink to visitors. His eyes roved over them with ill-concealed curiosity as he placed the pot on the bench next to his mistress. Shale was polite, and took the infusion and savouries Amethyst offered, but held himself in abeyance.

She waited until Jomat left before asking, "So what is this story?"

"Can I trust you?" he countered. The look he gave her was steady.

She treated the question seriously, aware that he expected nothing less. "Not entirely, perhaps. For a start, everybody has their price. Everybody, no matter how good their intentions are."

He nodded, as if in agreement, but did not ask for further guarantees. "I am here because I don't know where else to turn and I have to trust Terelle's judgement. I am fleeing a man who had my sister and parents killed and my brother enslaved. Taquar, Highlord of Scarcleft. I need to escape from him, from this city, and I need a place to go."

She was stilled, her breath catching in her throat, her

heart pounding. Taquar? *Oh Watergiver save me, you have come to the wrong person!*

"I had heard that the reeves were looking for a youth," she said cautiously. "It was the talk of the bazaars a few days ago. They put up posters. Was that you?" *He's so self-contained*, she thought. *So young to be so in command of himself. Does he ever break, I wonder?*

He said, "Yes, that was me. I have been hiding with Russet. We thought it better to let the search die down a bit before I ventured out."

"Why does Taquar seek you?"

"He wishes to use my water-powers for his own ends. He is no stormlord, but he wants to control a stormlord's power."

Her breath caught. "You are a *stormlord*?" she asked, incredulous. *A Gibberman a stormlord?*

By way of answer, the contents of the hot-water pot shot into the air through the spout and moulded themselves into the shape of a face. Taquar's face. Terelle squeaked and clapped a hand over her mouth.

"I'm more than a rainlord, not yet quite a stormlord," he said.

Amethyst suppressed a shudder. "Put it back," she said sharply. Shale obeyed without, it seemed, any effort at all. "You had better tell me how you and Taquar came to cross paths. And speak softly, young man."

Amethyst still did not know what to make of him: he was precise and logical, telling a tale of death and betrayal as if he spoke of everyday matters. Then she noticed: he had fire within, and a heart, this youth—no, this man on the verge of full maturity. When he spoke of his sister's death and his brother's probable enslavement, rage was there in his voice and grief in his eyes. She found herself feeling for him, even as she admired his control.

He finished by saying, "Terelle and Russet tell me people say Highlord Taquar is the Quartern heir. We have to change that. I have to get to the Cloudmaster in Breccia City, to tell him what kind of man Highlord Taquar is. I did try to get a message to Breccia through an Alabaster trader, but I don't think it arrived."

She almost laughed at his audacity. "You think to change the succession?" When neither of them answered, she asked, "What do you want from me?"

It was Terelle who replied. "It might be difficult for Shale to join a caravan with everyone looking for him. The disguise may not hold up. So we thought of sending a message to the Cloudmaster about Shale. Then he could send someone to fetch him. Trouble is, if we send such a message, who will bother to read it and who will believe it? And then I thought of you. People know of Arta Amethyst the dancer. A message closed with your seal would be taken seriously in Breccia Hall."

"You don't know what you ask of me. Have you *any* idea of what Taquar would do if he thought I was disloyal?"

"He wouldn't ever find out—"

"No? What if the message was intercepted? If the messenger I chose was not trustworthy? Taquar has spies everywhere, even here in my home. Don't be stupid, child! Who do you think the rainlord was who helped me when I was young?"

Terelle stared at the dancer in horror. "That was Highlord Taquar? You were the highlord's . . ."

"Whore? Yes! Until he wearied of me. And being

Taquar, that was not the end of it, you can be sure of that. He has spies everywhere making sure that there is no other man in my life, even though he himself tired of me long ago. Shale is right in what he has just said: Taquar loves control and power. He wears a mask of civility and polish—charm, even. He is not a man who glories in cruelty, but he is dangerous and ruthless beyond measure when crossed. There is no humanity in him then, just a cold and pitiless heart. He punishes disloyalty. Always."

Shale sat still, his dark eyes considering her without expression.

Terelle looked stricken. She glanced at Shale and laid a hand on his arm. "I'm sorry," she whispered. "I didn't know."

He shrugged. "Will you betray me to him?" he asked Amethyst, his voice still cool and steady.

She marvelled at his lack of outward fear. *Ah*, she thought, *I know where that comes from. When you live within Taquar's world, you learn to hide your true feelings deep. And this youth has spent almost four years seeing no one but the rainlord, Watergiver help him. He has courage.*

She tried to be honest. He deserved that much. "Not—not willingly. But what of Jomat? He has seen you."

Anxiety flared in his eyes. "He spies for Highlord Taquar?"

"I have never asked." *Never wanted to be sure.* "But—yes, I have always believed so. Let's hope he doesn't make the connection between a young Reduner and the youth the reeves are looking for. Because if he does—" She considered. "If Taquar wants your skills enough, he may keep you alive, I suppose."

Terelle flicked an anxious look towards the door and the stairs.

Shale's gaze steadied. "Will you help me?" he asked. "Or at least advise me?"

"You would trust me?"

He shrugged again. "You hate Taquar as much as I do."

"I also fear him," she snapped, frightened that he had read her so easily.

Neither of them said anything. Terelle looked hurt; Shale was still expressionless.

"All right, all right, I will send the message. It is easily enough done. My patroness in Breccia Hall is Cloudmaster Granthon's wife, Lady Ethelva. I have danced for her several times. I will send the message to her using the normal letter service; that's probably the safest way to do it."

"Can you do that without Jomat knowing?" Terelle asked.

"Even if he found out I sent a letter, he wouldn't know to whom or what was in it. But it won't go until the next caravan leaves, which might not be for days. Can Shale stay hidden all that while?"

"Artisman Russet has offered me a place with him and Terelle until I leave Scarcleft, if I stay inside the room. It will be no hardship for me; I am used to it. I will keep this Reduner disguise on as well, just in case I am seen."

There was no change in his voice, but something told Amethyst he lied. He hated the confinement; perhaps he always had. She shivered and wondered whether her worry for him was necessary. He had inner strength, this man, and one day it might be Taquar who would need to beware. She looked away and said, "I will send a message to you when I hear something. You had better go now.

And try to keep your face averted from Jomat on your way out, Shale. The less he sees of you, the better."

"Maybe we can just show ourselves out," Terelle suggested.

"No. Do nothing that is unusual." Amethyst rang the bell on the table and waited for Jomat to make his ponderous way upstairs.

As soon as they were in the street again and Jomat had closed the door, Shale said, "That man really is repulsive."

"Yes," Terelle said. "I loathe him. Shale, I'm sorry. I was stupid taking you to Amethyst. I had forgotten she said she once had a relationship with a rainlord." She took a deep breath. "Fortunately Jomat rarely goes out anywhere. He's too fat. He gets the delivery boys to come to the house or he sends the servants out, so it's unlikely he's seen any posters of you."

Shale said nothing.

She looked at him, her eyes wide with curiosity. "Don't you ever get scared, Shale? Or even angry?"

He stared back, not understanding. Whenever he thought of Taquar, he was terrified. He was in the highlord's city, surrounded by his guards and reeves and enforcers. In his heart, he knew Amethyst was right: Taquar was a cold, ruthless man. When he thought of being captured again, his mouth dried up, it was hard to get words out, and his stomach cramped. He was afraid, of course he was. Wasn't it obvious?

When he didn't reply, she turned away and started off down the street. "You don't have any feelings," she said.

Inside the house, Jomat lowered his bulk into his favourite chair—one of the few that didn't creak when he sat—and mulled over what had happened. There was something going on, he was sure of it. They were frightened, Amethyst and that slut of a girl with her uncanny eyes. But why?

He tapped podgy fingers on the arm of the chair and tried to think of anything that would explain the association between Terelle and a Reduner. It was so unlikely. And it was strange, anyway, that a Reduner so young was in Scarcleft. Those heathens always sent experienced traders and envoys, not youths still growing their teeth.

One thing was for sure: he would get to the bottom of this eventually.

Just before he dozed off in the chair, he noticed smudging across the stone flooring. There was red dust tramped in from the front door and up the stairs. "Dirty barbarian lout," he muttered.

CHAPTER THIRTY

Once again Shale put away all thought of the desert, of the sky, of feeling the wind on his cheek or Gibber pebbles beneath his feet. As it was useless to taunt himself with what he could not have, he sealed his need for freedom inside him. He still had days of confinement ahead. And anyway, there was part of himself—the part that liked looking at Terelle—that did not mind so much. Better still, she was becoming a friend. The concept was new. The closest he'd ever had to friendship was his relationship with Mica, but a brother was different. When Terelle told him her story, he realised they were both people displaced by events beyond their control trying to find a place to call their own. She knew how he felt; he understood her predicament. There was something comforting in that.

To his amazement, he found Russet was both able and willing to help him further his water skills. "You're a rainlord!" he exclaimed after the waterpainter explained an easier way to control water vapour by a trick of concentration.

"Not so," the old man said, stabbing at Shale with a gnarled finger. "I be waterpainter. Different skill. Manipulate water through time, changing future being. Superior art to movement of water from one place to another! Waterpainters be *artists*." His glare softened as he shrugged and added, "Watergivers understand moving water. If not, how we be Watergivers?"

For a moment, Shale thought the old man had accidentally mixed up the terms "waterpainter" and "Watergiver". But then Terelle looked up from her spot on the floor near the fireplace, where she was putting the finishing touches to a painting, and asked, "Why do you always keep on referring to yourself as a Watergiver? There's only one Watergiver. That's what the priests say. His name was Ashsomething and he came as an emissary from the Sunlord to show water sensitives how to manipulate the clouds."

He laughed, giving an unpleasant cackle of mockery and derision that Shale was learning to hate. "Terelle, ye know nothing of world. More Watergivers be walking this earth than red drovers on dunes, Alabasters in Whiteout and priests in Breccia combined."

"You're saying you're a Watergiver?" Shale asked. Did the man think he was an immortal being? Shale wouldn't have been surprised if he did; there was something mad about him, mad and malevolent. "An emissary of the Sunlord?"

Russet merely shot a sly smile in Terelle's direction. It was Terelle who answered. "Of course he's not saying that."

"And what ye be thinking I mean?" Russet asked her.

"I think it's the name your people give yourselves because you worship the Watergiver."

Shale didn't say anything, but he didn't think that was what Russet had meant at all. He sighed inwardly. Russet's secrets and air of mystery drove Terelle crazy, but she usually restrained her irritation. He thought he knew why she never pressed Russet to give answers that made sense. When you were totally dependent on someone else for water, there were times when you bit your tongue.

The morning after the visit to Amethyst's, Russet and Terelle spent a long time talking in the hallway. Russet was explaining a new painting technique to her. Shale stayed inside, but he heard snatches of conversation.

"Be very particular about the measurements."

"*All* the agates?"

"No, not *that* grey—this one. Flax-grey that be called, or gridelin. Has violet tinge—without it, motley not right."

"Oh. Like this?"

Eventually Russet came in, muttering under his breath. Terelle stayed outside painting until middmorning, when she stuck her head around the door and said, "I've finished, Artisman. Do you want to see?"

Shale watched from the doorway, first using his water senses to make sure there was no one else around. Terelle had painted a street scene featuring a gateway set into a brown daub wall. The wooden gate, studded with slices of red and white agate in a swirling pattern, was brightly coloured as if it had caught the rays of the morning sun, while the remainder of the street was still in shadow.

Russet asked, "Ye sure it be true?"

"I remember it exactly—the patterns, the colours, the shadows." She looked at Shale. "It's right, isn't it?"

"That's Amethyst's house? I don't remember the details. Do you? Really? All those swirls?"

She nodded.

Intrigued by her certainty, he waved a hand at the painting. "Even how many pieces of agate there were?"

She waved a hand at the painting. "That many."

"You *counted* them?"

"No, I just remember."

"Nobody's that good."

"I am." She indicated the floating picture. "That's how the arta's street gate looks, right down to the patterns in the individual agates."

"Blood runs true," Russet said complacently. "Now watch. Amethyst's message sent to Breccia, but how we know they send rainlord to protect Shale? We make sure! Remember I be doing this for ye, Gibberman."

"Really? Why? If Taquar finds out, you'll never sell another painting in Scarcleft. You'll be thrown out of the gates tomorrow. Or worse." More likely worse.

But whatever Russet's motives were, the old man was not going to explain them. He ignored Shale's question and sat cross-legged on the floor in front of the tray. Terelle knelt next to him. Neither of them said anything, but Shale had an idea Terelle was apprehensive about what was going to happen. He wanted to warn her, but didn't know what the warning should be. For one wild moment he wanted to grab her by the hand and pull her away, take her downstairs and out into the safety of the street.

Except the street wasn't safe.

The old man took up a paint spoon and started to apply colour to the area near the doorway. He worked quickly, almost carelessly, not worrying too much about detail or clear-cut edges. He was painting two figures, both men, and the arm and shoulder of a third, who was standing off to the left. The two full figures stood in the shadow. One could only be seen in profile. He was a lean man wearing nondescript riding clothes; his face was clearly defined, and his features were vaguely familiar to Shale. The other man, taller and more muscular, was reaching out to pull the bell. His face was also sharply depicted. The third man, whose arm and shoulder only were pictured, was wearing what appeared to be a uniform. Livery.

Terelle frowned, and the frown deepened as ripples advanced across the surface of the painting and it began to change. For a moment, Shale thought that Russet had knocked the tray, but the painter was motionless.

The painted figures were changing, clarifying. The edges sharpened. Shale gasped. *How had the water-painter done that?*

"Highlord Nealrith Almandine of Breccia," Russet said, pointing to the man painted in profile.

"How do you know what he looks like?" Terelle asked, troubled.

"Met him. I did paintings for Breccia Hall." Pointing at the painting, he turned to address Shale. "Now Nealrith comes in answer to Amethyst's message. Other man pulling the bell: Kaneth Carnelian, warrior rainlord. Two rainlords—ye be safe, no?"

"Taquar mentioned Kaneth to me. I don't think Taquar likes him much. But how is putting them into a painting going to ensure they come?" Shale asked, not bothering to hide his scorn. He had to believe that the man could alter a painting without touching it, because he had just seen it happen; he'd manipulated the water, obviously. It was quite another thing to think that a painting could influence the future.

Russet turned fierce eyes on him. "Ye lords be not only ones with water-powers. Watergivers of my people—once Russet Kermes be finest of them—bring more than water through space *and* time, by painting."

"Are you trying to tell us the rainlords Nealrith and Kaneth stand right now at Amethyst's gate?" he asked.

"If they be in Breccia, yes. But they must be riding here first, no?" He waved a hand at the picture. "I put future into paint, they obey. No choice."

Shale was still scornful. "Then why get Amethyst to write a letter?"

"Quicker, better, if they have reason to be coming. Letter give them good reason—to find new stormlord." He turned back to Terelle. "Ye must practise this art, over and over. But remember, ye get what ye be asking, so no more watersellers on roof. Understand?"

She appeared troubled, but she nodded.

He continued with his instructions. "Art not accurate, nothing happens. Must be having much detail right. Ye be blessed with waterpainter's memory—yet detail not always desirable." He indicated the painting in front of them. "Nealrith and Kaneth's face in detail. Door perfect detail. But only suggestion of lords' tunics. Back view of Breccia guard's uniform."

"Why?" Terelle asked.

"If paint tunic in detail for Nealrith, but he be not owning tunic like that? What then? Maybe he be delaying trip till he get one. Suggest what ye not know; detail what ye do. Understand?"

"I think so."

"And then?" Shale asked. "What then? There is detail there now. The tunics and trousers, the guard—"

"Water to water—my water, to water in the tray, to water in Nealrith and Kaneth—plus power of a Water-giver. That be all I need. I picture them both at Amethyst's gate. Picture them, move water and the paint to make it so. Who servant be, what clothes Nealrith and Kaneth wear, that decided by what possible, what probable."

He gestured at the painting once more. "I paint dark blue tunic, brown trousers. Common colours. Power of water decides which blue tunic in Nealrith's wardrobe. Same with trousers. He be wearing them day he knocks at Amethyst's door. I not make it so—it just be so, and therefore be so in painting." He raised his eyes to look at Terelle. "Power of water, artistry, waterpainter, all working together, that be real power. Can do many things. Can kill. Can enslave."

The wilted bastard, Shale thought, *he's like Taquar. He wants power, but finding it, he'd misuse it.* If he was so powerful that he could bring Nealrith to him across the fissured land of the Scarpen Quarter, then why was he just a waterpainter on the thirty-sixth level of Scarcleft, living hand to mouth in a miserable rented room?

"If that were so, you could be a stormlord and supply us with storms," he said aloud. "All you'd have to do is paint rain."

Russet looked disconcerted and did not answer.

Looking at him now, Shale thought the old man didn't look powerful; he looked sick. When he rose to his feet, he staggered and almost fell.

He leaned against the wall for a moment, flexing stiff joints, and then said, "One such painting a day from ye,

Terelle. Harmless portraits. House gecko falling off shelf, that sort of thing. I be going to lie down for a while. We need more white paint. Mix some." He gathered up his colourful wrap, tucked in the ends firmly about him and disappeared back inside the room.

Shale said in a whisper, "He's sun-fried."

"No, he's not," she said quietly from where she sat. "I can do it, too."

He stared at her. She was not looking at him; her eyes were downcast, as if she was ashamed. She continued, "I can do what he did. Make the details of a figure come up through the painted picture by manipulating the tiny spots of paint below, fashioning them using the power of the water. I don't know how. But I can." She lifted her eyes to meet his, and they were pooled with misery. "You remember that man on the roof?"

"Of course."

"I did that. I didn't believe anything would happen, you see, so I painted a suggestion of him up there. Vato the waterseller. Then I pulled the details up through the paint and made him—no, not *him*: his future—I made his future real. I made his future to be sitting on the roof. And a few moments later, he was there, perched on . . ." Her words trailed away. "It's something that happens when the water and paint passes through the picture. It is as Russet said: a combination of water, art and the mind."

Shale sat still, saying nothing. Was it possible? He had seen the man on the roof. And Terelle believed it.

She went on, "I spoke to him about it yesterday. The waterseller. I asked him how he came to be on the roof. He said he just had this urge to climb up there, and so he did. He didn't know why, and he was helpless to resist. If he'd fallen, it would have been my fault. And people stole his water while he was away." A tear ran down her face. "I didn't know it was going to be like this when I became Artisman Russet's apprentice. Is it evil to do this sort of thing, Shale? To ensure a particular future?"

He thought about that before replying, and after a long silence said, "If what you say is true, then yes, I think it is."

She looked so woebegone, he felt compelled to add an explanation. "If putting a person into a painting has forced him to do something that he would not have done willingly, it is evil. Imagine how such power could be used. Or misused. You could make a painting of someone giving you a costly gift, which he would then proceed to do, whether he really wanted to or not. Would that be any different from stealing his water tokens?" He had to turn away from her grief. "I wouldn't trust Russet's motives, not for a moment. Leave him, Terelle."

"How?" she whispered. "I am waterless. I don't have the skills to steal water like you do. Without him I have nothing."

He flushed. He had been unaware that she noticed his surreptitious thefts, drop by drop, of water from water jars or the steam from cooking pots in the neighbourhood. His own misuse of power. He said hastily, "You have a skill now. You can paint on water. And you know how to make the paints. You could make a living." He hesitated. "Terelle, you couldn't make it rain with your painting, could you?"

"I did think about that. But what if I just made a stormlord's cloud drop its water in the wrong place? We'd be worse off, not better. Russet told me it's hard to influence something inanimate, anyway, unless a person or an animal is involved in the process. To make it rain in a particular place would be tough; to influence a stormlord to drop his rain would be easier."

He thought about that and then said, "Terelle, come with me to Breccia."

Her whole face lit up, but her smile vanished as quickly as it had come, to be replaced by a haunted look that tore through his heart.

"What's the matter?" he asked.

"I can't. Besides, you don't even like me."

His flush deepened. "I never said that," he protested. The look she gave him then told him he had failed her. She had wanted him to say something else, but what? He had no idea. He rushed on. "You should leave. I don't trust Russet. He's . . . not a nice man. He is using you. I don't know why, but I do know that much." He added, "I know about being used."

She considered that. "You think he and Highlord Taquar are the same?"

"Yes. No. Taquar is cold. Calculating. Clever. Russet is none of those things. But he is sly." He struggled to express what he sensed. "He is . . . greedy. Can't you see the way he looks at you? As though you are—are something to eat. He wants something from you. You just don't know what yet. I suspect, though, that what he wants is the same thing that Taquar wanted from me: power."

"Russet has his own power."

"Does he? Or is he growing weaker as the years go by? Is he perhaps watching his power diminish and wondering just how to survive? He hasn't been truthful with you. It's obvious you both come from the same place, wherever that is. You have the same eyes, and you say you have the same ability with waterpainting the future. He has spoken of your mother as if he knew her. Why won't he tell you where he comes from?"

"I'm from the Gibber."

"No, you're not. I've never seen Gibber folk with green eyes like yours. I've never seen anyone with eyes like yours. Except Russet."

She had started to clean up the paints, turning her back to him as she worked, flinging things noisily into the sand basin, wiping up splashes of paint on the floor with dried leaves. "You don't know everything, Shale sand-grubber. In fact, I don't think you know *anything*."

As she began to scour the paint spoons with sand, he retreated, aware that he had just made her angry. He had only been trying to help and did not fully understand just where he had gone wrong.

Only much later, after they had been wrenched apart, did it occur to him that she had wanted him to say he cared for more than her welfare. She had wanted to hear him say that he cared for *her*. By then, it was too late.

Shale knew little about girls. There had been none around his own age in the shanties of Wash Drybone, and the girls who lived in proper houses in the settle certainly had nothing at all to do with the family of Galen the sot. Terelle didn't simper or giggle as the settle girls often had, and he was grateful for that, but she did have the knack of making him thick-tongued and clumsy. He even found himself flushing simply because of the way she sometimes looked at him: with eyebrows raised and an expression that said, "You can't really be as stupid as *that*, can you?"

He was never able to predict just what would prompt that reaction in her. She did it when he told her one of her paintings was pretty. She did it when he said that just because they didn't like Jomat, it didn't necessarily mean he was evil. She did it when he remarked that Nealrith was lucky because he was married to someone who must surely be the loveliest woman in all the Quarter. She did it when he said that he couldn't see anything wrong with owning ziggers. Sometimes, the more logical the statement was to him, the higher her eyebrows went. Even when he tried to pay her a compliment, it could go awry. When he said one of her tunics suited her, she said scathingly, "*This?* You think I look good in *this*?"

Still, there were other times when he thought she was better company than Mica had ever been. She laughed more. She made him laugh. Without his being actively aware of it, she insinuated herself into his waking thoughts and night-time dreams, and the results were pleasant. Just thinking about her stirred his body. He found himself looking forward to her company. He was happier when she was in the room than when she wasn't. He wanted to touch her but never dared.

One day he told her as much as he could remember about Mica and then asked, "Do you—do you think it would be possible for you to paint him? I mean, a picture where—where he and I meet up again, or something?"

She thought about that. "I don't know what he looks like," she said finally. "Even if you were to describe him . . . No, I'm sorry, Shale; I don't think it would work. I'll ask Russet, though."

He nodded, resigned. He had not really expected anything else.

"You cheated!"
"I did not!"

Shale tilted his head in disbelief. "There were four shells in that hollow. You dropped another in and then transferred them. You could skip the lady's hollow because of the purple shell, but you had to have five shells, which means the last one had to—"

She started to laugh. She had taught him how to play a board game called Lords and Shells, which involved trying to collect all your opponent's shells from the many hollows on their side of the carved board and distribute them into your own hollows, using strategy that involved farsighted interpretation of how the game was going to go. They argued long and hard about just how much luck was involved and how much of the outcome was indeed due to planning; sometimes a single game would go on well into the night. It helped to pass the time. No, more than that, it was *fun*. And it was hard to get angry with Terelle when she tried to get the better of him by cheating. She would look so innocent and wide-eyed, he always knew she must have done *something*, but sometimes it was hard trying to work out exactly what. That, he decided, was one of the things he liked about her: she was never dull. Her company made the waiting, the necessity of his Reduner disguise and his virtual imprisonment bearable.

The news she relayed from Vato the waterseller and the bazaars was worrying. There was unrest everywhere. Searches and harassment had become a part of life on their level, and people did not like it. When the waterless lived on the sufferance of those above, they kept many secrets. Spot searches and sudden raids had an uncomfortable way of uncovering them. According to Vato, rumour said the red dunes were divided and at war, with one side led by a woman warrior called Vara Redmane, who had once been a sandmaster's wife. Besides fighting this rebellion against his rule, Davim ran raids into the White Quarter, seized quarried salt and harried the Alabasters.

Terelle frowned over that. "But that's silly," she said. "If the 'Basters don't get any profit from selling salt because the Reduners always steal it first, then they won't quarry it."

Shale thought about that before replying. "Davim will force them," he said finally. "Quarry salt, or die. He intends to rule the north. Just as Taquar aimed to rule the whole of the Scarpen and the Gibber."

"Taquar did? Using what forces?"

"Reduners, I reckon. Davim's men. In exchange for water . . . which I was supposed to supply. Taquar wanted to control the Gibber gem, mineral and resin trade as well as the whole of the Scarpen. Davim wanted control of the north: the Reduners and the Alabasters." In his anger, his voice deepened. "An evil pact between two evil men."

"Taquar told you that?"

"In a sort of roundabout way, yes. Only he said it was someone else, not him. Highlord Nealrith or Rainlord Kaneth. And I believed him. Blighted eyes, Terelle, I saw what happened to Wash Drybone Settle, and he could look me straight in the eye and talk about the wickedness of the rogue rainlord, when all the time it was *him*."

She sat quietly, watching him. "And now? After Taquar has lost you?"

"Davim may not know that yet. I can only guess what Taquar will do, but knowing him, he will keep it quiet as long as he can, hoping all the while he'll find me again. He will never give up. Never. There's no place I'll ever be safe in Scarcleft."

"Cloudmaster Granthon and Highlord Nealrith will protect you," she said softly. "All you have to do is get to them. They *need* you. The whole of the Quartern needs you."

Her words didn't cheer him, but he accepted their truth and prepared himself to accept all they implied about his future.

Both Taquar and Feroze had told Shale that Cloudmaster Granthon had stopped sending regular storms to both the White and the Gibber Quarters, and tendrils of rumour saying the same thing had insinuated themselves into the bazaar gossip. The rumour was confirmed when one of the waterpriests gave an official explanation from the pulpit. Storms were still being sent to the two quarters, he said, whenever possible. Unfortunately, they would not be enough to sustain the present level of population.

Terelle came back from the market with the news. She was tight-lipped, but that only lasted until she saw Shale. "What will happen to all those people?" she raged. "What do they mean, 'present level of population'?"

Russet entered the room behind her, his arms full of parcels, and he replied before Shale could think of anything to say. "Settles with water saved in cisterns soon be fighting off those with none. Raids, marauders—groves robbed, destroyed. The Gibber be finished. The settles soon be as barren as the plains themselves." His tone contained a distasteful avidity that sickened Shale.

Terelle's frown hardened; she couldn't accept what he said. "Are people really so stupid?" she asked Shale as she sat down at the table and started to unwrap her parcels.

"Don't waste your water," Russet said, regarding the

beginning of tears in Terelle's eyes. "They be not worthy of it."

"My family are Gibber people," she protested.

The laugh he gave was harsh with sarcasm. "Ye don't have a drop of Gibber blood, ye silly frip."

"My father—" she began.

"Ye be already living within your mother before that Gibberman find her. Ye be Watergiver through and through."

There was a long silence. Then, "It is time you told me who I am, *if* you really know."

"Of course I know. Scoured the Quartern looking for your mother. My mistake. I shuffled her likeness into waterpaintings, thinking to bring her to me, not knowing she be dead. I thought she be using her power to resist the power of the painting. I wasted years." He gave a grunt of frustration. "Your mother foolish, headstrong, wilful, stupid."

"Who am I?"

Shale stared at Terelle, his eyes widening. Her voice contained a hardness he had never heard before.

"And what do you mean, calling me Watergiver?"

Russet shrugged. "Nothing. Name of people, that be all. Just as ye talk of Scarpermen and Gibbermen and Reduner."

"What people?" Shale asked.

"People of Khromatis. My land."

"I've never heard of it."

"Khromatis lies on roof of Variega mountains. Beyond your comprehension, Gibberman. Past the Alabaster Whiteout. My home." He looked at Terelle. *"Your* home."

"Why were you looking for my mother? Who is my father? My real father. Does he live?"

"No."

The word was stark, uncompromising, but she would not be diverted. "His name?"

"Erith." He spat it out, his voice twisting with unpleasant emotion. "Erith Grey. Name better forgotten. Stole your mother from her people and fled the mountains. Took her because she had power. And he be having none. He be neither waterpainter nor watershifter. An eel-catcher!" His contempt was thick and unpleasant. "No true Watergiver. Peasant from salt marshes of borderlands."

She stared at him, her face a mask behind which she hid her turmoil. "And you?" she whispered finally. "What are you to me?"

"Kin," he said at last. "Trying to be bringing her back. Your mother."

"You spent so many *years* looking for her? From—from before my birth until you met me? That was fourteen years!"

"Yes."

"And now that you know she's dead?"

"Ye be taking her place, of course."

She stared. "To do what?"

"When ye ready, I take ye to Khromatis. Soon—"

She scrambled to her feet so suddenly she upturned her chair. "And have I no say in all this? What am I—a shell to be moved from one hollow to another on the board at another's whim? I'll go *nowhere* without knowing a lot more than this, old man."

With that deliberate rudeness, she turned on her heel, picked up her hat from the peg at the door and left.

"As wilful as her mother," Russet growled at Shale.

Shale, only too aware that he owed his safety to this man's sanctuary, could say nothing; he gritted his teeth in his frustration at being unable to speak his mind. *The sandblighted old bastard*, he thought. *In his own way, he's as evil as Taquar. And I'm damned if I will allow him to do this to Terelle. I will find a way to get her out of this. I must.*

CHAPTER THIRTY-ONE

Scarpen Quarter
Scarcleft City
Artisman Russet's room, Level 36

Terelle returned to Russet's room an hour or so later.

There was nowhere else to go. And as always, when her mind schemed rebellion, her body suffered. She sweated; her stomach cramped.

In one part of her mind and heart she had always known that Russet was not a gentle, kindly old man with an altruistic interest in her wellbeing. She just hadn't wanted to see the extent of his nastiness and greed, even in the privacy of her thoughts.

She scowled, thinking, *That was so childish.*

At least she knew her true name now: Terelle Grey. And if Russet was telling the truth, Viviandra's father, who had sold her to a Reduner caravan, had only been her stepfather. She was glad of that, too.

She shivered slightly. The thought of journeying to a land so far away that no one had even heard of it scared her. *Watergivers.* Even the name was outlandish, as if they were all gods. Or blasphemous, as if they all thought of themselves as gods. Yet she didn't know if she was prepared to confront Russet and demand answers, or to give ultimatums. What if he painted a worse future for her? Perhaps he could restrict her still further, tighten his grip on her small freedoms. How would she bear it? It was bad enough as it was. In her heart, she ached to go with Shale. She trusted him. She liked him. When she was with him, she felt content. No, more than that: safe. Happy. When she thought of him walking out of her life, she went cold all over. But how to tear free of Russet when even thinking about it made her feel so ill?

Sunlord help me, how long do I have to spend with that old man? I hate him!

For the next few days, she kept practising her waterpainting skills, including the ability to influence the future.

"We call it shuffling," Russet said. "Ye shuffle up new picture from base paint, or ye shuffle the future—make it happen."

She experimented by manipulating things that she hoped were trivial, but the more she trained her hand and her mind, the more she was frightened by the scope of what she was able to do. "If ye be having details, then only two limits to power of waterpainting, Terelle," Russet said. "Ye can't shuffle up yourself into a painting. Meaning ye can't make your own future. Second thing, ye can't ask impossible—can't be bringing dead back to life or making someone fly like bird."

"It wouldn't be possible for me to ensure that Shale and Mica meet again, would it?" she asked, wanting to be sure she had been right about that.

"Your heart and mind must have picture of Mica, so how? Ye can't."

Shale, practising his water skills alongside her, looked away without commenting. His innate disapproval of waterpainting was like a smothering blanket.

Her fear grew. Her sense of rebellion was being slowly snuffed out, spark by spark. It had nothing to do with Shale, everything to do with Russet. And there was nothing she could do to stop it.

As a snuggery madam, Opal considered the girls' reading of poetry or writing of loving missives to favoured clients to be part of their entertainment value. Consequently, both Terelle and Vivie had been taught to read. However, Terelle had never read the kind of books that Shale had in his possession. A book about Scarcleft and the people who had once ruled the Scarpen. A book on the geography of the Quartern. A book describing plants and animals and gemstones. A book detailing the dynamics of water.

"I never knew reading could be so—so interesting!" she said. "Where did you get them all?"

"I took them from the mother cistern. There were lots of books there when I arrived, children's books mostly, and Taquar brought me more later."

"Books in a mother cistern? Why?" she asked.

"What?"

"Why? Why on earth did Taquar keep books at a cistern? And why children's books? Did he take them there for you?"

He paused, thinking. "No, I don't think so. Most of them were stacked away and dusty. There were all sorts of odd things there. Toys. Children's clothes of different sizes, for girls. Women's clothing, too. As if . . ."

"As if?"

"As if other people had been living there before me."

"*Children?*" She was disbelieving.

He was silent so long she thought he was not going to answer.

Then he said softly, "I'm stupid. I never really thought about it, but of course it wasn't like that. It was one child, growing up. Getting bigger, older."

"That doesn't make sense."

"Yes, it does. If she was like me."

She stared at him, not comprehending, and then with growing horror as she did. "A water sensitive," she said at last. "A potential stormlord. Kidnapped. Living there alone for *years*? Growing *up* there? Until she was a woman?"

"A prisoner." He could barely get the words out. "Taquar's prisoner. Like me. Maybe she was looked after by a woman. There were no clothes to fit a child older than about ten. Maybe he took her away before she got any older than that."

"Or maybe she died then."

He went to rummage through his bag. Russet, who had been brewing more of his paints at the fireplace, looked over at him curiously, but he ignored the old man and held up what he had been looking for: the gold bracelet he had found in the mother cistern. "I found this there. There's a word on it, but I wasn't sure what it meant." He handed it to her.

Before she had time to examine it, Russet had reached over her shoulder and taken it from her. "Vymeth? No, Lyneth."

"It's a girl's name," Terelle said.

Russet considered. "Familiar. Lyneth. Yes, I remember. Two rainlords lost daughter in desert. Lyneth. Stormlord, folk said. Father be still looking for her, even now. Sandcrazy man with limp. His name? Ianin? Iani, that be it. Husband to Moiqa, Highlord of Qanatend. Their daughter."

"Not a lost child," Shale said. "A kidnapped child. She must have died, of illness perhaps. Otherwise he would not have needed me."

"Taquar maybe killed her if she not stormlord he wanted," Russet said.

"Maybe she just went crazy," Terelle whispered. "All those years shut away . . ."

"Here." Russet gave the bracelet back to Shale. "Give to Cloudmaster when ye meet." He sounded more gleeful than touched by the tragedy it represented.

Shale's expression was one of revulsion. "You would like to see Breccia and Scarcleft fighting one another," he said. "Why?"

Russet's face twitched. "I be owing them nothing," he said. "Asked them for help, all those years ago. Nealrith, Granthon, Taquar, Moiqa, others, too—not one help get me what rightfully mine. Not one."

"What was it that was rightfully yours?" Shale asked.

But the old man left the room for the hallway without replying.

"My mother," Terelle said quietly. "He means my mother. He asked them to help him find her."

He thought about that and whispered back, "At least we can guess now why he's helping me. He wants to stir up trouble between the cities. Between Nealrith and Taquar."

Terelle wanted to argue, wanted to deny it, but she couldn't bring herself to utter the words. It could have been true. She settled for changing the subject. "If Taquar finds you, but thinks you won't cooperate, he could have you killed. We heard today that they were conducting a house-to-house search on the other side of our level. And that some of the streets were blocked off."

"Were they looking for me?"

"I don't know. Nobody was allowed over there to find out what was going on."

"Terelle, you need to be careful. Anyone who helps me could be in danger."

"Let him try to hurt me," she said, half-amused, half-rattled by the concern in his voice. "He'd have to override waterpainting magic first. You see, Russet has painted me older than I am now." Her amusement vanished with her next thought. When she had left the snuggery, she had sworn she would be free to do as she wanted. And yet Russet now as good as owned her. She wasn't even able to *think* of leaving him.

She, who had so valued her freedom, had lost all the freedom she'd ever had.

Every day after that, enforcers searched a different sector of the level and then carefully screened everyone who entered the searched areas afterwards.

"Only a matter of time before they get here," Shale said. "And still too soon to be expecting Highlord Nealrith." It was hard to curb his impatience to be gone.

Russet's advice was to let them come. "They never be looking for a Reduner," he said.

"What reason would a Reduner be here, in our room?" Terelle asked. "It would seem so odd to an enforcer, surely. I mean, Reduners don't mix with Scarcleft folk."

"Reduner caravanners be selling goods to anyone, just like 'Baster caravanners. Can sell waterpainters red pigment, no?"

They prepared themselves by getting rid of anything that tied Shale to his past: the books, his clothes, the cloth bag. Then they made paint-powder in different shades of red and wrapped each in red cloth.

"I'm in trouble if an enforcer speaks to me in the Reduner tongue," Shale said. "I know all the more common words, and I understand quite a bit, but that's all."

Russet grunted. "Scarpen folk be too arrogant to learn other tongues," he said, dismissing Shale's concerns with an airy wave of his hand.

He has to be the most irritating man I've ever met, Shale thought.

As far as he knew, no one was aware that Russet's room had an extra person. Terelle had no need to buy him water, and whenever his water-senses told him there was anyone around, he spoke only in a whisper and avoided using the communal outhouse at the end of the hallway. The secrecy was tiresome but bearable. When Vato warned Terelle the search had started in their area, Russet announced that if the enforcers took Shale, he—Russet—must be free to paint him out of trouble. With that, he disappeared with his paints and trays.

"Oooh!" Terelle cried after he'd gone. "Sometimes I want to push his face right into the middle of one of his paintings while the paint is still wet! He's leaving us to face the enforcers alone, the—the sand-blighted misbegotten son of a—"

Shale grinned sympathetically as words failed her. "It doesn't matter. We can do this alone. At least we know he would do his best to help *you* afterwards if anything went wrong."

They heard the commotion in the street first. People wailing, shouts. It was past midday, though, before Shale sensed strangers coming up their stairs. "A party of six. All men," he said.

Terelle tensed. "Is it them?"

"Probably."

"I'm scared," she whispered.

"Don't be. We've rehearsed all this. And we have got rid of everything that ties me to Taquar." That wasn't quite true. Hidden in the hem of his tunic was Lyneth's bracelet, but he wasn't going to remind her of that. "How do I look?"

She surveyed him critically. "Like a Reduner. But belt on your scimitar."

He grabbed the weapon up, cursing himself for forgetting it, and did up the sword belt. She reached up to arrange his red braids so that some fell in front of his ears and were clearly visible.

They left the door open and were therefore forced to listen to the sounds of their neighbours being bullied. Terelle paled. Shale smiled encouragement, but she didn't look any happier.

When the enforcers and a reeve arrived, she was calmly counting tokens into Shale's outstretched hand. The paint-powder was on the table, with several of the cloths untied to show the heaps of colour.

She looked up as the men appeared. "Yes?" she asked.

They ignored her question and all of them entered the room. Four of them began searching, throwing belongings around without care. The reeve and the enforcer in charge stood either side of the doorway.

"Your name and work?" the reeve asked.

"Terelle Grey, apprentice waterpainter. I live here with my, um, grandfather, Russet, who does the waterpaintings for the upper levels." She dug into her pocket and pulled out the uplevel pass Russet had left with her.

The reeve looked at it, then passed it back and turned his attention to Shale.

Shale stared back, with arrogant calm, or so he hoped.

"And who are you?" the reeve asked.

"Evrim, caravanner of Dune Pebblered," Shale said, imitating a heavy Reduner accent.

One of the searchers slashed the pallets so that he could feel through the teased fibres inside. Terelle winced when she saw what he was doing.

"Why are you here?" the reeve asked Shale.

"Trading," he answered.

"We buy red paint from his dune," Terelle added and indicated the powder on the table in front of her. "And is it really necessary to make such a mess?" An enforcer had started to rake through the ashes in the hearth, sending up billows of dust.

"I didn't know there was a Reduner caravan in," the enforcer by the door said. He had been watching his men, but now his gaze held Shale's.

Shale glared. "You spy?" he asked suspiciously. "Spy on me?" His hand dropped to the handle of his scimitar.

Terelle looked horrified. She made an involuntary gesture of negation.

"No, no," the enforcer said hurriedly. His right hand hovered around the hilt of his weapon, but he did not look happy at the prospect of a fight against a Reduner.

"We have no quarrel with you," the reeve said to Shale. "Finish your business, pedeman, and be on your way."

Grateful for the reputation Reduners had for being quick and deadly in battle, Shale took his hand away from the scimitar. He drew himself up and folded his arms instead. "Reduner warrior never leave woman alone with *rakui* men!" he said. "I wait!"

The reeve and the enforcer exchanged glances. The reeve shrugged. "We've finished anyway," he said.

Terelle and Shale waited in silence while the men filed out. When they heard them descend the stairs, Terelle let out the breath she had been holding.

"Oh, you—you—dryhead! I thought I was going to die of fright! What if he'd pulled his sword?"

Shale grinned at her. "At least it never occurred to him that I was the Gibber youth they were looking for."

"And what does *rakui* mean?"

"Not sure. It's an insult of some sort."

She rolled her eyes at him. "You're impossible. I'd better check on Lilva and anyone else who's around. If I don't, they'll only come here to find out how I am. Behave yourself."

She left, closing the door behind her. He sat down at the table and stared at his hands, which seemed to have suddenly developed a tremor, wondering if he'd been out of his mind.

Russet was out again on the day the Breccian rainlords arrived in Scarcleft.

Terelle was painting, while Shale watched. She was seated on the old man's mat near the open door where the light was best, while he sat at the table and wished he still had his books.

As she gently tapped powdered colour from an application spoon onto the surface of the water, he asked, "Have you ever met an Alabaster?"

She finished what she was doing before she replied. "An Alabaster? I once saw one up close. The day I first met Russet." She frowned. "Russet said something odd about that. He said that he, the Alabaster, was drawn to me because of my tears. I weep tears when I feel sad, you see. Russet said the Alabaster felt them. And the Alabaster, he raised his hand in blessing towards me. I don't know why."

Shale thought about that. "You shed tears when you don't have something in your eye? I've never met anyone else who did that."

"I think it is how Russet found me. From a distance, no one would know I was not Gibber. You have to be close up to realise my eyes are green. It was my tears that betrayed me." She sounded matter-of-fact. "Maybe it is something that these people from Khromatis do. Waste water on grief."

He was silent for a moment, pondering. It was the first time she had actually acknowledged that she was indeed one of Russet's people. "If the Alabaster realised that—"

He paused, thinking things through. "Maybe if you were to ask one, they might be able to tell you more about who you are. Or at least about who the mountain people are."

"You could be right. Only there aren't any Alabasters around any more. I guess they got to hear what happened to that man you told us about. What was his name?"

"Feroze Khorash."

"You believe he's dead, don't you?"

He nodded abruptly, not wanting to think about it. "Terelle, if Highlord Nealrith comes, please say you'll come with me to Breccia."

She was silent so long, he knew something was wrong. "What is it?" he asked.

"Russet won't let me go. Whatever it is he plans, he needs me for it."

"He can't stop you."

"Shale, he can shuffle up a future in which I don't go with you to Breccia. He can paint you out of my life. He might have already done so. He has certainly already influenced my future."

He stared at her, trying to think through the implications, not certain if he believed what she was trying to tell him.

She started fiddling with her paint jars, turning from him so he could not see her face. "You don't understand, do you? He controls me through his waterpainting. He has concocted his version of the future and placed me there, doing the things he has planned for me. I don't think I even had a chance to refuse his offer of apprenticeship. I didn't realise it then, of course. And now I want to choose another way, I can't. He's taken away my choices, Shale. I don't have any. I think I never did."

Something inside him lurched painfully. "You're trapped *inside* his paintings?" he asked, incredulous.

She continued. "In a way. They pull me. I know that I want to go with you. That I ought to go. That I will be safer with you, better off in Breccia. I know all those things in my head, but I don't *feel* that I want to go. Just the opposite. I am being drawn to a different future. The one he has painted." She looked away from him and back at her painting. "I can't go with you, and I'm sorrier than I can say."

He was shocked by her certainty. By the fact that she accepted it. "That's coercion. It's not right. It's worse than slavery."

She was silent.

"What future has been painted for you?"

"I've seen pictures of me in what is probably the White Quarter, and also in a green place, where water flows on the land. Maybe it won't be so bad. If I am his kin, if he takes me back to where I belong, at least I'll find out about my real mother and father. Perhaps I have other family—"

"It's not right to be forced."

"No. But I can't help myself."

The words were whispered, despairing, so unlike her that he was shocked. "Yes, you can! Remember what Russet said? He said that he thought he couldn't find your mother because she resisted the pull of his waterpainting! It must be possible to resist, to pull away, to stand against it. Otherwise he would not have believed she could do it."

"He was talking about my *mother*, not me. She was powerful in these water arts, or so he has implied. I'm just an apprentice."

"I can't believe that you are just going to give up! *You*?" He stood up and came over to where she was still seated on the mat. "You struggled so long to find a way to escape the snuggery and now you are just going to allow yourself to be enslaved again? By someone you don't even *like*? Terelle, you've got to fight it!"

His passion broke through into his voice and she looked up at him, startled. He dropped to his knees beside her. "Terelle, I'll speak to Highlord Nealrith. Maybe he can help. What if you do your own painting? There's got to be a way!"

"I can't paint myself, remember? And Russet's so much more powerful than I am."

"*Is* he? If that was so, then he wouldn't need you so much! Terelle, don't give up. Please—" He stopped, astonished by his own reaction to being parted from her. It *mattered*. He couldn't bear to lose another person. Especially not Terelle. He opened his mouth to protest further but didn't have the words to express what he wanted, what he thought. All that would come out was a pathetic, "Please don't give up. Not like this."

His passion had shaken her, he could see that. She looked at him uncertainly, then her eyes filled with tears. And suddenly she was in his arms, crying, and he was patting her awkwardly on the back.

He took a deep breath and forced himself to say the things he had been holding inside. "Terelle, other than Mica, you're the only friend I've ever had. I thought after Taquar that I'd never trust anyone again." He was grateful she had her face buried in his shoulder and was not watching him as he stumbled on, wading through a welter of raw emotion. "For nearly four years I never spoke to anyone but Taquar, and that not often. So if I'm not making sense, I'm sorry. I'm not good at saying things. But I want to tell you I don't want to lose you. And that I'll look after you, if I can. You'll never want for water, I swear. And I'll keep you safe."

She pulled back then, to look at him, wiping her face with the back of her hand. She managed to appear amazed and bemused and delighted, all at the one time.

"But you've got to fight Russet's power first. I can't do that for you," he added.

And something died in her expression, even as she said, "I'll try. I promise I'll try."

CHAPTER THIRTY-TWO

Scarpen Quarter
Scarcleft City
Scarcleft Hall, Level 2

The seneschal of Scarcleft Hall, Harkel Tallyman, was a thin, small-framed man, nondescript in appearance and deceptively harmless in his manner. As a consequence, he was often overlooked. Yet after the highlord himself, Harkel was the most powerful man in Scarcleft, maintaining his position through a network of spies, assassins, thieves, blackmailers, water sensitives and informants. Trusted with the running of the city when Taquar was absent—which was frequently—his loyalty to the highlord was unswerving and unquestioning.

It had surprised him, then alarmed him, when it took so long to find Shale the Gibber youth. He had grown unused to failure. He had been at fault, he acknowledged to himself; he hadn't taken the search seriously enough at first, assuming the enforcers would soon find one lone young man, newly arrived and naive in the ways of the city.

The last time he had been face-to-face with Taquar, he had seen a deep anger in the rainlord's eyes, the first directed his way in more than ten years. It had unsettled him. He knew Taquar better than anybody, and he knew just how utterly ruthless the rainlord could be when cold rage overtook careful strategy as his driving force.

At last, however, the fickle winds of luck were at last gusting Harkel's way, and he was relieved to be able to go to the highlord with news of Shale Flint from several different sources.

Taquar was going through a pile of paperwork when Harkel entered his room, but he pushed that aside immediately and acknowledged the seneschal with a terse nod. "What is it?"

"A possibility, lord. One of my informants saw someone who may have been the Gibber youth, Shale, some time ago at a residence on Level Ten. Unfortunately, he only realised this more recently, when he saw one of the posters. I have put a watch on the house, and one of my men is courting the maidservant."

The rainlord did not move a muscle, yet Harkel was aware of how taut he was. How close to lashing out in a lethal rage. "Go on."

"My informant—his name is Jomat—is the steward for an arta, Amethyst the dancer. I understand that my lord is acquainted with the lady."

"Watch your tongue, Harkel."

Harkel's mouth went dry. "Yes, my lord. I mean no disrespect. The young man was disguised as a Reduner. He came to Amethyst's house with a Gibber girl who is an apprentice to the outlander waterpainter Russet Kermes. Her name is Terelle. It is possible that the boy is hiding in the waterpainter's room. I have men out tracing the exact building, but I am treading carefully. The house must have been searched before, but somehow he was not found then. Perhaps he was warned. This time, we are being more careful.

"Jomat tells me that shortly after seeing Shale, the dancer wrote a letter to someone. I had men inquire at the tenth level's letter repository, and they found that it had already been dispatched to Breccia Hall, addressed to Lady Ethelva. I do not know if these two events are connected."

Taquar interrupted. "Yes. They are. Of course they are." His fingers drummed on the desk, betraying unaccustomed agitation. Taquar continued, "Someone has given him good advice. He has applied to Breccia Hall for help." Anger smouldered like a dampened fire about to break through. "I shall want everyone dead, Harkel. Except Shale."

"Including the dancer?"

"Especially the dancer. But don't you worry about her. I'll attend to that myself. First, we must make sure we have Shale safe. Do nothing until he is physically in your hands."

"I have another piece of news which may be connected. An informant in Breccia Hall sent a message to me via a myriapede rider. Highlord Nealrith has left Breccia with a small entourage. Eleven men altogether."

"Bound for Scarcleft?"

"No one knows for sure, but my informant checked the amount of water the party took with them and the gate they left by. Both fit a journey to Scarcleft. And the timing is right for them to have left in response to the letter Amethyst sent."

"Ah. When are they due?"

"My informant's messenger travelled as fast as he could, but I don't imagine that he is as much as a day ahead. It's likely Nealrith and party will arrive sometime later today."

Taquar stopped his drumming. "He will probably go straight to Amethyst. She will then send for Shale. Nealrith will wait at Amethyst's for him, and then they'll leave."

"I could have my men intercept them at the gate. On the way out, I mean."

"Don't be stupid. That's too risky. Can you have forgotten you would be dealing with a rainlord of power? No, I think it is up to me to intercept Nealrith. You must go after Shale before the two of them meet. Follow Amethyst's messenger to find out for sure where he is. Once you have Shale spirited away to Scarcleft Hall, kill the waterpainters, the messenger, anyone else who looks as if they know anything. I will deal with Nealrith and Amethyst." He smiled. "You seem to have done something right in this matter at last, Harkel. Which is well for you."

Harkel stilled the fear that soaked him. "As you say, m'lord."

Taquar smiled yet again. "It is a pity that I am not yet ready for an open confrontation with Nealrith, but nonetheless, I shall enjoy thwarting him."

"Highlord—" Harkel hesitated.

Taquar raised his eyebrows in question.

"The boy's abilities. I know he can move water—the reeves from the city's waterhall told me that much. But I need to know if he can kill . . . in the rainlord manner."

"No. That I never taught him. And I have reason to believe he would find it difficult. You should have no problems dealing with him." He sat down again. "Let us discuss the details of this plan, Harkel. There must be no mistake. Shale must be safe and unhurt in my hands, and all those who know about him must die." He looked up and fixed an unwavering gaze on the seneschal. "There can be no other result. Do you understand me?"

Harkel nodded calmly. "Of course, m'lord. And I apologise for my former missteps in this matter. It won't happen again."

Taquar smiled. "I'm sure it won't."

Harkel did not feel reassured.

CHAPTER THIRTY-THREE

Scarpen Quarter
Scarcleft City
Level 36

"Someone's coming along the hallway," Shale said.

Terelle moved out of his arms, spilling water from her painting tray in her hurry. "I'll *never* get used to you being able to do that."

"Four men."

"Let's hope it's the rainlords. But get out of sight, just in case."

He stepped behind the curtain that surrounded her sleeping pallet, and a moment later heard a man's voice saying, "We are looking for Terelle, the apprentice to the waterpainter."

Terelle's reply was steady. "That's me."

"Amethyst the dancer sent us here to fetch your friend. Nealrith, Highlord of Breccia City, asks for his presence."

At last. Shale stepped out from behind the curtain and nodded to Terelle. She stood back to allow the men to enter and then closed the door behind them. They were all large, and they made the room seem small. The oldest, a formidable man in his thirties with a hook nose and a scar running down the side of his face, carried a pike. Two others, both young, had scimitars at their belts. The leader of the group, a muscular, tanned man with lazy blue eyes, wore a sword.

He spoke first, directing his words to Shale, "Who are you?"

"Shale Flint."

"A *Reduner*?"

"It seemed a sensible disguise."

"Ah. No one warned me. I'm Kaneth Carnelian, a rainlord of Breccia City." He indicated the man with the scar. "Elmar, pikeman of the Breccia Hall guard. Highlord Nealrith is at the house of Arta Amethyst. He asked me to bring you to him."

Shale's heart was pounding fast, but he tried not to show that he was edgy. He turned to Terelle. "Come with me."

She hesitated.

He wanted to tell her so many things, but the words dried up in his mouth.

The rainlord was saying, "Fetch all your things. You won't be returning here."

To Shale's relief, Terelle began to shovel her paint pots into a woven bag. As she grabbed up her clothes to stuff them on top, Lord Kaneth watched with a raised eyebrow but didn't say anything. When Shale had gathered together his own meagre belongings, one of the men took them from him, saying, "I'm Soltar. Gadri here will carry this for you." He tossed the bundle over to the fourth man, who grinned at Shale but didn't say anything.

"We need to hurry," Lord Kaneth said, frowning at Terelle. "We want to be out of Scarcleft before Taquar knows we've arrived."

"Why not leave the city now, from here? It would be safer. Enforcers are looking for me. The south gate is only a few moments' walk," Shale said.

Lord Kaneth looked at him in surprise. "Are you questioning Highlord Nealrith's orders? I do not think that anyone will challenge our right to escort you anywhere." He tapped the insignia on Soltar's tunic, a monogram of entwined letters. "That stands for Breccia Hall," he said.

"I didn't recognise it. And neither will the people in the street out there," Terelle told him. "And here on the thirty-sixth, they won't much care, either. All people care about now is water, and the reward offered for Shale's capture is a lifetime allotment. True, he's posed as a Reduner once out on the streets, but since then there's been a lot more searches and trouble. People are more alert."

Lord Kaneth surveyed Shale. "The disguise is a good one. We're not likely to have trouble."

"I agree with Terelle," Shale said. "Going up to the tenth would be foolish. Lord Nealrith can't understand the mood of the people of this level or know how dangerous Lord Taquar is."

The Breccian pikeman with the scar, Elmar, interrupted. "You speak of two highlords, young fellow. Keep a civil tongue behind your teeth!"

"He speaks of a man who killed his family!" Terelle rapped back. "Doesn't Highlord Nealrith know what is at stake?"

"Listen!" Shale cried suddenly. Strangers, men running up the stairs—he could sense them.

Kaneth misunderstood and ignored him. "All we know

is an unsubstantiated story that may well malign a fellow rain—" he began. He did not get any further.

Shale shouted a warning. At the same moment, the door was pulled open. Terelle, who had been leaning against it, fell flat on her back, half in and half out of the doorway. Her head slammed onto the floor. A burly man wearing the uniform of the enforcers trampled over her, followed by seven or eight others. The room suddenly bristled with blades. Shale went to dive through them to get to Terelle, but Lord Kaneth grabbed his arm to jerk him back behind the table.

Elmar swung his pike up into a defensive position, attempting to bar the intruders from reaching Shale and the rainlord. "What is this?" he asked, puffing up in indignation. "Who dares to challenge the Cloudmaster's men? What do you want?"

"We have come to take the youth," the first man replied. "He is a wanted criminal."

Lord Kaneth stepped in front of Shale. "We have precedence in this matter, I think," he said. There was nothing lazy or slow about him now. "I am here representing Cloudmaster Granthon, who has given orders for this man to be brought before him."

"Highlord Taquar rules in Scarcleft. Not you." The sneer in the voice of the enforcer was an insult in itself. He turned to the men behind him. "Take the youth. If anyone tries to prevent you, kill them."

The enforcers moved forward as a block, one of them thrusting his pike across the table at Lord Kaneth to push him out of the way.

In an instant, Shale felt as if he had just been transported to the eye of a spindevil. The room exploded into a fury of action. Elmar swung his pike to slice into the arm of the enforcer threatening Lord Kaneth. Another blade flashed within inches of Shale's cheek—Kaneth's—and it sliced into the unprotected side of an assailant. Elmar swung his pike again, with lethal effect. One of the intruders fell, his head nearly severed by the pike blade, and blood squirted impossibly far, spraying everyone in the room.

Terelle was still on the floor. Every time she struggled to get up, someone trod on her.

Unexpectedly, Lord Kaneth jumped up onto the table and just stood there, no longer using his sword. Gadri was locked in hand-to-hand battle with another man; Soltar used his scimitar to hold off two others. The room was filled with noise: Terelle, still in the doorway, squealed as someone's heel came down on her hand. A man who'd had his face slashed was screaming and trying to hold the edges of his cheek together. Metal dashed on metal; men gasped and grunted. Familiar smells mingled in an unfamiliar mix: sweat, blood, bodily waste. Someone was shouting orders—a thin man in the doorway—but no one could hear him. Certainly no one took any notice.

Entirely forgetting that he was wearing a scimitar, Shale grabbed at the nearest article he could find to use as a weapon: the iron spit from the fireplace. He swung it hard at the head of the nearest Scarcleft enforcer. The man dropped, groaning. Someone slashed out with a scimitar at one of the intruders, and more blood sprayed across the room, catching Shale in a swathe of droplets. His stomach heaved as he wiped his face on his sleeve. He headed for the door to help Terelle, reckoning he was reasonably safe. It was unlikely that Taquar wanted him dead.

Terelle had given up trying to haul herself to her feet
and was crawling out of the door, wincing in pain. The
thin man standing there wrenched at the arm of one of the
Scarcleft enforcers. "Kill her!" he ordered and pointed at
Terelle. Shale yelled at her to run. She took one look at
the man bearing down on her, scrambled to her feet and
fled, vanishing from Shale's sight.

Another Scarcleft enforcer grabbed at him but then
screamed, a hideous high-pitched sound. Shale saw something he would never forget as long as he lived: the man's
eyes shrivelled up like dried bab fruits in the sun, their water
pouring down his face. The man sank to his knees, wailing
and clutching at his eyes. Shale looked wildly around the
room: Elmar and Soltar were still fighting on, apparently
unharmed, but Gadri was down on the floor, lying in a pool
of blood. A disproportionate number of Scarcleft enforcers
were out of the fight, either wounded by pike or scimitar
slashes, or clutching their eyes and moaning.

Lord Kaneth remained standing on the table, untouched, surveying the room with a cold gaze. When his
glance met that of the thin man, still standing in the doorway, he roared at him, "Stop the fighting!"

Elmar and Soltar stepped back immediately, and their
opponents looked at the thin man for guidance. He held
up his hand in agreement. "The fight is ours, I think," he
said softly to the rainlord. "You are outnumbered. You are
in our jurisdiction, Lord Kaneth, and I order you in the
name of the Highlord of Scarcleft to surrender Shale Flint
to me."

"I think not, Harkel" Kaneth said. "Look around at your
men. How many of them are still in fighting condition?"

Before Harkel could reply, the Scarcleft enforcer closest to Shale grabbed him in a headlock from behind. Shale gasped, choking, as the man's arm tightened around his throat. The fellow had abandoned his sword for a knife, which now pricked Shale's ribs.

The balance had changed, yet Harkel hesitated before he said, "Surrender, or the lad dies."

Lord Kaneth smiled, unperturbed. "I suspect your orders were to take him alive and unharmed."

The arm at Shale's throat went into spasm then hardened; the grip loosened. Water soaked Shale's back and dripped onto the floor. One moment he was crushed against his captor's chest, the next he was jammed up against something as hard and as uneven as a rough stone wall. He looked down at the enforcer's forearm, and the hairs on his neck rose. The wrist that emerged from the sleeve of the uniform was as thin as a broom handle; white skin was now deep brown, like that of an animal carcass dried out in a desert sun. Water soaked Shale's tunic and breeches. The knife in the man's other hand dropped from rigid bony fingers. Shale yelped in shock and struggled, still caught in the man's unyielding clasp. A pool of water widened at his feet. The man's body, hard and almost without weight, bumped at his back. Horrified, Shale felt himself clutched in a lifeless embrace. The man had died wordlessly, before he could utter a cry, still standing.

"Our game, I think," Lord Kaneth drawled, still calm. "Unless you wish to join your enforcer as skin and bone and a pool of water on the floor."

In frantic horror, Shale thrust violently against the arm at his throat until the joints snapped. The body, a shrunken parody of a human being, released him and fell away into the water that had once given it life. Shale backed away, his revulsion total, his whole body shaking.

Seneschal Harkel stood motionless.

Lord Kaneth said softly, "Shame your men did not recognise me as a rainlord. There was no need for them to suffer this. Step into the room, Harkel. And tell your men to throw their weapons out of the door."

Harkel did not move. Then, ashen, he looked down at his sandaled feet. From his ankles downwards, sweat was seeping out through his skin, to dribble onto the floor. "No," he said in a strangled whisper. "Don't do this."

"Your choice."

The seneschal's face was ashen. "You'll make an enemy for life in Taquar," he warned, but his voice wavered.

"Is this the way you want to die?" Kaneth asked.

No one moved. All eyes were turned to watch the slow seepage of water from the seneschal's feet. Even Shale felt a nauseated fascination: this was a slow version of how the other man had died. Repelled, he turned away, his stomach queasy.

The seneschal gave a harsh laugh. "Taquar will kill me anyway if I lose here."

Kaneth shrugged. "It doesn't make much difference to me," he said casually. "I am happy enough to kill you all." He smiled pleasantly at Harkel. "But then perhaps this is an easier death than the one Taquar will give you. Goodbye, Seneschal."

"*No!*" Harkel took a deep breath. "No." He gestured to the enforcers. "Do as he asks."

Sullenly, those men still standing disposed of their weapons outside in the hallway.

Lord Kaneth jumped down from the table and said, "Outside, Shale."

Shale tripped over his feet in his anxiety to leave the room. He looked along the hallway to the stairs, but Terelle had vanished—and so had the enforcer who had followed her out with orders to kill her.

Soltar followed him, bringing along Shale's bundle. He stopped, briefly, to mutter a farewell and touch Gadri's body in passing. Lord Kaneth left next, with Elmar guarding his back. He pushed the door closed, with all the enforcers and Harkel inside the room. There was no bar and no lock on the outside, but that didn't faze Kaneth. He stared at the door for a moment, and the bab panels dampened and swelled until the door was jammed in place.

I'll be pissing waterless, Shale thought. *He used their water, the water of the dead.* He wanted to vomit.

"That should keep them in for a while," Kaneth said, still coldly calm. "Soltar, Shale, Elmar, throw their weapons onto the roof of that building over there." He was already walking away.

They did as he asked and then hurried to catch up. "You get your wish, Shale," Kaneth said when they reached the bottom of the stairs. "We won't be going uplevel. We'll go straight out of the gates to the livery where we left our mounts. Fortunately, I already asked to have them loaded with enough water to get us back to Breccia."

"I can't go with you! Terelle—" Shale began, stricken at the thought of leaving her behind. "I have to find her first."

Kaneth ignored his protest and, staggering slightly, turned to Soltar, saying, "It will be up to you to get to the tenth level, back to the dancer's house. Think you can do it?"

"Yes, my lord," the guard said, but he looked grim.

"As fast as you can. You have to tell Nealrith what happened here. Tell him I am going straight back to the rendezvous camp, and we'll wait out the night there. If he doesn't arrive by dawn, we'll ride for Breccia."

Elmar interrupted, "But, Lord Kaneth, we can't leave the highlord—"

"Yes, we can. And must." He looked down at Shale. "If Taquar wants this lad from the Gibber so much that he sends his seneschal to get him, at the risk of starting a battle with the Cloudmaster's guards, he must be important. Nealrith would agree with my decision. Soltar—go."

Soltar threw Shale's bundle to Elmar and left at a run.

"But what about Terelle?" Shale said, hanging back. Desperately he cast about for any sign of her water, but she must have been too far away, because he couldn't sense her. "My friend. I can't just leave her. I promised—"

Kaneth grabbed his arm and pulled him along. "Oh yes, you can. It will only be a matter of moments before they break down that door. Your friend is not important; you are. And she's probably fine, anyway." He was breathing heavily and stumbling, as if he had been running, but his hold on Shale only tightened.

"There was a guard after her," Shale protested. "I can't—"

"You can, and you will," Kaneth rasped at him, all pretence of drawling good humour gone. "*Move*—and that is an order, Shale. Uttered in my capacity as a representative of the Highlord of Breccia City, and through him, the Cloudmaster of the Quartern. Do you understand me?" He pulled Shale after him, dragging him down the street.

Shale shook off Kaneth's hand. "She's important to me! Would *you* abandon a friend?"

Kaneth stopped. "Ah," he said, "I see." He drew in a ragged breath before adding, "Probably not. But *I* am not the Quartern's best hope for any kind of future. Look, I'll hunt for her. I promise. But later. Now your safety is all that matters, to her, to us, to this land. Harkel just convinced me of that. If Terelle has any sense, she will have headed straight for Amethyst's house on the tenth. She will meet up with Nealrith and Soltar, and they will bring her with them when they come to meet us." Then he repeated his previous question, even more sharp-edged this time. "Do you understand me?"

They stared at one another, and Kaneth's stare was uncompromising.

Shale nodded miserably.

"If she doesn't turn up there, then you have my promise I will look for her," Kaneth added as they turned to push their way into the level's crowded main thoroughfare.

Once they were slowed down by the throng, Elmar said, "We were damned lucky you were with us, my lord, or we'd have all been slaughtered like Gadri back there."

"Thank Nealrith, not me. He was the one who insisted on having another rainlord along on this trip."

Around them, the crowd swirled and a whisper started, brushing its way from person to person like the soft touch of a breeze. "Look, a Reduner!" . . . "Hey, isn't that blood?" . . . "Who are they?"

Elmar made a menacing movement with his pike. "Make way for Breccia City's highlord!" he cried, blithely promoting Kaneth. "Make way!" He poked an insistent beggar hard in the ribs with the shaft of the pike, and the crowd nervously edged back.

Kaneth gave a twisted smile. "Are you really a rain-lord, young man?" he asked Shale.

"I—I guess so."

"A stormlord?"

"I don't know yet."

Kaneth exchanged a glance with Elmar. "Strange how things turn out, eh, Elmar? One day both you and I might be on our knees before Shale here, pledging our allegiance to a new cloudmaster. Just as well it's a whole lot easier to leave a city than enter it."

"Not for me," Shale argued. "They have been watching for me for weeks, and when they entered Russet's room they were looking for a Reduner."

"Ah. Yes. You're right. They weren't surprised, were they? Let's find a quiet spot." He turned into a dead-end lane stacked with seaweed briquettes. Several traders guarding the wares eyed them with open suspicion. Spattered with blood and armed, they didn't look like customers.

Elmar bared his teeth at them. One by one they looked away as if they had far more interesting matters of concern.

Kaneth said, "Elmar, give Shale the pike to carry and exchange tunics with him. Shale, I'm sorry about this."

"Sorry about wha—" He had the question answered for him before he finished it. Casually, Kaneth drew his sword and began to hack off all of Shale's beaded braids.

"Ow!" Shale yelled.

"Sorry. It's the quickest way. Then you can wear my palmubra to hide the rest of your red hair." When the last of the braids was dropped into the dust at their feet, he dug his crumpled headgear out of his belt pouch and held it up. "Quick, get changed. Pull the hat well down to hide that red face of yours. Nothing much you can do about your hands. I'll try to concentrate the guards' attention elsewhere." He leaned against a wall as he waited.

"Are you all right, m'lord?" Elmar asked, after he had gamely struggled into Shale's Reduner clothes. The breeches were far too small.

Shale shot a quick look at the rainlord. Elmar's words had made him realise just how weak Kaneth was.

"Nothing that a week or two's rest won't cure," the rainlord said with a wan smile and a hint of dry humour. "Moving water out of men is a bloody tiring business." He looked at Shale. "Remember, it's much easier just to disable someone by withdrawing the water from their eyes than to do it to the whole body. Takes less out of you. Now, can you try to look like a guardsman instead of a potter's boy hunched over his wheel? Shoulders back, that's it. I am going to make a scene at the gate so everyone looks at me, not you. Understand?"

"Yes, lord."

There was still no hint of Terelle's water in his consciousness. Wherever she was, it was not close by. Kaneth was right. She would have gone to Level Ten. She was safe. And then he remembered how difficult it might be for Terelle to get up to the tenth, with all the reeves and enforcers on the lookout for the waterless, and he despaired all over again.

Kaneth turned and looked once more at the briquette traders. "If you are wise, you didn't see a thing," he called out to them. He dug into his pouch, extracted a handful of tokens and launched them into the air so that they scattered over the piles of briquettes.

"That should give them something else to think about for a while," he muttered as they headed for the city's southern wall once more.

He stumbled again as they reached the gate, and this time it was one of the city guards who grabbed him by the elbow. He was berated for his trouble, as Kaneth indignantly launched into a tale of how he had been assaulted in the bazaar by a pack of waterless Gibbermen and would not have escaped with his life if not for his valiant Breccian armsmen. Glowering, he jabbed a finger into the guard's chest, demanding to know what sort of law they had in Scarcleft. How was an attack on a visiting rainlord even possible? Especially one sent by the Cloudmaster of the Quartern! It was outrageous!

Shale skulked behind Elmar's bulk, his head lowered. Every now and then, he glanced behind. There was no sign of pursuit. By the time Kaneth had finished with the Scarcleft gate guards, they were only too grateful to see the rainlord and his party pass on through.

Shale took one last despairing look over his shoulder as they left the city. *I'm sorry, Terelle*, he thought. *I'm so, so sorry. Everything happened so fast.*

He gulped, trying to hold back the horror inside him. Please let her not be dead, too. Not Terelle.

CHAPTER THIRTY-FOUR

Scarpen Quarter
Scarcleft City
Arta Amethyst's house, Level 10

Nealrith sipped the hot tea served in a stylish glass with a silver handle. Resin plant seeds floated on top, a Gibber product much sought after in the Scarpen.

In spite of Amethyst's hospitality, he shifted uncomfortably in his chair. He did not feel at ease in Scarcleft. Old fears stirred deep within; Taquar Sardonyx unsettled him. He always had. It dated back to their boyhood, to the odd times when Taquar had sought a subtle revenge of one kind or another, usually in answer to a perceived slight. He had been good at that, planning with cold vindictiveness to achieve a rival's humiliation.

In their adult years, Taquar had given him less reason to worry; he'd not even appeared to resent Nealrith's marriage to Laisa, the woman he had once courted himself. He'd given his congratulations with an amused smile, remarking that he thought them entirely well suited. But Nealrith had just walked into the city past the remains of men and women nailed—still alive—to the city gates for offences concerning water. He was glad he had four armed men wearing the Breccia Hall monogram waiting for him in the anteroom.

Nonetheless, he found it hard to believe that any rainlord, even Taquar, would hide the presence of a potential stormlord from the only man who could train him properly: his father, Granthon. He had not fully believed the message his mother had received from Amethyst. There must, he decided, be some kind of rational explanation. He and Ethelva had talked it over with Kaneth, and they had all decided not to trouble Granthon with the story until they'd had time to investigate. His father was in no condition to have his hopes raised and dashed once again.

Yes, Nealrith had believed that Taquar had been to blame—by his lack of effective leadership—for the deaths of the two young rainlords in the desert decades ago, but he had never thought him capable of *murder*. And yet here was Amethyst telling him a story of collusion with Reduner killers, of the destruction of a whole settle, of betrayal so great it was beyond horror.

He had always disliked Taquar, yes, but this was something else. This was treason of the highest order. Moreover, it was *stupid*. And Taquar was not stupid.

He took another sip of tea and asked carefully, "Do you think Taquar capable of these things?" In the distance, he heard the gate bell ring and suppressed an urge to get up and see if Kaneth was back at last.

"I do, and I know him better than most. I was his mistress for ten years."

Nealrith cleared his throat, embarrassed. "I did hear that, yes. And the boy? Is he honest?"

"I believe so. And don't think of him as a boy, Highlord. Shale is beyond childhood. Anyway, he's not all that young in years, either. Eighteen, possibly. A little socially inept—because of his history, perhaps—but surprisingly well educated, self-contained, capable of mature thought and analysis. He doesn't strike me as particularly imaginative, yet his tale would have required great imagination if it wasn't true. He described the details of rainlord training, for example, just as I have told you. Were those accurate?"

He nodded reluctantly. "And he saw the man who destroyed his settle speaking with Taquar?"

"So he says. Davim, from Dune Watergatherer." She stopped as Jomat came to the door. "Yes?"

"Madam, a visitor."

"I told you we were not to be disturbed."

"Not even by me, my dear?" Taquar stepped around Jomat's bulk and closed the door in the steward's face. "Why, I'll be waterless! Nealrith. Such an *unexpected* pleasure to see you here. What is it that brings you to Scarcleft? And unannounced, too. That's a breach of protocol, I believe. A highlord's visit to another city should always be preceded by a request for an invitation, is that not so?"

Nealrith curbed his anger. "I am not here in any official capacity, Taquar. I merely bring a request from my mother for Arta Amethyst to dance for her in Breccia City."

"That's carrying the job of dutiful son to extremes, is it not?"

"I was on my way to Pediment on the Cloudmaster's business, as it happens."

"I hope this was not an urgent request on the part of

Lady Ethelva. Amethyst has a full schedule for the next several weeks, I believe."

The dancer had stood up as soon as Taquar had entered the room. Now, pale faced, she said woodenly, "Not to my knowledge."

Taquar raised an eyebrow and smiled. "Rebellion, my dear?" Then he looked over at Nealrith, and the smile disappeared. "Leave my city, Rith. Now. You are not welcome here."

Nealrith gritted his teeth, even more enraged. "As you wish," he said tightly and rose to his feet. He stooped to pick up his water skin. "Oh, one other thing. There's a whisper on the wind about a young water sensitive with potential right here in Scarcleft. Perhaps it would be a good idea if I took him back to Breccia City with me."

"But you just told me you are on your way to Pediment. Anyway, you should not listen to rumours. There is a half-mad boy who has been living in the tunnel and stealing our water, but he is no water sensitive. Merely sandcrazy and highly imaginative. He has been spreading an imbecilic story far and wide about how I killed his family, kidnapped him, held him prisoner, all so that I could prevent the Quartern from having another stormlord. Now does that sound likely? Watergiver only knows why that would be an aim of mine. I am not suicidal. I like to have water in my dayjar, too, and it is clear your father is unable to make that a certainty." He looked Nealrith straight in the eye. "I assure you that looking for the lad will be a waste of your time."

Nealrith hesitated, wrestling with his own doubt as he tried to keep his voice even and confident. "Oh? You have examined him yourself?"

"Of course not. I leave that sort of thing up to the people I employ. After all, I already know his story to be a midden heap of untruths, don't I?" Taquar smiled blandly. "Jomat, show the rainlord out, please."

Amethyst made a choking noise, and they both looked at her.

"My dear, you do not sound well, and you are exceptionally pale," Taquar said. "Why do you not rest?"

"I wish to accompany Highlord Nealrith to Breccia City," she said, her voice barely above a whisper. "Lady Ethelva has asked for me."

"And I say you will not go."

Nealrith interrupted to say, "Taquar, you can hardly stop her."

"Of course I can. This is my city, and all I have to do is forbid the guards at the gates to allow her through."

Nealrith paused, looking from one to the other, his frustration at his situation warring with his idea of what was legal and proper for a man in his position. Taquar was still smiling affably; Amethyst was as white as sun-bleached salt.

"Don't leave me," she said to Nealrith. The despair in her eyes pleaded.

"I have twenty men out in the street," Taquar said, staring right at Nealrith. "And you have *no* jurisdiction here. Even Granthon cannot command me in any matters except those that pertain to external water supply or to the security of the Quartern, or other matters that concern more than just this city. I should not have to tell you that."

Oh Sunlord, Nealrith thought, his stomach churning as he heard the hidden message and its mockery. *This Shale Flint is telling the truth. But even if we find him, how will we ever prove it? And if we prove it, what will we ever be able to do about it?* "I would advise you to reconsider," he said finally. "I will send a message to the Cloudmaster. I feel certain that he would be profoundly upset if anything were to prevent the arta's arrival there within, let's say, ten days."

Amethyst gave a sound that could have been a sob and turned her face away.

Taquar inclined his head. "I will take the Cloudmaster's emotional state into consideration. Now be so good as to leave, and take your guards with you. I repeat: you are not welcome in Scarcleft. My men will escort you all to the city gates."

Nealrith turned on his heel and left the room. His own guards fell in behind him, but he scarcely noticed. He was still seeing the blank horror on Amethyst's face.

Terelle fled, the terror behind propelling her forward with blind dedication—and speed. She had no destination in mind, no plan beyond escaping the guard. That horrible man's order still rang in her ears. *Kill her.* Not "Kill her if she runs" or "Kill her if she doesn't cooperate," but simply "Kill her." She didn't know who he was, but he could command the enforcers, and his callous indifference made her feet fly. There was no alternative. If she lost this race, then she died.

She tore down the stairs three at a time, swung around the corner at the bottom and hurtled into the main thoroughfare. There were people there—too many. She was forced to slow, to push her way on, feeling all the while the prickling between her shoulders as if a blade was about to strike. She guessed her eyes reflected her fear, because people stared at her. She expected someone to stop her, to seize her, to hand her over to the guard. But, unlike Shale, there was no price on her head, and instead of hindering her, several of the level's less reputable citizens took it upon themselves to delay her pursuer. A youth carrying a bundle of bab palm fronds swung around, seemingly by accident, so that the stalks whacked the guard behind his knees. He crashed with a thud. Immediately after he regained his feet and resumed the chase, Ba-ba came out of nowhere pushing a wheelbarrow full of sinucca leaves into his path. By the time he had scrambled up again, Terelle was out of sight.

She continued on, terrified. Sick with worry for Shale. As she skirted the city's base at a run, she kept remembering her last glimpse of the chaos in Russet's room. There had been blood everywhere. And dead people. And blind people clutching their eyes. Shale had been in the middle of it all, trying to get to her. And he wasn't a warrior! He had no idea how to use the scimitar he wore. Blighted eyes, he hadn't even pulled it out of its scabbard! She bit her lip, scaring herself just thinking about it.

She ran out of breath and slowed to a walk. She looked back over her shoulder. There was no disturbance behind, nothing that indicated she was still being chased.

Now what? she asked herself. She considered warning Russet, but had no idea where he had gone. No, best she get to Amethyst's. Highlord Nealrith was there, and he could protect her. Besides, that was her only chance of meeting up with Shale again. Anyway, the arta and the Breccian highlord needed to be warned about the attack on Kaneth.

She hurried uplevel as quickly as she could without

drawing too much attention to herself. It wasn't easy: reeve representatives were more alert than ever, looking out for lowlevellers who had no reason to come uplevel. She was stopped several times and produced Russet's uplevel pass. Because she was neatly dressed and well spoken, she succeeded where other lowlevellers might have failed.

Once on the tenth level, however, she was lost: she had never been at that end of the level before. It took time to find her way through a maze of shops and residential streets to Amethyst's lane.

When she arrived at the gate, she found it ajar.

She hesitated, then gave it a tentative push with her fingers. It swung wider to reveal the small unroofed outer courtyard. She looked around. Jomat was nowhere to be seen, and the house was deathly quiet. A faint, unpleasant smell drifted on the air. The main door to the house also stood ajar. She tiptoed into the entrance hall, only to trip over Jomat because she was looking around instead of down.

He lay on the flagstone floor, obviously dead. He had been sliced open across the abdomen and lay in a pool of foul-smelling liquid. A sagging hole penetrated layers of yellow fat, and his guts spilled out in an obscene tangle. His hands still clutched at them, as if he had tried to tuck them back where they belonged. His face was frozen in a dying rictus of surprise and betrayal and pain. He had not expected to die, and his unbelief was still there in the eyes that stared sightlessly at her.

She gagged and had to cover her mouth and look away. Highlord Nealrith wouldn't have done this, would he? But if not, then who?

She dithered. Should she flee? But where to? She had expected help, and now there was none. And then her next thought: *Amethyst.* Where was the arta?

Oh, please, let her be all right!

Without thinking too much—because if she did, she knew she'd be too terrified—she ran up the stairs two at a time. Once again she found an open door. There was no one in the outer chamber, no one in the sitting room. She ran through into the bedroom. Amethyst lay on the canopied bed, her hands clasped at her waist. She appeared to be sleeping. Terelle approached, her heart hammering in her throat, the roaring rush in her ears blocking sound. It wasn't until she was at the edge of the bed, looking down, that she saw the knife. It was angled upwards from below Amethyst's left breast, jammed in as far as the hilt. But there was hardly any blood. If she had not been so unnaturally still, Terelle might have thought that she still lived.

A slight sound broke through her shock, bringing her back to a sense of her own danger. She raised her eyes from Amethyst's body and saw a man emerging from the adjoining water-room. He was wiping his sword on a towel, which he then casually dropped on the floor. The weapon he kept in his hand. He was tall and lean, a handsome man, with dark hair neatly tied at his nape. His eyes were a deep grey and held an intensity that made her instantly fearful. She knew who he was: Taquar, Highlord of Scarcleft.

"Let me guess," he said softly, "you must be Terelle."

She nodded, unable to do anything else in the face of his menace.

"Are you alone?"

She nodded again and looked down at the bed. "Did she kill herself?"

"No, I did that. She knew she was about to die, so she attacked me with that knife. Brave, but futile. Why are you here?"

"I came to see Amethyst," she whispered. "The door was open." She began to back away.

Casually he reached into his cloth belt and withdrew an object he had secreted there. He brought it up until it was level with his shoulders and pointed it in her direction. "And do you know what this is?"

She halted, the last of her courage draining away. "It—it's a zigtube."

"It is also loaded. Hear that whining? All I have to do is tap this little catch here, twice"—he indicated the spot—"and the barrier between the zigger and freedom will drop, and the zigger will fly out. You know what will happen then?"

Donnick the doorman, clutching at his throat, writhing on the courtyard paving, taking time to die. She nodded again.

"They can follow you around corners, did you know that? Bloodlust drives them. They go for the soft parts of the body. Your eye, perhaps. Or maybe up a nostril and straight into the brain, and as they burrow, they exude their toxins. No one has ever been able to tell us if it is painful, but I assure you, it has always looked that way to me. The victims just go on screaming until they die. Is this the way you want to end your life, Terelle?"

She shook her head, incapable of any other movement.

"Then kneel on the floor—slowly—and put your hands behind you."

She hesitated, then shook her head. "You're going to kill me, just like you killed Amethyst."

"A justifiable deduction, but not necessarily accurate. I most definitely won't kill you until I have Shale in my hands. And maybe I won't even then. Maybe I could use you to ensure his cooperation. Is he fond of you?"

She met his eyes. "I'm hardly going to say no to that, am I?"

He gave a slight smile. "You *are* a surprising girl."

She clamped her lips together tightly to stop her chin quivering.

He took up the towel he had been using to wipe his sword and cut it into strips which he knotted together to make a rope. She watched him, waiting for a moment's inattention, but his gaze flicked her way constantly, and the zigtube was now on the bed within his easy reach. When he'd finished the rope to his satisfaction, he used it to tie her hands together, leaving one end trailing down. Then he tied this long end around one of her ankles in such a way that she had to stoop slightly. Like that, there was no way she could run, or even walk without stumbling.

He tucked the zigtube away, saying, "Now we'll go and sit downstairs while we wait for the seneschal and his men to return with Shale." He gestured to her, indicating that she should precede him down the stairs.

She faltered a little but made it to the bottom. There, he sat in one of the chairs in the hall and indicated the floor in front of him. "Sit there."

Wordlessly, she obeyed and for some time they sat in silence. He continued to polish his sword, using the throw cover of the chair he sat in. The reek of Jomat's body wafted by intermittently. She wondered what had happened to Amethyst's other staff: there had been a maid and a cook, she knew. She listened for sounds from the kitchen area, but all was quiet.

Amethyst. Terelle wanted to grieve, but couldn't; shock held her emotions immobile. "Why did you kill her?" she asked, her voice as thin as a child's.

"She betrayed me. She betrayed me by helping Shale escape, when she should have told me about him."

"And why did you kill Jomat? Amethyst thought he spied for you."

"For Seneschal Harkel, yes. I just didn't want anyone left alive who knows about my interest in Shale Flint."

"So you *are* going to kill me. I would really rather you didn't."

He stared at her, surprised. Then he laughed. "You have backbone, I'll give you that. How did you meet Amethyst? Who are you, Terelle? I've never met anyone with eyes quite like yours."

"I came to Arta Amethyst to take dance lessons."

"And how did you meet Shale?"

"We bumped into each other. Accidentally. He was running from some of the enforcers . . ." Her voice shook and trailed off.

"And you were living with a waterpainter, an old outlander. A relative of yours?"

"I don't know."

"That's an odd answer."

"Well, I don't know."

He laid his blade aside and leaned forward. "Shale told you about what happened to him, didn't he?"

"Happened to him when?"

"He told you about me."

She shook her head. "I don't even know who you are."

"I think you do."

She did not reply.

He picked up his sword and put the tip of the blade under her chin. He tilted her face upwards, forcing her to look at him. "I think you know very well. Don't play games with me, Terelle, or you may regret it. How old are you?"

Instinctively, she lied. "Fourteen. Just last week."

"You are tall for that age."

"I can't help it!" she wailed. Anything to convince him she was a child still. "I just keep growing!"

He laughed at her. "In another couple of years, you will be very desirable. There may be a place for you in Scarcleft Hall."

"If you want a waterpainter."

He smiled and went back to polishing the handle of his sword.

CHAPTER THIRTY-FIVE

Scarpen Quarter
Scarcleft City to Breccia City

A circular depression, with a scree-scattered scarp rising on one side and a low natural rock wall on the other, formed a perfect camp site. The sun had just set, and darkness gathered in the depression like a dusky mist. No one would see the camp fires unless they climbed the surrounding slope and looked down into the scoop. Yet it could also be a trap, Shale realised, as their myriapedes flowed over the rim and he gazed down into the gloom.

He shivered slightly, aware that Scarcleft was just an hour's ride away to the north and that Taquar was not the kind of man who would meekly surrender his ambition. Worse, a rainlord could track people by the water within them, especially out in the dry country of the Skirtings.

He saw a few tents before him, a couple of myriapedes and only two more people. One turned out to be Kaneth's wife, another rainlord, but still, he had expected more. He had thought that the Highlord of Breccia, who was also the son of the Cloudmaster, would travel with a large escort.

Lord Ryka he didn't remember at all, although she told

him she was part of the group that had come to Wash Dry-bone. When he looked at her now, he wondered how he could have forgotten her. It wasn't that she was beautiful but rather that she unsettled the space around her, like a spindevil wind. He liked her right from the start. She didn't ply him with questions but set about finding him some better-fitting Scarpen clothes to wear and a meal to eat. Worried about Terelle, he wasn't hungry but forced some food down to please Lord Ryka while they waited for the highlord. He arrived an hour later, together with Soltar, who had met him on the street as the rainlord was being escorted to the gate. He had only another four men with him.

And no Terelle.

Shale stared. Ten men and a woman. They rode from Breccia to Scarcleft with eleven people, and only three of them rainlords. *They don't know Taquar*, he thought miserably. *And Terelle is still there, somewhere in his city.*

"Come, Shale," Kaneth said as the newcomers dismounted wearily. "You must meet Nealrith." He led Shale forward to where Lord Ryka had just taken hold of the reins of Nealrith's pede as he dismounted. "This is the man, Rith. Shale Flint. He tells me he's from Wash Dry-bone Settle, Gibber Quarter."

"Welcome, Shale. And good work, Kaneth. Although Soltar tells me we lost Gadri."

"I'm afraid so. You didn't see the young waterpainter woman, did you, the one Shale has been staying with? Terelle?"

"No. Was she supposed to come to Amethyst's?"

"We were hoping," Lord Kaneth said with a sympathetic look at Shale. "We thought she might have gone there for help, and to warn you."

"I could have done with the warning. Soltar found me only after we left the arta's house. Sunlord forgive me, I left Amethyst with Taquar."

Even in the dim light, Shale glimpsed a haunted look in the rainlord's eyes. *Taquar will kill her*, he thought with certainty. *And Lord Nealrith knows it. Yet he isn't going to do a thing.*

Nealrith turned his attention to him. "Wash Drybone Settle?" he asked. "We went there, must be four years ago now. I don't remember you." He gripped Shale's shoulder. "Come, let's go and sit down by the fire where I can see you better, and you can tell us the whole story."

The guards brought them food and water as Shale recounted his history. When he skimped on the telling, trying to gloss over the details to avoid the pain of memory, it was Lord Ryka who teased the full tale out of him. Useless, he decided, to hide anything from her; she had a mind that could race ahead of his and a personality that would not rest until the truth was known. In the end, the only thing he didn't touch on was what he knew about the power of waterpainting.

He said, by way of ending, "I think Lord Taquar's the one who stole the storm that came down our wash. I believe he kidnapped Lyneth. And that it's even possible he killed the other young rainlords who rivalled him."

The rainlords exchanged startled glances. Lord Nealrith said, "He kidnapped *Lyneth*? What do you know of her? Dear sweet water, she's not still *alive*, is she?"

Shale shook his head. "I shouldn't think so." He told them about the clothes at the mother cistern and how he had guessed who had once worn them. He showed them Lyneth's bracelet.

Nealrith fingered it, his face ashen, and passed it to Kaneth. "I remember this. It was a present from Iani." He looked back at Shale. "You will have to tell him of what you have learned, when you meet him. Lyneth's father. And her mother, too, Lord Moiqa."

Kaneth gave the bracelet to Ryka to look at, and she handled it with an expression of profound grief on her face. "No end is too horrible for that man," she said at last, almost spitting out the words in her disgust. She handed the bracelet back to Shale. "None."

Kaneth looked startled at her vehemence but didn't comment. "It can't have been a coincidence that Taquar was at the dancer's house, can it?" he asked.

"That stinking steward of hers must have betrayed us," Shale said. "Amethyst thought he was Taquar's spy. I wish I knew what happened to Terelle."

Nealrith looked at Kaneth. "Sandblast it, how can we rainlords have been so blind to Taquar's perfidy? Is he withering insane, dealing with a scorpion like Davim and stirring up trouble from one end of the Quartern to the other?"

It was Ryka who replied. "Power mad. How we get rid of him is the problem. We are hardly prepared to declare war on another Scarpen city, especially not on one that has zigger-armed guards."

"The Council of Rainlords could vote him out of power," Nealrith said, "just as it once voted to back the Cloudmaster's decision to give him the rule of Scarcleft."

"Don't be ridiculous. He is long past listening to the

council," Kaneth said with heavy scorn. "It will take force to dislodge him now."

"He's the Cloudmaster's *heir*," Nealrith reminded them in anguished tones. "And my father thinks he's the nearest thing we have to a solution to our problems." He turned his attention back to Shale. "You say Taquar trained you in the use of water-powers?"

"Yes."

"Can you shift water?"

"Yes."

"How far? From here to the rim up there?"

Shale glanced upwards. "Yes." Nealrith frowned sharply, and Shale knew he had heard the element of hesitation in his voice. He added, "Further. It's not shifting water that is my difficulty. It's separating it from impurities. I can't get fresh water from salty."

"Oh!" Nealrith thought that over before asking, "But Taquar thought you were a stormlord?"

"He was hoping I'd learn how to be, in time. I'm not so sure it's possible. I never seem to get any better."

In the flickering light of the fire, Nealrith's cheeks looked sunken and gaunt. "Damn it, if we'd taken you to my father four years ago . . . That man may have destroyed any chance we have."

"He has to be stopped," Kaneth said.

"I thought you would support him," Nealrith said.

"That's unjust, Rith. True, I want a firm hand in Breccia ruling over the Quartern, but no sane man would hanker after a power-hungry tyant who would ally himself with a murderous band of renegade Reduners."

Nealrith looked back at Shale. "Will you come to Breccia with us and learn the art of a stormlord? It will be hard work, and it will mean heavy responsibilities. In return, you will never want for anything, as long as you live. You will be honoured as a stormlord of the Quartern, or at the very least as a rainlord, and will have all the privileges that go with that rank. One day, you may even rule this land."

Shale stared at him. "You are *asking* me?"

"Yes, that's right."

"Uh—I mean, can I refuse?"

"Yes, you can refuse."

Annoyed, Lord Kaneth made an exasperated sound of protest, but Lord Nealrith held up his hand to quiet him.

Shale shuffled his feet, disturbed, and shot a glance at Kaneth before asking Nealrith, "What happens if I say no?"

"Nothing. I will still take you with us to Breccia. You can live there, under the protection of the city, if that is what you wish. We don't turn people away from our gates."

"I—no one has ever given me a choice before."

"I'm not sure it's much of a choice now, either," Lord Ryka said. "If you don't learn to stormshift and cloud-break, in all probability we will die, you included."

"You don't have to say yes yet," Nealrith said. "Right now, I think we should ride on through the night. Taquar will be searching outside the walls for us now that Shale has escaped." He waved Elmar over. "Break camp. We ride out at once, and we don't stop until the pedes are exhausted. Shale, best you ride behind Soltar, I think, even though we do have a spare pede now."

"And Terelle?" Shale cut in. "She ran, but one of Taquar's men went after her with orders to kill her. Kaneth promised to go back and look for her."

Kaneth nodded. "And I will, right now. I'd like to get Amethyst out of there, too, if I can."

Ryka frowned. "You're tired," she said.

"Going back could be dangerous," Nealrith added.

"I doubt Taquar wants me dead that badly. True, his men were trying to kill me earlier, but that was only because they didn't know who I was. Once Harkel had control of the situation, we sorted things out."

Nealrith took a moment to consider, then said, "All right. But your safety is paramount. A rainlord's life is more important than a dancer's or an apprentice waterpainter's; remember that." He walked away towards his pede.

Ryka stared at Kaneth. "Yes. You remember that," she said. She sounded snappish.

Bitterness surfaced somewhere inside Shale. That was always the way of it. Some people were more important than others. Terelle would have said it wasn't fair, and she would have been right.

Kaneth turned to Shale, his voice blade-sharp when he spoke, "Ryka was right earlier. The idea of choice is an illusion. You don't have a choice."

Shale looked at him solemnly. "I know. But at least Highlord Nealrith let me have the illusion." He turned away.

"Louse of a lad," Kaneth muttered to Ryka, but he was grinning.

It took them well over a day to arrive in Breccia. It was an unpleasant journey. They rode at a punishing pace, and anxiety about Terelle's safety made Shale feel ill much of the time. During their brief rest stops, he found it difficult to eat and even harder to nap. So, evidently, did Nealrith, who used the time to question him concerning Amethyst's relationship to Taquar, betraying his own battle with guilt. To Shale, Ryka appeared tense and worried. The guards were grieving the death of Gadri and did not talk much. The only good news was that there was no sign of pursuit.

It was a relief to arrive in the city, although Nealrith gave Shale no time to rest. He was taken straight to the Cloudmaster's quarters, in Breccia Hall.

Shale stared at Granthon, shocked. His first meeting with the Cloudmaster, and all he could think of was how ill the man looked. Wasted, a fragile shell, so weak he could scarcely stand. When Shale was ushered in, Lady Ethelva was spoon-feeding him something soft and mushy, as though he was a toothless babe.

"Father," Nealrith said after introductions and a brief explanation, "I'd like Shale to tell you his story." He didn't wait for the Cloudmaster to reply but said to Shale, "Tell him everything you told me, starting with the first day you met Taquar."

As Shale related his tale yet again, the Cloudmaster continued eating, although his gaze never left Shale's face. Ethelva drew in a shocked breath several times. At Shale's description of Citrine's death, she clamped her free hand over her lips. Once again, Shale skipped any mention of the power of waterpainting, deciding he would bring that up later. He was heartened to note a light of hope gleaming in the Cloudmaster's eyes by the time he finished, and when Granthon spoke, his voice contained a sharpness that revealed the continued acuteness of his mind.

"At last!" he said. "Another stormlord."

"We don't know that for sure, yet," Nealrith warned.

"I will undertake his initial assessment if you wish. And train him, too, if I can, until he's ready for you."

"Yes, do, do," Granthon said and turned his eyes back to the sea. "Hurry, Nealrith. I am not sure how much longer I can last."

"And Taquar? What of him?"

"What of him?" Granthon repeated. "You may not agree with his methods, Nealrith, but at least he was willing to seize the chance to make something of this young man. He was motivated by his own desire for power, but he thought to build a new nation on a new stormlord."

"But his *methods*!"

"Doubtless, he did what he thought was best at the time. Leave Taquar to his own problems and his own city." Suddenly weary again, he lay back on his divan. The gleam in his eyes dulled, as if he was too weak to sustain even that.

Nealrith, his jaw twisting in his anger, persisted. "And what of this alliance of his with the Reduner rebel, Davim? He probably stole your storm in an attempt to impress the man."

"You've no proof of that. And Reduners have no cause to join Davim. I never stopped sending them storms. Sandmaster Davim will fade away in time. Just a foolish hothead."

Shale's control crumbled. Ethelva, who was sitting next to him, reached out and gripped his arm, clearly signalling him to be silent, but he refused to obey. "My sister didn't die on the whim of a hothead, Cloudmaster," he said. "She was killed, brutally and deliberately."

Nealrith intervened, diverting Granthon's irritation towards himself. "Indeed, the news we have suggests

Shale is right. Davim is no hothead but an unscrupulous and murderous leader. Think, Father. We have not heard from Bejanim in far too long. Nor from his brother, Sandmaster Makdim. Reports from the Red Quarter suggest Davim controls most of the tribes and that he slaughtered the drovers of Dune Scarmaker. We hear Makdim's wife, Vara Redmane, leads a nomadic resistance to Davim. We hear Davim leads murderous raids into the White Quarter and even parts of the Gibber. Kaneth and his men have been doing their best to stop them, but they are too few."

Granthon sighed. "I know. And we have that delegation from the White Quarter awaiting my decision with regard to aid."

"They told us Samphire City has sent to us for help no less than four times, yet none of the previous delegations ever arrived here," Nealrith explained to Shale. "They disappeared on their way."

Shale felt sick. "There was an Alabaster trader named Feroze Khorash who rode out from Scarcleft about, oh, fifty days ago," he said. "He wanted to see you. Did he ever get here?"

Granthon shook his head. "No, these are the first Alabasters we've seen in some time."

Nealrith groaned. "Another man lost! And we do *nothing*?"

Granthon frowned at him, his white brows drooping across the top of his nose in an expression that was part weariness, part glower. "And what do you suggest we do, Nealrith? Send out an army to fight the Reduners? What army? They are the ones who have all the pedes, who have the warriors, who have the ziggers. All we ever had was rainlords and stormlords to keep them in check.

Once, even the threat of our power was enough. Now? With so few of us?

"And if I send the few rainlords we do have, what do you think will happen here, in all of our cities, as water becomes more and more scarce? We need our rainlords here, to quell the coming riots simply by being present— or even by giving a few well-placed demonstrations of their killing power, if need be. Or do you think our guards are sufficient to put down huge crowds of thirsty and hungry citizens by themselves? Even Kaneth's roaming the Quartern after Reduner marauders must stop. He's needed here."

"Riots?"

"You heard me. People will not sit quietly while they thirst and their children die. You had better bring Shale into his powers soon, Rith. And you, Shale, had better work hard to realise your full potential. Otherwise, this nation dies, quarter by quarter. We are already ailing." His voice cracked, and he lay back, breathing heavily.

Ethelva glared at her son, but he would not be silenced.

"Then what about this evidence Shale has concerning the fate of Lyneth?"

"What evidence? A bracelet bearing a name? She was not the only lass to be called Lyneth." He coughed, and Ethelva held a glass of water to his lips. He drank and lay back. "Taquar would never kill a potential stormlord. The idea is ridiculous. He did not kill Shale, did he? And by the young man's own admission, he was treated well. Better than he had been by his own family." He closed his eyes.

Shale stared at him, appalled, unwilling to believe that he had heard correctly.

Nealrith sent a despairing glance to his mother. She indicated with a jerk of the head that they should go, and she led them both out.

"He seems worse," Nealrith said. "And not rational. Mother, we can't let Taquar get away with this!"

"He *is* worse. He does nothing except create storms whenever he can, which is nowhere near often enough. He spends his days and nights reclining in front of the open shutters, waiting for his body to gather sufficient strength for one more storm. And then for another one. And another." She bit her bottom lip. "He lives against all odds, and he brings the storms to the Warthago Range and the Red Quarter against all odds. Sometimes he even sends them to the White Quarter and the Gibber. Nealrith, you will not burden him with troubles that will drain him of what little strength he has."

"I don't *want* to! If I had my way, he would allow me to deal with these problems while he concentrates on storm-shifting. I do my best, but without his signature I can't legally issue directives that concern the Quartern. Worse, the whole Quartern knows that he intends Taquar to rule after him. Mother, how can we stand by and allow our land to fall into the hands of a traitor? It is unthinkable!"

"Be warned, Nealrith, if you press this, he may publicly give the administrative powers to Taquar now." She looked at Shale, and her tone softened. "At least in you we have a potential alternative. But we will speak of these matters another time. Shale, I will pray to the Sunlord that you are indeed a stormlord. And I will request water sacrifices for your success from the waterpriests as well."

Shale wasn't comforted. In fact, he felt sick. He had thought all his problems would be over if he came to the Cloudmaster. He'd thought Taquar would be stripped of his ruling power. Instead, the man was still the heir. Which meant that if Granthon died . . . No, he didn't even want to think about what would happen then.

As he left with Nealrith, he asked, "*Can* you teach me to be a stormlord?"

Nealrith drew in a ragged breath, an action that stripped him of all rainlord mystique. "I know the exercises, yes. My father taught both me and Ryka all a stormlord needs to know, long ago, in case he died. I know the theory of it. I know the teaching techniques. I can pass it on. When you are ready, Granthon will teach you how to put it into practice."

Sandblast it, Shale thought, *he is just a man, battling with problems too large for him. And he's ashamed of his father. I'm the fool, for expecting so much more.*

"I'm sorry, Shale, if he has disappointed you."

Shale shrank from the bitterness he heard. Salted damn, dealing with other people was like trying to walk the crumbling surface where the Gibber Plains were hollow below. Put a foot wrong and it went through the crust into some old mine workings. Say the wrong thing and your words went places you had never meant them to penetrate.

CHAPTER THIRTY-SIX

Scarpen Quarter
Breccia City
Level 2 and Level 3

Shale thrashed on the bed, fighting the rigid arms that hugged him. Death had come, clad in rags, limbs blackened, sinews as tough as hemp, clasping him in an embrace that could end only when his last breath was choked from him.

He woke, entangled in the sheet. A sheet that was finer than any cloth he had ever touched before, as smooth and as soft as water. Breathless, he dragged it from his throat and sat on the edge of his bed. A bed that was much higher than the one at the Scarcleft mother cistern, and he wasn't sure he liked it. He hadn't slept well on his first night, thinking he would roll over and fall to the floor.

Breccia Hall. It took his breath away, all of it. The polish of the patterned stones of the floors, the gleam of the fine bab-wood furniture, the beauty of the painted ceramic water jars in every room, the smooth taste of the food on the table at mealtimes, the extravagance of library shelves lined with books and scrolls. Water everywhere for the taking. No one to say you'd had your allotment for the day. No one to chide you for drinking too much. He'd read about these things, or Taquar had told him, but experiencing the reality was different.

He lay there a moment, trying to comprehend it all, to absorb the change in his life. His dream resurfaced, impinging on his reality. The dead man embracing him. The man Kaneth had killed to save him. Real, but also a nightmare.

He padded across the room to the shutters. He flung them open, and the starlight streamed in. That at least was the same: the brilliance of a night sky that contained little or no water vapour, pure light from swirls of stars that gave night its blue sheen. He walked out onto the balcony and looked down on the sleeping city, on the spill of buildings spreading outwards and downwards to the foot of the escarpment, like a giant's staircase that widened as it went. The natural pale sienna colour of the mud-brick had turned purple in the starlight, and the canyons of the streets, inlaid with stone paving, were the deepest of blue-blacks.

There was a smell of citrus flowers in the air, from the blossoming of the potted trees at the edge of the balcony. The fruit of the pomegranate bushes were already bursting, their fecundity cracking them open. He touched the nearest fruit, running a finger over its plump redness, but could not bring himself to pick it.

It all seemed profligate. Would he ever feel at home with this abundance? With this luxury? He remembered too many things. The days when he and Mica went hungry. The nights when he fell asleep sucking on a pebble to quell his thirst. The whores of Scarcleft's thirty-sixth level selling their bodies for a drink of water. The children husking bab fruit in the groves for a pittance in tinny tokens. The boys shovelling pede pellets off the streets to take home and burn in their cooking fires because they couldn't afford the imported seaweed briquettes. Terelle, who'd had to fight so hard to find some kind of life.

Terelle. He couldn't get her out of his mind. The way she laughed, full-throated, as he had never learned to do. The way she teased him. The way the slimness of her body and the gentle roundness of her curves brought him a sensual pleasure when she moved. Even the regal way she had of looking him up and down and raising an eyebrow, as if he'd just said something so stupid she couldn't believe her ears.

And he'd left her in Scarcleft. Just ridden away and left her there, at the mercy of Taquar's enforcers, or—if she escaped them—at the mercy of Russet's plans for her. Just as he'd been forced to leave Mica to the mercy of Davim's Reduners.

He slammed his palm down on the balustrade, hurting his hand, welcoming the pain that shot up to his elbow.

On the first day of the journey to Breccia, when they'd ridden the pedes hard in their hurry to escape the risk of pursuit, he'd thought of making her safety a condition of his cooperation. But he'd scrapped that idea as soon as it had been born. It hadn't felt right. Instead, he'd made a request: if Kaneth didn't bring her back with him, could they please at least find out what happened to her and try to help her? Nealrith and Ryka had agreed, but Nealrith had added regretfully, "You must understand that none of us have any official powers in Scarcleft. My father has certain powers as Cloudmaster, it's true, and there are a great many laws concerning trade and water rights and travelling which Taquar and Scarcleft must adhere to, but there is nothing that gives us the right to interfere with the way in which Scarcleft treats its citizens."

The words sank into Shale's mind with the dead weight of a boulder, and his anger rippled outwards in response. "Then there ought to be," he said. "It's not right that Taquar can get away with what he has done."

Nealrith hadn't replied, leaving Shale raging with impotent fury.

And now he watched and waited for the dawn, waited for news of Kaneth and Terelle. Servants came in the morning to take him to Nealrith for his first lessons. Another thing to get used to: having people around him whose sole job was to fetch and carry for him or to conduct him around the hall until he could find his own way. Their service embarrassed him.

That morning, however, as he trailed behind a man named Morion, who was to be his personal servant, he was grateful for the guidance. He didn't know how he would ever find his way through the network of passages and connecting stairs of Breccia Hall; they all looked the same. He had trouble orienting himself, because he could not see the sky.

When he entered Nealrith's quarters, it was to find Kaneth there as well. The two men were standing just inside the door, as if Kaneth was already on his way out. He was still dust-covered from his journey and obviously tired. He shook his head when he saw Shale. "No sign of her, I'm sorry. And Amethyst's definitely dead. Killed in her house, together with her servants."

"Taquar?" Shale gritted his teeth. "Will he get away with it?"

"He already has. I went back to the old man's room as well," Kaneth added, "but neither Russet nor Terelle were there. No one had seen them." He touched Shale's arm in sympathy. "I'm sorry. I have asked some friends of mine to make some discreet inquiries. If there is any news, they'll let me know. And I've let it be known among the people who lived in Russet's building that anyone who turns up here in Breccia with Terelle will be well rewarded. The news will spread."

"Sandblast him to a waterless death," Nealrith said quietly. "There was no need for him to kill Amethyst."

"It must have been just moments after you left," Kaneth said, making Nealrith wince. "I am hellishly weary. I must go. I haven't been home yet."

"Thank you for trying," Shale said.

"We won't give up on her," Kaneth replied, heading for the door. "I promise."

After he'd gone, Shale sank down into one of the chairs, in gloomy silence.

Nealrith sighed. "I followed the law I am bound to follow as highlord, as my father's son. And Amethyst died." He went to stand at the open shutters, to look down on the city. He was silent for a long while, then said, "There are so many ironies in my life of late. My father taught me never to forget my humanity. I have tried incentive and reasoning to persuade people to conserve water, rather than force and punishment. I was only behaving as he taught me to, with compassion. As a consequence, I have been called weak, and my father turned to another to rule the Quartern."

"Can someone who is not a stormlord rule the Quartern?"

"Not in normal times. But what other choice is there now? There is you, but you are young. You were not brought up to rule. And more than that, you will be the Quartern's *only* stormlord. Just to supply water to the nation will take most of your waking moments."

Shale froze, unable to believe what he was hearing. "Even if I was a stormlord, Taquar would still rule the land?"

"I think that is what my father would like, yes. He expects to die soon. You are too inexperienced to take on the responsibility, and I am too weak, or so he believes. He thinks that only Taquar will be able to force people to save water, only Taquar will be able to rein in the Reduners." He snorted.

Shale shook his head, his denial vehement. "But it was Taquar who urged the Reduners to rebellion!"

"Irony upon irony."

"When Taquar could tell the Reduners he had a future stormlord, he had a way of controlling Davim. Now he has nothing."

"I doubt he is going to tell Davim that. Davim has seen you with his own eyes. Seen how easily you shift water. Taquar will have told him he has taken you to Scarcleft for your final training."

Shale struggled with his shock. With his betrayal. Again. With his burgeoning horror. *Waterless damnation, one day I am going to be returned to Taquar's power!*

Nealrith continued, "My hope is that if you can learn to bring us storms, there won't be any need for a man such as Taquar to rule, and my father will change his mind."

"He *must* change his mind. Highlord Nealrith, he doesn't understand Taquar."

"No, he doesn't. He thinks you exaggerate. That is another irony. You want to know my father, Shale? As he used to be? Then look at me. Granthon Almandine is me, too weak to rule this land in time of trouble. He will not believe the worst of Taquar because he himself would never be capable of such crimes. Believe me, I have tried to convince him. He accuses me of petty spite."

"Perhaps if I was to talk to him." Even as he said the words, Shale wondered at his temerity. Who was he to speak to rulers about who had the right to rule? He was still just Shale Flint, one of the washfolk of Drybone Settle.

"No. He has heard your story once. My father needs to have faith in you, and you will not earn that faith by appearing to be greedy for power—or by showing lack of judgement by supporting any tenuous claim of mine."

Shale was silent, thinking things through. Finally he said, "You're not going to tell anyone you have me, are you? Because Granthon wouldn't want that news to get to Davim. Taquar won't tell him and you don't want the sandmaster to know, either."

Nealrith smiled, appreciative. "You're no fool, are you? If Davim thinks Taquar has you, he will wait and Taquar can control him. Better that than a horde of Reduners rampaging across the land."

Shale shook his head. *Taquar does not have control over Davim, and he never did, for all that he* thought *he did.*

"I want you to use another name for a while," Nealrith continued. "And to pretend you're just another water sensitive we found in the Gibber."

Shale found it hard to give voice to his thoughts. He had lived so long keeping all he believed within his heart, not blurting it out like water from a spigot. Still, he knew he had to try to speak his thoughts; if he didn't, then how could he expect people to know what he knew? How could he share his understanding? He took a deep breath. "If Taquar becomes the ruler of the Quartern, I may be safe—but one of the first things he will do is have you killed. Anyone who believes differently is a fool. Or they don't know Taquar."

Nealrith nodded. "I know that now. But my father is not dead yet. Things can change."

They looked at each other and Shale knew they were thinking the same thing: they had much in common. They had both been betrayed by people they'd respected. Shale said quietly, "We're just shells in a game, aren't we? To be moved about on the board, to be collected as part of the spoils and discarded at will when not needed. I thought things were going to be better here—but they're no different." He tilted his head in a gesture of defiance. "Lord Nealrith, I will not stay, you know. If Scarpen rule is handed over to Lord Taquar, I will leave. I will not serve that man. *Ever.*"

Nealrith gave a rare smile. "We'll leave together, then," he said. "I'll do my best for you, Shale, no matter what, because you are the only hope we have. Whatever happens, I promise you that much."

Shale nodded, almost believing him. Nealrith reached out and laid a hand on his shoulder. "I swear it, Shale. And I am not Taquar. Nor am I my father." Shale nodded again, this time with more certainty. "And you shouldn't address me by my title, not in private. We rainlords are all equals. I am Nealrith or Rith; you are Shale. Or whatever your new name is. Have you decided?"

He remembered Galen, blinded by avarice and drink. Remembered Citrine, seeing only the beauty of a piece of bloodstone in her last happy moment of life. What had Taquar called the gem? The martyr's stone. The familiar knotted feeling welled up inside him. The same feeling he had every time he thought of Citrine. Or Mica. Or of the burden he carried: to be a stormlord. To save a land from thirst. The burden of responsibility.

The true horror of being a stormlord.

"Jasper Bloodstone," he said.

"We call that the martyr's stone." Nealrith sounded dubious. "I hope that's not a prophetic choice."

"It's a better name than the one I had." *Shale Flint the Gibber boy was a dupe. I have to leave him behind.* The man who would cope with what was to come was Jasper Bloodstone. That was the face the world must see. A man who wouldn't trust again so foolishly.

Nealrith shrugged. "As you wish. And now we must start your exercises. The ones Taquar would not teach you, because they enable you to kill in the rainlord manner. If you can master these, you will not have any trouble in extracting fresh water vapour from salt water. But before we begin, I want you to meet my wife, Laisa, and my daughter, Senya. She is younger than you are, fifteen. I hope you will be friends. Come, I'll take you through to my private rooms."

Shale blinked, trying to assimilate the difference between private rooms and the one they were in. The extravagance of any family having so much space shocked him. He followed Nealrith, momentarily overwhelmed, reflecting wryly that Jasper Bloodstone had a lot to learn before he stopped being Shale Flint.

He remembered how Mica had spoken of Laisa's beauty with awe—and of her desirability with a more basic crudity. She was everything that Mica had said she was: sensual and lovely. Her eyes, though, were knowing, and there was no gentleness in her gaze as she welcomed him to Breccia City.

"There is much riding on your shoulders, young man," she told him. "I trust you have the fortitude to take on such a burden. I have always found Gibber-grubbers to be more feckless than hardworking, myself."

"I am sure we will have no complaints with Sh—Jasper," Nealrith said. "Jasper Bloodstone."

Laisa's eyebrows shot up. "A gemstone from a Gibber rock, eh? Well, we will see."

The girl at her side giggled. Shale was damned if he was going to blush; he was Jasper now. He switched his gaze to her without colouring up. Senya was shorter and less elegant than her mother, but her face was just as beautiful. Right then, though, as her amusement faded, lines of distaste marred her prettiness. He recognised that look. He'd seen it on the faces of some of the settlefolk when they looked at the washfolk of the shanties.

"This is Senya," Nealrith said. "I trust the two of you will be good friends."

She eyed him with a curl of her lip; Jasper gave her the same flat stare he'd used on uppity settlefolk. Life in Breccia City, he decided, was not going to be so different from what he was used to, after all.

"I am sure we will," he said, and knew he lied.

"So, have you had second thoughts about supporting Taquar as the next ruler of the Quartern?" Ryka asked, handing Kaneth a wet towel. They did not bathe any more; water was too precious. A wet towel was all they allowed themselves. Even the public baths were closed.

He stripped off the last of his undergarments and stood naked, wiping himself down.

Watergiver help me, she thought, trying not to show her appreciation of the muscular curves of his thighs and buttocks. *Why does his body excite me so? I feel like a silly eighteen-year-old lusting after the local hero.*

Maybe he was the hero at that. The pikeman, Elmar Waggoner, had told her with open admiration all the details of the fight in the waterpainter's room. Kaneth had cleverly made the best use of his water-powers and defeated a much larger group of attackers to save them all. But it hadn't been pretty. Battle, she guessed, rarely was, in spite of the written epics that told stories of glory. She shivered at the thought of the blind men Kaneth had left behind.

"Second thoughts?" he asked. "No, I haven't. And I won't, not until Jasper starts bringing in rain-soaked clouds. Nothing has changed, Ryka. Not yet."

"Don't be silly, of course it has! We have evidence that Taquar has connived at murder and kidnapped children. And this is the man you want to rule this land? Are you mad? You and Granthon both?" She faced him, hands on hips, enraged. "Kaneth, how can you?"

"How can I what? I'm not doing anything, except trying to get the sand out of my hair."

"Don't play games with me! You have been backing Granthon in this, against Nealrith, who is supposed

to be your best friend. You've been agreeing with the
Cloudmaster that Taquar is the best person to rule the
Quartern, but now we know he most certainly is not.
Blighted eyes, Kaneth, we have evidence to suggest he
took Iani and Moiqa's daughter and imprisoned her for
years, until she died. And this is the man whom you
would have rule us?"

"We don't know that about Lyneth, not for sure. And
even if it is true, what choice do we have? I don't *like* it,
you know. Do you think I don't know how much I have
hurt Nealrith by what he sees as disloyalty? But the alternative is a bloodbath in the streets, with our people battling one another over a water jar."

"Rubbish. People are more sensible than you give them
credit for. And for all that I don't particularly like priests
or their reliance on a Sunlord who palpably lost interest
in our welfare after sending us the Watergiver a thousand
years ago, we in the Scarpen are a people who believe in
what our religion promotes: generosity and compassion
and sacrifice and rules designed for the greater good."

Kaneth shook his head. "We are a land of hypocrites
who cynically manipulate rules based on the inherent in-
feriority of each level of the city to the one above."

"That's a horrible way of looking at life."

"It's honest."

"Tell me, if we did have a baby on the way, and the
child was born without water sensitivity, what would you
do if Taquar—as ruler of the Quartern—decreed such
children should be slaughtered for the greater good of us
all? Would you oblige him?"

"You're being ridiculous. That would never happen."

"Wouldn't it? Have you heard some of the things the

man has been doing to keep the number of water drinkers at a minimum in Scarcleft?"

"He's unnecessarily unpleasant, I agree. Nonetheless, Nealrith should impose some sort of tough regime here. But he won't, which means we could all be dead by the end of the next star cycle, long before Jasper comes into his powers. Ryka, we *have* to be tough. Quite frankly, it's my belief that rainlords are the only people who should be producing children now. We ought to be enforcing a no-child policy on everyone else, until such time as we have a competent, strong stormlord in Breccia Hall. Or more than one stormlord."

"And just how would you do that? Drag pregnant women into the waterhalls to be stripped of their babies, the way Taquar does it? He's murdering the unborn, Kaneth! And often inadvertently killing the mothers as well."

"They were warned. He told them what would happen if they chose not to dose themselves with sinucca. And they should know by now that Taquar is a man who keeps his word about things like that."

"Accidents happen to any woman! I can't believe you would countenance—"

He raised his voice to interrupt her. "It's either unborn children or a whole city!"

"I don't believe that." She blinked, hating the feeling at the back of her eyes of tears that would never fall. To express her rage, she threw the clean wet towel at him, hitting him in the face. "It's not going to happen that way!"

He plucked the towel away and used it to wipe his back. "All right then, if you want to believe in the innate goodness of a mob of thirsty people, go ahead. But they will still die, Ryka. *You* will still die. Because our water won't last so long if we keep sharing it with a new generation of children."

"You're a monster, just like Taquar. And to think I thought you had a kind heart! Here's something you had better believe, Kaneth Carnelian. I will not bed you *ever* again. We are done with trying to have a child. And I am done with you!"

She didn't give him a chance to reply. She ran into their adjacent bedroom, slamming the door behind her, and flung herself down on the bed to bury her swollen and aching eyes in the pillow.

I don't love him, she thought. *I can't love a man like that.*

But if she didn't love him, why did she feel this way? His hardness hurt her so.

She lay still, steadying her breath. *Because you always will love him*, her inner voice whispered. *In spite of everything. There's no reason; it just is.*

Slowly she slipped her hand down to cover her lower abdomen and feel again the presence of a tiny bundle of water.

It's nothing, she thought. *I'm imagining it. I'm not even late yet. It's nothing.*

And then, *It can't be right to be cruel, can it?*

She punched her pillow with impotent rage until her anger and confusion faded into grief.

CHAPTER THIRTY-SEVEN

Scarpen Quarter
Breccia City
Breccia Hall, Level 2

Every night, before going to bed, Jasper—as he now thought of himself—extinguished his lamp and went to stand on the balcony of his room. There, bathed in starlight, shivering with the cold of the desert night, he thought of Terelle. It was a ritual, pointless in itself, yet providing a way to remember her, even if the memory brought the pain of grief. He had hinged part of himself to her, to the thought of her. He did not know if it was love—there had not been much love in his life and he was not sure that he would recognise it—but now she wasn't there and he was diminished, just as he had been diminished by Mica's absence, by Citrine's death. Her absence *hurt*.

He heaved a sigh. There were so many things he didn't want to think about.

For fifteen days he'd studied with Nealrith. The exercises were more precise and detailed than those Taquar had taught him; unfortunately, they'd had as little success. To kill by drawing out a living creature's water sounded simple; after all, it was just a movement of water, and he could do that. But first he had to separate the water from the living tissue.

They started with flies. All he had to do was remove a drop of water. Half a drop, in fact. And he couldn't do it. His ability to move and shape and manipulate plain water did improve, but he could no more extract water from a fly than he could raise a rain cloud from the sea.

Ryka and Kaneth were in the highlord's rooms when Jasper arrived for his morning lesson with Nealrith the next day. He hesitated with his hand on the door when he heard his name mentioned.

". . . not as strong as you hoped?" Kaneth was asking. He sounded incredulous.

"The initial problem remains," Nealrith replied. "He cannot extract vapour from anything as salty as the sea. He can't take the water out of an orange, and he can't take it from blood and tissue."

"The waterhall reeves said he lifted a whole cistern of water when you asked him to!" Kaneth's protest was comically indignant.

"They shouldn't have been talking about it, but yes, he can. However, that was pure water. Father thinks Jasper's flaw is a result of coming too late to training."

"Sunlord save us. What does that mean for our future?"

"I've thought of trying to work out a way we can use my rainlord strength to give him the added boost he needs, just in case Father dies. After all, any of us can extract fresh water from salt."

Kaneth gave a wry laugh. "Yeah. A cupful at a time.

With a little luck, you should be able to water a pot plant or two."

"Maybe Taquar could do better," Nealrith said, acknowledging a bitter truth. "He's stronger than any of us, that's obvious. And he always was good at making vapour when we were students. Perhaps if he could be persuaded to work with Father to stormbring . . ." His voice trailed away unhappily.

"His price would be more than you want to pay," Ryka said.

"No. It is one we *should* pay," Kaneth contradicted. "What is more important than cloudmaking? You're right, Rith. He *was* good at pulling vapour out of water. But useless at keeping it together, I remember. Do you recall that time he lost control and his cloud condensed all over the ceiling at the academy? Water dripping everywhere, and old Master Rockdale was furious."

"Granthon did ask him last year if he would help," Nealrith said. "Before we knew what he was up to, of course. He refused."

"He *refused*?" Ryka was astonished.

"Said his skills weren't up to it," Nealrith said wearily.

"More likely he just didn't want to spend his time so tediously," Ryka said.

There was a long silence, broken finally by Kaneth. "So we have found ourselves a talented mover of water, and he is flawed. Waterless skies!"

"Poor Shale," Ryka said softly. "What a burden for him. Ah, Jasper, I should say."

There was a sudden silence, then a whisper he didn't hear.

They've finally sensed my water, he thought. He knocked at the door and entered. Nealrith waved him into an empty chair.

"I'm sorry if you heard what I said, Jasper," Kaneth said. "I was preoccupied and wasn't aware anyone was out there. I wasn't blaming you."

He shrugged, trying not to care. "It was no more than the truth." No one said anything to that, so he asked, "Have any of you heard anything from Scarcleft about Terelle?"

"I haven't," Nealrith said.

"Neither have we," Ryka said, and from the compassion in her glance, he guessed that she thought there was little chance anyone ever would.

"There is something about her that I haven't told you," he said. "She—she could be of value to you. To us." Three pairs of eyes fixed him with looks of polite disbelief.

"She is a Watergiver," he said. "Not an intermediary from the Sunlord, of course, but one of a people from the mountains on the far side of the White Quarter. That's what they call themselves apparently, Watergivers. Russet Kermes is one."

The three rainlords continued to stare at him, faces blank.

He struggled on. "She is also a waterpainter. Waterpainters have certain, um, powers. They can influence the future with their art. They can paint something to ensure it happens. Russet did that to make Nealrith go to Scarcleft. Perhaps Terelle could paint rain clouds or something. I think she would be willing to try."

Nealrith interrupted. "What are you talking about? Russet told you I came as a result of *sorcery*?"

"Well, magic. Waterpainting."

"What the pickled pede do you mean? I went to Scarcleft because of Amethyst's letter, to find another stormlord, not because of any sorcery."

"I saw that magic at work," he said stubbornly. "He painted you going to Amethyst's house. I should have told you earlier, but I was afraid you wouldn't believe me. Besides, I don't like it. The power, it's horrible. Russet trapped Terelle by his paintings, for a start. He drew her future and took away her choices. If she tried to leave him, she was ill." He drew another deep breath. "Although perhaps his plans have gone awry now. He's old; maybe his magic doesn't work well any more. In fact, I'm sure it doesn't; that's why he needs Terelle."

When he faltered, Nealrith said snappishly, "Make sense, Jasper. We used to have a waterpainting. Laisa ordered several of them, in fact. Might even have been Russet who did them. I ordered the last one removed not so long ago because it had to be kept topped up with water, and I thought it a waste. There was nothing special about it that I could see."

"What the painter can do with the power—if he wants—is horrible. Unthinkable. But to save Terelle or Mica, I'd do anything, even try to get you interested in using such power. Russet made waterpaintings to determine the future, and Terelle can, too. They can *make* things happen. Imagine: perhaps she could paint a future that ensured the defeat of Davim, or maybe the birth of more stormlords or something. If you brought her here, and told her what was needed—"

Nealrith's face flushed dark. "I have never heard of anything more ridiculous. You have been deceived by some kind of trickery, Jasper. There are shams and fraudsters everywhere, and all you've told me about this Russet indicates he is one of them."

"Terelle is no fraudster," he said, not trying to hide his rage. "I *saw* her make a man climb onto a rooftop. Why won't you believe in that, when you will believe in the magic that enables a stormlord to move water from the sea into clouds, that enables him to bring those clouds to the hills, to force them upwards so that they break and the rain falls?"

Ryka quickly smothered an involuntary laugh. Kaneth's face went studiously blank. Nealrith, however, was so shocked he was almost speechless. He had to swallow hard before he could say, "Cloudmaking and stormshifting are not *sorcery*! Jasper, how could you ever *think* such a thing! Stormshifting is the goodness of the Sunlord's powers manifested in a stormlord, the Holy One's blessing to us, the people of the Quartern. He sent an intermediary to us from his realm a thousand years ago, in the form of a man called Ash Gridelin, now known to us as the Watergiver, to tell us how to use that God-given power. How can you equate such a holy gift, and the knowledge to use it, with *magic*? That is blasphemy. And the Watergiver was the Sunlord's true emissary, not some—some fake from a market stall!"

Jasper stared at him helplessly. He wanted to ask, *If the Sunlord is so powerful, why did he need a human as an intermediary?* But he suspected he would not receive an answer that satisfied him. He couldn't see much difference between magic and the Sunlord's gift, but he had a suspicion that arguing the point with Nealrith would get him nowhere.

Ryka laid a hand on Nealrith's arm. "Rith, you can

hardly blame Jasper for the gaps in his religious knowledge. You remember what the remoter areas of the Gibber were like, including his. They were so ignorant of Scarpen faith that some thought we were gods."

The highlord drew in a calming breath. "I remember. I can certainly see that his religious education has been inadequate."

"I can teach him," she offered.

"You? Would I use a cistern of water to bring life to embers? I will arrange with Lord Gold for him to have private lessons at the temple with a waterpriest teacher." He glanced at Jasper. "Lord Gold is the highest-ranking priest. The Quartern's Sunpriest."

"And Terelle?" Jasper asked. "Won't you send someone to look for her?"

"Our informants can't find her, and if they can't, I'm sure we couldn't. I don't think we should try. I'm sorry."

Buffeted by guilt and worry, he subsided into a miserable silence as Nealrith continued. "Let's deal with the reason—reasons—I asked Ryka and Kaneth in this morning. Firstly, the gaps in your education, Jasper. Besides the religious ones, I mean. I think you do not have sufficient time to attend the Water Sensitives Academy on Level Three, as we all did—not with the water exercises you have to practise. So I'd like you to work with Ryka."

Jasper swallowed his irritation and hid a scowl. He liked Ryka, but it would have been nicer to have been asked rather than told.

Nealrith continued, unheeding. "Another gap is in your ability to protect yourself. If you can't kill the rainlord way, then you need to learn swordplay. That's where you come in, Kaneth. I want you to teach him."

"Sword or scimitar?"

"Both."

"There's a difference in the way you use them?" Jasper asked.

Kaneth nodded. "Scimitars work better for slashing, and slashing works better when you are riding a pede. But Rith, why don't you ask a professional sword master? I may be both skilled and experienced, but like any rainlord, I rely on my water skills in a real fix."

"Because I don't want too many people to know that Jasper is special. Nothing must get back to Davim that would make him wonder if Jasper and Shale are the same person. Give your lessons inside Breccia Hall—the reception room is big enough."

Kaneth shrugged. "All right." He grinned at Jasper. "Don't worry, I do know the basics. It'll be fun. Granthon doesn't want me out looking for Reduner marauders any more anyway, and teaching you beats spending my time checking for leaks along the tunnel."

"Good," Nealrith said. "I will take the mornings for water skills. You two share the afternoons. Work out a schedule and get back to me. And you'll have religious classes and driving lessons on alternate days."

Jasper brightened. "Oh! I can learn to drive a pede?"

"Well, I wasn't talking about a donkey." When Jasper looked blank, he added, "It's a rare animal they use a lot for carrying loads in the land across the Giving Sea. They have some in Pediment." He smiled suddenly, banishing his habitual look of worry. "Let's go down to the hall stable. I want to show you something."

* * *

They all left the room together, but Kaneth and Ryka headed home while Nealrith led Jasper through a network of courtyards, archways and passageways to the stables. When they arrived there, Jasper looked around with widening eyes. There were six myriapedes, each with its own immaculate stall. Several stable boys were busy grooming one of the animals while it tore and masticated a mixture of saltbush and desert root, its numerous pairs of mouthparts audibly grinding and ripping the vegetation into smaller and smaller pieces.

Waterless damn, Jasper thought, *these pedes live better than even Palmier Rishan did back in Wash Drybone!*

"Some of our animals are out being used, of course," Nealrith said. "And our packpedes are always stabled outside the city walls. Anyway, this is the beast I want you to have a look at." He pointed to the end stall, where a half-grown male myriapede looked out over the door of its stall. "He's for you."

"For me to ride?"

"More than that—he's yours."

Jasper blinked in amazement. "To *own*? You're *giving* me a pede?"

"Not me, personally. Every rainlord has his own, bought with Quartern taxes. This one will be fully mature in about two years, but he is ready to be ridden and trained now."

"You bought it for me?"

Nealrith's gaze flicked away as if he was embarrassed. "Er, no. Not originally. I bought it for Senya. But she has shown no interest in it and does not want to learn to drive. Tomorrow morning, be here at dawn and you can have your first lesson."

Jasper turned back to the pede. He extended his right

hand, slowly, towards the animal's mouthparts, giving it time to accustom itself to his smell. The feelers whipped forward, the sensitive tips seeking him out, running over his face, his hands, his clothing.

"Thank you," he said to Nealrith, his delight shining through the restraint of his reply. "I have never really owned anything before. Unless you count my clothes, of course." *And once I had a piece of bloodstone.*

He was stroking the pede and saw neither the pity, nor the ache that immediately followed it, on the highlord's face.

"Why do you think the Gibber folk are darker skinned and poorer than Scarpen city folk?"

Ryka's question stymied him, as her questions often did. She stimulated and challenged him, goaded him to think, really *think* about things, especially about why the Quartern was the way it was.

"I don't know," he said, feeling foolish because he had never thought about it before.

"History, Jasper. History. Listen: once, when the Giving Sea was no more than a gully, our ancestors, yours and mine, were outlanders who came here from the places on the Other Side. When they came, they pushed out the folk who were here first, forcing them north."

He was astonished. "You mean Reduners once *owned* the Scarpen?"

"The Scarpen *and* the Gibber. Most Scarpen folk won't believe that, but I think it is true. The people who came, they wanted the wealth of the land—the minerals and the gemstones—and they were willing to fight to get it. There were many more of them than there were Reduners, and in those days the Reduners had neither pedes nor ziggers.

Back then, there was always water to be found, because it rained at certain times of the star cycle, and the gullies and washes ran with water every year for tens of days at a time without fail. Even in between the rains, there were pools to be found. There was no need of stormlords, or so the myths and legends say.

"Then something went wrong. We don't know what. The rains began to disappear, year by year, yet the Giving Sea rose up and flooded the land between us and the places we had come from. The waterpriests tell us it was punishment for our sins. On the Other Side, cities were washed away by the ocean. People there died in the thousands, their cities ruined and drowned. For a long time, we aren't sure how long exactly, we were cut off. Here the land was so dry that many—perhaps most—people died. Those who were left became nomads, copying the Reduners. They adapted. This became known as the Time of Random Rain.

"But most of our history was lost. Life was hard. The only memory people held on to, because it was important to them, was that once they had been miners and traders in minerals. They called themselves by the names of the rocks and the stones and the gems, so that they would never forget. Gibber folk were, I think, more miners than traders; Scarpen Quarter folk more traders. It was from Portennabar and Portfillik that the ancient routes ran across what is now the Giving Sea to the Other Side.

"It was during the Time of Random Rain that the Reduners—then living in the dunes—tamed the pedes and ziggers they'd found there. Because of those, they dominated the Quartern and built a culture based on slavery of the conquered. The Time of Random Rain lasted until the

Watergiver came and taught some water sensitives how to be stormlords and rainlords."

"How do we know the Watergiver was real?"

"The waterpriests have religious texts that tell the story. They say the texts were inspired by the Sunlord and therefore must be true." She smiled slightly. "That's an argument based on its own circular logic, of course, but don't tell them I said that. How are you enjoying your religious classes, by the way?"

He pulled a face. "Not much. I—I find it hard to believe all the things Lord Basalt tells me. He says I should have faith, but he doesn't really *explain* things. Then he gets angry if I ask *why*." He considered the matter. "Terelle always used to make libations to the Sunlord. I thought it was a waste of water. She said it was easier to believe than to question and that it made her happier to believe than to doubt, but for me it's the other way around."

"If there is one thing I have discovered," she said, "it's this: it is impossible to force belief on yourself. It doesn't work, any more than someone with a deep faith can suddenly throw it all away because someone asks them to. Nealrith *never* doubts. You doubt all the time. And so do I. Kaneth doesn't think about it and isn't interested. By the sound of it, Terelle doesn't think about it much, either—but she does the opposite: she accepts. There is room for us all, but unhappily, the really religious feel obligated to save the endangered souls they are sure the rest of us have, without realising how impossible it is to believe when you just don't. I am not sure who is to be most pitied, those troubled by our damnation or we who have to live believing we end with death."

She touched his hand in commiseration. "If I were you,

I'd play the hypocrite. Pretend you believe; it makes them happier. One day, who knows, maybe it will all make sense to you, but if it doesn't, you will at least be in a position to tell them you think it's all about as real as a sand-dancer."

He pulled a wry face and decided she was right. "We've got off the subject," he said. "About why the Gibber is so much poorer than the Scarpen."

"Not entirely. It's connected. The priests say it was because the Watergiver went first to the Gibber, but they laughed at him and drove him out. So the Sunlord punished them by making the sun hotter and the washes of the Gibber the last places to be given regular water."

She laughed at Jasper's disgusted face and continued, "It took generations for the stormlords and the rainlords to refine their skills, to nourish enough water sensitives to bring the Scarpen back from the edge of disaster. At the same time, they had to battle the Reduners for their freedom. In the meantime, the Gibber suffered. The Reduners raided the Gibber Plains, too, just to make it worse.

"Eventually there was controlled rain, and the Other Siders built ships to come to us, so there was trade once more. We defeated the Reduners, and there were no more raids, but by that time, your people were so poor that you've never quite caught up."

"And our darker skin colour?"

"The religious texts say it was the Sunlord's mercy, to save you from his burning heat, since you had to spend so much of your time looking for food on the plains and fossicking for resin and minerals to trade."

Religion again, he thought with a sigh. *Things would be so much easier if I could believe it all.*

She continued, "If we believe the priests, it was the Watergiver who changed everything for the better in the Scarpen. He not only showed us how to use a water sensitive's power to make and break the clouds, he gave us the skill to kill using our water-powers. That gave us the edge we needed to send the Reduners back to the dunes. The pedemen of the Red Quarter have hated us ever since."

He stared at her, not bothering to hide his astonishment. "But that must have been almost a thousand years ago! They still hate us after all that time?"

"Men have long memories for slighted pride."

That's ridiculous, he thought. Then he remembered the bitter dislike in Davim's eyes. The cold core of fear inside him grew. Confound Ryka; the more he learned from her, the more uneasy he felt. Nothing was as simple as it had been once, when all he had to do was keep out of the reach of Galen's fists and somehow earn or steal enough food and water to fill his belly.

"The Reduners don't believe in the Sunlord, of course," Ryka continued. "They have their dune gods, one for each dune. They say their gods speak to the tribes, using a language only the shamans understand."

Jasper snorted. "So a dune shaman could be a very powerful man."

"Indeed," she agreed blandly. They exchanged a smile.

"What about the Alabasters? Where do they come from?"

"Ah. There you have an intriguing mystery. No one knows. The Reduners call them the forbidden people, but they can't say why. And the Alabasters themselves don't say. Or won't. I have interviewed many of them, trying to find out, and I have the feeling that they do know. We have a saying here, 'to keep a secret as well as a 'Baster.'"

"What do *you* think?"

"They have their own language, although they don't speak it any more. They use it to read and write, though. To me that means they were one of the original people, like the Reduners. I think they know far more than they say. They are cultured, and I suspect they have a written history they don't care to share. But I am just guessing."

"You like them."

"Yes, I do. They are gentle and generous. We need more people like them, not fewer." Her tone was troubled as she added, "Ah, Jasper, sometimes I think the world we are heading towards needs much more than we know how to give."

His lessons with Kaneth were exhausting, but fun because they were unpredictable. Better still, he found he had a talent for combat. He enjoyed the physicality of it and liked nothing more than repeating moves over and over until they were graceful and instinctive.

Sometimes Ryka or Nealrith would come to watch the lessons. Nealrith evaluated his progress with a practised eye and offered advice. Ryka just watched Kaneth.

And Jasper wondered about the dread he sometimes glimpsed in her gaze when she looked at her husband. He didn't think anyone else noticed, but he was an expert at seeing fear in a woman's eyes. He'd seen it in his mother's gaze when she looked at Galen. He'd seen it in Terelle when she looked at Russet. But Ryka didn't fear that Kaneth would hurt her, surely.

So why those flickers of panic?

He had no idea. Another complication he didn't understand.

The days bled into one another, one hardly different from the next. Yet each day made him a slightly different person. More competent, more knowledgeable, a better rainlord, a little closer to being a stormlord, a little further away from Terelle, from Mica, from the rawness of Citrine's death. More Jasper and less Shale. Then, when he had been in Breccia for just over seventy days, Nealrith took him back to Granthon.

"You are needed now," the highlord told Jasper. "Even another day might be too late."

"But I still can't extract pure water—or vapour—from water as salty as the sea!" It was the one area where he had made no progress.

"My father will cloudmake," Nealrith said. "You will cloudshift." The tone he used brooked no protest.

The Cloudmaster looked weaker than ever. Jasper concealed his despair at the man's decline. He listened carefully as Granthon took him step by step through what he needed to know. Granthon would devote all his strength to the separation of fresh water from salt and its conversion to vapour. The moment the water vapour rose from the surface of the sea, Jasper was to take over. Nealrith would tell him where to send the clouds, and Granthon would help him break them.

And so he started shifting clouds, taking what the weakened stormlord made and teasing them across the sky at Nealrith's direction. At first he found it especially hard to do once a cloud moved out of sight across the Sweepings, to the north of the city. But as the days passed, that became easier, too. He could use his senses to track and guide the unseen cloud to force it higher and higher above the Warthago Range, until it finally broke and released its life-giving water.

After that, he and Granthon worked alone, raising at least two storms every day.

Even though he still could not extract water from the sea, he was making a difference, and he was proud of that. Granthon would live longer because of him. The Quartern would survive longer.

He knew who he was now. Jasper Bloodstone, rainlord. Useful, talented—but still an imperfect vessel, doing no more than postponing the Quartern's day of reckoning.

He knew that, ultimately, his failure to do more would condemn them all.

CHAPTER THIRTY-EIGHT

Scarpen Quarter
Breccia City
Level 3 and Level 2

Lord Basalt, High Waterpriest of Breccia and second in the hierarchy of the Quartern's one true faith, stood on the suntower that rose above the Sun Temple and watched as Jasper, on his way home after his religion lesson, threaded his way through the crowd on the streets of Level Three. Several guards, dressed as ordinary citizens, unobtrusively followed.

I hate him, Basalt thought, surprising himself by the degree of venom he felt. *I hate the Quartern's next stormlord. He's a dirty Gibber sand louse with the soul of an unbelieving lowleveller. In front of me he pretends to worship the Sunlord, but I can see through him, even if Lord Gold does not.*

In Basalt's opinion, the Quartern Sunpriest—who, following a long tradition, had taken on the name of Lord Gold for the colour of the sun—was far too gullible and forgiving, and too old for the job, as well. He was wizened, and shrivelled more with each passing day. Already his vigils under the Sunlord's face were weakening him.

Basalt allowed himself to daydream a little, visualising the Sunpriest's body laid out in the House of the Dead so that the rainlords could transfer his water to the libations cistern. Basalt would take pleasure in sprinkling that water on the ground when he was the new Lord Gold.

An unbecoming thought, he acknowledged. He pulled himself back to the present.

He could still see Jasper below, lingering at the edge of a crowd gathered around some street performers when he should have been on his way uplevel to Breccia Hall. Basalt could have sworn the Gibber youth was taller, more muscular and less wiry than when he had come for his first lesson barely one hundred days earlier. He would never have the height that Kaneth or Nealrith commanded, but he was already taller than most Gibbermen. When he walked the streets now, the girls turned their heads to look. Doubtless he revelled in their attention, blast him.

I know a lying hypocrite when I see one, he thought. *And Jasper Bloodstone will be the greatest enemy the faith has, unless we curb him now.* But how to convince Lord Gold of that?

Lord Basalt's hands clenched the balustrade. One day, he would prove to everyone that Jasper was as unworthy of the position he sought as he was of that pretentious name, Bloodstone. The bastard was no stormlord. He wasn't even a rainlord.

"Your feelings do you no credit, Basalt," a calm voice remarked.

Basalt jumped, startled. He'd been so intent on the

desert-grubber that the Sunpriest had come to stand beside him, without his even being aware of the man's water.

"Ah. Lord Gold."

"I have found that if one wishes to impress the young with the righteousness of our beliefs, it is best to treat them with respect. It is our duty to guide them, not look down on them. Our vocation is to set an example of compassion, not condemnation. Even mild antipathy has no place in the heart of a priest."

He calmed the pounding of his heart with a few deep breaths. "Yet a priest should hate sin, Lord Gold."

"Sin? That young man has not a spare moment in his day to commit a sin!"

"His sins are not of the body. They reside in his heart and mind. He denigrates the Sunlord with his lack of belief."

"He has not expressed any such heresy, has he? Perhaps he doubts, but is that not a simple human failing? Have you never doubted, Basalt?"

He was shocked. "*Never!*"

"Then you are luckier than most. When I questioned Rainlord Jasper, at your suggestion, his comments were all that is proper."

"He lied."

"You cannot know that."

"He is not even a proper stormlord."

"Yet he is shifting clouds, and has been for the past thirty days or so."

His shock deepened. "You did not tell me!"

"It was not something you needed to know, and the Cloudmaster wishes us to keep gossip about your pupil to a minimum, as you know. You may not trust the young man, but he is our next stormlord, possibly the future ruler of the Quartern. You owe him your respect."

"But you told me he cannot extract fresh water from the sea!"

"Not yet, no. The Cloudmaster is still doing that. But it is young Jasper who brings the clouds to be broken. Ah, the sun sets. Would you commence the evening prayers, my lord?"

Obediently, Basalt lifted his hands, but just as he opened his mouth to begin, Lord Gold leaned forward to look down at the street below. "Wait. Some kind of commotion down there," he remarked. "Can you hear what they are shouting?"

Basalt bent over the balustrade. "It's a pede. I think that's Rainlord Iani on its back. He's in a tearing hurry, asking for people to clear the way." He frowned. "Wasn't he back in Qanatend?"

"As far as I know, yes."

"His pede is missing a feeler. And some legs, too, by the gait."

They stared at each other.

"Pray this doesn't involve that godless heathen of a sandmaster. The one they call Davim," Basalt growled.

"We'll know soon enough," Gold murmured. "No point in speculating." But as he spoke, he took his water skin from inside his robe and sacrificed the rest of his day's water allowance on the sun symbol recessed in the hard mud-bricks beneath his feet. Staring into the heart of the setting sun, he prayed for the Sunlord's intercession on behalf of Qanatend.

*   *   *

Jasper returned to Breccia Hall through the main gate, deep in thought. No matter how much he tried, he could not like the High Waterpriest. Basalt was so sure of his own righteousness that he had no understanding of another's failings. Worse, his was a religion of punishment for transgressions, and the more Jasper learned, the less he liked it. If he had not had several conversations with the older, milder Lord Gold, if he had not observed the gentle, unwavering faith of Highlord Nealrith, he would have despised the one true faith. As it was, he was learning to fear Basalt. The man's dislike was so strong that Jasper felt threatened.

Watergiver save me, Jasper thought with deliberate irreverence. *He's as unreasonable as Galen in a drunken temper*. But it wasn't drink that drove Basalt; it was religious fervour.

As he crossed the forecourt to the main door of the hall, sudden shouts behind him made him stop and look back.

"Make way! Make way!"

A single rider on a myriapede, moving in fast mode, entered the court. Jasper leaped to the side. The tips of the tens of feet clattered like water running down a slot as the beast shot past. To his astonishment, it didn't slow, but flowed up the front steps to the main entrance. For a moment, Jasper thought the rider was going to urge the beast inside, but one of the guards grabbed the reins, and the man leaped off. He almost fell, and the guard moved quickly to steady him.

"What is it, m'lord?" the guard asked.

"Reduners have attacked Qanatend," the man said. He

gathered himself together and half-ran, half-limped the rest of the way inside.

"Who was that?" Jasper said when he reached the top of the steps.

"Rainlord Iani Potch, Reeve Jasper," the guard replied. Like most people, he was unaware that Jasper had any talents beyond those of a reeve.

Lord Iani the sandcrazy. His wife, Moiqa, was the Highlord of Qanatend.

As Jasper strode on, he pictured in his mind one of the maps he had been studying with Nealrith to learn where clouds were to be broken. Qanatend was the only Scarpen city on the far side of the Warthago Range, which meant it was the closest city to the Red Quarter. And now it was under attack.

Davim. It had to be Davim. He'd tired of waiting for Taquar to produce Shale Flint, the stormlord.

Jasper felt sick. Everything would change now.

And he had to tell Iani about the bracelet. He wasn't looking forward to that, either.

CHAPTER THIRTY-NINE

Scarpen Quarter
Breccia City
Breccia Hall, Level 2

Morion came to tell Jasper to join Nealrith and his family in their private dining room that evening. When he did, he found neither Granthon nor Nealrith nor Ethelva was there. Instead, Rainlord Laisa and her daughter, Senya, were seated with Iani, who was still dusty and travel-stained.

Laisa looked up as soon as he entered. "Ah, there you are. Come meet Lord Iani. He has just come from a meeting with Granthon and Nealrith. They have excused him to have a meal. Poor man has not eaten properly since leaving Qanatend. You have heard the news, I suppose? I have dismissed the servants so I can talk to him freely. Help yourself to the food and drink on the side tables."

She then resumed her conversation, giving Jasper no chance to reply. He went to select his food, and sneaked a look at Iani while he helped himself. The rainlord was grey-haired and stooped. One side of his face was drawn downwards, out of kilter with the other.

When he went to join them at the table, it was Iani

who spoke first. "So you're Jasper Bloodstone. Nealrith mentioned you."

Iani's speech was slightly slurred, and Jasper—reminded of his father's drunken mumbling—was for a moment repulsed. Then he saw that half of Iani's face did not move as the other half did. A trail of dribble trickled out of one side of his mouth; the man was partially palsied. He waved a spoon at Jasper. "Sit down, sit down. Nealrith said that Taquar was involved."

"Taquar found him," Laisa said by way of explanation as Jasper sat and stabbed at his meal with his spoon. He avoided looking at her because he wasn't sure if he could stop staring. She was wearing a loose robe that clung to different parts of her anatomy with disturbing effect, revealing more than it concealed. She continued, "Our estimable friend kept the boy a prisoner while he taught him the rudiments of watershifting."

"It seems unbelievable! Whatever was he intending?" He addressed Jasper once more: "Nealrith says that you are a stormlord."

"No, he's not," Senya interrupted. She smiled at Jasper.

"No, not yet," he agreed, controlling his wince. "Not really."

"My daughter Lyneth also had the potential to be a stormlord," Iani said.

"So I heard, m'lord."

"Iani, Iani, Iani. Call me Iani. She was beautiful, you know. Lyneth."

Jasper's face flooded with colour, and he changed the subject. "I heard you tell the guard that Qanatend is under attack by Reduners?"

"Yes. I rode for help. I was not in the city when they came; I was inspecting the tunnel. And looking for her, you know. Lyneth. My daughter. I always look for her." Jasper tackled his meal, but all the while he was thinking frantically. Had Nealrith spoken to Iani about Lyneth's bracelet? He thought it unlikely. This was the first time Iani had come to Breccia since Jasper had arrived, and there were more urgent things to consider right now.

"Is—is the attack serious?" he asked. "Or just a quick raid by marauders?"

"Oh, it is serious all right." Iani's tone was grim. "They surround the city. They have our groves and the mother cistern in the hills above. They control our water tunnel. When I left, Moiqa was holding them off at the city walls. I couldn't get back in. I wanted to find Lyneth for her, you know. Can you conceive what it is like for a mother to lose her only child and never to know what happened to her?"

Jasper shook his head and stopped eating. He suddenly had no appetite.

Iani continued, "The city will be all right for a while, with rationing. I sent some men to ask Pediment and Scarcleft for help, and I came here. It will take twice as long to get back with reinforcements. And several days to organise it all first. Supplies. Water. Got to bring their own water. Problem, that. But we can take the mother cistern back first." He swirled the hot honeyed tea in his mug. "Who knows if they can last long enough? The city, I mean."

"What do the Reduners want? Why would they raid a Scarpen city?" Senya asked, her eyes bright with interest.

"You tell me, dear child."

She pouted, apparently not liking to be called a child, and didn't answer, so Iani turned to Jasper. "You tell me."

"I don't know, although I suppose I could make a few guesses."

Iani looked interested, Laisa scornful, Senya disbelieving. "Such as?" Laisa asked.

"Sandmaster Davim of Watergatherer has united most of the dunes but needs to prove to them that he can lead— and that means getting them enough water."

Laisa made an impatient gesture. "Get to the point."

"Davim believed Taquar could supply the Red Quarter, if he wanted, through my cloudshifting powers. At a guess, Taquar told him I am a lot better than I really am and hasn't told him that he doesn't have me any more. So Davim tells Taquar to supply water to make up Granthon's shortfall. When he doesn't get it, he makes good on a threat. 'Fool with me, Taquar, and I'll destroy the Scarpen cities you want to rule one day. Careful, or I'll leave you with nothing.' And so he starts with Qanatend, which is the city closest to the Red Quarter."

"So much wisdom in one so young," Laisa drawled. "Where *do* you get your ideas from?"

Senya giggled.

Iani paused, his drink halfway to his lips. "Explain yourself," he said at last. "You think Davim and Taquar plotted treason *together*?"

"I saw them together. Taquar had me demonstrate my water skills to Davim."

Iani almost dropped his drink. "Do you mean to tell me you think Moiqa's city is under siege simply because this Reduner wants *to teach Taquar a lesson*?"

"That, and maybe it's a way for the Reduners to get more water, at least for as long as water flows into the mother cistern. They have the pedes necessary to transport it. I would say they are already doing their best to steal it from Qanatend."

Iani looked aghast. "This fellow, Davim—he must believe that Granthon won't send rain to the Red Quarter's waterholes now that he has raided a Scarpen city. So he would be entirely dependent on Taquar, whom you say he does not trust? He would not be so foolish, surely! He must have some other plan, something we are not aware of."

"He's gambling," replied Jasper.

"That's sandcrazy!" said Iani.

"No, because he doesn't think he can lose. If Taquar doesn't start supplying the water Davim needs, then he will simply attack more Scarpen cities until he does. Of course, he doesn't know Taquar doesn't have me any more. Each time he gains a city, he seizes more water. He thinks the Reduner tribes will be increasingly angry with the Scarpen, and happier with him."

"You are contradicting yourself," Laisa said. "You said they are already united behind him."

"Yes, most of the dune tribes are," Jasper agreed, "but at the moment he has their support only because they fear his power. He has been threatening them, and most have succumbed. But it's hard to win a battle with reluctant warriors. He needs the sandmasters of the other dunes to support him willingly. And one way to do that is to provide them with a common enemy. Who better than the people who stopped sending them water? He would then have a huge force of mounted tribesmen with ziggers. Enough to conquer the whole of the Quartern, if he wanted."

"And leave their families at home without water," Iani pointed out.

"Not exactly. There would still be water in most of the Reduner waterholes for a while. And he would be sending water back to them all the time."

Laisa looked at him, frowning. Senya more rudely asked, "How can you possibly know that stuff? You're just a Gibberman who never went to the academy."

Jasper flushed but continued doggedly, "I don't *know* anything. Rainlord Iani just asked my opinion, and I gave it. And I am hardly untutored. Cloudmaster Granthon tells me things he thinks I ought to know and gives me texts to read. So does Highlord Nealrith. I study with Rainlord Ryka. And I had nothing else to do but read when I was imprisoned. I even corresponded with Scarcleft teachers. Being caged gives you a lot of time to read and learn."

Laisa gave him a hard stare. "Well," she said, "who would have thought *you* would have all the answers. How do you explain the limited nature of this plan of Davim's? He must realise that sooner or later he will run out of water to steal."

"Once he has sufficient water stored in Reduner water holes to last a couple of years, he will rid himself of every rainlord in the Quartern, including Taquar, Granthon and me. He hates rainlords and stormlords. Random rain will then return. The Red Quarter will survive; we won't."

"Why can they be powerful in a time of random rain and we can't?" Senya asked.

It was her mother who answered. "They have pedes by the hundred. They are hunters. Their sandmasters and tribemasters and shamans are water sensitives who can find desert waterholes filled by random rain. We rainlords and reeves could, too, I suppose, but all of us in the Scarpen and the Gibber are linked too irrevocably to our groves and our cities and settles to prosper without them."

Iani all but choked with rage. "And Taquar allied himself with a monster such as this?"

"You have to admire his effrontery," Laisa said. "And it's not the worst thing he has done. Tell Iani about the bracelet you found, Jasper."

Jasper did look at her then. Her face was faultless, her eyes rimmed with cosmetics, her lips reddened. She appeared unaware of the enormity of what she was asking him to say. He had wanted to speak to Iani in his own time, if he had to, not like this. Not now, not in front of her. She cocked her head at him and raised a pencilled eyebrow, encouraging him to go on. Jasper found himself hating her.

He cleared his throat. "This may not be something you'd like to hear, Lord Iani." He dug into his belt pouch and drew out the bracelet. "I found this at the Scarcleft mother cistern, which is where Taquar was keeping me prisoner. There were clothes there, too, for a little girl." He handed him the bracelet and looked away, not wanting to see the expression on that ravaged face.

In the end, the prolonged silence of the rainlord forced him to look back. Senya was staring at the bracelet in a mixture of fascination and horror. Iani held it in hands that shook, and rubbed the name with fingers that trembled. His face was stark with pain. Jasper looked away.

"It is hers," the rainlord said at last, his voice so low Jasper had to strain to hear. "You are saying *he* took her? Because he wanted a stormlord?"

"I think so."

"What—what happened to her? What happened to my little Lyneth?"

"I don't know."

"Is she—is she—"

"If he still had her, he would not have needed me."

Another long silence, and then, in a whisper: "All those years, all those years of looking me in the face and pretending sympathy." He looked up from the bracelet, straight at Jasper. "How long did she live?"

"There were clothes there to fit a child of nine or ten."

"She wasn't yet six when she disappeared."

"I know."

Iani dragged in a deep breath and tried to still his shaking hands. "What—what do you think happened to her?"

"I don't know. He would not have hurt her or mistreated her physically, you know. He never mistreated me." He thought of a six-year-old child locked up at the mother cistern and repressed a shudder. Iani did not need to hear the details. "Her death would have been a disaster for his plans. An—an illness perhaps. There were other clothes there, too. For at least one adult woman. I suspect he had someone to look after her. Lyneth would not have been alone the way I was."

Laisa, who had continued to eat her meal, said between mouthfuls, "Of course, this is all speculation. I find it hard to believe that Taquar is capable of villainy such as that."

"Do you, my dear?" Nealrith said. "I don't find it hard at all."

Jasper looked up, startled. Too intent on their conversation, he had neither seen nor felt Nealrith enter.

"I will *kill* the bastard," Iani said. "Sunlord help me, I *swear* I will kill him!"

"Only if you are the first to get the opportunity," Nealrith said, sitting down next to him. "Before he is finished, there is going to be a long line of people wanting to effect his demise. I am sorry, my old friend. More sorry than I can say. We have all been blind."

"Perhaps you should have acted when Jasper first told us about all this," Laisa told her husband.

"And done what? Gone to war with another of our own cities? With a man supported by the Cloudmaster as Quartern heir, whose guards use ziggers when we have none?"

"What did Granthon say about Iani's news?" Laisa asked, pouring herself some more tea from the pot on the table. "Get me some more seeds, will you, Jasper?" He rose to do her bidding, bringing the cruet of resin seeds to the table from the sideboard. She sprinkled some on her drink, apparently oblivious to the emotional turmoil of those around her. Jasper, annoyed with himself, had to drag his eyes away from the sheer attractiveness of her languor. Senya watched him with a catlike stare.

"He says we cannot send guards to Qanatend," Nealrith said in answer.

Iani's head jerked up. "*What?*"

"He says it would leave Breccia City vulnerable to attack. And we don't have the numbers, anyway. He's right about that, Iani. By your own account, there were some seven or eight thousand tribesmen besieging Qanatend. We have barely thirty packpedes and thirty-five myriapedes at our disposal at the best of times, although we could seize those belonging to traders and individuals, I suppose. We have only five hundred permanent guardsmen. Father ordered me to send most of them to guard our mother cistern and the tunnel."

"Every man in Qanatend—and half the women and children—will fight. They were fighting when I left. What Qanatend needs now is rainlords!"

"I know, my friend. I know. But by the time we got there, the fighting would be over. You know that. Qanatend has probably already fallen."

Iani stood, knocking his chair over, and looked down on them all. "Do any of you know what it is like to abandon the groves outside your gates, which have been your city's *life* for fifty generations? Do you know what it is like to hear the ziggers coming over the city walls and know that they will not rest until they have found a victim? Do you know what it is like to feel you cannot sleep, because you are one of too few rainlords to defend your city? Moiqa knows! Then she had to watch while I fled for my life, pursued by Reduner warriors and too many ziggers to count. She can have no idea if I even survived."

Jasper stood and righted Iani's chair. The man sat down again, trembling, and added with a disturbing coldness, "I came across people caught outside the walls. People who had torn their own flesh trying to rip the ziggers out. People who had dropped in the midst of their tasks, dead. I saw a baby slaughtered in his mother's arms, with a zigger hole through his cheek. They like babies, you know. Because of the softness of their skin." He stopped and looked at the bracelet still clenched tight in his hand. "My poor, poor Lyneth. I couldn't find a way back into the city to help. I couldn't find my sweet Lyneth, either."

"And is Granthon at least going to stop all the storms to the Red Quarter now?" Laisa asked, sipping her tea.

Nealrith shook his head. "No. It would unite the rest of the tribes in opposition."

Iani cried out, his misshapen mouth distorting the words. "They are already united!"

"It doesn't matter which of you is right," Laisa said. "What is important is that having no water would kill the tribesmen, a favourable result for us, surely." Beside her, Senya's gaze flicked from speaker to speaker in fascinated interest.

"Not fast enough to save Qanatend. Or us," Nealrith said quietly. "They have supplies for months and would become more determined than ever to steal water from our cities. Thirst also kills the innocent. Granthon thinks to court the moderates and to use water supply as leverage. He wants to support the resistance under the leadership of Vara Redmane—"

For the first time, Laisa lost her calm. "Granthon is not fit to rule. He won't fight to save us, nor will he stop supplying water to our enemies! What shall we do: sit here and wait for them to come riding across the Sweepings to our walls?" She made a gesture of disgust. "Are there no *men* in your line, Nealrith?"

"Granthon has decided it is time to send a team of negotiators to Davim, to tell him we have Shale Flint. We will threaten to stop the storms to the Red Quarter unless they withdraw. When Davim discovers his unholy plot with Taquar is missing the most important element, he will be forced to obey. As long as we have Jasper, we are safe."

"Rubbish," Laisa spat at him. "What if Davim doesn't mind going back to random rain, as Jasper says? What if he comes in search of Jasper? We should at least send a couple of rainlords to assassinate this blighted sandmaster. Without its head, this unity of tribes may fall apart."

Nealrith didn't answer. Instead, he said, "All rainlords are going to be ordered to Breccia City."

Iani scrambled to his feet again. "You are ordering rainlords *here*? Not to Qanatend to help Moiqa?"

"Forgive us, Iani. Those are Granthon's orders. And he is right: his safety, and Jasper's, is of more importance than—"

But Iani didn't let him finish. Enraged, he hooked his hands under the edge of the table and heaved it upwards. Laisa leaped to her feet out of the way as dishes and mugs and food slid to the floor. Senya squealed. The table crashed on its side.

"More important than Qanatend?" Iani shouted at Nealrith. "Maybe you're right. But it's not just about Qanatend or my Moiqa! It's about all the other cities, too. And my Lyneth. It's about justice. And compassion. And children dying. It's about our *honour*!" He stood for a moment, gasping, then added, "I never thought I would live to see this day." And he walked unsteadily to the door and left the room.

Jasper, feeling foolish sitting where he was when his meal was on the floor, stood up. Senya, surveying the mess, put a hand over her mouth to stifle a giggle.

Laisa looked on dispassionately. "I'm surprised," she said. "I would not have thought he could do that with a crippled hand." She glanced to where Nealrith still sat. "You are a dreamer, Rith. Your awakening will be a rude one. To protect the whole tunnel system is impossible, you know that. We may be able to protect the mother cistern for a while with rainlords, but the many miles of tunnel? It is not possible."

"We may not have warriors like the Reduners, but we

do have rainlords who can kill both men and ziggers. And who can sense men and pedes in the desert from afar. Davim will discover that rainlords are not to be trifled with if he comes here."

"If the rainlords are here."

"What do you mean?"

She turned on him in a swirl of flowing sleeves and skirt. "Do you *really* think that the cities of the Scarpen will give up their rainlords so easily in order to protect *us*?"

"Of course they will! Without a stormlord, they can't survive. They must protect us; they must save Granthon and Jasper—or they won't have water in the future."

"Tell people to think about the future when the present is threatening them, Rith, and see what happens."

"People are not so foolish," he muttered, as she walked away.

Jasper, righting a chair, was not so sure. He remembered the irrationality of the attack on Feroze, the Alabaster salt trader. Did it make any sense to condemn him to certain death and to kill his mounts simply because he was an Alabaster? Sooner or later everyone needed salt. He sighed. *People can be so unbelievably stupid.*

Nealrith clapped a hand to his back, adding, "Don't worry, Jasper. There's no way Taquar would countenance an attack on Breccia by Davim. He wants to rule here, rule a *city*, not a heap of smoking ruins. He will stop Davim. Or kill him if necessary. Anyway, I have a number of things to do right now. Orders to give. We are going to give priority to protecting the mother cistern and the tunnel and to keeping a watch. Your classes with Kaneth and Ryka will have to be put on hold. I need the rainlords.

You can still take the religion classes, though, and I will get another swordsman to teach you, as well."

"I'd rather forget the classes with the High Waterpr—" Jasper began, but he was speaking to himself. Nealrith had already gone.

Senya smirked at him as she rose to go. "Don't you like religious studies, Jasper? I suppose that's because you Gibber folk are all heathens."

He watched her leave, not even bothering to reply, his thoughts elsewhere. Everyone was making decisions based on guesses. Who really knew what motivated Davim the drover? Or what he would do next? To even consider that the Reduner might take any notice of an instruction from Taquar was ludicrous. One thing Jasper did know: Davim took orders from no one. Nor was he a man to be scared by threats from the Cloudmaster.

He wondered if killing the sandmaster would solve the problem. Would the tribes go back to arguing with one another if they did not have his leadership? It was worth a try, although maybe Davim was grooming an heir. A son perhaps.

He sat down again in the chair he had put to rights. How could he know more than men like Nealrith and Granthon? It wasn't how things were supposed to be.

But I do, he thought, exasperated. *They are wrong, and I am right, and no one will listen to me.*

CHAPTER FORTY

Scarpen Quarter
Scarcleft City
Scarcleft Hall, Level 2

Terelle paced her room like a desert cat in a cage.

She could hardly believe that this had happened to her, and she had not the faintest idea of how much longer she would be able to stand it. Sixteen paces one way, fourteen the other. A bed, a chair, a rug on the stone-tiled floor. A closet-privy built into the corner. A dayjar, filled for her at dawn every day. And nothing to do. Nothing. It was worse than being a handmaiden in a snuggery and spending the day primping and preening, and she had always thought that was the most boring thing she could imagine.

She had been locked in the one room for not quite half a year—she wasn't sure of the exact number of days, but she knew it was close to one hundred and fifty—and she thought she was going sandcrazy. The fact that it happened to be the loveliest room she had ever slept in was irrelevant; it was still a prison. Her view of the world was what she could glimpse through the openwork carving of the locked shutters that separated her from the outside. If she placed her face to the carved holes, she could see the sky; if she pressed hard enough to indent the patterns onto her skin, she could just see the lower-level courtyard of the building, one floor below, with armed guards on patrol every hour of the day and night.

She knew where she was. Scarcleft Hall, villa of the Highlord of Scarcleft, Taquar Sardonyx. Just thinking his name was enough to conjure up an image of horror, the casual wiping of blood from a sword, the touch of his blade under her chin, the dagger driven so deep under Amethyst's breast.

She had done her best to fill her time, making up dances and performing them as she hummed the music; painting on the walls with paint made from bread and water and oil, coloured with fruit and vegetable juice—all from her food trays; unpicking the cover of her bed and then weaving it again with a different pattern.

The only distractions in otherwise eventless days were the delivery of water and the arrival of meals, but the servants responsible were disinclined to talk and were always accompanied by a guard. All Terelle's attempts to be friendly or to seek information were met with stony silence.

At first, her hope centred on Russet. He had already made paintings of her future, and they didn't include her being imprisoned in Scarcleft Hall, so surely that meant she was going to be freed. If he could just make a waterpainting of her free and somewhere else, then she could count on being released sooner rather than later. Or having an opportunity to escape. Or something. But as the days passed and nothing happened, she began to wonder if Russet was still alive. Perhaps he had returned to his room only to be arrested and killed. Perhaps once a water-painter was dead, the magic of their paintings dissipated. Hadn't he once said something like that? That when he was dead, she would be free to do what she liked?

And free to be killed.

The thought that he might be dead was . . . what? Certainly not devastating in the way Amethyst's death had been. She hated him for the way he had tethered her with his painted magic, for the secretiveness that deliberately obscured her origins. She disliked the sly pleasure he took in other people's troubles. His death would not sadden her, but she grieved that it might sever the only connection she had to a distant family she had never known. Her thoughts of Russet's fate were not the worst that plagued her, though.

The worst moments of each day came when her thoughts returned—again and again—to Shale. Her last glimpse of him had been of his face, pale and grim, surrounded by a swirl of fighting men, a spray of blood dappling his skin and clothes. Apart from that, her most vivid memories of those moments were of the noise: the clash of blades, the heart-wrenching keening of wounded men, the confused shouting and grunting, the cold voice saying "Kill her."

She still did not know how the fight had ended. Taquar had never told her what the outcome was. When Taquar's men had not returned that day to Amethyst's house as quickly as he had expected, he had locked Terelle in the water-room and left the house. She had tried furiously to escape, clawing and battering at the door with the only implement she had—the wooden water scoop—without success. Several hours later, some enforcers had come for her and escorted her to Scarcleft Hall. She had been locked in the room she now occupied and had not seen Taquar again. No one told her if Shale had escaped with Kaneth, or indeed if Nealrith and Kaneth had succeeded in leaving the city. No one told her anything, and every question she asked was ignored.

The idea that Shale might be dead gnawed at her, hour after hour, but she had to accept that it was possible. Anything was possible, and it was the not knowing that was the worst. She and Shale: they had squabbled, he with reasoned coolness and she more with hotheaded passion, but part of her had revelled in the joy of the relationship, in the wonder of her first good friend. Nor had she been blind to the way he looked at her sometimes, with the hint of something more than friendship if only she would give the word. Haunted by memories of the lust of men who came to the snuggery, she had hesitated. And now it was too late.

Part of her had been deeply touched by his last promise, no matter that it had been rendered ineffective just moments later. He had said he would look after her, that she would never want for water.

And now? Now the days dragged by in boredom and in fear of a future she could not foretell.

It was a relief when Taquar finally came to see her.

Yet she had never met anyone who frightened her as much as the rainlord did. The cold flatness of his eyes, the calculation in his gaze. He was handsome, true, and sensual, but in a way that disturbed rather than attracted, and there was no heart there, none.

*Waterless souls, how could Shale have lived with only
this man for company for so long?*

She faced him from the far side of the room, at first
unable, in her terror, to speak. Behind him, two other men
entered carrying a small desk, a chair and some writing
implements. They placed these at Taquar's side and left
the room. "I want you to write a letter for me," he said
without preamble.

She ran her tongue over her dry lips. "Who—who to?"
She put her hands behind her back to hide the way they
shook, and wondered if he carried a knife like the one he
had used on Amethyst.

"To your friend Shale Flint."

Her relief was so intense she nearly dropped where she
stood. Shale was alive. And Taquar did not have him.

When she did not move or speak, he beckoned her to
the chair. "Sit down. You can write, I believe?"

She had started to move forward, but stopped dead
then. "How—how can you know that?" Her fear was so
tangible she was wearing it like an extra skin.

"There is little I don't know about you, child. I have
even spoken to your sister. Viviandra, is it?"

"She's not my sister."

"No? She seems to think she is."

"Her parents took me in. No more than that." *Have you
hurt her?* She did not dare ask the question aloud. For
Vivie's sake, she did not dare show an interest.

"Hmm. No matter." He indicated the chair. "Sit. This
is not a hard letter to write, because every bit will be the
truth. You can put it in your own words. I don't care how
you say it."

She sat and pulled the parchment towards her. "And if

I refuse?" She had to put her hands flat on the desktop to stop their trembling. Her palms left damp marks on the bab wood. *Once I write it, will you kill me?*

"It matters little. I could write it myself, saying the same things. I just thought that if you put pen to parchment, it might have a little more immediacy. I want you to tell Shale that you are my prisoner. Tell him how that came about. Tell him that I have told you that I will kill you slowly and unpleasantly unless he finds some way to escape Breccia City and come to me. Make it sound a little dramatic, if you would. Then tell him that a man called Bankor, an apothecary on the tenth level of Breccia, will help him escape if he needs help. I think that's all." He gave her a faint smile that was bone-chilling in its indifference. "Simple."

"Why haven't you done this before?" she asked. Anything to defer the moment of decision as to whether to acquiesce or not.

He blinked in surprise at her temerity. "That is none of your business!"

She stared back.

He chuckled. "Ah, why not? I wanted Granthon to teach him cloudshifting first. Once he knows how, he is of use to me. And I have heard that Granthon now has help shifting clouds, so I assume Shale is now a stormlord. It is time to get him back."

"He won't take any notice of a letter," she said, amazed that she sounded so matter-of-fact. The thumping of her heart was painful; the sound of it drummed in her body. Surely he could hear it. "Why should he? I scarcely know him."

"We shall see."

"Well," she said, "I hope you don't really mean it. It is not particularly nice to be told that you are going to be tortured to death. Shale won't care, but I do." Bravado. Stupid. It wouldn't get her anywhere.

He laughed again. "Not nice? I am not a particularly *nice* man, Terelle."

"Where's Russet?" she asked. "Did you kill him?"

He shrugged. "I have no interest in him as long as he lies quiet. My seneschal will kill him if he turns up, though—just to tidy things up."

He reached out and touched her cheek with his fingertips. She drew her head back sharply, but the idea of standing up again, of moving out of his reach, died when she saw the look in his eyes. Huckman. It was Huckman all over again. The horror of having her first-night sold. The revulsion and the terror back again.

He brushed her hair away from her face, sliding his hand down her cheek, outlining her lips with his thumb. This time she did not move, other than letting her eyes fall to the sheet of paper on the desk. When his fingers dropped away—an eternity later—she opened the ink well, dipped in the pen and began to write. As she worked, he stood at her shoulder and played with a lock of her hair. His touch slid up and down, feather light, stroking the strands over his forefinger, turning her hair this way and that so that the rich brown of it was burnished by morning sunlight patching through the latticework. To sit still and not flinch away took all her will; but she had nothing left for resistance. Nothing.

I'm not brave, she thought. *I don't even know how to begin to be brave.*

And so she wrote the letter exactly as he had asked

for it to be written. When she had finished, she handed it to him wordlessly, with a shaking hand. And part of her expected to dic violated, there in that room. Against her will, her glance flickered to the bed. Then back to the sword he wore.

He read the letter through and smiled once more. "Your spelling is original," he remarked, "but it is a good letter. I like the wobbly writing; it will be good for him to see your fear. We will see if it has the desired result."

She shook her head. "I just told you it won't." She remained seated, staring at the desktop. "Shale is not a fool, and he doesn't care about me."

"Stand up, Terelle," he said.

She did as he asked, without looking at him. She knew she was trembling but was unable to control it.

"Look at me," he commanded.

Reluctantly, she raised her head, to find that if she stared straight ahead, she was gazing at his mouth. *When did I get so tall?* she asked herself in inane surprise. *I don't remember growing up.*

He put his hands on either side of her face and raised her chin so her gaze met his. "I am not a cruel man, Terelle, only a ruthless one. I get no particular pleasure from hurting others and will not do so unless it brings me profit. I would rather keep you here until you have grown up a little more, to an age when I would find pleasure in your company. When you are old enough to understand your own sensuality." He bent and kissed her full on the mouth.

She did not know what to do. She wanted to step away from him, wanted to express her revulsion, but was held in place by terror, by an upbringing that had taught her not to cheek her elders, to be respectful to those in positions of power and to pander to men who came to enjoy favours. One certainly didn't slap their faces. But when his tongue pressed against her teeth, seeking entry to her mouth, she clenched them hard. He stopped the kiss immediately and stepped back.

"I—I don't know what—what you mean," she faltered. It was a lie; of course she knew what he meant. She had spent seven years of her childhood listening to handmaidens talk of their nights; she had lived another four next to a woman who daily rented out her children as whore and catamite. She knew *exactly* what he meant.

"No? Hmm. You will understand soon, I promise you," he said, releasing her. He folded the letter and tucked it away in his pouch. "I suspect Shale is far too decent to abandon you, my dear. I should not worry too much if I were you."

"And what am I to do in the meantime?" she asked, sharpening her fear to asperity with an effort. "Sit here with nothing to do all day while I grow up?" Silently she blessed the obvious: Vivie had not told him her real age.

"I certainly do not trust you enough to let you loose."

"Could you at least let me have my waterpaints? Then I could do some paintings for you, for the palace. It would give me something to do. I am very good, you know." *Watergiver's heart, I sound like a wheedling brat.*

He laughed outright. "I was correct—you are an extraordinary girl. And I wonder if you are as young as you say you are. I do not think I have been spoken to like this in years, not since Amethyst in her younger days. Very well. I believe everything that was in Russet's room was brought here. I'll see if the paints can be located, and I'll have them brought to you. You can paint to your heart's content, if it keeps you happy."

For a breathless moment the name Amethyst hung in the air between them, then she said woodenly, "Thank you, my lord."

He laughed again. "I'll visit every now and then," he promised and left her, without taking away the chair and table.

She collapsed onto her bed and gave way to gasping sobs. Her emotions had been rent and then flung in all directions. There was joy that Shale was safe in Breccia City, fear that he would indeed be idiot enough to take notice of her letter, terror that Taquar would torture her to death or simply kill her "to tidy things up," tremulous delight that she would have her paints once more and therefore—perhaps—a way of escape.

And through all that tumult of reaction, she could still feel the slide of his fingers up and down her hair. The taste of him, of his lips, his tongue. The smell of him, of his lust, lingered in her nostrils.

Taquar was as good as his word.

That afternoon, Terelle's waterpaints, together with eight picture trays and some of her personal belongings, were delivered to her prison. When she unpacked, she fingered the mirror Vivie had given her and choked with unexpected emotion. She had not thought about it since she had run out of Russet's rooms, yet now that she had it back, she felt a wash of tenderness for her sister and for a childhood that no longer existed.

At the bottom of the bag, there was a scroll of paintings.

Russet's portraits of her future, all of them. Taquar's men had brought her the very paintings that trapped her within Russet's plans for her life. She had her waterpaints and the possibility of freedom. She had Russet's painted future for her. Surely there must be something she could do to escape both of the men who sought to command her life.

It was only later, when she began to think about how to do it, that she realised liberty was not going to be as easy as she had first thought.

You can't put yourself into the future, Russet had said. He was right, she found. She did try. She tried to shuffle up a picture of herself standing on the thirty-sixth level—and nothing happened. Nothing at all. Her sharpened image did not appear; the paint did not move. It remained static; it looked lifeless; it felt dead. She could not influence her own future, at least not by projecting herself there.

What else could she do?

Kill Taquar.

The thought was suddenly there in her head. *Paint him dead.*

Picture him lying on the ground with a gaping wound in his chest, lots of blood. Leave his clothes indistinct, but make his face detailed. And then shuffle the future up to make it real.

Russet had never confirmed that it was possible to kill with waterpainting, but he had not denied it, either, when she had asked. And it would be so easy to try. Would they let her go if Taquar was dead? Possibly. She could save Shale from Taquar's clutches, for certain.

But to murder a man, any man?

She shivered, the icy finality of that thought going right

through to her heart. It would be so . . . cold-blooded. So deliberate.

I will think about it. She'd have to be very certain before she did something like that.

She contemplated Russet's paintings. Maybe she could change her destiny if she altered them, changed the background, for example, or removed all trace of Russet by scraping off the paint or painting over the top? She tried that on one of them but could not shuffle up anything. The shuffling had been done, and the future was fixed, no matter what she did to the paint.

She thought of altering her appearance, her real appearance. Scarring her face, perhaps. Cutting her hair very short so that she never looked like the woman in the paintings. But when she thought of doing that, the magic asserted itself and her stomach roiled and her hands shook. She would never be able to do it.

She thought of just destroying them. Tearing them up. Setting fire to them. But what if that killed her, as Russet had said? She remembered Shale had put his foot into the painting of Vato up on the rooftop, ruining it, and Vato had not been hurt. But then, the damage to the painting hadn't stopped him from climbing up onto the roof, either.

Besides, she thought, *maybe these paintings are all that is keeping me alive right now. If Russet hadn't painted my older self, maybe the enforcer would have caught up with me and killed me. Or maybe Taquar would have killed me after I wrote that letter.* Instead, he was keeping her, apparently for the day when he would regain control of Shale and be able to use her as a hostage, to assure Shale's good behaviour.

She sighed, rolled them up and put them away.

She started on an ordinary waterpainting instead, something she thought Taquar might appreciate: a portrait of himself riding a myriapede, as she had first seen him from the roof of the snuggery, a lifetime ago. She thought she captured the essence of the man well: his pride, his sensual menace, his handsome arrogance, his assurance. The magnificence of his mount. The image was engraved on her mind, down to the last details, so that part was not hard. More difficult was the challenge of eliminating the fear she felt creating his painted image.

While she worked on the portrait, she pondered what other pictures she could paint to benefit her future.

Useless just to paint the door to her prison swung open and an empty room beyond. That might mean anything: that she was moved to another part of Scarcleft Hall, for example. She thought about depicting Russet's room and then shuffling up into that picture something that was now with her—her clothes, perhaps. After all, if her clothes were on the thirty-sixth level, she would be, too, wouldn't she? Then she thought of other scenarios that might account for her clothes being down in the thirty-sixth—and her imagination supplied a few unpleasant possibilities.

When she finished the portrait, she left it on the floor next to her dayjar. If Taquar came back before she was ready for him, at least she had something inoffensive to show him.

On the following day, she prepared a tray with a base of motley. She painted Taquar again, this time lying on roughly depicted ground. Dead eyes stared blankly out of a dead face. A wound in his chest looked as if it might have been caused by a spear that had pierced him and then been roughly wrenched free. Just to make it clear he was dead, she painted a copious amount of spilled blood and portrayed his head lying at an odd angle.

She stared at it a long time. All she had to do was shuffle it up, and sometime in the future, Taquar would die. But how long would it take? She had no way of knowing.

And it was so sandblasted horrible to decide to do it. Cold-blooded murder . . .

But if I don't, Shale might be imprisoned once more. I must do this. I must. For him.

She gripped both sides of the tray. She stared at the paint and connected to the motley, felt the magic, the power within her. Started to ease the water-motley upwards. Thought of the change she wanted to wreak. The death she wanted to make real. The *murder*.

And faltered. She lost her hold, lost her concentration, lost her determination.

She slumped, unnerved. The painting had not moved. It was still ordinary, Taquar's clothes and the ground still not detailed or real. She was shaking, her forehead beaded with sweat.

Sunlord help me, she thought. *I can't do it.*

With the picture still unaltered, she hid the tray under her bed. If she was in danger from Taquar, she might want to try shuffling again, might be *able* to shuffle, so she kept it as surety. She turned her thoughts to other methods of escape, and finally, several days later, she had an idea.

She painted a picture of a place she knew well: the open hallway outside Russet's room. Depicting the section of wall between his door and Lilva's, she captured the detail as she remembered it: the cracks, the crumbling mud-brick, the edge of the bab-wood doors, all seen in the reddish light of dawn. It took her a while to correctly paint the long morning shadow cast by the balustrade, but the perfection of her waterpainter's memory guided her paint spoon. When she was satisfied that she had everything exactly as it should be, she put the paint tray aside and waited till nightfall.

Her jailers had supplied her with candles and the means to light them. That night, she spent considerable time moving the desk and candle around, trying to get the best placement for what she wanted: her shadow profiled on the wall. Once she had it just right, she angled Vivie's mirror so that she could see the shadowed profile. She was struck by a sense of unfamiliarity: it was the silhouette of a mature woman, not of a child. The nose was strong and long, the chin determined, the forehead straight and high. Her bust line was a woman's; her waist was defined by the swell of a woman's mature hips.

She stared, absorbing the details, the proportions, of this person she was beginning to understand. She knew now what Taquar had seen and what he had anticipated. He had seen a mature body; what she had lacked for him was her own knowledge of it. He had held back because he had still seen a child in her gaze, in her directness, and he had not wanted a child in his bed, but a woman. She shuddered in the realisation of the closeness of her escape. She could so easily have become another Amethyst. And somewhere deep inside, she knew that the next time he looked he would see what he wanted. He had awakened the very thing he was seeking, awakened it not by his sensuality but by the fear it engendered.

She took a deep breath and focused once more on the task at hand. *Do the rough sketch of the profiled shadow, a suggestion, a whisper of what is to come. Concentrate on the painting. Feel the motley below. Look once more in the mirror at my shadow on the wall. Attach the paint grains to the water, move the water, shuffle up the image . . .*

She felt the water shiver in response to the image in her mind; she felt the shift—the rip—in time. She closed her eyes. The nausea, the knowledge that there had been a profound change in fundamental truth. She felt it all.

She opened her eyes.

There, on the painting in front of her, was the shadow she had depicted. From the lower body, which threw its dark image across the floor of the hallway, it was impossible to tell who was casting that shadow. But where the shadow hit the wall between the two doors, the profile of a head and torso was undeniably her own. She had not shuffled up herself, but her shadow. She had tricked the magic.

She allowed herself the beginnings of a smile.

And that was the moment when she was shaken, as if a giant had twisted the floor beneath her and then kicked the chair she was sitting on. She crashed over onto her back. Stunned, she lay there, unable to react. Slowly the desk toppled towards her, not pulled by her, but of its own volition, spilling paints and water from her paint tray, splashing her with water and colour.

She was so shocked, she didn't even scream.

CHAPTER FORTY-ONE

Scarpen Quarter
Breccia City
Level 3

When Jasper emerged from the Sun Temple on the third level after the annual Gratitudes ceremony, a person brushed close by him and pressed something into his hand. Startled, he looked to see who it was, but in the mass of people, he could not single out the giver. He was surrounded by a swarm of worshippers from all levels, hemmed in by officials and reeves and guards, pestered by a number of street boys darting in and out to see how close they could get to the rainlords. It could have been any one of them; he had no way of knowing. He looked down at the item he clutched. A letter of some kind. There was no chance to look at it just then, so he shoved it deep into the wrap-over of his ceremonial robe.

As he glanced around, he felt uncomfortable. Everyone was staring at him, whispering among themselves. He knew why, of course. Granthon had just declared Jasper Bloodstone a stormlord of the Quartern, by grace of the Sunlord and virtue of his proven power to move and break clouds.

Praise to the Life Giver of the Quartern, thanks be His name, and all praise to His intermediary, the Holy Watergiver.

The robe they had then pulled over his head, with its gold embroidered hem and neckline, was heavy and hot, and it scratched. And it was all a lie. He wasn't a stormlord. Not really. Unaided, he would have been incapable of creating a single cloud from sea water, let alone one sufficiently laden to carry rain. Oh, he could feel Granthon's power. The way it reached out to suck up the water in the sea like dry desert soil thirsting after a man's piss. It tingled, that power, coursing through his blood, stinging the inside of his nose and mouth and throat. But he couldn't emulate it.

All he could do was move clouds. At that he was an expert, sending them across the sky with an ease that baffled Nealrith. He didn't need to see them; feeling their water was enough. Guided by maps and his feel for fixed areas of water—the distant cities, the mother cisterns, the mother wells, the tunnels—he could shift clouds to the designated destinations with an accuracy that impressed even the old stormlord.

But it was Granthon—weak, half-crazy Granthon—who created the storms, even as he died, inch by inch. Without Jasper, Granthon was a stormlord with insufficient strength to move a cloud. Without Granthon to free the water from the sea to make a storm cloud, Jasper was no stormlord.

The ceremony in the temple had been a lie to give people hope.

Far better than the public acknowledgement of Jasper's skill was Granthon's equally public withdrawal of his endorsement of Taquar as his heir. Jasper knew whom he had to thank for that: Lady Ethelva. Afraid for the safety of her son, she had finally managed to convince her husband that any man who had done what Taquar had done to Jasper and Lyneth was unfit to rule a city, let alone a nation. Jasper had not been present at the conclusive argument on the issue—no one had except Granthon—but the servants had been full of it for days. Normally gentle Ethelva, who protected her husband from every stress, had made her opinion heard in a voice that had resonated from behind two sets of closed doors. And Granthon had caved in like a pebblemouse hole under pede feet. He had changed his recommended succession and confirmed it publicly. What he had not done was propose someone else. The Quartern was once again without a recognised heir.

"Come," Kaneth was saying in his ear, "let's get out of this crush." He took Jasper by the elbow and shepherded him back in the direction of the palace, signalling for the guards to close in around them. "What did you think of your first Temple Gratitudes?"

Jasper gave a snort. "We wouldn't waste water like that in Wash Drybone. Just pouring it into the ground as a sacrifice to the Sunlord?" He shook his head. "I don't think the priests have any idea of what it's like to go thirsty."

"Probably not, at least not on this level. Some priests on lower levels often share their water, or so I'm told."

"When did you get back?" Jasper asked. Kaneth had been away, riding the Sweepings with his men, searching for any evidence of further infiltration of the Scarpen by Reduners.

"Last night. A tame spying trip, not as exciting as chasing marauders off the White and Gibber Quarters."

They caught up with Nealrith and Ryka. Ahead of them, Ethelva, Laisa and Senya accompanied Granthon's litter. "What's the news from Qanatend?" Kaneth asked, laying a hand on the highlord's shoulder as they all walked up the stepped street towards the closest entry to the hall. "I heard there were messengers in this morning."

Nealrith nodded unhappily. "No news. The spies couldn't get through. The Reduners continue to hold the northern side of Pebblebag Pass through the Warthago Range. All we know for certain is that the city fell about ten days after the siege started. We guess it is still occupied and the Reduners are still helping themselves to the water."

"Any word of Moiqa and Iani and the other rainlords?"

"Nothing. I've no way of knowing whether Iani even made it as far as Qanatend."

Kaneth's lips tightened. "We can ill afford to lose another rainlord. He should never have gone back."

"And just how could we stop him from going to the rescue of his wife and her city?" Ryka snapped. "Bad enough that we did nothing to help them."

Jasper did not want to hear any more. To him, it was unconscionable that Qanatend had received no aid, and the thought of a city fighting Davim while others watched and waited was acid in his gut. "What happens now?" he asked. They had reached the main gate of Breccia Hall, and the guards snapped to attention, disconcerting him. It felt strange to be the object of such formal respect. "How long will they stay in Qanatend?"

"The Reduners have a distaste for roofs over their heads," Nealrith replied, nodding an acknowledgement to the guards, "so I doubt it will be permanent. More likely their intention is to stay awhile, rest their mounts, replenish their supplies, eat well, drink well, sleep with new women and then return to the Red Quarter."

Kaneth snorted, disbelieving. "Slim chance. More likely they'll move on to the next city. If they are generous, they will just kill the guards and the water sensitives and leave each city intact. If they aren't so generous, then they will destroy the groves and the cisterns as well."

"Without groves and cisterns, everyone would die," Ryka said in protest.

"You have met Davim, Jasper. Do you think that would bother him?" Kaneth asked.

Jasper shook his head.

"He knows we have Shale now," Nealrith said. "He knows Jasper is Shale, because we've told him. There's no point in him trying to threaten Taq—"

"He refused to negotiate with the mediators you sent," Kaneth pointed out. "Face it, Nealrith. He wants his Time of Random Rain."

"What can we do other than train more guards, as we are doing?" Nealrith asked. "If only we had more stormlords, we could still salvage the situation . . ." The words trailed away, as futile as the desire to have them come true.

Jasper's insides lurched. Always, always, it came down to a stormlord's power. The power that he had to have, and have soon. Everything depended on him. Everything.

Ryka said softly, "Iani will never forgive us for not going to Qanatend. He loved that city."

"Iani is doubtless dead," Kaneth said. "Moiqa, too."

"There has been yet another deputation of Alabasters bringing more news of what has been happening in the White Quarter," Nealrith said. "More requests for help against Reduner raids." He looked away, and there was real pain in the words that followed. "We can't even help ourselves, and they want aid from us!"

"Davim must be stretching his resources," Kaneth remarked. "Which seems foolish."

Jasper thought about that, remembering the red man, remembering the heat of his gaze. Impatient to the point of recklessness sometimes, perhaps—but a fool? They might not comprehend his ambition for a Time of Random Rain; his desire for a different future might be ridiculous in their eyes—but that did not mean he was stupid.

"Are we going to do nothing except guard our side of the Pebblebag Pass?" Kaneth asked. "What if they find a way to bypass our guards? Or launch a full-scale attack with ziggers? We have only a handful of rainlords up there. And there must be other ways through." He looked at Jasper. "Tell me, by any chance, could you sense the water of an army on pedes descending on us?"

He hesitated. "If I was looking for it, yes. Most of the time, though, I close down my senses, otherwise I get overwhelmed by all the water in the city—people, tunnels, cisterns, plants, dayjars, the groves . . ."

Nealrith nodded glumly. "I do the same thing."

"If they scatter their forces rather than bunch together," Jasper added, "that would make it difficult to sense them. Do they know enough about rainlord or stormlord powers to know that?"

"Probably," Nealrith said.

"So," Kaneth drawled, "the question remains: is Davim going to try to seize both Breccia City and Jasper—and if he tries, how do we stop him?"

Nealrith returned the salute of more guards as they passed into the forecourt of the Hall. "I don't know how to fight such idiocy. We may all perish in such a conflict. If they destroy the tunnels and cisterns and slots, they could bring down our whole civilisation! The Reduners would be the only ones to survive. Damn Taquar to a waterless death for ever starting this."

Jasper shivered.

"Do you think Taquar truly did kill the talented among us, Nealrith, as Jasper believes?" Ryka asked. "Eliminating the competition?"

"Oh, he did it all right," Nealrith said. "All the really talented ones. Kaneth and me, he didn't bother about."

"Me, neither," added Ryka with a hollow laugh.

Kaneth nodded. "At that time, he thought he would be a stormlord, and he wanted to make sure he was the only one. He destroyed our future by murder."

Ryka shook her head, not in negation but in grief. "And later, when he realised he didn't have the skills of a stormlord but Lyneth probably would . . . That poor little girl."

Kaneth glanced at Jasper. "Rith, the sooner you marry this youth off to your Senya, the better. They have to produce children of talent, and quickly. We need more stormlords, and they are our best chance."

Marry Senya? Jasper's jaw dropped. His stomach twisted and knotted; his heart pounded at his throat. Marry *Senya*? That spoiled, manipulative bitch? Every time he met her, he was exposed to her contempt, her childish sulks and her brainless remarks. He gaped at them, speechless.

"That reminds me, Jasper," Kaneth added, not noticing his consternation, "someone gave you something down in front of the temple. What was it?" Jasper put his hand into his robe and pulled out the parchment. He turned it over to see the inscription on the outside fold. "It's a letter."

"Who gave it to you?" Nealrith asked sharply.

"I don't know. I didn't see." He broke the seal and unfolded the sheet. Slowly he read the words written there—and felt the blood drain from his face, leaving him light-headed. "It's from Terelle. Taquar has her. He says I've got to get back to him, otherwise—otherwise—"

Kaneth twitched the letter from his hand, glanced at it and handed it on to Nealrith. "This time he's making sure Jasper knows."

"That's mine," Jasper said in agonised protest. "It is addressed to me." He stopped. Then, "*This* time?" His gaze shifted from one to the other as his mind raced in disbelief. They had known she was alive and hadn't told him?

"I'm sorry," Nealrith said when he had finished scanning the sheet. "Kaneth, see that the apothecary Bankor that's mentioned here is dealt with."

Kaneth nodded and walked away. Ryka watched him go, biting her lip, then walked briskly after him.

When Nealrith went to continue up the steps into the hall, Jasper—outraged—stayed where he was. "This time? You *knew*?" he accused. "You already *knew* that he had Terelle?"

Nealrith paused and turned back. "Not at first. But a while back Taquar tried to send you a message, and it was intercepted. He said he had her, but we had no way of knowing whether it was true, so we didn't tell you. There is no question of your leaving Breccia, Jasper," he added gently. "The idea of you going back to Taquar is unthinkable. You know that."

"She is my—my friend." *The only one I've ever had.*

"I know. And I'm sorry. I'm sorrier still for her."

Jasper took a shuddering breath. *Sandblast them all. She is nothing to them!*

Aloud he said, "You don't understand. I made her a promise. I said I would look after her." He shoved his hands behind his back so Nealrith did not see his fists clenching in anger. "I had a little sister once. I promised myself that no one would ever harm her. And they slaughtered her in front of my eyes, throwing her around from spear to spear until she wasn't recognisable as anything but a piece of meat. And I had a brother taken as a slave. I made myself another promise about him, too. I promised I'd free him. I'm very good at making promises, Lord Nealrith. I'm just not good at keeping them. Do you understand what that's like?"

Terelle, ah, Terelle—be brave. I haven't forgotten you, I swear.

"Look." Nealrith took him by the shoulders and roughly turned him to face the entrance hallway, where Granthon's litter had just arrived and the Cloudmaster was laboriously climbing out. "He should not have gone to the temple today. But he needs to be seen. People need to know he is still alive, still able to read the prayer of sacrifice as he did today. His presence gives them hope and comfort, so he went. And now he will go back to his room and call up another cloud for you to move. That's what sacrifice is, Jasper. That is what is required of us all."

"It's not *my* sacrifice I'm worrying about. It's all the people who trust me to fulfil my promises to them, only to have me discard them as if they are no more than zigger fodder. Do you know what that's *like*?"

"Of course I do! Iani has been closer to me than my own father—and look what we did to him. And to Moiqa. Their whole city!" Nealrith's voice cracked. "I pray every day that the Sunlord will forgive me, Jasper, because I can't forgive myself. I have so much blood on my hands I don't know how I can ever wash them clean."

They stood there in the entranceway, staring deep into each other's souls. Nealrith put a hand on Jasper's shoulder, and Jasper felt the message there. A seeking of understanding, a request for respect, a sharing of pain so deep that it was inexpressible any other way. Jasper knew Nealrith wanted a sign from him, a sign that he understood what they shared.

He withheld the indication.

Nealrith took a deep breath. "If I were to send anyone except a rainlord to free Terelle, they would simply die in the attempt. Taquar's guards use ziggers, remember. And I can't afford to send a rainlord. Not now. Not when our own safety is in jeopardy. If I had sufficient rainlords, I would send them to the defence of Qanatend and other cities, not to rescue a single young woman in Scarcleft."

"Then I will ask this of Granthon."

"I forbid you to worry him with this."

"Today in the temple, Granthon proclaimed me a stormlord, Nealrith. You cannot forbid me a voice. Besides, it is still your father who rules the Quartern, not you."

Nealrith drew in a sharp breath, but it wasn't anger Jasper saw on his face; it was grief, that and despair. "Speak to him, then. It will make no difference to the outcome. Your friend Terelle must look after herself. For you to put her safety before your own would be a terrible misjudgement of what is important. The life of no individual can be more important than your safety, Jasper. *None.* You are the only hope for the Quartern. Don't you understand that?"

Jasper came close to slamming a clenched fist into Nealrith's jaw. He halted the movement in time, and let his anger explode in words instead.

"Even if she was just ordinary, she's in trouble because she helped me. That makes me responsible. On top of that, I have been trying to tell you that Terelle is important. Perhaps even more important than I am. You just aren't listening."

"There is no such thing as magic, Jasper. I don't know what you saw, but it was just trickery."

"You think I am lying?"

"No, just misguided."

"Oh—a fool, then."

"You are being ridiculous."

Jasper choked back his words. He could not trust himself to speak.

"Do I have your word that you will not try to leave Breccia City in some misguided attempt to rescue her?"

Jasper hesitated, gritting his teeth in angry frustration. Citrine, Mica, now Terelle. Was he bound to betray everyone he had ever cared for? "Yes," he snapped, his bitterness spilling out in words. "You have my word. Without me, Granthon would not manage another rain cloud. Without me, there would be no rains anywhere. I know my value. It's a pity you can't recognise hers."

"I'm sorry," Nealrith said again.

Jasper snorted and walked into the hall. Grief spilled from his every pore, and every step felt as if it left its imprint of pain behind. The beat inside his head repeated the same words over and over: *betrayer of friendship, betrayer, betrayer . . .*

CHAPTER FORTY-TWO

Scarpen Quarter
Scarcleft City

Had she screamed? She couldn't remember. If she had,
then the sound would have been lost in the noise that saturated the air anyway. A deep groaning from a tormented
earth. Screams of naked terror from outside. Crashing,
creaking, cracking. Unidentifiable explosive sounds.
Things falling, bursting, breaking. Then the candle tumbling, going out, so that when the outer wall crumbled,
she saw it only as a darkness that disappeared into choking dust.

When it was all over, she continued to lie where she
had fallen, unable, in her shock, to move. Everything was
suddenly awfully, unnaturally quiet. Dust settled around
her, coating her skin with grit, sifting into her hair and
silting through her clothes. She moved then, to cough, to
retch, to grope around for a cloth so that she could cover
her nose and mouth. She found her bedcover, already
ripped by a falling shutter, and tore a piece from that.

When she had control of her breathing, she was able

to think. Yet her thoughts made no sense. What had happened?

In the distance, someone shouted into the silence. There was another far-off crash. She lay and thought about it, forced her wits to work. The building. Something had happened to Scarcleft Hall. Part of it had fallen down, that was it. There was a hole in the wall. She had no idea why, and didn't want to know, but one idea was as clear as water in a cistern: she had to get out while she had the chance.

She scrambled up, coughing in the swirls of powdered mud-brick. In the darkness she couldn't see much, and the air was as thick as a spindevil wind full of desert dust. She groped her way over to the dayjar, toppled but still stoppered, in the corner. The idea of leaving her prison without a supply of water was tough to accept, but there was no alternative. The jar was too heavy and cumbersome to lug far, and she didn't have a water skin. She found her mug and poured herself a drink, and then another and another, until she could drink no more. Extravagantly, she used the last to wash away the grime and wet the cloth that covered her face. Once that was done and she could breathe more easily, she felt around for what was left of her paint jars and brushes. There was no way she would leave those behind. She made a bundle of the rest of the bedcover and tucked the painting things, Russet's paintings of her, Viviandra's mirror and a spare suit of clothes into it. Everything was covered in dust.

Only then did she feel her way along to where she had seen the outer wall crumble. Fine dust particles still hung in the air, making her cough. She could feel it in her nasal passages, in her throat, abrasive, choking. If she looked upwards, she could catch glimpses of stars where once there had been a windowless wall. The outer side of her room no longer existed.

She stared into the darkness at her feet and could just make out a slope of rubble extending downwards. It was steep and unstable, and she couldn't be sure how far it went or where it went or how safe it was, but she held on to the image she had in her mind of her shadow on a wall on the thirty-sixth. She would escape unhurt. She must. Gingerly she slid a foot outwards onto the tumble of mud-brick blocks.

She could not see more than a few paces, and if there were holes she could fall into, if the debris was precarious, if one small misstep meant a fall to instant death—well, she had no idea.

Don't think about it, you sun-shrivelled idiot. One step at a time. Don't think.

Most of the time she crept backwards on all fours, hampered by her pack, feeling with hands and feet for secure places that would take her weight. Once she started a landslip and almost went with it, whimpering in terror; only a piece of firmly wedged stone pillar kept her from a worse fall. All the while, she imagined that there would be a hue and cry, that guards would loom up out of the darkness to catch hold of her. But there was no one. She could hear shouts and screams and cries for help in the distance, but close by, there was only the silence of an eerie solitude. Sandblast it, what had happened?

When she finally scrambled upright on flat ground, she could see a little better. The dust had mostly settled, and there were torch flames and lamps casting light from doorways at the bottom of a set of steps going down to the next level. She continued on, to find herself not far from the sun tower of the Sun Temple on Level Three. It must have lost a few bricks from the top because the edge silhouetted against the sky was jagged.

There were people about, but no one paid attention to her. A woman staggered past with blood in runnels down her face; a man stood, dazed, covered in dust; two or three people grouped around someone lying on the ground. Further along, a family sat huddled together, rocking to and fro like one entity, crying in one voice.

Terelle started to jog, her bundle bumping on her back, intent only on distancing herself from Scarcleft Hall. Speed was not possible; the street was littered with the debris from fallen walls and buildings. A few homes were on fire, the flame-lit scenes a cameo of tragedy and destruction—but Scarcleft's mud-brick structures were strongly built, and with walls as thick as a man's arm was long, most had suffered no more than overturned furniture and broken dayjars. In less-fortunate dwellings there had been deaths. She saw the body of a boy crumpled in his mother's arms. The woman sat in her gateway, rocking back and forth, and her cries skirled through the smoky night air.

Terelle averted her eyes and hurried on.

On the twentieth, water was flowing out of a break in the level's cistern. Reeves and their enforcers were organising people with water jars and other containers to salvage what they could. Terelle ran through a puddle, wetting her bare feet, and shuddered at the waste.

The thirty-sixth level was ablaze long before she arrived. Many people had fled the city altogether, and she glimpsed them standing about in the groves beyond the open gate, waiting for the flames to die down. Within the walls, a few hardier inhabitants tried to salvage what they could—whether their own belongings or other people's was not clear—and a few had simply decided to stay put in order to guard the little they had. The number who fought the fire was smaller still. There was not much point. The larger mud-brick buildings would probably not burn, no matter what happened, while the lean-tos and shanties made of woven palm leaves could never be saved.

Terelle hesitated a moment. The sensible thing to do was follow the exodus and leave the city. To wait out the end of the fire. Yet something turned her feet the other way, towards Russet's room. She had no idea of what she would find and no idea why she felt the need to be there right then. Her feet were leaden, yet they moved of their own accord, past the pot-seller's stand where pots lay in shards, past the corner where the whores usually advertised their wares with deft glimpses of leg or breast, past the rag-pickers' lean-to, which was now no more than ash, to the building where she and Russet had lived. A group of looters ran by, wearing pilfered clothing over their own garments and carrying a cooking pot; by the smell, they had lifted it straight from the stove.

Ba-ba the humpback and his wife, Fipiah, Lilva and her family, Cilla the mat weaver, Qatoo the madman and his son—all were grouped together at the foot of the stairs that led up to the top rooms. Ba-ba looked furious, his wife resigned. Qatoo was naked, as usual, but for once his son was not nagging him to wear his clothing. Instead the lad sat, shaking and wide-eyed with fear, with his arms wrapped around his thin body. Their lean-to—ignited by a flying spark—was burning; a few meagre belongings were piled at the foot of the stairs. The son sat between their most precious possessions: their two dayjars. The rest of the group, still shocked by what had happened, watched the lines of flame consume the sinucca leaves Ba-ba had hung out across the street to dry. The main building remained untouched.

It was Cilla the mat weaver who saw and recognised Terelle first. She gave a toothless grin and said, "My, look who's back. You wanna watch it, girl, you and that old man. You are bad smells to the enforcers, and they'll come sniffin' around at your stink again before long."

"Is he here?" Terelle demanded. "Russet?"

"Oh, ay, he is that," Lilva said with a shudder. "Poor Vato died, flattened when part of a building fell on him over there"—she waved her hand at some rubble down the street—"but that bastard of a waterpainter came sneaking back tonight, as untouched as can be, first time we seen him since you left. Came in just after the shaking stopped."

"Vato died?"

"Squashed as flat as a bab fruit sat on by a pede. Saw it happen."

For a moment Terelle could not move. Vato.

No, it's just a coincidence. I mean, it's been almost half a year since I painted him and Shale trod on his likeness.

She went up the stairs, her cloth clamped to her nose to filter out the flying ash. Her feet were driven by an urgency she couldn't comprehend, and her mind was mired in incoherence.

Only once she was outside Russet's room did she come to a halt. Only then did her understanding flood back and her thoughts become her own.

Her shadow was cast on the wall. She had thought to paint herself in the light of dawn, but it wasn't the sun that cast the shadow, it was fire. She had painted a picture illuminated by flame. In reality, her shadow danced on the wall, writhing in tune with the burning of a palm-woven building behind her.

Sweet waters, she thought, and panic saturated her mind. *I did this? I caused the buildings to fall, the fires to start? This is what I drew! Oh Sunlord, forgive me, how many people did I kill tonight?*

Her panicked horror brought her to her knees. *No. No.*

The door in front of her opened, and Russet was standing there, framed by the dim light in the room behind. "Well, don't just be grovelling there like a sanctimonious waterpriest," he said irritably. "Come in. Safe enough here. For now, anyway."

She rose and moved forward automatically, her mind still crying out against the truth she did not want to accept. A lamp burned inside, and he waved her over to the table. He was not wearing his colourful wrap, but threadbare worker's clothes. To be inconspicuous, she guessed. She dumped her bundle on the floor and sat down on one of the two chairs; the backs of both were broken. There was a deep gouge in the table, too, a scimitar slash gone awry. There were waterpaintings there as well, rolled up and tied with twine.

"I came back," he said. "I be thinking ye'd come."

"You knew I'd escape tonight?" she asked, bewildered.

"Painted ye escaping. I painted ye here, too."

"It was so long," she said, and the words sounded distant, unemotional, as if someone else had uttered them.

"I thought you must be dead because you didn't paint me out of there."

"Oh, but I did," he said. He undid the twine and unrolled a painting. "See?"

She spread it out on the table, and the colours sprang into life under the lamplight. A barbed mixture of relief and renewed horror shredded any remaining equilibrium as she stared. "*You* did this? You did this deliberately?"

He had painted a street by night, and a good part of the building portrayed had crumbled into the roadway. She was in the painting, only her face clearly lit, as she clambered over the darkened rubble. "What did you do?" she barked at him, aghast.

He shrugged, his small green eyes mocking her. "Nothing. Nothing without you. No longer be having power to start a quake. Told ye once, not be easy to influence nonliving objects."

"A quake?"

"A ground-shaking, hard enough to be bringing buildings down. In Variega mountains it be common enough." He grimaced and gestured at the painting. "Painted immediately after ye were taken."

"What do you mean, you didn't have the power to start the earth quaking? I felt it. It tossed me on the floor, and then the walls fell down." *It wasn't my fault. He did this.*

"Told ye—be painting this soon after ye be taken. Nothing happened."

She took a deep breath, trying to still the helpless fluttering of a heart that didn't want to hear the truth he would eventually tell her. "You just said you painted me here. Wasn't that enough?"

He shrugged. "Ye be imprisoned. Couldn't be answering the call."

She thought: *He's lying. He tried lots of things and none of them worked. Until I did my painting. It was me.*

He continued, gesturing at the painting, "So I be thinking of this. A quake with ye escaping."

She was silent, sifting through a jumble of thoughts, wondering which one to pick up and say.

"I be old, end of my days," he said suddenly. He sounded sullen, reluctant to admit an approximation of the truth. "Gratitudes be five days back, so must be hundred and fifty days ago since I paint the quake. My power be too weak. Nothing happened."

"Until tonight. Why now?"

"Ye be painting something. Ye must have. With your power in your waterpainting, my poor effort be made real, too . . . be method of your escape. Ye did, yes? Ye be painting something. The fools let ye have your paints."

She was silent.

He changed the subject. "We must go now, tonight. Leave Scarcleft. They be hunting me down since that day. Tomorrow they be hunting ye too. A myriapede to ride, supplies—everything be arranged at livery outside the walls." When she looked incredulous, he added, "It be a standing arrangement. Just in case."

"Can we go to Breccia?"

"No. No, it's time ye be going home. To Khromatis. Ye be a Watergiver, now true waterpainter. Time to claim what be yours."

No hint of *asking* her first. She remembered the pull that had drawn her back to this building, to Russet. There was more than one way to imprison a person.

"Claim? Claim what? What exactly is mine? And just who are you to me?"

He considered her carefully; she guessed he was assessing her stubbornness. She put on her best stubborn look. He shrugged, capitulating. "Ye be my great-granddaughter. Your mother, Sienna, my granddaughter. Her mother, Magenta, my daughter. She married the Pinnacle."

"Who is . . . ?"

"The Pinnacle be . . . well, ruler. I be father-in-law to most powerful man in Khromatis, so had power myself. But Magenta died. Then your mother, my granddaughter Sienna, be running off. The silly frip! She be her father's heir—Pinnacle one day if she be winning approval of Watergiver Council. Instead she thinks herself in love. Man have no powers. An eel-catcher. A wanderer. A nothing. Erith Grey. Pah!"

His anger at something that had happened so long ago was still enough to make his hands shake. Terelle stared, mesmerised by the way the patterns on his skin, lit by the lamplight, moved with each tremble as if they were living creatures crawling down his arms from under his wrap.

"Sienna's father, the Pinnacle, furious. Pinnacle's heir must be marrying someone of power, get children of power." He shook his head, part in anger, part in puzzlement. "She and lover, they left mountains without permission. That be forbidden. They reached White Quarter, me at their heels. Wanted to bring her back. But some 'Basters gave them passage across the salt to the Gibber. I caught up with them there."

"You killed him, didn't you? You killed my father!" She was certain of it.

He shrugged. "Be him or me. And I be waterpainter."

"But *why*?" she asked, outraged. "Why go after her like that anyway? You ended up being responsible for the deaths of them both!"

"She family. Her behaviour shamed me. Ye not understand—I be revered as great waterpainter of our time. But be getting old. Powers lessening. For family to have position, must be power in next generation, no? Sienna have that power. She was stormshifter. What you call stormlord, and she threw it all away."

"Because she wanted to marry an ordinary man? So what?"

"Not just that. She not be wanting power. She refused to study. I chased her to bring her back. Find her in the Gibber. She told me she be having baby, a girl she be going to call Terelle." He glared at her. "We be naming our children with colours. Match a child to their real colour, then they be the finest of waterpainters. But the name Terelle? Means exile. Nothing to do with colour. Her way of telling me she never be coming back."

She shook her head, distraught, touched for a moment by the love of a mother she had never known. Unable to speak, she gestured with a hand that he was to continue.

He said, "The eel-catcher fight. He died. I be making sure of that with my painting. She fled into storm she made—"

"And you never found her."

"No."

"So why didn't you go back to Khromatis?"

"What be point? My powers vanishing, Sienna gone, Pinnacle blaming me. So I keep looking, hoping she be still alive and one day I find her in a place where I painted her. I be travelling all over the Quartern looking. Gibber first, then Scarpen. And one day I be lucky: I followed your tears. You be having the look of her: proud and stubborn."

Terelle's outrage poured from her. "You killed my parents! You *can't* think to take me back so that I can restore you to your position of power. That's ridiculous."

He didn't answer.

"What do you think would happen, anyway? That they'd welcome you back after so many years? What, almost nineteen years—no, I suppose more like almost twenty, all told? And then what? They'll make *me* the next Pinnacle? Do you think your people would allow a woman from the Gibber to lead them? I am nothing! I'm not really a Watergiver; I know nothing of your people or your customs or your language. And I don't care to learn!"

"Ye be having great power; that be enough. Terelle, not be safe here for you. I painted ye at nineteen—after that, ye have no protection."

"I'd be safe in Breccia."

"Ye know, ye not be having much choice." The smile he gave her was self-satisfied.

"Your paintings have no power any more," she pointed out, but her heart was thumping, and she feared she was wrong. "You can no longer trap me in them. They weren't enough to stop Taquar taking me prisoner. They weren't enough to free me."

The smile broadened, feral in its sly triumph. "Your fate be decided the moment I laid eyes on ye, foolish girl, and ye know it. Painted your future then, while I strong. Enough to make ye stay with me. Enough to point your feet in right direction—direction *I* want ye to take."

"What if the paintings are already destroyed?" she asked. They were still in her bundle; she could burn them.

"They aren't, or ye'd be dead," he said. "I told ye that. They be your future, Terelle. Into them, I put last water-painting magic I truly had."

She didn't reply. She suspected he told the truth, but she would never really know for sure. *Did Vato die because Shale planted his foot on my painting of him?*

One thing she did know for sure: she had no choice. She already felt the tug of his paintings. She'd already experienced the penalty for resisting her future.

"Pick up your bundle," he said. "We be leaving right now for White Quarter and Khromatis."

Yet my mother resisted the paintings, I know she did.

That thought was followed by another, far more chilling. Rather than go back to Russet, her mother had become the mistress of a brutish Gibberman who would one day sell his own child into a brothel.

Then another thought, puzzling rather than frightening. If her mother had been a stormshifter, why had she stayed with a man like Yagon and lived in water penury? The explanation, when it came to her, was damning. It was Viviandra who had unwittingly given her the answer. "I think she was weak and ill most of the time," she had said, speaking of Sienna.

Terelle's mother, giving birth without a midwife, had died. Perhaps her resistance to the power of her grandfather's paintings had left her too tired and ill and exhausted to live.

Terelle went cold with terror. If she chose to resist, she might die.

She picked up her bundle and followed Russet out.

In the doorway, she stopped to look back at the room. She and Shale had forged a friendship there. That link to him had been torn by her imprisonment, and the idea that it was about to be sundered entirely by her journey to an unknown land broke her heart.

A single tear gathered in the corner of her eye, but didn't fall. *Oh Shale*, she thought.

Then, lifting her chin, *I shall come back. I'll find a way. Somehow I'll find a way, I swear it.*

CHAPTER FORTY-THREE

Scarpen Quarter
Breccia City

Kaneth wasn't happy. Right then, though, he couldn't have said which irritation in his life worried him the most.

It might have been the sand-ticks crawling up into his groin or the stones digging into his stomach as he lay at the top of a ridge in the foothills of the Warthago Range. It might have been the way the frost forming on the plants in front of his nose reminded him of the cold eating deep into his bones. Or perhaps the monotonous booming of that sandblighted night-parrot calling from its burrow entrance like a demented dune god. Or the fact that he believed Breccia's attempts to train sufficient guards for its defence were too few and too late. Or the unsettled feeling he had that someone was out there in the dark in front of him, someone who had no right to be there.

Or annoyance at his own shortcomings as a rainlord. If Jasper had been with him, he would have identified the unknowns, counted how many pedes and how many people and how far off—and all Kaneth had was a nebulous feeling.

Or, then again, it might have been memories of saying goodbye to Ryka three days ago, soon after the Gratitudes festival. Her farewell had been formal, polite—and somehow sad.

Ryka. He didn't know where to start when he thought of her. It was hard to admit, but he loved her in the idiotic manner of a youth twenty years younger. And she dodged him with the skill of a desert pebblemouse. When he walked into the room, she left. She hadn't been in his bed for so long he had almost forgotten what she looked like naked. She had even taken to wearing unattractive baggy clothing, as if she was warning him off. Strangely enough, that didn't help, either; it just made him yearn for her all the more.

Everything about her puzzled him lately. Several times he had felt she wanted to speak to him, tell him something that mattered, but every time she had backed off at the last moment. Once, she would have insisted on coming with him on a job like this, hunting for Reduners infiltrating the Sweepings to the south of the Warthago. Once, Ryka the scholar had also been Ryka the risk-taker, someone who liked adventure. This time, she had stayed behind to teach the water sensitives they had brought back from the Gibber, to try to turn them into skilled rainlords. Watergiver knew, they needed as many as they could train and as quickly as possible, but most of them were no longer in the city, anyway. They had been spread out over all the other Scarpen cities—except Scarcleft—because Nealrith had been loath to "put all our gems in one jewel box," as he had put it.

Kaneth sighed and pushed his thoughts away from Ryka to Davim. His gut feeling told him the sandmaster wanted Jasper. Kaneth just wasn't sure whether it was to make use of Jasper's abilities in order to appease other dune tribes—or to kill him, to ensure the return of a Time of Random Rain. One thing Kaneth knew for sure: Davim was not going to stay in Qanatend forever. Granthon might believe the sandmaster would return to the Red Quarter; Kaneth was not so optimistic.

He felt Pikeman Elmar Waggoner coming up the slope from their camp behind him, so he slid down just below the lip of the ridge and rolled over onto his back. He could see their camp fire below and the occasional outline of one of the other ten guards as they passed in front of the flame.

"Something to eat, m'lord," Elmar said, settling down beside him and handing over a packet of food. "You want to get some rest? I can get a couple of the men to relieve you."

"No. This job is one for a rainlord. There's something out there, I feel it. That valley running into the heart of the range is as black as a tunnel at midnight now. None of your men would see a thing." He unwrapped the packet and peered at the contents. "I can't even see what I am about to eat." He took a tentative bite.

"So what is out there?" Elmar asked, scratching idly at the large scar that marred his face, reminder of a long-ago skirmish.

"Living water of some kind. Blighted eyes, what is this stuff?" He took another bite. It didn't pay to be fussy out in the desert. "Something a dung beetle dragged in?"

Elmar did not even deign to acknowledge the complaint. "Want me to send someone with a message to the city?"

"No, not yet. It could just be a couple of Scarpen fossickers, after all, and not Reduner warriors riding to battle."

"Reckon they can't get packpedes anywhere over the Warthago except at the Pebblebag Pass, anyway. Those hills are as cut up with gorges and gullies as your granny's cheeks are with wrinkles."

"Elmar, how long has it been since Qanatend fell?"

"Must be sixty-five, seventy days, I reckon."

"And we have the pass blocked up with our men and rainlords on our side, and so do they on their side. We can't get down to Qanatend, and the Reduners can't get through to us. So what do you reckon Davim's been doing all that time?" He didn't wait for an answer but gave his own. "He's either riding around the end of the range, through Fourcross Tell—and that's a long way to take an army without a source of water—or he's looking for a way through that doesn't involve Pebblebag Pass. By travelling the length of one of those wrinkles you mentioned, in fact. With access to a water supply right behind him, the Qanatend mother cistern."

He ate the rest of the food, without ever identifying its origins. "There's something alive out there."

"A pair of randy horned cats fucking themselves silly?"

"Elmar, I love the way you regard your rainlord's water-powers with *such* respectful awe."

Elmar's teeth gleamed white in his face.

Kaneth licked his fingers and edged up to the ridge top again. And gasped as the feel of water on the move hit him with the force of a rockslide.

"*Pedeshit!*"

"What is it?" Elmar edged up beside him, peering into the darkness. "I can't see a bleeding thing."

"Neither can I," Kaneth said, but he slid back down the

slope towards the camp in a hurry. "I don't have to! Elmar, tell the men to get the camp struck and packed as fast as they know how." He scrambled to his feet and began to run, calling over his shoulder as he went. "The Scarpen has just been invaded. There's a couple of thousand men riding like a spindevil wind up that valley towards us." His thought was an even more horrified: *And Reduners have pedes that make our hacks look like cripples on crutches.*

When Jasper opened the door to leave Granthon's study after cloudshifting, Senya was waiting outside. She tilted her head at him as he closed the door firmly. "Your grandfather is too tired to be disturbed," he said.

"He's dying," she said with a careless shrug, "but it doesn't matter so much now that you're here."

He stared, disliking her even while his body betrayed him and responded to her physical presence. Like her mother, she was so sunblasted beautiful. Blond curls and full lips, long lashes, nipples outlined by the thin cloth of her tunic, thighs that curved, just so—all saying things his mind didn't want to hear even as his body did.

Blighted eyes, how can she do that to me? he pondered. *I don't want to marry her; I'd rather marry Terelle.* At least he didn't flush around Terelle, like a settle boy caught thieving pomegranates, as he was doing right now.

Senya tilted her head and surveyed him rather as a pede seller might regard a prospective buyer for one of his mounts. Her next words made him wonder if she was reading his thoughts. "My parents want us to marry. They think we would have a good chance of raising stormlord children. I just wanted to tell you that I can't imagine anything worse."

"I probably could," he said, face expressionless. "But only with a great deal of thought. However, it's nice to know we do agree on something." To his amazement, she was taken aback, as if it had never occurred to her that *he* might not want to marry *her*. "You didn't imagine that I would—" he began, and then stopped. "Oh, you really did, didn't you? You thought I would *want* to wed you."

"Everyone wants to marry me," she said.

"Not this sand-grubber. I may be a dolt from the Gibber, but I'm not so sandcrazy that I would want to marry a bad-tempered spoiled brat, even if she is passably pretty."

He realised he'd gone too far when he saw the flash of fire in her eyes, pure hate. She stalked off, anger smouldering in every line of her body, leaving him regretting his words.

As if I don't already have enough enemies, he thought. *Waterless wells, you're a fool, Jasper.*

"You do have to marry her," a voice behind him said.

He spun around to come face-to-face with Laisa.

Amused by his startled surprise, she said, "You really should practise keeping part of your senses tuned to your surroundings, you know. People should not be able to sneak up on you."

"You were sneaking, Laisa?" he asked, unsmiling.

She ignored that. "You and Senya *will* marry. Make no mistake about that. You have no choice. And soon. We need other stormlords born, and a union of you two is our best chance."

"She's too young."

"She's just turned sixteen. Old enough."

The only emotion he could feel right then was grief. He turned on his heel, and headed for his room.

That evening he did not join the Almandine family for dinner. One part of him might have happily bedded Senya, but he found it hard to face her across the table. And the thought that he might have to do that every day of his life appalled him.

"Wake up! Wake up, my lord!"

Jasper stirred sleepily. Since he'd been shifting water, he slept so heavily it was hard to wake. It wasn't until Morion grabbed him by the shoulder and roughly shook him that he roused.

"Whaddisit?" he muttered, opening a sleepy eye.

"We're about to be attacked!"

That brought him to his feet in an instant. The world beyond his open shutters was alive with noise: indistinct shouts, running footsteps, banging doors. "What's happening?" he asked.

"Quick, get dressed." Morion, his eyes stark with fear, shoved some clothes into his arms. "Those sandgrubbing Reduner bastards are attacking the city. Or they will be by dawn. Lord Kaneth and Elmar rode in a while back. They've been riding two straight days with Reduners right on their heels sending ziggers after them."

"Are they all right?"

"Heard they were the only two left. There were twelve of them when they set out."

Jasper winced. Ten men dead, just like that?

He looked down at the tunic and trousers as he tried to absorb the news. "Travelling clothes?" he asked.

"Highlord Nealrith's orders for any emergency. Hurry, m'lord." He flung a pack down on the bed. "This is to take with you. There's food inside, a change of clothes, tokens, some instructions—"

Jasper scrambled, the sense of urgency having finally penetrated his senses, even as he protested. "I'm not going anywhere, Morion. How can I leave if we are being attacked? It is my duty to help defend—"

"That it is not," a voice interrupted, and Jasper looked up, startled. Kaneth entered, haggard and dirty. There was dust on his clothes, and dried blood. Yet his voice was steady, his gaze cool, his words as pragmatic and as cynical as usual. "If Davim enters this city, my guess is the first person he'll be asking after is you. And you wouldn't enjoy the meeting. Your duty, above all else, is to get to a place of safety. If anything happens to you, none of us have a future." Then his eyes spied the open shutters, and he momentarily lost his calm. "And what the pedepiss are you doing leaving the shutters open? There'll be thousands of ziggers out there soon!" He dived across the room and slammed them closed.

"I'm supposedly a stormlord—how can I run away?" Jasper asked.

"And just how many ziggers can you kill if you can't draw out their water?" Kaneth asked.

Jasper flushed and fell silent as he pulled on his trousers.

"Nealrith just asked me to make sure you know what you have to do. Laisa, Granthon, Ethelva and Senya will be going with you. You'll head south to the coast and Portennabar. Laisa will be your protection. Her rainlord skills are not too bad. You're to meet in Granthon's rooms. I'll take you there."

He grabbed up Jasper's pack and sword and hustled

him out of the door towards the Cloudmaster's quarters. Jasper was still trying to tie his tunic.

"Morion said you had a hard time getting back here. What happened?" he asked, running to catch up. Two women servants hurried past in the opposite direction, wide-eyed and worried.

Kaneth said, "The advance guard were trying to cut us off. They didn't want us to warn the city. Most of my men were killed. Ziggers. Damn, but I loathe those whining winged bastards!"

"How much time do we have?"

Kaneth gave a hollow laugh. "The first of their warriors were on our heels. Maybe half the run of a sandglass behind us. That's all. Oh, the full army won't be here until tomorrow, but there'll be ziggers over the walls any time now. I doubt that everyone will hear the warning in time. I'm not sure we can even get you out before they get here."

They halted outside Granthon's door. It was open and the Cloudmaster's room was crowded with people. Servants had brought in a litter, and the Cloudmaster was sitting on the edge of it, about to lie down. He was glowering at everybody. Ethelva hovered nearby, her grey hair loose and untidily ruffled. Lord Gold was flicking water onto Granthon's head, murmuring a prayer at the same time. A couple of armed guards and a manservant stood next to the shuttered windows, silent and watchful.

Laisa and Senya had just entered, clutching water skins, packs and a lantern. Laisa regarded the scene calmly, her travelling clothes neat and practical, yet flattering; Senya was wide-eyed with a mixture of fright and excitement and looked as if she had dressed in a hurry. She was, as usual, wearing a calf-length skirt and frilly over-blouse. Jasper had never seen her dressed any other way.

"I'm off to my post on the walls," Kaneth said quietly to Jasper. "Zigger-killing. You take care, Jasper." He hesitated, as if he didn't quite know what to say. Finally, he settled for, "You deserve better than this, but it's all you've got. I'm sorry."

The lump in Jasper's throat was painful. "I know," he said. "Don't worry, I know."

Kaneth nodded, and then he was gone. Jasper entered the room, just in time to hear Granthon mutter, "A stormlord shouldn't have to leave his city."

"I know, dear," Ethelva said. "But you have to live for us all to survive. Now lie down, and these good men will carry you down to the pede."

"I don't feel well," he said.

"Then lie down," she repeated.

Instead, he doubled over. His hands clutched at his upper body and his face contorted. Then, silently, he toppled from the litter onto the floor. Ethelva tried to catch him but wasn't strong enough to break his fall. She ended up on her knees beside him.

Jasper stared. Granthon's eyes were wide open in a sightless gaze.

Oh waterless damn, he thought, aghast. *That* can't *have just happened.*

Before anyone reacted, there was a high-pitched whine outside the window. Lord Gold glanced that way, then knelt at the Cloudmaster's side.

"Is Grandpa dead?" Senya asked, her eyes large and round.

"I rather think so," Laisa said, sounding more exasperated than upset. "And those are ziggers whining at the shutters."

"Lady Ethelva, his spirit has left him," Gold confirmed.

Ethelva looked at him blankly.

Jasper remained stunned with horror. *The Cloudmaster of the Quartern is dead.* Which meant he, Jasper, was now the only stormlord the land had. He pushed away the terror of that. His heart thudded in his chest.

Later, I'll think about it later.

Laisa moved to touch Ethelva on the shoulder. "We should go," she said.

Ethelva looked up at her, not understanding. "Go? And leave him? I cannot do that."

"There is nothing you can do here." Laisa pointed out with calm logic. "He is dead. And he would want you safe in Portennabar."

Ethelva, leaning heavily on Lord Gold's arm, stood up. She said, with heartbreaking dignity, "My husband has just died. I will do my best for his city, and I will attend to the proper disposal of his water. That is my duty. It is yours to protect the next generation, Laisa." She beckoned to Senya and dropped a kiss on her cheek. "Be the best rainlord you know how to be, my dear." Then she turned back to Lord Gold. "Can you protect us from the ziggers while we accompany the body downlevel to the House of the Dead? I wish the ceremonies to take place there, as is customary."

Laisa shrugged and turned to Jasper. "You ready?"

He returned her look numbly. "The ziggers?"

Senya gave him a scornful look. "We don't have to go out into the street. Don't you know *anything*?"

"Nealrith had all contingencies covered," Laisa said. "Follow me."

"My father has had this planned for ages," Senya told him smugly as they hurried along the passage. "An escape route we can use if there are ziggers in the city. The waterhall first, then down through a tunnel to the thirtieth level. There's a secret room there where we can hide until the fighting is over and we've won."

He blinked, wondering if she could believe that. *Won?* Could a handful of rainlords and a few hundred guards win against hordes of Reduners with ziggers? And didn't she even care her grandfather had just died?

In the waterhall, lit by an extravagance of oil lamps, workmen were constructing a stone wall to block most of the tunnel leading to the mother cistern in the Warthago Range. A hole at the bottom of the barrier allowed water to pour through. The waterhall's two reeves watched the workers in a worried fashion. Ryka Feldspar was leaning against a wall with her eyes closed. A number of guards lounged about, fidgeting in edgy boredom.

"Are there Reduners out there?" Laisa asked, addressing her question to Ryka.

Ryka looked up wearily. "Not now. At least not within range of my powers. Their damn ziggers killed three of my men, though." She indicated the floor, and Jasper saw that the flagstones were littered with dried-up zigger bodies.

"Where's your father?" Laisa asked.

"Up on the North Wall. Trying to kill ziggers before they cross the wall into the city." She shrugged. "Not easy in the dark." She glanced at a wall niche where sand sifted through a sandglass. "Another two runs till dawn. I don't know that he'll make it. He's not alone, but there are only four of them up there." She meant four rainlords. "Four for the whole of the Level One wall, plus the Level Two escarpment wall." She smiled wanly. "I don't think they are going to make all that much difference, do you?"

Jasper licked dry lips.

Laisa didn't comment. She was already turning to the nearest of the guards, asking him to open the trapdoor in the floor close to where the man stood. "Disguise the entrance after us," she added to one of the reeves as the guard pulled up the cover. He nodded, as if he had been briefed on that already.

Nealrith planned for all this, Jasper thought. *The wall across the tunnel, our escape routes, every rainlord knowing where to go and what to do. Even the pack I carry was prepared for me beforehand. And yet they scorn Rith as a weak ruler.*

Ryka asked Jasper, "Kaneth? Did you see Kaneth?"

He nodded. "He went to the walls. I don't know which part."

She nodded, as if that was what she had expected to hear. Jasper turned away, unable to face the panicked expression in her eyes. *She really cares for him*, he thought in surprise. *She's sick with worry, but it's for him, not herself.*

With the lantern in her hand, Laisa climbed into the hole and Senya followed, fussing about her skirts. Jasper climbed down after her and found himself in a dry brick tunnel. The reeve shut the trapdoor after him.

"It leads to the groves with one exit between," Laisa told him, "on the thirtieth level. We aren't going to bump into anyone coming up the other way. At least I hope not, because that would mean that the Reduners have found the outside entrance in the groves."

"They won't, will they?" Senya asked. Any semblance of scornful superiority had vanished. The sight of the dead ziggers had shaken her.

"Unlikely," her mother said. "The entrance is under the water in one of the grove cisterns."

"I don't like this," Jasper said. "We shouldn't be running away. If the Reduners are using ziggers, only rainlords—you and Senya included—can stop them."

Laisa turned on him in a fury. "Do you think I want to run? If we don't win tonight, I lose everything I've ever worked to have. I'd rather be up there killing ziggers than down here hiding. But you and Senya are the future, the only future we have. And I've been elected the one to secure that future. If Breccia City loses the battle tonight—tomorrow—I'm the one who has to escort you to safety. Now get going."

He paused, torn. She walked away down the tunnel, taking the lantern with her. Senya trailed behind, white-faced.

Jasper thought, *Laisa believes we will lose.* Sighing, he followed.

It was a long and silent trek, often steeply downhill, sometimes stepped. Jasper pondered his options as he went. He could not spend too long hiding underground. He was the only stormlord the Quartern had now. He didn't think he could make clouds at all without Granthon, but he had to try. Perhaps, in Portennabar, close to the sea . . . If he could see the water, reach out to it.

Deep inside, he knew it was unlikely.

At last they came to a manhole lid in the bricked floor of the passage that had the figure 30 painted on it.

"This is it," Laisa said. "Open it up, Jasper."

He did as she asked, and she knelt to lower the lantern inside. He peered in. A ladder went down a cistern wall into water deep enough to be over his head.

"I don't want to go in there," Senya protested. "I'll get wet."

"You're a rainlord, you fool girl," her mother said, her contempt scathing. "Who ever heard of a rainlord getting wet if they didn't want to? Jasper, you go first. Here, take the lantern. We'll follow. Go down to the bottom and walk to your right along the cistern wall. There is a watertight metal door at the end. That leads into our hiding place."

Senya continued to protest, but Jasper didn't wait to hear. He climbed down, pushing the water gently away from his body to form an encircling bubble of air. He arrived still dry at the bottom. He followed Laisa's directions, creating his own tunnel of air as he went. When he reached the entrance she had mentioned, he cleared it of water and studied the configuration of the water lock of the heavy metal door. It was a simpler version of the Scarcleft mother cistern grille, easy enough to manipulate. He soon had it open, only to find another door, unlocked, immediately behind it. Just in case the first leaked, he guessed. He opened it and stepped through, careful to hold back the water behind him.

It was a large room, much larger than he had anticipated. There were no windows and no other doors. Fresh air entered through several ventilation shafts set high in the walls. Pallets were piled in one corner; chairs and table sat in the centre; a fireplace—with kettle and pots on the hob—had been built into one wall, under a hooded chimney. The other walls were lined with cupboards and shelves and dayjars. He entered, still maintaining the wall of water so that it didn't spill into the room. He put his pack and the lantern on the table and opened one of the cupboards. It was filled with sacks and jars of preserved food, bowls and plates. Another contained a pile of compressed seaweed briquettes, an earthenware jar of lamp oil and several lanterns.

When he turned to face the door, Senya was just entering. She was half-soaked, and her skirt flapped wetly around her calves. Laisa came in behind her. "Oh, for goodness' sake, Senya, if you would only practise your water skills more, that wouldn't happen. Now get rid of all that water before I close the doors."

Sulkily, Senya did as she was told and sent the water back into the cistern. It was clumsily done and left Jasper thinking that she really didn't have much talent. He kept his expression bland. Laisa closed the doors behind her and reset the water lock. Jasper released his hold on the contents of the cistern and heard the water slap up against the outer door.

"Who knows about this place?" he asked.

"All the rainlords, including the waterpriests and Lord Gold. The seneschal. That's all."

Jasper thought: *And all it would take for Davim to find us would be one man tortured into telling.*

Senya looked around in horror. "There's no windows! I can't stay here."

"You don't have much choice," Laisa said unsympathetically. "Either this or ziggers. Take your pick."

"At least I could try to kill ziggers," she muttered.

"From the exhibition you just gave of water control, I'm not too sure you could."

"I could if someone would just teach me how to kill the rainlord way!"

"When you display the kind of maturity necessary to make good judgements, perhaps they might," said Laisa, hanging the lantern from a hook in the ceiling. She looked around the room with a sigh. "What do you know about ziggers, Jasper?"

"Quite a lot. I used to care for Taquar's. The Reduners would want to be quite sure all their ziggers are satiated and back in their cages before they themselves venture inside the city walls. They want no accidents caused to their own men by an improperly trained zigger."

Senya plonked herself down at the table, looking forlorn. Laisa, fidgeting, paced back and forth as she spoke. "They lost the element of surprise, thanks to Kaneth. And their mad rush from the Warthago Range means they and their beasts must be exhausted. It gives our rainlords a chance."

Jasper thought, *She's as furious about this as a scorpion taken out of its hole.* Aloud he said, "There's too few of them to protect a whole city."

"Yes. Fifteen without counting us but including the waterpriest rainlords. Most of them with no fighting experience, like the priests, or incompetent, like Merqual and Ryka, or just plain old."

"The other cities should have sent their rainlords," Senya said, "like Grandfather asked them to."

Jasper ignored that and said, "Fifteen rainlords to fight—what, two thousand Reduners? Ten thousand?"

"I've no idea. Iani said the force that struck at

Qanatend was about seven or eight thousand mounted pedemen. Kaneth couldn't give an estimate of those he saw." She laughed. "He said he didn't stop to count them."

"What is this room?"

"It has existed since the city was built, I expect. Our forebears were always quarrelling between cities, quite viciously, I understand, until the idea of Scarpen unity was imposed on them. I suppose they once thought they needed secret tunnels and hiding places."

"What's our plan?" He was sure there was one.

"Several myriapedes are secreted away in a hidden gully along the escarpment to the west. They are kept loaded and saddled under the care of a pedeman, waiting for us if the city falls. All we have to do is get to them unseen and then flee to Portennabar, on the coast."

"If the Reduners besiege us, we could be here a long time. Even Qanatend held out for ten days."

"We are to leave the moment the walls are breached. In the heat of battle, in effect. The reeve on this level will let us know the right moment."

"How will he tell us?" Senya asked. "No reeve can open water locks to get in here."

Her mother indicated the two ventilation shafts. "The one on the left goes to the outside. The right-hand one opens into the level's Cistern Chambers. All the reeve has to do is speak down it, and we will hear. Anyway, let's light the fire and have a hot drink."

She took up the kettle to fill it from the water jar. Jasper fetched some briquettes for a fire.

"How long do we have to stay here?" Senya whined. "When's Daddy coming?"

Laisa ignored the question.

Jasper stared at Senya, nonplussed. She sounded like a girl half her age. "There's no way we can know the answer to that," he said finally.

"I don't like it in here."

"Neither do I much." He was about to say something else placating when he heard a whine, a sharp buzzing hum like the sound of a stone-cutter's saw. He knew what it was, and he knew it was in the room with them. He and Laisa both shouted at the same moment: "Zigger!"

Jasper acted without thinking. He grabbed up the nearest thing to hand, intending to swat the beast once he'd worked out where it was. At the same time, he pulled water out of the open water jar as a backup. He spun around, searching. The zigger was perching on the edge of the left-hand ventilator shaft, the one that led to the outside.

Senya screamed and jumped to her feet. Attracted by the movement, the zigger streaked towards her, its wings a blur. She dodged, her shrieks escalating in pitch and volume. At the last moment, she flicked her head sideways in a desperate attempt to escape. Her long hair swept around her face, netting the creature. Shrieking hysterically, flinging herself around, she gave Jasper no chance to hit the zigger and Laisa no chance to use her power without endangering her daughter.

Jasper flung the shaft of water like a spear. Half of it smacked Senya in the face; the rest tore the zigger out of her hair. Stunned and soggy, it fell to the floor. He stomped on it. When he lifted his sandaled foot, there was a splatter of red blood underneath.

Senya fell to her knees, still screaming. With a controlled calm, Laisa stepped up to her and slapped her face.

She picked the dead zigger up by a wing and waved it under her daughter's nose. "Dead, see?"

The screams faded into heaving sobs interspersed with indistinct complaints. "In my hair . . . could have died . . . horrid . . . Jasper *wet* me."

"Yes, and you should thank him for it. He saved your life. Sunlord above, Senya, it's time you learned to behave like the rainlord you are. It is time you learned to *be* one."

Jasper turned away, embarrassed and shaken. He didn't like Senya, but he didn't like the way Laisa treated her daughter, either.

He glanced down and found he had a seaweed briquette in his hand.

Salted hells, he mused, *just as well I didn't clobber Senya with that. She'd never have let me forget it.* He said, "I'll find a bit of cloth to put across the opening of the shaft, but it was probably just sheer chance. It was looking for a way back to its cage." He pointed at the floor. "Ziggers don't have red blood. It had already eaten its fill."

Laisa casually threw the remains into the fireplace. "Revolting things," she said.

As he turned back to the task of laying the fire, Jasper considered what he had just done. He'd killed a zigger. He pondered that, and his thoughts were a revelation.

I've been a withering idiot, he thought. *There is more than one way to eat a bab fruit.*

And he smiled.

CHAPTER FORTY-FOUR

Scarpen Quarter
Breccia City
Level 40

At sunset on the first day of the attack, Nealrith stood on the wall near the South Gate and felt a moment's brief satisfaction. He hadn't really believed the Reduners would come, but ever since Qanatend had fallen he had prepared for it anyway, and he thought they had all done well.

Considering everyone's lack of experience, not bad at all.

His gaze roved up and down, searching out any activity on the part of the besieging red warriors. Most were hidden among the bab palms of the groves or behind the buildings outside the gates, well out of range of his power to seize their water.

Mistake, that, he thought, *to allow the livery stables and the smelters and so many other noisy and grimy workshops to build so close to the walls. Bad strategy for defence of a city. They should have been sited further away.*

And now it was too late.

He glanced along the wall at the line of guards. Too

few of them, but still, more than he'd expected. Ordinary citizens, determined to do their best, had joined them. They'd be useless under real attack, but armed with butterfly nets, they didn't do too badly against ziggers.

He allowed himself a smile. Ryka's idea, that. The nets, soaked in bab oil, were designed to catch the butterflies that came to lay eggs on the green bab fruit, but they were effective against ziggers. Once the little stinkers were caught, their soft hind wings stuck to the oil and they couldn't fly. Helpless, they were easy to squash. Breccia had not lost as many people as he had feared, even at night, when it was hard to see ziggers.

At intervals along the wall's walkway were catapults, another idea of Ryka's. Inspired by a child's toy, they provided a way of launching fireballs to illuminate what was happening beyond the walls at night, or to heave rocks during the day.

"You sent for me, Rith?"

He turned to look into the street below. Kaneth, mounted on the back of a myriapede, greeted him with a wave. Watergiver damn, but the man looked exhausted. He couldn't have had much sleep in three or four days, and he'd made a ride that would go down in history—if there was anyone left to write it after this was all over.

"Yes," he said. "Wait there; I'll come down." He turned to the overman standing next to him. "I'm going to grab a bite to eat. Let me know immediately if there's any change."

"Yes, m'lord."

By the time he was down in the street, Kaneth had dismounted. Nealrith clapped him on the back, saying,

"You've got to snatch some sleep. But come and eat with me first. How are things on the north wall?"

"Quiet. I think the red bastards are sleeping. At a guess, we can expect an attack about two hours before dawn."

"Make sure you get some sleep between now and then." He guided Kaneth towards the guardroom across the street. "But you know, they need not attack at all. They could just maintain a siege and send ziggers in until there are too few of us left to defend the walls."

"They are Reduner warriors hankering after their supposedly more glorious times as nomadic raiders. They'll attack. And I bet they know a lot more about our vulnerabilities than they did before they took Qanatend."

Nealrith grimaced. "You're probably right, unfortunately. I suppose it means we don't have to worry too much about our water supply or our food stores, because those will last longer than we do. Seen Davim at all?"

"Who knows which one he is? They all look alike from up on the wall. And he's probably too damned canny to make himself a target."

"We've done well with killing their ziggers. I'm proud of the men of Breccia."

Kaneth gave a lopsided grin. "Better mention the women, too, or you'll have Ryka punching you on the nose. She's just spent the day keeping ziggers and Reduners out of the waterhall. They've been attacking through the tunnel."

Nealrith nodded. He knew they had lost both the mother cistern and the tunnel to the invaders.

When they entered the nearby guardroom, the aroma of hot food drifted from covered dishes on the table. "Sunlord above," Nealrith said, "that smells good. I don't think I've eaten today, come to think of it, which is foolish of me." He spooned some food into an empty plate. "You heard about my father, didn't you?"

"Yes. I'm sorry, and not just because he was our Cloudmaster."

"I loved the stubborn old goat. I haven't had time to take it all in yet, let alone grieve. I couldn't go to his water gifting. I haven't even seen my mother since he died. I hear she's refusing to leave the city with the others. Sunlord damn it, it's hard to take. All of it." He shook his head wearily. "Eat something, my friend. That's an order. You need it." He watched while Kaneth piled up his plate, then asked, "We are going to lose this one, aren't we? Eventually."

"I . . . hmm. Yes, I think so. Well, the city anyway. But as long as we get Jasper and Senya out of here safely, there's hope for . . . something. Jasper is special, Rith. If he stays free, the Quartern has a future."

Nealrith looked at him in surprise. "So says Kaneth the cynic, who always takes the gloomy view?"

Kaneth smiled. "Oh, I think my view is sufficiently dark to please the worst pessimist. It's not weeping likely either you or I will live to see many more sunrises. I just wish . . ."

"What?"

"That I could save Ryka."

"Ah." He didn't know what to say. *I'm lucky*, he thought. *Senya and Laisa might live through this.* He said, "You really love her, then?"

"Sandblast it, Rith," he burst out, "you should see her. Those bastards have been battering at the barrier into the waterhall. Every time they dislodge a brick, they send in more sodding ziggers, and she deals with them until her men get the hole covered. Ryka, who's half blind! She can scarcely see the little stinkers, yet she deals with them, and I can't even stay to help because it's more important I'm out on the walls." He was silent. Finally he threw up his hands. "Yes, I love her. How's that for a sodding joke? Kaneth the tomcat of Level Three, tamed by the edge of the sharpest mind and the barbs of the sharpest tongue in the city, hankering after a woman most men would call plain."

Nealrith was silent.

"You know what will really make you laugh?" Kaneth added, and his voice softened. "To me, she's wise, not shrewish. To me, she's the most beautiful woman in Breccia, not the plainest." He gave a laugh, half amused, half bitter. "And she hasn't let me near her in nearly half a year."

Nealrith snatched a nap up on the wall, wrapped in a blanket. All too soon, one of the guards was shaking him awake.

"Highlord," he said, "There's some kind of activity out there."

Nealrith scrambled to his feet and looked over the parapet. "Pedeshit," he whispered, then roared, "Sound the alarm! Get some fireballs out there for light. *Move* it!"

Little could be seen in the darkness, but what he sensed heaped the terror in his soul. There was a solid line of pedes moving towards the wall. Each carried too many people for him to count. A fireball lobbed over the wall a moment later illuminated the scene. A running pede shied away from the burning ball of woven palm leaves doused in oil, but the others kept on coming, tens of animals, each packed with chalamen and bladesmen.

Nealrith bellowed for a continuous stream of fireballs.

He shouted a message to his pede riders within the city to relay to the other rainlords elsewhere. Behind him, the warning drums started thrumming, the sound picked up by the drums of other levels, one after the other up through the city.

He took the water from the face of the nearest pede driver and wished he had enough power to drain the pede itself through its carapace. Useless to waste power blinding it; their eyesight was poor, anyway. They relied on their feelers, not their eyes.

Too hard to target human eyes at this distance. *Faces, just grab water from their faces.* That one. Another. A third. Then another. Other riders took over the reins from the affected, damn them. A fifth, sixth. That one there. He lost count.

No ziggers. Which meant they intended to scale the walls.

And then there was no more time.

The first of the packpedes leaped at the wall. Spears flew from both sides. Men scrambled. The pede dug the points of its feet into the sheer face of the wall and hauled itself upwards, a giant centipede climbing a rock. It was so huge its back segments were still on the ground when its mouthparts crunched into the top of the wall. The men it carried crawled up its body and over its head to the parapet. One part of Nealrith's mind—the cool, unruffled part that refused to listen to his fear or hear his despair—noted that they had screwed more handles than usual into the pede segments to help them climb.

Pedes all along the wall now, scrabbling to raise their enormous bodies. Living, armoured ladders. The Reduners' mode of entry into the city.

They learned a thing or two, the calm part thought, *in Qanatend. Now I know how the city fell.*

He used his power again and again, until he had none left. On either side of him, his men died. And were replaced. Fought. And died. Until the man next to him was a grinning Reduner and he had to use his sword to fight a red bladesman whose joy was battle. He knew before he started he was unlikely to win. But he had to try.

And not long afterwards, he was falling, falling. Off the wall. Down, his bloodied sword still in his hand and Senya calling out to him, in that cool part of his head, *Don't die, Papa! Don't die!*

He woke into a darkness so profound he thought it was death. Pain soon told him a different truth. He hurt so much there was no way he could be dead. Something jabbed him in the genitals, sending waves of agony to drown the rest of the pain. He groaned then, and light filtered through the dark of his vision.

He was lying on his back in the street, where he had fallen. He was surrounded by men. Red faces, red clothes, red braided hair. Zigger stink. One of them was holding a spear far too close to his privates. He couldn't move. Everything ached too much and his shaken body would not respond. Waves of pain made nonsense of his thoughts.

From a long way off, he heard a voice speaking in an accent so thick he wasn't sure he understood.

"I, Sandmaster Davim the drover. You, rainlord, son of stormlord. Nealrith, your men say. My men say you no power more. Your men dead now."

His mind struggled with that—and then found an explanation he didn't like. Davim had tortured his men into identifying him and then killed them. The monstrous ache inside him prevented a reply.

"Where stormlord?"

Nealrith looked up at Davim through a haze. "Dead," he said finally. "Died even before the battle started. You'll find his body, what's left of it, in the House of the Dead. You can pay your respects there, to the man who brought you the water you drank every day of your life."

Father. I wanted to say goodbye. Oh, Mother, don't be there when the Reduners arrive! I cannot save you. Maybe Father was the lucky one.

He tried to focus on the sandmaster. Not a large man; he'd expected someone taller. But he reeked of power for all that.

Senya. She will have gone by now. Laisa, too. That was the arrangement: for them to flee the moment the walls were breached.

He tried to reach the man with his power. Tried to take his water. But he had nothing left, nothing. And maybe it wouldn't have made any difference if he'd still had power. Davim was water sensitive, surely, and must have known enough to keep his own water safe.

The withered bastard was smiling, amused.

He knows I tried. Did it tickle him, perhaps? He feels safe now, the rotting piece of shit.

"And the youth? Shale Flint?" Davim asked. His eyes glittered in the flame of a burning torch.

It was night still, then. His own eyes were behaving oddly. He couldn't focus. And his head ached. But then, so did everything else.

"Shale Flint?" The spear poked at him again.

Pedeshit, that hurt! "Jasper left the city. I sent him away."

"Where? When?"

"Sorry. Can't remember. My head hurts. I think I fell off the wall."

An upwards quirk of the lips, a flash of ire in those black eyes: they promised horrors.

Davim turned to the man with the spear and spoke in his own tongue. Then he turned back to Nealrith. "This man cut Nealrith's eye. Give to his zigger. Then number two eye. You no see. Then number one ball, then number two. You no have more children. Then he cut your pleasure stick, feed to cat. You no more pleasure women. You still no say where Shale Flint, he cut tongue. Then you no more tell anyone anything. Understand?"

"I think so. Sounds plain enough."

"Where Shale? You say, I kill you now. All finish quickly then. No hurt more."

Nealrith drifted away from the pain, then deliberately brought himself back. He battled for coherence. It seemed important, although he was no longer sure why. "I have seen all I ever wanted to see. I have the child I desired." *Senya, oh, Senya.* "There can be no more pleasure when my city is in your hands." *Laisa, I wish you could have loved me.*

He fought to stay lucid. "To help you find Jasper Bloodstone would be a greater agony. Do your damnedest, Davim the drover, and may your heart shrivel in the waterless land you'll leave behind you."

Davim unsheathed a knife and rapped out a command. Men grabbed Nealrith's arms and legs and held him hard to the ground. He didn't struggle.

No point, he thought. *No point to anything now.*

Davim leaned over and held the eyelid of Nealrith's left eye open with the fingers of one hand.

I must really have riled him, he thought with grim humour. *He's going to do it himself.*

Then Davim stuck his knife into the eyeball and cut it out. Agony lanced deep into Nealrith's brain like a stream of molten fire. He struggled then, and screamed. He hadn't known what pain was till then. Blood poured down his face and into his mouth.

Davim straightened up and pushed the eye through the bars of the zigger cage he wore at his belt.

Nealrith didn't see, and no longer cared.

CHAPTER FORTY-FIVE

Scarpen Quarter
Breccia City

Past noon, and the reeve at the Cistern Chambers on Level
Six was still alive and still on duty. He unlocked the door
to the main water tunnel for Lord Kaneth and fifteen exhausted, wounded men.

"They are killing reeves," Kaneth said as the man lit
a candle lantern for them to use in the tunnel. "Level by
level. Come with us to Breccia Hall. If you stay here at
the waterhall, you'll die."

"It's hard to walk away from your duty," the reeve replied, shaking his head. "My father was the reeve here
before me. And his father before him. I grew up here."
He sighed. "I shall probably die here. What else is there
for me?"

Kaneth looked away. *Honour*, he thought, *comes at a
terrible price*. He had seen too many good men die this
day. Aloud he resorted to ritual words. "May the Sunlord
send you solace."

"Take care, my lord."

Kaneth urged his small group of guards uplevel. Tired

as they were, bleeding and bruised and limping, they found it a tough dimb. Worse, there were grilles blocking the tunnel on every level, each with a water lock to be opened and closed, which meant Kaneth had to find power somewhere inside himself to manipulate them. He had never been so close to dropping with exhaustion. Blighted eyes, but he was tired!

He had used up most of his power on the walls hours before, just after dawn. The drums had told him to expect the worst, and the worst had come with the forced opening of the gates—by Reduners already on the inside. Since then, Kaneth had been fighting in the streets. No more ziggers, though, thank the Sunlord. Or maybe thank the Reduner reluctance to risk dying in the frenzy from their own bastard weapons. Still, men died, overwhelmed by the sheer numbers of chalamen and bladesmen. They'd had to flee and regroup.

He'd known they were doomed. Known he was a dead man refusing to give up. It made no difference to his decisions. He had rallied as many guards as he could find, and they'd held off the invaders for a time on Level Ten. He and Elmar had fought side by side, two men sealing a long camaraderie with a deeper bond of two warriors who believed they were about to die. As the day wore on, more and more men dropped. Elmar saved Kaneth several times; Kaneth returned the favour, flashing a smile at the pikeman. For a while, they seemed charmed, a duo that could hold death at bay.

On Level Eight, their small group made another stand and held their position with the aid of an ageing water-priest rainlord who had not yet used up all his power. In the end, the man died, speared from behind, and the group splintered as they were charged by Reduner warriors. Kaneth led those who stuck with him to the Level Six Cistern Chambers. He knew it was time to abandon the streets to the Reduners.

When he scanned the men remaining with him, Elmar was no longer among them. He spared a moment to grieve.

They arrived at the Breccia Hall entrance almost a sandglass run later, and a water reeve opened the door for them. Kaneth continued up to the waterhall on Level One, leaving the guards behind at the hall.

He emerged straight into chaos. The defensive wall that had been erected across the tunnel leading from the mother cistern had been partially torn down. Everywhere he looked there were bodies of the dead or dying. At one end of the hall, half a dozen guards and a reeve were fighting still, close to being overwhelmed by eight or nine Reduners. At first glance, Kaneth couldn't see Ryka, and his heart clenched with the unthinkable fear that she was dead. Then he saw her, lying against the wall, out of the way of the fighting.

Not dead, but wounded. Her thigh was roughly bandaged; blood showed through the cloth. She faced the skirmishing, propping herself up on an elbow. From the intensity of her stare, he guessed she was using her waterpowers. He raced across the room, sword drawn, reaching for the dregs of his power as he ran. Halfway across, he sucked water from the nearest Reduner. The man collapsed, shrieking. Entering the fray, Kaneth trod on the man's face. The next man he ran through with his blade. The impact almost wrenched his sword out of his hand.

Kaneth came up behind a warrior advancing on Ryka and tossed him face first into the nearest cistern. He pushed the man's head under the water. A younger warrior leaped at Kaneth with a roar of rage and a swinging scimitar. Kaneth ducked, parried—and blinded his attacker without losing his hold on the drowning man. He released his grip only when the Reduner stilled under his hand.

Panting, Kaneth resorted to water-power again and blinded two more Reduners before they realised their danger. Another turned to flee towards the exit tunnel, only to have Ryka snatch up a sword and swing it into the back of his knees. He collapsed. She finished him off by extracting the water from his throat. He died opening and closing his mouth in silence, like a fish out of water.

Kaneth looked around for someone else to kill, but the remaining Reduners were already dead. He lowered his sword and turned to the Breccian guards. They were all wounded, but still upright. "Good work," he said with a satisfied nod. "Check all the bodies to make sure they are dead. If not, kill them. And get that dead fellow out of our drinking water. Then start to block the entrance to the tunnel again before the next lot come."

The men obeyed wordlessly. One of them plunged his head into the open cistern. When he lifted it out again, dripping, he drank deeply from his cupped hands. To Kaneth, it was an action that said more than anything else; in a single day, something that once would have been a crime had ceased to mean anything at all.

He looked at Ryka. She was on her feet, bloodied, dirty, weary, her sword slipping from her grasp. And he was certain, as never before, what was important—and how stupid he had been not to have seen it years earlier. *How ironic*, he thought, his heart aching. *It took a war.*

"How badly are you hurt?" he asked, striding to her side.

"Shallow cut. Bloody, but nothing serious."

"Your father?"

"I heard he died up on the walls."

The pain in her eyes unmanned him. He couldn't speak. It was she who came to him, standing up and reaching out in answer to what she read in his eyes. "I thought you might be dead, too," she whispered. "I thought I'd lost you."

He enfolded her in his embrace, clutched her tight, buried his face in her hair. They stood like that, momentarily shut off from the world, while the men dealt out death around them. When he did speak, he said the first thing that came into his head.

"There haven't been any hussies. Or snuggery jades. Not since the day we married. Not even once." *Oh shit*, he thought. *Did I really have to mention that now?*

Her arms tightened around him. "Not even since I left your bed?" she asked.

"Not even then. I didn't want them any more, not after you." He eased his hold so that he could see her face, meet her eyes. When he spoke, there was pain behind every word he uttered, and he neither tried nor wanted to hide it. "Ryka, the truth is you have to come through this alive. Because without you, I won't have a reason to live. It's taken me half a lifetime to see that you are all that matters, all I want, all I need. I'm so sorry you were forced into a marriage you didn't want. So very, very sorry."

She sighed as if he had said something excessively stupid. "You are the only man I ever wanted to marry since I was fourteen years old, you dryhead."

He tried to make sense of that, but it was too difficult. Emotion uncurled inside him, but he couldn't untangle the strands: love, hope and shining joy entwined with dark knots of despair and grief.

"There's no need to say it," she said gently and laid a finger to his lips. "I've already heard the only thing I needed to hear. I love you, Kaneth Carnelian, and I always have. Always."

The day passed unbearably slowly down in the hidden room on the thirtieth level. They measured time by the run of a sandglass and the faint light that entered through the ventilator from the outside. The day had, in fact, begun for them before dawn, when they had heard the distant drumbeats that signalled an attack on the walls. The level's reeve had spoken to them then, using the other ventilator shaft, his voice echoing strangely. He had told them he would go out into the streets to find out what was happening and they were not to move until he came back.

He had not returned yet.

Senya slept most of the time; Laisa paced; Jasper tried to read by lantern light. He'd opened the pack he had been given, to find that it contained the tables and maps he had studied with Cloudmaster Granthon. They detailed all the areas throughout the Quartern where rain was supposed to fall, and when, and how to get it there. Some of this Jasper had already learned in a practical sense from Granthon. Granthon and Nealrith had done their best to pour as much knowledge into him in the time they'd had, but it had not been enough. Here, in written form, was all he needed to know, if he ever had the chance to study it. If ever he grew enough in power to apply it. The size of the task was monumental.

Those papers weren't the only things in the pack: there were food supplies, a blanket, a palmubra hat and water skins, as yet empty. All things he would need on a journey.

He looked up, watching Laisa's shadow on the wall as she paced with unending restlessness. *What drives her?* he wondered. Not love, he was sure of that. He looked away from the shadow to her face, to the reality. Her brows were drawn together into a deep furrow, and the lines around her lips were tight with irritation.

We are all about to lose the lives we have led, he thought. And then, brightening slightly, *Never mind. Maybe I can search for Terelle at last. Maybe I can find Mica.*

But though he tried to find hope in that, he was thinking of a land without rain. Of a Quartern that was about to die because he couldn't bring it water, because he was the last stormlord and couldn't make a storm cloud.

Terelle. Maybe she could help with her painting. That was another reason to find her.

As if I needed another one! I must find her. We have to find a way.

We must.

The reeve did not return to speak to them again.

Some time after midnight, Kaneth came, but a different Kaneth to the well-groomed man Jasper knew. He was dirty, tired, unshaven. There was blood on his clothing, and he reeked of sweat and crushed ziggers and death. He was so exhausted, Jasper had to hold back the water while he entered or they would all have been inundated.

Senya wrinkled her nose and said, "You stink, Lord Kaneth!"

They all ignored her. Laisa asked, her voice unusually rough, "What's the news?"

Jasper poured him a drink of amber as the rainlord replied: "The worst. They're in the city. In fact, I expected to find you gone. I thought I had better check, just to be sure you'd got out."

"The reeve never told us anything. We haven't heard from him since before dawn, just after the drums started," Laisa said.

"Ah. He was one of the casualties, I expect. And if there was a backup plan in case something went wrong, that also failed you. You should have gone just before dawn. That's when they entered the city."

"They've taken Breccia?" Jasper asked.

"We still hold the waterhall and Breccia Hall. Level One and Level Two. Mix some water with that, Jasper—I don't want to lose my edge. And get me some food. I need to build up my power." He sat down with a sigh. "There are so many Breccian dead. The guard is shattered. Lord Gold is dead. Other rainlords died. Merqual and the waterpriest Foqat for sure. I haven't seen Lord Selbat or Lord Meridan or Lord Porfrey or Lord Tourmaline, and nor has anyone else, so they are missing, too."

He took the mug and looked at Laisa. She read the look and said calmly, "He's dead?"

"Not—not yet. That I know of. But they do have him. He did a brilliant job, you know," Kaneth said.

"Who are you talking about?" Senya asked petulantly. "Who's captured?"

"They paraded him under the walls of Breccia Hall," Kaneth said. "He was, um, still alive. I'm sorry."

For the first time, Jasper saw Laisa lose her composure. Her face whitened. He understood then the double meaning in Kaneth's words and had to turn away to hide the dry heave that rose through him.

"You mean Papa?" Senya asked. "But he's a rainlord! They couldn't take him prisoner. He'd just suck the water out of them!"

No one said anything. Senya looked from one to another, then started to cry. For once, Laisa showed some compassion for her daughter. She reached out and gently pulled the girl to her, burying Senya's face in her shoulder.

"How many people do we have safe in Breccia Hall and the waterhall?" she asked after a pause. To Jasper's ears, she sounded inhumanly calm.

"About five or six thousand adults. It's packed up there. Too many are not fighters. There are so many children. It was hard to turn anyone away. We can hold out for a while. With a smaller area to defend, the rainlords still alive have a better chance."

"What's happening in the rest of the city?" Jasper asked, bringing a selection of food to Kaneth.

"The Reduners are telling people to stay indoors. If they don't, they are killed. They are slaughtering all reeves as soon as they identify them. And any Breccian guards, of course." He helped himself to some flat cakes stuffed with bab fruit.

Laisa tapped her fingernails impatiently on Senya's back. "There's something else you are not saying, Kaneth," she said.

"I'm getting to that. We had a message from Davim.

He says that he will spare the city, leave entirely, even give us back Nealrith . . . if we give him Jasper."

"Oh!" Senya exclaimed, tears forgotten. "Then we can do that! What does it matter? Jasper can go with the Reduners. They need a stormlord, so they won't hurt him. And he can still bring us rain."

Jasper shot her a look, then turned away. Neither Laisa nor Kaneth spoke. Kaneth doggedly continued eating. The silence dragged on.

Finally Jasper asked, "And if I don't go to him?"

"Nealrith dies, and Davim starts bringing out the city folk, ten at a time, to feed the ziggers. Ten people every hour."

"Did he give a deadline for the decision?"

"Sunset tomorrow. I've no idea why he gave us so long."

"He's probably smart enough to realise that it's something that would require some debate," Laisa said. "And by then he will have shown you in other ways that you can't win."

"He'll have his answer tomorrow," Jasper added tightly.

"No!" Senya cried. "It's not your decision, Jasper! It's ours! We can give you up if we like."

Jasper whipped around to face her. He said coldly, "With the death of your grandfather, I am now Cloudmaster, and you will not treat me with disrespect. Do I make myself clear?" His voice sounded confident and calm to his ears, but inside, both his resolution and his courage trembled. The blood burned in his cheeks.

Who am I trying to fool?

She stared at him, defiant. "You may be *a* stormlord,

but Grandfather didn't appoint you as his heir. You're not the Cloudmaster, Shale Flint! Taquar was to be the high ruler, not you. You're just a dirty Gibber rat!"

"Taquar's claim to the position was revoked at the Gratitudes festival," he said.

"But Grandfather died without naming anyone else," she pointed out triumphantly. "And Mama said that means it could revert to the last named heir—Taquar."

Her words gored him. Whatever had given him his moment of strength, of resolution, was ripped apart by her words. He turned to Laisa and Kaneth, unwilling to believe. "Is that true?"

Laisa nodded. Kaneth demurred. "Only if the Council of Rainlords agrees," he said.

Jasper went taut, every part of him strained with anger and betrayal, as if there was something inside him that was too big to be contained.

The look Laisa gave him was one of pity. "Jasper, Granthon had a point. You are very young to rule. And to be the Quartern's one and only stormlord at the same time?" She shrugged. "You know how tiring it is." He heard her unspoken taunt. *How inadequate you are.*

He was silent.

She continued, "You will have Taquar's power to back you. You may be able to call up storms with his help. You will be the most revered of the Quartern's citizens, its stormshifter. There won't be any question this time of Taquar keeping you imprisoned in some mother cistern somewhere."

He was silent long enough to control his rage, to be able to say quietly, "I doubt that Davim has included Taquar in his present plans. For myself, I don't care too much about whether I rule as Cloudmaster, but I will not take orders from Taquar or Davim. Not *ever*. And until such time as Davim takes power in Breccia City, *I* will make the decisions here, at least the ones that concern me and the ones that concern water." He looked back at Senya. "And my name is Jasper Bloodstone."

For a moment, he thought she was going to defy him. Then all her bravado drained away, and he was reminded that she was, after all, just a spoiled girl whose world was breaking up around her, who had just been told that her father was a hostage to a desert warrior not known for his compassion. She nodded, subdued and sulky.

Wonderful, he thought. *The first thing you do with your authority is lord it over a silly half-grown girl.*

He looked at Laisa. "Rainlord?"

She shrugged indifferently. "As you wish."

"Kaneth?"

The rainlord gave an ironical bow. The curve of his lips, the knowing smile, told Jasper that he wasn't fooling the man. Kaneth knew exactly how he quaked inside, how inadequate he felt. How inadequate he *was*.

Jasper said, "I need to know everything from now on, no matter what."

His mouth full, Kaneth waved a half-eaten flat cake indicating his acquiescence. He swallowed and said, "You can't surrender yourself to Davim, anyway. He could kill you, and then we'd be as good as gutted."

"I am aware of that," Jasper said. He was ashamed of his relief. Struggling to hide it, he added, "My death would be the best way to ensure another era of random rain and a new age of the nomad."

Laisa made an exasperated noise. "Watergiver's heart!

None of that matters much now. What we have to do is decide when to leave."

"Best wait until tomorrow," Kaneth said. "At sunset. Davim will be at the gates of the Hall, and so will most of his men. They will have fewer guards on the periphery then, and you'll have a better chance of escape. We'll prolong the discussion, try to bargain with him. Then we'll tell him you've already gone—a fact you will have to make obvious to the guards in the groves as you leave."

Jasper turned and went to stand by the fireplace. He kicked at a still-glowing coal that had rolled onto the hearth. Six thousand people. Plus who knows how many children. People like Ryka. City folk, ten at a time, to feed the ziggers. And who had the chance to walk away from all this? Jasper Bloodstone. Not to mention Laisa and Senya.

When he turned back to face the three of them, he felt old, as ancient and as harshly sculptured as Wash Drybone. He said, "Yes, I agree. Come back here tomorrow to tell us if there's any change."

Kaneth nodded. There was pity in the rainlord's eyes as he turned towards the door.

"I'll open it," Jasper said. "You conserve your strength." He walked Kaneth to the bottom of the ladder. "About Rith," he said softly. "Where did they take him? Is there any chance he'll live?"

"He was in—in poor shape. Tortured. Someone must have told them that a weakened man can't renew his power. Even if they gave him back to us, I don't think he'd live. I heard from one of the reeves who came through the tunnel later that they put him in some kind of cage and strung it up over the South Gate."

They exchanged a glance, sharing their grief. *He's known Rith since they were children,* Jasper thought. *His closest friend.* The pain of his loss, the agony of knowing there was no way of going back—it was written there on his face.

"Cloudmaster," Kaneth said and inclined his head; and because he was Kaneth, there was raillery mixed with the respect. Jasper smiled slightly and watched as the rainlord climbed to the manhole above.

When he returned to the room, Laisa said, "You've come a long way, Jasper Bloodstone, late of Wash Drybone Settle. It was kind of Kaneth not to mention your lack of cloudmaking abilities." The eyes were beautiful, but the look she gave him was hard. "And apart from that, you're only, what, eighteen maybe? Nineteen at the outside. What do you know of ruling? Of war? Of the affairs of men?" She was patronising him still, but she was wary of him now, in a way she had never been before.

"More than some learn in a lifetime, Laisa. Believe me, I have learned fast of late."

"If you die, my lord, so does a land. That is quite a responsibility."

"I know."

Dear Watergiver, I know.

CHAPTER FORTY-SIX

Scarpen Quarter
Breccia City

"Where do you think you are going?"

Jasper swallowed a sigh. He might have known his manipulating of the water lock would wake Laisa, even if lighting the lantern hadn't.

"Out," he said.

"After what I said about responsibility?" she asked. "You can't take water from a man or a zigger! How will you survive out there? Are you sandcrazy?"

"I found out yesterday that I don't have to take water out of a zigger to kill it. And you know what? I think rainlords have got so used to doing things the one way, the same way, year after year, that they have forgotten just how powerful water is. I will take no risks that I cannot handle. None, I promise."

She looked over her shoulder to make sure Senya was asleep and dropped her voice to a furious whisper. "Jasper, if you are going after Nealrith, remember this: you are much more important than he is. Let it be, for all our sakes."

"He's your husband! The father of your daughter. How can you be so uncaring?"

"Don't be a fool. I care. I am the wife of a city's ruler. I do not give that up easily, believe me. But I am first and foremost a rainlord and a pragmatic woman. What happens to Nealrith is of no importance when compared to what happens to you. He would be the first to say so. And if you were to die rescuing him, he would never forgive you the stupidity."

"You have made your point," he said. "And I know it, anyway."

Behind her, Senya stirred and raised herself on one elbow. "Is it morning?" she asked sleepily.

Laisa ignored her. "I don't suppose I can stop you. You can't go back to the same tunnel we used before, you know. It doesn't have an opening into the city."

"I know." He would have to use the tunnel that supplied the cistern with its water. The entrance to that, a lidded hole, was in the middle of the cistern roof, out of reach. And there was no ladder, either.

He opened both the doors with care, his mind focusing on the water beyond. It was odd to stand there and look into the water, knowing that if his concentration slipped it would come crashing into the room. His forehead furrowed, he pushed the wall of water away with his power until the level in the centre of the room rose. When it was close to touching the roof, he stopped. Laisa stood beside him in the doorway, studying his handiwork.

"Ingenious," she said, her respect reluctant.

He dived sideways into the water, using part of his concentration to keep the lantern dry, even though he himself had to get wet because he needed to swim upwards to reach the manhole in the ceiling. Once there, he found it wasn't easy to open up the cover from underneath. His sword hindered him; his saturated clothes became heavier by the moment; the lighted lantern in one hand was an encumbrance. He began to sink.

Idiot, he thought. *Use your power.*

He made a pillar of water and pushed it against the lid until it flew open. He surfaced once more, reached up and placed the lantern on the floor of the supply tunnel, and hoisted himself out. He looked back down into the cistern to make sure that Laisa had shut the door to the room, before allowing the water to find its own level once more. Sitting on the edge of the hole, he removed the water from his clothing. When he was dry once more, he stood up and raised the lamp to look around. The door to the Cistern Chambers of the thirtieth level was directly opposite him. Leaving the cistern lid lying where it had been tossed by the pillar of water, he went to try the handle.

The door was unlocked.

Back in the room, Laisa remarked, "That man is a great deal stronger in power than we have been giving him credit for."

Senya pouted. "He's a sunfried Gibber grubber. And I don't want to marry him!"

"You fool!" Laisa exclaimed. "Have you no common sense?"

"I don't know what you mean."

"Jasper is your future, you stupid child. Alienate him and you're lost, because your power is barely scraping through to rainlord level. It won't get you anywhere, and neither will your looks if all you ever do is whine and complain and pout." Restlessly she paced the floor. "Can't you see? It doesn't *matter* if he was once a Gibber brat. It doesn't matter if he doesn't know how to use a fingerbowl or doesn't want to wear perfume. What matters is that he is the only person approaching stormlord status in the Quartern. Power, Senya, *power*. That's what it's all about. With power you can have wealth and comfort and riches and control. Without it, you might lose all those things. Marry him and *you* will have power."

"Comfort? Riches? We have already lost those things," Senya wailed. "We're stuck in this room hiding and scared, and by now there's probably Reduners in my bedroom pawing all my things. Jasper's a nobody—worse than a nobody! He's going to die, just like Daddy and Grandpa! And then where will we be?" She dissolved into a storm of weeping.

Her mother made no effort to comfort her.

The man who lay in front of the Cistern Chamber's main door to the street wore a tunic with a reeve's insignia. He had been speared in the back. Jasper was overwhelmed with the stench; the man must have been dead some time, lying out in the heat until nightfall.

Out in the darkened city, there was an odd smell in the air, all-pervading: a strong mix of rot, cooking meat, smoke and acridity. Jasper coughed as he stepped into the street, but there was no one to hear him. He stood still for a moment, pushing his water senses ahead. It was difficult; at a distance, all water tended to merge. Was that a man in a nearby house or someone walking in the street parallel? He couldn't tell.

He sent his powers back to the cistern to change water

to vapour—easy enough when he was not dealing with salt water—then wisped it out through the doors and into the open air. A cloud formed, white and damp and thick. He wrapped it around himself as he descended towards the lowest level, so that he trailed mist like an ethereal spirit from another world or a shimmering sand-dancer, perhaps, walking the deserted streets.

When he reached the thirty-seventh level, he took an outside staircase going up to a rooftop. Even though there was no light, he sensed there were people there, including children. That, he decided, ruled out the possibility of Reduners. Nonetheless, he was cautious and paused before setting foot on the walled flat rooftop. His lamp revealed a couple and two children aged about six and eight. They were huddled together sleeping, well wrapped in rough bab-fibre blankets against the bitter cold of a desert night. All Scarpen people, by their colouring. No one to fear. He released some of his hold on the vapour, allowing it to disperse and become less obvious in the night air.

They feared him, though, when he woke them. They stared, their eyes round and terrified, their arms clutching at one another. "There's no need to be frightened of me," he said softly. He held the lantern up so that they could see his face. "Do you know who I am?"

The man shook his head.

"I'm a rainlord," Jasper said. "I've come because I want to know what is happening in the lower levels of the city."

"Rainlord!" The man looked shocked. He knelt, scrambling out of his blankets. "Please, m'lord, don't stand there like a practice butt for the spearing. They may see you!"

He spread the blanket out on the rooftop. "If the lord'll sit hisself—" He turned to his wife. "A drink, a drink!"

She rose to obey, too shocked to speak. Jasper knew enough to be aware that he must accept the water they gave him, no matter if they could ill afford to spare it. He sat and inclined his head in acceptance. "Your name?"

"Chellis, rainlord, shoveller at the smelters, outside the walls."

Jasper gave a swift look around. There was no furniture, none. Just the blackened mud-bricks at one end of the roof that served as a fireplace, the four dayjars, the woven sleeping mats that doubled as shelter from the sun when strung from balustrade to balustrade. A man so poor he could only afford a rooftop for his family, but at least he had water entitlement. He worked, and he had the right to live on the thirty-seventh level.

"I want something other than water," Jasper said softly. "Information. I want to know everything that happened today."

In the end, Jasper was surprised to find out just how much the man did know. The townsfolk had found numerous ways to exchange information, the linked houses and common rooftops having become news routes. Streets were left to the Reduners, but the townsfolk commanded the rooftops, and those who could read and write would throw a note across the road to the house opposite, passing on information.

The first part of the attack had been bad, even though they'd had warning. When the ziggers came, Chellis and his family had pulled the bab matting over themselves. Successive waves of ziggers buzzed them for the next few hours, defeated by the tough matting. Eventually they left the petrified family alone to find easier prey.

By mid-morning of the next day, Chellis had heard Reduners in the streets, shouting in their strange accents. One of them came up the stairs and dragged Chellis out to help clear the streets of bodies, and that was what he'd done for the rest of the day. It had been a horrible job. Not everyone had heard the warning. Not everyone had heeded it. Many of the dead were his neighbours, people he had known all his life. Many were children, killed when ziggers entered windows through open shutters.

The corpses had to be piled up on the back of packpedes and carted outside the city, where they were burned on a pyre.

Jasper felt sick. "Oh—oh, sweet water, that's what I can smell!" Human flesh *cooking*.

Chellis nodded, then continued with his tale. He told of how he had seen fighting, of how he had seen the last of the city's guard overwhelmed by frightening numbers of Reduner warriors and their ferocious mounts in the streets of the city itself, right to the walls of Breccia Hall. "Must of been rainlords there," he said. "I saw Reduners fall with the water sucked out of 'em. Saw 'em with dried-up eyes—hundreds of 'em, as blind as sand-leeches in their holes. The Reduners kill 'em, y'know, the blind ones. Slaughter 'em, their own tribesmen."

"Have you seen the rainlord prisoner?"

"The highlord? They strung 'im up in a cage over the South Gate. Every time we went out with the bodies and came back in, we had to go under 'im. Could hear him moanin'. And I saw blood drippin'. Then by nightfall, didn't hear no more. Reckon he died."

Jasper shook his head. *No. Not Nealrith.* He refused to believe it. "Where are all the Reduners now?" he asked.

"Big camp outside the walls. Hear tell they don't like roofs over their heads, Reduners. Then there's a ring of guards along the city walls and a second ring around Breccia Hall and the waterhall. They haven't broken into Level Two yet. And none of us can leave the city 'cept under guard to work for them red bastards."

Jasper thanked the man for his information and hid some tokens from his purse under the mat he was seated on. As he stood up to go, Chellis pointed to his lantern. Jasper had turned the wick down low, but it still burned. "Careful with that, my lord. Don't know why 'tis, but the ziggers like the light."

"What makes you say that?"

"I saw a lot of bodies today, my lord. More than one should see in a whole lifetime, I reckon. Most of them had zigger holes. But time and again, I saw more ziggers burned up against a lamp glass than holes in the man that had held the lantern. So many of the little buggers! I reckon they got attracted by the light. Be careful."

"I'll bear that in mind. Thank you, both of you. You have served the Scarpen and Breccia well today." Formal language, suitable for a ruler. All he had to offer, but perhaps it helped.

Back on the street again, he headed for the fortieth level and the South Gate.

It was exactly as Chellis had described: a cage swinging in the gateway, just high enough for a man to walk under without ducking his head. At this time of night, of course, the gate was closed. Several Reduner guards lounged by the postern, clearly visible in the light of the torches in the wall brackets. Harder to see, but present nonetheless, were the guards at their posts along the top of the wall, two men every thirty paces or so, silhouetted against the starlit sky. So *many* of them. And not, surely, because they expected attack from outside; these were to keep Scarpermen from leaving the city, to stop rainlords and reeves escaping.

To stop Jasper Bloodstone.

His lamp extinguished, his mist dissipated so he could watch, he flattened himself against the wall of a house at the corner of the street, until he was sure he had seen or sensed all there was to know nearby. The guards were inattentive, talking about the day's events in the language of the Quartern, describing how this one had died or how they themselves had killed. Laughing about the man swinging in his cage. One of them jabbed his chala spear through the bars. "Is dead, you think?"

"Dune gods prevent, hope not," another replied in a thick Reduner accent. "Sandmaster wanted bastard alive long time. Likes to see enemies in pain, not dead and dried, he does."

A third man stirred uneasily as he looked up at the cage. "I don't know 'bout that meself. What's t'stop this shrivelled water-waster from suckin' the water out of our eyes like he did with all th'others?" The accent was pure Gibber, not Reduner, which might have explained why the two Reduners were not speaking their own tongue. Jasper thought instantly of Mica, and the physical pain almost brought him to his knees.

But Mica would never have joined the Reduners. Never.

He stared hard at the man nonetheless, and was relieved to see he was much older than Mica would have been.

"Too weak," the second man replied. "Bleed them, make hungry, and lords too weak to use powers."

"Sandmaster Davim's not cruel just to hurt," the first man added. "This"—he waved a hand at the cage—"teach Scarpermen lesson they never forget: men of the dunes are powerful! Can put rainlord in cage like animal. Can rip out rainlord's tongue or throw away highlord's balls, no trouble."

Jasper's rage ploughed through him, to shred his fear into oblivion. He gathered the vapour, teasing mist around him like softened bab fibres onto a spindle. It swirled in damp eddies, laid its tendrils against his skin, coated his hair with moisture. The sensual pleasure of being in a cloud, of the feel of water in the air about him, of the unaccustomed dampness—it stirred his anger to a cutting fury. And he stepped out onto the open street.

"What the—! Look!" one of the men said, in Reduner this time. He added a string of Reduner vulgarities Jasper remembered from his childhood.

Jasper smiled. He thickened the mist in front of him to obscure his form as he walked forward, leaving only a small hole unobstructed so he could see. "Smoke?" the Gibberman suggested, more puzzled than worried.

"Don't smell like no smoke."

The two Reduners exchanged agitated glances. The first of the mist trailed across their faces.

"It's wet!" one cried, and added something in Reduner.

Jasper's power poured through his anger to seize more water from the air, from the dew on the trees beyond the wall, from wherever he could find it. He had to stop them calling for help. His idea was as coldly merciless as it was clear. He couldn't take someone's water, but he could drown them.

They didn't understand at first, of course. Each had a ball of water clamped across his mouth and nose, and nothing, nothing would dislodge it. They tried to bat it away, scoop it off, scrape it from them, but their hands just ran through the water without effect. They didn't breathe it in either, because Jasper moulded it to hold its shape. They couldn't breathe at all.

As they sank to their knees, choking, eyes bulging, terror blinding them to anything except survival, Jasper cleared the vapour away so they could see him. "I will let you breathe," he said quietly, "but don't try to run or shout for help—or you will die. I am a rainlord, and you know my power." His voice grated in his ears, allowing no promise of pity. He peeled back the water from their faces and bundled it into individual globes that hovered by the cheek of each man. "I want you to lower the cage to the ground."

One of the men, gasping for air, reached for the loaded zigtube hooked into his belt. In one fluid movement, he had it pointed at Jasper. He tapped the side.

Nothing happened. "It's already dead," Jasper said. "I drowned it."

The man stared at the tube. It dripped water.

"Do you want to die that way yourself? Or would you rather end up a dried-out husk?" Jasper brushed the globe against the man's cheek, rolling it across his nose to the other side of his face. It left a trail of wetness behind.

The man trembled and shook his head.

"Then lower the cage."

They untied the rope from the wall and eased it through the pulley, a simple job for several men to do together. Their stricken gaze flicked from water globe to the task and back again. Even in the cool of the night, they sweated. One tried to speak, so Jasper jammed the water ball in his mouth. It squashed, but he couldn't spit it out. Only when he choked did Jasper take pity on him.

"I told you not to speak," he said.

The cage reached the ground. Jasper stepped forward—and saw the horror in detail then. A man once. Tortured beyond comprehension until his humanity was blurred. Alive, yes, but not living. Existing only in a welter of hopeless pain.

The cage had no door; it had been soldered together. The space was too small for a grown man to sit or lie or stand. The thing inside could only hunch with his head bowed down. He still wore a tunic, but no trousers.

It was Nealrith . . . but not the Nealrith that Jasper knew. His eye sockets gaped, half-filled with congealed blood; there were no eyeballs. His lower face was swollen and torn. His mouth sagged open; there was no tongue. There was blood on the floor of the cage. A lot of it. And body wastes and a water skin.

Jasper knelt beside the bars.

"Rith?" he asked. His tone was assured, calm. He did not know how he could sound like that.

Hearing his voice, Nealrith started, but only barely.

"It's me, Jasper. I've come to get you out." Soothing. Reasonable. *Lies*.

Nealrith made a movement of his hand, a gesture of rejection.

"I'm all right, don't worry." Jasper knelt beside the cage. "You," he said to a Reduner, "bring one of the torches here." The tight fury in his voice had the man scuttling to do as he was bidden, especially as the water globe remained tethered to his cheek.

The added light revealed more injuries to Nealrith's body. The blood had dried, and his tunic had stuck to his skin, so it was impossible to see what had happened, but Jasper thought he knew anyway: the rainlord had been castrated. Or worse.

He raised his gaze to the three men cowering from him near the wall. "And you could laugh about this," he said. "What kind of men are you?" His voice was soft, yet his rage thundered from him, carrying the fullness of his fury. They knew better than to reply. He reached in and took Nealrith's hand. "I can get you out of here," he said. He had no idea how.

Nealrith moved his head, a slight shake. Painfully, he raised a hand and drew it across his throat. Then he pointed to himself. There could be no doubt what he meant.

"No!" *Please don't ask that of me*. He said, desperate, begging, "We can fight on, Rith. You will always have your water-sense. You can use it to see."

The hand he held gripped him tightly, squeezing, hurting him. Once more the rainlord gestured for his own death. And then his hand dropped away, groping across the bottom of the cage. When he touched the stickiness of the blood there, he used a finger to trace out: "Senya?"

"She's safe. So is Laisa."

More letters drawn in blood. "Marry. Children, hope."

Jasper swallowed, unable to say quite what Nealrith wanted to hear. "I will take care of her, I promise you."

"My city?" the highlord scrawled.

He couldn't tell the whole truth. "The waterhall and Breccia Hall hold yet. I will leave with Senya and Laisa soon, just in case. And you can come with us."

The finger moved in the blood again, tracing letters over those he had already written. "Dying. Pain. Please." Then he tapped the bars. The implication was clear: how would Jasper free him, anyway?

Jasper sat back on his heels, trying to rid himself of the choking lump in his throat. He could choose not to do it. Once again, a choice that was no choice at all.

Nealrith, I can't—

As if he had heard the unspoken words, Nealrith traced more letters in his own spilled blood: "You can." His other hand tightened on Jasper's.

Jasper struggled to give voice to what he needed to say, the heartfelt truth. "I wish—I wish we had known each other in better times, my lord. I understand what you tried to do, the way you tried to rule your city, and why. I wish you could have been my father. Although I would have been a poor son."

A smile ghosted on the tortured mouth, and Nealrith's hand patted his. He mouthed and gestured to make the words clear: "You will father my grandchildren."

Jasper bit his lip and struggled to find the right words of ritual. "You are a true rainlord," he said finally. "Your water is precious to us." He licked his dry lips. "I will be safe, I promise, and Taquar will never rule this land. Never. And neither will Davim."

The wounded man nodded.

"Are you ready, Highlord Nealrith of Breccia?" But as he spoke the words, he hesitated. *I can't.*

And then, with his last strength, Nealrith gathered vapour from the air to form letters, as if this was his last defiance, his last action as a mover of water, his last benediction. Lighted by the flickering torches, the letters danced red in the air in front of the cage: *Farewell, Cloudmaster*. And his ravaged mouth smiled. It was a travesty, a rictus of blood, but he did it for Jasper.

Jasper braced himself against his own revulsion. "Goodbye, Rith," he said. The huskiness of his voice made him sound old. He sought the comforting words of the funeral ritual the waterpriests had taught him: "Go back to the living water. Be at one with life."

Nealrith indicated his readiness.

And Jasper thrust his sword into the cage and slit the rainlord's throat. Nealrith fell forward against the bars. Blood pulsed, then slowed. A hand went into spasm, then was still.

The first man he had ever killed, and it had to be the man he had come to most honour, to most admire. A man he would have liked to call father. And he couldn't even take his water in a final gesture of respect. He'd had to use his sword.

There was a sharp intake of breath from one of the Reduners, and the Gibberman doubled over, retching. All that was left of Nealrith hardly looked human any more. Jasper struggled to rise.

"I could kill you all now," he told the guards from between gritted teeth. It was true; his revulsion at Nealrith's death had banished all compassion. And they believed him. The Gibberman tried to speak, but Jasper slapped the water over his mouth, gagging him. He struggled to speak anyway. None of the sounds made any sense. The

Reduner beside him glared. The Gibberman sagged to his knees, gesturing, grunting.

Jasper knew what he was trying to say: I am a Gibberman like you. Not one of them. The Reduner lashed out and sent the grovelling man sprawling in the dust. The tribesman glared at Jasper and folded his arms in defiance. The second Reduner moaned and huddled against the wall, trying to make himself look small. Jasper gagged both of them as well, but refrained from covering their noses this time. Then he stumbled away, sickened.

Just before reaching the street that led upwards, he turned back. The Gibberman scrambled up on his knees. They stared at each other across the space, and for a moment Jasper knew they were thinking the same thing: there had been a time when they were not much different. Grubby Gibber brats from a drywash town somewhere, eking out an existence as best they could.

"Did you ever meet a man called Mica?" Jasper asked him. "About the same age as me? From—"

He stopped. The man's expression told Jasper he was torn, trying to decide whether a yes or a no would bring him most benefit.

There was no way to know if the answer was going to be honest. Jasper turned to walk away. A desperate grunting made him glance back over his shoulder. The man uttered a few more guttural sounds without opening his mouth, and then repeated them. Jasper stood, rooted, wanting to hear, wanting to believe. He decided to give the man a chance to speak. He allowed the water to peel away from the Gibberman's mouth. But instead of speaking, he shrieked and dropped. Behind him, the defiant Reduner stood swaying: he'd jammed a knife into the hapless Gibberman's ribs. Without thinking, Jasper expanded the water to cover the tribesman's nose as well as his mouth.

Someone shouted from the top of the wall. Voices responded. A Reduner on the wall pointed in Jasper's direction. Hurriedly, Jasper clutched the mist around himself once more, grabbed up his lantern and left at a shambling run. It was all he could manage.

By the time additional tribesmen arrived at the gate, he was no more than a white patch rolling upwards, misty gossamer in the dimness of starlight. The newcomers looked from the bloodied cage, to the dead Gibberman, to the guard dying as he gasped for air he could not find, to the other Reduner with water held, impossibly, over his mouth—and then to that unearthly shape.

Not one of them chose to follow in pursuit.

Jasper blundered on, hearing over and over the name he was sure the Gibberman had tried to utter: *Wash Drybone. Wash Drybone.*

The man had known a man named Mica from Wash Drybone Settle.

CHAPTER FORTY-SEVEN

Scarpen Quarter
Breccia City

"What happened?" Kaneth asked. His normal insouciance was gone; what had replaced it was hard-edged and angry.

"He insisted on going out alone. When he came back he was like this." Laisa looked down at the sleeping form on the pallet. "Absolutely exhausted."

"He almost drowned us all," Senya said. It had happened hours before, but her words still crackled with indignation.

"He came stumbling through the door," Laisa explained, "and collapsed where he is now. He let go of his hold on the water in the cistern, and if I hadn't been quick, it would have come pouring in the door with the force of a rush down a Gibber wash."

"And all he could say was that Nealrith was dead?"

"He said that much, and then he just wasn't here any more. At first, I wasn't sure if he was asleep or unconscious, but I think it's just sleep."

Kaneth knelt at the edge of the pallet and shook Jasper's shoulder, hard.

Jasper stirred restlessly, muttering. "I killed him." His head tossed from side to side. "I killed him."

"Come on, Jasper, wake up."

Jasper's eyes flew open. For a long moment, he didn't know where he was. For a moment, the horror of the dream seemed unreal; then he remembered. It wasn't a dream. He had killed Nealrith.

"Kaneth . . ." he said, but couldn't go on.

"Are you all right?" Kaneth asked.

Jasper sat up slowly and replied even more slowly. "Yes," he said at last. "Tired. Very, very tired."

"You should eat," Kaneth reached out a hand and helped him heave himself to his feet. "You should eat a lot. You've been over-using your water-powers."

"Oh, Kaneth," he groaned, "I thought I could save Nealrith. But they had him in a cage that had no door. And they had—" He stopped, suddenly aware that he was also talking within the hearing of Nealrith's wife and daughter. "I am sorry, Laisa, Senya. He died. I was holding his hand."

Laisa raised an eyebrow. "You killed him?"

Senya's eyes grew round. "You *killed* him? You killed my father?"

Jasper was silent.

"He asked you to?" Laisa suggested.

"He knew he did not have long to live, and no man would want to live another moment like that . . ." He trailed off. "It was his wish."

Senya glared at him with righteous hatred, her chin quivering. Her mother stepped in, gripped her arm tightly, and said without expression, "I am sure you did what was best, Jasper."

"*Best?*" Senya's fury was about to explode, but Laisa

tightened her hold in warning, and Senya took refuge in a storm of hysterical tearless weeping instead.

Jasper and Kaneth sat in awkward silence at the table. Jasper hunted for something to say, but it was Kaneth who spoke first. "That took courage. Would that we all could have such friends at the last. You will make a fine Cloudmaster, Jasper."

Jasper winced. "Is that what makes a good ruler? The ability to kill when you need to? Anyway, I'm not even a stormlord. We all know that." His stomach heaved. "What time of day is it?" he asked. Anything not to remember. Not to feel the grief swelling unasked in his throat.

"Midday."

"What's the situation?"

"Not much different. We are holding them off from Breccia Hall and the water hall still. The rest of the city is theirs. We have been in contact with the lower city, and many reeves have been killed, at least the ones they could find. The guards were wiped out, except for the one hundred or so men we have with us. Reduners have tried a few times to break in through the tunnels, without success so far. We haven't lost any more rainlords, and we've managed to blind about another hundred of them. It's not pretty."

"How much longer can you hold out?"

"It depends on what they do. They could maintain a siege to spare their warriors an assault on the walls. We could last for half a cycle if they did that, but patience is not their strong point. I think they will try to persuade us to surrender by killing the townsfolk in front of our eyes instead. We could try to save as many ordinary citizens as possible by surrendering the city on agreed terms."

"Could we trust a Reduner to hold to such an agreement?" Laisa asked.

"Probably not. If we don't agree to their terms, then my feeling is they'll gather everything they have and storm the walls and tunnels at the same time. As long as they don't mind losing a lot of men, they will win in a day or two." He went to one of the cupboards and took out a jar, broke the seal and poured some stewed grain and palm sugar into a bowl, which he set in front of Jasper. "You must eat."

To his surprise, Jasper was suddenly ravenous. He ate, hardly bothering to note what it was. "How much do we know about what happened in Qanatend after they entered it?" he asked.

"Nothing. No one got through to us. Ryka says they have a past history of offering children from about eight to sixteen a choice between being made slaves, or becoming Reduner wives or whores or warriors. Adults are either killed or ignored."

"Slavery is banned," Senya pointed out. She had stopped crying; now her eyes just glowered at Jasper, smouldering in outrage.

Kaneth raised an eyebrow. "Do you seriously think a Quartern law is a barrier to Davim's endorsement of slavery?"

When she didn't reply, it was Jasper who explained, curbing his irritation. "The Reduners were always the ones who liked the end of slavery least. Tribal wars always ended with people of one tribe being slaves of another. Easy enough to return to old ways, if they shake off the rule of the Cloudmaster."

"How can you possibly know all that?" Senya asked.

He ignored her scorn and said to Kaneth, "I had hoped I would be strong enough to—to do more."

Kaneth shook his head. "You shouldn't have gone, Jasper. You are too valuable to risk." He gave a bitter laugh. "It is hardly your fault that you don't have the strength to take on an armed force of thousands. Any change in your plan?"

Laisa raised an eyebrow. "Are we to let this untried youth suggest the strategy now, Kaneth?"

The two men ignored the comment. Jasper answered Kaneth, saying, "No. Sunset tonight, I will make it clear to the Reduners that Jasper Bloodstone is leaving the city." He gave an agitated gesture with one hand. "Before they start killing the hostages, you must start to negotiate surrender terms. You and any other rainlords and reeves who are still alive must try to leave through the tunnels at the moment of surrender. And Lady Ethelva. She is still alive, I hope."

"I heard she was in Breccia Hall. I haven't seen her, though." Kaneth took a deep breath. "We've talked about it, Jasper. All of us. And we've decided that no matter what, we rainlords must stay."

Jasper stared at him in dismay. "But *why*? I need you. The Scarpen needs you. We need every rainlord we have—we need your children, even."

"This is my city. I wasn't born here, but I've been a rainlord here since I was much younger than you are now. How can I turn my back and walk away from the people of Breccia? It would be like saying they don't mean anything to me. That my life is more important than theirs."

"Kaneth, *it is*. Sandblast you, isn't that what you have all been saying to me since I got here? Rainlords are valuable! Anyway, the ordinary citizens have a chance of getting through this alive. You don't, unless you leave. That's a fundamental difference."

Kaneth shrugged. "Too bad. We are the rainlords of Breccia, and we must be seen to fight for the people of our city, or surrender with them. It is as simple as that."

"They'll kill you. They can't afford to let a rainlord live!"

"Probably. Jasper, our guess is that they will offer no terms of surrender, certainly not one that includes a rainlord. Davim is a warrior, and he wants to take us by storm. Even if we handed you over, he would still storm our walls. That, to him, is glory."

"And Ryka?"

Pain flitted across his face, and then was gone. "I cannot make decisions for her. We have argued about this, I will admit, but she won't leave, either. She's as stubborn as granite is hard, that woman."

"If I order you, as your Cloudmaster?"

Kaneth gave a lopsided smile. "Ah, Jasper, I'd hate to think that the first time you gave me a direct order, I would disobey it."

"You ask *me* to do what you will not do yourself: live for the Quartern rather than die for it." Frustrated, he glared at the rainlord.

"Yes, I know. I was always fond of irony."

"If we go back to a Time of Random Rain, the watersense of every rainlord will be needed. And what about Ethelva? She is not a rainlord."

"Do you really imagine *she* would leave?" Kaneth asked gently. "None of us are desperate to die, you know. We will do our best to escape in the end, I promise you.

And some of us doubtless will—we know the tunnels and water locks of this city as they do not. But in the meantime, we will fight until we have nothing more to give. The fall of Breccia will cost the Red Quarter more than they can spare. They will mourn more warriors than they ever dreamed of losing, and perhaps, just perhaps, those losses will stop them from attacking another city."

"It would be different if I was already a cloudmaster with power enough to bring the storms," Jasper said bitterly. If the rainlords believed there was a stormlord who could supply water to the Quartern, then they would believe in a future. And they might therefore decide that it was their duty to live to serve their people. As it was, they had no faith in Jasper's ability, and no hope. And so they would die fighting.

Jasper sighed and thought of Terelle and how she had always wanted life to be fair. "I'll make you all a promise, Kaneth. Rainlords will rule here again one day. *I* will rule here one day. Not Taquar. Not Davim. Me. And everyone who fought here will be remembered."

Kaneth gave a laugh, but there was no amusement there. "Just make sure it's for my death, Jasper, not the way I lived. That was nothing spectacular, as I am sure you have realised. The only wise thing I ever did was marry Ryka, and I almost ruined my chances with her by behaving like a withering waste of water." He glanced at Laisa, who was watching them both with folded arms and a bemused expression. "Beware of Laisa. She is indubitably a beautiful woman and a highly intelligent one. She is also quite amoral."

"Thank you, Kaneth, for that," she said, inclining her head in mock deference. "I don't believe you will be any great loss to the world, either."

Kaneth ignored her. "Cloudmaster Jasper Bloodstone, may the waters always be sweet to your taste."

He picked up his lamp, and Jasper went to open the door and clear the water for him.

Afterwards, Laisa remarked, "Who would have thought? Kaneth, of all people. A hero."

"Don't mock him," Jasper snapped. "None of them. Not ever."

Jasper crawled out of the grove cistern onto its flat covered roof and tried to sense what lay beyond without raising his head to see.

People. Far too many people. And animals. Pedes. Carefully he tried to build a picture from the water he could feel out there. Reduner pedemen everywhere. Mostly sitting in groups. And the pedes were in lines, which probably meant they were tied up. He rolled over onto his side as Laisa and Senya arrived beside him. Senya's skirt was wet again. Impatient with the way it hampered her movements, he sent the water back to where it belonged. When Laisa went to close the cistern lid, he stopped her.

"I will need the water," he said.

She nodded, understanding.

"There are people everywhere," he continued. "There's a camp, a huge Reduner camp all the way along the grove. We've got to be quiet."

Laisa raised her head to look. "A diversion?" she suggested a moment later.

"Yes. Which direction do we have to go in?"

She pointed. "That way. Up the scarp, but at an angle, cutting across, towards the west. Not too close to the city wall. Our pedes are in a hidden gully near the top of the escarpment, about two hours' walk. Maybe more in the dark."

"There's no danger that they will have been found? No chance we will walk into a trap?"

She didn't bother to answer. It had been a stupid question, of course. She couldn't possibly know the answer to the first part, but they could sense a trap before it was sprung. They were water sensitives, after all.

He crawled to the edge of the roof and peered over. "We can jump down, no problem." He eyed Senya's skirt in distaste. "You should have worn travelling clothes; however can you run in a skirt?"

"I don't *like* trousers," she said. "I'm not a man."

"Get ready to jump and run," he said, smothering a sigh. "Don't wait for me. Laisa, can you take my pack and water?"

"They have to see you leave," Laisa said, pointing out the obvious as she took his things.

"They will. The sun's setting, but it won't be fully dark for a while."

And let's hope they don't kill the hostages anyway. They might, Jasper knew that. But he had no choice. He had to stay alive, in the hope that he would eventually find a way to bring water to the Quartern.

He reached out with his water-power and sucked some water out of the cistern. Carefully raising his head to peep, he sent the water in a thin line through the gloaming to one of the palms near a camp fire at the far end of the camp. Once it was there, he dumped it on the old palm fronds sagging from the bab palm's underskirt. One by one, under the sudden weight of water, the fronds snapped at the base and fell to the ground. Several Reduners sitting beneath the tree were hit, and the fronds were heavy. Someone yelled, and men shouted warnings as more sodden branches came crashing down. All heads swung in that direction. "Now," he said to Laisa and Senya. "Jump!"

They both obeyed. Jasper repeated his trick with another tree. This time, the fronds dropped into a camp fire, and there was a billow of smoke. Then he himself jumped and ran. Behind him, there was pandemonium as more wet branches fell and put a camp fire out. The line of tethered myriapedes baulked and twisted and reared, screaming their panic in ululating wails. The sound made the hairs stand up on Jasper's neck, but he didn't look back.

Even as he ran, he· pulled water out of the cistern, twisting it through the trees after him like a tail, just as he had done when he'd freed the Alabaster Feroze. There were more yells and answering replies; he'd been seen. He ran on, pursued by water, pursued by men. A spear whistled through the air, but it fell short. He dodged behind a tree and paused there while he assessed the pursuit. Just men on foot, he decided. No one was mounted. He turned the line of water and pounded a stream hard into the faces of the closest pursuers, the force of it knocking them off their feet. He drove the water into their noses and mouths and eyes and ears. Then he sent a twist of water, the length of several pedes, slapping into the faces of the rest of the men following him. They tried to duck and weave, but the water pursued them, whipping around and reforming after every stinging blow. The pursuit faltered as those behind ran into the men on the ground, their faces bruised, most of them barely alive.

Jasper called out to them from the gathering dusk,

"Tell Davim that Cloudmaster Jasper Bloodstone is leaving Breccia now. Tell him that I still command the water of the Quartern." And he spun the water into a funnel, sending it gyrating into the midst of the Reduners, a wet spindevil that tore at their clothes and their weapons, that knocked them off their feet and flung them down like dust in a wind.

After that, there was no effective pursuit.

Jasper had lost sight of Laisa and Senya. He left the groves, put his back to the camp fires, kept the city walls far to his right and headed up the escarpment after the two women, following traces of their water. He hurried, but made no attempt to catch up with them. He was glad to be alone in the drylands again. No one demanding his time. No one asking him to do something. For a while, he could pretend to be just Shale the Gibber-born, out collecting resin, not the Quartern's last stormlord whose failure would mean the death of a land. Not a young man commanded to marry a girl-woman for whom he had little but contempt. Not a man who had killed one of the few people who had ever cared about him or a cloudmaster who had failed to be the saviour of the land.

He pushed those thoughts away to concentrate on this night world of the desert. He had no need of any light; the star-shine and his water-sense were enough. Once, he startled a pebblemouse and smiled at its frantic fright as it somersaulted head over heels, diving for its burrow. A little later, he came across a flock of night-parrots as they chewed their way through grass tufts full of seeds. They watched him warily with their huge eyes but never halted their incessant and noisy feeding.

I want to go home, he thought, and it was the Gibber he

meant. And then he wondered at himself. What was there in the Gibber for him? What had he ever had there that was of value, except perhaps the love of his brother and sister—neither of whom was there any more? He didn't *have* a home.

One day, I will, I swear, he said to himself. *A place where I belong, which is truly mine. I will build it myself, for me and those I love.*

He paused to look back. Far below, he could see the camp fires of the Reduners. In front of the flames, he could see men scurrying about. Some were saddling pedes, others lighting torches. The foot of the escarpment was alive with moving flickers of red, the burning brands of the searchers. They were spreading up the hill like sparks scattered by a gusting wind. He could feel the water of pedes as well, but none were close as yet. He smiled. They were as obvious to him as an eagle in the noonday sky. They would never find him.

To his right, the city was mostly dark. He traced the outline of the waterhall at the top, then Breccia Hall, and thought of Nealrith and Kaneth and Ryka and Ethelva. He thought of Terelle the last time he had seen her, fleeing for her life through the streets of Scarcleft. He thought of Mica, enslaved. Or dead. He thought of Citrine, the piece of jasper clasped in her hand just before she died.

"Davim," he whispered. "You did this. You and Taquar. And one day you both will pay."

CHAPTER FORTY-EIGHT

Scarpen Quarter
Breccia City

Ryka wondered, not for the first time, if she'd done the right thing. She'd denied Kaneth her body, moved out of his bed, avoided him as much as possible. She had concealed her thickening waist to punish the man she loved. It all seemed horribly childish now. She could hardly remember why she'd done it in the first place.

Perhaps the baby in her womb, almost half grown now, would be a stormlord. Perhaps he might be the future of the land, and she ought to hide herself away to keep her baby safe. And what right had she to deny Kaneth the knowledge of his baby's existence? She'd been thinking all along that she wouldn't have to tell him, that he would realise. That he would sense the baby's water. But he never had. That had hurt, had made her even angrier with him. How could he not feel his own son, there under his nose?

Yet if she told Kaneth, he would never rest until he had sent her to safety. And she couldn't live without him.

I can't.

He was sleeping, sprawled out on the stone tiles of the waterhall floor. She sat opposite, back to the wall, and drank in the sight of him: long, lanky, lean. Tousled hair, worry lines on his face smoothed away by exhausted sleep, snatching rest while he still could.

It wouldn't be long now before the Reduners realised Jasper had escaped. The next attack, when it came, would be vicious; she knew enough about Reduners to be sure of that, enough to know that any attempt at negotiation would be ignored.

She glanced over at the others in the waterhall. The remaining reeve and surviving guards had been reinforced by another eight guards, all that could be spared from the thinly stretched forces that remained to defend both the waterhall and Breccia Hall. She looked around at them. One of them, Pikeman Elmar Waggoner, was now replenishing the oil in the lamps in the wall niches and placing extra ones around the edge of the cisterns. His face resembled a battle-scarred tomcat, yet when his gaze lit on Kaneth, it softened to a gentleness at variance with his tough exterior. Earlier, both had thought the other dead, and their meeting in the waterhall had been a bright moment in an otherwise dark day.

She thought of her father, who had died fighting on the city wall. She wondered if her mother and Beryll were safe inside the hall somewhere. That exasperating, teasing sister who drove her sandcrazy—now Ryka would have given everything she owned to have Beryll live through this siege safely.

Something overhead started to thump, and dust sifted into the air from the hairline cracks that webbed their way along the daub ceiling. She frowned, watching. They were in the highest building in the city, the top of the escarpment. There was nothing above them.

The thump continued. Her hand crept to her womb, to rest protectively over the child within. Her mouth went dry.

When her gaze returned to Kaneth, she found he was staring at her, at where she had placed her hand. "They are coming through the roof," she said. "The Level One wall must be breached." *So soon.*

"Ryka," he whispered, "do you have something to tell me?" Around them the guards were waking, looking upwards to where the thump continued to pound. Men reached for their weapons and stood. No one spoke. Faces tilted towards the ceiling. The air thrummed with tension, with sound, with fear.

Ryka had eyes only for Kaneth, and his did not waver from hers. She nodded.

He paled. "Oh, Watergiver's heart! Ryka, why didn't you tell me earlier? You should not be here." He grabbed her wrist and pulled her to her feet. He moved towards the concealed trapdoor, the one that led to the hidden room, tugging her after him. Someone had covered the entrance with a stone slab.

She pulled against him. "No. No time. If they were to break through now and see it open— What if Jasper and Laisa and Senya haven't left yet?"

He halted, in agony. Torn. "A child is our hope for the future, Ryka. Everyone's future. How could you endanger him? Or is it a her? How could you not tell me?"

"A boy, I think, but I could yet be wrong. And he would die of thirst long before he learned to cloudshift. Leave it, Kaneth."

Still he hesitated, his anguish a tangible thing between them.

"It's too late," she whispered, knowing she had made a horrendous mistake, but the words were drowned in shattering sound as the roof at one end of the waterhall collapsed. Several of the guards died on the spot, hit by falling debris. The rest were swamped in a cloud of dust. Kaneth grabbed Ryka with one hand and drew his sword with the other.

And out of the dust the Reduners came, ululating their war cry to their dune god.

There were too many of them, Ryka saw that at a glance, and they kept on coming, leaping down through the hole in the roof. Kaneth dropped her hand, and they placed their backs to the wall, side by side, and groped in their tired bodies for the water-power to make men blind.

I wonder if Kaneth was right about Taquar? Ryka reflected. *Would things have been different if he had ruled here? Because the rest of us made such a mess of it.*

But there was no time to consider what might have been. To her despair, she realised the Reduners were using new tactics. They held chala spears, not scimitars.

She and Kaneth blinded the first few men who tried to throw them, but there were just too many chalamen. The guards began to fall under the onslaught. More and more blinded men groped their way through the battling warriors, until Ryka had no more power to call on. She clutched her sword, preparing for the first of the Reduners to reach her, but Kaneth grabbed her hand and yanked her away from the wall. He raced along the walkway between the open cisterns, towards the waterhall door, pulling her with him. Elmar, ever ready to follow his lord, pounded down a parallel walkway, heading in the same direction.

Kaneth yelled to the guards, ordering them out, too, although Ryka doubted many of them would make it—or even hear.

She didn't see the spear that hit him, but she saw his head jerk back, felt him stagger. Another spear tore at her tunic, pulling her off balance as it ripped the fabric and sliced a thin line across her skin. She flailed and fell backwards into the cistern. And Kaneth dropped face down on top of her, blood pouring from his head. He clutched her as they fell, his grip hard and tight.

She closed her eyes as his weight bore them both to the bottom. The water was cold. She felt stonework under her back and panicked. Instinct told her to surface. Rational thought told her all that waited there was death.

And then she was breathing air. She opened her eyes, to look directly into Kaneth's only a finger's length from her own. And there was nothing but air between them, a small pocket he had cleared for them to breathe. He winked and mouthed, "Don't move." They drifted upwards through the water, and at the surface he let her go. His arms floated on either side of her head, keeping her sunken beneath the protection of his body.

Waterless hell, she thought, *he knows there's a good chance someone is going to plunge a spear into his back to make sure he's dead. How can he be so brave?*

They were going to die, and she was flooded with regret. They should have run. They should have tried to save their child. Death was forever. *I was wrong*, she thought.

"Live," she said to Kaneth, just the tiniest whisper into

the air between them so no one else would hear. "Live, for the three of us."

The water around their heads reddened with his blood. She could see it running from his wound, a crease through his scalp, a deep furrow that must have reached the bone. The edges of the air pocket weakened as the last of his power drained. She used her senses to feel its dimensions: just enough to cover their faces, with a narrow pipe running from the edge to emerge on the surface, hidden in the floating tangle of her hair. She shored up the sides by pushing water away. Sandblast, she was so weak. Only the faintest dregs of her power remained. How long could she keep the water at bay?

He must have felt her power take over from his, because his eyes closed, and she felt him slip away somewhere she could not follow. His last conscious action had been to protect her and their child.

She wanted to hold him. She wanted to tell him she loved him. And most of all, she wanted to reach out and pinch his wound closed with her fingers to stop the bleeding that leached his life away. *Live*, she told him silently. *Live.*

Yet she could do nothing. A single movement, a single sound would betray them both and bring certain death. She had to play dead. A slim chance, but the only one they had. *So much blood . . .*

Think, woman! she shouted in her mind, berating herself. *You are a rainlord. You can stop the bleeding if you can find enough within you . . .* As she floated there in a sea of his blood, her heart breaking, she searched for a fragment of power to dry his wound, to seal it with dry scabbing. Just a fragment, that's all she needed.

Oh, Kaneth, love, please don't die on me, not now.

Motionless and silent, she searched for power—and wondered, if he died, whether she would sense the moment his life left him.

"Mother?" Senya asked, breathless after the climb. "What do we do next? I mean, if we go to Portennabar, Davim will just go there, too, and exactly the same thing will happen. We can't fight, because we don't have ziggers or enough rainlords or enough pedes."

"I'm glad to see you are finally thinking, child. Ah, here's the gully. I can sense the pedes, right where they should be."

"So what are we going to do?"

Laisa smiled in the darkness. "Don't worry, Senya. We are *not* going to Portennabar." She lowered her voice to a conspiratorial whisper. "Have you ever known your mother not to have a spare water jar in the cupboard? We have the Quartern's only stormlord. So we will go where there are fighters and ziggers and pedes and a *man* with guts enough to lead us to power and victory."

Senya's eyes widened. Then she began to smile.

ACKNOWLEDGEMENTS

My heartfelt thanks to all the wonderful people around the world who helped to make this a better book. I know how much I owe you. To name just some of you:

my beta readers Alena, Mark, Marcus, Mitenae, Phill, Donna, Karen, Russell, Jason;

my agent Dorothy Lumley;

my editors and copy editor at HarperCollins Voyager Australia and Orbit Books UK.

extras

orbit

meet the author

Glenda is an Australian who now lives in Malaysia, where she works on the two great loves of her life: writing fantasy and the conservation of rainforest avifauna. She has also lived in Tunisia and Austria, and has at different times in her life worked as a housemaid, library assistant, school teacher, university tutor, medical correspondence course editor, field ornithologist and designer of nature interpretive centers. Along the way she has taught English to students as diverse as Korean kindergarten kids and Japanese teenagers living in Malaysia, Viennese adults in Austria, and engineering students in Tunis. If she has any spare time (which is not often), she goes birdwatching; if she has any spare cash (not nearly often enough), she visits her daughters in the United States and her family in Western Australia. Find out more about the author at www.glendalarke.com.

introducing

If you enjoyed **THE LAST STORMLORD**,
look out for

STORMLORD RISING

Stormlord: Book Two

by Glenda Larke

Scarpen Quarter
Breccia City, Breccia Hall, Level Two

The man lying next to Lord Ryka Feldspar was dead.

His eyes stared upward past her shoulder, sightless, sad,
the vividness of their blue already fading. For a while, his
blood had seeped from his wounded chest onto her tunic,
but that had slowed, then stopped. She did not know his
name, although she had known him by sight. He'd been
a guard at Breccia Hall. Younger than she was. Eighteen,
twenty?

Too young to die.

The man on top of her was dead, too. He was a Reduner. His head lay on her chest and the beads threaded onto his red braids pressed uncomfortably into her breast, but she didn't dare move. Not yet. Around her she heard Reduner voices still; men, heaving bodies onto packpedes, talking among themselves. Making crude jokes about the dead. Coping, perhaps, with the idea that it could so easily have been them. To die or to survive: Even for the victors, the outcome was often as unpredictable as the gusting of a desert wind.

Reduners. Red men from a land of red sand dunes, flesh-devouring zigger beetles, and meddles of black pedes. Drovers and nomads and warriors who hankered after a past they thought was noble: a time when rain had been random and they ruled most of the Quartern with their tribal savagery. A people who had recently returned to a time of slave raids, living under laws decided by the strength of a man's arm and dispensed with a scimitar or a zigtube.

She had been a scholar once, and she spoke their tongue well. She could understand them now as they chatted. "Those withering bastard rainlords," one was saying, his tone bitter and angry. "They took the water from Genillid's eyes while he was fighting next to me. Left his eyeballs like dried berries in their sockets! Blind as a sandworm."

"What did you do?" another asked, a youngster by the sound of him.

"For Genillid? Killed him. That was Sandmaster Davim's orders. Reckon he was right, too. What's left for a dunesman if he can't see?"

"I heard he went among the men afterward and killed everyone who was like to lose a hand or leg as well. 'No place for a cripple on the dunes,' he said."

Ryka felt no pity. They had taken her city. Killed her people. Cloudmaster Granthon Almandine, the Quartern's ruler and its bringer of water and its only true stormlord, was dead; she knew that. His son Highlord Nealrith, the city's ruler, had been taken and tortured. He'd died in a cage swung over one of the city gates. She knew that, too. She'd heard Jasper Bloodstone had killed him to save him the agony of a slow death.

Poor Jasper. She'd seen the respect and affection in his eyes when he'd spoken to the Highlord.

Gentle, kindly Nealrith. She had grown up with him, gone to Breccia Academy with him, attended his wedding to that bitch, Lord Laisa. *Oh Sunlord receive you into his sunfire, Rith. You did not deserve your end.*

"Did we get all them bastards?" the same youth asked.

"The rainlords? Reckon so. I hear exhaustion finally sapped their powers, leaving them defenseless. My brother killed one of them rainlord priests. Still, not even a sandmaster can tell one from an ordinary city grubber. They don't look no different."

"I heard some of them are women."

The first man gave a bark of laughter. "One thing for sure, we can slaughter any force that has to use women to fight a battle!"

Ryka wanted to grit her teeth, but she couldn't risk even that slight movement. *Blast Davim's sun-blighted eyes.* The tribes of the Red Quarter had been leaving their violent past behind until he'd come along to twist their view of the history.

Sandmaster Davim, with his vicious hatreds and his brutal desire for power, had taken away that scholarly life of hers. He'd shattered the Quartern's peace, mocked the cultures not his own, destroyed the learning, all in a couple of star cycles. His men had killed her father. Watergiver only knew what had happened to her sister and her mother. And Kaneth?

No, you mustn't think he is dead. You mustn't lose hope.

Strange even to think of the life she'd had because it was all gone now, spun away on the invader's swords and the shimmering wings of their ziggers, like sand whirled into the desert on a spindevil wind. A wisp of her hair tickled her cheek. She ignored it. She mustn't move. Not even a twitch. She had to live through this, for the baby. For Kaneth.

Sunlord, I know I don't really believe in you, but let him be alive, that wonderful, gentle bladesman-warrior of mine. Father of my child. She longed to raise her head and look for him. Perhaps he lay somewhere beneath her, still alive. Or dead. Her hand longed to move to cover her abdomen where their son stirred. She knew his water and thus his maleness. *Oh Kaneth, we had so little time . . .*

The memory of her last moments with him replayed over and over. The battle in the waterhall. His last conscious act had been to protect her with his body. Could she have done more? Done something differently? She had used the last of her power to stop his bleeding, to dry the horrible wound exposing the bone of his scalp as he floated face down, senseless in the cistern. She had kept pure the bubble of air around their faces so they could both breathe. But mostly she'd just had to float there, eyes almost closed, hoping the invaders would leave the waterhall and she could pull Kaneth out of the water and take him to safety.

A futile hope, easily splintered. The Reduners had slung them both out of the cistern. They had dumped Kaneth, unconscious—or dead—on the floor; the sound of his body thudding onto the paving echoed in her head still. She'd landed on top of him a moment later. It had taken all her courage to allow herself to fall like a dead body. Not to stretch out a hand to break her landing. Not to open her eyes, not to touch him, not to look to see if his wound was bleeding again.

More waiting then, more futile praying that the Reduners would leave the waterhall, more begging a boon of a Sunlord she didn't believe in. A little joy, too, when she'd felt the baby stir within her.

She'd tried speaking to Kaneth, whispered words of encouragement and love, but he had not replied. She thought she'd felt the movement of his breath faint against her cheek, but she couldn't be sure.

Several runs of the sandglass later, the guards had received fresh orders. She'd heard and understood: "Take the dead outside. Load them onto a pede and dump them outside the walls."

Her heart had leaped within her. A chance. A chance for both her and Kaneth—if he lived. *Please, let it be so . . .*

More rough handling when she was thrown over a man's shoulder, carried, her face bumping against his back, only to be dumped once more, onto this heap of the dead. She wasn't outside the city walls; she knew that much. Cracking open an eyelid, she'd recognized one of the Breccia Hall courtyards. Hampered by her confounded short-sightedness blurring the details of anything farther than ten paces away, she saw enough to know that the last bastion against the invaders had fallen. They had lost the city to the Reduners.

And so it was she now lay motionless, cushioned by lifeless bodies, her clothes drying out in the heat of an afternoon sun, as she listened and awaited her time to move.

Sunlord, but she was tired! She needed to eat, and eat well. Without food, she had no energy; without energy, she had no water-power, no way of fighting back. Her sword was gone and she doubted she could have lifted it anyway.

Some more desultory conversation, laughter, and then a voice answering an unheard question. "No. That's the dead burning outside the city all you can smell."

The words sent fear stabbing into her bowels. They were burning bodies.

"Are we eating them now?" someone asked, amused.

"You sand-tick, Ankrim! The sandmaster ordered all the dead burned as soon as possible. Easier, I suppose, than burying them, when we have all those bab palms to fuel the pyres."

"Nah. More to teach a lesson to the living, I reckon. Here, let's get this pede loaded."

She stopped listening. *Burned! Sandblast the bastards —if Kaneth was unconscious, then* . . . Being taken outside the wall began to sound like a rotten idea.

The packpede was loaded, but no one approached the heap of dead she was on. The nearby voices were gone, leaving only far-off screams and shouting. She risked opening her eyes. No one. Cautiously, she raised her head and looked around. She was in front of the main entrance to the pede stables adjoining Breccia House, and as far as she could see, there was no one in sight. As she climbed down, bodies squelched under her sandaled feet and the odors of death intensified. Rot, shit, piss, blood. She gagged.

Boys, some of them. Not all soldiers, either . . .

In death, there was little to choose between those who had their skin stained red by desert dust, and the fair-skinned Scarpen folk like herself.

Her feet reached the gravel surface of the courtyard and she stood up. She was sore all over, and stiff. She moved like an old woman. After another swift glance around to make sure she was unobserved, she poked through the piled corpses. The Reduners she ignored, and those wearing a guard uniform. Kaneth had never been one for uniforms. "If I am going to fight, I want to be comfortable," he'd said, as he'd chosen his oldest tunic and trousers. She'd joked that he looked like a brass worker from Level Twenty, but she had followed his lead and worn clothes more suited to a laborer than a woman of her class.

She couldn't find him. Tall, broad shouldered, muscular, long limbed—he was hard to miss. And that sun-streaked fair hair he kept tied at the nape, it would stand out among the Reduners.

She searched again, even more carefully. He wasn't there. There had been a second pile of bodies, but it had disappeared. If he'd been among those . . .

Panicking and weak and thirsty, she swallowed back a surge of dizzying nausea.

"Looking for something?"

The voice, and the accompanying sound of a weapon being drawn from its scabbard, dulled her fear for Kaneth, smothered it in more immediate terror. Her heart skipped, pounded. Slowing its beating by force of will, she turned to face the speaker. A Reduner man, for all he spoke the Quartern tongue with a strong Gibber accent. He'd just stepped out of the stables. Slim, athletic, armed, his red skin streaked with dust and blood. His dark red braids were untidy with beads missing or broken. His sword was blood drenched.

The darkness of his eyes contained no hint of mercy, no hint of anything. She guessed he was at least ten cycles younger than she was, but he carried himself with assurance. His belted robe was elaborately embroidered, so she knew why: He came from a wealthy and important family.

Probably learned his Quartern tongue from Gibber slaves, she thought, her bitterness deep. Reduners had been raiding the Gibber, almost with impunity, for more than four years. Kaneth and his men had done their best to curtail such raids, but their success had been limited.

"My husband," she said, keeping her voice level and respectful—but not meek; she would not grovel, even though she knew she was a finger's breadth away from death. Or worse.

He held his scimitar up and took a step toward her, the blade pointed at her chest. She did not move.

"Find him?" he inquired, his tone deceptively mild, if the sword was to be believed.

"No."

"You're supposed t'be in the big room." He waved his free hand toward the hall. "In there. How did y'get out?"

The point of the scimitar came within a whisker of her left nipple. She refused to look down and held his gaze instead. "A woman will risk much to serve her husband."

Something flared in his eyes then, but she wasn't sure she could read it. "Not in my experience," he said, his lip curling in cynicism. "These folk," he added, indicating the heap of bodies, "came out of the waterhall. Your husband—guard, was he? Fighting up there?"

"He was up there," she said, "but he wasn't a guard. He was a brass worker from downlevel. He went to help." She did not have to feign grief; she knew it was written on her face and captured in her voice for anyone to see and hear. "He brought me up here for safety. He knew nothing about fighting."

"Then I think you can be certain he's snuffed it. Everyone in the waterhall died."

No, they didn't. I'm here.

She didn't move. Every piece of her being concentrated on not showing fear. Reduners valued courage and despised weakness, even in their women. Not, of course, that he would think twice about lopping off her head with his blade if it pleased him. "Doubtless you're right," she said, fighting her nausea, "but I would like to know one way or the other."

"What's your name?"

I shan't make you a present of that, you bastard. If he realized she was a rainlord, she was dead—and someone among the Reduners might know the name Ryka Feldspar. "Who wants to know?"

He stared at her, as if he couldn't believe his ears. "My name's Ravard," he said finally. "But what should count with you, woman, is the weapon I hold t'your body. *What's your name?*" The blade tip brushed her nipple this time and then traced a pattern up to her throat.

"Garnet," she said, appropriating the name of the cook in Carnelian House and then adding another gemstone at random: "Garnet Prase."

"Dangerous for a woman t'be out on the streets after a battle," he remarked with heavy mockery. "You never know what nasty thing might happen. There's men wanting their rewards for a battle well fought, and they'll take it anyhow they please."

"So your men are out of control already?" she asked, and then bit her tongue. Why could she never learn to keep silent when it counted!

His eyes narrowed. "You play a dangerous game, woman, with your Scarpen arrogance. Perhaps you care nothing for yourself." The sword point dropped to her abdomen. "But what about the brat you carry?"

This time she couldn't control her shock. "How—" she began, and then closed her mouth firmly, though her hand dropped to cover the roundness of her belly, as if she could protect her son from his weapon. *If only I had my water-power—*

"I have eyes in me head," he said. "Suggest you keep a still tongue in yours, Garnet, less you want t'lose your life and your man's get, as well. I'll take you t'other women in there. Tonight, you sleep with a man who's not your husband, or you'll lose more than your man. Think on it."

He turned her roughly and started her walking in front of him toward the hall's main door. She hugged her arms about her to stop her trembling.

A complete stranger works out I'm pregnant at a glance? It took Kaneth nearly half a cycle to wake up to it! This fellow was strange.

She slipped in a patch of blood on the gravel and he grabbed her by the arm, wrenching her upright before she hit the ground. "Careful, sweet lips," he said in her ear. "We want you undamaged, don't we?"

She gasped in pain. The sword cut on her upper leg— not deep, but raw and throbbing nonetheless—had opened up. He hadn't noticed it before because the cut in her trousers had been almost covered by her tunic, but he saw the fresh blood now. He gave an exasperated grunt.

"Why didn't y'tell me you were hurt?" he asked.

"It's nothing."

He pulled up the hem of the tunic and looked at the wound. There had been a makeshift bandage around her thigh once, but it had long since come loose and fallen off. "Humph. Maybe not, but needs covering nonetheless, t'stop that bleeding."

He left her where she was and went back to the heaped-up dead. With his scimitar, he slashed at a dead man's tunic and brought back a piece of the cloth. She wanted to take it from him, but he ignored her gesture and knelt to wrap it around her thigh himself, over the top of her trousers. She braced herself for an intimate touch, a leer, or a sneering remark, but all he did was bandage her.

As he tied off the ends, he said, "When you get a chance, wash the wound 'n' put a clean cloth 'bout it. Even a small cut like that can kill you, if it gets dirty."

Perhaps that would be best anyway, she thought. *To die.*

The thought must have been reflected on her face because he said harshly, "Listen t'me, you water-soft city groveller. Living's what counts, understand? Your man's dead. Probably your whole withering family's been snuffed. Your city's fallen. Your rainlords are rotting in the sun. Soon there'll be no more water in your skyless city. Take your chance with us. We've not got rainlords, but our sandmasters and tribemasters can sense water on the wind. Our dune gods protect us." He pointed to her abdomen. "That young'un of yours? It can grow up Reduner, a warrior or a woman of the tribe. Reduners don't make no difference 'tween folk. Out there on the dunes, we're all red soon enough. Being alive? That's all that matters. That's *all*."

She stood facing him. Wasn't there more to life than that? Yes, of course, there was—but you had to be alive to achieve it. *Sandblast it,* she thought, despairing. *How did we Breccians ever come to this?*

She nodded to the man. "Yes," she said. "You are right."

"Now, get going, Garnet. I don't have time t'waste on you."

Kaneth, I will be strong. I promise, for the sake of our son. You're on your own, wherever you are. And so, dammit, am I.

And then, just a whisper in her mind, to a man who was probably dead: *I love you.*